PENGUIN CLASSICS

OLIVER TWIST

CHARLES DICKENS was born in Portsmouth on 7 February 1812, the second of eight children. Dickens's childhood experiences were similar to those depicted in *David Copperfield*. His father, who was a government clerk, was imprisoned for debt and Dickens was briefly sent to work in a blacking warehouse at the age of twelve. He received little formal education, but taught himself shorthand and became a reporter of parliamentary debates for the *Morning Chronicle*. He began to publish sketches in various periodicals, which were subsequently republished as *Sketches by Boz*. *The Pickwick Papers* was published in 1836–7, after a slow start it became a publishing phenomenon and Dickens's characters the centre of a popular cult. Part of the secret of his success was the method of cheap serial publication he adopted; thereafter, all Dickens's novels were first published in serial form. He began *Oliver Twist* in 1837, followed by *Nicholas Nickleby* (1838) and *The Old Curiosity Shop* (1840–41). After finishing *Barnaby Rudge* (1841) Dickens set off for America; he went full of enthusiasm for the young republic but, in spite of a triumphant reception, he returned disillusioned. His experiences are recorded in *American Notes* (1842). *A Christmas Carol*, the first of the hugely popular *Christmas Books*, appeared in 1843, while *Martin Chuzzlewit*, which included a fictionalized account of his American travels, was first published over the period 1843–4. During 1844–6 Dickens travelled abroad and he began *Dombey and Son* while in Switzerland. This and *David Copperfield* (1849–50) were more serious in theme and more carefully planned than his early novels. In later works, such as *Bleak House* (1853) and *Little Dorrit* (1857), Dickens's social criticism became more radical and his comedy more savage. In 1850 Dickens started the weekly periodical *Household Words*, succeeded in 1859 by *All the Year Round*; in these he published *Hard Times* (1854), *A Tale of Two Cities* (1859) and *Great Expectations* (1860–61). Dickens's health was failing during the 1860s and the physical strain of the public readings which he began in 1858 hastened his decline, although *Our Mutual Friend* (1865) retained some of his best comedy. His last novel, *The Mystery of Edwin Drood*, was never completed and he died on 9 June 1870. Public grief at his death was considerable and he was buried in the Poets' Corner of Westminster Abbey.

PHILIP HORNE was educated at Cambridge University and is Professor of English Literature at University College London. He has published *Henry James and Revision: The New York Edition* (1990), and edited the acclaimed *Henry James: A Life in Letters* (Penguin, 1999), James's *A London Life & The Reverberator* and the Penguin edition of *The Tragic Muse*.

CHARLES DICKENS

OLIVER TWIST,
or, The Parish Boy's Progress

Edited with an Introduction and Notes by
PHILIP HORNE

PENGUIN BOOKS

PENGUIN BOOKS

Published by the Penguin Group
Penguin Books Ltd, 80 Strand, London WC2R 0RL, England
Penguin Putnam Inc., 375 Hudson Street, New York, New York 10014, USA
Penguin Books Australia Ltd, 250 Camberwell Road, Camberwell, Victoria 3124, Australia
Penguin Books Canada Ltd, 10 Alcorn Avenue, Toronto, Ontario, Canada M4V 3B2
Penguin Books India (P) Ltd, 11, Community Centre, Panchsheel Park, New Delhi – 110 017, India
Penguin Books (NZ) Ltd, Cnr Rosedale and Airborne Roads, Albany, Auckland, New Zealand
Penguin Books (South Africa) (Pty) Ltd, 24 Sturdee Avenue, Rosebank 2196, South Africa

Penguin Books Ltd, Registered Offices: 80 Strand, London WC2R 0RL, England

First published 1837–8
Published in Penguin Classics 2002

1

Set in 10.75/12.5 pt Monotype Fournier
Typeset by Rowland Phototypesetting Ltd, Bury St Edmunds, Suffolk
Printed in England by Clays Ltd, St Ives plc

CONTENTS

LIST OF ILLUSTRATIONS

ACKNOWLEDGEMENTS

I have debts to many scholars, critics, editors and annotators, in particular Katherine Tillotson, Peter Fairclough, David Paroissien, Stephen Gill.

Also, for help and encouragement of various kinds: John Allen, Rosemary Ashton, Mark Ford, Dan Jacobson, Danny Karlin, Alison Light, Karl Miller, Adrian Poole, Yopie Prins, Neil Rennie, Tom Staley, Susan Stead, John Sutherland, Peter Swaab, David Trotter, Sarah Wintle, Henry Woudhuysen; and in particular Judith Hawley.

I have special debts to a succession of editors at Penguin over a number of years: to Tim Bates, who commissioned the edition; to Robert Mighall, a dauntingly authoritative Dickens scholar as well as a demanding close reader, who did his best to keep me up to the mark; and to Laura Barber, an astute and sympathetic presence. I am also indebted to Lindeth Vasey, who has been a friendly, thoroughly demanding and entirely helpful copy-editor; and Penguin's sharp proof-readers Michael Paul and Karin Barry.

The edition is dedicated to Michael Slater, whose practical help and generous encouragement have been invaluable.

1812   *7 February* Charles John Huffam Dickens born at Portsmouth, where his father is a clerk in the Navy Pay Office. The eldest son in a family of eight, two of whom die in childhood.

1817   Family move to Chatham.

1822   Family move to London.

1824   Dickens's father in Marshalsea Debtors' Prison for three months. Dickens employed in a blacking warehouse, labelling bottles. Attends Wellington House Academy, a private school, 1824–7.

1827   Becomes a solicitor's clerk.

1832   Becomes a parliamentary reporter after mastering shorthand. In love with Maria Beadnell, 1830–33.

1833   First published story, 'A Dinner at Poplar Walk', in the *Monthly Magazine*. Further stories and sketches in this and other periodicals, 1834–5.

1834   Becomes reporter on the *Morning Chronicle*.

1835   Engaged to Catherine Hogarth, daughter of editor of the *Evening Chronicle*.

1836   *Sketches by Boz*, First and Second Series, published. Marries Catherine Hogarth. Meets John Forster, his literary adviser and future biographer.

1837   *The Pickwick Papers* published in one volume (issued in monthly parts, 1836–7). Birth of a son, the first of ten children. Death of Mary Hogarth, Dickens's sister-in-law. Edits *Bentley's Miscellany*, 1837–9.

1838   *Oliver Twist* published in three volumes (serialized monthly in *Bentley's Miscellany*, 1837–9). Visits Yorkshire schools of the Dotheboys type.

1839   *Nicholas Nickleby* published in one volume (issued in monthly parts, 1838–9).

1841 Declines invitation to stand for Parliament. *The Old Curiosity Shop* and *Barnaby Rudge* published in separate volumes after appearing in weekly numbers in *Master Humphrey's Clock*, 1840–41. Public dinner in his honour at Edinburgh.

1842 *January–June* First visit to North America, described in *American Notes*, two volumes.

1843 *December A Christmas Carol* appears.

1844 *Martin Chuzzlewit* published in one volume (issued in monthly parts, 1843–4). Dickens and family leave for Italy, Switzerland and France. Dickens returns to London briefly to read *The Chimes* to friends before its publication in December.

1845 Dickens and family return from Italy. *The Cricket on the Hearth* published at Christmas. Writes autobiographical fragment, ?1845–6, not published until included in Forster's *Life* (three volumes, 1872–4).

1846 Becomes first editor of the *Daily News* but resigns after seventeen issues. *Pictures from Italy* published. Dickens and family in Switzerland and Paris. *The Battle of Life* published at Christmas.

1847 Returns to London. Helps Miss Burdett Coutts to set up, and later to run, a 'Home for Homeless Women'.

1848 *Dombey and Son* published in one volume (issued in monthly parts, 1846–8). Organizes and acts in charity performances of *The Merry Wives of Windsor* and *Every Man in His Humour* in London and elsewhere. *The Haunted Man* published at Christmas.

1850 *Household Words*, a weekly journal 'Conducted by Charles Dickens', begins in March and continues until 1859. Dickens makes a speech at first meeting of Metropolitan Sanitary Association. *David Copperfield* published in one volume (issued in monthly parts, 1849–50).

1851 Death of Dickens's father. Further theatrical activities in aid of the Guild of Literature and Art, including a performance before Queen Victoria. *A Child's History of England* appears at intervals in *Household Words*, published in three volumes (1852, 1853, 1854).

1853 *Bleak House* published in one volume (issued in monthly parts,

1852–3). Dickens gives first public readings (from *A Christmas Carol*).

1854 Visits Preston, Lancashire, to observe industrial unrest. *Hard Times* appears weekly in *Household Words* and is published in book form.

1855 Speech in support of the Administrative Reform Association.

1856 Dickens buys Gad's Hill Place, near Rochester.

1857 *Little Dorrit* published in one volume (issued in monthly parts, 1855–7). Dickens acts in Wilkie Collins's melodrama *The Frozen Deep* and falls in love with the young actress Ellen Ternan. *The Lazy Tour of Two Idle Apprentices*, written jointly with Wilkie Collins about a holiday in Cumberland, appears in *Household Words*.

1858 Publishes *Reprinted Pieces* (articles from *Household Words*). Separation from his wife followed by statement in *Household Words*. Dickens's household now largely run by his sister-in-law Georgina.

1859 *All the Year Round*, a weekly journal again 'Conducted by Charles Dickens', begins. *A Tale of Two Cities*, serialized both in *All the Year Round* and in monthly parts, appears in one volume.

1860 Dickens sells London house and moves family to Gad's Hill.

1861 *Great Expectations* published in three volumes after appearing weekly in *All the Year Round* (1860–61). *The Uncommercial Traveller* (papers from *All the Year Round*) appears; expanded edition, 1868. Further public readings, 1861–3.

1863 Death of Dickens's mother, and of his son Walter (in India). Reconciled with Thackeray, with whom he had quarrelled, shortly before the latter's death. Publishes 'Mrs Lirriper's Lodgings' in Christmas number of *All the Year Round*.

1865 *Our Mutual Friend* published in two volumes (issued in monthly parts, 1864–5). Dickens severely shocked after a train accident when returning from France with Ellen Ternan and her mother.

1866 Begins another series of readings. Takes a house for Ellen at Slough. 'Mugby Junction' appears in Christmas number of *All the Year Round*.

1867   Moves Ellen to Peckham. Second journey to America. Gives readings in Boston, New York, Washington and elsewhere, despite increasing ill-health. 'George Silverman's Explanation' appears in *Atlantic Monthly* (then in *All the Year Round*, 1868).

1868   Returns to England. Readings now include the sensational 'Sikes and Nancy' from *Oliver Twist*; Dickens's health further undermined.

1870   Farewell readings in London. *The Mystery of Edwin Drood* issued in six monthly parts, intended to be completed in twelve. *9 June* Dies, after collapse at Gad's Hill, aged fifty-eight. Buried in Westminster Abbey.

Stephen Wall, 1995

INTRODUCTION

*(New readers are advised that this Introduction makes the
details of the plot explicit.)*

The first instalment of *Oliver Twist, or, The Parish Boy's Progress* by
Boz appeared in *Bentley's Miscellany* in February 1837, four months
before the death of King William IV and the accession of Queen
Victoria. This grimmer, slimmer second novel by Dickens, in a new
magazine of which he was editor, initially came as a shock to many of
those who were still enjoying *The Pickwick Papers*, the fat comic serial
he had been bringing out since April 1836, and would not complete
till November 1837. The genial adventures of the plump, accident-
prone, comfortably-off Mr Pickwick and his cockney servant Sam
Weller had caught the public imagination, and the circulation of the
monthly parts had swollen forty-fold to 20,000. But Dickens was now
deliberately shifting social and moral focus: the nearest equivalent
to Mr Pickwick in *Oliver Twist*, Mr Brownlow, a well-meaning old
gentleman and Oliver's benefactor, is hardly among the book's half-
dozen most memorable or artistically successful characters. The new
work would take its public off the mainly cheerful coaching high-
ways of *Pickwick* into some darker and more dangerous dens and
alleys.

Lord Melbourne, the young Queen Victoria's prime minister and
mentor, was an early reader of the novel. His response, as she told her
diary, was revulsion: 'It's all among Workhouses, and Coffin Makers,
and Pickpockets . . . I don't *like* those things; I wish to avoid them; I
don't like them in reality, and therefore I don't wish them represented.'
The new queen herself found it 'excessively interesting'.[1] There was
moreover something new about the *way* such low scenes were represented by Dickens. Pierce Egan's bestselling *Life in London*, of 1821,
dedicated to George IV, and illustrated, like *Oliver Twist*, by the

great George Cruikshank (together with his father and brother), had established a fashionable, thrilling but cosy image of the unrespectable underworld. Taking his heroes Tom and Jerry slumming on 'Rambles and Sprees through the Metropolis', Egan introduced the public to the 'flash' world of the criminal and sporting fraternities, but in a comic spirit and always with a safe escape route back to the comforts of the West End. When his well-to-do heroes end up in the Bow Street magistrates' court after a brawl, it is for a sentimental episode in which they witness a magistrate being moved to pity by the plight of a penniless girl, the victim of a cruel seducer. The reassuring moral is thus that 'Justice was never seen to greater advantage.' The magistrate's court in which Oliver Twist finds himself after being wrongly arrested is a different place altogether, the domain of the insulting and brutally punitive Mr Fang, a 'Justice' who – with others – plays each day 'enough fantastic tricks', Dickens says, 'to make the angels weep thick tears of blood' (Book the First, Chapter the Eleventh, hereafter as 'I, 11'). For a pocket-picking he has not committed, Oliver is summarily sentenced by Fang to three months' hard labour, like Bulwer-Lytton's hero in *Paul Clifford* (1830). A witness happens to arrive and exonerate Oliver; but it is an ordeal after which he collapses, 'his face a deadly white, and a cold tremble convulsing his whole frame'. Dickens's harsh, rapid, sardonic manner, his note of charged understatement, drawing on his experience in reportage with *Sketches by Boz* (1836–7), insists on the shocking plausibility of such injustice in an England that makes scant provision for those without friends in high places or funds in the bank.

Another contributor to *Bentley's Miscellany*, indeed Bentley's life-long friend and paid literary adviser, the Revd R. H. Barham, found the start of *Oliver Twist* politically unsettling: 'By the way,' he told a friend in April 1837, 'there is a sort of Radicalish tone about *Oliver Twist* which I don't altogether like. I think it will not be long till it is remedied, for Bentley is loyal to the backbone himself.'[2] Barham's remark tallies with the comment of the modern critic Steven Marcus that 'The socially radical impulse behind the moral idea in *Oliver Twist* is revealed in the fact that it is written from a point of view which . . . regards society from without.' At no point in the novel is the orphaned

Oliver shown as being able to appeal for sympathy or vindication to public institutions, charitable or legal.

At least to begin with *Oliver Twist* is not a 'Victorian novel'. The police at the end cry out to open up 'In the King's name', and the England in which it takes place was only in the process of becoming what we might recognize as 'modern'. Perhaps the most strikingly alien of its features is the looming prospect of capital punishment, which informs the entire book, and whose implications deserve close consideration. When we first meet the new-born Oliver in the workhouse he is lying 'gasping on a little flock mattress' (I, 1), and we soon learn he is in danger of having his hard-won breath cut off by society. Says the gentleman in the white waistcoat, 'That boy will be hung' (I, 2). Nothing seems likelier than an end on the gallows for Dickens's small, socially excluded hero, in the world of Bumbles, Sowerberrys and Fagins his creator sets before him. Oliver's very surname, given him by Bumble, suggests not only perversity but also its likely fate: one slang sense of 'twisted' was 'hanged' – the usage deriving, Eric Partridge (see Appendix C) tells us, in the vivid way of such terms, from 'twisting as one swings on the rope'.

The gallows-haunted world into which Dickens thrusts us, moreover, is true to the extreme severity of the law at the time. Between 1801 and 1835, 103 death-sentences were passed on children under the age of fourteen for theft (though sensibilities were changing and not one was carried out). Lest it be thought that the ranks of the hanged would dwindle naturally with the onward march of progress, it must be registered that twice as many people were hanged in the first thirty years of the nineteenth century as in the last fifty of the eighteenth. This gruesome increase can be associated with the social unsettlement caused by the Napoleonic Wars, industrialization and urban growth, and with fear of the lower orders among the propertied classes after the French Revolution. In the year 1830 there had been an extraordinary 18,017 felony prosecutions under the capital (or 'bloody') code (probably reflecting the judicial repression of the discontent of agricultural labourers as expressed in the 'Swing Riots'). Two-thirds of the 671 hangings in the 1820s, as V. A. C. Gatrell's horrifying *The Hanging*

Tree: Execution and the English People, 1770–1868 reports, were for property crime, only one-fifth for murder. The situation would alter drastically over the very period of *Oliver Twist*'s serialization; Dickens as usual had an acute sense of change in the air; thanks to a series of reforms, 438 were sentenced to death in 1837, only 56 in 1839 – and few of those were actually hanged.

The executions were a major social phenomenon in more than a symbolic sense. They were public, and their audiences were frequently vast (crowds of up to 100,000 were recorded). Dickens told his friend and publisher John Macrone in a letter of 1835 why he would not follow up the success of his 'Boz' sketch of Newgate prison, which included a visit to the death cell, with one about the House of Correction at Coldbath-Fields, which he had just visited: 'You cannot throw the interest over a years imprisonment, however severe, that you can cast around the punishment of death. The Tread-Mill will not take the hold on men's feelings that the Gallows does . . .' Several criminals often went to the gallows in one go; a few decades earlier as many as eighteen or twenty had been dispatched per session. Oliver having arrived at the London lair of Fagin, his newest pro-tector, on a Sunday night, it is to one of these Monday morning rituals, we gather, that the Dodger and Charley Bates go off to 'make pocket-handkerchiefs' by picking pockets while Oliver dozes. On their return Fagin starts softening up Oliver for the same line of work, but then 'changed the subject', as Dickens ironically says, 'by asking whether there had been much of a crowd at the execution that morning'. Of course Fagin's real subject remains the same – crime and punish-ment – and we see where Oliver may be heading under his tutelage. Earlier, Fagin has been muttering to himself, 'What a fine thing capital punishment is!', for some of the hanged have been members of his own gang, who have gone to their deaths without betraying him, though it seems that he has betrayed them for the rewards. He is profiting by the hangings in several ways; and Dickens is comprehen-sively challenging the notion of the deterrent effect of the gallows. The novel ties together in an unobtrusive symbolic knot the handkerchiefs criminally picked from pockets, those sported as neckwear, the hempen 'cravat' of the hangman and all the vicissitudes that throats or 'windpipes' are heir to, of choking, strangling, clasping, tearing and cutting. Its low characters all seem to breathe on sufferance.

What the gallows crowd went for was a matter of some controversy, though Dickens was in little doubt. He wrote to Macvey Napier in 1845, recalling with some horror having attended the execution of the murderer François Courvoisier in 1840, that 'robbery and obscenity and callous indifference are of no commoner occurrence anywhere, than at the foot of the Scaffold'. And in February 1846 (while carefully revising *Oliver Twist* for a new issue in ten monthly parts), he wrote about the same event in an extended letter to the *Daily News* against capital punishment:

From the moment of my arrival, when there were but a few score boys in the street, and those all young thieves . . . – down to the time when I saw the body with its dangling head, being carried on a wooden bier into the gaol – I did not see one token in all the immense crowd; at the windows, in the streets, on the house-tops, anywhere; of any one emotion suitable to the occasion. No sorrow, no salutary terror, no abhorrence, no seriousness; nothing but ribaldry, debauchery, levity, drunkenness, and flaunting vice in fifty other shapes. I should have deemed it impossible that I could have ever felt any large assemblage of my fellow-creatures to be so odious.[3]

A similar horror permeates *Oliver Twist*: Fagin's Old Bailey trial ends with the courtroom shaken by 'deep loud groans . . . like angry thunder', the sound of 'a peal of joy from the populace outside, greeting the news that he would die on Monday' (III, 14).

One sees the thinking that led Dickens at Courvoisier's send-off to look down on his 'fellow-creatures' from an upper room; and the alienation he expresses here contrasts potently with the response of his colleague and rival novelist William Makepeace Thackeray, whom he recognized below, rubbing shoulders with the crowd. Thackeray's 1840 essay about the experience, 'On Going to See a Man Hanged', makes a point of saying that 'the mob was extraordinarily gentle and good-humoured', and expressing 'wonder at the vigorous, orderly good sense, and intelligence of the people'. On the other hand, he goes on to confess that his own response is 'an extraordinary feeling of terror and shame', to describe the whole crowd as swayed by 'that hidden lust after blood which influences our race', and to say 'that I came away down Snow Hill that morning with a disgust for murder, but it was for *the murder I saw done*'. Dickens in his 1845 letter to Napier asked 'whether ignorant and dissolute persons . . . , seeing that murder done, and not having seen the other, will not, almost of necessity sympathize with the man who dies before them; especially as he is shewn, a Martyr to their fancy'. There was often much sympathy with the condemned; the case of Fagin and his hostile audience seems exceptional.

Dickens still hiding the wound of his period of family abandonment and social despair in Warren's blacking factory, and so predominantly self-taught and self-made, came to Newgate on an impulse, at the last minute, and may have had cause to doubt the purity of his own motives. Already in *Pickwick Papers*, though there farcically treated, mobs were an object of suspicion and fear, liable to unjust and violent surges of caprice. But since, on your own, you could not beat a mob, you might all too easily end by joining it, as the timorous Pickwick whispers to his comrades, 'Don't ask any questions. It's always best on these occasions to do what the mob do' (ch. 13). In 'The Hospital Patient', one of the *Sketches by Boz*, first published in August 1836 (the same month as that chapter of *Pickwick*), Dickens records how strolling through Covent Garden he saw a pickpocket being taken to a police office, and found that 'Somehow we can never resist joining a crowd, so we turned back with the mob, and entered the office.' Oliver Twist too is pursued through the streets of London as a pickpocket, to cries of 'Stop thief! stop thief!', in a thrilling set-piece. But then Dickens turns on himself and us to point out that the object of the chase here is 'One wretched, breathless child, panting with exhaustion, terror in his looks, agony in his eye'. Dickens's feelings are involved on both sides, and it is this vertiginous doubleness of sympathy, with the violent and the victimized, that informs the many great passages and chapters of what is at once a flawed and a magnificent, startling novel.

Dickens's friend and biographer John Forster famously wrote of the romantic glamour and excitement that drew Dickens even as a ten-year-old boy to various areas of London, and particularly the criminal ones known as 'rookeries': 'But, most of all, he had a profound attraction of repulsion to St Giles's.' That the striking phrase here is Dickens's own we can be sure; for he uses it in the 1846 letter already quoted, to the *Daily News*, expanding on 'the horrible fascination' of the death penalty 'in the minds . . . of good and virtuous and well-conducted people': 'The attraction of repulsion being as much a law of our moral nature, as gravitation is in the structure of the visible world, operates in no case (I believe) so powerfully, as in this case of the punishment of death.'[4] The 'horrible fascination' both of the criminal underworld and of 'the punishment of death', formulated here as a psychological theory some years after *Oliver Twist*, deeply informs the imaginative construction of the novel, not least in the nightmare logic by which, as Richard Maxwell has put it, 'Oliver gets back to safety, no matter how great his peril; peril threatens no matter how great his safety.' And the chief peril for Oliver is that he should be driven into the criminal life that points to the gallows. Critics have been misled, I think, by Dickens's declaration after the event, in his 1841 Preface, that 'I wished to show, in little Oliver, the principle of Good surviving through every adverse circumstance, and triumphing at last.' This need not be taken as saying that he is a spotless goody-goody: 'the principle of Good' survives in him, it isn't necessarily that he is an allegorical embodiment of it. We shall not undergo the full experience of the book if we knowingly decide to feel no suspense about whether he will end up as an object of 'the hideous apparatus of death' (III, 14).

In *Tom Jones* (1749), the masterpiece of Henry Fielding, we are told of the foundling hero that 'it was the universal Opinion of all *Mr Allworthy's* Family, that he was certainly born to be hanged' (Bk. III, ch. 2). If in *Oliver Twist* we fail to register the first prediction that 'That boy will be hung', we get more chances, for as a ward of the parish Oliver is proverbial gallows-fodder. The sneaking bully Noah Claypole taunts Oliver by stating 'his intention of coming to see him hung whenever that desirable event should take place' (I, 6), adding that if Oliver's mother had not died in childbirth *she* would most likely have been hung. Oliver responds with a fury resembling those we see later in Bill Sikes, a reaction that is both understandable and a seeming confirmation of the prediction: he 'seized Noah by the throat, shook him in the violence of his rage till his teeth chattered in his head, and, collecting his whole force into one heavy blow, felled him to the ground'. Cue the gentleman in the white waistcoat, reiterating that 'I felt a strange presentiment from the very first, that that audacious young savage would come to be hung' (I, 7). When Oliver is wounded and captured after the attempted housebreaking at the Maylies' house in Chertsey, one of his captors administers first aid, solicitously trying 'to restore Oliver, lest he should die before he could be hung' (II, 7) – a likely prospect for anyone involved in an armed attempt at housebreaking (during which Sikes has fired his pistol). The conspiracy between Monks and Fagin against Oliver chimes with the general doom-mongering about him; they mean to use the law to kill him, 'by driving him through every jail in town, and then hauling him up for some capital felony' – dragging him, as Monks says later, 'to the very gallows-foot' (III, 3, 13).

I have mentioned Dickens's formative period in Warren's blacking factory at the age of ten, of which he told no one until he confided it to Forster in the spring of 1847 in a fragment of autobiography. Its impact seems to have driven *Oliver Twist* (and the later parts of *Pickwick Papers*) before being more explicitly treated in *David Copperfield* (1849–50). A relative's offer of the humbling, menial job in 'a crazy, tumble-down old house . . . literally overrun with rats' was 'accepted very willingly by my father and mother', Dickens bitterly recorded, to help the disastrous family finances – which not long afterwards landed the father in Marshalsea Prison for debt. The boy himself experienced this ready abandonment of his education for the sake of six shillings a week as a parental betrayal and a blighting of his future, feeling 'my early hopes of growing up to be a learned and distinguished man crushed in my breast'. All the more that soon the family home was broken up and Dickens '(small Cain that I was, except that I had never done harm to any one)' was left alone 'as a lodger to a reduced old lady'.

He remembers his own hungry loungings about the streets after work: 'But for the mercy of God, I might easily have been, for any care that was taken of me, a little robber or a little vagabond.' This presents the young novelist-to-be as another little Oliver barely escaping – providentially – a Fagin's ultimately murderous sponsorship. That treacherous guardian is indeed foreshadowed too. Young Dickens *does* have a Fagin, in fact his benefactor, looking after him: 'on the first Monday morning' at Warren's one of the older boys came 'to show me the trick of using the string and tying the knot. His name was Bob Fagin; and I took the liberty of using his name, long afterwards, in *Oliver Twist*.' Not only his name, though: Oliver's Fagin also starts to show him the tricks of a sullying trade on his first morning. In the blacking warehouse Dickens anxiously protected his shaky title as 'the young gentleman' with the help of the kindly Bob Fagin, who also looked after him when he was ill; but Dickens would recall 'the secret agony of my soul as I sunk into this companionship', and there is no little ingratitude in the liberty he takes by using the name for his wickedest villain. He seems later to have recognized this himself, to judge by the poignantly outgrown protector-figure of Joe Gargery in *Great Expectations* (1860–61), whom he even has visit a blacking warehouse when he comes to London.

One must agree with John Bayley in his essay on *Oliver Twist* when he comments, 'No wonder Fagin the criminal is such an ambivalent figure when the real Fagin's kindness had, so to speak, threatened to inure Dickens to the hopeless routine of the wage-slave.' This seems kinder and truer than the blunt instrument of John Carey's joky sarcasm in *The Violent Effigy* about the parts of the book where Oliver falls among thieves: 'We should realize . . . that Dickens is simply reasserting, in this part of the novel, the distinction between himself and the low boys in the blacking warehouse. It is a hymn to the purity of the middle-class soul.' The novel should indeed make us feel uneasy about the relation between class and virtue, enforcing as it does the recognition that accidents of exposure, of 'adverse circumstance', as well as the intrinsic innocence or strength of character which we prefer to think about, may determine which individuals can resist temptation, and which of us become corrupted.

'*Oliver Twist*', as the great Dickensian Humphry House once noted, 'is intensely topical to the time of its publication.' For a start, the famous incident in the workhouse at the end of the first instalment, where Oliver holds out his bowl and scandalously announces, 'Please, sir, I want some more' (I, 2), promptly points to the urgent contemporary relevance of the question of the poor. Much has been written on the withering treatment of the workhouse and apprenticeship systems in the first part of the book, and on the question of how that opening relates to what follows in London with Fagin and Mr Brownlow. Dickens seems to be satirizing the then-controversial 'New Poor Law' created by the Poor Law Amendment Act of 1834, a measure of Utilitarian inspiration – carried through, that is, by followers of Jeremy Bentham – on the basis that it has caused, in House's words, 'a rejuvenation of abuses in a more unpleasant form'. He may also be targeting 'faults of the old law allowed to continue under the new', for individual parishes were allowed considerable leeway in their application of the new rules.

At any rate, as K. J. Fielding has argued, Dickens is directing his ethical criticism at the bleakly inhuman (or, in practice, brutally selfish) doctrines of political economy not only in their application to the legislative and public-administrative fields, but also as he sees their extended application in such matters of private morality as the supposed tradition of honour among thieves. Mr Bumble, the beadle, grandly declares that 'political economy' (I, 4) – a tag which for him functions as an euphemism for calculated parsimony – is something those outside the workhouse do not understand. Equally, when the Dodger and Charley Bates save themselves by joining in the mob's pursuit of Oliver for their own theft, Dickens shifts into the high ironic mode of Henry Fielding in *Tom Jones* or *Joseph Andrews* to draw a mock-Utilitarian moral:

. . . this strong proof of their anxiety for their own preservation and safety goes to corroborate and confirm the little code of laws which certain profound and sound-judging philosophers have laid down as the mainsprings of all Madam Nature's deeds and actions . . . putting entirely out of sight any considerations of heart, or generous impulse and feeling . . . (I, 13)

And later, more vividly, in Fagin's superb witty homily to 'Morris Bolter', *alias* Noah Claypole, explaining why crude self-interest must be slightly modified, Dickens parodies the reductive Utilitarian conception of human life and society in a way that clarifies the central concerns of the novel:

'Every man's his own friend . . . Some conjurors say that number three is the magic number, and some say number seven. It's neither, my friend, neither. It's number one.'

'Ha! ha!' cried Mr Bolter. 'Number one for ever!'

'In a little community like ours,' said the Jew, who felt it necessary to qualify this position, 'we have a general number one; that is, you can't consider yourself as number one without considering me too as the same, and all the other young people.'

'Oh, the devil!' exclaimed Mr Bolter. (III, 6)

Noah epitomizes treacherous selfishness, and Fagin has to spell out that if he breathes a word against the gang then Fagin will have to 'blow upon' him, as the phrase is, for his (capital) crime of stealing from Sowerberry, a crime which 'would put the cravat round your throat that's so very easily tied, and so very difficult to unloosen, – in plain English, the halter!' For now, the warning has the desired effect: 'Mr Bolter put his hand to his neckerchief, as if he felt it inconveniently tight, and murmured an assent . . .' And Fagin draws his conclusion:

'. . . so we come at last to what I told you at first – that a regard for number one holds us all together, and must do so, unless we would all go to pieces in company.'

It is part of Dickens's vision of applied political economy, and his vindication of 'considerations of heart, or generous impulse and feeling' (I, 13), that such selfish reasoning does not hold them all together, and that it is Noah who fatally 'peaches' upon Fagin at the last.

The vertiginous suddenness of the young author's huge success at this time – he only turned twenty-five in February 1837 – is hard to take in. As *Oliver Twist* began its *Bentley's Miscellany* run Dickens had only one *book* as such to his credit – not to his name, but his pseudonym – the First and Second Series of *Sketches by Boz*, published in February and December 1836 with forty illustrations by George Cruikshank, collecting pieces of journalism from as far back as December 1833. But there was a revised reissue in monthly parts from November 1837 to June 1839, thus coinciding with most of the serial run of *Oliver Twist*, and providing chapter and verse for many of the observations of London life that glinted in the novel's darkness.

More remarkably, when *Oliver Twist* started its run, and for ten months, it also overlapped with the runaway success *Pickwick Papers*, published in monthly parts from April 1836 to November 1837. *Pickwick*'s parts, published on their own, were on average twice the length of the roughly 9,000-word instalments of *Oliver Twist*: Dickens would write the intense *Oliver* batches first, then cheer himself up with the expansiveness of *Pickwick*. One gets some idea of the almost unmanageable wave of popularity Dickens was trying to surf at the period of *Oliver Twist* from the fact that his third novel, *Nicholas Nickleby*, began appearing in March 1838 and ran till October 1839, an overlap of thirteen months. This is not to mention (during the *Oliver Twist* period alone) a successful play, *Is She His Wife? or, Something Singular!*, put on in March 1837 at the St James's Theatre. And Dickens's market value was shooting up all the time: the long-delayed *Barnaby Rudge*, initially valued at £200 for outright copyright, had risen in less than four years, by mid 1840, to £3,000 for an outright lease. It was mainly his swelling success, and Forster's encouragement, that incited him to resign as *Bentley's* editor – once *Oliver Twist* had been written – after a final quarrel about terms and conditions with the interfering and imprudently mean-spirited Richard Bentley, the 'Burlington Street Brigand' (who was, however, legally in the right).[5]

The repeated transfers of creative engagement between works seem to have been cross-fertilizing. They did not sap, but positively inspired Dickens. It was not till three months after little Oliver had escaped from the frying pan of the workhouse into the hellfire of Fagin's den in May 1837 that poor Mr Pickwick left the bustling world of inns, coaches and embarrassing scrapes, quixotically entering the reality of the Fleet debtors' prison, to encounter its squalid, debasing regime and its gaunt, isolated, desperate inmates. Pickwick is shocked, and Dickens denounces 'the just and wholesome law which declares that the sturdy felon shall be clothed, and that the penniless debtor shall be left to die of starvation and nakedness. This is no fiction' (ch. 42). The sarcasm here is, as Steven Marcus observes, 'the kind of social satire with which *Oliver Twist* is launched'; so that, as he brilliantly says, 'Dickens is that unique instance – a novelist whose first book might be said to have been influenced by his second.'

And, we might also say, his second by his third. The first episode of *Nicholas Nickleby* gives Dickens a dry run for the end of *Oliver Twist*, anticipating the trial and execution of Fagin, which was not written till later that year. The wandering Nicholas is chilled at the sudden sight of the exterior of Newgate, and has a vision of the deaths of men in the past – 'when curious eyes have glared from casement, and house-top, and wall and pillar, and when, in the mass of white and up-turned faces, the dying wretch, in his all-comprehensive look of agony, has met not one – not one – that bore the impress of pity or compassion'. This seems to recover through an anguish of identification something of the nightmare of Dickens's memory of the blacking factory, where he and Bob Fagin worked at a street window, 'so brisk at it, that the people used to stop and look in. Sometimes there would be quite a little crowd there. I saw my father coming in at the door one day when we were very busy, and I wondered how he could bear it.' The triggers of association were thus primed for use in Fagin's trial scene, with its court 'paved from floor to roof with human faces', 'a firmament all bright with beaming eyes' where 'in no one face . . . could he read the faintest sympathy with him' (III, 14).

It sharpens our appreciation of *Oliver Twist*, then, to see it as a thrilling triumph of improvisation, the work of a novelist discovering himself again – finding this time, deeper down than *Pickwick*, a more darkly imagined kind of novel. There has been disagreement among critics as to how far Dickens had worked out in advance the plot of the book; indeed, whether when he started he knew he was going to write a novel at all. We can in this edition read the work in its first, serial form – with a few rough edges, and moments of emotional overflow mostly stirred by his distress at the death in May 1837 of his beloved sister-in-law Mary Hogarth. Using this text gives us, so to speak, a ticket to the excitement of the première, a live performance, and allows us to get closer to the experience of Dickens's first readers. Only in *Bentley's Miscellany* is the town of Oliver's birth named, as

'Mudfog' (as if readers of *Bentley's* were simply receiving another of Dickens's occasional humorous 'Mudfog Chronicles'); only in *Bentley's* do we get some Fieldingesque paragraphs from the narrator on the topic of benevolence and self-interest, or a digression on digressions; and only in *Bentley's* is Nancy presented, more pertly and ironically, as 'Miss Nancy', still wearing the tartily 'gorgeous' attire of 'red gown, green boots, and yellow curl-papers' (I, 13), which is in later texts whisked off her, as it were, and draped instead on her colleague Bet.

Dickens had not yet written a tightly plotted novel, only a picaresque one, and so he had not developed the careful system of 'number-plans' that permitted the intricate hints, links and foreshadowings of such later works as *Bleak House* (tightness of plotting was in any case uncommon in the spacious, often serialized, fiction of the nineteenth century). The Dickensian scholar Burton M. Wheeler points out some examples of what he sees as a more freewheeling plotting technique adapted to serial publication, where you could not go back and change things as you wanted. Dickens, he says, leaves himself hints that are open for later development – as on the first morning in Fagin's den, where the old fence takes out one trinket 'so small that it lay in the palm of his hand. There seemed to be some very minute inscription on it, for the Jew . . . pored over it long and earnestly' (I, 9). In the event we never hear of this trinket again; it seems quite possible that Dickens planted it there in case he wanted to develop something from it later – perhaps to make it jewellery from the dead Agnes.

Another aspect of the spontaneity of *Oliver Twist* comes in with the involvement of the illustrator, whose contribution caused the young Henry James to remember the book as 'more Cruikshank's than Dickens's; it was a thing of such terribly vivid images'. Late in life, after Dickens's death, George Cruikshank would indeed claim, not very plausibly, that the idea for *Oliver Twist* was his. Yet he did play a crucial role, and not only because, as Baudelaire described it, his characteristic violent style involves a theatricality that chimes with Dickens's own – 'All his little characters are furiously and turbulently miming away like actors in a pantomime' – and is grim or cartoonish: 'The grotesque is habitual with him.'[6] When Dickens had his material well in hand, Cruikshank would receive each month's chapters to work from; but sometimes Dickens could only send a description by note or word of mouth. In 'Is Oliver Dreaming?', John Sutherland ingeniously but persuasively speculates that this arrangement may have been responsible for the bizarre and seemingly inexplicable episode at the Maylies' country house in II, 11, where Oliver, dozing at the window, seems to be having a nightmare in which he is back at Fagin's, only to wake and find Fagin and Monks right outside the window, really staring in at him – the image Cruikshank memorably fixes as 'Monks and the Jew'. They then vanish bafflingly, without trace – as if not real after all. Sutherland suggests that before actually writing the instalment, 'Dickens foresaw an abduction or murder attempt on Oliver, and duly instructed Cruikshank to go ahead with the villains-at-the-window illustration, preparatory to that scenario' – only to decide at short notice on a different tack, too late to replace the illustration, thus having to make the scene a possible hallucination.

Sutherland's theory intriguingly shows a symbolic or psychological complexity in the work – the question of Oliver's post-traumatic capacity for life without fear – arising out of a mundane accident of the collaborative circumstances of serial publication. The fact that it *could* be true, moreover, accentuates the perceptiveness of Richard Maxwell's comment that Cruikshank's interpretation of Dickens's story 'has a unique advantage. It can point up possibilities to the author as well as the reader; it can enter into the making of the work on which it comments.' Maxwell notes, for example, how Dickens picks up on suggestions in Cruikshank's plate of 'Oliver introduced to the respectable Old Gentleman' in the first chapter he wrote after approving it. The artist puts over the fireplace a broadsheet, unmentioned by Dickens, depicting three hanged criminals on the gallows, and works in a moral design, with a purposeful diagonal leading from the handkerchief filled with belongings in Oliver's hand to the kerchief round the Dodger's neck, then to the one knotted on Fagin's head and finally to the triple noose on the wall (stolen handkerchiefs are piled over a clotheshorse in the background). This is the path to the gallows Oliver is in danger of treading. Dickens seems freshly inspired by this when in I, 9 Fagin soliloquizes on capital punishment, on the 'Fine fellows' hanged that morning whom he apparently had employed and denounced. 'Five of them strung up in a row' answers (with two extra victims) Cruikshank's broadsheet, and suggests the likely fate of Fagin's young gang, which they choose to ignore in the delusive fug of their pipes and strong drink.

This is only one of the many kinds of meaning that Dickens's novel rolls up into itself as it gathers momentum. Writing *Oliver Twist* was an addiction; supposedly taking a break from it in Brighton in November 1837, Dickens had 'great difficulty keeping [his] hands off Fagin and the rest of them'. To read his letters of early October 1838, when, in a concentrated burst, with his door shut and callers told he had left town, he pushed through the breathtaking last chapters – Nancy's murder, the pursuit of Sikes, Fagin's final anguish – is to feel an author being carried along in a heightened state of possession, possession of but also possession *by* his material. While writing 'with greater power than I have been able to bring to bear on anything yet', Dickens fires curt dispatches to his confidant Forster, darkly humorous side-blasts from the forge: 'Hard at work still. – Nancy is no more. I shewed what I have done to Kate last night who was in an unspeakable "*state*", from which and my own impression I augur well. When I have sent Sikes to the Devil, I must have yours.' The murder of Nancy brings out something in Dickens that quite understandably puts his readers and hearers, starting with his wife, in a 'state' – as it still would years later when he began to perform 'Sikes and Nancy', or as he called it in 1869 'commit the murder', in his fatal, all-out theatrical readings. And after that horror and the harrowing quasi-accidental public hanging of Sikes, there still remained the trial and last hours of Fagin, which he may have written next, slightly out of sequence. He told Forster in a letter of October 1838 of 'not yet having disposed of the Jew who is such an out and outer that I don't know what to make of him'. Painfully, punitively imagining the numb horror of Fagin's final stunned days, what he later called 'the flush and fever of that flying interval between the Warrant and the Noose',[7] Dickens's sentences find an unadorned brevity that anticipates the sharpest early Hemingway: 'The jailer touched him on the shoulder. He followed mechanically to the end of the dock, and sat down on a chair. The man pointed it out, or he should not have seen it' (III, 14). And the jury's verdict some moments later is done as if in the note-form of a court-reporter: 'Perfect stillness ensued – not a rustle – not a breath – Guilty.' There is much that is as good as, but nothing *better* than these passages in all the rest of Dickens.

Oliver Twist is throughout an electrifying discovery of technique for the young novelist. When the Dodger approaches the desperate Oliver in Barnet and says, 'Hullo! my covey, what's the row?' (I, 8), Dickens's inventive prose doubles back to fill us in with a full paragraph on his strange appearance before catching itself up and repeating the line. Similarly, Bill Sikes first manifests himself as a deep, growling voice in an angry speech before being physically described. The writing is studded with gems of piercing detail, as later when Fagin hushes the noisy Sikes, in case someone hears their plan for the Chertsey crib: '"Let 'em hear!" said Sikes; "I don't care." But as Mr Sikes *did* care, upon reflection, he dropped his voice as he said the words, and grew calmer' (I, 19). 'As he said the words': we read them first as defiantly loud, but then are made to hear them – the way Sikes inwardly does – as imprudent, and thus with an instantaneous drop in volume. The contradiction between Sikes's violence and his self-interest, which ultimately undoes him, is precisely and unshowily rendered. Dickens's contemporary G. H. Lewes, later to be consort to George Eliot, remarked nicely in a review on the constant 'drollery' that 'his language, even on the most trivial points, has, from a peculiar collocation of the words, or some happy expression', attributing the effect to a 'fine . . . association of idea'. John Carey notes a lovely instance where the newly arrived Oliver 'washed himself and made everything tidy, by emptying the basin out of the window, agreeably to the Jew's directions' (I, 9). As he says, '"Agreeably to", which looks an innocent adverbial construction, makes a disdainful comment, in passing, about people who pour dirty water out of windows.' The verbal wit and life is often beyond 'drollery', as on the night after Fagin has learned from Noah of Nancy's supposed treachery, and sits biting his nails in passionate meditation, gazing into a candle – 'which, with long-burnt wick drooping almost double, and hot grease falling down in clots upon the table, plainly showed that his thoughts were busy elsewhere' (III, 9). 'Plainly showed' means, punningly, both that he neglects to trim it, and that its light makes plainly visible the sinister concentration on his face. We may not consciously register such intricate verbal ingenuities as we read, but they inevitably inform our sense of the novel's imagined world.

Behind the 1841 'Author's Introduction to the Third Edition', one of Dickens's fullest critical statements and printed here as Appendix A, there lies the notorious 'Newgate' controversy. In his second captivity Oliver is left a book by Fagin, 'a history of the lives and trials of great criminals', whose 'terrible descriptions were so vivid and real, that the sallow pages seemed to turn red with gore' (I, 20). The *Newgate Calendar*, the principal literary document of English crime, first published in 1728, which leaves Oliver in 'a paroxysm of fear', was the focus of the controversy over the sensationalism of the 'Newgate Novel', which, to Dickens's great disgust, caught up *Oliver Twist* in its toils a little after its first appearance. The popular press of the 1830s was strong stuff, as Louis James has shown in *English Popular Literature 1819–1851*, evoking a counterblast from organs like *Livesey's Moral Reformer*, which groaned in 1833 that 'Rapes and every obscenity are published to pander to the corrupt tastes of their readers.' Further upmarket, Edward Bulwer's (later Bulwer-Lytton's) criminal excursions – in particular *Paul Clifford* (written against capital punishment) and *Eugene Aram* in 1832 (the story of a real case of a scholar–murderer), both with some radical political undercurrent – had provoked Tory critics. In a different vein, the bestselling *Rookwood* in 1834, by William Harrison Ainsworth, who became a friend of Dickens in 1835, was a less politically-earnest historical romance, indeed a preposterously sensational ride into the eighteenth-century world of crime and criminals, a frenzied, sexy and violent melodrama of illegitimacy, tombs, oaths, curses, poison, disputed inheritances and concealed identities, with a jolly, glamorous Dick Turpin and a 'Canting Crew' of Gypsies thrown in. Ainsworth is nostalgic for that legendary age of crime ('we are sadly in want of highwaymen', he laments) in a way that Dickens – despite his friendship with the author, his enjoyment of the book, his borrowing of much of its cant terminology (thieves' slang) and perhaps his conscious tweaking of its hatred between a legitimate and an illegitimate brother – appears to be directly rejecting in the harsh modernities of *Oliver Twist*.

When Ainsworth wrote a new Preface to *Rookwood* in October 1837, he praised the delineation of London life in the early instalments of *Oliver Twist*; and Dickens became all too clearly associated with the sensational side of the 'Newgate Novel' when Ainsworth's next big hit, *Jack Sheppard*, based on the exploits of a notorious eighteenth-century thief, overlapped in *Bentley's Miscellany* (of which Ainsworth took over as editor in February 1839) with the last four instalments of *Oliver Twist* – which it exceeded in popularity. Robert Patten tells us that, just in case anyone was in danger of missing the connection, Bentley, cashing in on his copyrights after his quarrel with Dickens, would make a point of announcing the book-form of Ainsworth's shocker as 'uniform in size and price with *Oliver Twist*'. Early in 1840, Dickens told his friend R. H. Horne in a letter that 'I am by some jolter-headed enemies most unjustly and untruly charged with having written a book after Mr Ainsworth's fashion. Unto these jolter-heads [thick-heads] and their intensely concentrated humbug, I shall take an early opportunity of temperately replying.'

One of these alleged 'jolter-heads' was Thackeray, older by a year than Dickens but his junior in the world of books, whose indignation had inspired his first novel, *Catherine*, written under the pseudonym of 'Ikey Solomons Jr' (after a well-known Jewish fence till recently thought to be the original of Dickens's Fagin). *Catherine* started in May 1839 in the overtly political (Tory) *Fraser's Magazine* and ran parallel to *Jack Sheppard* as a parodic, mock-Newgate, commentary (its sordid, deliberately unsympathetic story came straight from the *Newgate Calendar*). In one of many asides in this intemperate attack, not reprinted in his lifetime, Thackeray declared: 'don't let us have any juggling and thimblerigging with vice and virtue, so that, at the end of three volumes, the bewildered reader shall not know which is which'. Refusing to accept characters in whom good and bad were mixed, and irritated by the double binds of Victorian self-censorship, Thackeray denounced Dickens's serious moral ambivalence as well as Ainsworth's thrill-seeking equivocation. According to Thackeray, in the February 1840 instalment of *Catherine*, responding doubtless to the rush of no fewer than six theatrical versions of *Oliver Twist* even before its serialization had finished, the reader was caused:

Breathless to watch all the crimes of Fagin, tenderly to deplore the errors of Nancy, to have for Bill Sikes a kind of pity and admiration, and an absolute love for the society of the Dodger . . . We had better pass them by in decent silence; for, as no writer can or dare tell the *whole* truth concerning them, and faithfully explain their vices, there is no need to give *ex-parte* statements of their virtues.

And what came of *Oliver Twist*? The public wanted something more extravagant still, more sympathy for thieves, and so *Jack Sheppard* makes his appearance.

The controversy intensified when on 5 May 1840, Courvoisier, a valet, murdered his 72-year-old master, Lord William Russell, subsequently proclaiming – allegedly anyway (Ainsworth disputed it) – 'that the idea of the crime had come to him upon reading *Jack Sheppard*'.[8] On 6 July, he was hanged before a crowd of about 30,000 which included, as we have seen, Dickens and Thackeray themselves – interested parties.

Thackeray's thrillingly unpredictable essay describing that occasion, 'On Going to see a Man Hanged', manages at one point a jab at *Oliver Twist* which extends his attack in *Catherine*. Among the teenage girls in the waiting crowd was 'one that Cruikshank and Boz might have taken as a study for Nancy. The girl was a young thief's mistress evidently.' She 'made no secret . . . as to her profession and means of livelihood'. Despite her shamelessness about being a prostitute, Thackeray declares, 'there was something good about the girl' in her reckless 'candour and simplicity'. She is with a friend.

I was curious to look at them, having, in late fashionable novels, read many accounts of such personages. Bah! what figments these novelists tell us! Boz, who knows life well, knows that his Miss Nancy is the most unreal fantastical personage possible; no more like a thief's mistress, than one of Gessner's shepherdesses[9] resembles a real country wench. He dare not tell the truth concerning such young ladies. They have, no doubt, virtues like other human creatures . . . But on these an honest painter of human nature has no right to dwell; not being able to paint the whole portrait, he has no right to present one or two favourable points as characterising the whole; and therefore, in fact, had better leave the picture alone altogether.

We have to pay attention to this line of attack. The logic of Thackeray's response echoes and extends Lord Melbourne's 'I don't *like* those things . . . in reality, and therefore I don't wish them represented.' Showing the full 'reality' is ruled out by censorship; showing anything less is cheating or glamorizing. Dickens's novel certainly leaves out some of the more sensational aspects of the criminal milieux of the time. Edward Gibbon Wakefield's chapter on 'Nurseries of Crime', in his remarkable non-fiction *Facts Relating to the Punishment of Death in the Metropolis* (1831), describes the use of girls by criminals like Fagin to draw boys, often as young as twelve, into thieving through 'the precocious excitement and gratification of the sexual passion'. That way of corrupting Oliver is omitted – as is the less dramatic method used by fences, apparently just as effective, of encouraging boys to borrow freely and plunge themselves so far into debt they had no choice but to thieve. Nancy's activity as a prostitute (her beat, clients, economic arrangements) is also completely left out, or at any rate left to our imagination. Even so, Thackeray's all-or-nothing argument seems askew, with its apparent fear that imaginative representations of the human complexity of crime will dangerously corrupt readers by breaking down the official barricades between the virtuous and the vicious.

When Dickens got his 'opportunity of temperately replying' in the Introduction to the Third Edition in April 1841, he produced the word missing from the novel: 'the girl is a prostitute'. He implicitly refused Thackeray's lumping of *Oliver Twist* with 'late fashionable novels', aligning his own clarity about the 'miserable reality' of contemporary urban criminal lives with Hogarth's and against the 'allurements and fascinations' of most criminal fictions, whose thieves are 'seductive fellows'. It may be a side-blow at some of the unauthorized theatrical versions of *Oliver Twist* when he contrasts the insupportability for fashionable audiences of 'a Sikes in fustian' with the glamour they find in a 'Massaroni in green velvet' – Massaroni being the 'very gentlemanly brigand, full of chivalry and romance', the 'Italian Robin Hood' (thus glorified in the play's introductory 'Remarks') of J. R. Planché's stage hit of 1829, *The Brigand: A Romantic Drama*. Dickens sees himself as attempting to reveal the barrenness of the supposedly thrilling life of crime, 'to dim the false glitter surrounding something which really did exist, by showing it in its unattractive and repulsive truth'. Putting, that is, the repulsion back into 'the attraction of repulsion'. And to Thackeray's argument that 'no writer can or dare tell the *whole* truth', Dickens answers with a different emphasis:

I endeavoured, while I painted it in *all* its fallen and degraded aspect, to banish from the lips of the lowest character I introduced, any expression that could by possibility offend; and rather to lead to the unavoidable inference that its existence was of the most debased and vicious kind, than to prove it elaborately by words and deeds.

Dickens is in one sense equivocating with 'I painted it in *all* its fallen and degraded aspect', since he *isn't* showing everything, all the 'words and deeds': offensive expressions are banished, Wakefield's 'gratification of the sexual passion' is mostly absent. But one could justify the claim to mean, in contrast with the Massaroni tradition, 'stripped of spurious glamour, reduced to its true moral squalor'. And the only significant sexual relation, between Sikes and Nancy, is an 'unavoidable inference' for the reader, just before the murder, when Sikes returns to 'his own room' to find Nancy lying on 'the bed' that – it goes without saying – they share. What he does with her there is shown in shocking explicitness.

In representing 'something which really did exist', only in a new harsher aspect, Dickens inevitably covers some of the same ground as the 'Newgate Novel' and the heroic criminal tradition. Half his terms of thieves' cant occur also in Ainsworth's *Rookwood* – but except in one place (I, 19) he eschews Ainsworth's footnote-translations with their learnedly witty, clubbish air. The presence of the 'green' Oliver usually means explanation can occur within the action, as when Charley Bates indicates 'by a lively pantomimic representation that scragging and hanging were one and the same thing' (I, 18). The comedy here of Charley's self-blinding gallows humour, like the humour of the

Dodger's entertaining courtroom defiance (based on the performance of a young pickpocket whose committal Dickens had witnessed), is part of the real delusive mentality of criminal life. And a novel on this subject must take a procedural interest in the techniques and arrangements of the criminal career, for, as Mayhew says in *The Criminal Prisons of London*, 'in order to obtain a regular living by criminal courses, it is necessary that the same apprenticeship should be served to the different forms of that business, as to any other trade'. Oliver's intended role in the Chertsey burglary is in fact an authentic 'rig', or trick, one not named in *Oliver Twist* but defined in Francis Grose's *Classical Dictionary of the Vulgar Tongue*: 'LITTLE SNAKES-MAN. A little boy who gets into a house through the sink-hole, and then opens the door for his accomplices; he is so called, from writhing and twisting like a snake, in order to work himself through the narrow passage.'

What distinguishes Dickens's vision of crime is the quality and intensity of his imagination, shown in the altogether appropriate alternation of comedy and serious grimness in his treatment of the criminal life. He sees beyond the apprenticeable trades of the underworld to something more universally human. As the Night-Inspector says in *Our Mutual Friend*, 'Burglary or pocket-picking wanted 'prenticeship. Not so, murder. We were all of us up to that' (ch. 3). In *Pickwick Papers* Dickens could have Sam Weller joke marvellously on the topic: 'Business first, pleasure arterwards, as King Richard the Third said ven he stabbed the t'other king in the Tower, afore he smothered the babbies' (ch. 25). There is no protective comic shield in *Oliver Twist*. Sikes crosses from the brutalizing habit of mere 'professional' crime into the spiritual horror of the murderer, shunned and self-tormented – a state Dickens so intimately recreates that he can think to record things one hopes he never saw: 'the reflection of the pool of gore that quivered and danced in the sunlight on the ceiling'; 'The very feet of the dog were bloody' (III, 10). And Nancy's murder confronts the book's materialists and mechanistic Utilitarians with the question of the soul. When her conscience is awakened Sikes comments that in her pallor, 'You look like a corpse come to life again' (III, 3); she is born again, fatally, as her not quite deadened spirit (and what Dickens calls 'the woman's original nature' (III, 3)) makes her turn painfully against the whole course of her life. This image of the revived corpse is punitively revised when Sikes is haunted by her on his terrible flight into the country: her figure follows him 'like a corpse endowed with the mere machinery of life' (III, 10). As John Bayley says, Sikes starts as an animal and 'murder turns him into a kind of man'. The minor thieves are horrified into 'shrinking off' from him (III, 11), and the hitherto frivolous Charley Bates is so 'appalled by Sikes's crime' he turns serious (III, 15), risking his life by attacking him. Later Charley actually reforms. Such deep moral antipathies and reverses, with their implicit rebuke to fictional indulgence, do not sit comfortably in the Newgate genre.

Dickens was evidently stung by the easy cynicism of Thackeray's announcement that 'his Miss Nancy is the most unreal fantastical personage possible', and the 1841 Introduction concludes with the impassioned claim about Nancy's character and conduct, her devotion to Sikes and risking of herself for Oliver, that 'IT IS TRUE.' The whole book is fascinating in its contradictory, thematically central, images of 'the woman's original nature': Mrs Bumble and Mrs Bedwin, Mrs Sowerberry and Mrs Maylie and, above all, Nancy and Rose Maylie. In a letter of November 1837 Dickens was particularly glad Forster liked I, 16 – where Nancy, instrumental in Oliver's recapture, turns on Fagin in instinctive rebellion when he strikes the boy, and flings his club 'into the fire with a force that brought some of the glowing coals whirling out into the room'. 'I hope to do great things with Nancy,' Dickens said. 'If I can only work out the idea I have formed of her, and of the female who is to contrast with her, I think I may defy Mr Hayward and all his works.' Abraham Hayward, reviewing Dickens's whole output in the October *Quarterly Review*, had praised the early numbers of *Oliver Twist* but saw a danger, if the young star continued to write so much, that having 'risen like a rocket, . . . he will come down like the stick'. Dickens indeed did not 'come down like the stick'; Nancy's trajectory, once Oliver is removed the second time into the bosom of the middle class, carries us deeper inside the thieves' world. We can see how powerfully Dickens imagined the span of Nancy's story in the ghastly echo, noted by John Carey, of this initial fiery 'whirling', when, after her murder, Sikes puts *his* club in the fire. 'There was human hair upon the end which blazed and shrunk into a light cinder, and, caught by the air, whirled up the chimney' (III, 10). The clubs and fires and whirlings mark the beginning and end of a tragic process.

In his 1898 study of Dickens, George Gissing, who in his youth had married a prostitute, implicitly disagreed with Thackeray: 'Nancy herself becomes credible by force of her surroundings and in certain scenes (for instance, that of her hysterical fury in Chapter XVI [I, 16]) is life itself.' Her sacrifice on Oliver's behalf, and yet her refusal to save herself by accepting Mr Brownlow's offer of refuge because 'I am chained to my old life' (III, 8), dramatizes the book's whole painful understanding of just how far – nearly all the way, but not quite – immersion in unchosen circumstances can dictate one's moral fate. The ineluctability of her death touches Shakespeare's *Othello* for tragic details: the handkerchief (Rose Maylie's, and redemptively a gift rather than a theft by poor from rich), the bedroom, the brutal overreaction of a deceived man of action. And then Sikes's fate draws on *Macbeth*: for the stress on the quantity of blood, the guilty hallucinations, the way he bears 'a charmed life' (III, 10) until the violent public death in the manner of a legal penalty. The echoes, unforced, do not impede our violent onrush to disaster.

It must be confessed that much in the book fails to reach Shakespearean heights. Gissing, though an admirer of *Oliver Twist*, put his finger on 'the two blemishes of the book': 'Monks with his insufferable (often ludicrous) rant, and his absurd machinations', and 'the feeble idyllicism of the Maylie group'. And much of the plotting, especially later on – probably because of Dickens's inexperience and the improvisatory nature of the writing – seems clumsily contrived, or at least seems clumsily revealed because ill prepared. Its accumulated coincidences are extraordinary, as a mere sample will indicate. The pocket picked by Charley and the Dodger when Oliver first goes out from Fagin's happens to be that of Mr Brownlow, the oldest friend of Oliver's father, and once in love with Oliver's aunt (now dead), who happens to have on his wall a portrait of Oliver's mother, which so resembles Oliver Mr Brownlow is awestruck. When Sikes takes Oliver after his recapture to commit his second crime, at Chertsey, hours away from London, it turns out to be the house where Oliver's other aunt, Rose Maylie, lives. Oliver's father's will, destroyed by the father's wife, happens to have stipulated that Oliver inherits only if 'in his minority he should never have stained his name with any public act of dishonour, meanness, cowardice, or wrong' (III, 13) – such a stain is just what falling into Fagin's hands puts Oliver at risk of; Oliver's legitimate but wicked brother Edward Leeford ('Monks') happens to be the only one to know of this will, *and* to see and recognize Oliver, whom he has never seen (this time by his uncanny resemblance to their common father), on the one occasion he is away from Fagin's (and rescued by Mr Brownlow). Somehow Monks connects him with, and somehow finds, Fagin, whom he employs to recapture and criminalize him. All this contrivance is amazing, when runaway boys were routinely sucked into London crime by Fagins anyway, as the book vividly illustrates with Noah Claypole.

But such an enumeration makes plain that, as K. J. Fielding says, 'our grasp on *Oliver Twist* depends on not trying to read it as if it were "realistic"' – at least in these sections. Even if one reflects that Oliver's dual resemblance to father and mother is not an impossible phenomenon, and grants some other links, the demands made of the reader's credulity seem excessive unless one takes seriously Dickens's invocation of what Mr Brownlow calls 'a stronger hand than chance' (III, 11 – and not just the author's own manipulations, either). The alliterative subtitle, 'The Parish Boy's Progress', invokes the religious allegory of Bunyan's providential *Pilgrim's Progress* (1678) – which makes sense, given the preoccupation with the soul in the more artistically successful parts of the novel. Or, if we wish to understand this closed world of intricately knitted meanings as pointing to a more modern or secular subjectivity, we can think ahead to Franz Kafka and the dreamlike paranoid encounters of *The Trial* (1925), where figures met seemingly by chance have repeatedly some uncanny personal relation to the hero, Josef K.

In a sense we are paying, in the delayed and thus weakened

explanations that occur in some later parts of the book, and paying too in the ravings and machinations of Monks, for the hypnotic power of the first half. The power, for instance, of the magnificently unmotivated, and thus apparently satanic, malignity of Fagin towards Oliver. With 'his face wrinkled into an expression of villany perfectly demoniacal' (I, 19), the devilish 'old gentleman' seems to need no contrived motive, beyond evil's congenital hatred of innocence, to want Oliver to be 'ours, – ours for his life!' (I, 19). It is intoxicatingly full-blooded. There is, however, a sinister side to the initial mythic effect Fagin makes before the complicating, somewhat deflating explanations kick in. We must be uneasy about the anti-Semitic legends of child-killing which Dickens irresponsibly allows to colour or 'naturalize' a phrase like 'the wily old Jew had the boy in his toils' (I, 18); Fagin's red hair, miserliness, resemblance to the devil, inhuman air of a 'goblin' or 'hideous phantom' or 'loathsome reptile' (III, 5, 9; I, 19), and general malevolence, all have some invidious connection with racial stereotype. Further on in his career Dickens, himself by habit not more than a casual anti-Semite, was to make partial amends when a Jewish lady he knew protested against his encouragement of 'a vile prejudice against the despised Hebrew', by creating the virtuous Riah in *Our Mutual Friend*.[10] Dickens's defence that Fagin was Jewish 'because it unfortunately was true of the time to which that story refers, that that class of criminal almost invariably *was* a Jew' is inadequate justification of the array of stereotypical stage properties with which he adorns his old crook (the most notorious Jewish fence of the time, Ikey Solomons, was brown-haired and beardless, and wore smart modern dress). The strongest mitigating circumstance may be Dickens's intense relish of and twisted identification with this unforgettable embodiment of self-interest, especially at the end when Fagin faces the gallows. Although the musical *Oliver!* (1960; filmed 1969), really a celebration of cockney life in the 1960s as it was collapsing, is by some measures a crude neutering and jollification of the novel, the fun its Jewish East-End composer Lionel Bart finds in his hero Fagin, displacing the serious evil on to Sikes, does correspond to something true about the novel – Dickens's uninhibited imaginative investment in his most antisocial characters. The modern reader of *Oliver Twist*, however pained by the constant references to 'the Jew', is bound to find Fagin *as a character* weakened, artistically, by his compromising link with Monks: Fagin is unconvincingly made to lament being 'bound . . . to a born devil that only wants the will, and has got the power to, to—' (II, 4). Dickens is unable to make Monks live up to this billing; we can't easily believe in Monks's 'power to' harm Fagin. Maybe, though, we *should*, as the mere weasel Noah Claypole can bring him to the gallows. Perhaps, indeed, the conception of Monks's tireless, cowardly malice and diseased, depraved nature – combined with his money – does have a greater force than is usually acknowledged as a picture of human evil, especially if we can adjust to the melodramatic idiom in which he is presented.

In his movements between high and low, Monks represents the book's most concrete connection between the bourgeois overworld and the criminal underworld, but there is another sense in which Dickens offers Oliver and us no real escape from Fagin and Sikes, in which even the artistic weakness of the good characters contributes to the novel's power. Henry James comments stimulatingly on his childhood experience of *Oliver Twist* through Cruikshank's illustrations that

the offered flowers or goodnesses, the scenes and figures intended to comfort and cheer, present themselves under his hand as but more subtly sinister, or more suggestively queer, than the frank badness and horrors. The nice people and the happy moments, in the plates, frightened me almost as much as the low and the awkward.

It is not just the plates that can provoke this disturbed reaction. The cosiness of the refuges offered by Mr Brownlow and the Maylies, their perfection as an obverse to captivity in the workhouse and Fagin's perch in the rookery, strike many readers as too good to be true, too convenient to be real – as if the whole action were a dream, a mere acting-out of wishes and fears. John Bayley puts this view forcefully: 'Even the apparent contrast between Fagin's world and that of Rose Maylie and Mr Brownlow is not a real one, and this is not because the happy Brownlow world is rendered sentimentally and unconvincingly by Dickens, but because the two do in fact co-exist in consciousness:

they are twin sides of the same coin of fantasy, not two real places that exist separately in life.' This seems borne out by the rhyming of Fagin and Brownlow as 'old gentlemen' (with Fagin seeming to imitate Brownlow in the pickpocketing game even before we see him), or the way the scene between Rose and Nancy 'bore more the semblance of a rapid dream than an actual occurrence' (III, 3) – and by the comparative lack in the Brownlow–Maylie scenes of what Henry James in his essay 'The Art of Fiction' (1884) would call 'solidity of specification', of street names, quirky details, relish in the language. The unsettling of realistic logic gives access to a profounder significance. G. K. Chesterton said it beautifully: 'As a nightmare, the work is really admirable. Characters which are not very clearly conceived as regards their own psychology are yet, at certain moments, managed so as to shake to its foundations our own psychology.' For much of the action, moreover, Oliver is ill or convalescent – confused, faint, delirious, woozy or actually unconscious – which grounds and partly justifies the lurid heightening of perception in Dickens's prose.

Another aspect of what has been called the book's 'Manichean' vision is that its 'good' bourgeois world is emphatically unofficial, operates quite apart from, and more efficiently than, the institutions of the state and their hierarchies. Mr Brownlow has to defy the magistrate Fang in order to save Oliver; Dr Losberne bullies the servants into backing his lies to the Bow Street Runners, again in order to save Oliver, after the Chertsey burglary. There is another challenging rhyme, suggesting an even darker sense of the benevolent conspiracy on Oliver's behalf: between the £25 bribe with which Losberne rewards the servant Giles for colluding in the lie that deceives the police, and the £25 bribe paid by Monks to Mrs Bumble for information about Oliver. The 'good' characters form a private 'committee' in the end, acting without reference to the law, and effectively kidnap Monks in order to torment and threaten him into submission (their easy success may well surprise us). They do this because they believe Oliver's story of his innocence, despite his inability to produce any evidence of it (which means he cannot have recourse to the official world that requires provable facts). Oliver's unbelievability, in fact, is part of his nightmare; we might connect his inability to vindicate himself with his illegitimacy as another mark of the outcast. Dr Losberne comments that 'he can only prove the parts that look bad' (II, 8), and perhaps this is the chief point of the seeming hallucination of Fagin and Sikes at the window, or the bizarre episode with the raving hunchback at the house by Chertsey Bridge, where Losberne does not lose faith in his young protégé despite the fact that 'not an article of furniture, not a vestige of anything, animate or inanimate, not even the position of the cupboards, answered Oliver's description!' (II, 9).

Oliver's experience of exclusion, then, and Nancy's, enforces on readers of the novel a view of society from the outside, and an understanding of the passionate necessity of having 'friends', a word that formerly could mean kinsmen or near relations. Nancy says to Rose (herself thought illegitimate, but luckier), 'Thank Heaven upon your knees, dear lady, . . . that you had friends to care for and keep you in your childhood' (III, 3). Oliver's desolate early years in the workhouse world as what Mr Bumble calls 'a naughty orphan which nobody can love' leave him emotionally scarred (I, 3). In *Bentley's Miscellany* he gives a harrowing statement of how he feels (cut down in subsequent editions) which forces even Bumble to cover his residual human response with husky-voiced coughing:

'So lonely, sir – so very lonely,' cried the child. 'Everybody hates me. Oh! sir, don't be cross to me. I feel as if I had been cut here, sir, and it was all bleeding away;' and the child beat his hand upon his heart, and looked into his companion's face with tears of real agony. (I, 4)

That 'Everybody hates me' is not quite true, but for practical purposes it's often true enough in the bleak England Dickens shows us. We find it so in the gratuitous meanness of the coach passengers to the starving Oliver as he limps towards London, or in the perversity of Brownlow's friend Grimwig as he sends Oliver on an errand he hopes will show him to be a liar and thief, or in the instant prejudiced approval of the onlookers in the street ('It'll do him good!') for the violent blows Bill Sikes delivers to Oliver's head as he recaptures the boy for Fagin (I, 15). 'Tears of real agony' are hardly an excessive reaction. It is as a guard against such raw, wounded solitude and its dangers that the cosy surrogate families and makeshift communities of Dickens's novels are constructed. The lonely are vulnerable to temptation, as we see in Oliver's second captivity at Fagin's, where after days of solitary confinement he is only 'too happy to have some faces, however bad, to look upon' (I, 18), and, in his relief at being in company, much enjoys Fagin's droll retelling of robberies he has committed: he 'could not help laughing heartily, and showing that he was amused in spite of all his better feelings'. Dickens knows the limits of resistance, and we should sense here how possible it is that Oliver may enter the life of crime and fulfil the prediction of the gentleman in the white waistcoat. When we learn of Oliver's mother's dying prayer for her baby, it is a statement of what we could see as the book's great yearning, an impulse born of Dickens's own childhood and constituting the serious ground of all the imaginative life and energy and humour of *Oliver Twist*: she asks God 'to raise up some friends for it in this troubled world, and take pity upon a lonely desolate child abandoned to its mercy!' (II, 2).

NOTES

1. Reprinted in *Charles Dickens: The Critical Heritage*, ed. Philip Collins. For details of this and other works cited in the Introduction, see 'Further Reading'. I have used notes only where sources of quotations are not obvious.

2. Quoted in *The Letters of Charles Dickens*, ed. Madeline House and Graham Storey, I, p. 279 (hereafter '*Letters*'). As a humorist and social observer, Barham himself, later a friend of Dickens, would touch on a central concern of *Oliver Twist* in 'The Execution: A Sporting Anecdote', a scathing 1840 account of an Egan-like aristocratic excursion to witness a public execution included in his popular comic verse-tale collection *The Ingoldsby Legends*. The vacuous, thrill-seeking Lord Tomnoddy believes that

> To see a man swing, at the end of a string,
> With his neck in a noose, will quite a new thing.

He hires a first-floor room in a public house, the Magpie and Stump, opposite the gallows at the front of Newgate Prison for himself and his friends. But they eat and drink too much the night before, and sleep through the event.

3. Dated 28 February 1846, reprinted in *The Law as Literature: An Anthology*

of Great Writing in and about the Law, ed. Louis Blom-Cooper, p. 385. These feelings of revulsion persisted in Dickens: 'Coming here from the Station this morning, I met, coming from the execution of the Walworth Murderer, such a tide of ruffians as never could have flowed from any point but the Gallows. Without any figure of speech, it turned one white and sick to behold them' (1860; *Letters*, IX, p. 303).

4. The phrase is implicit in *Oliver Twist*, II, 4, where the Three Cripples' clients' countenances 'irresistibly attracted the attention by their very repulsiveness'.

5. Robert L. Patten, *Charles Dickens and his Publishers*, p. 86; *Letters*, I, p. 619. Dickens's friend W. C. Macready confided to his diary his real sense of the rights and wrongs of the dispute: '[Dickens] makes a contract, which he considers advantageous at the time, but subsequently finding his talent more lucrative than he had supposed, he refused to fulfil the contract' (quoted in *Charles Dickens and his Publishers*, p. 85).

6. Charles Baudelaire, quoted in J. Hillis Miller, 'The Fiction of Realism: *Sketches by Boz*, *Oliver Twist* and Cruikshank's Illustrations', p. 141.

7. Kathleen Tillotson, 'A Letter from Dickens on Capital Punishment' (from the *Daily News*, 23 February 1846), *Times Literary Supplement*, 12 August 1965, p. 704.

8. Quoted in Keith Hollingsworth, *The Newgate Novel 1830–1847: Bulwer, Ainsworth, Dickens, and Thackeray*, p. 143. Dickens in the letter of 28 February 1846 calls this 'his wicked defence' (*The Law as Literature*, ed. Blom-Cooper, p. 385).

9. Salomon Gessner (1730–88) was a German pastoral poet.

10. See *Charles Dickens and His Jewish Characters*, ed. Cumberland Clark, p. 18. See also note 9 to I, 8. Dickens also revised many of the references to 'the Jew' in the 1867 'Charles Dickens' edition. See 'Selected Textual Variants'.

FURTHER READING

DICKENS'S WORKS

Sketches by Boz, ed. Dennis Walder (London: Penguin Classics, 1995).
The Pickwick Papers, ed. Mark Wormald (London: Penguin Classics, 1999).
Nicholas Nickleby, ed. Mark Ford (London: Penguin Classics, 1999).

The Letters of Charles Dickens, ed. Madeline House and Graham Storey (assoc. edr. Kathleen Tillotson), The Pilgrim Edition, 10 vols. to date (Oxford: Clarendon Press, 1965–).
Letter to *The Daily News*, 23 February 1846. Reprinted by Kathleen Tillotson, 'A Letter from Dickens on Capital Punishment', *Times Literary Supplement*, 12 August 1965, p. 704.
Letter to *The Daily News*, 28 February 1846. Reprinted in *The Law as Literature: An Anthology of Great Writing in and about the Law*, ed. Louis Blom-Cooper (London: Bodley Head, 1961), pp. 382–7.

Dickens' Journalism, ed. Michael Slater, 4 vols. (London: J. M. Dent, 1993–).
The Annotated Dickens, ed. Edward Guiliano and Philip Collins, 2 vols. (New York: Clarkson N. Potter, 1986).
Kathleen Tillotson, ed., *Oliver Twist* (in the Clarendon Dickens) (Oxford: Clarendon Press, 1966).

DICKENS'S CONTEMPORARIES

William Harrison Ainsworth, *Rookwood*, 3 vols. (London: Richard Bentley, 1834).
——, *Jack Sheppard*, 3 vols. (London: Richard Bentley, 1840).

R. H. Barham, 'The Execution: A Sporting Anecdote', in *The Ingoldsby Legends* (London: Richard Bentley, 1843).

Thomas Beames, *The Rookeries of London* (1850, 2nd edn, 1852; reprinted London: Frank Cass, 1970).

Edward Bulwer-Lytton, *Paul Clifford*, 3 vols. (London: H. Colburn & R. Bentley, 1830).

——, *Eugene Aram* (1832).

Pierce Egan, *Life in London: or, the Day and Night Scenes of Jerry Hawthorn, Esq. and his Elegant Friend Corinthian Tom, Accompanied by Bob Logic, the Oxonian, in their Rambles and Sprees through the Metropolis* (London: Sherwood, Neely & Jones, 1821; reprinted London: Methuen, 1904).

John Forster, *The Life of Charles Dickens* (1872–4; reprinted London: Chapman & Hall, n.d).

[Abraham Hayward], anonymous review, 'The Pickwick Papers etc.', *Quarterly Review* 59 (October 1837), 484–518.

Louis James, *English Popular Literature 1819–1851* (New York: Columbia University Press, 1976).

G. H. Lewes, review of Dickens's early work (1837). Reprinted in Collins, *Charles Dickens: The Critical Heritage*.

[Thomas H. Lister], review of 'Dickens's *Tales*', *Edinburgh Review* 68 (October 1838), 75–97.

Henry Mayhew and John Binny, *The Criminal Prisons of London* (London: Griffin, Bohn, 1862).

William Makepeace Thackeray, *Catherine*, *Fraser's Magazine* 19–21 (May 1839 to February 1840).

——, 'On Going to See a Man Hanged' *Fraser's Magazine* 22 (August 1840).

Edward Gibbon Wakefield, *Facts Relating to the Punishment of Death in the Metropolis* (London: E. Wilson, 1831).

LATER SCHOLARS AND CRITICS

Peter Ackroyd, *Dickens* (London: Sinclair-Stevenson, 1990).

Regina Barreca, '"The Mimic Life of the Theatre": The 1838

Adaptation of *Oliver Twist*', in *Dramatic Dickens*, ed. Carol Hanbery MacKay (New York: St Martin's Press, 1989).

John Bayley, 'Oliver Twist: "things as they really are"', in *Dickens and the Twentieth Century*, ed. John Gross and Gabriel Pearson (London: Routledge & Kegan Paul, 1962), pp. 49–64.

John Carey, *The Violent Effigy: A Study of Dickens' Imagination* (London: Faber, 1973; 2nd edn, 1991).

G. K. Chesterton, *Appreciations and Criticisms of the Works of Charles Dickens* (London: J. M. Dent, 1911).

Kathryn Chittick, *Dickens and the 1830s* (Cambridge: Cambridge University Press, 1990).

Cumberland Clark (ed.), *Charles Dickens and his Jewish Characters* (London: Chiswick Press, 1918).

Philip Collins, *Dickens and Crime* (1962; Bloomington: Indiana University Press, 1968).

—— (ed.), *Charles Dickens: The Critical Heritage* (London: Routledge & Kegan Paul, 1971).

K. J. Fielding, 'Benthamite Utilitarianism and *Oliver Twist*: A Novel of Ideas', *Dickens Quarterly* 4 (1987), 49–65.

George H. Ford, *Dickens and his Readers: Aspects of Novel-Criticism since 1836* (Princeton: Princeton University Press, 1955).

V. A. C. Gatrell, *The Hanging Tree: Execution and the English People 1770–1868* (Oxford: Oxford University Press, 1994).

George Gissing, *Charles Dickens* (1898; reprinted New York: Haskell House, 1974).

Graham Greene, 'The Young Dickens' (1950), in *Dickens: Modern Judgements*, ed. A. E. Dyson (London: Macmillan, 1968).

Keith Hollingsworth, *The Newgate Novel 1830–1847: Bulwer, Ainsworth, Dickens, and Thackeray* (Detroit: Wayne State University Press, 1963).

Humphry House, *The Dickens World*, 2nd edn (Oxford: Oxford University Press, 1942).

Henry James, *A Small Boy and Others* (1913), in *Henry James: Autobiography*, ed. F. W. Dupee (New York: Criterion Books, 1956).

Steven Marcus, *Dickens: From Pickwick to Copperfield* (London: Chatto & Windus, 1965).

Richard Maxwell, *The Mysteries of Paris and London* (Charlottesville and London: University of Virginia Press, 1992).

Robert Mighall, *A Geography of Victorian Gothic Fiction* (Oxford: Clarendon Press, 1999).

J. Hillis Miller, 'The Fiction of Realism: *Sketches by Boz*, *Oliver Twist* and Cruikshank's Illustrations', in *Dickens Centennial Essays*, ed. Ada B. Nisbet and Blake Nevius (Berkeley: University of California Press, 1971), pp. 85–153.

Norman Page, *A Dickens Chronology* (London: Macmillan Press, 1988).

David Paroissien, *Oliver Twist: An Annotated Bibliography* (New York and London: Garland, 1986).

——, *The Companion to 'Oliver Twist'* (Edinburgh: Edinburgh University Press, 1992).

Robert L. Patten, *Dickens and his Publishers* (Oxford: Clarendon Press, 1978).

Adrian Poole, 'The Shadow of Lear's "Houseless" in Dickens', *Shakespeare Survey 53: Shakespeare and Narrative*, ed. Peter Holland (Cambridge: Cambridge University Press, 2000), pp. 103–13.

F. S. Schwarzbach, *Dickens and the City* (London: Athlone Press, 1979).

F. W. H. Sheppard, *London, 1808–71: The Infernal Wen* (London: Secker & Warburg, 1971).

Michael Slater, *Dickens and Women* (London: J. M. Dent, 1983).

Richard L. Stein, *Victoria's Year: English Literature and Culture, 1837–1838* (New York: Oxford University Press, 1987).

Harry Stone, 'Dickens and the Jews', *Victorian Studies* 2 (1959), 223–53.

John Sutherland, 'Is Oliver Dreaming?', in *Is Heathcliff a Murderer: Great Puzzles in Nineteenth-Century Literature* (Oxford: World's Classics, 1996), pp. 35–45.

——, 'Why is Fagin Hanged and Why isn't Pip Prosecuted?', in *Can Jane Eyre Be Happy? More Puzzles in Classic Fiction* (Oxford: World's Classics, 1997), pp. 52–63.

——, 'Does Dickens Lynch Fagin?', in *Who Betrays Elizabeth Bennet? Further Puzzles in Classic Fiction* (Oxford: World's Classics, 1999), pp. 44–8.

Kathleen Tillotson, 'Introduction', *Oliver Twist*, The Clarendon Dickens (Oxford: Clarendon Press, 1966), pp. xv–xlvii.

——, 'Oliver Twist', *Essays and Studies*, 12 (1959), 87–105.

——, '*Oliver Twist* in Three Volumes', *The Library* 18 (June 1963), 113–32.

J. J. Tobias, *Crime and Industrial Society in the Nineteenth Century* (London: Bateford, 1967).

——, 'Ikey Solomons – a real-life Fagin', *Dickensian* 65: 3 (September 1969), 171–5.

Burton M. Wheeler, 'The Text and Plan of Oliver Twist', *Dickens Studies Annual*, 12 (1983), 41–61.

Edmund Wilson, 'Dickens: The Two Scrooges', in *The Wound and the Bow: Seven Studies in Literature* (1941; reprinted London: Methuen, 1961), pp. 1–93.

A NOTE ON THE TEXT

This is the first critical edition to take as copy-text the original periodical version of *Oliver Twist, or, The Parish Boy's Progress* in *Bentley's Miscellany*, which ran from February 1837 to April 1839 in twenty-four instalments (with no instalments in May 1837, October 1837 or September 1838). Dickens was himself the editor of *Bentley's Miscellany* until the last of several clashes with its publisher Richard Bentley, about money, editorial control, etc., led to his resignation on 31 January 1839. The public's first opportunity to read the last nine chapters came with Bentley's rapid publication of the novel in three-volume form at 25 shillings on 9 November 1838 – before the end of its serial appearance. Dickens had given the printers the text for the complete novel on 20 October 1838 (consisting of the *Bentley's Miscellany* instalments up to that of October 1838 – he made some revisions subsequently on the proof – and of manuscript for the last eleven chapters). The divisions between magazine instalments are marked in this text with an asterisk (*).

The editor of what Dickens saw as his first real novel is confronted with several difficult choices when it comes to the text. The main textual sources are: the *Bentley's Miscellany* text, set from manuscript up to November 1838 and thereafter from the first book-edition (hereafter *Bentley's*); the November 1838 Bentley first book-edition in three volumes (hereafter *1838*), which was the basis for several reissues including the 1841 'third edition'; the major 1846 revised edition (hereafter *1846*), issued in ten monthly parts and then a single volume (frequently reprinted and the basis of Kathleen Tillotson's 1966 Clarendon Press edition); the 1850 'Cheap Edition'; and the last lifetime edition, the 'Charles Dickens' of 1867. (There is in addition the incomplete manuscript, surviving in the Victoria & Albert Museum, from which some readings are given in the Selected Textual Variants.)

The choice of *Bentley's Miscellany*, which is unavailable outside

1

research libraries, as a copy-text may be controversial, but Richard Altick, in his review of the Clarendon edition, cites Tillotson's judgement that 'the text achieves stability only in 1846', and comments persuasively:

Little complaint can be made of this rationale; yet it seems to me that there is an equally good argument for choosing an earlier text, either that of the serialization in *Bentley's Miscellany* or that of the first book-form publication, the Bentley edition of 1838. If, to invoke what is by now a critical common-place, the totality of a literary work as we now have it embraces and is significantly affected by the history of its reception, one may plead that a text which faithfully represents the book in its pristine form has at least as much value as one which embodies the results of the author's second thoughts. It represents the work as it was at the most critical moment of its life. In a case like Dickens's, in the history of whose career the factor of immediate and immense popularity is so important, such an argument seems to me to have especial validity.

1838 was produced in some haste (in order to be on the market early enough to tempt impatient readers from the serial), and the last portion in manuscript was delivered to the printer no earlier than 20 October, leaving little time before publication on 9 November (and Dickens went to Wales for the crucial last eleven days). Its setting, like that of the earlier part of the novel from *Bentley's*, was divided between two printers (though this was not unusual at the time). Dickens saw proof of much (and just possibly, at the last minute, of all) of the book, and he refined details of phrasing, as well as attempting to iron out wrinkles in the timing of the plot; but there was no large-scale revision.

Bentley's gives us a slightly longer book; in the early stages of composition, as Tillotson points out, 'Dickens made some quite considerable *cuts* – the three-volume version is slightly shorter than the *Miscellany* version, and that is considerably shorter than the manuscript version' ('*Oliver Twist* in Three Volumes'). There are thus some long passages which now appear in the novel for the first time in a critical edition. *Bentley's* is also, famously, the only text in which the town where Oliver is born and raised in the workhouse is named, as 'Mudfog'. The division of chapters between the three (unequal) Books of *Bentley's* (22, 14 and 15 chapters respectively) is lost in all subsequent editions. In *1838*, chapters are simply numbered up to fifty-one, with no division of Books; in *1846*, the divisions are slightly different (helping to fit the text into ten parts), and there are 53 chapters.

Another decisive factor in the present choice of copy-text is that as editor of *Bentley's Miscellany*, which was an elegantly produced gentlemen's magazine (not particularly aimed at a 'family' readership), Dickens was responsible for revising and correcting all articles accepted, and for correcting proof. He thus seems to have closely supervised the *Bentley's* appearance of *Oliver Twist* at least up until his resignation from the editorship (and Tillotson notes, 'There is also some evidence of Dickens's proof-correction of *Bentley's* instalments after December'). The involvement of the author, the care that was taken over the *Bentley's* text in its handsome page and the generally accepted view that in Tim Cribb's words 'awareness of the instalment form should be an essential part in the normal experience of reading Dickens', have all weighed heavily in the selection of the serial text.

I have aimed at producing a clear reading text, with a minimum of alteration or emendation of *Bentley's*. In a few places I have felt forced to emend self-evident errors affecting the sense and thus the flow of reading; I have signalled emendations in the list of Selected Textual Variants and one or two in the Notes. In accordance with usual Penguin Classics house style, double quotation marks have become single; m-dashes have become spaced n-dashes (and 2m-dashes m's); and titles (e.g. Mr, Mrs) have lost their full stop. The chapter titles are in capitals (as in *Bentley's* and later editions), but are in italics here.

The illustrations by George Cruikshank (see Introduction, pp. xxiii, xxvi–xxvii) appeared in *Bentley's Miscellany* and most subsequent illustrated editions.

At the end of this edition there is a list of 'Selected Textual Variants', which is designed to give readers a general sense of the significant differences between the texts, and to show that they can be interesting.

For a full history of the novel's composition and text, readers should consult Tillotson's Introduction to her Clarendon edition, and her '*Oliver Twist* in Three Volumes'; and also Burton M. Wheeler's subsequent and fiendishly imaginative account of the work's evolution in 'The Text and Plan of Oliver Twist'. Dickens's fraught relations with Bentley, whom he called in 1840 'the Burlington Street Brigand', are carefully but fascinatingly detailed in Robert L. Patten's *Charles Dickens and His Publishers*, and also in Kathryn Chittick's *Dickens and the 1830s*. Significant contributions to the debate over editorial approach were made in reviews of the Clarendon edition by: Richard D. Altick, in *Victorian Studies* 11 (March 1968), 415–16; Fredson Bowers, in *Nineteenth Century Fiction* 23 (September 1968), 226–39; and Timothy Cribb, in *Review of English Studies* 19 (February 1968), 87–91.

OLIVER TWIST,

OR, THE PARISH BOY'S PROGRESS.

BY BOZ.
ILLUSTRATED BY GEORGE CRUIKSHANK.

CHAPTER THE FIRST

TREATS OF THE PLACE WHERE OLIVER TWIST WAS BORN, AND OF THE CIRCUMSTANCES ATTENDING HIS BIRTH

Among other public buildings in the town of Mudfog,[1] it boasts of one which is common to most towns great or small, to wit, a workhouse;[2] and in this workhouse there was born on a day and date which I need not trouble myself to repeat, inasmuch as it can be of no possible consequence to the reader, in this stage of the business at all events, the item of mortality[3] whose name is prefixed to the head of this chapter. For a long time after he was ushered into this world of sorrow and trouble, by the parish surgeon,[4] it remained a matter of considerable doubt whether the child would survive to bear any name at all; in which case it is somewhat more than probable that these memoirs would never have appeared, or, if they had, being comprised within a couple of pages, they would have possessed the inestimable merit of being the most concise and faithful specimen of biography extant in the literature of any age or country. Although I am not disposed to maintain that the being born in a workhouse is in itself the most fortunate and enviable circumstance that can possibly befal a human being, I do mean to say that in this particular instance it was the best thing for Oliver Twist that could by possibility have occurred. The fact is, that there was considerable difficulty in inducing Oliver to take upon himself the office of respiration, – a troublesome practice, but one which custom has rendered necessary to our easy existence, – and for some time he lay gasping on a little flock mattress, rather unequally poised between this world and the next, the balance being decidedly in favour of the latter. Now, if during this brief period Oliver had been surrounded by careful grandmothers, anxious aunts, experienced nurses, and doctors of profound wisdom, he would most inevitably and indubitably have been killed in no time. There being nobody by, however, but a pauper old woman, who was rendered rather misty by an unwonted allowance of beer, and a parish surgeon who did such matters by contract, Oliver and nature fought out the point between them. The result was, that, after a few struggles, Oliver breathed, sneezed, and proceeded to advertise to the inmates of the workhouse the fact of a new burden having been imposed upon the parish, by setting up as loud a cry as could reasonably have been expected from a male infant who had not been possessed of that very useful appendage, a voice, for a much longer space of time than three minutes and a quarter.

As Oliver gave this first testimony of the free and proper action of his lungs, the patchwork coverlet, which was carelessly flung over the iron bedstead, rustled; the pale face of a young female was raised feebly from the pillow; and a faint voice imperfectly articulated the words 'Let me see the child, and die.'

The surgeon had been sitting with his face turned towards the fire, giving the palms of his hands a warm, and a rub, alternately; but as the young woman spoke, he rose, and, advancing to the bed's head, said with more kindness than might have been expected of him –

'Oh, you must not talk about dying, yet.'

'Lor bless her dear heart, no!' interposed the nurse, hastily depositing in her pocket a green glass bottle, the contents of which she had been tasting in a corner with evident satisfaction. 'Lor bless her dear heart, when she has lived as long as I have, sir, and had thirteen children of her own, and all on 'em dead except two, and them in the wurkus with me, she'll know better than to take on in that way, bless her dear heart! Think what it is to be a mother, there's a dear young lamb, do.'

Apparently this consolatory perspective of a mother's prospects failed in producing its due effect. The patient shook her head, and stretched out her hand towards the child.

The surgeon deposited it in her arms. She imprinted her cold white lips passionately on its forehead, passed her hands over her face, gazed wildly round, shuddered, fell back – and died. They chafed her breast, hands, and temples; but the blood had frozen for ever. They talked of hope and comfort. They had been strangers too long.

'It's all over, Mrs Thingummy,' said the surgeon, at last.

'Ah, poor dear; so it is!' said the nurse, picking up the cork of the green bottle which had fallen out on the pillow as she stooped to take up the child. 'Poor dear!'

'You needn't mind sending up to me, if the child cries, nurse,' said the surgeon, putting on his gloves with great deliberation. 'It's very likely it *will* be troublesome. Give it a little gruel[5] if it is.' He put on his hat, and, pausing by the bed-side on his way to the door, added, 'She was a good-looking girl too; where did she come from?'

'She was brought here last night,' replied the old woman, 'by the overseer's order.[6] She was found lying in the street; – she had walked some distance, for her shoes were worn to pieces; but where she came from, or where she was going to, nobody knows.'

The surgeon leant over the body, and raised the left hand. 'The old story,' he said, shaking his head: 'no wedding-ring, I see. Ah! good night.'

The medical gentleman walked away to dinner; and the nurse, having once more applied herself to the green bottle, sat down on a low chair before the fire, and proceeded to dress the infant.

And what an excellent example of the power of dress young Oliver Twist was! Wrapped in the blanket which had hitherto formed his only covering, he might have been the child of a nobleman or a beggar; – it would have been hard for the haughtiest stranger to have fixed his station in society. But now he was enveloped in the old calico robes, that had grown yellow in the same service; he was badged and ticketed, and fell into his place at once – a parish child – the orphan of a workhouse – the humble, half-starved drudge – to be cuffed and buffeted through the world, despised by all, and pitied by none.

Oliver cried lustily. If he could have known that he was an orphan, left to the tender mercies of churchwardens and overseers, perhaps he would have cried the louder.

CHAPTER THE SECOND

TREATS OF OLIVER TWIST'S GROWTH, EDUCATION, AND BOARD

For the next eight or ten months, Oliver was the victim of a systematic course of treachery and deception – he was brought up by hand.[1] The hungry and destitute situation of the infant orphan was duly reported by the workhouse authorities to the parish authorities. The parish authorities inquired with dignity of the workhouse authorities, whether there was no female then domiciled in 'the house' who was in a situation to impart to Oliver Twist the consolation and nourishment of which he stood in need. The workhouse authorities replied with humility that there was not. Upon this, the parish authorities magnanimously and humanely resolved, that Oliver should be 'farmed,' or, in other words, that he should be despatched to a branch-workhouse some three miles off, where twenty or thirty other juvenile offenders against the poor-laws[2] rolled about the floor all day, without the inconvenience of too much food, or too much clothing, under the parental superintendence of an elderly female who received the culprits at and for the consideration of sevenpence-halfpenny per small head per week. Sevenpence-halfpenny's worth per week is a good round diet for a child; a great deal may be got for sevenpence-halfpenny – quite enough to overload its stomach, and make it uncomfortable. The elderly female was a woman of wisdom and experience; she knew what was good for children, and she had a very accurate perception of what was good for herself. So, she appropriated the greater part of the weekly stipend to her own use, and consigned the rising parochial generation to even a shorter allowance than was originally provided for them; thereby finding in the lowest depth a deeper still,[3] and proving herself a very great experimental philosopher.

Everybody knows the story of another experimental philosopher, who had a great theory about a horse being able to live without eating,[4] and who demonstrated it so well, that he got his own horse down to a straw a day, and would most unquestionably have rendered him a very spirited and rampacious animal upon nothing at all, if he hadn't died, just four-and-twenty hours before he was to have had his first comfortable bait of air. Unfortunately for the experimental philosophy of the female to whose protecting care Oliver Twist was delivered over, a similar result usually attended the operation of *her* system; for just at the very moment when a child had contrived to exist upon the smallest possible portion of the weakest possible food, it did perversely happen in eight and a half cases out of ten, either that it sickened from want and cold, or fell into the fire from neglect, or got smothered by accident; in any one of which cases, the miserable little being was usually summoned into another world, and there gathered to the fathers which it had never known in this.

Occasionally, when there was some more than usually interesting inquest upon a parish child who had been overlooked in turning up a bedstead, or inadvertently scalded to death when there happened to be a washing, (though the latter accident was very scarce, – anything approaching to a washing being of rare occurrence in the farm,) the jury would take it into their heads to ask troublesome questions, or the parishioners would rebelliously affix their signatures to a remonstrance: but these impertinencies were speedily checked by the evidence of the surgeon, and the testimony of the beadle;[5] the former of whom had always opened the body, and found nothing inside (which was very probable indeed), and the latter of whom invariably swore whatever the parish wanted, which was very self-devotional. Besides, the board[6] made periodical pilgrimages to the farm, and always sent the beadle the day before, to say they were coming. The children were neat and clean to behold, when *they* went; and what more would the people have?

It cannot be expected that this system of farming would produce any very extraordinary or luxuriant crop. Oliver Twist's eighth birth-day[7] found him a pale, thin child, somewhat diminutive in stature, and decidedly small in circumference. But nature or inheritance had implanted a good sturdy spirit in Oliver's breast: it had had plenty of room to expand, thanks to the spare diet of the establishment; and perhaps to this circumstance may be attributed his having any eighth birth-day at all. Be this as it may, however, it *was* his eighth birth-day; and he was keeping it in the coal-cellar with a select party of two other young gentlemen, who, after participating with him in a sound threshing,[8] had been locked up therein, for atrociously presuming to be hungry, when Mrs Mann, the good lady of the house, was unexpectedly startled by the apparition of Mr Bumble the beadle, striving to undo the wicket of the garden-gate.

'Goodness gracious! is that you, Mr Bumble, sir?' said Mrs Mann, thrusting her head out of the window in well-affected ecstasies of joy. '(Susan, take Oliver and them two brats up stairs, and wash 'em directly.) – My heart alive! Mr Bumble, how glad I am to see you, sure-ly!'

Now Mr Bumble was a fat man, and a choleric one; so, instead of responding to this open-hearted salutation in a kindred spirit, he gave the little wicket a tremendous shake, and then bestowed upon it a kick, which could have emanated from no leg but a beadle's.

'Lor, only think,' said Mrs Mann, running out, – for the three boys had been removed by this time, – 'only think of that! That I should have forgotten that the gate was bolted on the inside, on account of them dear children! Walk in, sir; walk in, pray, Mr Bumble; do, sir.'

Although this invitation was accompanied with a curtsey that might have softened the heart of a churchwarden, it by no means mollified the beadle.

'Do you think this respectful or proper conduct, Mrs Mann,' inquired Mr Bumble, grasping his cane, – 'to keep the parish officers a-waiting at your garden-gate, when they come here upon porochial business connected with the porochial orphans? Are you aware, Mrs Mann, that you are, as I may say, a porochial delegate, and a stipendiary?'

'I'm sure, Mr Bumble, that I was only a-telling one or two of the dear children as is so fond of you, that it was you a-coming,' replied Mrs Mann with great humility.

Mr Bumble had a great idea of his oratorical powers and his import-ance. He had displayed the one, and vindicated the other. He relaxed.

'Well, well, Mrs Mann,' he replied in a calmer tone; 'it may be as you say; it may be. Lead the way in, Mrs Mann; for I come on business, and have got something to say.'

Mrs Mann ushered the beadle into a small parlour with a brick floor, placed a seat for him, and officiously deposited his cocked hat and cane on the table before him. Mr Bumble wiped from his forehead the perspiration which his walk had engendered, glanced complacently at the cocked hat, and smiled. Yes, he smiled: beadles are but men, and Mr Bumble smiled.

'Now don't you be offended at what I'm a-going to say,' observed Mrs Mann with captivating sweetness. 'You've had a long walk, you know, or I wouldn't mention it. Now will you take a little drop of something, Mr Bumble?'

'Not a drop – not a drop,' said Mr Bumble, waving his right hand in a dignified, but still placid manner.

'I think you will,' said Mrs Mann, who had noticed the tone of the refusal, and the gesture that had accompanied it. 'Just a *leetle* drop, with a little cold water, and a lump of sugar.'

Mr Bumble coughed.

'Now, just a little drop,' said Mrs Mann persuasively.

'What is it?' inquired the beadle.

'Why it's what I'm obliged to keep a little of in the house, to put in the blessed infants' Daffy[9] when they ain't well, Mr Bumble,' replied Mrs Mann as she opened a corner cupboard, and took down a bottle and glass. 'It's gin.'

'Do you give the children Daffy, Mrs Mann?' inquired Bumble, following with his eyes the interesting process of mixing.

'Ah, bless 'em, that I do, dear as it is,' replied the nurse. 'I couldn't see 'em suffer before my very eyes, you know, sir.'

'No,' said Mr Bumble approvingly; 'no, you could not. You are a humane woman, Mrs Mann.' – (Here she set down the glass.) – 'I shall take an early opportunity of mentioning it to the board, Mrs Mann.' – (He drew it towards him.) – 'You feel as a mother, Mrs Mann.' – (He stirred the gin and water.) – 'I – I drink your health with cheerfulness, Mrs Mann;' – and he swallowed half of it.

'And now about business,' said the beadle, taking out a leathern pocket-book. 'The child that was half-baptised,[10] Oliver Twist, is eight years old to-day.'

'Bless him!' interposed Mrs Mann, inflaming her left eye with the corner of her apron.

'And notwithstanding an offered reward of ten pound, which was afterwards increased to twenty pound, – notwithstanding the most superlative, and, I may say, supernat'ral exertions on the part of this parish,' said Bumble, 'we have never been able to discover who is his father, or what is his mother's settlement, name, or condition.'[11]

Mrs Mann raised her hands in astonishment; but added, after a moment's reflection, 'How comes he to have any name at all, then?'

The beadle drew himself up with great pride, and said, 'I inwented it.'

'You, Mr Bumble!'

'I, Mrs Mann. We name our foundlin's in alphabetical order. The last was a S, – Swubble: I named him. This was a T, – Twist: I named *him*. The next one as comes will be Unwin, and the next Vilkins. I have got names ready made to the end of the alphabet, and all the way through it again, when we come to Z.'

'Why, you're quite a literary character, sir!' said Mrs Mann.

'Well, well,' said the beadle, evidently gratified with the compliment; 'perhaps I may be; perhaps I may be, Mrs Mann.' He finished the gin and water, and added, 'Oliver being now too old to remain here, the Board have determined to have him back into the house; and I have come out myself to take him there, – so let me see him at once.'

'I'll fetch him directly,' said Mrs Mann, leaving the room for that purpose. And Oliver having by this time had as much of the outer coat of dirt which encrusted his face and hands removed as could be scrubbed off in one washing, was led into the room by his benevolent protectress.

'Make a bow to the gentleman, Oliver,' said Mrs Mann.

Oliver made a bow, which was divided between the beadle on the chair and the cocked hat on the table.

'Will you go along with me, Oliver?' said Mr Bumble in a majestic voice.

Oliver was about to say that he would go along with anybody with great readiness, when, glancing upwards, he caught sight of Mrs Mann, who had got behind the beadle's chair, and was shaking her fist at him with a furious countenance. He took the hint at once, for the fist had been too often impressed upon his body not to be deeply impressed upon his recollection.

'Will *she* go with me?' inquired poor Oliver.

'No, she can't,' replied Mr Bumble; 'but she'll come and see you, sometimes.'

This was no very great consolation to the child; but, young as he was, he had sense enough to make a feint of feeling great regret at going away. It was no very difficult matter for the boy to call the tears into his eyes. Hunger and recent ill-usage are great assistants if you want to cry; and Oliver cried very naturally indeed. Mrs Mann gave him a thousand embraces, and, what Oliver wanted a great deal more, a piece of bread and butter, lest he should seem too hungry when he got to the workhouse. With the slice of bread in his hand, and the little brown-cloth parish cap upon his head, Oliver was then led away by Mr Bumble from the wretched home where one kind word or look had never lighted the gloom of his infant years. And yet he burst into an agony of childish grief as the cottage-gate closed after him. Wretched as were the little companions in misery he was leaving behind, they were the only friends he had ever known; and a sense of his loneliness in the great wide world sank into the child's heart for the first time.

Mr Bumble walked on with long strides; and little Oliver, firmly grasping his gold-laced cuff, trotted beside him, inquiring at the end of every quarter of a mile whether they were 'nearly there,' to which interrogations Mr Bumble returned very brief and snappish replies; for the temporary blandness which gin and water awakens in some bosoms had by this time evaporated, and he was once again a beadle.

Oliver had not been within the walls of the workhouse a quarter of an hour, and had scarcely completed the demolition of a second slice of bread, when Mr Bumble, who had handed him over to the care of an old woman, returned, and, telling him it was a board night, informed him that the board had said he was to appear before it forthwith.

Not having a very clearly defined notion of what a live board was, Oliver was rather astounded by this intelligence, and was not quite certain whether he ought to laugh or cry. He had no time to think about the matter, however; for Mr Bumble gave him a tap on the head with his cane to wake him up, and another on the back to make him lively, and, bidding him follow, conducted him into a large whitewashed room, where eight or ten fat gentlemen were sitting round a table, at the top of which, seated in an arm-chair rather higher than the rest, was a particularly fat gentleman with a very round, red face.

'Bow to the board,' said Bumble. Oliver brushed away two or three tears that were lingering in his eyes, and seeing no board but the table, fortunately bowed to that.

'What's your name, boy?' said the gentleman in the high chair.

Oliver was frightened at the sight of so many gentlemen, which made him tremble; and the beadle gave him another tap behind, which made him cry; and these two causes made him answer in a very low and hesitating voice; whereupon a gentleman in a white waistcoat said he was a fool, which was a capital way of raising his spirits, and putting him quite at his ease.

'Boy,' said the gentleman in the high chair; 'listen to me. You know you're an orphan, I suppose?'

'What's that, sir?' inquired poor Oliver.

'The boy *is* a fool – I thought he was,' said the gentleman in the white waistcoat, in a very decided tone. If one member of a class be blessed with an intuitive perception of others of the same race, the gentleman in the white waistcoat was unquestionably well qualified to pronounce an opinion on the matter.

'Hush!' said the gentleman who had spoken first. 'You know you've got no father or mother, and that you are brought up by the parish, don't you?'

'Yes, sir,' replied Oliver, weeping bitterly.

'What are you crying for?' inquired the gentleman in the white waistcoat; and to be sure it was very extraordinary. What *could* he be crying for?

'I hope you say your prayers every night,' said another gentleman in a gruff voice, 'and pray for the people who feed you, and take care of you, like a Christian.'

'Yes, sir,' stammered the boy. The gentleman who spoke last was unconsciously right. It would have been *very* like a Christian, and a marvellously good Christian, too, if Oliver had prayed for the people who fed and took care of *him*. But he hadn't, because nobody had taught him.

'Well, you have come here to be educated, and taught a useful trade,' said the red-faced gentleman in the high chair.

'So you'll begin to pick oakum[12] to-morrow morning at six o'clock,' added the surly one in the white waistcoat.

For the combination of both these blessings in the one simple process of picking oakum, Oliver bowed low by the direction of the beadle, and was then hurried away to a large ward, where, on a rough hard bed, he sobbed himself to sleep. What a noble illustration of the tender laws of this favoured country! they let the paupers go to sleep!

Poor Oliver! He little thought, as he lay sleeping in happy unconsciousness of all around him, that the board had that very day arrived at a decision which would exercise the most material influence over all his future fortunes. But they had. And this was it: —

The members of this board were very sage, deep, philosophical men; and when they came to turn their attention to the workhouse, they found out at once, what ordinary folks would never have discovered, — the poor people liked it! It was a regular place of public entertainment for the poorer classes, — a tavern where there was nothing to pay, — a public breakfast, dinner, tea, and supper, all the year round, — a brick and mortar elysium where it was all play and no work. 'Oho!' said the board, looking very knowing; 'we are the fellows to set this to rights; we'll stop it all in no time.' So they established the rule, that all poor people should have the alternative (for they would compel nobody, not they,) of being starved by a gradual process in the house, or by a quick one out of it. With this view, they contracted with the water-works to lay on an unlimited supply of water, and with a corn-factor to supply periodically small quantities of oatmeal; and issued three meals of thin gruel a-day, with an onion twice a week, and half a roll on Sundays. They made a great many other wise and humane regulations having reference to the ladies,[13] which it is not necessary to repeat; kindly undertook to divorce poor married people, in consequence of the great expense of a suit in Doctors' Commons;[14] and, instead of compelling a man to support his family as they had theretofore done, took his family away from him, and made him a bachelor! There is no telling how many applicants for relief under these last two heads would not have started up in all classes of society, if it had not been coupled with the workhouse. But they were long-headed men, and they had provided for this difficulty. The relief was inseparable from the workhouse and the gruel; and that frightened people.

For the first three months after Oliver Twist was removed, the system was in full operation. It was rather expensive at first, in consequence of the increase in the undertaker's bill, and the necessity of taking in the clothes of all the paupers, which fluttered loosely on their wasted, shrunken forms, after a week or two's gruel. But the number of workhouse inmates got thin, as well as the paupers; and the board were in ecstasies.

The room in which the boys were fed, was a large, stone hall, with a copper at one end,[15] out of which the master, dressed in an apron for the purpose, and assisted by one or two women, ladled the gruel at meal-times; of which composition each boy had one porringer, and no more, – except on festive occasions, and then he had two ounces and a quarter of bread besides. The bowls never wanted washing – the boys polished them with their spoons, till they shone again; and when they had performed this operation (which never took very long, the spoons being nearly as large as the bowls), they would sit staring at the copper with such eager eyes as if they could devour the very bricks of which it was composed; employing themselves meanwhile in sucking their fingers most assiduously, with the view of catching up any stray splashes of gruel that might have been cast thereon. Boys have generally excellent appetites: Oliver Twist and his companions suffered the tortures of slow starvation for three months; at last they got so voracious and wild with hunger, that one boy, who was tall for his age, and hadn't been used to that sort of thing, (for his father had kept a small cook's shop,) hinted darkly to his companions, that unless he had another basin of gruel *per diem*,[16] he was afraid he should some night eat the boy who slept next him, who happened to be a weakly youth of tender age. He had a wild, hungry eye, and they implicitly believed him. A council was held; lots were cast who should walk up to the master after supper that evening, and ask for more; and it fell to Oliver Twist.

The evening arrived: the boys took their places; the master in his cook's uniform stationed himself at the copper; his pauper assistants ranged themselves behind him; the gruel was served out, and a long grace was said over the short commons. The gruel disappeared, and the boys whispered each other and winked at Oliver, while his next neighbours nudged him. Child as he was, he was desperate with hunger and reckless with misery. He rose from the table, and advancing, basin and spoon in hand, to the master, said, somewhat alarmed at his own temerity –

'Please, sir, I want some more.'

The master was a fat, healthy man, but he turned very pale. He gazed in stupified astonishment on the small rebel for some seconds, and then clung for support to the copper. The assistants were paralysed with wonder, and the boys with fear.

'What!' said the master at length, in a faint voice.

'Please, sir,' replied Oliver, 'I want some more.'

The master aimed a blow at Oliver's head with the ladle, pinioned him in his arms, and shrieked aloud for the beadle.

The board were sitting in solemn conclave when Mr Bumble rushed into the room in great excitement, and addressing the gentleman in the high chair, said, –

'Mr Limbkins, I beg your pardon, sir; – Oliver Twist has asked for more.' There was a general start. Horror was depicted on every countenance.

'For *more!*' said Mr Limbkins. 'Compose yourself, Bumble, and answer me distinctly. Do I understand that he asked for more, after he had eaten the supper allotted by the dietary?'

'He did, sir,' replied Bumble.

'That boy will be hung,' said the gentleman in the white waistcoat; 'I know that boy will be hung.'

Nobody controverted the prophetic gentleman's opinion. An animated discussion took place. Oliver was ordered into instant confinement; and a bill was next morning pasted on the outside of the gate, offering a reward of five pounds to anybody who would take Oliver Twist off the hands of the parish: in other words, five pounds and Oliver Twist were offered to any man or woman who wanted an apprentice to any trade, business, or calling.

'I never was more convinced of anything in my life,' said the

Oliver asking for more

gentleman in the white waistcoat, as he knocked at the gate and read the bill next morning, – 'I never was more convinced of anything in my life, than I am that that boy will come to be hung.'

As I propose to show in the sequel whether the white-waistcoated gentleman was right or not, I should perhaps mar the interest of this narrative, (supposing it to possess any at all,) if I ventured to hint just yet, whether the life of Oliver Twist will be a long or a short piece of biography.

*

CHAPTER THE THIRD

RELATES HOW OLIVER TWIST WAS VERY NEAR GETTING A PLACE, WHICH WOULD NOT HAVE BEEN A SINECURE

For a week after the commission of the impious and profane offence of asking for more, Oliver remained a close prisoner in the dark and solitary room to which he had been consigned by the wisdom and mercy of the board. It appears, at first sight, not unreasonable to suppose, that, if he had entertained a becoming feeling of respect for the prediction of the gentleman in the white waistcoat, he would have established that sage individual's prophetic character, once and for ever, by tying one end of his pocket handkerchief to a hook in the wall, and attaching himself to the other. To the performance of this feat, however, there was one obstacle, namely, that pocket-handkerchiefs being decided articles of luxury, had been, for all future times and ages, removed from the noses of paupers by the express order of the board in council assembled, solemnly given and pro-nounced under their hands and seals. There was a still greater obstacle in Oliver's youth and childishness. He only cried bitterly all day; and when the long, dismal night came on, he spread his little hands before his eyes to shut out the darkness, and crouching in the corner, tried to sleep, ever and anon waking with a start and tremble, and drawing himself closer and closer to the wall, as if to feel even its cold hard surface were a protection in the gloom and loneliness which surrounded him.

Let it not be supposed by the enemies of 'the system,' that, during the period of his solitary incarceration, Oliver was denied the benefit of exercise, the pleasure of society, or the advantages of religious consolation. As for exercise, it was nice cold weather, and he was allowed to perform his ablutions every morning under the pump, in a stone yard, in the presence of Mr Bumble, who prevented his catching cold, and caused a tingling sensation to pervade his frame, by repeated applications of the cane; as for society, he was carried every other day into the hall where the boys dined, and there sociably flogged as a public warning and example; and, so far from being denied the advantages of religious consolation, he was kicked into the same apartment every evening at prayer-time, and there permitted to listen to, and console his mind with, a general supplication of the boys, containing a special clause therein inserted by the authority of the board, in which they entreated to be made good, virtuous, contented, and obedient, and to be guarded from the sins and vices of Oliver Twist, whom the supplication distinctly set forth to be under the exclusive patronage and protection of the powers of wickedness, and an article direct from the manufactory of the devil himself.

It chanced one morning, while Oliver's affairs were in this auspicious and comfortable state, that Mr Gamfield, chimney-sweeper, was wending his way adown the High-street, deeply cogitating in his mind, his ways and means of paying certain arrears of rent, for which his landlord had become rather pressing. Mr Gamfield's most sanguine calculation of funds could not raise them within full five pounds of the desired amount; and, in a species of arithmetical desperation, he was alternately cudgelling his brains and his donkey, when, passing the workhouse, his eyes encountered the bill on the gate.

'Woo!' said Mr Gamfield, to the donkey.

The donkey was in a state of profound abstraction, – wondering, probably, whether he was destined to be regaled with a cabbage-stalk or two, when he had disposed of the two sacks of soot with which the little cart was laden; so, without noticing the word of command, he jogged onwards.

Mr Gamfield growled a fierce imprecation on the donkey generally, but more particularly on his eyes; and, running after him, bestowed a blow on his head which would inevitably have beaten in any skull but a donkey's; then, catching hold of the bridle, he gave his jaw a sharp wrench, by way of gentle reminder that he was not his own master: and, having by these means turned him round, he gave him another blow on the head, just to stun him till he came back again; and, having done so, walked up to the gate to read the bill.

The gentleman with the white waistcoat was standing at the gate with his hands behind him, after having delivered himself of some profound sentiments in the board-room. Having witnessed the little dispute between Mr Gamfield and the donkey, he smiled joyously when that person came up to read the bill, for he saw at once that Mr Gamfield was just exactly the sort of master Oliver Twist wanted. Mr Gamfield smiled, too, as he perused the document, for five pounds was just the sum he had been wishing for; and, as to the boy with which it was encumbered, Mr Gamfield, knowing what the dietary of the workhouse was, well knew he would be a nice small pattern, just the very thing for register stoves. So he spelt the bill through again, from beginning to end; and then, touching his fur cap in token of humility, accosted the gentleman in the white waistcoat.

'This here boy, sir, wot the parish wants to 'prentis,'[1] said Mr Gamfield.

'Yes, my man,' said the gentleman in the white waistcoat, with a condescending smile, 'what of him?'

'If the parish vould like him to learn a light, pleasant trade, in a good 'spectable chimbley-sweepin' bisness,' said Mr Gamfield, 'I wants a 'prentis, and I'm ready to take him.'

'Walk in,' said the gentleman with the white waistcoat. And Mr Gamfield having lingered behind, to give the donkey another blow on the head, and another wrench of the jaw as a caution not to run away in his absence, followed the gentleman with the white waistcoat, into the room where Oliver had first seen him.

Oliver escapes being bound apprentice to the Sweep

'It's a nasty trade,' said Mr Limbkins, when Gamfield had again stated his wish.

'Young boys have been smothered in chimneys, before now,' said another gentleman.

'That's acause they damped the straw afore they lit it in the chimbley to make 'em come down again,' said Gamfield; 'that's all smoke, and no blaze; vereas smoke ain't o' no use at all in makin' a boy come down; it only sinds him to sleep, and that's wot he likes. Boys is wery obstinit, and wery lazy, gen'lm'n, and there's nothink like a good hot blaze to make 'em come down vith a run; it's humane too, gen'lm'n, acause, even if they've stuck in the chimbley, roastin' their feet makes 'em struggle to hextricate theirselves.'

The gentleman in the white waistcoat appeared very much amused with this explanation; but his mirth was speedily checked by a look from Mr Limbkins. The board then proceeded to converse among themselves for a few minutes; but in so low a tone that the words 'saving of expenditure,' 'look well in the accounts,' 'have a printed report published,' were alone audible: and they only chanced to be heard on account of their being very frequently repeated with great emphasis.

At length the whispering ceased, and the members of the board having resumed their seats, and their solemnity, Mr Limbkins said,

'We have considered your proposition, and we don't approve of it.'

'Not at all,' said the gentleman in the white waistcoat.

'Decidedly not,' added the other members.

As Mr Gamfield did happen to labour under the slight imputation of having bruised three or four boys to death, already, it occurred to him that the board had perhaps, in some unaccountable freak, taken it into their heads that this extraneous circumstance ought to influence their proceedings. It was very unlike their general mode of doing business, if they had; but still, as he had no particular wish to revive the rumour, he twisted his cap in his hands, and walked slowly from the table.

'So you won't let me have him, gen'lmen,' said Mr Gamfield, pausing near the door.

'No,' replied Mr Limbkins; 'at least, as it's a nasty business, we think you ought to take something less than the premium we offered.'

Mr Gamfield's countenance brightened, as, with a quick step he returned to the table, and said,

'What'll you give, gen'lmen? Come, don't be too hard on a poor man. What'll you give?'

'I should say three pound ten was plenty,' said Mr Limbkins.

'Ten shillings too much,' said the gentleman in the white waistcoat.

'Come,' said Gamfield; 'say four pound, gen'lmen. Say four pound, and you've got rid of him for good and all. There!'

'Three pound ten,' repeated Mr Limbkins, firmly.

'Come, I'll split the difference, gen'lmen,' urged Gamfield. 'Three pound fifteen.'

'Not a farthing more,' was the firm reply of Mr Limbkins.

'You're desp'rate hard upon me, gen'lmen,' said Gamfield, wavering.

'Pooh! pooh! nonsense!' said the gentleman in the white waistcoat. 'He'd be cheap with nothing at all, as a premium. Take him, you silly fellow! He's just the boy for you. He wants the stick now and then; it'll do him good; and his board needn't come very expensive, for he hasn't been overfed since he was born. Ha! ha! ha!'

Mr Gamfield gave an arch look at the faces round the table, and, observing a smile on all of them, gradually broke into a smile himself. The bargain was made, and Mr Bumble was at once instructed that Oliver Twist and his indentures were to be conveyed before the magistrate[2] for signature and approval, that very afternoon.

In pursuance of this determination, little Oliver, to his excessive astonishment, was released from bondage, and ordered to put himself into a clean shirt. He had hardly achieved this very unusual gymnastic performance, when Mr Bumble brought him with his own hands, a basin of gruel, and the holiday allowance of two ounces and a quarter of bread; at sight of which Oliver began to cry very piteously, thinking, not unnaturally, that the board must have determined to kill him for some useful purpose, or they never would have begun to fatten him up in this way.

'Don't make your eyes red, Oliver, but eat your food, and be thankful,' said Mr Bumble, in a tone of impressive pomposity. 'You're a-going to be made a 'prentice of, Oliver.'

'A 'prentice, sir!' said the child, trembling.

'Yes, Oliver,' said Mr Bumble. 'The kind and blessed gentlemen which is so many parents to you, Oliver, when you have none of your own, are a-going to 'prentice you, and to set you up in life, and make a man of you, although the expence to the parish is three pound ten! – three pound ten, Oliver! – seventy shillin's! – one hundred and forty sixpences! – and all for a naughty orphan which nobody can love.'

As Mr Bumble paused to take breath after delivering this address, in an awful voice, the tears rolled down the poor child's face, and he sobbed bitterly.

'Come,' said Mr Bumble, somewhat less pompously; for it was gratifying to his feelings to observe the effect his eloquence had produced. 'Come, Oliver, wipe your eyes with the cuffs of your jacket, and don't cry into your gruel; that's a very foolish action, Oliver.' It certainly was, for there was quite enough water in it already.

On their way to the magistrate's, Mr Bumble instructed Oliver that all he would have to do, would be to look very happy, and say, when the gentleman asked him if he wanted to be apprenticed, that he should like it very much indeed; both of which injunctions Oliver promised to obey, the more readily as Mr Bumble threw in a gentle hint, that if he failed in either particular, there was no telling what would be done to him. When they arrived at the office, he was shut up in a little room by himself, and admonished by Mr Bumble to stay there, until he came back to fetch him.

There the boy remained with a palpitating heart for half an hour, at the expiration of which time Mr Bumble thrust in his head, unadorned with the cocked-hat, and said aloud,

'Now, Oliver, my dear, come to the gentleman.' As Mr Bumble said this, he put on a grim and threatening look, and added in a low voice, 'Mind what I told you, you young rascal.'

Oliver stared innocently in Mr Bumble's face at this somewhat contradictory style of address; but that gentleman prevented his offering any remark thereupon, by leading him at once into an adjoining room, the door of which was open. It was a large room with a great window; and behind a desk sat two old gentlemen with powdered heads, one of whom was reading the newspaper, while the other was perusing, with the aid of a pair of tortoise-shell spectacles, a small piece of parchment which lay before him. Mr Limbkins was standing in front of the desk, on one side; and Mr Gamfield, with a partially washed face, on the other; while two or three bluff-looking men in top-boots were lounging about.

The old gentleman with the spectacles gradually dozed off, over the little bit of parchment; and there was a short pause after Oliver had been stationed by Mr Bumble in front of the desk.

'This is the boy, your worship,' said Mr Bumble.

The old gentleman who was reading the newspaper raised his head for a moment, and pulled the other old gentleman by the sleeve, whereupon the last-mentioned old gentleman woke up.

'Oh, is this the boy?' said the old gentleman.

'This is him, sir,' replied Mr Bumble. 'Bow to the magistrate, my dear.'

Oliver roused himself, and made his best obeisance. He had been wondering, with his eyes fixed on the magistrates' powder, whether all boards were born with that white stuff on their heads, and were boards from thenceforth, on that account.

'Well,' said the old gentleman,' I suppose he's fond of chimney-sweeping?'

'He dotes on it, your worship,' replied Bumble, giving Oliver a sly pinch, to intimate that he had better not say he didn't.

'And he *will* be a sweep, will he?' inquired the old gentleman.

'If we was to bind him to any other trade to-morrow, he'd run away simultaneously, your worship,' replied Bumble.

'And this man that's to be his master, – you, sir, – you'll treat him well, and feed him, and do all that sort of thing – will you?' said the old gentleman.

'When I says I will, I means I will,' replied Mr Gamfield doggedly.

'You're a rough speaker, my friend, but you look an honest, open-hearted man,' said the old gentleman, turning his spectacles in the direction of the candidate for Oliver's premium, whose villanous countenance was a regular stamped receipt for cruelty. But the magistrate was half blind, and half childish, so he couldn't reasonably be expected to discern what other people did.

'I hope I am, sir,' said Mr Gamfield with an ugly leer.

'I have no doubt you are, my friend,' replied the old gentleman, fixing his spectacles more firmly on his nose, and looking about him for the inkstand.

It was the critical moment of Oliver's fate. If the inkstand had been where the old gentleman thought it was, he would have dipped his pen into it and signed the indentures, and Oliver would have been straightway hurried off. But, as it chanced to be immediately under his nose, it followed as a matter of course that he looked all over his desk for it, without finding it; and happening in the course of his search to look straight before him, his gaze encountered the pale and terrified face of Oliver Twist, who, despite all the admonitory looks and pinches of Bumble, was regarding the very repulsive countenance of his future master with a mingled expression of horror and fear, too palpable to be mistaken even by a half-blind magistrate.

The old gentleman stopped, laid down his pen, and looked from Oliver to Mr Limbkins, who attempted to take snuff[3] with a cheerful and unconcerned aspect.

'My boy,' said the old gentleman, leaning over the desk. Oliver started at the sound, – he might be excused for doing so, for the words were kindly said, and strange sounds frighten one. He trembled violently, and burst into tears.

'My boy,' said the old gentleman,' you look pale and alarmed. What is the matter?'

'Stand a little away from him, beadle,' said the other magistrate, laying aside the paper, and leaning forward with an expression of some interest. 'Now, boy, tell us what's the matter: don't be afraid.'

Oliver fell on his knees, and, clasping his hands together, prayed that they would order him back to the dark room, – that they would starve him – beat him – kill him if they pleased – rather than send him away, with that dreadful man.

'Well!' said Mr Bumble, raising his hands and eyes with most impressive solemnity, – 'Well! of *all* the artful and designing orphans that ever I see, Oliver, you are one of the most bare-facedest.'

'Hold your tongue, beadle,' said the second old gentleman, when Mr Bumble had given vent to this compound adjective.

'I beg your worship's pardon,' said Mr Bumble, incredulous of his having heard aright, – 'did your worship speak to me?'

'Yes – hold your tongue.'

Mr Bumble was stupified with astonishment. A beadle ordered to hold his tongue! A moral revolution.

The old gentleman in the tortoise-shell spectacles looked at his companion: he nodded significantly.

'We refuse to sanction these indentures,' said the old gentleman, tossing aside the piece of parchment as he spoke.

'I hope,' stammered Mr Limbkins, – 'I hope the magistrates will not form the opinion that the authorities have been guilty of any improper conduct, on the unsupported testimony of a mere child.'

'The magistrates are not called upon to pronounce any opinion on the matter,' said the second old gentleman sharply. 'Take the boy back to the workhouse, and treat him kindly. He seems to want it.'[4]

That same evening the gentleman in the white waistcoat most positively and decidedly affirmed, not only that Oliver would be hung, but that he would be drawn and quartered into the bargain. Mr Bumble shook his head with gloomy mystery, and said he wished he might come to good; to which Mr Gamfield replied, that he wished he might come to him, which, although he agreed with the beadle in most matters, would seem to be a wish of a totally opposite description.

The next morning the public were once more informed that Oliver Twist was again to let, and that five pounds would be paid to anybody who would take possession of him.

CHAPTER THE FOURTH

OLIVER, BEING OFFERED ANOTHER PLACE, MAKES HIS FIRST ENTRY INTO PUBLIC LIFE

In great families, when an advantageous place cannot be obtained, either in possession, reversion, remainder, or expectancy,[1] for the young man who is growing up, it is a very general custom to send him to sea. The board, in imitation of so wise and salutary an example, took counsel together on the expediency of shipping off Oliver Twist in some small trading vessel[2] bound to a good unhealthy port, which suggested itself as the very best thing that could possibly be done with him; the probability being, that the skipper would either flog him to death, in a playful mood, some day after dinner, or knock his brains out with an iron bar – both pastimes being, as is pretty generally known, very favourite and common recreations among gentlemen of that class. The more the case presented itself to the board, in this point of view, the more manifold the advantages of the step appeared; so they came to the conclusion that the only way of providing for Oliver effectually, was to send him to sea without delay.

Mr Bumble had been despatched to make various preliminary inquiries, with the view of finding out some captain or other who wanted a cabin-boy without any friends; and was returning to the workhouse to communicate the result of his mission, when he encountered just at the gate no less a person than Mr Sowerberry, the parochial undertaker.

Mr Sowerberry was a tall, gaunt, large-jointed man, attired in a suit of threadbare black, with darned cotton stockings of the same colour, and shoes to answer. His features were not naturally intended to wear a smiling aspect, but he was in general rather given to professional jocosity; his step was elastic, and his face betokened inward pleasantry, as he advanced to Mr Bumble and shook him cordially by the hand.

'I have taken the measure of the two women that died last night, Mr Bumble,' said the undertaker.

'You'll make your fortune, Mr Sowerberry,' said the beadle, as he thrust his thumb and forefinger into the proffered snuff-box of the undertaker, which was an ingenious little model of a patent coffin. 'I say you'll make your fortune, Mr Sowerberry,' repeated Mr Bumble, tapping the undertaker on the shoulder in a friendly manner, with his cane.

'Think so?' said the undertaker in a tone which half admitted and half disputed the probability of the event. 'The prices allowed by the board are very small, Mr Bumble.'

'So are the coffins,' replied the beadle, with precisely as near an approach to a laugh as a great official ought to indulge in.

Mr Sowerberry was much tickled at this, as of course he ought to be, and laughed a long time without cessation. 'Well, well, Mr Bumble,' he said at length, 'there's no denying that, since the new system of feeding has come in, the coffins are something narrower and more shallow than they used to be; but we must have some profit, Mr Bumble. Well-seasoned timber is an expensive article, sir; and all the iron handles come by canal from Birmingham.'[3]

'Well, well,' said Mr Bumble, 'every trade has its drawbacks, and a fair profit is of course allowable.'

'Of course, of course,' replied the undertaker; 'and if I don't get a profit upon this or that particular article, why, I make it up in the long run, you see – he! he! he!'

'Just so,' said Mr Bumble.

'Though I must say,' – continued the undertaker, resuming the current of observations which the beadle had interrupted – 'though I must say, Mr Bumble, that I have to contend against one very great disadvantage, which is, that all the stout people go off the quickest – I mean that the people who have been better off, and have paid rates for many years, are the first to sink when they come into the house; and let me tell you, Mr Bumble, that three or four inches over one's calculation makes a great hole in one's profits, especially when one has a family to provide for, sir.'

As Mr Sowerberry said this, with the becoming indignation of an ill-used man, and as Mr Bumble felt that it rather tended to convey a reflection on the honour of the parish, the latter gentleman thought it advisable to change the subject; and Oliver Twist being uppermost in his mind, he made him his theme.

'By the bye,' said Mr Bumble, 'you don't know anybody who wants a boy, do you – a porochial 'prentis, who is at present a dead-weight – a millstone,[4] as I may say – round the porochial throat? Liberal terms, Mr Sowerberry – liberal terms;' – and, as Mr Bumble spoke, he raised his cane to the bill above him, and gave three distinct raps upon the words 'five pounds,' which were printed therein in Roman capitals of gigantic size.

'Gadso!' said the undertaker, taking Mr Bumble by the gilt-edged lappel of his official coat; 'that's just the very thing I wanted to speak to you about. You know – dear me, what a very elegant button this is, Mr Bumble; I never noticed it before.'

'Yes, I think it is rather pretty,' said the beadle, glancing proudly downwards at the large brass buttons which embellished his coat. 'The die is the same as the parochial seal, – the Good Samaritan healing the sick and bruised man.[5] The board presented it to me on New-year's morning, Mr Sowerberry. I put it on, I remember, for the first time, to attend the inquest on that reduced tradesman who died in a doorway at midnight.'

'I recollect,' said the undertaker. 'The jury brought in "Died from exposure to the cold, and want of the common necessaries of life," – didn't they?'

Mr Bumble nodded.

'And they made it a special verdict, I think,' said the undertaker, 'by adding some words to the effect, that if the relieving officer[6] had —'

'Tush – foolery!' interposed the beadle angrily. 'If the board attended to all the nonsense that ignorant jurymen talk, they'd have enough to do.'

'Very true,' said the undertaker; 'they would indeed.'

'Juries,' said Mr Bumble, grasping his cane tightly, as was his wont when working into a passion, – 'juries is ineddicated, vulgar, grovelling wretches.'

'So they are,' said the undertaker.

'They haven't no more philosophy or political economy[7] about 'em than that,' said the beadle, snapping his fingers contemptuously.

'No more they have,' acquiesced the undertaker.

'I despise 'em,' said the beadle, growing very red in the face.

'So do I,' rejoined the undertaker.

'And I only wish we'd a jury of the independent sort in the house for a week or two,' said the beadle; 'the rules and regulations of the board would soon bring their spirit down for them.'

'Let 'em alone for that,' replied the undertaker. So saying, he smiled approvingly to calm the rising wrath of the indignant parish officer.

Mr Bumble lifted off his cocked-hat, took a handkerchief from the inside of the crown, wiped from his forehead the perspiration which his rage had engendered, fixed the cocked-hat on again; and, turning to the undertaker, said in a calmer voice,

'Well; what about the boy?'

'Oh!' replied the undertaker; 'why, you know, Mr Bumble, I pay a good deal towards the poor's rates.'

'Hem!' said Mr Bumble. 'Well?'

'Well,' replied the undertaker, 'I was thinking that if I pay so much towards 'em, I've a right to get as much out of 'em as I can, Mr Bumble; and so – and so – I think I'll take the boy myself.'

Mr Bumble grasped the undertaker by the arm, and led him into the building. Mr Sowerberry was closeted with the board for five minutes, and then it was arranged that Oliver should go to him that evening 'upon liking,' – a phrase which means, in the case of a parish apprentice, that if the master find, upon a short trial, that he can get enough work out of a boy without putting too much food in him, he shall have him for a term of years, to do what he likes with.

When little Oliver was taken before 'the gentlemen' that evening, and informed that he was to go that night as general house-lad to a coffin-maker's, and that if he complained of his situation, or ever came back to the parish again, he would be sent to sea, there to be drowned, or knocked on the head, as the case might be, he evinced so little emotion, that they by common consent pronounced him a hardened young rascal, and ordered Mr Bumble to remove him forthwith.

Now, although it was very natural that the board, of all people in the world, should feel in a great state of virtuous astonishment and horror at the smallest tokens of want of feeling on the part of anybody, they were rather out, in this particular instance. The simple fact was, that Oliver, instead of possessing too little feeling, possessed rather too much, and was in a fair way of being reduced to a state of brutal stupidity and sullenness for life, by the ill usage he had received. He heard the news of his destination in perfect silence, and, having had his luggage put into his hand, – which was not very difficult to carry, inasmuch as it was all comprised within the limits of a brown paper parcel, about half a foot square by three inches deep, – he pulled his cap over his eyes, and once more attaching himself to Mr Bumble's coat cuff, was led away by that dignitary to a new scene of suffering.

For some time, Mr Bumble drew Oliver along, without notice or remark, for the beadle carried his head very erect, as a beadle always should; and, it being a windy day, little Oliver was completely enshrouded by the skirts of Mr Bumble's coat as they blew open, and disclosed to great advantage his flapped waistcoat and drab plush knee-breeches. As they drew near to their destination, however, Mr Bumble thought it expedient to look down and see that the boy was in good order for inspection by his new master, which he accordingly did, with a fit and becoming air of gracious patronage.

'Oliver!' said Mr Bumble.

'Yes, sir,' replied Oliver, in a low, tremulous voice.

'Pull that cap off of your eyes, and hold up your head, sir.'

Although Oliver did as he was desired at once, and passed the back of his unoccupied hand briskly across his eyes, he left a tear in them when he looked up at his conductor. As Mr Bumble gazed sternly upon him, it rolled down his cheek. It was followed by another, and another. The child made a strong effort, but it was an unsuccessful one; and, withdrawing his other hand from Mr Bumble's, he covered his face with both, and wept till the tears sprung out from between his thin and bony fingers.

'Well!' exclaimed Mr Bumble, stopping short, and darting at his little charge a look of intense malignity, – 'well, of *all* the ungratefullest, and worst-disposed boys as ever I see, Oliver, you are the —'

'No, no, sir,' sobbed Oliver, clinging to the hand which held the well-known cane; 'no, no, sir; I will be good indeed; indeed, indeed, I will, sir! I am a very little boy, sir; and it is so – so –'

'So what?' inquired Mr Bumble in amazement.

'So lonely, sir – so very lonely,' cried the child. 'Everybody hates me. Oh! sir, don't be cross to me. I feel as if I had been cut here, sir, and it was all bleeding away;' and the child beat his hand upon his heart, and looked into his companion's face with tears of real agony.

Mr Bumble regarded Oliver's piteous and helpless look with some astonishment for a few seconds, hemmed three or four times in a husky manner, and, after muttering something about 'that troublesome cough,' bid Oliver dry his eyes and be a good boy; and, once more taking his hand, walked on with him in silence.

The undertaker had just put up the shutters of his shop, and was making some entries in his day-book[8] by the light of a most appropriately dismal candle, when Mr Bumble entered.

'Aha!' said the undertaker, looking up from the book, and pausing in the middle of a word; 'is that you, Bumble?'

'No one else, Mr Sowerberry,' replied the beadle. 'Here, I've brought the boy.' Oliver made a bow.

'Oh! that's the boy, is it?' said the undertaker, raising the candle above his head to get a full glimpse of Oliver. 'Mrs Sowerberry! will you come here a moment, my dear?'

Mrs Sowerberry emerged from a little room behind the shop, and presented the form of a short, thin, squeezed-up woman, with a vixenish countenance.

'My dear,' said Mr Sowerberry, deferentially, 'this is the boy from the workhouse that I told you of.' Oliver bowed again.

'Dear me!' said the undertaker's wife, 'he's very small.'

'Why, he *is* rather small,' replied Mr Bumble, looking at Oliver as if it were his fault that he wasn't bigger; 'he *is* small, – there's no denying it. But he'll grow, Mrs Sowerberry, – he'll grow.'

'Ah! I dare say he will,' replied the lady pettishly, 'on our victuals, and our drink. I see no saving in parish children, not I; for they always cost more to keep, than they're worth: however, men always think they know best. There, get down stairs, little bag o' bones.' With this, the undertaker's wife opened a side door, and pushed Oliver down a steep flight of stairs into a stone cell, damp and dark, forming the ante-room to the coal-cellar, and denominated 'the kitchen,' wherein sat a slatternly girl in shoes down at heel, and blue worsted stockings very much out of repair.

'Here, Charlotte,' said Mrs Sowerberry, who had followed Oliver down, 'give this boy some of the cold bits that were put by for Trip: he hasn't come home since the morning, so he may go without 'em. I dare say he isn't too dainty to eat 'em, – are you, boy?'

Oliver, whose eyes had glistened at the mention of meat, and who was trembling with eagerness to devour it, replied in the negative; and a plateful of coarse broken victuals was set before him.

I wish some well-fed philosopher, whose meat and drink turn to gall within him, whose blood is ice, and whose heart is iron, could have seen Oliver Twist clutching at the dainty viands that the dog had neglected, and witnessed the horrible avidity with which he tore the bits asunder with all the ferocity of famine: – there is only one thing I should like better; and that would be to see him making the same sort of meal himself, with the same relish.

'Well,' said the undertaker's wife, when Oliver had finished his supper, which she had regarded in silent horror, and with fearful auguries of his future appetite, 'have you done?'

There being nothing eatable within his reach, Oliver replied in the affirmative.

'Then come with me,' said Mrs Sowerberry, taking up a dim and dirty lamp, and leading the way up stairs; 'your bed's under the counter. You won't mind sleeping among the coffins, I suppose? – but it doesn't much matter whether you will or not, for you won't sleep any where else. Come; don't keep me here, all night.'

Oliver lingered no longer, but meekly followed his new mistress.

*

CHAPTER THE FIFTH

OLIVER MINGLES WITH NEW ASSOCIATES, AND, GOING TO A FUNERAL FOR THE FIRST TIME, FORMS AN UNFAVOURABLE NOTION OF HIS MASTER'S BUSINESS

Oliver, being left to himself in the undertaker's shop, set the lamp down on a workman's bench, and gazed timidly about him with a feeling of awe and dread, which many people a good deal older than Oliver will be at no loss to understand. An unfinished coffin on black tressels, which stood in the middle of the shop, looked so gloomy and death-like, that a cold tremble came over him every time his eyes wandered in the direction of the dismal object, from which he almost expected to see some frightful form slowly rear its head to drive him mad with terror. Against the wall were ranged in regular array a long row of elm boards cut into the same shape, and looking in the dim light like high-shouldered ghosts with their hands in their breeches-pockets. Coffin-plates, elm-chips, bright-headed nails, and shreds of black cloth, lay scattered on the floor; and the wall above the counter was ornamented with a lively representation of two mutes[1] in very stiff neckcloths, on duty at a large private door, with a hearse drawn by four black steeds approaching in the distance. The shop was close and hot, and the atmosphere seemed tainted with the smell of coffins. The recess beneath the counter in which his flock-mattress was thrust, looked like a grave.

Nor were these the only dismal feelings which depressed Oliver. He was alone in a strange place; and we all know how chilled and desolate the best of us, will sometimes feel in such a situation. The boy had no friends to care for, or to care for him. The regret of no recent separation was fresh in his mind; the absence of no loved and well-remembered face sunk heavily into his heart. But his heart *was* heavy, notwithstanding; and he wished, as he crept into his narrow bed, that that were his coffin, and that he could be laid in a calm and lasting sleep in the churchyard ground, with the tall grass waving gently above his head, and the sound of the old deep bell to soothe him in his sleep.

Oliver was awakened in the morning by a loud kicking at the outside of the shop-door, which, before he could huddle on his clothes, was repeated in an angry and impetuous manner about twenty-five times; and, when he began to undo the chain, the legs left off their volleys, and a voice began.

'Open the door, will yer?' cried the voice which belonged to the legs which had kicked at the door.

'I will directly, sir,' replied Oliver, undoing the chain, and turning the key.

'I suppose yer the new boy, a'nt yer?' said the voice, through the key-hole.

'Yes, sir,' replied Oliver.

'How old are yer?' inquired the voice.

'Eleven, sir,' replied Oliver.

'Then I'll whop yer when I get in,' said the voice; 'you just see if I don't, that's all, my work'us brat!' and, having made this obliging promise, the voice began to whistle.

Oliver had been too often subjected to the process to which the very expressive monosyllable just recorded, bears reference, to entertain the smallest doubt that the owner of the voice, whoever he might be, would redeem his pledge most honourably. He drew back the bolts with a trembling hand, and opened the door.

For a second or two, Oliver glanced up the street, and down the street, and over the way, impressed with the belief that the unknown, who had addressed him through the key-hole, had walked a few paces off to warm himself, for nobody did Oliver see but a big charity-boy[2] sitting on the post in front of the house, eating a slice of bread and butter, which he cut into wedges the size of his mouth with a clasp-knife, and then consumed with great dexterity.

'I beg your pardon, sir,' said Oliver, at length, seeing that no other visitor made his appearance; 'did you knock?'

'I kicked,' replied the charity-boy.

'Did you want a coffin, sir?' inquired Oliver, innocently.

At this the charity-boy looked monstrous fierce, and said that Oliver would stand in need of one before long, if he cut jokes with his superiors in that way.

'Yer don't know who I am, I suppose, work'us?' said the charity-boy, in continuation; descending from the top of the post, meanwhile, with edifying gravity.

'No, sir,' rejoined Oliver.

'I'm Mister Noah Claypole,' said the charity-boy, 'and you're under me. Take down the shutters, yer idle young ruffian!' With this Mr Claypole administered a kick to Oliver, and entered the shop with a dignified air, which did him great credit: it is difficult for a large-headed, small-eyed youth, of lumbering make and heavy countenance, to look dignified under any circumstances; but it is more especially so, when, superadded to these personal attractions, are a red nose and yellow smalls.

Oliver having taken down the shutters, and broken a pane of glass in his efforts to stagger away beneath the weight of the first one to a small court at the side of the house in which they were kept during the day, was graciously assisted by Noah, who, having consoled him with the assurance that 'he'd catch it,' condescended to help him. Mr Sowerberry came down soon after, and, shortly afterwards, Mrs Sowerberry appeared; and Oliver having 'caught it,' in fulfilment of Noah's prediction, followed that young gentleman down stairs to breakfast.

'Come near the fire, Noah,' said Charlotte. 'I saved a nice little piece of bacon for you from master's breakfast. Oliver, shut that door at Mister Noah's back, and take them bits that I've put out on the cover of the bread-pan. There's your tea; take it away to that box, and drink it there, and make haste, for they'll want you to mind the shop. D'ye hear?'

'D'ye hear, work'us?' said Noah Claypole.

'Lor, Noah!' said Charlotte, 'what a rum creature you are! Why don't you let the boy alone?'

'Let him alone!' said Noah. 'Why everybody lets him alone enough, for the matter of that. Neither his father nor mother will ever interfere with him: all his relations let him have his own way pretty well. Eh, Charlotte? He! he! he!'

'Oh, you queer soul!' said Charlotte, bursting into a hearty laugh, in which she was joined by Noah; after which they both looked scornfully at poor Oliver Twist, as he sat shivering upon the box in the coldest corner of the room, and ate the stale pieces which had been specially reserved for him.

Noah was a charity-boy, but not a workhouse orphan. No chance-child was he, for he could trace his genealogy back all the way to his parents, who lived hard by; his mother being a washerwoman, and his father a drunken soldier, discharged with a wooden leg and a diurnal pension of twopence-halfpenny and an unstateable fraction. The shop-boys in the neighbourhood had long been in the habit of branding Noah in the public streets with the ignominious epithets of 'leathers,' 'charity,' and the like; and Noah had borne them without reply. But now that fortune had cast in his way a nameless orphan, at whom even the meanest could point the finger of scorn, he retorted on him with interest. This affords charming food for contemplation. It shows us what a beautiful thing human nature is, and how impartially the same amiable qualities are developed in the finest lord and the dirtiest charity-boy.

Oliver had been sojourning at the undertaker's some three weeks or a month, and Mr and Mrs Sowerberry, the shop being shut up, were taking their supper in the little back-parlour, when Mr Sowerberry, after several deferential glances at his wife, said,

'My dear –' He was going to say more; but, Mrs Sowerberry looking up with a peculiarly unpropitious aspect, he stopped short.

'Well!' said Mrs Sowerberry, sharply.

'Nothing, my dear, nothing,' said Mr Sowerberry.

'Ugh, you brute!' said Mrs Sowerberry.

'Not at all, my dear,' said Mr Sowerberry, humbly. 'I thought you didn't want to hear, my dear. I was only going to say—'

'Oh, don't tell me what you were going to say,' interposed Mrs Sowerberry. 'I am nobody; don't consult me, pray. *I* don't want to intrude upon your secrets.' And, as Mrs Sowerberry said this, she gave an hysterical laugh, which threatened violent consequences.

'But, my dear,' said Sowerberry, 'I want to ask your advice.'

'No, no, don't ask mine,' replied Mrs Sowerberry, in an affecting manner; 'ask somebody else's.' Here there was another hysterical laugh, which frightened Mr Sowerberry very much. This is a very common and much-approved matrimonial course of treatment, which is often very effective. It at once reduced Mr Sowerberry to begging as a special favour to be allowed to say what Mrs Sowerberry was most curious to hear, and, after a short altercation of less than three quarters of an hour's duration, the permission was most graciously conceded.

'It's only about young Twist, my dear,' said Mr Sowersberry. 'A very good-looking boy that, my dear.'

'He need be, for he eats enough,' observed the lady.

'There's an expression of melancholy in his face, my dear,' resumed Mr Sowerberry, 'which is very interesting. He would make a delightful mute, my dear.'

Mrs Sowerberry looked up with an expression of considerable wonderment. Mr Sowerberry remarked it, and, without allowing time for any observation on the good lady's part, proceeded,

'I don't mean a regular mute to attend grown-up people, my dear, but only for children's practice. It would be very new to have a mute in proportion, my dear. You may depend upon it that it would have a superb effect.'

Mrs Sowerberry, who had a good deal of taste in the undertaking way, was much struck by the novelty of the idea; but, as it would have been compromising her dignity to have said so under existing circumstances, she merely inquired with much sharpness why such an obvious suggestion had not presented itself to her husband's mind before. Mr Sowerberry rightly construed this as an acquiescence in his proposition: it was speedily determined that Oliver should be at once initiated into the mysteries of the profession, and, with this view, that he should accompany his master on the very next occasion of his services being required.

The occasion was not long in coming; for, half an hour after breakfast next morning, Mr Bumble entered the shop, and supporting his cane against the counter, drew forth his large leathern pocket-book, from which he selected a small scrap of paper which he handed over to Sowerberry.

'Aha!' said the undertaker, glancing over it with a lively countenance; 'an order for a coffin, eh?'

'For a coffin first, and a porochial funeral afterwards,' replied Mr Bumble, fastening the strap of the leathern pocket-book, which, like himself, was very corpulent.

'Bayton,' said the undertaker, looking from the scrap of paper to Mr Bumble; 'I never heard the name before.'

Bumble shook his head as he replied, 'Obstinate people, Mr Sowerberry, very obstinate; proud, too, I'm afraid, sir.'

'Proud, eh?' exclaimed Mr Sowerberry with a sneer. – 'Come, that's too much.'

'Oh, it's sickening,' replied the beadle; 'perfectly antimonial,[3] Mr Sowerberry.'

'So it is,' acquiesced the undertaker.

'We only heard of them the night before last,' said the beadle; 'and we shouldn't have known anything about them then, only a woman who lodges in the same house made an application to the porochial committee for them to send the porochial surgeon to see a woman as was very bad. He had gone out to dinner; but his 'prentice, which is a very clever lad, sent 'em some medicine in a blacking-bottle, off-hand.'

'Ah, there's promptness,' said the undertaker.

'Promptness, indeed!' replied the beadle. 'But what's the consequence; what's the ungrateful behaviour of these rebels, sir? Why, the husband sends back word that the medicine won't suit his wife's complaint, and so she shan't take it – says she shan't take it, sir. Good, strong, wholesome medicine, as was given with great success to two Irish labourers and a coalheaver only a week before – sent 'em for nothing, with a blacking-bottle in, – and he sends back word that she shan't take it, sir.'

As the flagrant atrocity presented itself to Mr Bumble's mind in full force, he struck the counter sharply with his cane, and became flushed with indignation.

'Well,' said the undertaker, 'I ne – ver – did –'

'Never did, sir!' ejaculated the beadle, – 'no, nor nobody never did; but, now she's dead, we've got to bury her, and that's the direction, and the sooner it's done, the better.'

Thus saying, Mr Bumble put on his cocked-hat wrong side first, in a fever of parochial excitement, and flounced out of the shop.

'Why, he was so angry, Oliver, that he forgot even to ask after you,' said Mr Sowerberry, looking after the beadle as he strode down the street.

'Yes, sir,' replied Oliver, who had carefully kept himself out of sight during the interview, and who was shaking from head to foot at the mere recollection of the sound of Mr Bumble's voice. He needn't have taken the trouble to shrink from Mr Bumble's glance, however; for that functionary on whom the prediction of the gentleman in the white waistcoat had made a very strong impression, thought that now the undertaker had got Oliver upon trial, the subject was better avoided, until such time as he should be firmly bound for seven years, and all danger of his being returned upon the hands of the parish should be thus effectually and legally overcome.

'Well,' said Mr Sowerberry, taking up his hat, 'the sooner this job is done, the better. Noah, look after the shop. Oliver, put on your cap, and come with me.' Oliver obeyed, and followed his master on his professional mission.

They walked on for some time through the most crowded and densely inhabited part of the town, and then striking down a narrow street more dirty and miserable than any they had yet passed through, paused to look for the house which was the object of their search. The houses on either side were high and large, but very old; and tenanted by people of the poorest class, as their neglected appearance would have sufficiently denoted without the concurrent testimony afforded by the squalid looks of the few men and women who, with folded arms and bodies half doubled, occasionally skulked like shadows along. A great many of the tenements had shop-fronts; but they were fast closed, and mouldering away: only the upper rooms being inhabited. Others, which had become insecure from age and decay, were prevented from falling into the street by huge beams of wood which were reared against the tottering walls, and firmly planted in the road; but even these crazy dens seemed to have been selected as the nightly haunts of some houseless wretches,[4] for many of the rough boards which supplied the place of door and window, were wrenched from their positions to afford an aperture wide enough for the passage of a human body. The kennel was stagnant and filthy;[5] the very rats that here and there lay putrefying in its rottenness, were hideous with famine.

There was neither knocker nor bell-handle at the open door where Oliver and his master stopped; so, groping his way cautiously through the dark passage, and bidding Oliver keep close to him and not be afraid, the undertaker mounted to the top of the first flight of stairs, and, stumbling against a door on the landing, rapped at it with his knuckles.

It was opened by a young girl of thirteen or fourteen. The undertaker at once saw enough of what the room contained, to know it was the apartment to which he had been directed. He stepped in, and Oliver followed him.

There was no fire in the room; but a man was crouching mechanically over the empty stove. An old woman, too, had drawn a low stool to the cold hearth, and was sitting beside him. There were some ragged children in another corner; and in a small recess opposite the door there lay upon the ground something covered with an old blanket. Oliver shuddered as he cast his eyes towards the place, and crept involuntarily closer to his master; for, though it was covered up, the boy *felt* that it was a corpse.

The man's face was thin and very pale; his hair and beard were grizzly, and his eyes were bloodshot. The old woman's face was wrinkled, her two remaining teeth protruded over her under lip, and her eyes were bright and piercing. Oliver was afraid to look at either her or the man, – they seemed so like the rats he had seen outside.

'Nobody shall go near her,' said the man, starting fiercely up, as the undertaker approached the recess. 'Keep back! d–n you, keep back, if you've a life to lose.'

'Nonsense! my good man,' said the undertaker, who was pretty well used to misery in all its shapes, – 'nonsense!'

'I tell you,' said the man, clenching his hands, and stamping furiously on the floor, – 'I tell you I won't have her put into the ground. She couldn't rest there. The worms would worry – not eat her, – she is so worn away.'

The undertaker offered no reply to this raving, but producing a tape from his pocket, knelt down for a moment by the side of the body.

'Ah!' said the man, bursting into tears, and sinking on his knees at the feet of the dead woman; 'kneel down, kneel down – kneel round her every one of you, and mark my words. I say she starved to death. I never knew how bad she was, till the fever came upon her, and then her bones were starting through the skin. There was neither fire nor candle; she died in the dark – in the dark. She couldn't even see her children's faces, though we heard her gasping out their names. I begged for her in the streets, and they sent me to prison.[6] When I came back, she was dying; and all the blood in my heart has dried up, for they starved her to death. I swear it before the God that saw it, – they starved her!' – He twined his hands in his hair, and with a loud scream rolled grovelling upon the floor, his eyes fixed, and the foam gushing from his lips.

The terrified children cried bitterly; but the old woman, who had hitherto remained as quiet as if she had been wholly deaf to all that passed, menaced them into silence; and having unloosened the man's cravat, who still remained extended on the ground, tottered towards the undertaker.

'She was my daughter,' said the old woman, nodding her head in the direction of the corpse, and speaking with an idiotic leer, more ghastly than even the presence of death itself. – 'Lord, Lord! – well, it *is* strange that I who gave birth to her, and was a woman then, should be alive and merry now, and she lying there, so cold and stiff! Lord, Lord! – to think of it; – it's as good as a play – as good as a play!'

As the wretched creature mumbled and chuckled in her hideous merriment, the undertaker turned to go away.

'Stop, stop!' said the old woman in a loud whisper. 'Will she be buried to-morrow – or next day – or to-night? I laid her out, and I must walk, you know. Send me a large cloak – a good warm one, for it is bitter cold. We should have cake and wine, too, before we go! Never mind: send some bread – only a loaf of bread and a cup of water. Shall we have some bread, dear?' she said eagerly, catching at the undertaker's coat, as he once more moved towards the door.

'Yes, yes,' said the undertaker, 'of course; anything, everything.' He disengaged himself from the old woman's grasp, and, dragging Oliver after him, hurried away.

The next day, (the family having been meanwhile relieved with a half-quartern loaf[7] and a piece of cheese, left with them by Mr Bumble himself,) Oliver and his master returned to the miserable abode, where Mr Bumble had already arrived, accompanied by four men from the workhouse, who were to act as bearers. An old black cloak had been thrown over the rags of the old woman and the man; the bare coffin having been screwed down, was then hoisted on the shoulders of the bearers, and carried down stairs into the street.

'Now, you must put your best leg foremost, old lady,' whispered Sowerberry in the old woman's ear; 'we are rather late, and it won't do to keep the clergyman waiting. Move on, my men, – as quick as you like.'

Thus directed, the bearers trotted on, under their light burden, and the two mourners kept as near them as they could. Mr Bumble and Sowerberry walked at a good smart pace in front; and Oliver, whose legs were not as long as his master's, ran by the side.

There was not so great a necessity for hurrying as Mr Sowerberry had anticipated, however; for when they reached the obscure corner of the churchyard in which the nettles grew, and the parish graves[8] were made, the clergyman had not arrived, and the clerk, who was sitting by the vestry-room fire, seemed to think it by no means improbable that it might be an hour or so before he came. So they set the bier down on the brink of the grave; and the two mourners waited patiently in the damp clay with a cold rain drizzling down, while the ragged boys, whom the spectacle had attracted into the churchyard, played a noisy game at hide-and-seek among the tombstones, or varied their amusements by jumping backwards and forwards over the coffin. Mr Sowerberry and Bumble, being personal friends of the clerk, sat by the fire with him, and read the paper.

At length, after the lapse of something more than an hour, Mr Bumble, and Sowerberry, and the clerk, were seen running towards the grave; and immediately afterwards the clergyman appeared, putting on his surplice as he came along. Mr Bumble then threshed a boy or two, to keep up appearances; and the reverend gentleman, having read as much of the burial service as could be compressed into four minutes, gave his surplice to the clerk, and ran away again.

'Now, Bill,' said Sowerberry to the grave-digger, 'fill up.'

It was no very difficult task, for the grave was so full that the uppermost coffin was within a few feet of the surface. The grave-digger shovelled in the earth, stamped it loosely down with his feet, shouldered his spade, and walked off, followed by the boys, who murmured very loud complaints at the fun being over so soon.

'Come, my good fellow,' said Bumble, tapping the man on the back, 'they want to shut up the yard.'

The man, who had never once moved since he had taken his station by the grave side, started, raised his head, stared at the person who had addressed him, walked forward for a few paces, and then fell down in a fit. The crazy old woman was too much occupied in bewailing the loss of her cloak (which the undertaker had taken off) to pay him any attention: so they threw a can of cold water over him, and when he came to, saw him safely out of the churchyard, locked the gate, and departed on their different ways.

'Well, Oliver,' said Sowerberry, as they walked home, 'how do you like it?'

'Pretty well, thank you, sir,' replied Oliver, with considerable hesitation. 'Not very much, sir.'

'Ah, you'll get used to it in time, Oliver,' said Sowerberry. 'Nothing when you *are* used to it, my boy.'

Oliver wondered in his own mind whether it had taken a very long time to get Mr Sowerberry used to it; but he thought it better not to ask the question, and walked back to the shop, thinking over all he had seen and heard.

CHAPTER THE SIXTH

OLIVER, BEING GOADED BY THE TAUNTS
OF NOAH, ROUSES INTO ACTION, AND
RATHER ASTONISHES HIM

It was a nice sickly season just at this time. In commercial phrase, coffins were looking up; and, in the course of a few weeks, Oliver had acquired a great deal of experience. The success of Mr Sowerberry's ingenious speculation exceeded even his most sanguine hopes. The oldest inhabitants recollected no period at which measles had been so prevalent, or so fatal to infant existence; and many were the mournful processions which little Oliver headed in a hat-band reaching down to his knees, to the indescribable admiration and emotion of all the mothers in the town. As Oliver accompanied his master in most of his adult expeditions too, in order that he might acquire that equanimity of demeanour and full command of nerve which are so essential to a finished undertaker, he had many opportunities of observing the beautiful resignation and fortitude with which some strong-minded people bear their trials and losses.

For instance, when Sowerberry had an order for the burial of some rich old lady or gentleman, who was surrounded by a great number of nephews and nieces, who had been perfectly inconsolable during the previous illness, and whose grief had been wholly irrepressible even on the most public occasions, they would be as happy among themselves as need be – quite cheerful and contented, conversing together with as much freedom and gaiety as if nothing whatever had happened to disturb them. Husbands, too, bore the loss of their wives with the most heroic calmness; and wives, again, put on weeds for their husbands, as if, so far from grieving in the garb of sorrow, they had made up their minds to render it as becoming and attractive as possible. It was observable, too, that ladies and gentlemen who were in passions of anguish during the ceremony of interment, recovered almost as soon as they reached home, and became quite composed before the tea-drinking was over. All this was very pleasant and improving to see; and Oliver beheld it with great admiration.

That Oliver Twist was moved to resignation by the example of these good people, I cannot, although I am his biographer, undertake to affirm with any degree of confidence; but I can most distinctly say, that for some weeks he continued meekly to submit to the domination and ill-treatment of Noah Claypole, who used him far worse than ever, now that his jealousy was roused by seeing the new boy promoted to the black stick and hat-band, while he, the old one, remained stationary in the muffin-cap and leathers. Charlotte treated him badly because Noah did; and Mrs Sowerberry was his decided enemy because Mr Sowerberry was disposed to be his friend: so, between these three on one side, and a glut of funerals on the other, Oliver was not altogether as comfortable as the hungry pig was, when he was shut up by mistake in the grain department of a brewery.

And now I come to a very important passage in Oliver's history, for I have to record an act, slight and unimportant perhaps in appearance, but which indirectly produced a most material change in all his future prospects and proceedings.

One day Oliver and Noah had descended into the kitchen, at the usual dinner-hour, to banquet upon a small joint of mutton – a pound and a half of the worst end of the neck; when, Charlotte being called out of the way, there ensued a brief interval of time, which Noah Claypole, being hungry and vicious, considered he could not possibly devote to a worthier purpose than aggravating and tantalising young Oliver Twist.

Intent upon this innocent amusement, Noah put his feet on the table-cloth, and pulled Oliver's hair, and twitched his ears, and expressed his opinion that he was a 'sneak,' and furthermore announced his intention of coming to see him hung whenever that desirable event should take place, and entered upon various other topics of petty annoyance, like a malicious and ill-conditioned charity-boy as he was. But, none of these taunts producing the desired effect of making Oliver cry, Noah attempted to be more facetious still, and in this attempt did what many small wits, with far greater reputations than Noah notwithstanding, do to this day when they want to be funny; – he got rather personal.

'Work'us,' said Noah, 'how's your mother?'

'She's dead,' replied Oliver; 'don't you say anything about her to me!'

Oliver's colour rose as he said this; he breathed quickly, and there was a curious working of the mouth and nostrils, which Mr Claypole thought must be the immediate precursor of a violent fit of crying. Under this impression he returned to the charge.

'What did she die of, work'us?' said Noah.

'Of a broken heart, some of our old nurses told me,' replied Oliver, more as if he were talking to himself than answering Noah. 'I think I know what it must be to die of that!'

'Tol de rol lol lol, right fol lairy, work'us,' said Noah, as a tear rolled down Oliver's cheek. 'What's set you a snivelling now?'

'Not *you*,' replied Oliver, hastily brushing the tear away. 'Don't think it.'

'Oh, not me, eh?' sneered Noah.

'No, not you,' replied Oliver, sharply. 'There; that's enough. Don't say anything more to me about her; you'd better not!'

'Better not!' exclaimed Noah. 'Well! better not! work'us; don't be impudent. *Your* mother, too! She was a nice 'un, she was. Oh, Lor!' And here Noah nodded his head expressively, and curled up as much of his small red nose as muscular action could collect together for the occasion.

'Yer know, work'us,' continued Noah, emboldened by Oliver's silence, and speaking in a jeering tone of affected pity – of all tones the most annoying – 'Yer know, work'us, it carn't be helped now, and of course yer couldn't help it then, and I'm very sorry for it, and I'm sure we all are, and pity yer very much. But yer must know, work'us, your mother was a regular right-down bad 'un.'

'What did you say?' inquired Oliver, looking up very quickly.

'A regular right-down bad 'un, work'us,' replied Noah, coolly; 'and it's a great deal better, work'us, that she died when she did, or else she'd have been hard labouring in Bridewell, or transported,[1] or hung, which is more likely than either, isn't it?'

Crimson with fury, Oliver started up, overthrew chair and table, seized Noah by the throat, shook him in the violence of his rage till his teeth chattered in his head, and, collecting his whole force into one heavy blow, felled him to the ground.

A minute ago the boy had looked the quiet, mild, dejected creature that harsh treatment had made him. But his spirit was roused at last; the cruel insult to his dead mother had set his blood on fire. His breast heaved, his attitude was erect, his eye bright and vivid, and his whole person changed, as he stood glaring over the cowardly tormentor that lay crouching at his feet, and defied him with an energy he had never known before.

'He'll murder me!' blubbered Noah. 'Charlotte! missis! here's the new boy a-murdering me! Help! help! Oliver's gone mad! Char – lotte!'

Noah's shouts were responded to, by a loud scream from Charlotte, and a louder from Mrs Sowerberry; the former of whom rushed into the kitchen by a side-door, while the latter paused on the staircase till she was quite certain that it was consistent with the preservation of human life to come further down.

'Oh, you little wretch!' screamed Charlotte, seizing Oliver with her utmost force, which was about equal to that of a moderately strong man in particularly good training, – 'Oh, you little un-grate-ful, mur-de-rous, hor-rid villain!' and between every syllable Charlotte gave Oliver a blow with all her might, and accompanied it with a scream for the benefit of society.

Charlotte's fist was by no means a light one; but, lest it should not be effectual in calming Oliver's wrath, Mrs Sowerberry plunged into the kitchen, and assisted to hold him with one hand, while she scratched his face with the other; and in this favourable position of affairs Noah rose from the ground, and pummeled him from behind.

This was rather too violent exercise to last long; so, when they were all three wearied out, and could tear and beat no longer, they dragged Oliver, struggling and shouting, but nothing daunted, into the dust-cellar, and there locked him up; and this being done, Mrs Sowerberry sunk into a chair, and burst into tears.

'Bless her, she's going off!' said Charlotte. 'A glass of water, Noah, dear. Make haste.'

'Oh, Charlotte,' said Mrs Sowerberry, speaking as well as she could

Oliver plucks up a spirit

through a deficiency of breath and a sufficiency of cold water, which Noah had poured over her head and shoulders, – 'Oh, Charlotte, what a mercy we have not been all murdered in our beds!'

'Ah, mercy, indeed, ma'am,' was the reply. 'I only hope this'll teach master not to have any more of these dreadful creatures that are born to be murderers and robbers from their very cradle. Poor Noah! he was all but killed, ma'am, when I came in.'

'Ah, poor fellow!' said Mrs Sowerberry, looking piteously on the charity-boy.

Noah, whose top waistcoat-button might have been somewhere on a level with the crown of Oliver's head, rubbed his eyes with the inside of his wrists while this commiseration was bestowed upon him, and performed some very audible tears and sniffs.

'What's to be done!' exclaimed Mrs Sowerberry. 'Your master's not at home, – there's not a man in the house, – and he'll kick that door down in ten minutes.' Oliver's vigorous plunges against the bit of timber in question rendered this occurrence highly probable.

'Dear, dear! I don't know, ma'am,' said Charlotte, 'unless we send for the police-officers.'

'Or the millingtary,' suggested Mr Claypole.

'No, no,' said Mrs Sowerberry, bethinking herself of Oliver's old friend; 'run to Mr Bumble, Noah, and tell him to come here directly, and not to lose a minute; never mind your cap, – make haste. You can hold a knife to that black eye as you run along, and it'll keep the swelling down.'

Noah stopped to make no reply, but started off at his fullest speed; and very much it astonished the people who were out walking, to see a charity-boy tearing through the streets pell-mell, with no cap on his head, and a clasp-knife at his eye.

*

CHAPTER THE SEVENTH

OLIVER CONTINUES REFRACTORY

Noah Claypole ran along the streets at his swiftest pace, and paused not once for breath until he reached the workhouse-gate. Having rested here, for a minute or so, to collect a good burst of sobs and an imposing show of tears and terror, he knocked loudly at the wicket, and presented such a rueful face to the aged pauper who opened it, that even he, who saw nothing but rueful faces about him at the best of times, started back in astonishment.

'Why, what's the matter with the boy?' said the old pauper.

'Mr Bumble! Mr Bumble!' cried Noah, with well-affected dismay, and in tones so loud and agitated that they not only caught the ear of Mr Bumble himself who happened to be hard by, but alarmed him so much that he rushed into the yard without his cocked hat, – which is a very curious and remarkable circumstance, as showing that even a beadle, acted upon by a sudden and powerful impulse, may be afflicted with a momentary visitation of loss of self-possession, and forgetfulness of personal dignity.

'Oh, Mr Bumble, sir!' said Noah; 'Oliver, sir, – Oliver has —'

'What? what?' interposed Mr Bumble, with a gleam of pleasure in his metallic eyes. 'Not run away: he hasn't run away; has he, Noah?'

'No, sir, no; not run away, sir, but he's turned wicious,' replied Noah. 'He tried to murder me, sir; and then he tried to murder Charlotte, and then missis. Oh, what dreadful pain it is! such agony, please sir!' and here Noah writhed and twisted his body into an extensive variety of eel-like positions; thereby giving Mr Bumble to understand that, from the violent and sanguinary onset of Oliver Twist, he had sustained severe internal injury and damage, from which he was at that speaking suffering the acutest torture.

When Noah saw that the intelligence he communicated perfectly paralysed Mr Bumble, he imparted additional effect thereunto, by bewailing his dreadful wounds ten times louder than before: and, when he observed a gentleman in a white waistcoat crossing the yard, he was more tragic in his lamentations than ever, rightly conceiving it highly expedient to attract the notice, and rouse the indignation, of the gentleman aforesaid.

The gentleman's notice was very soon attracted; for he had not walked three paces when he turned angrily round, and inquired what that young cur was howling for, and why Mr Bumble did not favour him with something which would render the series of vocular exclamations so designated, an involuntary process.

'It's a poor boy from the free-school, sir,' replied Mr Bumble, 'who has been nearly murdered – all but murdered, sir – by young Twist.'

'By Jove!' exclaimed the gentleman in the white waistcoat, stopping short. 'I knew it! I felt a strange presentiment from the very first, that that audacious young savage would come to be hung!'

'He has likewise attempted, sir, to murder the female servant,' said Mr Bumble, with a face of ashy paleness.

'And his missis,' interposed Mr Claypole.

'And his master, too, I think you said, Noah?' added Mr Bumble.

'No, he's out, or he would have murdered him,' replied Noah. 'He said he wanted to –'

'Ah! said he wanted to – did he, my boy?' inquired the gentleman in the white waistcoat.

'Yes, sir,' replied Noah; 'and, please sir, missis wants to know whether Mr Bumble can spare time to step up there directly, and flog him, 'cause master's out.'

'Certainly, my boy; certainly,' said the gentleman in the white waistcoat, smiling benignly, and patting Noah's head, which was about three inches higher than his own. 'You're a good boy – a very good boy. Here's a penny for you. Bumble, just step up to Sowerberry's with your cane, and see what's best to be done. Don't spare him, Bumble.'

'No, I will not, sir,' replied the beadle, adjusting the wax-end which was twisted round the bottom of his cane[1] for purposes of parochial flagellation.

'Tell Sowerberry not to spare him, either. They'll never do anything with him, without stripes and bruises,' said the gentleman in the white waistcoat.

'I'll take care, sir,' replied the beadle. And, the cocked hat and cane having been by this time adjusted to their owner's satisfaction, Mr Bumble and Noah Claypole betook themselves with all speed to the undertaker's shop.

Here the position of affairs had not at all improved, for Sowerberry had not yet returned, and Oliver continued to kick with undiminished vigour at the cellar-door. The accounts of his ferocity, as related by Mrs Sowerberry and Charlotte, were of so startling a nature that Mr Bumble judged it prudent to parley before opening the door: with this view, he gave a kick at the outside, by way of prelude, and then, applying his mouth to the keyhole, said, in a deep and impressive tone,

'Oliver!'

'Come; you let me out!' replied Oliver, from the inside.

'Do you know this here voice, Oliver?' said Mr Bumble.

'Yes,' replied Oliver.

'Ain't you afraid of it, sir? Ain't you a-trembling while I speak, sir?' said Mr Bumble.

'No!' replied Oliver, boldly.

An answer so different from the one he had expected to elicit, and was in the habit of receiving, staggered Mr Bumble not a little. He stepped back from the keyhole, drew himself up to his full height, and looked from one to another of the three bystanders in mute astonishment.

'Oh, you know, Mr Bumble, he must be mad,' said Mrs Sowerberry. 'No boy in half his senses could venture to speak so to you.'

'It's not madness, ma'am,' replied Mr Bumble, after a few moments of deep meditation; 'it's meat.'

'What!' exclaimed Mrs Sowerberry.

'Meat, ma'am, meat,' replied Bumble, with stern emphasis. 'You've overfed him, ma'am. You've raised a artificial soul and spirit in him, ma'am, unbecoming a person of his condition, as the board, Mrs Sowerberry, who are practical philosophers, will tell you. What have paupers to do with soul or spirit either? It's quite enough that we let 'em have live bodies. If you had kept the boy on gruel, ma'am, this would never have happened.'

'Dear, dear!' ejaculated Mrs Sowerberry, piously raising her eyes to the kitchen ceiling. 'This comes of being liberal!'

The liberality of Mrs Sowerberry to Oliver had consisted in a profuse bestowal upon him, of all the dirty odds and ends which nobody else would eat; so that there was a great deal of meekness and self-devotion in her voluntarily remaining under Mr Bumble's heavy accusation, of which, to do her justice, she was wholly innocent in thought, word, or deed.

'Ah!' said Mr Bumble, when the lady brought her eyes down to earth again. 'The only thing that can be done now, that I know of, is to leave him in the cellar for a day or so till he's a little starved down, and then to take him out, and keep him on gruel all through his apprenticeship. He comes of a bad family – excitable natures, Mrs Sowerberry. Both the nurse and doctor said that that mother of his, made her way here against difficulties and pain that would have killed any well-disposed woman weeks before.'

At this point of Mr Bumble's discourse, Oliver just hearing enough to know that some further allusion was being made to his mother, recommenced kicking with a violence which rendered every other sound inaudible. Sowerberry returned at this juncture, and Oliver's offence having been explained to him, with such exaggerations as the ladies thought best calculated to rouse his ire, he unlocked the cellar-door in a twinkling, and dragged his rebellious apprentice out by the collar.

Oliver's clothes had been torn in the beating he had received; his face was bruised and scratched, and his hair scattered over his forehead. The angry flush had not disappeared, however; and when he was pulled out of his prison, he scowled boldly on Noah, and looked quite undismayed.

'Now, you are a nice young fellow, ain't you?' said Sowerberry, giving Oliver a shake, and a sound box on the ear.

'He called my mother names,' replied Oliver, sullenly.

'Well, and what if he did, you little ungrateful wretch?' said Mrs Sowerberry. 'She deserved what he said, and worse.'

'She didn't!' said Oliver.

'She did!' said Mrs Sowerberry.

'It's a lie!' said Oliver.

Mrs Sowerberry burst into a flood of tears.

This flood of tears left Sowerberry no alternative. If he had hesitated for one instant to punish Oliver most severely, it must be quite clear to every experienced reader that he would have been, according to all precedents in disputes of matrimony established, a brute, an unnatural husband, an insulting creature, a base imitation of a man, and various other agreeable characters too numerous for recital within the limits of this chapter. To do him justice, he was, as far as his power went, – it was not very extensive, – kindly disposed towards the boy; perhaps because it was his interest to be so, perhaps because his wife disliked him. The flood of tears, however, left him no resource; so he at once gave him a drubbing, which satisfied even Mrs Sowerberry herself, and rendered Mr Bumble's subsequent application of the parochial cane rather unnecessary. For the rest of the day he was shut up in the back kitchen, in company with a pump and a slice of bread; and, at night, Mrs Sowerberry, after making various remarks outside the door, by no means complimentary to the memory of his mother, looked into the room, and, amidst the jeers and pointings of Noah and Charlotte, ordered him up stairs to his dismal bed.

It was not until he was left alone in the silence and stillness of the gloomy workshop of the undertaker, that Oliver gave way to the feelings which the day's treatment may be supposed likely to have awakened in a mere child. He had listened to their taunts with a look of dogged contempt; he had borne the lash without a cry, for he felt that pride swelling in his heart which would have kept down a shriek to the last, if they had roasted him alive. But, now that there were none to see or hear him, he fell upon his knees on the floor, and, hiding his face in his hands, wept such tears as, God send for the credit of our nature, few so young may ever have cause to pour out before him.

For a long time Oliver remained motionless in this attitude. The candle was burning low in the socket when he rose to his feet, and having gazed cautiously round him, and listened intently, gently undid the fastenings of the door and looked abroad.

It was a cold dark night. The stars seemed to the boy's eyes further from the earth than he had ever seen them before; there was no wind, and the sombre shadows thrown by the trees on the earth looked sepulchral and death-like, from being so still. He softly reclosed the door, and, having availed himself of the expiring light of the candle to tie up in a handkerchief the few articles of wearing apparel he had, sat himself down upon a bench to wait for morning.

With the first ray of light that struggled through the crevices in the shutters Oliver rose, and again unbarred the door. One timid look around, – one moment's pause of hesitation, – he had closed it behind him, and was in the open street.

He looked to the right and to the left, uncertain whither to fly. He remembered to have seen the waggons as they went out, toiling up the hill; he took the same route, and arriving at a footpath across the fields, which he thought after some distance led out again into the road, struck into it, and walked quickly on.

Along this same footpath, Oliver well remembered he had trotted beside Mr Bumble, when he first carried him to the workhouse from the farm. His way lay directly in front of the cottage. His heart beat quickly when he bethought himself of this, and he half resolved to turn back. He had come a long way though, and should lose a great deal of time by doing so. Besides, it was so early that there was very little fear of his being seen; so he walked on.

He reached the house. There was no appearance of its inmates stirring at that early hour. Oliver stopped, and peeped into the garden. A child was weeding one of the little beds; and, as he stopped, he raised his pale face, and disclosed the features of one of his former companions. Oliver felt glad to see him before he went, for, though younger than himself, he had been his little friend and playmate; they had been beaten, and starved, and shut up together, many and many a time.

'Hush, Dick!' said Oliver, as the boy ran to the gate, and thrust his thin arm between the rails to greet him. 'Is any one up?'

'Nobody but me,' replied the child.

'You mustn't say you saw me, Dick,' said Oliver; 'I am running away. They beat and ill-use me, Dick; and I am going to seek my fortune some long way off, I don't know where. How pale you are!'

'I heard the doctor tell them I was dying,' replied the child with a faint smile. 'I am very glad to see you, dear; but don't stop, don't stop.'

'Yes, yes, I will, to say good-b'ye to you,' replied Oliver. 'I shall see you again, Dick; I know I shall. You will be well and happy.'

'I hope so,' replied the child, 'after I am dead, but not before. I know the doctor must be right, Oliver; because I dream so much of heaven, and angels, and kind faces that I never see when I am awake. Kiss me,' said the child, climbing up the low gate, and flinging his little arms round Oliver's neck. 'Good-b'ye, dear! God bless you!'

The blessing was from a young child's lips, but it was the first that Oliver had ever heard invoked upon his head; and through all the struggles and sufferings of his after life, through all the troubles and changes of many weary years, he never once forgot it.

CHAPTER THE EIGHTH

OLIVER WALKS TO LONDON, AND ENCOUNTERS ON THE ROAD A STRANGE SORT OF YOUNG GENTLEMAN

Oliver reached the stile at which the by-path terminated, and once more gained the high-road. It was eight o'clock now; and, though he was nearly five miles away from the town, he ran, and hid behind the hedges by turns, till noon, fearing that he might be pursued and overtaken. Then he sat down to rest at the side of a mile-stone, and began to think for the first time where he had better go and try to live.

The stone by which he was seated, bore in large characters an intimation that it was just seventy miles from that spot to London. The name awakened a new train of ideas in the boy's mind. London! – that great large place! – nobody – not even Mr Bumble – could ever find him there. He had often heard the old men in the workhouse, too, say that no lad of spirit need want in London, and that there were ways of living in that vast city which those who had been bred up in country parts had no idea of. It was the very place for a homeless boy, who must die in the streets unless some one helped him. As these things passed through his thoughts, he jumped upon his feet, and again walked forward.

He had diminished the distance between himself and London by full four miles more, before he recollected how much he must undergo ere he could hope to reach his place of destination. As this consideration forced itself upon him, he slackened his pace a little, and meditated upon his means of getting there. He had a crust of bread, a coarse shirt, and two pairs of stockings in his bundle; and a penny – a gift of Sowerberry's after some funeral in which he had acquitted himself more than ordinarily well – in his pocket. 'A clean shirt,' thought Oliver, 'is a very comfortable thing, – very; and so are two pairs of darned stockings, and so is a penny; but they are small helps to a sixty-five miles' walk in winter time.' But Oliver's thoughts, like those of most other people, although they were extremely ready and active to point out his difficulties, were wholly at a loss to suggest any feasible mode of surmounting them; so, after a good deal of thinking to no particular purpose, he changed his little bundle over to the other shoulder, and trudged on.

Oliver walked twenty miles that day; and all that time tasted nothing but the crust of dry bread, and a few draughts of water which he begged at the cottage-doors by the road-side. When the night came, he turned into a meadow, and, creeping close under a hay-rick, determined to lie there till morning. He felt frightened at first, for the wind moaned dismally over the empty fields, and he was cold and hungry, and more alone than he had ever felt before. Being very tired with his walk, however, he soon fell asleep and forgot his troubles.

He felt cold and stiff when he got up next morning, and so hungry that he was obliged to exchange the penny for a small loaf in the very first village through which he passed. He had walked no more than twelve miles, when night closed in again; for his feet were sore, and his legs so weak that they trembled beneath him. Another night passed in the bleak damp air only made him worse; and, when he set forward on his journey next morning, he could hardly crawl along.

He waited at the bottom of a steep hill till a stage-coach came up, and then begged of the outside passengers; but there were very few who took any notice of him, and even those, told him to wait till they got to the top of the hill, and then let them see how far he could run for a halfpenny. Poor Oliver tried to keep up with the coach a little way, but was unable to do it, by reason of his fatigue and sore feet. When the outsides saw this, they put their halfpence back into their pockets again, declaring that he was an idle young dog, and didn't deserve anything; and the coach rattled away, and left only a cloud of dust behind.

In some villages, large painted boards were fixed up, warning all persons who begged within the district that they would be sent to jail, which frightened Oliver very much, and made him very glad to get out of them with all possible expedition. In others he would stand about the inn-yards, and look mournfully at every one who passed; a proceeding which generally terminated in the landlady's ordering one of the post-boys[1] who were lounging about, to drive that strange boy out of the place, for she was sure he had come to steal something. If he begged at a farmer's house, ten to one but they threatened to set the dog on him; and when he showed his nose in a shop, they talked about the beadle, which brought Oliver's heart up into his mouth, – very often the only thing he had there, for many hours together.

In fact, if it had not been for a good-hearted turnpike-man,[2] and a benevolent old lady, Oliver's troubles would have been shortened by the very same process which put an end to his mother's; in other words, he would most assuredly have fallen dead upon the king's highway. But the turnpike-man gave him a meal of bread and cheese; and the old lady, who had a shipwrecked grandson wandering bare-footed in some distant part of the earth, took pity upon the poor orphan, and gave him what little she could afford – and more – with such kind and gentle words, and such tears of sympathy and compassion, that they sank deeper into Oliver's soul than all the sufferings he had ever undergone.

Early on the seventh morning after he had left his native place, Oliver limped slowly into the little town of Barnet.[3] The window-shutters were closed, the street was empty, not a soul had awakened to the business of the day. The sun was rising in all his splendid beauty, but the light only seemed to show the boy his own lonesomeness and desolation as he sat with bleeding feet and covered with dust upon a cold door-step.

By degrees the shutters were opened, the window-blinds were drawn up, and people began passing to and fro. Some few stopped to gaze at Oliver for a moment or two, or turned round to stare at him as they hurried by; but none relieved him, or troubled themselves to inquire how he came there. He had no heart to beg, and there he sat.

He had been crouching on the step for some time, gazing listlessly at the coaches as they passed through, and thinking how strange it seemed that they could do with ease in a few hours what it had taken him a whole week of courage and determination beyond his years to accomplish, when he was roused by observing that a boy who had passed him carelessly some minutes before, had returned, and was now surveying him most earnestly from the opposite side of the way. He took little heed of this at first; but the boy remained in the same attitude of close observation so long, that Oliver raised his head, and returned his steady look. Upon this, the boy crossed over, and, walking close up to Oliver, said,

'Hullo! my covey, what's the row?'

The boy who addressed this inquiry to the young wayfarer was about his own age, but one of the queerest-looking boys that Oliver had ever seen. He was a snub-nosed, flat-browed, common-faced boy enough, and as dirty a juvenile as one would wish to see; but he had got about him all the airs and manners of a man. He was short of his age, with rather bow-legs, and little sharp ugly eyes. His hat was stuck on the top of his head so slightly that it threatened to fall off every moment, and would have done so very often if the wearer had not had a knack of every now and then giving his head a sudden twitch, which brought it back to its old place again. He wore a man's coat, which reached nearly to his heels. He had turned the cuffs back halfway up his arm to get his hands out of the sleeves, apparently with the ultimate view of thrusting them into the pockets of his corduroy trousers, for there he kept them. He was altogether as roystering and swaggering a young gentleman as ever stood three feet six, or something less, in his bluchers.[4]

'Hullo, my covey, what's the row?' said this strange young gentleman to Oliver.

'I am very hungry and tired,' replied Oliver, the tears standing in his eyes as he spoke. 'I have walked a long way, – I have been walking these seven days.'

'Walking for sivin days!' said the young gentleman. 'Oh, I see. Beak's order, eh? But,' he added, noticing Oliver's look of surprise, 'I suppose you don't know wot a beak is, my flash com-pan-i-on.'

Oliver mildly replied, that he had always heard a bird's mouth described by the term in question.

'My eyes, how green!' exclaimed the young gentleman. 'Why, a beak's a madg'st'rate; and when you walk by a beak's order, it's not straight forerd, but always going up, and nivir coming down agen. Was you never on the mill?'

'What mill?' inquired Oliver.

'What mill! – why, *the* mill, – the mill as takes up so little room that it'll work inside a stone jug, and always goes better when the wind's low with people than when it's high, acos then they can't get workmen. But come,' said the young gentleman; 'you want grub, and you shall have it. I'm at low-water-mark – only one bob and a magpie; but, *as* far *as* it goes, I'll fork out and stump. Up with you on your pins. There: now then, morrice.'

Assisting Oliver to rise, the young gentleman took him to an adjacent chandler's shop, where he purchased a sufficiency of ready-dressed ham and a half-quartern loaf, or, as he himself expressed it, 'a fourpenny bran;' the ham being kept clean and preserved from dust by the ingenious expedient of making a hole in the loaf by pulling out a portion of the crumb, and stuffing it therein. Taking the bread under his arm, the young gentleman turned into a small public-house,[5] and led the way to a tap-room in the rear of the premises. Here, a pot of beer was brought in by the direction of the mysterious youth; and Oliver, falling to, at his new friend's bidding, made a long and hearty meal, during the progress of which the strange boy eyed him from time to time with great attention.

'Going to London?' said the strange boy, when Oliver had at length concluded.

'Yes.'

'Got any lodgings?'

'No.'

'Money?'

'No.'

The strange boy whistled, and put his arms into his pockets as far as the big-coat sleeves would let them go.

'Do you live in London?' inquired Oliver.

'Yes, I do, when I'm at home,' replied the boy. 'I suppose you want some place to sleep in to-night, don't you?'

'I do indeed,' answered Oliver. 'I have not slept under a roof since I left the country.'

'Don't fret your eyelids on that score,' said the young gentleman. 'I've got to be in London to-night, and I know a 'spectable old genelman as lives there, wot'll give you lodgings for nothink, and never ask for the change; that is, if any genelman he knows interduces you. And don't he know me? — Oh, no, — not in the least, — by no means, — certainly not.'

The young gentleman smiled, as if to intimate that the latter fragments of discourse were playfully ironical, and finished the beer as he did so.

This unexpected offer of shelter was too tempting to be resisted, especially as it was immediately followed up, by the assurance that the old gentleman already referred to, would doubtless provide Oliver with a comfortable place without loss of time. This led to a more friendly and confidential dialogue, from which Oliver discovered that his friend's name was Jack Dawkins, and that he was a peculiar pet and *protégé* of the elderly gentleman before mentioned.

Mr Dawkins's appearance did not say a vast deal in favour of the comforts which his patron's interest obtained for those whom he took under his protection; but as he had a somewhat flighty and dissolute mode of conversing, and furthermore avowed that among his intimate friends he was better known by the *sobriquet* of 'The artful Dodger,' Oliver concluded that, being of a dissipated and careless turn, the moral precepts of his benefactor had hitherto been thrown away upon him. Under this impression, he secretly resolved to cultivate the good opinion of the old gentleman as quickly as possible; and, if he found the Dodger incorrigible, as he more than half suspected he should, to decline the honour of his farther acquaintance.

As John Dawkins objected to their entering London before nightfall, it was nearly eleven o'clock when they reached the turnpike at Islington. They crossed from the Angel into St John's road, struck down the small street which terminates at Sadler's Wells theatre, through Exmouth-street and Coppice-row, down the little court by the side of the workhouse, across the classic ground which once bore the name of Hockley-in-the-hole, thence into Little Saffron-hill, and so into Saffron-hill the Great,[6] along which, the Dodger scudded at a rapid pace, directing Oliver to follow close at his heels.

Although Oliver had enough to occupy his attention in keeping sight of his leader, he could not help bestowing a few hasty glances on either side of the way as he passed along. A dirtier or more wretched place he had never seen. The street was very narrow and muddy, and the air was impregnated with filthy odours. There were a good many small shops; but the only stock in trade appeared to be heaps of children, who, even at that time of night, were crawling in and out at the doors, or screaming from the inside. The sole places that seemed to prosper amid the general blight of the place were the public-houses, and in them, the lowest orders of Irish (who are generally the lowest orders of anything)[7] were wrangling with might and main. Covered ways and yards, which here and there diverged from the main street, disclosed little knots of houses where drunken men and women were positively wallowing in the filth; and from several of the doorways, great ill-looking fellows were cautiously emerging, bound, to all appearance, upon no very well-disposed or harmless errands.

Oliver was just considering whether he hadn't better run away, when they reached the bottom of the hill: his conductor, catching him by the arm, pushed open the door of a house near Field-lane,[8] and, drawing him into the passage, closed it behind them.

'Now, then,' cried a voice from below, in reply to a whistle from the Dodger.

'*Plummy and slam!*' was the reply.

This seemed to be some watchword or signal that it was all right; for the light of a feeble candle gleamed upon the wall at the farther end of the passage, and a man's face peeped out from where a balustrade of the old kitchen staircase had been broken away.

'There's two on you,' said the man, thrusting the candle farther out, and shading his eyes with his hand. 'Who's the t'other one?'

'A new pal,' replied Jack, pulling Oliver forward.

'Where did he come from?'

'Greenland. Is Fagin up stairs?'

'Yes, he's a sortin' the wipes. Up with you!' The candle was drawn back, and the face disappeared.

Oliver, groping his way with one hand, and with the other firmly grasped by his companion, ascended with much difficulty the dark and broken stairs which his conductor mounted with an ease and expedition that showed he was well acquainted with them. He threw open the door of a back-room, and drew Oliver in after him.

The walls and ceiling of the room were perfectly black with age and dirt. There was a deal-table before the fire, upon which was a candle stuck in a ginger-beer bottle; two or three pewter pots, a loaf and butter, and a plate. In a frying-pan which was on the fire, and which was secured to the mantel-shelf by a string, some sausages were cooking; and standing over them, with a toasting-fork in his hand, was a very old shrivelled Jew,[9] whose villanous-looking and repulsive face was obscured by a quantity of matted red hair. He was dressed in a greasy flannel gown, with his throat bare, and seemed to be dividing his attention between the frying-pan and a clothes-horse, over which a great number of silk handkerchiefs were hanging. Several rough beds made of old sacks were huddled side by side on the floor; and seated round the table were four or five boys, none older than the Dodger, smoking long clay pipes and drinking spirits with all the air of middle-aged men. These all crowded about their associate as he whispered a few words to the Jew, and then turned round and grinned at Oliver, as did the Jew himself, toasting-fork in hand.

'This is him, Fagin,' said Jack Dawkins; 'my friend, Oliver Twist.'

The Jew grinned; and, making a low obeisance to Oliver, took him by the hand, and hoped he should have the honour of his intimate acquaintance. Upon this, the young gentlemen with the pipes came round him, and shook both his hands very hard, – especially the one in which he held his little bundle. One young gentleman was very anxious to hang up his cap for him; and another was so obliging as to

Oliver introduced to the respectable Old Gentleman

put his hands in his pockets, in order that, as he was very tired, he might not have the trouble of emptying them when he went to bed. These civilities would probably have been extended much further, but for a liberal exercise of the Jew's toasting-fork on the heads and shoulders of the affectionate youths who offered them.

'We are very glad to see you, Oliver, – very,' said the Jew. 'Dodger, take off the sausages, and draw a tub near the fire for Oliver. Ah, you're a staring at the pocket-handkerchiefs! eh, my dear? There are a good many of 'em, ain't there? We've just looked 'em out ready for the wash; that's all, Oliver; that's all. Ha! ha! ha!'

The latter part of this speech was hailed by a boisterous shout from all the hopeful pupils of the merry old gentleman, in the midst of which they went to supper.

Oliver ate his share; and the Jew then mixed him a glass of hot gin and water, telling him he must drink it off directly, because another gentleman wanted the tumbler. Oliver did as he was desired. Almost instantly afterwards, he felt himself gently lifted on to one of the sacks, and then he sunk into a deep sleep.

*

CHAPTER THE NINTH

CONTAINING FURTHER PARTICULARS CONCERNING THE PLEASANT OLD GENTLEMAN, AND HIS HOPEFUL PUPILS

It was late[1] next morning when Oliver awoke from a sound, long sleep. There was nobody in the room beside, but the old Jew, who was boiling some coffee in a saucepan for breakfast, and whistling softly to himself as he stirred it round and round with an iron spoon. He would stop every now and then to listen when there was the least noise below; and, when he had satisfied himself, he would go on whistling and stirring again, as before.

Although Oliver had roused himself from sleep, he was not thoroughly awake. There is a drowsy, heavy state, between sleeping and waking, when you dream more in five minutes with your eyes half open, and yourself half conscious of everything that is passing around you, than you would in five nights with your eyes fast closed, and your senses wrapt in perfect unconsciousness. At such times, a mortal knows just enough of what his mind is doing to form some glimmering conception of its mighty powers, its bounding from earth and spurning time and space, when freed from the irksome restraint of its corporeal associate.

Oliver was precisely in the condition I have described. He saw the Jew with his half-closed eyes, heard his low whistling, and recognised the sound of the spoon grating against the saucepan's sides; and yet the self-same senses were mentally engaged at the same time, in busy action with almost everybody he had ever known.

When the coffee was done, the Jew drew the saucepan to the hob, and, standing in an irresolute attitude for a few minutes as if he did not well know how to employ himself, turned round and looked at Oliver, and called him by his name. He did not answer, and was to all appearance asleep.

After satisfying himself upon this head, the Jew stepped gently to the door, which he fastened; he then drew forth, as it seemed to Oliver, from some trap in the floor, a small box, which he placed carefully on the table. His eyes glistened as he raised the lid and looked in. Dragging an old chair to the table, he sat down, and took from it a magnificent gold watch, sparkling with diamonds.

'Aha!' said the Jew, shrugging up his shoulders, and distorting every feature with a hideous grin. 'Clever dogs! clever dogs! Staunch to the last! Never told the old parson where they were; never peached upon old Fagin. And why should they? It wouldn't have loosened the knot, or kept the drop up a minute longer. No, no, no! Fine fellows! fine fellows!'

With these, and other muttered reflections of the like nature, the Jew once more deposited the watch in its place of safety. At least half a dozen more were severally drawn forth from the same box, and surveyed with equal pleasure; besides rings, brooches, bracelets, and other articles of jewellery, of such magnificent materials and costly workmanship that Oliver had no idea even of their names.

Having replaced these trinkets, the Jew took out another, so small that it lay in the palm of his hand. There seemed to be some very minute inscription on it, for the Jew laid it flat upon the table, and, shading it with his hand, pored over it long and earnestly. At length he set it down as if despairing of success, and, leaning back in his chair, muttered,

'What a fine thing capital punishment is! Dead men never repent; dead men never bring awkward stories to light. The prospect of the gallows, too, makes them hardy and bold. Ah, it's a fine thing for the trade! Five of them strung up in a row, and none left to play booty or turn white-livered!'

As the Jew uttered these words, his bright dark eyes which had been staring vacantly before him, fell on Oliver's face; the boy's eyes were fixed on his in mute curiosity, and, although the recognition was only for an instant – for the briefest space of time that can possibly be conceived, – it was enough to show the old man that he had been observed. He closed the lid of the box with a loud crash, and, laying his hand on a bread-knife which was on the table, started furiously up. He trembled very much though; for, even in his terror, Oliver could see that the knife quivered in the air.

'What's that?' said the Jew. 'What do you watch me for? Why are you awake? What have you seen? Speak out, boy! Quick – quick! for your life!'

'I wasn't able to sleep any longer, sir,' replied Oliver, meekly. 'I am very sorry if I have disturbed you, sir.'

'You were not awake an hour ago?' said the Jew, scowling fiercely on the boy.

'No – no, indeed, sir,' replied Oliver.

'Are you sure?' cried the Jew, with a still fiercer look than before, and a threatening attitude.

'Upon my word I was not, sir,' replied Oliver, earnestly. 'I was not, indeed, sir.'

'Tush, tush, my dear!' said the Jew, suddenly resuming his old manner, and playing with the knife a little before he laid it down; as if to induce the belief that he had caught it up in mere sport. 'Of course I know that, my dear. I only tried to frighten you. You're a brave boy. Ha! ha! you're a brave boy, Oliver!' and the Jew rubbed his hands with a chuckle, but looked uneasily at the box notwithstanding.

'Did you see any of these pretty things, my dear?' said the Jew, laying his hand upon it after a short pause.

'Yes, sir,' replied Oliver.

'Ah!' said the Jew, turning rather pale. 'They – they're mine, Oliver; my little property. All I have to live upon in my old age. The folks call me a miser, my dear, – only a miser; that's all.'

Oliver thought the old gentleman must be a decided miser to live in such a dirty place, with so many watches; but, thinking that perhaps his fondness for the Dodger and the other boys cost him a good deal of money, he only cast a deferential look at the Jew, and asked if he might get up.

'Certainly, my dear, – certainly,' replied the old gentleman. 'Stay. There's a pitcher of water in the corner by the door. Bring it here, and I'll give you a basin to wash in, my dear.'

Oliver got up, walked across the room, and stooped for one instant to raise the pitcher. When he turned his head, the box was gone.

He had scarcely washed himself and made everything tidy by emptying the basin out of the window, agreeably to the Jew's directions, than the Dodger returned, accompanied by a very sprightly young friend whom Oliver had seen smoking on the previous night, and who was now formally introduced to him as Charley Bates. The four then sat down to breakfast off the coffee and some hot rolls and ham which the Dodger had brought home in the crown of his hat.

'Well,' said the Jew, glancing slyly at Oliver, and addressing himself to the Dodger, 'I hope you've been at work this morning, my dears.'

'Hard,' replied the Dodger.

'As nails,' added Charley Bates.

'Good boys, good boys!' said the Jew. 'What have *you* got, Dodger?'

'A couple of pocket-books,' replied that young gentleman.

'Lined?' inquired the Jew with trembling eagerness.

'Pretty well,' replied the Dodger, producing two pocket-books, one green and the other red.

'Not so heavy as they might be,' said the Jew, after looking at the insides carefully; 'but very neat, and nicely made. Ingenious workman, ain't he, Oliver?'

'Very, indeed, sir,' said Oliver. At which Mr Charles Bates laughed uproariously, very much to the amazement of Oliver, who saw nothing to laugh at, in anything that had passed.

'And what have you got, my dear?' said Fagin to Charley Bates.

'Wipes,' replied Master Bates: at the same time producing four pocket-handkerchiefs.

'Well,' said the Jew, inspecting them closely; 'they're very good ones, – very. You haven't marked them well, though, Charley; so the marks shall be picked out with a needle, and we'll teach Oliver how to do it. Shall us, Oliver, eh? – Ha! ha! ha!'

'If you please, sir,' said Oliver.

'You'd like to be able to make pocket-handkerchiefs as easy as Charley Bates, wouldn't you, my dear?' said the Jew.

'Very much indeed, if you'll teach me, sir,' replied Oliver.

Master Bates saw something so exquisitely ludicrous in this reply that he burst into another laugh; which laugh meeting the coffee he was drinking, and carrying it down some wrong channel, very nearly terminated in his premature suffocation.

'He is so jolly green,' said Charley when he recovered, as an apology to the company for his unpolite behaviour.

The Dodger said nothing, but he smoothed Oliver's hair down over his eyes, and said he'd know better by-and-by; upon which the old gentleman, observing Oliver's colour mounting, changed the subject by asking whether there had been much of a crowd at the execution that morning.[2] This made him wonder more and more, for it was plain from the replies of the two boys that they had both been there; and Oliver naturally wondered how they could possibly have found time to be so very industrious.

When the breakfast was cleared away, the merry old gentleman and the two boys played at a very curious and uncommon game, which was performed in this way: – The merry old gentleman, placing a snuff-box in one pocket of his trousers, a note-case in the other, and a watch in his waistcoat-pocket, with a guard-chain[3] round his neck, and sticking a mock diamond pin in his shirt, buttoned his coat tight round him, and, putting his spectacle-case and handkerchief in the pockets, trotted up and down the room with a stick, in imitation of the manner in which old gentlemen walk about the streets every hour in the day. Sometimes he stopped at the fire-place, and sometimes at the door, making belief that he was staring with all his might into shop-windows. At such times he would look constantly round him for fear of thieves, and keep slapping all his pockets in turn, to see that he hadn't lost anything, in such a very funny and natural manner, that Oliver laughed till the tears ran down his face. All this time the two boys followed him closely about, getting out of his sight so nimbly every time he turned round, that it was impossible to follow their motions. At last the Dodger trod upon his toes, or ran upon his boot accidentally, while Charley Bates stumbled up against him behind; and in that one moment they took from him with the most extraordinary rapidity, snuff-box, note-case, watch-guard, chain, shirt-pin, pocket-handkerchief, – even the spectacle-case. If the old gentleman felt a hand in any one of his pockets, he cried out where it was, and then the game began all over again.

When this game had been played a great many times, a couple of young ladies came to see the young gentlemen, one of whom was called Bet and the other Nancy. They wore a good deal of hair, not very neatly turned up behind, and were rather untidy about the shoes and stockings. They were not exactly pretty, perhaps; but they had a great deal of colour in their faces, and looked quite stout and hearty. Being remarkably free and agreeable in their manners, Oliver thought them very nice girls indeed, as there is no doubt they were.

These visitors stopped a long time. Spirits were produced, in consequence of one of the young ladies complaining of a coldness in her inside, and the conversation took a very convivial and improving turn. At length Charley Bates expressed his opinion that it was time to pad the hoof, which it occurred to Oliver must be French for going out; for directly afterwards the Dodger, and Charley, and the two young ladies went away together, having been kindly furnished with money to spend, by the amiable old Jew.

'There, my dear,' said Fagin, 'that's a pleasant life, isn't it? They have gone out for the day.'

'Have they done work, sir?' inquired Oliver.

'Yes,' said the Jew; 'that is, unless they should unexpectedly come across any when they are out; and they won't neglect it if they do, my dear, depend upon it.'

'Make 'em your models, my dear, make 'em your models,' said the Jew, tapping the fire-shovel on the hearth to add force to his words; 'do everything they bid you, and take their advice in all matters, especially the Dodger's, my dear. He'll be a great man himself, and make you one too, if you take pattern by him. Is my handkerchief hanging out of my pocket, my dear?' said the Jew, stopping short.

'Yes, sir,' said Oliver.

'See if you can take it out, without my feeling it, as you saw them do when we were at play this morning.'

Oliver held up the bottom of the pocket with one hand as he had seen the Dodger do, and drew the handkerchief lightly out of it with the other.

'Is it gone?' cried the Jew.

'Here it is, sir,' said Oliver, showing it in his hand.

'You're a clever boy, my dear,' said the playful old gentleman, patting Oliver on the head approvingly; 'I never saw a sharper lad. Here's a shilling for you. If you go on in this way, you'll be the greatest man of the time. And now come here, and I'll show you how to take the marks out of the handkerchiefs.'

Oliver wondered what picking the old gentleman's pocket in play had to do with his chances of being a great man; but thinking that the Jew, being so much his senior, must know best, followed him quietly to the table, and was soon deeply involved in his new study.

CHAPTER THE TENTH

*OLIVER BECOMES BETTER ACQUAINTED
WITH THE CHARACTERS OF HIS NEW
ASSOCIATES, AND PURCHASES
EXPERIENCE AT A HIGH PRICE. BEING A
SHORT BUT VERY IMPORTANT CHAPTER
IN THIS HISTORY*

For eight or ten days Oliver remained in the Jew's room, picking the marks out of the pocket-handkerchiefs, (of which a great number were brought home,) and sometimes taking part in the game already described, which the two boys and the Jew played regularly every day. At length he began to languish for the fresh air, and took many occasions of earnestly entreating the old gentleman to allow him to go out to work with his two companions.

Oliver was rendered the more anxious to be actively employed by what he had seen of the stern morality of the old gentleman's character. Whenever the Dodger or Charley Bates came home at night empty-handed, he would expatiate with great vehemence on the misery of idle and lazy habits, and enforce upon them the necessity of an active life by sending them supperless to bed: upon one occasion he even went so far as to knock them both down a flight of stairs; but this was carrying out his virtuous precepts to an unusual extent.

At length one morning Oliver obtained the permission he had so eagerly sought. There had been no handkerchiefs to work upon, for two or three days, and the dinners had been rather meagre. Perhaps these were reasons for the old gentleman's giving his assent; but, whether they were or no, he told Oliver he might go, and placed him under the joint guardianship of Charley Bates and his friend the Dodger.

The three boys sallied out, the Dodger with his coat-sleeves tucked up and his hat cocked as usual, Master Bates sauntering along with his hands in his pockets, and Oliver between them, wondering where they were going, and what branch of manufacture he would be instructed in first.

The pace at which they went was such a very lazy, ill-looking saunter, that Oliver soon began to think his companions were going to deceive the old gentleman, by not going to work at all. The Dodger had a vicious propensity, too, of pulling the caps from the heads of small boys and tossing them down areas; while Charley Bates exhibited some very loose notions concerning the rights of property, by pilfering divers apples and onions from the stalls at the kennel sides, and thrusting them into pockets which were so surprisingly capacious, that they seemed to undermine his whole suit of clothes in every direction. These things looked so bad, that Oliver was on the point of declaring his intention of seeking his way back in the best way he could, when his thoughts were suddenly directed into another channel by a very mysterious change of behaviour on the part of the Dodger.

They were just emerging from a narrow court not far from the open square in Clerkenwell, which is called, by some strange perversion of terms, 'The Green,'[1] when the Dodger made a sudden stop, and, laying his finger on his lip, drew his companions back again with the greatest caution and circumspection.

'What's the matter?' demanded Oliver.

'Hush!' replied the Dodger. 'Do you see that old cove at the book-stall?'

'The old gentleman over the way?' said Oliver. 'Yes, I see him.'

'He'll do,' said the Dodger.

'A prime plant,' observed Charley Bates.

Oliver looked from one to the other with the greatest surprise, but was not permitted to make any inquiries, for the two boys walked stealthily across the road, and slunk close behind the old gentleman towards whom his attention had been directed. Oliver walked a few paces after them, and, not knowing whether to advance or retire, stood looking on in silent amazement.

The old gentleman was a very respectable-looking personage, with a powdered head[2] and gold spectacles; dressed in a bottle-green coat with a black velvet collar, and white trousers: with a smart bamboo cane under his arm. He had taken up a book from the stall, and there

Oliver amazed at the Dodger's mode of 'going to work'

he stood, reading away as hard as if he were in his elbow-chair in his own study. It was very possible that he fancied himself there, indeed; for it was plain, from his utter abstraction, that he saw not the book-stall, nor the street, nor the boys, nor, in short, anything but the book itself, which he was reading straight through, turning over the leaves when he got to the bottom of a page, beginning at the top line of the next one, and going regularly on with the greatest interest and eagerness.

What was Oliver's horror and alarm as he stood a few paces off, looking on with his eye-lids as wide open as they would possibly go, to see the Dodger plunge his hand into this old gentleman's pocket, and draw from thence a handkerchief, which he handed to Charley Bates, and with which they both ran away round the corner at full speed!

In one instant the whole mystery of the handkerchiefs, and the watches, and the jewels, and the Jew, rushed upon the boy's mind. He stood for a moment with the blood tingling so through all his veins from terror, that he felt as if he were in a burning fire; then, confused and frightened, he took to his heels, and, not knowing what he did, made off as fast as he could lay his feet to the ground.

This was all done in a minute's space, and the very instant that Oliver began to run, the old gentleman, putting his hand to his pocket, and missing his handkerchief, turned sharp round. Seeing the boy scudding away at such a rapid pace, he very naturally concluded him to be the depredator, and, shouting 'Stop thief!' with all his might, made off after him, book in hand.

But the old gentleman was not the only person who raised the hue and cry. The Dodger and Master Bates, unwilling to attract public attention by running down the open street, had merely retired into the very first doorway round the corner. They no sooner heard the cry, and saw Oliver running, than, guessing exactly how the matter stood, they issued forth with great promptitude, and, shouting 'Stop thief!' too, joined in the pursuit like good citizens.

Although Oliver had been brought up by philosophers, he was not theoretically acquainted with their beautiful axiom that self-preservation is the first law of nature. If he had been, perhaps he would have been prepared for this. Not being prepared, however, it alarmed him the more; so away he went like the wind, with the old gentleman and the two boys roaring and shouting behind him.

'Stop thief! stop thief!' There is a magic in the sound. The tradesman leaves his counter, and the carman his waggon; the butcher throws down his tray, the baker his basket, the milkman his pail, the errand-boy his parcels, the schoolboy his marbles, the paviour his pick-axe, the child his battledore: away they run, pell-mell, helter-skelter, slap-dash, tearing, yelling, and screaming, knocking down the passengers as they turn the corners, rousing up the dogs, and astonishing the fowls; and streets, squares, and courts re-echo with the sound.

'Stop thief! stop thief!' The cry is taken up by a hundred voices, and the crowd accumulate at every turning. Away they fly, splashing through the mud, and rattling along the pavements; up go the windows, out run the people, onward bear the mob: a whole audience desert Punch in the very thickest of the plot,' and, joining the rushing throng, swell the shout, and lend fresh vigour to the cry, 'Stop thief! stop thief!'

'Stop thief! stop thief!' There is a passion for *hunting something* deeply implanted in the human breast. One wretched, breathless child, panting with exhaustion, terror in his looks, agony in his eye, large drops of perspiration streaming down his face, strains every nerve to make head upon his pursuers; and as they follow on his track, and gain upon him every instant, they hail his decreasing strength with still louder shouts, and whoop and scream with joy 'Stop thief!' – Ay, stop him for God's sake, were it only in mercy!

Stopped at last. A clever blow that. He's down upon the pavement, and the crowd eagerly gather round him; each new comer jostling and struggling with the others to catch a glimpse. 'Stand aside!' – 'Give him a little air!' – 'Nonsense! he don't deserve it.' – 'Where's the gentleman?' – 'Here he is, coming down the street.' – 'Make room there for the gentleman!' – 'Is this the boy, sir?' – 'Yes.'

Oliver lay covered with mud and dust, and bleeding from the mouth, looking wildly round upon the heap of faces that surrounded him, when the old gentleman was officiously dragged and pushed into the circle by the foremost of the pursuers, and made this reply to their anxious inquiries.

'Yes,' said the gentleman in a benevolent voice, 'I am afraid it is.'

'Afraid!' murmured the crowd. 'That's a good un.'

'Poor fellow!' said the gentleman, 'he has hurt himself.'

'I did that, sir,' said a great lubberly fellow stepping forward; 'and preciously I cut my knuckle agin' his mouth. *I* stopped him, sir.'

The fellow touched his hat with a grin, expecting something for his pains; but the old gentleman, eyeing him with an expression of disgust, looked anxiously round, as if he contemplated running away himself; which it is very possible he might have attempted to do, and thus afforded another chase, had not a police officer (who is always the last person to arrive in such cases)[4] at that moment made his way through the crowd, and seized Oliver by the collar. 'Come, get up,' said the man roughly.

'It wasn't me indeed, sir. Indeed, indeed, it was two other boys,' said Oliver, clasping his hands passionately, and looking round: 'they are here somewhere.'

'Oh no, they ain't,' said the officer. He meant this to be ironical; but it was true besides, for the Dodger and Charley Bates had filed off down the first convenient court they came to. 'Come, get up.'

'Don't hurt him,' said the old gentleman compassionately.

'Oh no, I won't hurt him,' replied the officer, tearing his jacket half off his back in proof thereof. 'Come, I know you; it won't do. Will you stand upon your legs, you young devil?'

Oliver, who could hardly stand, made a shift to raise himself upon his feet, and was at once lugged along the streets by the jacket-collar at a rapid pace. The gentleman walked on with them by the officer's side; and as many of the crowd as could, got a little a-head, and stared back at Oliver from time to time. The boys shouted in triumph, and on they went.

CHAPTER THE ELEVENTH

TREATS OF MR FANG THE POLICE MAGISTRATE, AND FURNISHES A SLIGHT SPECIMEN OF HIS MODE OF ADMINISTERING JUSTICE

The offence had been committed within the district, and indeed in the immediate neighbourhood of a very notorious metropolitan police-office. The crowd had only the satisfaction of accompanying Oliver through two or three streets, and down a place called Mutton-hill, when he was led beneath a low archway and up a dirty court into this dispensary of summary justice,[1] by the back way. It was a small paved yard into which they turned; and here they encountered a stout man with a bunch of whiskers on his face, and a bunch of keys in his hand.

'What's the matter now?' said the man carelessly.

'A young fogle-hunter,' replied the man who had Oliver in charge.

'Are you the party that's been robbed, sir?' inquired the man with the keys.

'Yes, I am,' replied the old gentleman; 'but I am not sure that this boy actually took the handkerchief. I – I'd rather not press the case.'

'Must go before the magistrate now, sir,' replied the man. 'His worship will be disengaged in half a minute. Now, young gallows.'

This was an invitation for Oliver to enter through a door which he unlocked as he spoke, and which led into a small stone cell. Here he was searched, and, nothing being found upon him, locked up.

This cell was in shape and size something like an area cellar, only not so light. It was most intolerably dirty, for it was Monday morning, and it had been tenanted since Saturday night by six drunken people. But this is nothing. In our station-houses, men and women are every night confined on the most trivial *charges* – the word is worth noting – in dungeons, compared with which, those in Newgate, occupied by the most atrocious felons, tried, found guilty, and under sentence of death, are palaces! Let any man who doubts this, compare the two.

The old gentleman looked almost as rueful as Oliver when the key grated in the lock; and turned with a sigh to the book which had been the innocent cause of all this disturbance.

'There is something in that boy's face,' said the old gentleman to himself as he walked slowly away, tapping his chin with the cover of the book in a thoughtful manner, 'something that touches and interests me. *Can* he be innocent? He looked like – By the bye,' exclaimed the old gentleman, halting very abruptly, and staring up into the sky, 'God bless my soul! where have I seen something like that look before?'

After musing for some minutes, the old gentleman walked with the same meditative face into a back ante-room opening from the yard; and there, retiring into a corner, called up before his mind's eye a vast amphitheatre of faces over which a dusky curtain had hung for many years. 'No,' said the old gentleman, shaking his head; 'it must be imagination.'

He wandered over them again. He had called them into view, and it was not easy to replace the shroud that had so long concealed them. There were the faces of friends and foes, and of many that had been almost strangers, peering intrusively from the crowd; there were the faces of young and blooming girls that were now old women; there were others that the grave had changed to ghastly trophies of death, but which the mind, superior to his power, still dressed in their old freshness and beauty, calling back the lustre of the eyes, the brightness of the smile, the beaming of the soul through its mask of clay, and whispering of beauty beyond the tomb, changed but to be heightened, and taken from earth only to be set up as a light to shed a soft and gentle glow upon the path to Heaven.

But the old gentleman could recall no one countenance of which Oliver's features bore a trace; so he heaved a sigh over the recollections he had awakened; and being, happily for himself, an absent old gentleman, buried them again in the pages of the musty book.

He was roused by a touch on the shoulder, and a request from the man with the keys to follow him into the office. He closed his book hastily, and was at once ushered into the imposing presence of the renowned Mr Fang.[2]

The office was a front parlour, with a panneled wall. Mr Fang sat behind a bar at the upper end; and on one side the door was a sort of wooden pen in which poor little Oliver was already deposited, trembling very much at the awfulness of the scene.

Mr Fang was a middle-sized man, with no great quantity of hair; and what he had, growing on the back and sides of his head. His face was stern, and much flushed. If he were really not in the habit of drinking rather more than was exactly good for him, he might have brought an action against his countenance for libel, and have recovered heavy damages.

The old gentleman bowed respectfully, and, advancing to the magistrate's desk, said, suiting the action to the word, 'That is my name and address, sir.' He then withdrew a pace or two; and, with another polite and gentlemanly inclination of the head, waited to be questioned.

Now, it so happened that Mr Fang was at that moment perusing a leading article in a newspaper of the morning, adverting to some recent decision of his, and commending him, for the three hundred and fiftieth time, to the special and particular notice of the Secretary of State for the Home Department. He was out of temper, and he looked up with an angry scowl.

'Who are you?' said Mr Fang.

The old gentleman pointed with some surprise to his card.

'Officer!' said Mr Fang, tossing the card contemptuously away with the newspaper, 'who is this fellow?'

'My name, sir,' said the old gentleman, speaking *like* a gentleman, and consequently in strong contrast to Mr Fang, – 'my name, sir, is Brownlow. Permit me to inquire the name of the magistrate who offers a gratuitous and unprovoked insult to a respectable man, under the protection of the bench.' Saying this, Mr Brownlow looked round the office as if in search of some person who would afford him the required information.

'Officer!' said Mr Fang, throwing the paper on one side, 'what's this fellow charged with?'

'He's not charged at all, your worship,' replied the officer. 'He appears against the boy, your worship.'

His worship knew this perfectly well; but it was a good annoyance, and a safe one.

'Appears against the boy, does he?' said Fang, surveying Mr Brownlow contemptuously from head to foot. 'Swear him.'

'Before I am sworn I must beg to say one word,' said Mr Brownlow; 'and that is, that I never, without actual experience, could have believed—'

'Hold your tongue, sir!' said Mr Fang peremptorily.

'I will not, sir!' replied the spirited old gentleman.

'Hold your tongue this instant, or I'll have you turned out of the office!' said Mr Fang. 'You're an insolent impertinent fellow. How dare you bully a magistrate!'

'What!' exclaimed the old gentleman, reddening.

'Swear this person!' said Fang to the clerk. 'I'll not hear another word. Swear him!'

Mr Brownlow's indignation was greatly roused; but, reflecting that he might only injure the boy by giving vent to it, he suppressed his feelings, and submitted to be sworn at once.

'Now,' said Fang, 'what's the charge against this boy? What have you got to say, sir?'

'I was standing at a book-stall –' Mr Brownlow began.

'Hold your tongue, sir!' said Mr Fang. 'Policeman! – where's the policeman? Here, swear this man. Now, policeman, what is this?'

The policeman with becoming humility related how he had taken the charge, how he had searched Oliver and found nothing on his person; and how that was all he knew about it.

'Are there any witnesses?' inquired Mr Fang.

'None, your worship,' replied the policeman.

Mr Fang sat silent for some minutes, and then, turning round to the prosecutor, said, in a towering passion,

'Do you mean to state what your complaint against this boy is, fellow, or do you not? You have been sworn. Now, if you stand there, refusing to give evidence, I'll punish you for disrespect to the bench; I will, by—'

By what, or by whom, nobody knows, for the clerk and jailer coughed very loud just at the right moment, and the former dropped a heavy book on the floor; thus preventing the word from being heard – accidentally, of course.

With many interruptions, and repeated insults, Mr Brownlow contrived to state his case; observing that, in the surprise of the moment, he had run after the boy because he saw him running away, and expressing his hope that, if the magistrate should believe him, although not actually the thief, to be connected with thieves, he would deal as leniently with him as justice would allow.

'He has been hurt already,' said the old gentleman in conclusion. 'And I fear,' he added, with great energy, looking towards the bar, – 'I really fear that he is very ill.'

'Oh! yes; I dare say!' said Mr Fang, with a sneer. 'Come; none of your tricks here, you young vagabond; they won't do. What's your name?'

Oliver tried to reply, but his tongue failed him. He was deadly pale, and the whole place seemed turning round and round.

'What's your name, you hardened scoundrel?' thundered Mr Fang. 'Officer, what's his name?'

This was addressed to a bluff old fellow in a striped waistcoat, who was standing by the bar. He bent over Oliver, and repeated the inquiry; but finding him really incapable of understanding the question, and knowing that his not replying would only infuriate the magistrate the more, and add to the severity of his sentence, he hazarded a guess.

'He says his name's Tom White, your worship,' said this kind-hearted thief-taker.

'Oh, he won't speak out, won't he?' said Fang. 'Very well, very well. Where does he live?'

'Where he can, your worship,' replied the officer, again pretending to receive Oliver's answer.

'Has he any parents?' inquired Mr Fang.

'He says they died in his infancy, your worship,' replied the officer, hazarding the usual reply.

At this point of the inquiry Oliver raised his head, and, looking round with imploring eyes, murmured a feeble prayer for a draught of water.

'Stuff and nonsense!' said Mr Fang; 'don't try to make a fool of me.'

'I think he really is ill, your worship,' remonstrated the officer.

'I know better,' said Mr Fang.

'Take care of him, officer,' said the old gentleman, raising his hands instinctively; 'he'll fall down.'

'Stand away, officer,' cried Fang savagely; 'let him if he likes.'

Oliver availed himself of the kind permission, and fell heavily to the floor in a fainting fit. The men in the office looked at each other, but no one dared to stir.

'I knew he was shamming,' said Fang, as if this were incontestable proof of the fact. 'Let him lie; he'll soon be tired of that.'

'How do you propose to deal with the case, sir?' inquired the clerk in a low voice.

'Summarily,' replied Mr. Fang. 'He stands committed for three months, – hard labour³ of course. Clear the office.'

The door was opened for this purpose, and a couple of men were preparing to carry the insensible boy to his cell, when an elderly man of decent but poor appearance, clad in an old suit of black, rushed hastily into the office, and advanced to the bench.

'Stop, stop, – don't take him away, – for Heaven's sake stop a moment,' cried the new-comer, breathless with haste.

Although the presiding geniuses in such an office as this, exercise a summary and arbitrary power over the liberties, the good name, the character, almost the lives of his Majesty's subjects, especially of the poorer class, and although within such walls enough fantastic tricks are daily played to make the angels weep thick tears of blood, they are closed to the public, save through the medium of the daily press. Mr Fang was consequently not a little indignant to see an unbidden guest enter in such irreverent disorder.

'What is this? Who is this? Turn this man out. Clear the office,' cried Mr Fang.

'I will speak,' cried the man; 'I will not be turned out, – I saw it all. I keep the book-stall. I demand to be sworn. I will not be put down. Mr Fang, you must hear me. You dare not refuse, sir.'

The man was right. His manner was bold and determined, and the matter was growing rather too serious to be hushed up.

'Swear the fellow,' growled Fang with a very ill grace. 'Now, man, what have you got to say?'

'This,' said the man: 'I saw three boys – two others and the prisoner here – loitering on the opposite side of the way, when this gentleman was reading. The robbery was committed by another boy. I saw it done, and I saw that this boy was perfectly amazed and stupified by it.' Having by this time recovered a little breath, the worthy book-stall keeper proceeded to relate in a more coherent manner the exact circumstances of the robbery.

'Why didn't you come here before?' said Fang after a pause.

'I hadn't a soul to mind the shop,' replied the man; 'everybody that could have helped me had joined in the pursuit. I could get nobody till five minutes ago, and I've run here all the way.'

'The prosecutor was reading, was he?' inquired Fang, after another pause.

'Yes,' replied the man, 'the very book he has got in his hand.'

'Oh, that book, eh?' said Fang. 'Is it paid for?'

'No, it is not,' replied the man, with a smile.

'Dear me, I forgot all about it!' exclaimed the absent old gentleman, innocently.

'A nice person to prefer a charge against a poor boy!' said Fang, with a comical effort to look humane. 'I consider, sir, that you have obtained possession of that book under very suspicious and disreputable circumstances, and you may think yourself very fortunate that the owner of the property declines to prosecute. Let this be a lesson to you, my man, or the law will overtake you yet. The boy is discharged. Clear the office!'

'D—me!' cried the old gentleman, bursting out with the rage he had kept down so long, 'd—me! I'll—'

'Clear the office!' roared the magistrate. 'Officers, do you hear? Clear the office!'

The mandate was obeyed, and the indignant Mr Brownlow was conveyed out, with the book in one hand and the bamboo cane in the other, in a perfect phrenzy of rage and defiance.

He reached the yard, and it vanished in a moment. Little Oliver Twist lay on his back on the pavement, with his shirt unbuttoned and his temples bathed with water: his face a deadly white, and a cold tremble convulsing his whole frame.

'Poor boy, poor boy!' said Mr Brownlow bending over him. 'Call a coach, somebody, pray, directly!'

A coach was obtained, and Oliver, having been carefully laid on one seat, the old gentleman got in and sat himself on the other.

'May I accompany you?' said the book-stall keeper looking in.

'Bless me, yes, my dear friend,' said Mr Brownlow quickly. 'I forgot you. Dear, dear! I've got this unhappy book still. Jump in. Poor fellow! there's no time to lose.'

The book-stall keeper got into the coach, and away they drove.

*

CHAPTER THE TWELFTH

IN WHICH OLIVER IS TAKEN BETTER CARE OF, THAN HE EVER WAS BEFORE. WITH SOME PARTICULARS CONCERNING A CERTAIN PICTURE

The coach rattled away down Mount Pleasant and up Exmouth-street, over nearly the same ground as that which Oliver had traversed when he first entered London in company with the Dodger, – and, turning a different way when it reached the Angel at Islington, stopped at length before a neat house in a quiet shady street near Pentonville.[1] Here a bed was prepared without loss of time, in which Mr Brownlow saw his young charge carefully and comfortably deposited; and here he was tended with a kindness and solicitude which knew no bounds.

But for many days Oliver remained insensible to all the goodness of his new friends; the sun rose and sunk, and rose and sunk again, and many times after that, and still the boy lay stretched upon his uneasy bed, dwindling away beneath the dry and wasting heat of fever, – that heat which, like the subtle acid that gnaws into the very heart of hardest iron, burns only to corrode and to destroy. The worm does not his work more surely on the dead body, than does this slow, creeping fire upon the living frame.

Weak, and thin, and pallid, he awoke at last from what seemed to have been a long and troubled dream. Feebly raising himself in the bed, with his head resting on his trembling arm, he looked anxiously round.

'What room is this? – where have I been brought to?' said Oliver. 'This is not the place I went to sleep in.'

He uttered these words in a feeble voice, being very faint and weak; but they were overheard at once, for the curtain at the bed's head was hastily drawn back, and a motherly old lady, very neatly and precisely dressed, rose as she undrew it, from an arm-chair close by, in which she had been sitting at needlework.

'Hush, my dear,' said the old lady softly. 'You must be very quiet, or you will be ill again, and you have been very bad, – as bad as bad could be, pretty nigh. Lie down again, there's a dear.' With these words the old lady very gently placed Oliver's head upon the pillow, and, smoothing back his hair from his forehead, looked so kindly and lovingly in his face, that he could not help placing his little withered hand upon hers and drawing it round his neck.

'Save us!' said the old lady, with tears in her eyes, 'what a grateful little dear it is. Pretty creetur, what would his mother feel if she had sat by him as I have, and could see him now!'

'Perhaps she does see me,' whispered Oliver, folding his hands together; 'perhaps she has sat by me, ma'am. I almost feel as if she had.'

'That was the fever, my dear,' said the old lady mildly.

'I suppose it was,' replied Oliver thoughtfully, 'because Heaven is a long way off, and they are too happy there, to come down to the bedside of a poor boy. But if she knew I was ill, she must have pitied me even there, for she was very ill herself before she died. She can't know anything about me though,' added Oliver after a moment's silence, 'for if she had seen me beat, it would have made her sorrowful; and her face has always looked sweet and happy when I have dreamt of her.'

The old lady made no reply to this, but wiping her eyes first, and her spectacles, which lay on the counterpane, afterwards, as if they were part and parcel of those features, brought some cool stuff for Oliver to drink, and then, patting him on the cheek, told him he must lie very quiet, or he would be ill again.

So Oliver kept very still, partly because he was anxious to obey the kind old lady in all things, and partly, to tell the truth, because he was completely exhausted with what he had already said. He soon fell into a gentle doze, from which he was awakened by the light of a candle, which, being brought near the bed, showed him a gentleman, with a very large and loud-ticking gold watch in his hand, who felt his pulse, and said he was a great deal better.

'You *are* a great deal better, are you not, my dear?' said the gentleman.

'Yes, thank you, sir,' replied Oliver.

'Yes, I know you are,' said the gentleman: 'you're hungry too, an't you?'

'No, sir,' answered Oliver.

'Hem!' said the gentleman. 'No, I know you're not. He is not hungry, Mrs Bedwin,' said the gentleman, looking very wise.

The old lady made a respectful inclination of the head, which seemed to say that she thought the doctor was a very clever man. The doctor appeared very much of the same opinion himself.

'You feel sleepy, don't you, my dear?' said the doctor.

'No, sir,' replied Oliver.

'No,' said the doctor with a very shrewd and satisfied look. 'You're not sleepy. Nor thirsty, are you?'

'Yes, sir, rather thirsty,' answered Oliver.

'Just as I expected, Mrs Bedwin,' said the doctor. 'It's very natural that he should be thirsty – perfectly natural. You may give him a little tea, ma'am, and some dry toast without any butter. Don't keep him too warm, ma'am; but be careful that you don't let him be too cold; will you have the goodness?'

The old lady dropped a curtsey; and the doctor, after tasting the cool stuff, and expressing a qualified approval thereof, hurried away: his boots creaking in a very important and wealthy manner as he went down stairs.

Oliver dozed off again soon after this, and when he awoke it was nearly twelve o'clock. The old lady tenderly bade him good-night shortly afterwards, and left him in charge of a fat old woman who had just come, bringing with her in a little bundle a small Prayer Book and a large nightcap. Putting the latter on her head, and the former on the table, the old woman, after telling Oliver that she had come to sit up with him, drew her chair close to the fire and went off into a series of short naps, chequered at frequent intervals with sundry tumblings forward and divers moans and chokings, which, however, had no worse effect than causing her to rub her nose very hard, and then fall asleep again.

And thus the night crept slowly on. Oliver lay awake for some time, counting the little circles of light which the reflection of the rushlight-shade[2] threw upon the ceiling, or tracing with his languid eyes the intricate pattern of the paper on the wall. The darkness and deep stillness of the room were very solemn; and as they brought into the boy's mind the thought that death had been hovering there for many days and nights, and might yet fill it with the gloom and dread of his awful presence, he turned his face upon the pillow and fervently prayed to Heaven.

Gradually he fell into that deep tranquil sleep which ease from recent suffering alone imparts; that calm and peaceful rest which it is pain to wake from. Who, if this were death, would be roused again to all the struggles and turmoils of life, – to all its cares for the present, its anxieties for the future, and, more than all, its weary recollections of the past!

It had been bright day for hours when Oliver opened his eyes; and when he did so, he felt cheerful and happy. The crisis of the disease was safely past, and he belonged to the world again.

In three days' time he was able to sit in an easy-chair well propped up with pillows; and, as he was still too weak to walk, Mrs Bedwin had him carried down stairs into the little housekeeper's room, which belonged to her, where, having sat him up by the fireside, the good old lady sat herself down too, and, being in a state of considerable delight at seeing him so much better, forthwith began to cry most violently.

'Never mind me, my dear,' said the old lady; 'I'm only having a regular good cry. There, it's all over now, and I'm quite comfortable.'

'You're very, very kind to me, ma'am,' said Oliver.

'Well, never you mind that, my dear,' said the old lady; 'that's got nothing to do with your broth, and it's full time you had it, for the doctor says Mr Brownlow may come in to see you this morning, and we must get up our best looks, because the better we look, the more he'll be pleased.' And with this, the old lady applied herself to warming up in a little saucepan a basin full of broth strong enough to furnish an ample dinner, when reduced to the regulation strength, for three hundred and fifty paupers, at the very lowest computation.

'Are you fond of pictures, dear?' inquired the old lady, seeing that Oliver had fixed his eyes most intently on a portrait which hung against the wall just opposite his chair.

'I don't quite know, ma'am,' said Oliver, without taking his eyes from the canvass; 'I have seen so few that I hardly know. What a beautiful mild face that lady's is!'

'Ah,' said the old lady, 'painters always make ladies out prettier than they are, or they wouldn't get any custom, child. The man that invented the machine for taking likenesses³ might have known *that* would never succeed; it's a deal too honest, – a deal,' said the old lady, laughing very heartily at her own acuteness.

'Is – is that a likeness, ma'am?' said Oliver.

'Yes,' said the old lady, looking up for a moment from the broth; 'that's a portrait.'

'Whose, ma'am?' asked Oliver eagerly.

'Why, really, my dear, I don't know,' answered the old lady in a good-humoured manner. 'It's not a likeness of anybody that you or I know, I expect. It seems to strike your fancy, dear.'

'It is so very pretty: so very beautiful,' replied Oliver.

'Why, sure you're not afraid of it?' said the old lady, observing in great surprise the look of awe with which the child regarded the painting.

'Oh no, no,' returned Oliver quickly; 'but the eyes look so sorrowful, and where I sit they seem fixed upon me. It makes my heart beat,' added Oliver in a low voice, 'as if it was alive, and wanted to speak to me, but couldn't.'

Oliver recovering from the fever

'Lord save us!' exclaimed the old lady, starting; 'don't talk in that way, child. You're weak and nervous after your illness. Let me wheel your chair round to the other side, and then you won't see it. There,' said the old lady, suiting the action to the word; 'you don't see it now, at all events.'

Oliver *did* see it in his mind's eye as distinctly as if he had not altered his position, but he thought it better not to worry the kind old lady; so he smiled gently when she looked at him, and Mrs Bedwin, satisfied that he felt more comfortable, salted and broke bits of toasted bread into the broth with all the bustle befitting so solemn a preparation. Oliver got through it with extraordinary expedition, and had scarcely swallowed the last spoonful when there came a soft tap at the door. 'Come in,' said the old lady; and in walked Mr Brownlow.

Now, the old gentleman came in as brisk as need be; but he had no sooner raised his spectacles on his forehead, and thrust his hands behind the skirts of his dressing-gown to take a good long look at Oliver, than his countenance underwent a very great variety of odd contortions. Oliver looked very worn and shadowy from sickness, and made an ineffectual attempt to stand up, out of respect to his benefactor, which terminated in his sinking back into the chair again; and the fact is, if the truth must be told, that Mr Brownlow's heart being large enough for any six ordinary old gentlemen of humane disposition, forced a supply of tears into his eyes by some hydraulic process which we are not sufficiently philosophical to be in a condition to explain.

'Poor boy, poor boy!' said Mr Brownlow clearing his throat. 'I'm rather hoarse this morning, Mrs Bedwin; I'm afraid I have caught cold.'

'I hope not, sir,' said Mrs Bedwin. 'Everything you have had has been well aired, sir.'

'I don't know, Bedwin, – I don't know,' said Mr Brownlow; 'I rather think I had a damp napkin at dinner-time yesterday: but never mind that. How do you feel, my dear?'

'Very happy, sir,' replied Oliver, 'and very grateful indeed, sir, for your goodness to me.'

'Good boy,' said Mr Brownlow stoutly. 'Have you given him any nourishment, Bedwin? – any slops, eh?'[4]

'He has just had a basin of beautiful strong broth, sir,' replied Mrs Bedwin, drawing herself up slightly, and laying a strong emphasis on the last word, to intimate that between slops, and broth well compounded, there existed no affinity or connexion whatsoever.

'Ugh!' said Mr Brownlow, with a slight shudder; 'a couple of glasses of port wine would have done him a great deal more good, – wouldn't they, Tom White, – eh?'

'My name is Oliver, sir,' replied the little invalid with a look of great astonishment.

'Oliver!' said Mr Brownlow; 'Oliver what? Oliver White, – eh?'

'No, sir, Twist, – Oliver Twist.'

'Queer name,' said the old gentleman. 'What made you tell the magistrate your name was White?'

'I never told him so, sir,' returned Oliver in amazement.

This sounded so like a falsehood, that the old gentleman looked somewhat sternly in Oliver's face. It was impossible to doubt him; there was truth in every one of its thin and sharpened lineaments.

'Some mistake,' said Mr Brownlow. But, although his motive for looking steadily at Oliver no longer existed, the old idea of the resemblance between his features and some familiar face came upon him so strongly that he could not withdraw his gaze.

'I hope you are not angry with me, sir,' said Oliver, raising his eyes beseechingly.

'No, no,' replied the old gentleman. – 'Gracious God, what's this! Bedwin, look, look there!'

As he spoke, he pointed hastily to the picture above Oliver's head, and then to the boy's face. There was its living copy, – the eyes, the head, the mouth; every feature was the same. The expression was for the instant so precisely alike, that the minutest line seemed copied with an accuracy which was perfectly unearthly.

Oliver knew not the cause of this sudden exclamation, for he was not strong enough to bear the start it gave him, and he fainted away.

CHAPTER THE THIRTEENTH

*REVERTS TO THE MERRY OLD
GENTLEMAN AND HIS YOUTHFUL
FRIENDS, THROUGH WHOM A NEW
ACQUAINTANCE IS INTRODUCED TO THE
INTELLIGENT READER, AND CONNECTED
WITH WHOM VARIOUS PLEASANT
MATTERS ARE RELATED APPERTAINING
TO THIS HISTORY*

When the Dodger and his accomplished friend Master Bates joined in the hue and cry which was raised at Oliver's heels, in consequence of their executing an illegal conveyance of Mr Brownlow's personal property, as hath been already described with great perspicuity in a foregoing chapter, they were actuated, as we therein took occasion to observe, by a very laudable and becoming regard for themselves: and forasmuch as the freedom of the subject and the liberty of the individual are among the first and proudest boasts of a true-hearted Englishman, so I need hardly beg the reader to observe that this action must tend to exalt them in the opinion of all public and patriotic men, in almost as great a degree as this strong proof of their anxiety for their own preservation and safety goes to corroborate and confirm the little code of laws which certain profound and sound-judging philosophers have laid down as the mainsprings of all Madam Nature's deeds and actions; the said philosophers very wisely reducing the good lady's proceedings to matters of maxim and theory, and, by a very neat and pretty compliment to her exalted wisdom and understanding, putting entirely out of sight any considerations of heart, or generous impulse and feeling, as matters totally beneath a female who is acknowledged by universal admission to be so far beyond the numerous little foibles and weaknesses of her sex.

If I wanted any further proof of the strictly philosophical nature of the conduct of these young gentlemen in their very delicate predicament, I should at once find it in the fact (also recorded in a foregoing part of this narrative) of their quitting the pursuit when the general attention was fixed upon Oliver, and making immediately for their home by the shortest possible cut; for although I do not mean to assert that it is the practice of renowned and learned sages at all to shorten the road to any great conclusion, their course indeed being rather to lengthen the distance by various circumlocutions and discursive staggerings, like those in which drunken men under the pressure of a too mighty flow of ideas are prone to indulge, still I do mean to say, and do say distinctly, that it is the invariable practice of all mighty philosophers, in carrying out their theories, to evince great wisdom and foresight in providing against every possible contingency which can be supposed at all likely to affect themselves. Thus, to do a great right, you may do a little wrong,[1] and you may take any means which the end to be attained will justify; the amount of the right or the amount of the wrong, or indeed the distinction between the two, being left entirely to the philosopher concerned: to be settled and determined by his clear, comprehensive, and impartial view of his own particular case.

It was not until the two boys had scoured with great rapidity through a most intricate maze of narrow streets and courts, that they ventured to halt by common consent beneath a low and dark archway. Having remained silent here, just long enough to recover breath to speak, Master Bates uttered an exclamation of amusement and delight, and, bursting into an uncontrollable fit of laughter, flung himself upon a door-step, and rolled thereon in a transport of mirth.

'What's the matter?' inquired the Dodger.

'Ha! ha! ha!' roared Charley Bates.

'Hold your noise,' remonstrated the Dodger, looking cautiously round. 'Do you want to be grabbed, stupid?'

'I can't help it,' said Charley, 'I can't help it. To see him splitting away at that pace, and cutting round the corners, and knocking up against the posts, and starting on again as if he was made of iron as well as them, and me with the wipe in my pocket, singing out arter him – oh, my eye!' The vivid imagination of Master Bates presented the scene before him in too strong colours. As he arrived at this apostrophe, he again rolled upon the door-step and laughed louder than before.

'What'll Fagin say?' inquired the Dodger, taking advantage of the next interval of breathlessness on the part of his friend to propound the question.

'What!' repeated Charley Bates.

'Ah, what?' said the Dodger.

'Why, what should he say?' inquired Charley, stopping rather suddenly in his merriment, for the Dodger's manner was impressive; 'what should he say?'

Mr Dawkins whistled for a couple of minutes, and then, taking off his hat, scratched his head and nodded thrice.

'What do you mean?' said Charley.

'Toor rul lol loo, gammon and spinnage, the frog he wouldn't, and high cockolorum,'[2] said the Dodger with a slight sneer on his intellectual countenance.

This was explanatory, but not satisfactory. Mr Bates felt it so, and again said, 'What do you mean?'

The Dodger made no reply, but putting his hat on again, and gathering the skirts of his long-tailed coat under his arms, thrust his tongue into his cheek, slapped the bridge of his nose some half-dozen times in a familiar but expressive manner, and then, turning on his heel, slunk down the court. Mr Bates followed, with a thoughtful countenance.

The noise of footsteps on the creaking stairs a few minutes after the occurrence of this conversation roused the merry old gentleman as he sat over the fire with a saveloy and a small loaf in his left hand, a pocket-knife in his right, and a pewter pot on the trivet. There was a rascally smile on his white face as he turned round, and, looking sharply out from under his thick red eyebrows, bent his ear towards the door and listened intently.

'Why, how's this?' muttered the Jew, changing countenance; 'only two of 'em! Where's the third? They can't have got into trouble. Hark!'

The footsteps approached nearer; they reached the landing, the door was slowly opened, and the Dodger and Charley Bates entered and closed it behind them.

'Where's Oliver, you young hounds?' said the furious Jew, rising with a menacing look: 'where's the boy?'

The young thieves eyed their preceptor as if they were alarmed at his violence, and looked uneasily at each other, but made no reply.

'What's become of the boy?' said the Jew, seizing the Dodger tightly by the collar, and threatening him with horrid imprecations. 'Speak out, or I'll throttle you!'

Mr Fagin looked so very much in earnest, that Charley Bates, who deemed it prudent in all cases to be on the safe side, and conceived it by no means improbable that it might be his turn to be throttled second, dropped upon his knees, and raised a loud, well-sustained, and continuous roar, something between an insane bull and a speaking-trumpet.

'Will you speak?' thundered the Jew, shaking the Dodger so much that his keeping in the big coat at all seemed perfectly miraculous.

'Why, the traps have got him, and that's all about it,' said the Dodger sullenly. 'Come, let go o' me, will yer!' and, swinging himself at one jerk clean out of the big coat, which he left in the Jew's hands, the Dodger snatched up the toasting-fork and made a pass at the merry old gentleman's waistcoat, which, if it had taken effect, would have let a little more merriment out than could have been easily replaced in a month or two.

The Jew stepped back in this emergency with more agility than could have been anticipated in a man of his apparent decrepitude, and, seizing up the pot, prepared to hurl it at his assailant's head. But Charley Bates at this moment calling his attention by a perfectly terrific howl, he suddenly altered its destination, and flung it full at that young gentleman.

'Why, what the blazes is in the wind now!' growled a deep voice. 'Who pitched that 'ere at me? It's well it's the beer and not the pot as hit me, or I'd have settled somebody. I might have know'd as nobody but an infernal rich, plundering, thundering old Jew could afford to throw away any drink but water, and not that, unless he done the River company every quarter.³ Wot's it all about, Fagin. D—me if my neckankecher an't lined with beer. Come in, you sneaking warmint;

wot are you stopping outside for, as if you was ashamed of your master. Come in!'

The man who growled out these words was a stoutly-built fellow of about five-and-forty, in a black velveteen coat, very soiled drab breeches, lace-up half-boots, and grey cotton stockings, which enclosed a very bulky pair of legs, with large swelling calves, – the kind of legs which in such costume always look in an unfinished and incomplete state without a set of fetters to garnish them. He had a brown hat on his head, and a dirty belcher handkerchief[4] round his neck, with the long frayed ends of which, he smeared the beer from his face as he spoke; disclosing when he had done so, a broad heavy countenance with a beard of three days' growth, and two scowling eyes, one of which displayed various parti-coloured symptoms of having been recently damaged by a blow.

'Come in, d'ye hear?' growled this engaging-looking ruffian. A white shaggy dog, with his face scratched and torn in twenty different places, skulked into the room.

'Why didn't you come in afore?' said the man. 'You're getting too proud to own me afore company, are you. Lie down!'

This command was accompanied with a kick which sent the animal to the other end of the room. He appeared well used to it, however; for he coiled himself up in a corner very quietly without uttering a sound, and, winking his very ill-looking eyes about twenty times in a minute, appeared to occupy himself in taking a survey of the apartment.

'What are you up to? Ill-treating the boys, you covetous, avaricious, in-sa-ti-a-ble old fence?' said the man, seating himself deliberately. 'I wonder they don't murder you; *I* would if I was them. If I'd been your prentice I'd have done it long ago; and – no, I couldn't have sold you arterwards, though; for you're fit for nothing but keeping as a curiosity of ugliness in a glass bottle, and I suppose they don't blow them large enough.'

'Hush! hush! Mr Sikes,' said the Jew, trembling; 'don't speak so loud.'

'None of your mistering,' replied the ruffian; 'you always mean mischief when you come that. You know my name: out with it. I shan't disgrace it when the time comes.'

'Well, well, then, Bill Sikes,' said the Jew with abject humility. 'You seem out of humour, Bill.'

'Perhaps I am,' replied Sikes. 'I should think *you* were rather out of sorts too, unless you mean as little harm when you throw pewter pots about, as you do when you blab and—'

'Are you mad?' said the Jew, catching the man by the sleeve, and pointing towards the boys.

Mr Sikes contented himself with tying an imaginary knot under his left ear, and jerking his head over on the right shoulder; a piece of dumb show which the Jew appeared to understand perfectly. He then in cant terms, with which his whole conversation was plentifully besprinkled, but which would be quite unintelligible if they were recorded here, demanded a glass of liquor.

'And mind you don't poison it,' said Mr Sikes, laying his hat upon the table.

This was said in jest; but if the speaker could have seen the evil leer with which the Jew bit his pale lip as he turned round to the cupboard, he might have thought the caution not wholly unnecessary, or the wish, at all events, to improve upon the distiller's ingenuity not very far from the old gentleman's merry heart.

After swallowing two or three glassfuls of spirits, Mr Sikes condescended to take some notice of the young gentlemen; which gracious act led to a conversation in which the cause and manner of Oliver's capture were circumstantially detailed, with such alterations and improvements on the truth as to the Dodger appeared most advisable under the circumstances.

'I'm afraid,' said the Jew, 'that he may say something which will get us into trouble.'

'That's very likely,' returned Sikes with a malicious grin. 'You're blowed upon, Fagin.'

'And I'm afraid, you see,' added the Jew, speaking as if he had not noticed the interruption, and regarding the other closely as he did so, – 'I'm afraid that, if the game was up with us, it might be up with a good many more; and that it would come out rather worse for you than it would for me,[5] my dear.'

The man started, and turned fiercely round upon the Jew; but the old gentleman's shoulders were shrugged up to his ears, and his eyes were vacantly staring on the opposite wall.

There was a long pause. Every member of the respectable coterie appeared plunged in his own reflections, not excepting the dog, who by a certain malicious licking of his lips seemed to be meditating an attack upon the legs of the first gentleman or lady he might encounter in the street when he went out.

'Somebody must find out what's been done at the office,' said Mr Sikes in a much lower tone than he had taken since he came in.

The Jew nodded assent.

'If he hasn't peached, and is committed, there's no fear till he comes out again,' said Mr Sikes, 'and then he must be taken care on. You must get hold of him, somehow.'

Again the Jew nodded.

The prudence of this line of action, indeed, was obvious; but unfortunately there was one very strong objection to its being adopted; and this was, that the Dodger, and Charley Bates, and Fagin, and Mr William Sikes, happened one and all to entertain a most violent and deeply-rooted antipathy to going near a police-office on any ground or pretext whatever.

How long they might have sat and looked at each other in a state of uncertainty not the most pleasant of its kind, it is difficult to say. It is not necessary to make any guesses on the subject, however; for the sudden entrance of the two young ladies whom Oliver had seen on a former occasion caused the conversation to flow afresh.

'The very thing!' said the Jew. 'Bet will go; won't you, my dear?'

'Wheres?' inquired the young lady.

'Only just up to the office, my dear,' said the Jew coaxingly.

It is due to the young lady to say that she did not positively affirm that she would not, but that she merely expressed an emphatic and earnest desire to be 'jiggered' if she would; a polite and delicate evasion of the request, which shows the young lady to have been possessed of that natural good-breeding that cannot bear to inflict upon a fellow-creature the pain of a direct and pointed refusal.

The Jew's countenance fell, and he turned to the other young lady, who was gaily, not to say gorgeously attired, in a red gown, green boots, and yellow curl-papers.

'Nancy, my dear,' said the Jew in a soothing manner, 'what do *you* say?'

'That it won't do; so it's no use a trying it on, Fagin,' replied Nancy.

'What do you mean by that?' said Mr Sikes, looking up in a surly manner.

'What I say, Bill,' replied the lady collectedly.

'Why, you're just the very person for it,' reasoned Mr Sikes: 'nobody about here, knows anything of you.'

'And as I don't want 'em to, neither,' replied Miss Nancy in the same composed manner, 'it's rayther more no than yes with me, Bill.'

'She'll go, Fagin,' said Sikes.

'No, she won't, Fagin,' bawled Nancy.

'Yes she will, Fagin,' said Sikes.

And Mr Sikes was right. By dint of alternate threats, promises, and bribes, the engaging female in question was ultimately prevailed upon to undertake the commission. She was not indeed withheld by the same considerations as her agreeable friend, for, having very recently removed into the neighbourhood of Field-lane from the remote but genteel suburb of Ratcliffe,[6] she was not under the same apprehension of being recognized by any of her numerous acquaintance.

Accordingly, with a clean white apron tied over the red gown, and the yellow curl-papers tucked up under a straw bonnet, – both articles of dress being provided from the Jew's inexhaustible stock, – Miss Nancy prepared to issue forth on her errand.

'Stop a minute, my dear,' said the Jew, producing a little covered basket. 'Carry that in one hand; it looks more respectable, my dear.'

'Give her a door-key to carry in her t'other one, Fagin,' said Sikes; 'it looks real and genivine like.'

'Yes, yes, my dear, so it does,' said the Jew, hanging a large street-door key on the fore-finger of the young lady's right hand. 'There; very good, – very good indeed, my dear,' said the Jew, rubbing his hands.

'Oh, my brother! my poor, dear, sweet, innocent little brother!' exclaimed Miss Nancy, bursting into tears, and wringing the little basket and the street-door key in an agony of distress. 'What has become of him – where have they taken him to! Oh, do have pity, and tell me what's been done with the dear boy, gentlemen; do, gentlemen, if you please, gentlemen.'

Having uttered these words in a most lamentable and heartbroken tone, to the immeasurable delight of her hearers, Miss Nancy paused, winked to the company, nodded smilingly round, and disappeared.

'Ah! she's a clever girl, my dears,' said the Jew, turning to his young friends, and shaking his head gravely, as if in mute admonition to them to follow the bright example they had just beheld.

'She's a honor to her sex,' said Mr Sikes, filling his glass, and smiting the table with his enormous fist. 'Here's her health, and wishing they was all like her!'

While these and many other encomiums were being passed on the accomplished Miss Nancy, that young lady made the best of her way to the police-office; whither, notwithstanding a little natural timidity consequent upon walking through the streets alone and unprotected, she arrived in perfect safety shortly afterwards.

Entering by the back way, she tapped softly with the key at one of the cell-doors and listened. There was no sound within, so she coughed and listened again. Still there was no reply, so she spoke.

'Nolly, dear?' murmured Nancy in a gentle voice; – 'Nolly?'

There was nobody inside but a miserable shoeless criminal, who had been taken up for playing the flute,[7] and who – the offence against society having been clearly proved – had been very properly committed by Mr Fang to the House of Correction for one month, with the appropriate and amusing remark that since he had got so much breath to spare, it would be much more wholesomely expended on the treadmill[8] than in a musical instrument. He made no answer, being occupied in mentally bewailing the loss of the flute, which had been confiscated for the use of the county; so Miss Nancy passed on to the next cell, and knocked there.

'Well,' cried a faint and feeble voice.

'Is there a little boy here?' inquired Miss Nancy with a preliminary sob.

'No,' replied the voice; 'God forbid!'

This was a vagrant of sixty-five, who was going to prison for *not* playing the flute, or, in other words, for begging in the streets, and doing nothing for his livelihood. In the next cell was another man, who was going to the same prison for hawking tin saucepans without a licence, thereby doing something for his living in defiance of the Stamp-office.[9]

But as neither of these criminals answered to the name of Oliver, or knew anything about him, Miss Nancy made straight up to the bluff officer in the striped waistcoat, and with the most piteous wailings and lamentations, rendered more piteous by a prompt and efficient use of the street-door key and the little basket, demanded her own dear brother.

'I haven't got him, my dear,' said the old man.

'Where is he?' screamed Miss Nancy in a distracted manner.

'Why, the gentleman's got him,' replied the officer.

'What gentleman? Oh, gracious heavins! what gentleman?' exclaimed Miss Nancy.

In reply to this incoherent questioning, the old man informed the deeply affected sister that Oliver had been taken ill in the office, and discharged in consequence of a witness having proved the robbery to have been committed by another boy not in custody; and that the prosecutor had carried him away in an insensible condition to his own residence, of and concerning which all the informant knew was, that it was somewhere at Pentonville, he having heard that word mentioned in the directions to the coachman.

In a dreadful state of doubt and uncertainty the agonized young woman staggered to the gate, and then, – exchanging her faltering gait for a good swift steady run, returned by the most devious and complicated route she could think of, to the domicile of the Jew.

Mr Bill Sikes no sooner heard the account of the expedition delivered, than he very hastily called up the white dog, and, putting on his hat, expeditiously departed, without devoting any time to the formality of wishing the company good-morning.

'We must know where he is, my dears; he must be found,' said the Jew, greatly excited. 'Charley, do nothing but skulk about, till you bring home some news of him. Nancy, my dear, I must have him found: I trust to you, my dear, – to you and the Artful for every thing. Stay, stay,' added the Jew, unlocking a drawer with a shaking hand; 'there's money, my dears. I shall shut up this shop to-night: you'll know where to find me. Don't stop here a minute, – not an instant, my dears!'

With these words he pushed them from the room, and carefully double-locking and barring the door behind them, drew from its place of concealment the box which he had unintentionally disclosed to Oliver, and hastily proceeded to dispose the watches and jewellery beneath his clothing.

A rap at the door startled him in this occupation. 'Who's there?' he cried in a shrill tone of alarm.

'Me!' replied the voice of the Dodger through the keyhole.

'What now?' cried the Jew impatiently.

'Is he to be kidnapped to the other ken, Nancy says?' inquired the Dodger cautiously.

'Yes,' replied the Jew, 'wherever she lays hands on him. Find him, find him out, that's all; and I shall know what to do next, never fear.'

The boy murmured a reply of intelligence, and hurried down stairs after his companions.

'He has not peached so far,' said the Jew as he pursued his occupation. 'If he means to blab us among his new friends, we may stop his windpipe yet.'

*

CHAPTER THE FOURTEENTH

*COMPRISING FURTHER PARTICULARS OF
OLIVER'S STAY AT MR BROWNLOW'S,
WITH THE REMARKABLE PREDICTION
WHICH ONE MR GRIMWIG UTTERED
CONCERNING HIM, WHEN HE WENT OUT
ON AN ERRAND*

Oliver soon recovered from the fainting-fit into which Mr Brownlow's abrupt exclamation had thrown him; and the subject of the picture was carefully avoided, both by the old gentleman and Mrs Bedwin, in the conversation that ensued, which indeed bore no reference to Oliver's history or prospects, but was confined to such topics as might amuse without exciting him. He was still too weak to get up to breakfast; but, when he came down into the housekeeper's room next day, his first act was to cast an eager glance at the wall, in the hope of again looking on the face of the beautiful lady. His expectations were disappointed, however, for the picture had been removed.

'Ah!' said the housekeeper, watching the direction of Oliver's eyes. 'It is gone, you see.'

'I see it is, ma'am,' replied Oliver, with a sigh. 'Why have they taken it away?'

'It has been taken down, child, because Mr Brownlow said, that, as it seemed to worry you, perhaps it might prevent your getting well, you know,' rejoined the old lady.

'Oh, no, indeed it didn't worry me, ma'am,' said Oliver. 'I liked to see it; I quite loved it.'

'Well, well!' said the old lady, good-humouredly; 'you get well as fast as ever you can, dear, and it shall be hung up again. There, I promise you that; now let us talk about something else.'

This was all the information Oliver could obtain about the picture at that time, and as the old lady had been so kind to him in his illness, he endeavoured to think no more of the subject just then; so listened attentively to a great many stories she told him about an amiable and handsome daughter of hers, who was married to an amiable and handsome man, and lived in the country; and a son, who was clerk to a merchant in the West Indies, and who was also such a good young man, and wrote such dutiful letters home four times a year, that it brought the tears into her eyes to talk about them. When the old lady had expatiated a long time on the excellences of her children, and the merits of her kind good husband besides, who had been dead and gone, poor dear soul! just six-and-twenty years, it was time to have tea; and after tea she began to teach Oliver cribbage,[1] which he learnt as quickly as she could teach, and at which game they played, with great interest and gravity, until it was time for the invalid to have some warm wine and water, with a slice of dry toast, and to go cosily to bed.

They were happy days, those of Oliver's recovery. Everything was so quiet, and neat, and orderly, everybody so kind and gentle, that after the noise and turbulence in the midst of which he had always lived, it seemed like heaven itself. He was no sooner strong enough to put his clothes on properly, than Mr Brownlow caused a complete new suit, and a new cap, and a new pair of shoes, to be provided for him. As Oliver was told that he might do what he liked with the old clothes, he gave them to a servant who had been very kind to him, and asked her to sell them to a Jew,[2] and keep the money for herself. This she very readily did; and, as Oliver looked out of the parlour window, and saw the Jew roll them up in his bag and walk away, he felt quite delighted to think that they were safely gone, and that there was now no possible danger of his ever being able to wear them again. They were sad rags, to tell the truth; and Oliver had never had a new suit before.

One evening, about a week after the affair of the picture, as Oliver was sitting talking to Mrs Bedwin, there came a message down from Mr Brownlow, that if Oliver Twist felt pretty well, he should like to see him in his study, and talk to him a little while.

'Bless us, and save us! wash your hands, and let me part your hair nicely for you, child,' said Mrs Bedwin. 'Dear heart alive! if we had known he would have asked for you, we would have put you a clean collar on, and made you as smart as sixpence.'

Oliver did as the old lady bade him, and, although she lamented grievously meanwhile that there was not even time to crimp the little frill that bordered his shirt-collar, he looked so delicate and handsome, despite that important personal advantage, that she went so far as to say, looking at him with great complacency from head to foot, that she really didn't think it would have been possible on the longest notice to have made much difference in him for the better.

Thus encouraged, Oliver tapped at the study door, and, on Mr Brownlow calling to him to come in, found himself in a little back room, quite full of books, with a window looking into some pleasant little gardens. There was a table drawn up before the window, at which Mr Brownlow was seated reading. When he saw Oliver, he pushed the book away from him, and told him to come near the table and sit down. Oliver complied, marvelling where the people could be found to read such a great number of books as seemed to be written to make the world wiser, – which is still a marvel to more experienced people than Oliver Twist every day of their lives.

'There are a good many books, are there not, my boy?' said Mr Brownlow, observing the curiosity with which Oliver surveyed the shelves that reached from the floor to the ceiling.

'A great number, sir,' replied Oliver; 'I never saw so many.'

'You shall read them if you behave well,' said the old gentleman kindly; 'and you will like that, better than looking at the outsides, – that is, in some cases, because there *are* books of which the backs and covers are by far the best parts.'

'I suppose they are those heavy ones, sir,' said Oliver, pointing to some large quartos with a good deal of gilding about the binding.

'Not those,' said the old gentleman, patting Oliver on the head, and smiling as he did so; 'but other equally heavy ones, though of a much smaller size. How should you like to grow up a clever man, and write books, eh?'

'I think I would rather read them, sir,' replied Oliver.

'What! wouldn't you like to be a book-writer?' said the old gentleman.

Oliver considered a little while, and at last said he should think it would be a much better thing to be a bookseller;' upon which the old gentleman laughed heartily, and declared he had said a very good thing, which Oliver felt glad to have done, though he by no means knew what it was.

'Well, well,' said the old gentleman, composing his features, 'don't be afraid; we won't make an author of you, while there's an honest trade to be learnt, or brick-making to turn to.'

'Thank you, sir,' said Oliver; and at the earnest manner of his reply the old gentleman laughed again, and said something about a curious instinct, which Oliver, not understanding, paid no very great attention to.

'Now,' said Mr Brownlow, speaking if possible in a kinder, but at the same time in a much more serious manner than Oliver had ever heard him speak in yet, 'I want you to pay great attention, my boy, to what I am going to say. I shall talk to you without any reserve, because I am sure you are as well able to understand me as many older persons would be.'

'Oh, don't tell me you are going to send me away, sir, pray!' exclaimed Oliver, alarmed by the serious tone of the old gentleman's commencement; 'don't turn me out of doors to wander in the streets again. Let me stay here and be a servant. Don't send me back to the wretched place I came from. Have mercy upon a poor boy, sir; do!'

'My dear child,' said the old gentleman, moved by the warmth of Oliver's sudden appeal, 'you need not be afraid of my deserting you, unless you give me cause.'

'I never, never will, sir,' interposed Oliver.

'I hope not,' rejoined the old gentleman; 'I do not think you ever will. I have been deceived before, in the objects whom I have endeavoured to benefit; but I feel strongly disposed to trust you, nevertheless, and more strongly interested in your behalf than I can well account for, even to myself. The persons on whom I have bestowed my dearest love lie deep in their graves; but, although the happiness and delight of my life lie buried there too, I have not made a coffin of my heart, and sealed it up for ever on my best affections. Deep affliction has only made them stronger; it ought, I think, for it should refine our nature.'

As the old gentleman said this in a low voice, more to himself than to his companion, and remained silent for a short time afterwards, Oliver sat quite still, almost afraid to breathe.

'Well, well,' said the old gentleman at length in a more cheerful voice, 'I only say this, because you have a young heart; and knowing that I have suffered great pain and sorrow, you will be more careful, perhaps, not to wound me again. You say you are an orphan, without a friend in the world; and all the inquiries I have been able to make confirm the statement. Let me hear your story; where you came from, who brought you up, and how you got into the company in which I found you. Speak the truth; and if I find you have committed no crime, you will never be friendless while I live.'

Oliver's sobs quite checked his utterance for some minutes; and just when he was on the point of beginning to relate how he had been brought up at the farm, and carried to the workhouse by Mr Bumble, a peculiarly impatient little double-knock was heard at the street-door, and the servant, running up stairs, announced Mr Grimwig.

'Is he coming up?' inquired Mr Brownlow.

'Yes, sir,' replied the servant. 'He asked if there were any muffins in the house, and, when I told him yes, he said he had come to tea.'

Mr Brownlow smiled, and, turning to Oliver, said Mr Grimwig was an old friend of his, and he must not mind his being a little rough in his manners, for he was a worthy creature at bottom, as he had reason to know.

'Shall I go down stairs, sir?' inquired Oliver.

'No,' replied Mr Brownlow; 'I would rather you stopped here.'

At this moment there walked into the room, supporting himself by a thick stick, a stout old gentleman, rather lame in one leg, who was dressed in a blue coat, striped waistcoat, nankeen[4] breeches and gaiters, and a broad-brimmed white hat, with the sides turned up with green. A very small-plaited shirt-frill stuck out from his waistcoat, and a very long steel watch-chain, with nothing but a key at the end, dangled loosely below it. The ends of his white neckerchief were twisted into a ball about the size of an orange; – the variety of shapes into which his countenance was twisted defy description. He had a manner of screwing his head round on one side when he spoke, and looking out of the corners of his eyes at the same time, which irresistibly reminded the beholder of a parrot. In this attitude he fixed himself the moment he made his appearance; and, holding out a small piece of orange-peel at arm's length, exclaimed in a growling, discontented voice,

'Look here! do you see this? Isn't it a most wonderful and extraordinary thing that I can't call at a man's house but I find a piece of this cursed poor-surgeon's-friend on the staircase? I've been lamed with orange-peel once, and I know orange-peel will be my death at last. It will, sir; orange-peel will be my death, or I'll be content to eat my own head, sir!' This was the handsome offer with which Mr Grimwig backed and confirmed nearly every assertion he made; and it was the more singular in his case, because, even admitting, for the sake of argument, the possibility of scientific improvements being ever brought to that pass which will enable a gentleman to eat his own head in the event of his being so disposed, Mr Grimwig's head was such a particularly large one, that the most sanguine man alive could hardly entertain a hope of being able to get through it at a sitting, to put entirely out of the question a very thick coating of powder.

'I'll eat my head, sir,' repeated Mr Grimwig, striking his stick upon the ground. 'Hallo! what's that?' he added, looking at Oliver, and retreating a pace or two.

'This is young Oliver Twist, whom we were speaking about,' said Mr Brownlow.

Oliver bowed.

'You don't mean to say that's the boy that had the fever, I hope?' said Mr Grimwig, recoiling a little further. 'Wait a minute, don't speak: stop –' continued Mr Grimwig abruptly, losing all dread of the fever in his triumph at the discovery; 'that's the boy that had the orange! If that's not the boy, sir, that had the orange, and threw this bit of peel upon the staircase, I'll eat my head and his too.'

'No, no, he has not had one,' said Mr Brownlow, laughing. 'Come, put down your hat, and speak to my young friend.'

'I feel strongly on this subject, sir,' said the irritable old gentleman, drawing off his gloves. 'There's always more or less orange-peel on the pavement in our street, and I *know* it's put there by the surgeon's boy at the corner. A young woman stumbled over a bit last night, and fell against my garden-railings; directly she got up I saw her look towards his infernal red lamp with the pantomime-light. "Don't go to him," I called out of the window, "he's an assassin, – a man-trap!" So he is. If he is not—' Here the irascible old gentleman gave a great knock on the ground with his stick, which was always understood by his friends to imply the customary offer whenever it was not expressed in words. Then, still keeping his stick in his hand, he sat down, and, opening a double eye-glass which he wore attached to a broad black riband, took a view of Oliver, who, seeing that he was the object of inspection, coloured, and bowed again.

'That's the boy, is it?' said Mr Grimwig, at length.

'That is the boy,' replied Mr Brownlow, nodding good-humouredly to Oliver.

'How are you, boy?' said Mr Grimwig.

'A great deal better, thank you, sir,' replied Oliver.

Mr Brownlow, seeming to apprehend that his singular friend was about to say something disagreeable, asked Oliver to step down stairs, and tell Mrs Bedwin they were ready for tea, which, as he did not half like the visitor's manner, he was very happy to do.

'He is a nice-looking boy, is he not?' inquired Mr Brownlow.

'I don't know,' replied Grimwig, pettishly.

'Don't know?'

'No, I don't know. I never see any difference in boys. I only know two sorts of boys, – mealy boys, and beef-faced boys.'

'And which is Oliver?'

'Mealy. I know a friend who's got a beef-faced boy; a fine boy they call him, with a round head, and red cheeks, and glaring eyes; a horrid boy, with a body and limbs that appear to be swelling out of the seams of his blue clothes – with the voice of a pilot, and the appetite of a wolf. I know him, the wretch!'

'Come,' said Mr Brownlow, 'these are not the characteristics of young Oliver Twist; so he needn't excite your wrath.'

'They are not,' replied Grimwig. 'He may have worse.'

Here Mr Brownlow coughed impatiently, which appeared to afford Mr Grimwig the most exquisite delight.

'He may have worse, I say,' repeated Mr Grimwig. 'Where does he come from? Who is he? What is he? He has had a fever – what of that? Fevers are not peculiar to good people, are they? Bad people have fevers sometimes, haven't they, eh? I knew a man that was hung in Jamaica for murdering his master; he had had a fever six times; he wasn't recommended to mercy on that account. Pooh! nonsense!'

Now, the fact was, that, in the inmost recesses of his own heart, Mr Grimwig was strongly disposed to admit that Oliver's appearance and manner were unusually prepossessing, but he had a strong appetite for contradiction, sharpened on this occasion by the finding of the orange-peel; and inwardly determining that no man should dictate to him whether a boy was well-looking or not, he had resolved from the first to oppose his friend. When Mr Brownlow admitted that on no one point of inquiry could he yet return any satisfactory answer, and that he had postponed any investigation into Oliver's previous history until he thought the boy was strong enough to bear it, Mr Grimwig chuckled maliciously, and demanded, with a sneer, whether the house-keeper was in the habit of counting the plate at night; because, if she didn't find a table-spoon or two missing some sun-shiny morning, why, he would be content to—, et cetera.

All this Mr Brownlow, although himself somewhat of an impetuous gentleman, knowing his friend's peculiarities, bore with great good humour; and as Mr Grimwig, at tea, was graciously pleased to express his entire approval of the muffins, matters went on very smoothly, and Oliver, who made one of the party, began to feel more at his ease than he had yet done in the fierce old gentleman's presence.

'And when are you going to hear a full, true, and particular account of the life and adventures of Oliver Twist?' asked Grimwig of Mr Brownlow, at the conclusion of the meal: looking sideways at Oliver as he resumed the subject.

'To-morrow morning,' replied Mr Brownlow. 'I would rather he was alone with me at the time. Come up to me to-morrow morning at ten o'clock, my dear.'

'Yes, sir,' replied Oliver. He answered with some hesitation, because he was confused by Mr Grimwig's looking so hard at him.

'I'll tell you what,' whispered that gentleman to Mr Brownlow; 'he won't come up to you to-morrow morning. I saw him hesitate. He is deceiving you, my dear friend.'

'I'll swear he is not,' replied Mr Brownlow, warmly.

'If he is not,' said Mr Grimwig, 'I'll—' and down went the stick.

'I'll answer for that boy's truth with my life,' said Mr Brownlow, knocking the table.

'And I for his falsehood with my head,' rejoined Mr Grimwig, knocking the table also.

'We shall see,' said Mr Brownlow, checking his rising passion.

'We will,' replied Mr Grimwig, with a provoking smile; 'we will.'

As fate would have it, Mrs Bedwin chanced to bring in at this moment a small parcel of books which Mr Brownlow had that morning purchased of the identical bookstall-keeper who has already figured in this history; which having laid on the table, she prepared to leave the room.

'Stop the boy, Mrs Bedwin,' said Mr Brownlow; 'there is something to go back.'

'He has gone, sir,' replied Mrs Bedwin.

'Call after him,' said Mr Brownlow; 'it's particular. He's a poor man, and they are not paid for. There are some books to be taken back, too.'

The street-door was opened. Oliver ran one way, and the girl another, and Mrs Bedwin stood on the step and screamed for the boy; but there was no boy in sight, and both Oliver and the girl returned in a breathless state to report that there were no tidings of him.

'Dear me, I am very sorry for that,' exclaimed Mr Brownlow; 'I particularly wished those books to be returned to-night.'

'Send Oliver with them,' said Mr Grimwig, with an ironical smile; 'he will be sure to deliver them safely, you know.'

'Yes; do let me take them, if you please, sir,' said Oliver; 'I'll run all the way, sir.'

The old gentleman was just going to say that Oliver should not go out on any account, when a most malicious cough from Mr Grimwig determined him that he should, and by his prompt discharge of the commission prove to him the injustice of his suspicions, on this head at least, at once.

'You *shall* go, my dear,' said the old gentleman. 'The books are on a chair by my table. Fetch them down.'

Oliver, delighted to be of use, brought down the books under his arm in a great bustle, and waited, cap in hand, to hear what message he was to take.

'You are to say,' said Mr Brownlow, glancing steadily at Grimwig, – 'you are to say that you have brought those books back, and that you have come to pay the four pound ten I owe him. This is a five-pound note, so you will have to bring me back ten shillings change.'

'I won't be ten minutes,⁵ sir,' replied Oliver, eagerly; and, having buttoned up the bank-note in his jacket pocket, and placed the books carefully under his arm, he made a respectful bow, and left the room. Mrs Bedwin followed him to the street-door, giving him many directions about the nearest way, and the name of the bookseller, and the name of the street, all of which Oliver said he clearly understood; and, having super-added many injunctions to be sure and not take cold, the careful old lady at length permitted him to depart.

'Bless his sweet face!' said the old lady, looking after him. 'I can't bear, somehow, to let him go out of my sight.'

At this moment Oliver looked gaily round, and nodded before he turned the corner. The old lady smilingly returned his salutation, and, closing the door, went back to her own room.

'Let me see; he'll be back in twenty minutes, at the longest,' said Mr Brownlow, pulling out his watch, and placing it on the table. 'It will be dark by that time.'

'Oh! you really expect him to come back, do you?' inquired Mr Grimwig.

'Don't you?' asked Mr Brownlow, smiling.

The spirit of contradiction was strong in Mr Grimwig's breast at the moment, and it was rendered stronger by his friend's confident smile.

'No,' he said, smiting the table with his fist, 'I do not. The boy has got a new suit of clothes on his back, a set of valuable books under his arm, and a five-pound note in his pocket; he'll join his old friends the thieves, and laugh at you. If ever that boy returns to this house, sir, I'll eat my head.'

With these words he drew his chair closer to the table, and there the two friends sat in silent expectation, with the watch between them. It is worthy of remark, as illustrating the importance we attach to our own judgments, and the pride with which we put forth our most rash and hasty conclusions, that, although Mr Grimwig was not a bad-hearted man, and would have been unfeignedly sorry to see his respected friend duped and deceived, he really did most earnestly and strongly hope at that moment that Oliver Twist might not come back. Of such contradictions is human nature made up!

It grew so dark that the figures on the dial were scarcely discernible; but there the two old gentlemen continued to sit in silence, with the watch between them.

CHAPTER THE FIFTEENTH

SHEWING HOW VERY FOND OF OLIVER TWIST, THE MERRY OLD JEW AND MISS NANCY WERE

If it did not come strictly within the scope and bearing of my long-considered intentions and plans regarding this prose epic (for such I mean it to be,) to leave the two old gentlemen sitting with the watch between them long after it grew too dark to see it, and both doubting Oliver's return, the one in triumph, and the other in sorrow, I might take occasion to entertain the reader with many wise reflections on the obvious impolicy of ever attempting to do good to our fellow-creatures where there is no hope of earthly reward; or rather on the strict policy of betraying some slight degree of charity or sympathy in one particularly unpromising case, and then abandoning such weaknesses for ever. I am aware that, in advising even this slight dereliction from the paths of prudence and worldliness, I lay myself open to the censure of many excellent and respectable persons, who have long walked therein; but I venture to contend, nevertheless, that the advantages of the proceeding are manifold and lasting. As thus: if the object selected should happen most unexpectedly to turn out well, and to thrive and amend upon the assistance you have afforded him, he will, in pure gratitude and fulness of heart, laud your goodness to the skies; your character will be thus established, and you will pass through the world as a most estimable person, who does a vast deal of good in secret, not one-twentieth part of which will ever see the light. If, on the contrary, his bad character become notorious, and his profligacy a by-word, you place yourself in the excellent position of having attempted to bestow relief most disinterestedly; of having become misanthropical in conse- quence of the treachery of its object; and of having made a rash and solemn vow, (which no one regrets more than yourself,) never to help or relieve any man, woman, or child again, lest you should be similarly deceived. I know a great number of persons in both situations at this moment, and I can safely assert that they are the most generally respected and esteemed of any in the whole circle of my acquaintance.

But, as Mr Brownlow was not one of these; as he obstinately persevered in doing good for its own sake, and the gratification of heart it yielded him; as no failure dispirited him, and no ingratitude in individual cases tempted him to wreak his vengeance on the whole human race, I shall not enter into any such digression in this place: and, if this be not a sufficient reason for this determination, I have a better, and, indeed, a wholly unanswerable one, already stated; which is, that it forms no part of my original intention so to do.[1]

In the obscure parlour of a low public-house, situate in the filthiest part of Little Saffron-Hill, – a dark and gloomy den, where a flaring gas-light burnt all day in the winter-time, and where no ray of sun ever shone in the summer, – there sat, brooding over a little pewter measure and a small glass, strongly impregnated with the smell of liquor, a man in a velveteen coat, drab shorts, half-boots, and stockings, whom, even by that dim light, no experienced agent of police would have hesitated for one instant to recognise as Mr William Sikes. At his feet sat a white-coated, red-eyed dog, who occupied himself alternately in winking at his master with both eyes at the same time, and in licking a large, fresh cut on one side of his mouth, which appeared to be the result of some recent conflict.

'Keep quiet, you warmint! keep quiet!' said Mr Sikes, suddenly breaking silence. Whether his meditations were so intense as to be disturbed by the dog's winking, or whether his feelings were so wrought upon by his reflections that they required all the relief derivable from kicking an unoffending animal to allay them, is matter for argument and consideration. Whatever was the cause, the effect was a kick and a curse bestowed upon the dog simultaneously.

Dogs are not generally apt to revenge injuries inflicted upon them by their masters; but Mr Sikes's dog, having faults of temper in common with his owner, and labouring perhaps, at this moment, under a powerful sense of injury, made no more ado but at once fixed his teeth in one of the half-boots, and, having given it a good hearty shake, retired, growling, under a form: thereby just escaping the pewter measure which Mr Sikes levelled at his head.

'You would, would you?' said Sikes, seizing the poker in one hand, and deliberately opening with the other a large clasp-knife, which he drew from his pocket. 'Come here, you born devil! Come here! D'ye hear?'

The dog no doubt heard, because Mr Sikes spoke in the very harshest key of a very harsh voice; but, appearing to entertain some unaccountable objection to having his throat cut, he remained where he was, and growled more fiercely than before, at the same time grasping the end of the poker between his teeth, and biting at it like a wild beast.

This resistance only infuriated Mr Sikes the more; so, dropping upon his knees, he began to assail the animal most furiously. The dog jumped from right to left, and from left to right, snapping, growling, and barking; the man thrust and swore, and struck and blasphemed; and the struggle was reaching a most critical point for one or other, when, the door suddenly opening, the dog darted out, leaving Bill Sikes with the poker and the clasp-knife in his hands.

There must always be two parties to a quarrel, says the old adage;[2] and Mr Sikes, being disappointed of the dog's presence, at once transferred the quarrel to the new-comer.

'What the devil do you come in between me and my dog for?' said Sikes with a fierce gesture.

'I didn't know, my dear, I didn't know,' replied Fagin humbly – for the Jew was the new-comer.

'Didn't know, you white-livered thief!' growled Sikes. 'Couldn't you hear the noise?'

'Not a sound of it, as I'm a living man, Bill,' replied the Jew.

'Oh no, you hear nothing, you don't,' retorted Sikes with a fierce sneer, 'sneaking in and out, so as nobody hears how you come or go. I wish you had been the dog, Fagin, half a minute ago.'

'Why?' inquired the Jew with a forced smile.

''Cause the government, as cares for the lives of such men as you, as haven't half the pluck of curs, lets a man kill his dog how he likes,' replied Sikes, shutting the knife up with a very expressive look; 'that's why.'

The Jew rubbed his hands, and, sitting down at the table, affected to laugh at the pleasantry of his friend, – obviously very ill at his ease, however.

'Grin away,' said Sikes, replacing the poker, and surveying him with savage contempt; 'grin away. You'll never have the laugh at me, though, unless it's behind a nightcap. I've got the upper hand over you, Fagin; and, d– me, I'll keep it. There. If I go, you go;³ so take care of me.'

'Well, well, my dear,' said the Jew, 'I know all that; we – we – have a mutual interest, Bill, – a mutual interest.'

'Humph!' said Sikes, as if he thought the interest lay rather more on the Jew's side than on his. 'Well, what have you got to say to me?'

'It's all passed safe through the melting-pot,' replied Fagin, 'and this is your share. It's rather more than it ought to be, my dear; but as I know you'll do me a good turn another time, and—'

''Stow that gammon,' interposed the robber impatiently. 'Where is it? Hand over!'

'Yes, yes, Bill; give me time, give me time,' replied the Jew soothingly. 'Here it is – all safe.' As he spoke, he drew forth an old cotton handkerchief from his breast, and, untying a large knot in one corner, produced a small brown-paper packet, which Sikes snatching from him, hastily opened, and proceeded to count the sovereigns it contained.

'This is all, is it?' inquired Sikes.

'All,' replied the Jew.

'You haven't opened the parcel and swallowed one or two as you come along, have you?' inquired Sikes suspiciously. 'Don't put on a injured look at the question; you've done it many a time. Jerk the tinkler.'

These words, in plain English, conveyed an injunction to ring the bell. It was answered by another Jew, younger than Fagin, but nearly as vile and repulsive in appearance.

Bill Sikes merely pointed to the empty measure, and the Jew, perfectly understanding the hint, retired to fill it, previously exchanging a remarkable look with Fagin, who raised his eyes for an instant as if in expectation of it, and shook his head in reply so slightly that the action would have been almost imperceptible to a third person. It was lost upon Sikes, who was stooping at the moment to tie the boot-lace which the dog had torn. Possibly if he had observed the brief inter-change of signals, he might have thought that it boded no good to him.

'Is anybody here, Barney?' inquired Fagin, speaking – now that Sikes was looking on – without raising his eyes from the ground.

'Dot a shoul,' replied Barney, whose words, whether they came from the heart or not, made their way through the nose.

'Nobody?' inquired Fagin in a tone of surprise, which perhaps might mean that Barney was at liberty to tell the truth.

'Dobody but Biss Dadsy,' replied Barney.

'Miss Nancy!' exclaimed Sikes. 'Where? Strike me blind, if I don't honor that 'ere girl for her native talents.'

'She's bid havid a plate of boiled beef id the bar,' replied Barney.

'Send her here,' said Sikes, pouring out a glass of liquor; 'send her here.'

Barney looked timidly at Fagin, as if for permission; the Jew remaining silent, and not lifting his eyes from the ground, he retired, and presently returned ushering in Miss Nancy, who was decorated with the bonnet, apron, basket, and street-door key complete.

'You are on the scent, are you, Nancy?' inquired Sikes, proffering the glass.

'Yes, I am, Bill,' replied the young lady, disposing of its contents; 'and tired enough of it I am, too. The young brat's been ill and confined to the crib; and —'

'Ah, Nancy, dear!' said Fagin, looking up.

Now, whether a peculiar contraction of the Jew's red eye-brows, and a half-closing of his deeply-set eyes, warned Miss Nancy that she was disposed to be too communicative, is not a matter of much importance. The fact is all we need care for here; and the fact is, that she suddenly checked herself, and, with several gracious smiles upon Mr Sikes, turned the conversation to other matters. In about ten minutes' time, Mr Fagin was seized with a fit of coughing, upon which Miss Nancy pulled her shawl over her shoulders, and declared it was time to go. Mr Sikes, finding that he was walking a short part of her way himself, expressed his intention of accompanying her: and they went away together, followed at a little distance by the dog, who slunk out of a back-yard as soon as his master was out of sight.

The Jew thrust his head out of the room door when Sikes had left it, looked after him as he walked up the dark passage, shook his clenched fist, muttered a deep curse, and then with a horrible grin reseated himself at the table, where he was soon deeply absorbed in the interesting pages of the Hue and Cry.[4]

Meanwhile Oliver Twist, little dreaming that he was within so very short a distance of the merry old gentleman, was on his way to the bookstall. When he got into Clerkenwell he accidentally turned down a by-street which was not exactly in his way; but not discovering his mistake till he had got halfway down it, and knowing it must lead in the right direction, he did not think it worth while to turn back, and so marched on as quickly as he could, with the books under his arm.

He was walking along, thinking how happy and contented he ought to feel, and how much he would give for only one look at poor little Dick, who, starved and beaten, might be lying dead at that very moment, when he was startled by a young woman screaming out very loud, 'Oh, my dear brother!' and he had hardly looked up to see what the matter was, when he was stopped by having a pair of arms thrown tight round his neck.

'Don't!' cried Oliver struggling. 'Let go of me. Who is it? What are you stopping me for?'

The only reply to this, was a great number of loud lamentations

Oliver claimed by his affectionate friends

from the young woman who had embraced him, and who had got a little basket and a street-door key in her hand.

'Oh my gracious!' said the young woman, 'I've found him! Oh, Oliver! Oliver! Oh, you naughty boy, to make me suffer such distress on your account! Come home, dear, come. Oh, I've found him. Thank gracious goodness heavins, I've found him!' With these incoherent exclamations the young woman burst into another fit of crying, and got so dreadfully hysterical, that a couple of women who came up at the moment asked a butcher's boy, with a shiny head of hair anointed with suet, who was also looking on, whether he didn't think he had better run for the doctor. To which the butcher's boy, who appeared of a lounging, not to say indolent disposition, replied that he thought not.

'Oh, no, no, never mind,' said the young woman, grasping Oliver's hand; 'I'm better now. Come home directly, you cruel boy, come.'

'What's the matter, ma'am?' inquired one of the women.

'Oh, ma'am,' replied the young woman, 'he ran away near a month ago from his parents, who are hard-working and respectable people, and joined a set of thieves and bad characters, and almost broke his mother's heart.'

'Young wretch!' said one woman.

'Go home, do, you little brute,' said the other.

'I'm not,' replied Oliver, greatly alarmed. 'I don't know her. I haven't got any sister, or father and mother either. I'm an orphan; I live at Pentonville.'

'Oh, only hear him, how he braves it out!' cried the young woman.

'Why, it's Nancy!' exclaimed Oliver, who now saw her face for the first time, and started back in irrepressible astonishment.

'You see he knows me,' cried Nancy, appealing to the bystanders. 'He can't help himself. Make him come home, there's good people, or he'll kill his dear mother and father, and break my heart!'

'What the devil's this?' said a man, bursting out of a beer-shop, with a white dog at his heels; 'young Oliver! Come home to your poor mother, you young dog! come home directly.'

'I don't belong to them. I don't know them. Help! help!' cried Oliver, struggling in the man's powerful grasp.

'Help!' repeated the man. 'Yes; I'll help you, you young rascal! What books are these? You've been a stealing 'em, have you? Give 'em here!' With these words the man tore the volumes from his grasp, and struck him violently on the head.

'That's right!' cried a looker-on, from a garret window. 'That's the only way of bringing him to his senses!'

'To be sure,' cried a sleepy-faced carpenter, casting an approving look at the garret-window.

'It'll do him good!' said the two women.

'And he shall have it, too!' rejoined the man, administering another blow, and seizing Oliver by the collar. 'Come on, you young villain! Here, Bull's-eye, mind him, boy! mind him!'

Weak with recent illness, stupified by the blows and the suddenness of the attack, terrified by the fierce growling of the dog and the brutality of the man, and overpowered by the conviction of the bystanders that he was really the hardened little wretch he was described to be, what could one poor child do? Darkness had set in; it was a low neighbourhood; no help was near; resistance was useless. In another moment he was dragged into a labyrinth of dark, narrow courts, and forced along them at a pace which rendered the few cries he dared to give utterance to, wholly unintelligible. It was of little moment, indeed, whether they were intelligible or not, for there was nobody to care for them had they been ever so plain.

*   *   *   *   *

The gas-lamps[5] were lighted; Mrs Bedwin was waiting anxiously at the open door; the servant had run up the street twenty times, to see if there were any traces of Oliver; and still the two old gentlemen sat perseveringly in the dark parlour, with the watch between them.

*

CHAPTER THE SIXTEENTH

RELATES WHAT BECAME OF OLIVER TWIST, AFTER HE HAD BEEN CLAIMED BY NANCY

The narrow streets[1] and courts at length terminated in a large open space, scattered about which, were pens for beasts, and other indications of a cattle-market. Sikes slackened his pace when they reached this spot, the girl being quite unable to support any longer the rapid rate at which they had hitherto walked; and, turning to Oliver, commanded him roughly to take hold of Nancy's hand.

'Do you hear?' growled Sikes, as Oliver hesitated, and looked round.

They were in a dark corner, quite out of the track of passengers, and Oliver saw but too plainly that resistance would be of no avail. He held out his hand, which Nancy clasped tight in hers.

'Give me the other,' said Sikes, seizing Oliver's unoccupied hand. 'Here, Bull's-eye!'

The dog looked up, and growled.

'See here, boy!' said Sikes, putting his other hand to Oliver's throat, and uttering a savage oath; 'if he speaks ever so soft a word, hold him! D'ye mind?'

The dog growled again, and, licking his lips, eyed Oliver as if he were anxious to attach himself to his windpipe without any unnecessary delay.

'He's as willing as a Christian, strike me blind if he isn't!' said Sikes, regarding the animal with a kind of grim and ferocious approval. 'Now you know what you've got to expect, master, so call away as quick as you like; the dog will soon stop that game. Get on, young 'un!'

Bull's-eye wagged his tail in acknowledgment of this unusually endearing form of speech, and, giving vent to another admonitory growl for the benefit of Oliver, led the way onward.

It was Smithfield that they were crossing, although it might have been Grosvenor Square,[2] for anything Oliver knew to the contrary.

The night was dark and foggy, and it was just beginning to rain. The lights in the shops could scarcely struggle through the heavy mist, which thickened every moment, and shrouded the streets and houses in gloom, rendering the strange place still stranger in Oliver's eyes, and making his uncertainty the more dismal and depressing.

They had hurried on a few paces, when a deep church-bell struck the hour. With its first stroke his two conductors stopped, and turned their heads in the direction whence the sound proceeded.

'Eight o'clock, Bill,' said Nancy, when the bell ceased.

'What's the good of telling me that; I can hear, can't I?' replied Sikes.

'I wonder whether *they* can hear it,' said Nancy.

'Of course they can,' replied Sikes. 'It was Bartlemy time when I was shopped,[3] and there warn't a penny trumpet in the fair as I couldn't hear the squeaking on. Arter I was locked up for the night, the row and din outside made the thundering old jail so silent, that I could almost have beat my brains out against the iron plates of the door.'

'Poor fellows!' said Nancy, who still had her face turned towards the quarter in which the bell had sounded. 'Oh, Bill, such fine young chaps as them!'

'Yes; that's all you women think of,' answered Sikes. 'Fine young chaps! Well, they're as good as dead; so it don't much matter.'

With this consolation Mr Sikes appeared to repress a rising tendency to jealousy, and, clasping Oliver's wrist more firmly, told him to step out again.

'Wait a minute,' said the girl: 'I wouldn't hurry by, if it was you that was coming out to be hung the next time eight o'clock struck, Bill. I'd walk round and round the place till I dropped, if the snow was on the ground, and I hadn't a shawl to cover me.'

'And what good would that do?' inquired the unsentimental Mr Sikes. 'Unless you could pitch over a file and twenty yards of good stout rope, you might as well be walking fifty mile off, or not walking at all, for all the good it would do me. Come on, will you, and don't stand preaching there.'

The girl burst into a laugh, drew her shawl more closely round her, and they walked away. But Oliver felt her hand tremble; and, looking

Oliver's reception by Fagin and the boys

up in her face as they passed a gas-lamp, saw that it had turned a deadly white.

They walked on, by little-frequented and dirty ways, for a full half-hour, meeting very few people, for it now rained heavily, and those they did meet appearing from their looks to hold much the same position in society as Mr Sikes himself. At length they turned into a very filthy narrow street, nearly full of old-clothes shops;[4] and the dog, running forward as if conscious that there was now no further occasion for his keeping on guard, stopped before the door of a shop which was closed and apparently untenanted, for the house was in a ruinous condition, and upon the door was nailed a board intimating that it was to let, which looked as if it had hung there for many years.

'All right,' said Sikes, looking cautiously about.

Nancy stooped below the shutters, and Oliver heard the sound of a bell. They crossed to the opposite side of the street, and stood for a few moments under a lamp. A noise, as if a sash-window were gently raised, was heard, and soon afterwards the door softly opened; upon which Mr Sikes seized the terrified boy by the collar with very little ceremony, and all three were quickly inside the house.

The passage was perfectly dark, and they waited while the person who had let them in, chained and barred the door.

'Anybody here?' inquired Sikes.

'No,' replied a voice, which Oliver thought he had heard before.

'Is the old 'un here?' asked the robber.

'Yes,' replied the voice; 'and precious down in the mouth he has been. Won't he be glad to see you? Oh, no.'

The style of this reply, as well as the voice which delivered it, seemed familiar to Oliver's ears; but it was impossible to distinguish even the form of the speaker in the darkness.

'Let's have a glim,' said Sikes, 'or we shall go breaking our necks, or treading on the dog. Look after your legs if you do, that's all.'

'Stand still a moment, and I'll get you one,' replied the voice. The receding footsteps of the speaker were heard, and in another minute the form of Mr John Dawkins, otherwise the artful Dodger, appeared, bearing in his right hand a tallow candle stuck in the end of a cleft stick.

The young gentleman did not stop to bestow any other mark of recognition upon Oliver than a humorous grin; but, turning away, beckoned the visitors to follow him down a flight of stairs. They crossed an empty kitchen, and, opening the door of a low earthy-smelling room, which seemed to have been built in a small back-yard, were received with a shout of laughter.

'Oh, my wig, my wig!' cried Master Charles Bates, from whose lungs the laughter had proceeded; 'here he is! oh, cry, here he is! Oh, Fagin, look at him; Fagin, do look at him! I can't bear it; it is such a jolly game, I can't bear it. Hold me, somebody, while I laugh it out.'

With this irrepressible ebullition of mirth, Master Bates laid himself flat on the floor, and kicked convulsively for five minutes in an ecstasy of facetious joy. Then, jumping to his feet, he snatched the cleft stick from the Dodger, and, advancing to Oliver, viewed him round and round, while the Jew, taking off his night-cap, made a great number of low bows to the bewildered boy; the Artful meantime, who was of a rather saturnine disposition, and seldom gave way to merriment when it interfered with business, rifling his pockets with steady assiduity.

'Look at his togs, Fagin!' said Charley, putting the light so close to Oliver's new jacket as nearly to set him on fire. 'Look at his togs! – superfine cloth, and the heavy-swell cut! Oh, my eye, what a game! And his books, too; – nothing but a gentleman, Fagin!'

'Delighted to see you looking so well, my dear,' said the Jew, bowing with mock humility. 'The Artful shall give you another suit, my dear, for fear you should spoil that Sunday one. Why didn't you write, my dear, and say you were coming? – we'd have got something warm for supper.'

At this, Master Bates roared again, so loud that Fagin himself relaxed, and even the Dodger smiled; but as the Artful drew forth the five-pound note at that instant, it is doubtful whether the sally or the discovery awakened his merriment.

'Hallo! what's that?' inquired Sikes, stepping forward as the Jew seized the note. 'That's mine, Fagin.'

'No, no, my dear,' said the Jew. 'Mine, Bill, mine; you shall have the books.'

'If that ain't mine!' said Sikes, putting on his hat with a determined air, — 'mine and Nancy's, that is, — I'll take the boy back again.'

The Jew started, and Oliver started too, though from a very different cause, for he hoped that the dispute might really end in his being taken back.

'Come, hand it over, will you?' said Sikes.

'This is hardly fair, Bill; hardly fair, is it, Nancy?' inquired the Jew.

'Fair, or not fair,' retorted Sikes, 'hand it over, I tell you! Do you think Nancy and me has got nothing else to do with our precious time but to spend it in scouting arter and kidnapping every young boy as gets grabbed through you? Give it here, you avaricious old skeleton; give it here!'

With this gentle remonstrance, Mr Sikes plucked the note from between the Jew's finger and thumb; and, looking the old man coolly in the face, folded it up small, and tied it in his neckerchief.

'That's for our share of the trouble,' said Sikes; 'and not half enough, neither. You may keep the books, if you're fond of reading; and if not, you can sell 'em.'

'They're very pretty,' said Charley Bates, who with sundry grimaces had been affecting to read one of the volumes in question; 'beautiful writing, isn't it, Oliver?' and at sight of the dismayed look with which Oliver regarded his tormentors, Master Bates, who was blessed with a lively sense of the ludicrous, fell into another ecstasy more boisterous than the first.

'They belong to the old gentleman,' said Oliver, wringing his hands, — 'to the good, kind old gentleman who took me into his house, and had me nursed when I was near dying of the fever. Oh, pray send them back; send him back the books and money! Keep me here all my life long; but pray, pray send them back! He'll think I stole them; — the old lady, all of them that were so kind to me, will think I stole them. Oh, do have mercy upon me, and send them back!'

With these words, which were uttered with all the energy of passionate grief, Oliver fell upon his knees at the Jew's feet, and beat his hands together in perfect desperation.

'The boy's right,' remarked Fagin, looking covertly round, and knitting his shaggy eyebrows into a hard knot. 'You're right, Oliver, you're right; they *will* think you have stolen 'em. Ha! ha!' chuckled the Jew, rubbing his hands; 'it couldn't have happened better if we had chosen our time!'

'Of course it couldn't,' replied Sikes; 'I know'd that, directly I see him coming through Clerkenwell with the books under his arm. It's all right enough. They're soft-hearted psalm-singers, or they wouldn't have took him in at all, and they'll ask no questions arter him, fear they should be obliged to prosecute, and so get him lagged. He's safe enough.'

Oliver had looked from one to the other while these words were being spoken, as if he were bewildered and could scarcely understand what passed; but when Bill Sikes concluded, he jumped suddenly to his feet, and tore wildly from the room, uttering shrieks for help that made the bare old house echo to the roof.

'Keep back the dog, Bill!' cried Nancy, springing before the door, and closing it as the Jew and his two pupils darted out in pursuit; 'keep back the dog; he'll tear the boy to pieces.'

'Serve him right!' cried Sikes, struggling to disengage himself from the girl's grasp. 'Stand off from me, or I'll split your skull against the wall!'

'I don't care for that, Bill; I don't care for that,' screamed the girl, struggling violently with the man: 'the child shan't be torn down by the dog, unless you kill me first.'

'Shan't he!' said Sikes, setting his teeth fiercely. 'I'll soon do that, if you don't keep off.'

The housebreaker flung the girl from him to the further end of the room, just as the Jew and the two boys returned, dragging Oliver among them.

'What's the matter here?' said the Jew, looking round.

'The girl's gone mad, I think,' replied Sikes savagely.

'No, she hasn't,' said Nancy, pale and breathless from the scuffle; 'no, she hasn't, Fagin: don't think it.'

'Then keep quiet, will you?' said the Jew with a threatening look.

'No, I won't do that either,' replied Nancy, speaking very loud. 'Come, what do you think of that?'

Mr Fagin was sufficiently well acquainted with the manners and customs of that particular species of humanity to which Miss Nancy belonged, to feel tolerably certain that it would be rather unsafe to prolong any conversation with her at present. With the view of diverting the attention of the company, he turned to Oliver.

'So you wanted to get away, my dear, did you?' said the Jew, taking up a jagged and knotted club which lay in a corner of the fire-place; 'eh?'

Oliver made no reply, but he watched the Jew's motions and breathed quickly.

'Wanted to get assistance, – called for the police, did you?' sneered the Jew, catching the boy by the arm. 'We'll cure you of that, my dear.'

The Jew inflicted a smart blow on Oliver's shoulders with the club, and was raising it for a second, when the girl, rushing forward, wrested it from his hand, and flung it into the fire with a force that brought some of the glowing coals whirling out into the room.

'I won't stand by and see it done, Fagin,' cried the girl. 'You've got the boy, and what more would you have? Let him be – let him be, or I shall put that mark on some of you that will bring me to the gallows before my time!'

The girl stamped her foot violently on the floor as she vented this threat; and with her lips compressed, and her hands clenched, looked alternately at the Jew and the other robber, her face quite colourless from the passion of rage into which she had gradually worked herself.

'Why, Nancy!' said the Jew in a soothing tone, after a pause, during which he and Mr Sikes had stared at one another in a disconcerted manner, 'you – you're more clever than ever to-night. Ha! ha! my dear, you are acting beautifully.'

'Am I!' said the girl. 'Take care I don't overdo it: you will be the worse for it, Fagin, if I do; and so I tell you in good time to keep clear of me.'

There is something about a roused woman, especially if she add to all her other strong passions the fierce impulses of recklessness and despair, which few men like to provoke. The Jew saw that it would be hopeless to affect any further mistake regarding the reality of Miss Nancy's rage; and, shrinking involuntarily back, a few paces, cast a glance, half-imploring and half-cowardly, at Sikes, as if to hint that he was the fittest person to pursue the dialogue.

Mr Sikes thus mutely appealed to, and possibly feeling his personal pride and influence interested in the immediate reduction of Miss Nancy to reason, gave utterance to about a couple of score of curses and threats, the rapid delivery of which reflected great credit on the fertility of his invention. As they produced no visible effect on the object against whom they were discharged, however, he resorted to more tangible arguments.

'What do you mean by this?' said Sikes, backing the inquiry with a very common imprecation concerning the most beautiful of human features, which, if it were heard above, only once out of every fifty thousand times it is uttered below, would render blindness as common a disorder as measles; 'what do you mean by it? Burn my body! do you know who you are, and what you are?'

'Oh, yes, I know all about it,' replied the girl, laughing hysterically, and shaking her head from side to side with a poor assumption of indifference.

'Well, then, keep quiet,' rejoined Sikes with a growl like that he was accustomed to use when addressing his dog, 'or I'll quiet you for a good long time to come.'

The girl laughed again, even less composedly than before, and, darting a hasty look at Sikes, turned her face aside, and bit her lip till the blood came.

'You're a nice one,' added Sikes, as he surveyed her with a contemptuous air, 'to take up the humane and genteel side! A pretty subject for the child, as you call him, to make a friend of!'

'God Almighty help me, I am!' cried the girl passionately; 'and I wish I had been struck dead in the street, or changed places with them we passed so near to-night, before I had lent a hand in bringing him here. He's a thief, a liar, a devil, all that's bad, from this night forth; isn't that enough for the old wretch without blows?'

'Come, come, Sikes,' said the Jew, appealing to him in a remonstratory tone, and motioning towards the boys, who were eagerly attentive to all that passed; 'we must have civil words, – civil words, Bill!'

'Civil words!' cried the girl, whose passion was frightful to see.

'Civil words, you villain! Yes; you deserve 'em from me. I thieved for you when I was a child not half as old as this (pointing to Oliver). I have been in the same trade, and in the same service, for twelve years since;[5] don't you know it? Speak out! don't you know it?'

'Well, well!' replied the Jew, with an attempt at pacification; 'and, if you have, it's your living!'

'Ah, it is!' returned the girl, not speaking, but pouring out the words in one continuous and vehement scream. 'It is my living, and the cold, wet, dirty streets are my home; and you're the wretch that drove me to them long ago, and that'll keep me there day and night, day and night, till I die!'

'I shall do you a mischief!' interposed the Jew, goaded by these reproaches; 'a mischief worse than that, if you say much more!'

The girl said nothing more; but, tearing her hair and dress in a transport of phrensy, made such a rush at the Jew as would probably have left signal marks of her revenge upon him, had not her wrists been seized by Sikes at the right moment; upon which she made a few ineffectual struggles, and fainted.

'She's all right now,' said Sikes, laying her down in a corner. 'She's uncommon strong in the arms when she's up in this way.'

The Jew wiped his forehead, and smiled, as if it were a relief to have the disturbance over; but neither he, nor Sikes, nor the dog, nor the boys, seemed to consider it in any other light than a common occurrence incidental to business.

'It's the worst of having to do with women,' said the Jew, replacing the club; 'but they're clever, and we can't get on in our line without 'em. – Charley, show Oliver to bed.'

'I suppose he'd better not wear his best clothes to-morrow, Fagin, had he?' inquired Charley Bates.

'Certainly not,' replied the Jew, reciprocating the grin with which Charley put the question.

Master Bates, apparently much delighted with his commission, took the cleft stick, and led Oliver into an adjacent kitchen, where there were two or three of the beds on which he had slept before; and here, with many uncontrollable bursts of laughter, he produced the identical old suit of clothes which Oliver had so much congratulated himself upon leaving off at Mr Brownlow's, and the accidental display of which to Fagin by the Jew who purchased them, had been the very first clue received of his whereabout.

'Pull off the smart ones,' said Charley, 'and I'll give 'em to Fagin to take care of. What fun it is!'

Poor Oliver unwillingly complied; and Master Bates, rolling up the new clothes under his arm, departed from the room, leaving Oliver in the dark, and locking the door behind him.

The noise of Charley's laughter, and the voice of Miss Betsy, who opportunely arrived to throw water over her friend, and perform other feminine offices for the promotion of her recovery, might have kept many people awake under more happy circumstances than those in which Oliver was placed; but he was sick and weary, and soon fell sound asleep.

CHAPTER THE SEVENTEENTH

OLIVER'S DESTINY CONTINUING UNPROPITIOUS, BRINGS A GREAT MAN TO LONDON TO INJURE HIS REPUTATION

It is the custom on the stage in all good, murderous melodramas, to present the tragic and the comic scenes in as regular alternation[1] as the layers of red and white in a side of streaky, well-cured bacon. The hero sinks upon his straw bed, weighed down by fetters and misfortunes; and, in the next scene, his faithful but unconscious squire regales the audience with a comic song. We behold with throbbing bosoms the heroine in the grasp of a proud and ruthless baron, her virtue and her life alike in danger, drawing forth her dagger to preserve the one at the cost of the other; and, just as our expectations are wrought up to the highest pitch, a whistle is heard, and we are straightway transported to the great hall of the castle, where a grey-headed seneschal sings a funny chorus with a funnier body of vassals, who are free of all sorts of places from church vaults to palaces, and roam about in company, carolling perpetually.

Such changes appear absurd; but they are by no means unnatural. The transitions in real life from well-spread boards to death-beds, and from mourning weeds to holiday garments, are not a whit less startling, only there we are busy actors instead of passive lookers-on, which makes a vast difference; the actors in the mimic life of the theatre are blind to violent transitions and abrupt impulses of passion or feeling, which, presented before the eyes of mere spectators, are at once condemned as outrageous and preposterous.

As sudden shiftings of the scene, and rapid changes of time and place, are not only sanctioned in books by long usage, but are by many considered as the great art of authorship, – an author's skill in his craft being by such critics chiefly estimated with relation to the dilemmas in which he leaves his characters at the end of almost every chapter, – this brief introduction to the present one may perhaps be deemed unnecessary. But I have set it in this place because I am anxious to disclaim at once the slightest desire to tantalise my readers by leaving young Oliver Twist in situations of doubt and difficulty, and then flying off at a tangent to impertinent matters, which have nothing to do with him. My sole desire is to proceed straight through this history with all convenient despatch, carrying my reader along with me if I can, and, if not, leaving him to take some more pleasant route for a chapter or two, and join me again afterwards if he will. Indeed, there is so much to do, that I have no room for digressions, even if I possessed the inclination; and I merely make this one in order to set myself quite right with the reader, between whom and the historian it is essentially necessary that perfect faith should be kept, and a good understanding preserved. The advantage of this amicable explanation is, that when I say, as I do now, that I am going back directly to the town in which Oliver Twist was born, the reader will at once take it for granted that I have good and substantial reasons for making the journey, or I would not ask him to accompany me on any account.

Mr Bumble emerged at early morning from the workhouse gate, and walked, with portly carriage and commanding steps, up the

High-street. He was in the full bloom and pride of beadleism; his cocked hat and coat were dazzling in the morning sun, and he clutched his cane with all the vigorous tenacity of health and power. Mr Bumble always carried his head high, but this morning it was higher than usual; there was an abstraction in his eye, and an elevation in his air, which might have warned an observant stranger that thoughts were passing in the beadle's mind, too great for utterance.

Mr Bumble stopped not to converse with the small shopkeepers and others who spoke to him deferentially as he passed along. He merely returned their salutations with a wave of his hand, and relaxed not in his dignified pace until he reached the farm where Mrs Mann tended the infant paupers with a parish care.

'Drat that beadle!' said Mrs Mann, hearing the well-known impatient shaking at the garden gate. 'If it isn't him at this time in the morning! – Lauk, Mr Bumble, only think of its being you! Well, dear me, it *is* a pleasure this is! Come into the parlour, sir, please.'

The first sentence was addressed to Susan, and the exclamations of delight were spoken to Mr Bumble as the good lady unlocked the garden gate, and showed him with great attention and respect into the house.

'Mrs Mann,' said Mr Bumble, – not sitting upon, or dropping himself into a seat, as any common jackanapes would, but letting himself gradually and slowly down into a chair, – 'Mrs Mann, ma'am, good morning!'

'Well, and good morning to you, sir,' replied Mrs Mann, with many smiles; 'and hoping you find yourself well, sir?'

'So-so, Mrs Mann,' replied the beadle. 'A porochial life is not a bed of roses, Mrs Mann.'

'Ah, that it isn't indeed, Mr Bumble,' rejoined the lady. And all the infant paupers might have chorused the rejoinder with great propriety if they had heard it.

'A porochial life, ma'am,' continued Mr Bumble, striking the table with his cane, 'is a life of worry, and vexation, and hardihood; but all public characters, as I may say, must suffer prosecution.'

Mrs Mann, not very well knowing what the beadle meant, raised her hands with a look of sympathy, and sighed.

'Ah! You may well sigh, Mrs Mann!' said the beadle.

Finding she had done right, Mrs Mann sighed again, evidently to the satisfaction of the public character, who, repressing a complacent smile by looking sternly at his cocked hat, said,

'Mrs Mann, I am a going to London.'

'Lauk, Mr Bumble!' said Mrs Mann, starting back.

'To London, ma'am,' resumed the inflexible beadle, 'by coach; I, and two paupers, Mrs Mann. A legal action is coming on about a settlement, and the board has appointed me – me, Mrs Mann – to depose to the matter before the quarter-sessions at Clerkinwell;[2] and I very much question,' added Mr Bumble, drawing himself up, 'whether the Clerkinwell Sessions will not find themselves in the wrong box before they have done with me.'

'Oh! you mustn't be too hard upon them, sir,' said Mrs Mann coaxingly.

'The Clerkinwell Sessions have brought it upon themselves, ma'am,' replied Mr Bumble; 'and if the Clerkinwell Sessions find that they come off rather worse than they expected, the Clerkinwell Sessions have only themselves to thank.'

There was so much determination and depth of purpose about the menacing manner in which Mr Bumble delivered himself of these words, that Mrs Mann appeared quite awed by them. At length she said,

'You're going by coach, sir? I thought it was always usual to send them paupers in carts.'

'That's when they're ill, Mrs Mann,' said the beadle. 'We put the sick paupers into open carts in the rainy weather, to prevent their taking cold.'

'Oh!' said Mrs Mann.

'The opposition coach contracts for these two, and takes them cheap,' said Mr Bumble. 'They are both in a very low state, and we find it would come two pound cheaper to move 'em than to bury 'em, – that is, if we can throw 'em upon another parish, which I think we shall be able to do, if they don't die upon the road to spite us. Ha! ha! ha!'

When Mr Bumble had laughed a little while, his eyes again encountered the cocked hat, and he became grave.

'We are forgetting business, ma'am,' said the beadle; – 'here is your porochial stipend for the month.'

Wherewith Mr Bumble produced some silver money, rolled up in paper, from his pocket-book, and requested a receipt, which Mrs Mann wrote.

'It's very much blotted, sir,' said the farmer of infants; 'but it's formal enough, I dare say. Thank you, Mr Bumble, sir; I am very much obliged to you, I'm sure.'

Mr Bumble nodded blandly in acknowledgment of Mrs Mann's curtsey, and inquired how the children were.

'Bless their dear little hearts!' said Mrs Mann with emotion, 'they're as well as can be, the dears! Of course, except the two that died last week, and little Dick.'

'Isn't that boy no better?' inquired Mr Bumble. Mrs Mann shook her head.

'He's a ill-conditioned, vicious, bad-disposed porochial child that,' said Mr Bumble angrily. 'Where is he?'

'I'll bring him to you in one minute, sir,' replied Mrs Mann. 'Here, you Dick!'

After some calling, Dick was discovered; and having had his face put under the pump, and dried upon Mrs Mann's gown, he was led into the awful presence of Mr Bumble, the beadle.

The child was pale and thin; his cheeks were sunken, and his eyes large and bright. The scanty parish dress, the livery of his misery, hung loosely upon his feeble body; and his young limbs had wasted away like those of an old man.

Such was the little being that stood trembling beneath Mr Bumble's glance, not daring to lift his eyes from the floor, and dreading even to hear the beadle's voice.

'Can't you look at the gentleman, you obstinate boy?' said Mrs Mann.

The child meekly raised his eyes, and encountered those of Mr Bumble.

'What's the matter with you, porochial Dick?' inquired Mr Bumble with well-timed jocularity.

'Nothing, sir,' replied the child faintly.

'I should think not,' said Mrs Mann, who had of course laughed very much at Mr Bumble's exquisite humour. 'You want for nothing, I'm sure.'

'I should like –' faltered the child.

'Hey-day!' interposed Mrs Mann, 'I suppose you're going to say that you *do* want for something, now? Why, you little wretch—'

'Stop, Mrs Mann, stop!' said the beadle, raising his hand with a show of authority. 'Like what, sir; eh?'

'I should like,' faltered the child, 'if somebody that can write, would put a few words down for me on a piece of paper, and fold it up, and seal it, and keep it for me after I am laid in the ground.'

'Why, what does the boy mean?' exclaimed Mr Bumble, on whom the earnest manner and wan aspect of the child had made some impression, accustomed as he was to such things. 'What do you mean, sir?'

'I should like,' said the child, 'to leave my dear love to poor Oliver Twist, and to let him know how often I have sat by myself and cried to think of his wandering about in the dark nights with nobody to help him; and I should like to tell him,' said the child, pressing his small hands together, and speaking with great fervour, 'that I was glad to die when I was very young; for, perhaps, if I lived to be a man, and grew old, my little sister, who is in heaven, might forget me, or be unlike me; and it would be so much happier if we were both children there together.'

Mr Bumble surveyed the little speaker from head to foot with indescribable astonishment, and, turning to his companion, said, 'They're all in one story, Mrs Mann. That out-dacious Oliver has demoralised them all!'

'I couldn't have believed it, sir!' said Mrs Mann, holding up her hands, and looking malignantly at Dick. 'I never see such a hardened little wretch!'

'Take him away, ma'am!' said Mr Bumble imperiously. 'This must be stated to the board, Mrs Mann.'

'I hope the gentlemen will understand that it isn't my fault, sir?' said Mrs Mann, whimpering pathetically.

'They shall understand that, ma'am; they shall be acquainted with the true state of the case,' said Mr Bumble pompously. 'There; take him away. I can't bear the sight of him.'

Dick was immediately taken away, and locked up in the coal-cellar; and Mr Bumble shortly afterwards took himself away to prepare for his journey.

At six o'clock next morning, Mr Bumble having exchanged his cocked hat for a round one, and encased his person in a blue great-coat with a cape to it, took his place on the outside of the coach,[3] accompanied by the criminals whose settlement was disputed, with whom, in due course of time, he arrived in London, having experienced no other crosses by the way than those which originated in the perverse behaviour of the two paupers, who persisted in shivering, and complaining of the cold in a manner which, Mr Bumble declared, caused his teeth to chatter in his head, and made him feel quite uncomfortable, although he had a great-coat on.

Having disposed of these evil-minded persons for the night, Mr Bumble sat himself down in the house at which the coach stopped, and took a temperate dinner of steaks, oyster-sauce, and porter; putting a glass of hot gin-and-water on the mantelpiece, he drew his chair to the fire, and, with sundry moral reflections on the too-prevalent sin of discontent and complaining, he then composed himself comfortably to read the paper.

The very first paragraph upon which Mr Bumble's eyes rested, was the following advertisement.

'FIVE GUINEAS REWARD.

'WHEREAS a young boy, named Oliver Twist, absconded, or was enticed, on Thursday evening last, from his home at Pentonville, and has not since been heard of; the above reward will be paid to any person who will give such information as may lead to the discovery of the said Oliver Twist, or tend to throw any light upon his previous history, in which the advertiser is for many reasons warmly interested.'

And then followed a full description of Oliver's dress, person, appearance, and disappearance, with the name and address of Mr Brownlow at full length.

Mr Bumble opened his eyes, read the advertisement slowly and carefully three several times, and in something more than five minutes was on his way to Pentonville, having actually in his excitement left the glass of hot gin-and-water untasted on the mantel-piece.

'Is Mr Brownlow at home?' inquired Mr Bumble of the girl who opened the door.

To this inquiry the girl returned the not uncommon, but rather evasive reply of, 'I don't know – where do you come from?'

Mr Bumble no sooner uttered Oliver's name in explanation of his errand, than Mrs Bedwin, who had been listening at the parlour-door, hastened into the passage in a breathless state.

'Come in – come in,' said the old lady: 'I knew we should hear of him. Poor dear! I knew we should, – was certain of it. Bless his heart! I said so all along.'

Having said this, the worthy old lady hurried back into the parlour again, and, seating herself on a sofa, burst into tears. The girl, who was not quite so susceptible, had run up-stairs meanwhile, and now returned with a request that Mr Bumble would follow her immediately, which he did.

He was shown into the little back study, where sat Mr Brownlow and his friend Mr Grimwig, with decanters and glasses before them: the latter gentleman eyed him closely, and at once burst into the exclamation,

'A beadle – a parish beadle, or I'll eat my head!'

'Pray don't interrupt just now,' said Mr Brownlow. 'Take a seat, will you?'

Mr Bumble sat himself down, quite confounded by the oddity of Mr Grimwig's manner. Mr Brownlow moved the lamp so as to obtain an uninterrupted view of the beadle's countenance, and said with a little impatience,

'Now, sir, you come in consequence of having seen the advertisement?' – 'Yes, sir,' said Mr Bumble.

'And you *are* a beadle, are you not?' inquired Mr Grimwig.

'I am a porochial beadle, gentlemen,' rejoined Mr Bumble proudly.

'Of course,' observed Mr Grimwig aside to his friend. 'I knew he was. His great-coat is a parochial cut, and he looks a beadle all over.'

Mr Brownlow gently shook his head to impose silence on his friend, and resumed:

'Do you know where this poor boy is now?'

'No more than nobody,' replied Mr Bumble.

'Well, what *do* you know of him?' inquired the old gentleman. 'Speak out, my friend, if you have anything to say. What do you know of him?'

'You don't happen to know any good of him, do you?' said Mr Grimwig caustically, after an attentive perusal of Mr Bumble's features.

Mr Bumble caught at the inquiry very quickly, and shook his head with portentous solemnity.

'You see this?' said Mr Grimwig, looking triumphantly at Mr Brownlow.

Mr Brownlow looked apprehensively at Bumble's pursed-up countenance, and requested him to communicate what he knew regarding Oliver, in as few words as possible.

Mr Bumble put down his hat, unbuttoned his coat, folded his arms, inclined his head in a retrospective manner, and, after a few moments' reflection, commenced his story.

It would be tedious if given in the beadle's words, occupying as it did some twenty minutes in the telling; but the sum and substance of it was, that Oliver was a foundling, born of low and vicious parents, who had from his birth displayed no better qualities than treachery, ingratitude, and malice, and who had terminated his brief career in the place of his birth, by making a sanguinary and cowardly attack on an unoffending lad, and then running away in the night-time from his master's house. In proof of his really being the person he represented himself, Mr Bumble laid upon the table the papers he had brought to town, and, folding his arms again, awaited Mr Brownlow's observations.

'I fear it is all too true,' said the old gentleman sorrowfully, after looking over the papers. 'This is not much for your intelligence; but I would gladly have given you treble the money, sir, if it had been favourable to the boy.'

It is not at all improbable that if Mr Bumble had been possessed with this information at an earlier period of the interview, he might have imparted a very different colouring to his little history. It was too late to do it now, however; so he shook his head gravely, and, pocketing the five guineas, withdrew.

Mr Brownlow paced the room to and fro for some minutes, evidently so much disturbed by the beadle's tale, that even Mr Grimwig forbore to vex him further. At length he stopped, and rang the bell violently.

'Mrs Bedwin,' said Mr Brownlow when the housekeeper appeared, 'that boy, Oliver, is an impostor.'

'It can't be, sir; it cannot be,' said the old lady energetically.

'I tell you he is,' retorted the old gentleman sharply. 'What do you mean by "can't be"? We have just heard a full account of him from his birth; and he has been a thorough-paced little villain all his life.'

'I never will believe it, sir,' replied the old lady, firmly.

'You old women never believe anything but quack-doctors and lying story-books,' growled Mr Grimwig. 'I knew it all along. Why didn't you take my advice in the beginning; you would, if he hadn't had a fever, I suppose, – eh? He was interesting, wasn't he? Interesting! Bah!' and Mr Grimwig poked the fire with a flourish.

'He was a dear, grateful, gentle child, sir,' retorted Mrs Bedwin indignantly. 'I know what children are, sir, and have done these forty years; and people who can't say the same shouldn't say anything about them – that's my opinion.'

This was a hard hit at Mr Grimwig, who was a bachelor; but as it extorted nothing from that gentleman but a smile, the old lady tossed her head and smoothed down her apron, preparatory to another speech, when she was stopped by Mr Brownlow.

'Silence!' said the old gentleman, feigning an anger he was far from feeling. 'Never let me hear the boy's name again: I rang to tell you that. Never – never, on any pretence, mind. You may leave the room, Mrs Bedwin. Remember; I am in earnest.'

There were sad hearts at Mr Brownlow's that night. Oliver's sank within him when he thought of his good, kind friends; but it was well for him that he could not know what they had heard, or it would have broken outright.

*

CHAPTER THE EIGHTEENTH

HOW OLIVER PASSED HIS TIME IN THE IMPROVING SOCIETY OF HIS REPUTABLE FRIENDS

About noon next day, when the Dodger and Master Bates had gone out to pursue their customary avocations, Mr Fagin took the opportunity of reading Oliver a long lecture on the crying sin of ingratitude,[1] of which he clearly demonstrated he had been guilty to no ordinary extent in wilfully absenting himself from the society of his anxious friends, and still more in endeavouring to escape from them after so much trouble and expense had been incurred in his recovery. Mr Fagin laid great stress on the fact of his having taken Oliver in and cherished him, when without his timely aid he might have perished with hunger; and related the dismal and affecting history of a young lad whom in his philanthropy he had succoured under parallel circumstances, but who, proving unworthy of his confidence, and evincing a desire to communicate with the police, had unfortunately come to be hung at the Old Bailey[2] one morning. Mr Fagin did not seek to conceal his share in the catastrophe, but lamented with tears in his eyes that the wrong-headed and treacherous behaviour of the young person in question had rendered it necessary that he should become the victim of certain evidence for the crown, which, if it were not precisely true, was indispensably necessary for the safety of him (Mr Fagin), and a few select friends. Mr Fagin concluded by drawing a rather disagreeable picture of the discomforts of hanging, and, with great friendliness and politeness of manner, expressed his anxious hope that he might never be obliged to submit Oliver Twist to that unpleasant operation.

Little Oliver's blood ran cold as he listened to the Jew's words, and imperfectly comprehended the dark threats conveyed in them: that it was possible even for justice itself to confound the innocent with the guilty when they were in accidental companionship, he knew already; and that deeply-laid plans for the destruction of inconveniently-knowing, or over-communicative persons, had been really devised and carried out by the old Jew on more occasions than one, he thought by no means unlikely when he recollected the general nature of the altercations between that gentleman and Mr Sikes, which seemed to bear reference to some foregone conspiracy of the kind. As he glanced timidly up, and met the Jew's searching look, he felt that his pale face and trembling limbs were neither unnoticed nor unrelished by the wary villain.

The Jew smiled hideously, and, patting Oliver on the head, said that if he kept himself quiet, and applied himself to business, he saw they would be very good friends yet. Then taking his hat, and covering himself up in an old patched great-coat, he went out and locked the room-door behind him.

And so Oliver remained all that day, and for the greater part of many subsequent days, seeing nobody between early morning and midnight, and left during the long hours to commune with his own thoughts; which, never failing to revert to his kind friends, and the opinion they must long ago have formed of him, were sad indeed. After the lapse of a week or so, the Jew left the room-door unlocked, and he was at liberty to wander about the house.

It was a very dirty place; but the rooms up stairs had great high wooden mantel-pieces and large doors, with paneled walls and cornices to the ceilings, which, although they were black with neglect and dust, were ornamented in various ways; from all of which tokens Oliver concluded that a long time ago, before the old Jew was born, it had belonged to better people, and had perhaps been quite gay and handsome, dismal and dreary as it looked now.[3]

Spiders had built their webs in the angles of the walls and ceilings; and sometimes, when Oliver walked softly into a room, the mice would scamper across the floor, and run back terrified to their holes: with these exceptions, there was neither sight nor sound of any living thing; and often, when it grew dark, and he was tired of wandering from room to room, he would crouch in the corner of the passage by the street-door, to be as near living people as he could, and to remain there listening and trembling until the Jew or the boys returned.

In all the rooms the mouldering shutters were fast closed, and the bars which held them were screwed tight into the wood; the only light which was admitted making its way through round holes at the top, which made the rooms more gloomy, and filled them with strange shadows. There was a back-garret window, with rusty bars outside, which had no shutter, and out of which Oliver often gazed with a melancholy face for hours together; but nothing was to be descried from it but a confused and crowded mass of house-tops, blackened chimneys, and gable-ends. Sometimes, indeed, a ragged grizzly head might be seen peering over the parapet-wall of a distant house, but it was quickly withdrawn again; and as the window of Oliver's observatory was nailed down, and dimmed with the rain and smoke of years, it was as much as he could do to make out the forms of the different objects beyond, without making any attempt to be seen or heard, – which he had as much chance of being as if he had been inside the ball of St Paul's Cathedral.[4]

One afternoon, the Dodger and Master Bates being engaged out that evening, the first-named young gentleman took it into his head to evince some anxiety regarding the decoration of his person (which, to do him justice, was by no means an habitual weakness with him;) and, with this end and aim, he condescendingly commanded Oliver to assist him in his toilet straightway.

Oliver was but too glad to make himself useful, too happy to have some faces, however bad, to look upon, and too desirous to conciliate those about him when he could honestly do so, to throw any objection in the way of this proposal; so he at once expressed his readiness, and, kneeling on the floor, while the Dodger sat upon the table so that he could take his foot in his lap, he applied himself to a process which Mr Dawkins designated as 'japanning his trotter-cases,' and which phrase, rendered into plain English, signifieth cleaning his boots.

Whether it was the sense of freedom and independence which a rational animal may be supposed to feel when he sits on a table in an easy attitude, smoking a pipe, swinging one leg carelessly to and fro, and having his boots cleaned all the time without even the past trouble of having taken them off, or the prospective misery of putting them on, to disturb his reflections; or whether it was the goodness of the tobacco that soothed the feelings of the Dodger, or the mildness of

Master Bates explains a professional technicality

the beer that mollified his thoughts, he was evidently tinctured for the nonce with a spice of romance and enthusiasm foreign to his general nature. He looked down on Oliver with a thoughtful countenance for a brief space, and then, raising his head, and heaving a gentle sigh, said, half in abstraction, and half to Master Bates,

'What a pity it is he isn't a prig!'

'Ah!' said Master Charles Bates. 'He don't know what's good for him.'

The Dodger sighed again, and resumed his pipe, as did Charley Bates, and they both smoked for some seconds in silence.

'I suppose you don't even know what a prig is?' said the Dodger mournfully.

'I think I know that,' replied Oliver, hastily looking up. 'It's a th–; you're one, are you not?' inquired Oliver, checking himself.

'I am,' replied the Dodger. 'I'd scorn to be anythink else.' Mr Dawkins gave his hat a ferocious cock after delivering this sentiment, and looked at Master Bates as if to denote that he would feel obliged by his saying anything to the contrary. 'I am,' repeated the Dodger; 'so's Charley; so's Fagin; so's Sikes; so's Nancy; so's Bet; so we all are, down to the dog, and he's the downiest one of the lot.'

'And the least given to peaching,' added Charley Bates.

'He wouldn't so much as bark in a witness-box, for fear of committing himself; no, not if you tied him up in one, and left him there without wittles for a fortnight,' said the Dodger.

'That he wouldn't; not a bit of it,' observed Charley.

'He's a rum dog. Don't he look fierce at any strange cove that laughs or sings when he's in company!' pursued the Dodger. 'Won't he growl at all, when he hears a fiddle playing, and don't he hate other dogs as ain't of his breed! Winkin! Oh, no!'

'He's an out-and-out Christian,' said Charley.

This was merely intended as a tribute to the animal's abilities, but it was an appropriate remark in another sense, if Master Bates had only known it; for there are a great many ladies and gentlemen claiming to be out-and-out Christians, between whom and Mr Sikes's dog there exist very strong and singular points of resemblance.

'Well, well!' said the Dodger, recurring to the point from which they had strayed, with that mindfulness of his profession which influenced all his proceedings. 'This hasn't got anything to do with young Green here.'

'No more it has,' said Charley. 'Why don't you put yourself under Fagin, Oliver?'

'And make your fortun' out of hand?' added the Dodger, with a grin.

'And so be able to retire on your property, and do the genteel, as I mean to in the very next leap-year but four that ever comes, and the forty-second Tuesday in Trinity-week,' said Charley Bates.

'I don't like it,' rejoined Oliver timidly; 'I wish they would let me go. I – I – would rather go.'

'And Fagin would *rather* not!' rejoined Charley.

Oliver knew this too well; but, thinking it might be dangerous to express his feelings more openly, he only sighed, and went on with his boot-cleaning.

'Go!' exclaimed the Dodger. 'Why, where's your spirit? Don't you take any pride out of yourself? Would you go and be dependent on your friends, eh?'

'Oh, blow that!' said Master Bates, drawing two or three silk handkerchiefs from his pocket, and tossing them into a cupboard, 'that's too mean, that is!'

'*I* couldn't do it,' said the Dodger, with an air of haughty disgust.

'You can leave your friends, though,' said Oliver, with a half-smile, 'and let them be punished for what you did.'

'That,' rejoined the Dodger, with a wave of his pipe, – 'that was all out of consideration for Fagin, 'cause the traps know that we work together, and he might have got into trouble if we hadn't made our lucky; that was the move, wasn't it, Charley?'

Master Bates nodded assent, and would have spoken, but that the recollection of Oliver's flight came so suddenly upon him, that the smoke he was inhaling got entangled with a laugh, and went up into his head, and down into his throat, and brought on a fit of coughing and stamping about five minutes long.

'Look here!' said the Dodger, drawing forth a handful of shillings and halfpence. 'Here's a jolly life! what's the odds where it comes from? Here, catch hold; there's plenty more where they were took from. You won't, won't you? oh, you precious flat!'

'It's naughty, ain't it, Oliver?' inquired Charley Bates. 'He'll come to be scragged, won't he?'

'I don't know what that means,' replied Oliver, looking round.

'Something in this way, old feller,' said Charley. As he said it, Master Bates caught up an end of his neckerchief, and, holding it erect in the air, dropped his head on his shoulder, and jerked a curious sound through his teeth, thereby indicating, by a lively pantomimic representation that scragging and hanging were one and the same thing.

'That's what it means,' said Charley. 'Look how he stares, Jack; I never did see such prime company as that 'ere boy; he'll be the death of me, I know he will.' And Master Charles Bates having laughed heartily again, resumed his pipe with tears in his eyes.

'You've been brought up bad,' said the Dodger, surveying his boots with much satisfaction when Oliver had polished them. 'Fagin will make something of you, though; or you'll be the first he ever had that turned out unprofitable. You'd better begin at once, for you'll come to the trade long before you think of it, and you're only losing time, Oliver.'

Master Bates backed this advice with sundry moral admonitions of his own, which being exhausted, he and his friend Mr Dawkins launched into a glowing description of the numerous pleasures incidental to the life they led, interspersed with a variety of hints to Oliver that the best thing he could do, would be to secure Fagin's favour without more delay by the same means which they had employed to gain it.

'And always put this in your pipe, Nolly,' said the Dodger, as the Jew was heard unlocking the door above, 'if you don't take fogles and tickers—'

'What's the good of talking in that way?' interposed Master Bates; 'he don't know what you mean.'

'If you don't take pocket-hankechers and watches,' said the Dodger, reducing his conversation to the level of Oliver's capacity, 'some other cove will; so that the coves that lose 'em will be all the worse, and you'll be all the worse too, and nobody half a ha'p'orth the better, except the chaps wot gets them – and you've just as good a right to them as they have.'

'To be sure, – to be sure!' said the Jew, who had entered unseen by Oliver. 'It all lies in a nutshell, my dear – in a nutshell, take the Dodger's word for it. Ha! ha! he understands the catechism of his trade.'

The old man rubbed his hands gleefully together as he corroborated the Dodger's reasoning in these terms, and chuckled with delight at his pupil's proficiency.

The conversation proceeded no farther at this time, for the Jew had returned home accompanied by Miss Betsy, and a gentleman whom Oliver had never seen before, but who was accosted by the Dodger as Tom Chitling, and who, having lingered on the stairs to exchange a few gallantries with the lady, now made his appearance.

Mr Chitling was older in years than the Dodger, having perhaps numbered eighteen winters; but there was a degree of deference in his deportment towards that young gentleman which seemed to indicate that he felt himself conscious of a slight inferiority in point of genius and professional acquirements. He had small twinkling eyes, and a pock-marked face; wore a fur cap, a dark corduroy jacket, greasy fustian trousers, and an apron. His wardrobe was, in truth, rather out of repair; but he excused himself to the company by stating that his 'time' was only out an hour before, and that, in consequence of having worn the regimentals for six weeks past, he had not been able to bestow any attention on his private clothes. Mr Chitling added, with strong marks of irritation, that the new way of fumigating clothes up yonder[5] was infernal unconstitutional, for it burnt holes in them, and there was no remedy against the county; the same remark he considered to apply to the regulation mode of cutting the hair, which he held to be decidedly unlawful. Mr Chitling wound up his observations by stating that he had not touched a drop of anything for forty-two mortal long hard-working days, and that he 'wished he might be busted if he wasn't as dry as a lime-basket!'

'Where do you think the gentleman has come from, Oliver?' inquired the Jew with a grin, as the other boys put a bottle of spirits on the table.

'I – I – don't know, sir,' replied Oliver.

'Who's that?' inquired Tom Chitling, casting a contemptuous look at Oliver.

'A young friend of mine, my dear,' replied the Jew.

'He's in luck then,' said the young man, with a meaning look at Fagin. 'Never mind where I came from, young 'un; you'll find your way there soon enough, I'll bet a crown!'

At this sally the boys laughed, and, after some more jokes on the same subject, exchanged a few short whispers with Fagin, and withdrew.

After some words apart between the last comer and Fagin, they drew their chairs towards the fire; and the Jew, telling Oliver to come and sit by him, led the conversation to the topics most calculated to interest his hearers. These were, the great advantages of the trade, the proficiency of the Dodger, the amiability of Charley Bates, and the liberality of the Jew himself. At length these subjects displayed signs of being thoroughly exhausted, and Mr Chitling did the same (for the house of correction becomes fatiguing after a week or two); accordingly Miss Betsy withdrew, and left the party to their repose.

From this day Oliver was seldom left alone, but was placed in almost constant communication with the two boys, who played the old game with the Jew every day, – whether for their own improvement, or Oliver's, Mr Fagin best knew. At other times the old man would tell them stories of robberies he had committed in his younger days, mixed up with so much that was droll and curious, that Oliver could not help laughing heartily, and showing that he was amused in spite of all his better feelings.

In short, the wily old Jew had the boy in his toils; and, having prepared his mind by solitude and gloom to prefer any society to the companionship of his own sad thoughts in such a dreary place, was now slowly instilling into his soul the poison which he hoped would blacken it and change its hue for ever.

CHAPTER THE NINETEENTH

IN WHICH A NOTABLE PLAN IS DISCUSSED AND DETERMINED ON

It was a chill, damp, windy night, when the Jew, buttoning his great-coat tight round his shrivelled body, and pulling the collar up over his ears so as completely to obscure the lower part of his face, emerged from his den. He paused on the step as the door was locked and chained behind him; and having listened while the boys made all secure, and until their retreating footsteps were no longer audible, slunk down the street as quickly as he could.

The house to which Oliver had been conveyed was in the neighbour-hood of Whitechapel; the Jew stopped for an instant at the corner of the street, and, glancing suspiciously round, crossed the road, and struck off in the direction of Spitalfields.

The mud lay thick upon the stones, and a black mist hung over the streets; the rain fell sluggishly down, and everything felt cold and clammy to the touch. It seemed just the night when it befitted such a being as the Jew to be abroad. As he glided stealthily along, creeping beneath the shelter of the walls and doorways, the hideous old man seemed like some loathsome reptile, engendered in the slime and darkness[1] through which he moved, crawling forth by night in search of some rich offal for a meal.

He kept on his course through many winding and narrow ways until he reached Bethnal Green;[2] then, turning suddenly off to the left, he soon became involved in a maze of the mean dirty streets which abound in that close and densely-populated quarter.

The Jew was evidently too familiar with the ground he traversed, however, to be at all bewildered either by the darkness of the night or the intricacies of the way. He hurried through several alleys and streets, and at length turned into one lighted only by a single lamp at the farther end. At the door of a house in this street he knocked, and, having exchanged a few muttered words with the person who opened the door, walked up stairs.

A dog growled as he touched the handle of a door, and a man's voice demanded who was there.

'Only me, Bill; only me, my dear,' said the Jew, looking in.

'Bring in your body,' said Sikes. 'Lie down, you stupid brute! Don't you know the devil when he's got a great-coat on?'

Apparently the dog had been somewhat deceived by Mr Fagin's outer garment; for as the Jew unbuttoned it, and threw it over the back of a chair, he retired to the corner from which he had risen, wagging his tail as he went, to show that he was as well satisfied as it was in his nature to be.

'Well!' said Sikes.

'Well, my dear,' replied the Jew. 'Ah! Nancy.'

The latter recognition was uttered with just enough of embarrassment to imply a doubt of its reception; for Mr Fagin and his young friend had not met since she had interfered in behalf of Oliver. All doubts upon the subject, if he had any, were, however, speedily removed by the young lady's behaviour. She took her feet off the fender, pushed back her chair, and bade Fagin draw up his without saying any more about it, for it was a cold night, and no mistake. Miss Nancy prefixed to the word 'cold' another adjective, derived from the name of an unpleasant instrument of death, which, as the word is seldom mentioned to ears polite[3] in any other form than as a substantive, I have omitted in this chronicle.

'It *is* cold, Nancy dear,' said the Jew, as he warmed his skinny hands over the fire. 'It seems to go right through one,' added the old man, touching his left side.

'It must be a piercer if it finds its way through your heart,' said Mr Sikes. 'Give him something to drink, Nancy. Burn my body, make haste! It's enough to turn a man ill to see his lean old carcase shivering in that way, like a ugly ghost just rose from the grave.'

Nancy quickly brought a bottle from a cupboard in which there were many, which, to judge from the diversity of their appearance, were filled with several kinds of liquids; and Sikes, pouring out a glass of brandy, bade the Jew drink it off.

'Quite enough, quite, thankye Bill,' replied the Jew, putting down the glass after just setting his lips to it.

'What! you're afraid of our getting the better of you, are you?' inquired Sikes, fixing his eyes on the Jew; 'ugh!'

With a hoarse grunt of contempt Mr Sikes seized the glass and emptied it, as a preparatory ceremony to filling it again for himself, which he did at once.

The Jew glanced round the room as his companion tossed down the second glassful; not in curiosity, for he had seen it often before, but in a restless and suspicious manner which was habitual to him. It was a meanly furnished apartment, with nothing but the contents of the closet to induce the belief that its occupier was anything but a working man; and with no more suspicious articles displayed to view than two or three heavy bludgeons which stood in a corner, and a 'life-preserver' that hung over the mantelpiece.

'There,' said Sikes, smacking his lips. 'Now I'm ready.'

'For business – eh?' inquired the Jew.

'For business,' replied Sikes; 'so say what you've got to say.'

'About the crib at Chertsey,⁴ Bill?' said the Jew, drawing his chair forward, and speaking in a very low voice.

'Yes. What about it?' inquired Sikes.

'Ah! you know what I mean, my dear,' said the Jew. 'He knows what I mean, Nancy; don't he?'

'No, he don't,' sneered Mr Sikes, 'or he won't, and that's the same thing. Speak out, and call things by their right names; don't sit there winking and blinking, and talking to me in hints, as if you warn't the very first that thought about the robbery. D— your eyes! wot d'ye mean?'

'Hush, Bill, hush!' said the Jew, who had in vain attempted to stop this burst of indignation; 'somebody will hear us, my dear; somebody will hear us.'

'Let 'em hear!' said Sikes; 'I don't care.' But as Mr Sikes *did* care, upon reflection, he dropped his voice as he said the words, and grew calmer.

'There, there,' said the Jew coaxingly. 'It was only my caution – nothing more. Now, my dear, about that crib at Chertsey; when is it to be done, Bill, eh? – when is it to be done? Such plate, my dears, such plate!' said the Jew, rubbing his hands, and elevating his eyebrows in a rapture of anticipation.

'Not at all,' replied Sikes coldly.

'Not to be done at all!' echoed the Jew, leaning back in his chair.

'No, not at all,' rejoined Sikes; 'at least it can't be a put-up job, as we expected.'

'Then it hasn't been properly gone about,' said the Jew, turning pale with anger. 'Don't tell me!'

'But I will tell you,' retorted Sikes. 'Who are you that's not to be told? I tell you that Toby Crackit has been hanging about the place for a fortnight, and he can't get one of the servants into a line.'

'Do you mean to tell me, Bill,' said the Jew, softening as the other grew heated, 'that neither of the two men in the house can be got over?'

'Yes, I do mean to tell you so,' replied Sikes. 'The old lady has had 'em these twenty year; and, if you were to give 'em five hundred pound, they wouldn't be in it.'

'But do you mean to say, my dear,' remonstrated the Jew, 'that the women can't be got over?'

'Not a bit of it,' replied Sikes.

'Not by flash Toby Crackit?' said the Jew incredulously. 'Think what women are, Bill.'

'No; not even by flash Toby Crackit,' replied Sikes. 'He says he's worn sham whiskers and a canary waistcoat the whole blessed time he's been loitering down there, and it's all of no use.'

'He should have tried mustachios and a pair of military trousers, my dear,' said the Jew after a few moments' reflection.

'So he did,' rejoined Sikes, 'and they warn't of no more use than the other plant.'

The Jew looked very blank at this information, and, after ruminating for some minutes with his chin sunk on his breast, raised his head, and said with a deep sigh that, if flash Toby Crackit reported aright, he feared the game was up.

'And yet,' said the old man, dropping his hands on his knees, 'it's a sad thing, my dear, to lose so much when we had set our hearts upon it.'

'So it is,' said Mr Sikes; 'worse luck!'

A long silence ensued, during which the Jew was plunged in deep thought, with his face wrinkled into an expression of villany perfectly demoniacal. Sikes eyed him furtively from time to time; and Nancy, apparently fearful of irritating the housebreaker, sat with her eyes fixed upon the fire, as if she had been deaf to all that passed.

'Fagin,' said Sikes, abruptly breaking the stillness that prevailed, 'is it worth fifty shiners extra if it's safely done from the outside?'

'Yes,' said the Jew, suddenly rousing himself as if from a trance.

'Is it a bargain?' inquired Sikes.

'Yes, my dear, yes,' rejoined the Jew, grasping the other's hand, his eyes glistening and every muscle in his face working with the excitement that the inquiry had awakened.

'Then,' said Sikes, thrusting aside the Jew's hand with some disdain, 'let it come off as soon as you like. Toby and I were over the garden-wall the night afore last, sounding the panels of the doors and shutters: the crib's barred up at night like a jail, but there's one part we can crack, safe and softly.'

'Which is that, Bill?' asked the Jew eagerly.

'Why,' whispered Sikes, 'as you cross the lawn—'

'Yes, yes,' said the Jew, bending his head forward, with his eyes almost starting out of it.

'Umph!' cried Sikes, stopping short as the girl, scarcely moving her head, looked suddenly round and pointed for an instant to the Jew's face. 'Never mind which part it is. You can't do it without me, I know; but it's best to be on the safe side when one deals with you.'

'As you like, my dear, as you like,' replied the Jew, biting his lip. 'Is there no help wanted but yours and Toby's?'

'None,' said Sikes, ''cept a centre-bit and a boy; the first we've both got; the second you must find us.'

'A boy!' exclaimed the Jew. 'Oh! then it is a panel, eh?'

'Never mind wot it is!' replied Sikes; 'I want a boy, and he mustn't be a big un. Lord!' said Mr Sikes reflectively, 'if I'd only got that young boy of Ned, the chimbley-sweeper's! – he kept him small on purpose, and let him out by the job. But the father gets lagged, and then the Juvenile Delinquent Society[5] comes, and takes the boy away from a trade where he was arning money, teaches him to read and write, and in time makes a 'prentice of him. And so they go on,' said Mr Sikes, his wrath rising with the recollection of his wrongs, – 'so they go on; and, if they'd got money enough, (which it's a Providence they have not,) we shouldn't have half-a-dozen boys left in the whole trade in a year or two.'

'No more we should,' acquiesced the Jew, who had been considering during this speech, and had only caught the last sentence. 'Bill!'

'What now?' inquired Sikes.

The Jew nodded his head towards Nancy, who was still gazing at the fire; and intimated by a sign that he would have her told to leave the room. Sikes shrugged his shoulders impatiently, as if he thought the precaution unnecessary, but complied, nevertheless, by requesting Miss Nancy to fetch him a jug of beer.

'You don't want any beer,' said Nancy, folding her arms, and retaining her seat very composedly.

'I tell you I do!' replied Sikes.

'Nonsense!' rejoined the girl, coolly. 'Go on, Fagin. I know what he's going to say, Bill; he needn't mind me.'

The Jew still hesitated, and Sikes looked from one to the other in some surprise.

'Why, you don't mind the old girl, do you, Fagin?' he asked at length. 'You've known her long enough to trust her, or the devil's in it: she ain't one to blab, are you Nancy?'

'*I* should think not!' replied the young lady, drawing her chair up to the table, and putting her elbows upon it.

'No, no, my dear, – I know you're not,' said the Jew; 'but—' and again the old man paused.

'But wot?' inquired Sikes.

'I didn't know whether she mightn't p'raps be out of sorts, you know, my dear, as she was the other night,' replied the Jew.

At this confession Miss Nancy burst into a loud laugh, and, swallowing a glass of brandy, shook her head with an air of defiance, and burst into sundry exclamations of 'Keep the game a-going!' 'Never say die!' and the like, which seemed at once to have the effect of re-assuring both gentlemen, for the Jew nodded his head with a satisfied air, and resumed his seat, as did Mr Sikes likewise.

'Now, Fagin,' said Miss Nancy with a laugh, 'tell Bill at once about Oliver!'

'Ah! you're a clever one, my dear; the sharpest girl I ever saw!' said the Jew, patting her on the neck. 'It *was* about Oliver I was going to speak, sure enough. Ha! ha! ha!'

'What about him?' demanded Sikes.

'He's the boy for you, my dear,' replied the Jew in a hoarse whisper, laying his finger on the side of his nose, and grinning frightfully.

'He!' exclaimed Sikes.

'Have him, Bill!' said Nancy. 'I would if I was in your place. He mayn't be so much up as any of the others; but that's not what you want if he's only to open a door for you. Depend upon it he's a safe one, Bill.'

'I know he is,' rejoined Fagin; 'he's been in good training these last few weeks, and it's time he began to work for his bread; besides, the others are all too big.'

'Well, he is just the size I want,' said Mr Sikes, ruminating.

'And will do everything you want, Bill my dear,' interposed the Jew; 'he can't help himself, – that is, if you only frighten him enough.'

'Frighten him!' echoed Sikes. 'It'll be no sham frightening, mind you. If there's anything queer about him when we once get into the work, – in for a penny, in for a pound, – you won't see him alive again, Fagin. Think of that before you send him. Mark my words!' said the robber, shaking a heavy crowbar which he had drawn from under the bedstead.

'I've thought of it all,' said the Jew with energy. 'I've – I've had my eye upon him, my dears, close: close. Once let him feel that he is one of us; once fill his mind with the idea that he has been a thief, and he's ours, – ours for his life! Oho! It couldn't have come about better!' The old man crossed his arms upon his breast, and, drawing his head and shoulders into a heap, literally hugged himself for joy.

'Ours!' said Sikes. 'Yours, you mean.'

'Perhaps I do, my dear,' said the Jew with a shrill chuckle. 'Mine, if you like, Bill.'

'And wot,' said Sikes, scowling fiercely on his agreeable friend, – 'wot makes you take so much pains about one chalk-faced kid, when you know there are fifty boys snoozing about Common Garden[6] every night, as you might pick and choose from?'

'Because they're of no use to me, my dear,' replied the Jew with some confusion, 'not worth the taking; for their looks convict 'em when they get into trouble, and I lose 'em all. With this boy properly managed, my dears, I could do what I couldn't with twenty of them. Besides,' said the Jew, recovering his self-possession, 'he has us now if he could only give us leg-bail again; and he *must* be in the same boat with us; never mind how he came there, it's quite enough for my power over him that he was in a robbery, that's all I want. Now how much better this is, than being obliged to put the poor leetle boy out of the way, which would be dangerous, – and we should lose by it, besides.'

'When is it to be done?' asked Nancy, stopping some turbulent exclamation on the part of Mr Sikes, expressive of the disgust with which he received Fagin's affectation of humanity.

'Ah, to be sure,' said the Jew, 'when is it to be done, Bill?'

'I planned with Toby the night arter to-morrow,' rejoined Sikes in a surly voice, 'if he heard nothing from me to the contrairy.'

'Good,' said the Jew; 'there's no moon.'

'No,' rejoined Sikes.

'It's all arranged about bringing off the swag,* is it?' asked the Jew. Sikes nodded.

'And about—'

'Oh ah, it's all planned,' rejoined Sikes, interrupting him; 'never mind particulars. You'd better bring the boy here to-morrow night; I shall get off the stones an hour arter day-break. Then you hold your tongue, and keep the melting-pot ready, and that's all you'll have to do.'

After some discussion in which all three took an active part, it was decided that Nancy should repair to the Jew's next evening, when the night had set in, and bring Oliver away with her: Fagin craftily observing, that, if he evinced any disinclination to the task, he would be more willing to accompany the girl, who had so recently interfered

* Booty.

in his behalf, than anybody else. It was also solemnly arranged that poor Oliver should, for the purposes of the contemplated expedition, be unreservedly consigned to the care and custody of Mr William Sikes; and further, that the said Sikes should deal with him as he thought fit, and should not be held responsible by the Jew for any mischance or evil that might befal the boy, or any punishment with which it might be necessary to visit him, it being understood that, to render the compact in this respect binding, any representations made by Mr Sikes on his return should be required to be confirmed and corroborated, in all important particulars, by the testimony of flash Toby Crackit.

These preliminaries adjusted, Mr Sikes proceeded to drink brandy at a furious rate, and to flourish the crowbar in an alarming manner, yelling forth at the same time most unmusical snatches of song mingled with wild execrations. At length, in a fit of professional enthusiasm, he insisted upon producing his box of housebreaking tools, which he had no sooner stumbled in with, and opened for the purpose of explaining the nature and properties of the various implements it contained, and the peculiar beauties of their construction, than he fell over it upon the floor, and went to sleep where he fell.

'Good night, Nancy!' said the Jew, muffling himself up as before.

'Good night!'

Their eyes met, and the Jew scrutinised her narrowly. There was no flinching about the girl. She was as true and earnest in the matter as Toby Crackit himself could be.

The Jew again bade her good night, and, bestowing a sly kick upon the prostrate form of Mr Sikes while her back was turned, groped down stairs.

'Always the way,' muttered the Jew to himself as he turned homewards. 'The worst of these women is, that a very little thing serves to call up some long-forgotten feeling; and the best of them is, that it never lasts. Ha! ha! The man against the child, for a bag of gold!'

Beguiling the time with these pleasant reflections, Mr Fagin wended his way through mud and mire to his gloomy abode, where the Dodger was sitting up, impatiently awaiting his return.

'Is Oliver a-bed? I want to speak to him,' was his first remark as they descended the stairs.

'Hours ago,' replied the Dodger, throwing open a door. 'Here he is!'

The boy was lying fast asleep on a rude bed upon the floor, so pale with anxiety, and sadness, and the closeness of his prison, that he looked like death; not death as it shows in shroud and coffin, but in the guise it wears when life has just departed: when a young and gentle spirit has but an instant fled to heaven, and the gross air of the world has not had time to breathe upon the changing dust it hallowed.

'Not now,' said the Jew turning softly away. 'To-morrow. To-morrow.'

*

CHAPTER THE TWENTIETH

WHEREIN OLIVER IS DELIVERED OVER TO MR WILLIAM SIKES

When Oliver awoke in the morning, he was a good deal surprised to find that a new pair of shoes with strong thick soles had been placed at his bedside, and that his old ones had been removed. At first he was pleased with the discovery, hoping it might be the forerunner of his release; but such thoughts were quickly dispelled on his sitting down to breakfast alone with the Jew, who told him, in a tone and manner which increased his alarm, that he was to be taken to the residence of Bill Sikes that night.

'To – to – stop there, sir?' asked Oliver anxiously.

'No, no, my dear, not to stop there,' replied the Jew. 'We shouldn't like to lose you. Don't be afraid, Oliver; you shall come back to us again. Ha! ha! ha! We won't be so cruel as to send you away, my dear. Oh no, no!'

The old man, who was stooping over the fire toasting a piece of bread, looked round as he bantered Oliver thus, and chuckled as if to show that he knew he would still be very glad to get away if he could.

'I suppose,' said the Jew, fixing his eyes on Oliver, 'you want to know what you're going to Bill's for – eh, my dear?'

Oliver coloured involuntarily to find that the old thief had been reading his thoughts; but boldly said, Yes, he did want to know.

'Why, do you think?' inquired Fagin, parrying the question.

'Indeed I don't know, sir,' replied Oliver.

'Bah!' said the Jew, turning away with a disappointed countenance from a close perusal of Oliver's face. 'Wait till Bill tells you, then.'

The Jew seemed much vexed by Oliver's not expressing any greater curiosity on the subject; but the truth is, that, although he felt very anxious, he was too much confused by the earnest cunning of Fagin's looks, and his own speculations, to make any further inquiries just then. He had no other opportunity; for the Jew remained very surly and silent till night, when he prepared to go abroad.

'You may burn a candle,' said the Jew, putting one upon the table; 'and here's a book for you to read till they come to fetch you. Good-night!'

'Good-night, sir!' replied Oliver softly.

The Jew walked to the door, looking over his shoulder at the boy as he went, and, suddenly stopping, called him by his name.

Oliver looked up; the Jew, pointing to the candle, motioned to him to light it. He did so; and, as he placed the candlestick upon the table, saw that the Jew was gazing fixedly at him with lowering and contracted brows from the dark end of the room.

'Take heed, Oliver! take heed!' said the old man, shaking his right hand before him in a warning manner. 'He's a rough man, and thinks nothing of blood when his own is up. Whatever falls out, say nothing; and do what he bids you. Mind!' Placing a strong emphasis on the last word, he suffered his features gradually to resolve themselves into a ghastly grin; and, nodding his head, left the room.

Oliver leant his head upon his hand when the old man disappeared, and pondered with a trembling heart on the words he had just heard. The more he thought of the Jew's admonition, the more he was at a loss to divine its real purpose and meaning. He could think of no bad object to be attained by sending him to Sikes which would not be equally well answered by his remaining with Fagin; and, after meditating for a long time, concluded that he had been selected to perform some ordinary menial offices for the housebreaker, until another boy, better suited for his purpose, could be engaged. He was too well accustomed to suffering, and had suffered too much where he was, to bewail the prospect of a change very severely. He remained lost in thought for some minutes, and then, with a heavy sigh, snuffed the candle, and, taking up the book which the Jew had left with him, began to read.

He turned over the leaves carelessly at first, but, lighting on a passage which attracted his attention, soon became intent upon the volume. It was a history of the lives and trials of great criminals,[1] and the pages were soiled and thumbed with use. Here, he read of dreadful crimes that make the blood run cold; of secret murders that had been committed by the lonely wayside, and bodies hidden from the eye of man in deep pits and wells, which would not keep them down, deep as they were, but had yielded them up at last, after many years, and so maddened the murderers with the sight, that in their horror they had confessed their guilt, and yelled for the gibbet to end their agony. Here, too, he read of men who, lying in their beds at dead of night, had been tempted and led on by their own bad thoughts to such dreadful bloodshed as it made the flesh creep and the limbs quail to think of. The terrible descriptions were so vivid and real, that the sallow pages seemed to turn red with gore, and the words upon them to be sounded in his ears as if they were whispered in hollow murmurs by the spirits of the dead.

In a paroxysm of fear the boy closed the book and thrust it from him. Then, falling upon his knees, he prayed Heaven to spare him from such deeds, and rather to will that he should die at once, than be reserved for crimes so fearful and appalling. By degrees he grew more calm, and besought, in a low and broken voice, that he might be rescued from his present dangers: and that if any aid were to be raised up for a poor outcast boy, who had never known the love of friends or kindred, it might come to him now, when, desolate and deserted, he stood alone in the midst of wickedness and guilt.

He had concluded his prayer, but still remained with his head buried in his hands, when a rustling noise aroused him.

'What's that!' he cried, starting up, and catching sight of a figure standing by the door. 'Who's there?'

'Me – only me,' replied a tremulous voice.

Oliver raised the candle above his head, and looked towards the door. It was Nancy.

'Put down the light,' said the girl, turning away her head: 'it hurts my eyes.'

Oliver saw that she was very pale, and gently inquired if she were ill. The girl threw herself into a chair, with her back towards him, and wrung her hands; but made no reply.

'God forgive me!' she cried after awhile, 'I never thought of all this.'

'Has anything happened?' asked Oliver. 'Can I help you? I will if I can; I will indeed.'

She rocked herself to and fro, and then, wringing her hands violently, caught her throat, and, uttering a gurgling sound, struggled and gasped for breath.

'Nancy!' cried Oliver, greatly alarmed. 'What is it?'

The girl burst into a fit of loud laughter, beating her hands upon her knees, and her feet upon the ground, meanwhile; and, suddenly stopping, drew her shawl close round her, and shivered with cold.

Oliver stirred the fire. Drawing her chair close to it, she sat there for a little time without speaking, but at length she raised her head and looked round.

'I don't know what comes over me sometimes,' said the girl, affecting to busy herself in arranging her dress; 'it's this damp, dirty room, I think. Now, Nolly, dear, are you ready?'

'Am I to go with you?' asked Oliver.

'Yes; I have come from Bill,' replied the girl. 'You are to go with me.'

'What for?' said Oliver recoiling.

'What for!' echoed the girl, raising her eyes, and averting them again the moment they encountered the boy's face. 'Oh! for no harm.'

'I don't believe it,' said Oliver, who had watched her closely.

'Have it your own way,' rejoined the girl, affecting to laugh. 'For no good, then.'

Oliver could see that he had some power over the girl's better feelings, and for an instant thought of appealing to her compassion for his helpless state. But then the thought darted across his mind that it was barely eleven o'clock, and that many people were still in the streets, of whom surely some might be found to give credence to his tale. As the reflection occurred to him, he stepped forward, and said somewhat hastily that he was ready.

Neither his brief consideration nor its purport were lost upon his companion. She eyed him narrowly while he spoke, and cast upon him a look of intelligence which sufficiently showed that she guessed what had been passing in his thoughts.

'Hush!' said the girl, stooping over him, and pointing to the door as she looked cautiously round. 'You can't help yourself. I have tried hard for you, but all to no purpose. You are hedged round and round; and, if ever you are to get loose from here, this is not the time.'

Struck by the energy of her manner, Oliver looked up in her face with great surprise. She seemed to speak the truth; her countenance was white and agitated, and she trembled with very earnestness.

'I have saved you from being ill-used once, and I will again, and I do now,' continued the girl aloud; 'for those would have fetched you, if I had not, would have been far more rough than me. I have promised for your being quiet and silent; if you are not, you will only do harm to yourself and me too, and perhaps be my death. See here! I have borne all this for you already, as true as God sees me show it.'

She pointed hastily to some livid bruises upon her neck and arms, and continued with great rapidity.

'Remember this, and don't let me suffer more for you just now. If I could help you I would, but I have not the power: they don't mean to harm you; and whatever they make you do, is no fault of yours. Hush! every word from you is a blow for me: give me your hand — make haste, your hand!'

She caught the hand which Oliver instinctively placed in hers, and, blowing out the light, drew him after her up the stairs. The door was opened quickly by some one shrouded in the darkness, and as quickly closed when they had passed out. A hackney cabriolet[2] was in waiting; and, with the same vehemence which she had exhibited in addressing Oliver, the girl pulled him in with her, and drew the curtains close. The driver wanted no directions, but lashed his horse into full speed without the delay of an instant.

The girl still held Oliver fast by the hand, and continued to pour into his ear the warnings and assurances she had already imparted. All was so quick and hurried, that he had scarcely time to recollect where he was, or how he came there, when the carriage stopped at the same house to which the Jew's steps had been directed on the previous evening.

For one brief moment Oliver cast a hurried glance along the empty street, and a cry for help hung upon his lips. But the girl's voice was in his ear, beseeching him in such tones of agony to remember her, that he had not the heart to utter it; and while he hesitated, the opportunity was gone, for he was already in the house, and the door was shut.

'This way,' said the girl, releasing her hold for the first time. 'Bill!'

'Hallo!' replied Sikes, appearing at the head of the stairs with a candle. 'Oh! that's the time of day. Come on!'

This was a very strong expression of approbation, and an uncommonly hearty welcome, from a person of Mr Sikes's temperament; Nancy, appearing much gratified thereby, saluted him cordially.

'Bullseye's gone home with Tom,' observed Sikes as he lighted them up. 'He'd have been in the way.'

'That's right,' rejoined Nancy.

'So you've got the kid,' said Sikes, when they had all reached the room: closing the door as he spoke.

'Yes, here he is,' replied Nancy.

'Did he come quiet?' inquired Sikes.

'Like a lamb,' rejoined Nancy.

'I'm glad to hear it,' said Sikes, looking grimly at Oliver, 'for the sake of his young carcase, as would otherways have suffered for it. Come here, young 'un, and let me read you a lectur', which is as well got over at once.'

Thus addressing his new *protégé*, Mr Sikes pulled off his cap and threw it into a corner; and then, taking him by the shoulder, sat himself down by the table, and stood Oliver in front of him.

'Now first, do you know wot this is?' inquired Sikes, taking up a pocket-pistol which lay on the table.

Oliver replied in the affirmative.

'Well then, look here,' continued Sikes. 'This is powder, that 'ere's a bullet, and this is a little bit of a old hat for waddin'.'

Oliver murmured his comprehension of the different bodies referred to, and Mr Sikes proceeded to load the pistol with great nicety and deliberation.

'Now it's loaded,' said Mr Sikes when he had finished.

'Yes, I see it is, sir,' replied Oliver, trembling.

'Well,' said the robber, grasping Oliver's wrist tightly, and putting the barrel so close to his temple that they touched, at which moment the boy could not repress a shriek; 'if you speak a word when you're out o' doors with me, except when I speak to you, that loading will be in your head without notice – so, if you *do* make up your mind to speak without leave, say your prayers first.'

Having bestowed a scowl upon the object of this warning, to increase its effect, Mr Sikes continued.

'As near as I know, there isn't anybody as would be asking very partickler arter you, if you *was* disposed of; so I needn't take this devil-and-all of trouble to explain matters to you if it warn't for your own good. D'ye hear?'

'The short and the long of what you mean,' said Nancy, speaking very emphatically, and slightly frowning at Oliver, as if to bespeak his serious attention to her words, 'is, that if you're crossed by him in this job you have on hand, you'll prevent his ever telling tales afterwards, by shooting him through the head, and take your chance of swinging for it as you do for a great many other things in the way of business every month of your life.'

'That's it!' observed Mr Sikes approvingly; 'women can always put things in fewest words, except when it's blowing-up, and then they lengthens it out. And now that he's thoroughly up to it, let's have some supper, and get a snooze afore starting.'

In pursuance of this request, Nancy quickly laid the cloth, and, disappearing for a few minutes, presently returned with a pot of porter and a dish of sheeps' heads, which gave occasion to several pleasant witticisms on the part of Mr Sikes, founded upon the singular coincidence of 'jemmies' being a cant name common to them and an ingenious implement much used in his profession. Indeed, the worthy gentleman, stimulated perhaps by the immediate prospect of being in active service, was in great spirits and good-humour; in proof whereof it may be here remarked, that he humorously drank all the beer at a draught, and did not utter, on a rough calculation, more than fourscore oaths during the whole progress of the meal.

Supper being ended, – it may be easily conceived that Oliver had no great appetite for it, – Mr Sikes disposed of a couple of glasses of spirits and water, and threw himself upon the bed, ordering Nancy, with many imprecations in case of failure, to call him at five precisely. Oliver stretched himself, in his clothes, by command of the same authority, on a mattress upon the floor; and the girl, mending the fire, sat before it, in readiness to rouse them at the appointed time.

For a long time Oliver lay awake, thinking it not impossible that Nancy might seek that opportunity of whispering some further advice, but the girl sat brooding over the fire without moving, save now and then to trim the light: weary with watching and anxiety, he at length fell asleep.

When he awoke, the table was covered with tea-things, and Sikes was thrusting various articles into the pockets of his great-coat which hung over the back of a chair, while Nancy was busily engaged in preparing breakfast. It was not yet daylight, for the candle was still burning, and it was quite dark outside. A sharp rain, too, was beating against the window-panes, and the sky looked black and cloudy.

'Now, then!' growled Sikes, as Oliver started up; 'half-past five! Look sharp, or you'll get no breakfast, for it's late as it is.'

Oliver was not long in making his toilet; and, having taken some breakfast, replied to a surly inquiry from Sikes, by saying that he was quite ready.

Nancy, scarcely looking at the boy, threw him a handkerchief to tie round his throat, and Sikes gave him a large rough cape to button over his shoulders. Thus attired, he gave his hand to the robber, who, merely pausing to show him, with a menacing gesture, that he had the pistol in a side-pocket of his great-coat, clasped it firmly in his, and, exchanging a farewell with Nancy, led him away.

Oliver turned round for an instant when they reached the door, in the hope of meeting a look from the girl; but she had resumed her old seat in front of the fire, and sat perfectly motionless before it.

CHAPTER THE TWENTY-FIRST

THE EXPEDITION

It was a cheerless morning when they got into the street, blowing and raining hard, and the clouds looking dull and stormy. The night had been very wet, for large pools of water had collected in the road, and the kennels were overflowing. There was a faint glimmering of the coming day in the sky, but it rather aggravated than relieved the gloom of the scene, the sombre light only serving to pale that which the street-lamps afforded, without shedding any warmer or brighter tints upon the wet housetops and dreary streets. There appeared to be nobody stirring in that quarter of the town, for the windows of the houses were all closely shut, and the streets through which they passed noiseless and empty.

By the time they had turned into the Bethnal Green road the day had fairly begun to break. Many of the lamps were already extinguished, a few country waggons were slowly toiling on towards London, and now and then a stage-coach, covered with mud, rattled briskly by, the driver bestowing, as he passed, an admonitory lash upon the heavy waggoner, who, by keeping on the wrong side of the road, had endangered his arriving at the office a quarter of a minute after his time. The public-houses, with gas-lights burning inside, were already open. By degrees other shops began to be unclosed, and a few scattered people were met with. Then came straggling groups of labourers going to their work; then men and women with fish-baskets on their heads, donkey-carts laden with vegetables, chaise-carts filled with live-stock or whole carcases of meat, milkwomen with pails, and an unbroken concourse of people trudging out with various supplies to the eastern suburbs of the town. As they approached the City, the noise and traffic gradually increased; and, when they threaded the streets between Shoreditch and Smithfield, it had swelled into a roar of sound and bustle. It was as light as it was likely to be till night set in again, and the busy morning of half the London population had begun.

Turning down Sun-street and Crown-street, and crossing Finsbury-square, Mr Sikes struck, by way of Chiswell-street, into Barbican, thence into Long-lane, and so into Smithfield, from which latter place arose a tumult of discordant sounds that filled Oliver Twist with surprise and amazement.

It was market-morning. The ground was covered nearly ankle-deep with filth and mire; and a thick steam perpetually rising from the reeking bodies of the cattle, and mingling with the fog, which seemed to rest upon the chimney-tops, hung heavily above. All the pens in the centre of the large area, and as many temporary ones as could be crowded into the vacant space, were filled with sheep; and, tied up to posts by the gutter side, were long lines of beasts and oxen three or four deep. Countrymen, butchers, drovers, hawkers, boys, thieves, idlers, and vagabonds of every low grade, were mingled together in a dense mass: the whistling of drovers, the barking of dogs, the bellowing and plunging of beasts, the bleating of sheep, and grunting and squeaking of pigs; the cries of hawkers, the shouts, oaths, and quarrelling on all sides, the ringing of bells and roar of voices that issued from every public-house; the crowding, pushing, driving, beating, whooping, and yelling; the hideous and discordant din that resounded from every corner of the market; and the unwashed, unshaven, squalid, and dirty figures constantly running to and fro, and bursting in and out of the throng, rendered it a stunning and bewildering scene which quite confounded the senses.

Mr Sikes, dragging Oliver after him, elbowed his way through the thickest of the crowd, and bestowed very little attention upon the numerous sights and sounds which so astonished the boy. He nodded twice or thrice to a passing friend: and, resisting as many invitations to take a morning dram, pressed steadily onward until they were clear of the turmoil, and had made their way through Hosier-lane into Holborn.

'Now, young 'un!' said Sikes surlily, looking up at the clock of St Andrew's church,[1] 'hard upon seven! you must step out. Come, don't lag behind already, Lazy-legs!'

Mr Sikes accompanied this speech with a fierce jerk at his little companion's wrist; and Oliver, quickening his pace into a kind of trot, between a fast walk and a run, kept up with the rapid strides of the housebreaker as well as he could.

They kept on their course at this rate until they had passed Hyde-Park corner, and were on their way to Kensington, when Sikes relaxed his pace until an empty cart, which was at some little distance behind, came up: when, seeing 'Hounslow' written upon it, he asked the driver, with as much civility as he could assume, if he would give them a lift as far as Isleworth.

'Jump up,' said the man. 'Is that your boy?'

'Yes; he's my boy,' replied Sikes, looking hard at Oliver, and putting his hand abstractedly into the pocket where the pistol was.

'Your father walks rather too quick for you; don't he, my man?' inquired the driver, seeing that Oliver was out of breath.

'Not a bit of it,' replied Sikes, interposing. 'He's used to it. Here, take hold of my hand, Ned. In with you!'

Thus addressing Oliver, he helped him into the cart; and the driver, pointing to a heap of sacks, told him to lie down there, and rest himself.

As they passed the different milestones, Oliver wondered more and more where his companion meant to take him. Kensington, Hammersmith, Chiswick, Kew Bridge, Brentford, were all passed; and yet they kept on as steadily as if they had only begun their journey. At length they came to a public-house called the Coach and Horses,[2] a little way beyond which, another road appeared to turn off. And here the cart stopped.

Sikes dismounted with great precipitation, holding Oliver by the hand all the while; and, lifting him down directly, bestowed a furious look upon him, and rapped the side-pocket with his fist in a very significant manner.

'Good-b'ye, boy!' said the man.

'He's sulky,' replied Sikes, giving him a shake; 'he's sulky, – a young dog! Don't mind him.'

'Not I!' rejoined the other, getting into his cart. 'It's a fine day, after all.' And he drove away.

Sikes waited till he had fairly gone, and then, telling Oliver he might look about him if he wanted, once again led him forward on his journey.

They turned round to the left a short way past the public-house, and then, taking a right-hand road, walked on for a long time, passing many large gardens and gentlemen's houses on both sides of the way, and at length crossing a little bridge which led them into Twickenham; from which town they still walked on without stopping for anything but some beer, until they reached another town, in which, against the wall of a house, Oliver saw written up in pretty large letters 'Hampton.' Turning round by a public-house which bore the sign of the Red Lion, they kept on by the river side for a short distance, and then Sikes, striking off into a narrow street, walked straight to an old public-house[3] with a defaced sign-board, and ordered some dinner by the kitchen fire.

The kitchen was an old low-roofed room, with a great beam across the middle of the ceiling, and benches with high backs to them by the fire, on which were seated several rough men in smock-frocks, drinking and smoking. They took no notice of Oliver, and very little of Sikes; and, as Sikes took very little notice of them, he and his young comrade sat in a corner by themselves, without being much troubled by the company.

They had some cold meat for dinner, and sat here so long after it, while Mr Sikes indulged himself with three or four pipes, that Oliver began to feel quite certain they were not going any further. Being much tired with the walk and getting up so early, he dozed a little at first; and then, quite overpowered by fatigue and the fumes of the tobacco, fell fast asleep.

It was quite dark when he was awakened by a push from Sikes. Rousing himself sufficiently to sit up and look about him, he found that worthy in close fellowship and communication with a labouring man, over a pint of ale.

'So, you're going on to Lower Halliford, are you?' inquired Sikes.

'Yes, I am,' replied the man, who seemed a little the worse – or better, as the case might be – for drinking; 'and not slow about it either. My horse hasn't got a load behind him going back, as he had coming up in the mornin', and he won't be long a-doing of it. Here's luck to him! Ecod, he's a good 'un!'

'Could you give my boy and me a lift as far as there?' demanded Sikes, pushing the ale towards his new friend.

'If you're going directly, I can,' replied the man, looking out of the pot. 'Are you going to Halliford?'

'Going on to Shepperton,'4 replied Sikes.

'I'm your man as far as I go,' replied the other. 'Is all paid, Becky?'

'Yes, the other gentleman's paid,' replied the girl.

'I say!' said the man with tipsy gravity; 'that won't do, you know.'

'Why not?' rejoined Sikes. 'You're a-going to accommodate us, and wot's to prevent my standing treat for a pint or so, in return?'

The stranger reflected upon this argument with a very profound face, and, having done so, seized Sikes by the hand, and declared he was a real good fellow. To which Mr Sikes replied he was joking; as, if he had been sober, there would have been strong reason to suppose he was.

After the exchange of a few more compliments, they bade the company good-night, and went out: the girl gathering up the pots and glasses as they did so, and lounging out to the door, with her hands full, to see the party start.

The horse, whose health had been drunk in his absence, was standing outside, ready harnessed to the cart. Oliver and Sikes got in without any further ceremony, and the man, to whom he belonged, having lingered a minute or two 'to bear him up,' and to defy the hostler and the world to produce his equal, mounted also. Then the hostler was told to give the horse his head, and, his head being given him, he made a very unpleasant use of it, tossing it into the air with great disdain, and running into the parlour windows over the way; after performing which feats, and supporting himself for a short time on his hind-legs, he started off at great speed, and rattled out of the town right gallantly.

The night was very dark; and a damp mist rose from the river and the marshy ground about, and spread itself over the dreary fields. It was piercing cold, too; all was gloomy and black. Not a word was spoken, for the driver had grown sleepy, and Sikes was in no mood to lead him into conversation. Oliver sat huddled together in a corner of the cart bewildered with alarm and apprehension, and figuring strange objects in the gaunt trees, whose branches waved grimly to and fro, as if in some fantastic joy at the desolation of the scene.

As they passed Sunbury church, the clock struck seven. There was a light in the ferry-house window opposite, which streamed across the road, and threw into more sombre shadow a dark yew-tree with graves beneath it. There was a dull sound of falling water not far off, and the leaves of the old tree stirred gently in the night wind. It seemed like solemn quiet music for the repose of the dead.

Sunbury was passed through, and they came again into the lonely road. Two or three miles more, and the cart stopped. Sikes alighted, and, taking Oliver by the hand, they once again walked on.

They turned into no house at Shepperton, as the weary boy had expected, but still kept walking on in mud and darkness through gloomy lanes and over cold open wastes, until they came within sight of the lights of a town at no great distance. On looking intently forward, Oliver saw that the water was just below them, and that they were coming to the foot of a bridge.

Sikes kept straight on till they were close upon the bridge, and then turned suddenly down a bank upon the left. 'The water!' thought Oliver, turning sick with fear. 'He has brought me to this lonely place to murder me!'

He was about to throw himself on the ground, and make one struggle for his young life, when he saw that they stood before a solitary house all ruinous and decayed. There was a window on each side of the dilapidated entrance, and one story above; but no light was visible. It was dark, dismantled, and to all appearance uninhabited.

Sikes, with Oliver's hand still in his, softly approached the low porch, and raised the latch. The door yielded to his pressure, and they passed in together.

CHAPTER THE TWENTY-SECOND

THE BURGLARY

'Hallo!' cried a loud, hoarse voice, directly they had set foot in the passage.

'Don't make such a row,' said Sikes, bolting the door. 'Show a glim, Toby.'

'Aha! my pal,' cried the same voice; 'a glim, Barney, a glim! Show the gentleman in, Barney; and wake up first, if convenient.'

The speaker appeared to throw a boot-jack, or some such article, at the person he addressed, to rouse him from his slumbers; for the noise of a wooden body falling violently was heard, and then an indistinct muttering as of a man between asleep and awake.

'Do you hear?' cried the same voice. 'There's Bill Sikes in the passage, with nobody to do the civil to him; and you sleeping there, as if you took laudanum with your meals, and nothing stronger. Are you any fresher now, or do you want the iron candlestick to wake you thoroughly?'

A pair of slipshod feet shuffled hastily across the bare floor of the room as this interrogatory was put; and there issued from a door on the right hand, first a feeble candle, and next, the form of the same individual who has been heretofore described as labouring under the infirmity of speaking through his nose, and officiating as waiter at the public-house on Saffron Hill.

'Bister Sikes!' exclaimed Barney, with real or counterfeit joy; 'cub id, sir; cub id.'

'Here! you get on first,' said Sikes, putting Oliver in front of him. 'Quicker! or I shall tread upon your heels.'

Muttering a curse upon his tardiness, Sikes pushed Oliver before him, and they entered a low dark room with a smoky fire, two or three broken chairs, a table, and a very old couch, on which, with his legs much higher than his head, a man was reposing at full length, smoking a long clay pipe. He was dressed in a smartly-cut snuff-coloured coat with large brass buttons, an orange neckerchief, a coarse, staring, shawl-pattern[1] waistcoat, and drab breeches. Mr Crackit (for he it was) had no very great quantity of hair, either upon his head or face; but what he had was of a reddish dye, and tortured into long, corkscrew curls, through which he occasionally thrust some very dirty fingers ornamented with large common rings. He was a trifle above the middle size, and apparently rather weak in the legs; but this circumstance by no means detracted from his own admiration of his top-boots, which he contemplated in their elevated situation with lively satisfaction.

'Bill, my boy!' said this figure, turning his head towards the door, 'I'm glad to see you; I was almost afraid you'd given it up, in which case I should have made a personal wentur'. Hallo!'

Uttering this exclamation in a tone of great surprise as his eyes rested on Oliver, Mr Toby Crackit brought himself into a sitting posture, and demanded who that was.

'The boy – only the boy!' replied Sikes, drawing a chair towards the fire.

'Wud of Bister Fagid's lads,' exclaimed Barney, with a grin.

'Fagin's, eh!' exclaimed Toby, looking at Oliver. 'Wot an inwalable boy that'll make for the old ladies' pockets in chapels. His mug is a fortun' to him.'

'There – there's enough of that!' interposed Sikes impatiently; and, stooping over his recumbent friend, he whispered a few words in his ear, at which Mr Crackit laughed immensely, and honoured Oliver with a long stare of astonishment.

'Now,' said Sikes, as he resumed his seat, 'if you'll give us something to eat and drink while we're waiting, you'll put some heart in us, – or in me, at all events. Sit down by the fire, younker, and rest yourself; for you'll have to go out with us again to-night, though not very far off.'

Oliver looked at Sikes in mute and timid wonder, and, drawing a stool to the fire, sat with his aching head upon his hands, scarcely knowing where he was, or what was passing around him.

'Here,' said Toby, as the young Jew placed some fragments of food and a bottle upon the table, 'Success to the crack!' He rose to honour the toast, and, carefully depositing his empty pipe in a corner, advanced to the table, filled a glass with spirits, and drank off its contents. Mr Sikes did the same.

'A drain for the boy,' said Toby, half filling a wine-glass. 'Down with it, innocence!'

'Indeed,' said Oliver, looking piteously up into the man's face; 'indeed I —'

'Down with it!' echoed Toby. 'Do you think I don't know what's good for you? Tell him to drink it, Bill.'

'He had better,' said Sikes, clapping his hand upon his pocket. 'Burn my body! if he isn't more trouble than a whole family of Dodgers. Drink it, you perwerse imp; drink it!'

Frightened by the menacing gestures of the two men, Oliver hastily swallowed the contents of the glass, and immediately fell into a violent fit of coughing, which delighted Toby Crackit and Barney, and even drew a smile from the surly Mr Sikes.

This done, and Sikes having satisfied his appetite, (Oliver could eat nothing but a small crust of bread which they made him swallow,) the two men laid themselves down on chairs for a short nap. Oliver retained his stool by the fire; and Barney, wrapped in a blanket, stretched himself on the floor, close outside the fender.

They slept, or appeared to sleep, for some time; nobody stirring but Barney, who rose once or twice to throw coals upon the fire. Oliver fell into a heavy doze, imagining himself straying alone through the gloomy lanes, or wandering about the dark churchyard, or retracing some one or other of the scenes of the past day, when he was roused by Toby Crackit's jumping up and declaring it was half-past one.

In an instant the other two were on their legs, and all were actively engaged in busy preparation. Sikes and his companion enveloped their necks and chins in large dark shawls,[2] and drew on their great-coats; while Barney, opening a cupboard, brought forth several articles, which he hastily crammed into the pockets.

'Barkers for me, Barney?' said Toby Crackit.

'Here they are,' replied Barney, producing a pair of pistols. 'You loaded them yourself.'

'All right!' replied Toby, stowing them away. 'The persuaders?'

'I've got 'em,' replied Sikes.

'Crape, keys, centre-bit, darkies – nothing forgotten?' inquired Toby, fastening a small crowbar to a loop inside the skirt of his coat.

'All right!' rejoined his companion. 'Bring them bits of timber, Barney: that's the time of day.'

With these words he took a thick stick from Barney's hands, who, having delivered another to Toby, busied himself in fastening on Oliver's cape.

'Now then!' said Sikes, holding out his hand.

Oliver, who was completely stupified by the unwonted exercise, and the air, and the drink that had been forced upon him, put his hand mechanically into that which Sikes extended for the purpose.

'Take his other hand, Toby,' said Sikes. 'Look out, Barney!'

The man went to the door, and returned to announce that all was quiet. The two robbers issued forth with Oliver between them; and Barney, having made all fast, rolled himself up as before, and was soon asleep again.

It was now intensely dark. The fog was much heavier than it had been in the early part of the night, and the atmosphere was so damp that, although no rain fell, Oliver's hair and eyebrows within a few minutes after leaving the house had become stiff with the half-frozen moisture that was floating about. They crossed the bridge, and kept on towards the lights which he had seen before. They were at no great distance off; and, as they walked pretty briskly, they soon arrived at Chertsey.

'Slap through the town,' whispered Sikes: 'there'll be nobody in the way to-night to see us.'

Toby acquiesced; and they hurried through the main street of the little town, which at that late hour was wholly deserted. A dim light shone at intervals from some bed-room window, and the hoarse barking of dogs occasionally broke the silence of the night; but there was nobody abroad, and they had cleared the town as the church bell[3] struck two.

Quickening their pace, they turned up a road upon the left hand; after walking about a quarter of a mile, they stopped before a detached house surrounded by a wall,[4] to the top of which Toby Crackit, scarcely pausing to take breath, climbed in a twinkling.

'The boy next,' said Toby. 'Hoist him up: I'll catch hold of him.'

Before Oliver had time to look round, Sikes had caught him under the arms, and in three or four seconds he and Toby were lying on the grass on the other side. Sikes followed directly, and they stole cautiously towards the house.

And now, for the first time, Oliver, well-nigh mad with grief and terror, saw that housebreaking and robbery, if not murder, were the objects of the expedition. He clasped his hands together, and involuntarily uttered a subdued exclamation of horror. A mist came before his eyes, the cold sweat stood upon his ashy face, his limbs failed him, and he sunk upon his knees.

'Get up!' murmured Sikes, trembling with rage, and drawing the pistol from his pocket; 'get up, or I'll strew your brains upon the grass!'

'Oh! for God's sake let me go!' cried Oliver; 'let me run away and die in the fields. I will never come near London – never, never! Oh! pray have mercy upon me, and do not make me steal: for the love of all the bright angels that rest in heaven, have mercy upon me!'

The man to whom this appeal was made swore a dreadful oath, and had cocked the pistol, when Toby, striking it from his grasp, placed his hand upon the boy's mouth and dragged him to the house.

'Hush!' cried the man; 'it won't answer here. Say another word, and I'll do your business myself with a crack on the head that makes no noise, and is quite as certain and more genteel. Here, Bill, wrench the shutter open. He's game enough now, I'll engage. I've seen older hands of his age took the same way for a minute or two on a cold night.'

Sikes, invoking terrific imprecations upon Fagin's head for sending Oliver on such an errand, plied the crowbar vigorously, but with little noise; and, after some delay and some assistance from Toby, the shutter to which he had referred swung open on its hinges.

It was a little lattice window, about five feet and a half above the ground, at the back of the house, belonging to a scullery or small brewing-place at the end of the passage: the aperture was so small that the inmates had probably not thought it worth while to defend it more securely; but it was large enough to admit a boy of Oliver's size nevertheless. A very brief exercise of Mr Sikes's art sufficed to overcome the fastening of the lattice, and it soon stood wide open also.

'Now listen, you young limb!' whispered Sikes, drawing a dark lantern[5] from his pocket, and throwing the glare full on Oliver's face; 'I'm a-going to put you through there. Take this light, go softly up the steps straight afore you, and along the little hall to the street-door. Unfasten it, and let us in.'

'There's a bolt at the top you won't be able to reach,' interposed Toby. 'Stand upon one of the hall chairs; there are three there, Bill, with a jolly large blue unicorn and a gold pitchfork on 'em, which is the old lady's arms.'

'Keep quiet, can't you?' replied Sikes with a savage look. 'The room door is open, is it?'

'Wide,' replied Toby, after peeping in to satisfy himself. 'The game of that is that they always leave it open with a catch, so that the dog, who's got a bed in here, may walk up and down the passage when he feels wakeful. Ha! ha! Barney 'ticed him away to-night, so neat.'

Although Mr Crackit spoke in a scarcely audible whisper, and laughed without noise, Sikes imperiously commanded him to be silent, and to get to work. Toby complied by first producing his lantern, and placing it on the ground; and then planting himself firmly with his head against the wall beneath the window, and his hands upon his knees, so as to make a step of his back. This was no sooner done than Sikes, mounting upon him, put Oliver gently through the window, with his feet first; and, without leaving hold of his collar, planted him safely on the floor inside.

'Take this lantern,' said Sikes, looking into the room. 'You see the stairs afore you?'

Oliver, more dead than alive, gasped out, 'Yes;' and Sikes, pointing to the street-door with the pistol barrel, briefly advised him to take notice that he was within shot all the way, and that if he faltered he would fall dead that instant.

'It's done in a minute,' said Sikes in the same low whisper. 'Directly I leave go of you, do your work. Hark!'

'What's that?' whispered the other man.

They listened intently.

The Burglary

'Nothing,' said Sikes, releasing his hold of Oliver. 'Now!'

In the short time he had had to collect his senses, the boy had firmly resolved that, whether he died in the attempt or not, he would make one effort to dart up stairs from the hall and alarm the family. Filled with this idea, he advanced at once, but stealthily.

'Come back!' suddenly cried Sikes aloud. 'Back! back!'

Scared by the sudden breaking of the dead stillness of the place, and a loud cry which followed it, Oliver let his lantern fall, and knew not whether to advance or fly. The cry was repeated – a light appeared – a vision of two terrified half-dressed men at the top of the stairs swam before his eyes – a flash – a loud noise – a smoke – a crash somewhere, but where he knew not, – and he staggered back.

Sikes had disappeared for an instant; but he was up again, and had him by the collar before the smoke had cleared away. He fired his own pistol after the men, who were already retreating, and dragged the boy up.

'Clasp your arm tighter,' said Sikes as he drew him through the window. 'Give me a shawl here. They've hit him. Quick! Damnation, how the boy bleeds!'

Then came the loud ringing of a bell, mingled with the noise of fire-arms and the shouts of men, and the sensation of being carried over uneven ground at a rapid pace. And then the noises grew confused in the distance, and a cold deadly feeling crept over the boy's heart, and he saw or heard no more.

THE END OF THE FIRST BOOK

*

BOOK THE SECOND

CHAPTER THE FIRST

WHICH CONTAINS THE SUBSTANCE OF A PLEASANT CONVERSATION BETWEEN MR BUMBLE AND A LADY; AND SHOWS THAT EVEN A BEADLE MAY BE SUSCEPTIBLE ON SOME POINTS

The night was bitter cold; the snow lay upon the ground frozen into a hard thick crust, so that only the heaps that had drifted into by-ways and corners were affected by the sharp wind that howled abroad, which, as if expending increased fury on such prey as it found, caught it savagely up in clouds, and, whirling it into a thousand misty eddies, scattered it in air. Bleak, dark, and piercing cold, it was a night for the well-housed and fed to draw round the bright fire, and thank God they were at home; and for the homeless starving wretch to lay him down and die. Many hunger-worn outcasts close their eyes in our bare streets at such times, who, let their crimes have been what they may, can hardly open them in a more bitter world.

Such was the aspect of out-of-door affairs when Mrs Corney, the matron of the workhouse to which our readers have been already introduced as the birth-place of Oliver Twist, set herself down before a cheerful fire in her own little room, and glanced with no small degree of complacency at a small round table, on which stood a tray of corresponding size, furnished with all necessary materials for the most grateful meal that matrons enjoy. In fact, Mrs Corney was about to solace herself with a cup of tea: and as she glanced from the table to the fireplace, where the smallest of all possible kettles was singing a small song in a small voice, her inward satisfaction evidently increased, – so much so, indeed, that Mrs Corney smiled.

'Well,' said the matron, leaning her elbow on the table, and looking reflectively at the fire, 'I'm sure we have all on us a great deal to be grateful for – a great deal, if we did but know it. Ah!'

Mrs Corney shook her head mournfully, as if deploring the mental blindness of paupers who did *not* know it, and, thrusting a silver spoon (private property) into the inmost recesses of a two-ounce tin tea-caddy, proceeded to make the tea.

How slight a thing will disturb the equanimity of our frail minds! The black teapot, being very small and easily filled, ran over while Mrs Corney was moralizing, and the water slightly scalded Mrs Corney's hand.

'Drat the pot!' said the worthy matron, setting it down very hastily on the hob; 'a little stupid thing, that only holds a couple of cups! What use is it of to anybody? – except,' said Mrs Corney pausing, – 'except to a poor desolate creature like me. Oh dear!'

With these words the matron dropped into her chair, and, once more resting her elbow on the table, thought of her solitary fate. The small teapot and the single cup had awakened in her mind sad recollections of Mr Corney, (who had not been dead more than five-and-twenty years,) and she was overpowered.

'I shall never get another!' said Mrs Corney pettishly, 'I shall never get another – like him!'

Whether this remark bore reference to the husband or the teapot is uncertain. It might have been the latter; for Mrs Corney looked at it as she spoke, and took it up afterwards. She had just tasted her first cup, when she was disturbed by a soft tap at the room door.

'Oh, come in with you!' said Mrs Corney sharply. 'Some of the old women dying, I suppose; – they always die when I'm at meals. Don't stand there, letting the cold air in, don't! What's amiss now, eh?'

'Nothing, ma'am, nothing,' replied a man's voice.

'Dear me!' exclaimed the matron in a much sweeter tone, 'is that Mr Bumble?'

'At your service, ma'am,' said Mr Bumble, who had been stopping outside to rub his shoes clean, and shake the snow off his coat, and who now made his appearance, bearing the cocked-hat in one hand and a bundle in the other. 'Shall I shut the door, ma'am?'

The lady modestly hesitated to reply, lest there should be any impropriety in holding an interview with Mr Bumble with closed doors. Mr Bumble, taking advantage of the hesitation, and being very cold himself, shut it without farther permission.

'Hard weather, Mr Bumble,' said the matron.

'Hard, indeed, ma'am,' replied the beadle. 'Anti-porochial weather this, ma'am. We have given away, Mrs Corney, – we have given away a matter of twenty quartern loaves, and a cheese and a half, this very blessed afternoon; and yet them paupers are not contented.'[1]

'Of course not. When would they be, Mr Bumble?' said the matron, sipping her tea.

'When, indeed, ma'am!' rejoined Mr Bumble. 'Why, here's one man that, in consideration of his wife and large family, has a quartern loaf and a good pound of cheese, full weight. Is he grateful, ma'am, – is he grateful? Not a copper farthing's worth of it! What does he do, ma'am, but ask for a few coals, if it's only a pocket-handkerchief full, he says! Coals! – what would he do with coals? – Toast his cheese with 'em, and then come back for more. That's the way with these people, ma'am; – give 'em a apron full of coals to-day, and they'll come back for another the day after to-morrow, as brazen as alabaster!'

The matron expressed her entire concurrence in this intelligible simile, and the beadle went on.

'I never,' said Mr Bumble, 'see anything like the pitch it's got to. The day afore yesterday, a man – you have been a married woman, ma'am, and I may mention it to you – a man, with hardly a rag upon his back, (here Mrs Corney looked at the floor,) goes to our overseer's door when he has got company coming to dinner, and says he must be relieved, Mrs Corney. As he wouldn't go away, and shocked the company very much, our overseer sent him out a pound of potatoes and half a pint of oatmeal. "My God!" says the ungrateful villain, "what's the use of *this* to me? You might as well give me a pair of iron spectacles." – "Very good," says our overseer, taking 'em away again, "you won't get anything else here." – "Then I'll die in the streets!" says the vagrant. – "Oh no, you won't," says our overseer.'

'Ha! ha! – that was very good! – so like Mr Grannet, wasn't it?' interposed the matron. 'Well, Mr Bumble?'

'Well, ma'am,' rejoined the beadle, 'he went away, and *did* die in the streets. There's a obstinate pauper for you!'

'It beats anything I could have believed!' observed the matron emphatically. 'But don't you think out-of-door relief a very bad thing any way, Mr Bumble? You're a gentleman of experience, and ought to know. Come.'

'Mrs Corney,' said the beadle, smiling as men smile who are conscious of superior information, 'out-of-door relief, properly managed, – properly managed, ma'am, – is the porochial safe-guard. The great principle of out-of-door relief is to give the paupers exactly what they don't want, and then they get tired of coming.'

'Dear me!' exclaimed Mrs Corney. 'Well, that is a good one, too!'

'Yes. Betwixt you and me, ma'am,' returned Mr Bumble, 'that's the great principle; and that's the reason why, if you look at any cases that get into them owdacious newspapers, you'll always observe that sick families have been relieved with slices of cheese. That's the rule now, Mrs Corney, all over the country. – But, however,' said the beadle, stooping to unpack his bundle, 'these are official secrets, ma'am; not to be spoken of except, as I may say, among the porochial officers such as ourselves. This is the port wine, ma'am, that the board ordered for the infirmary, – real fresh, genuine port wine, only out of the cask this afternoon, – clear as a bell, and no sediment.'

Having held the first bottle up to the light, and shaken it well[2] to test its excellence, Mr Bumble placed them both on the top of a chest of drawers, folded the handkerchief in which they had been wrapped, put it carefully in his pocket, and took up his hat as if to go.

'You'll have a very cold walk, Mr Bumble,' said the matron.

'It blows, ma'am,' replied Mr Bumble, turning up his coat-collar, 'enough to cut one's ears off.'

The matron looked from the little kettle to the beadle, who was moving towards the door; and as the beadle coughed, preparatory to bidding her good-night, bashfully inquired whether – whether he wouldn't take a cup of tea?

Mr Bumble instantaneously turned back his collar again, laid his hat

Mr Bumble and Mrs Corney taking tea

and stick upon a chair, and drew another chair up to the table. As he slowly seated himself, he looked at the lady: she fixed her eyes upon the little teapot. Mr Bumble coughed again, and slightly smiled.

Mrs Corney rose to get another cup and saucer from the closet. As she sat down, her eyes once again encountered those of the gallant beadle; she coloured, and applied herself to the task of making his tea. Again Mr Bumble coughed, – louder this time than he had coughed yet.

'Sweet, Mr Bumble?' inquired the matron, taking up the sugar-basin.

'Very sweet, indeed, ma'am,' replied Mr Bumble. He fixed his eyes on Mrs Corney as he said this; and, if ever a beadle looked tender, Mr Bumble was that beadle at that moment.

The tea was made, and handed in silence. Mr Bumble, having spread a handkerchief over his knees to prevent the crumbs from sullying the splendour of his shorts, began to eat and drink, varying these amusements occasionally by fetching a deep sigh, which, however, had no injurious effect upon his appetite, but, on the contrary, rather seemed to facilitate his operations in the tea and toast department.

'You have a cat, ma'am, I see,' said Mr Bumble, glancing at one, who in the centre of her family was basking before the fire; 'and kittens too, I declare!'

'I am so fond of them, Mr Bumble, you can't think,' replied the matron. 'They're *so* happy, *so* frolicsome, and *so* cheerful, that they are quite companions for me.'

'Very nice animals, ma'am,' replied Mr Bumble approvingly; 'so very domestic.'

'Oh, yes!' rejoined the matron with enthusiasm; 'so fond of their home too, that it's quite a pleasure, I'm sure.'

'Mrs Corney, ma'am,' said Mr Bumble slowly, and marking the time with his teaspoon, 'I mean to say this, ma'am, that any cat or kitten that could live with you, ma'am, and *not* be fond of its home, must be an ass, ma'am.'

'Oh, Mr Bumble!' remonstrated Mrs Corney.

'It's no use disguising facts, ma'am,' said Mr Bumble, slowly flourishing the teaspoon with a kind of amorous dignity that made him doubly impressive; 'I would drown it myself with pleasure.'

'Then you're a cruel man,' said the matron vivaciously, as she held out her hand for the beadle's cup, 'and a very hard-hearted man besides.'

'Hard-hearted, ma'am!' said Mr Bumble, 'hard!' Mr Bumble resigned his cup without another word, squeezed Mrs Corney's little finger as she took it, and inflicting two open-handed slaps upon his laced waistcoat, gave a mighty sigh, and hitched his chair a very little morsel farther from the fire.

It was a round table; and as Mrs Corney and Mr Bumble had been sitting opposite each other, with no great space between them, and fronting the fire, it will be seen that Mr Bumble, in receding from the fire, and still keeping at the table, increased the distance between himself and Mrs Corney; which proceeding some prudent readers will doubtless be disposed to admire, and to consider an act of great heroism on Mr Bumble's part, he being in some sort tempted by time, place, and opportunity to give utterance to certain soft nothings, which, however well they may become the lips of the light and thoughtless, do seem immeasurably beneath the dignity of judges of the land, members of parliament, ministers of state, lord-mayors, and other great public functionaries, but more particularly beneath the stateliness and gravity of a beadle, who (as is well known) should be the sternest and most inflexible among them all.

Whatever were Mr Bumble's intentions, however, – and no doubt they were of the best, – whatever they were, it unfortunately happened, as has been twice before remarked, that the table was a round one; consequently Mr Bumble, moving his chair by little and little, soon began to diminish the distance between himself and the matron, and, continuing to travel round the outer edge of the circle, brought his chair in time close to that in which the matron was seated. Indeed, the two chairs touched; and, when they did so, Mr Bumble stopped.

Now, if the matron had moved her chair to the right, she would have been scorched by the fire, and if to the left, she must have fallen into Mr Bumble's arms; so (being a discreet matron, and no doubt foreseeing these consequences at a glance,) she remained where she was, and handed Mr Bumble another cup of tea.

'Hard-hearted, Mrs Corney?' said Mr Bumble, stirring his tea, and looking up into the matron's face; 'are *you* hard-hearted, Mrs Corney?'

'Dear me!' exclaimed the matron, 'what a very curious question from a single man! What can you want to know for, Mr Bumble?'

The beadle drank his tea to the last drop, finished a piece of toast, whisked the crumbs off his knees, wiped his lips, and deliberately kissed the matron.

'Mr Bumble,' cried that discreet lady in a whisper, for the fright was so great that she had quite lost her voice, 'Mr Bumble, I shall scream!' Mr Bumble made no reply, but in a slow and dignified manner put his arm round the matron's waist.

As the lady had stated her intention of screaming, of course she would have screamed at this additional boldness, but that the exertion was rendered unnecessary by a hasty knocking at the door, which was no sooner heard than Mr Bumble darted with much agility to the wine-bottles, and began dusting them with great violence, while the matron sharply demanded who was there. It is worthy of remark, as a curious physical instance of the efficacy of a sudden surprise in counteracting the effects of extreme fear, that her voice had quite recovered all its official asperity.

'If you please, mistress,' said a withered old female pauper, hideously ugly, putting her head in at the door, 'old Sally is a-going fast.'

'Well, what's that to me?' angrily demanded the matron. 'I can't keep her alive, can I?'

'No, no, mistress,' replied the old woman, raising her hand, 'nobody can; she's far beyond the reach of help. I've seen a many people die, little babes and great strong men, and I know when death's a-coming well enough. But she's troubled in her mind; and when the fits are not on her, – and that's not often, for she is dying very hard, – she says she has got something to tell which you must hear. She'll never die quiet till you come, mistress.'

At this intelligence the worthy Mrs Corney muttered a variety of invectives against old women who couldn't even die without purposely annoying their betters; and, muffling herself in a thick shawl which she hastily caught up, briefly requested Mr Bumble to stop till she came back, lest anything particular should occur, and bidding the messenger walk fast, and not be all night hobbling up the stairs, followed her from the room with a very ill grace, scolding all the way.

Mr Bumble's conduct, on being left to himself, was rather inexplicable. He opened the closet, counted the teaspoons, weighed the sugar-tongs, closely inspected a silver milk-pot to ascertain that it was of the genuine metal; and, having satisfied his curiosity upon these points, put on his cocked-hat cornerwise, and danced with much gravity four distinct times round the table. Having gone through this very extraordinary performance, he took off the cocked-hat again, and, spreading himself before the fire with his back towards it, seemed to be mentally engaged in taking an exact inventory of the furniture.

CHAPTER THE SECOND

TREATS OF A VERY POOR SUBJECT, BUT IS A SHORT ONE, AND MAY BE FOUND OF IMPORTANCE IN THIS HISTORY

It was no unfit messenger of death that had disturbed the quiet of the matron's room. Her body was bent by age, her limbs trembled with palsy, and her face, distorted into a mumbling leer, resembled more the grotesque shaping of some wild pencil than the work of Nature's hand.

Alas! how few of Nature's faces there are to gladden us with their beauty! The cares, and sorrows, and hungerings of the world change them as they change hearts, and it is only when those passions sleep, and have lost their hold for ever, that the troubled clouds pass off, and leave heaven's surface clear. It is a common thing for the countenances of the dead, even in that fixed and rigid state, to subside into the long-forgotten expression of sleeping infancy, and settle into the very look of early life; so calm, so peaceful do they grow again, that those who knew them in their happy childhood kneel by the coffin's side in awe, and see the angel even upon earth.

The old crone tottered along the passages and up the stairs, muttering some indistinct answers to the chidings of her companion; and, being at length compelled to pause for breath, gave the light into her hand, and remained behind to follow as she might, while the more nimble superior made her way to the room where the sick woman lay.

It was a bare garret-room, with a dim light burning at the farther end. There was another old woman watching by the bed, and the parish apothecary's apprentice[1] was standing by the fire, making a toothpick out of a quill.

'Cold night, Mrs Corney,' said this young gentleman as the matron entered.

'Very cold indeed, sir,' replied the mistress in her most civil tones, and dropping a curtsey as she spoke.

'You should get better coals out of your contractors,' said the apothecary's deputy, breaking a lump on the top of the fire with the rusty poker; 'these are not at all the sort of thing for a cold night.'

'They're the board's choosing, sir,' returned the matron. 'The least they could do would be to keep us pretty warm, for our places are hard enough.'

The conversation was here interrupted by a moan from the sick woman.

'Oh!' said the young man, turning his face towards the bed, as if he had previously quite forgotten the patient, 'it's all U. P. there, Mrs Corney.'

'It is, is it, sir?' asked the matron.

'If she lasts a couple of hours, I shall be surprised,' said the apothecary's apprentice, intent upon the toothpick's point.

'It's a break-up of the system altogether. Is she dozing, old lady?'

The attendant stooped over the bed to ascertain, and nodded in the affirmative.

'Then perhaps she'll go off in that way, if you don't make a row,' said the young man. 'Put the light on the floor, – she won't see it there.'

The attendant did as she was bidden, shaking her head meanwhile to intimate that the woman would not die so easily; and, having done so, resumed her seat by the side of the other nurse, who had by this time returned. The mistress, with an expression of impatience, wrapped herself in her shawl, and sat at the foot of the bed.

The apothecary's apprentice, having completed the manufacture of the toothpick, planted himself in front of the fire, and made good use of it for ten minutes or so, when, apparently growing rather dull, he wished Mrs Corney joy of her job, and took himself off on tiptoe.

When they had sat in silence for some time, the two old women rose from the bed, and, crouching over the fire, held out their withered hands to catch the heat. The flame threw a ghastly light on their shrivelled faces, and made their ugliness appear perfectly terrible, as in this position they began to converse in a low voice.

'Did she say any more, Anny dear, while I was gone?' inquired the messenger.

'Not a word,' replied the other. 'She plucked and tore at her arms for a little time; but I held her hands, and she soon dropped off. She hasn't much strength in her, so I easily kept her quiet. I ain't so weak for an old woman, although I am on parish allowance; – no, no.'

'Did she drink the hot wine the doctor said she was to have?' demanded the first.

'I tried to get it down,' rejoined the other; 'but her teeth were tight set, and she clenched the mug so hard, that it was as much as I could do to get it back again. So *I* drank it, and it did me good.'

Looking cautiously round to ascertain that they were not overheard, the two hags cowered nearer to the fire, and chuckled heartily.

'I mind the time,' said the first speaker, 'when she would have done the same, and made rare fun of it afterwards.'

'Ay, that she would,' rejoined the other; 'she had a merry heart. A many, many beautiful corpses she laid out, as nice and neat as wax-work. My old eyes have seen them, – ay, and these old hands touched them too; for I have helped her scores of times.'

Stretching forth her trembling fingers as she spoke, the old creature shook them exultingly before her face; and then, fumbling in her pocket, brought out an old time-discoloured tin snuff-box, from which she shook a few grains into the outstretched palm of her companion, and a few more into her own. While they were thus employed, the matron, who had been impatiently watching until the dying woman should awaken from her stupor, joined them by the fire, and sharply asked how long she was to wait.

'Not long, mistress,' replied the second woman, looking up into her face. 'We have none of us long to wait for Death. Patience, patience! he'll be here soon enough for us all.'

'Hold your tongue, you doting idiot!' said the matron sternly. 'You, Martha, tell me; has she been in this way before?'

'Often,' answered the first woman.

'But will never be again,' added the second one; 'that is, she'll never wake again but once, – and mind, mistress, that won't be for long.'

'Long or short,' said the matron snappishly, 'she won't find me here when she does, and take care, both of you, how you worry me again for nothing. It's no part of my duty to see all the old women in the house die, and I won't, – that's more. Mind that, you impudent old harridans! If you make a fool of me again, I'll soon cure you, I warrant you!'

She was bouncing away, when a cry from the two women, who had turned towards the bed, caused her to look round. The sick woman had raised herself upright, and was stretching her arms towards them.

'Who's that?' she cried in a hollow voice.

'Hush, hush!' said one of the women stooping over her, – 'lie down, lie down!'

'I'll never lie down again alive!' said the woman struggling. 'I *will* tell her! Come here – nearer. Let me whisper in your ear.'

She clutched the matron by the arm, and forcing her into a chair by the bedside was about to speak, when, looking round, she caught sight of the two old women bending forward in the attitude of eager listeners.

'Turn them away,' said the woman drowsily; 'make haste – make haste!'

The two old crones, chiming in together, began pouring out many piteous lamentations that the poor dear was too far gone to know her best friends, and uttering sundry protestations that they would never leave her, when the superior pushed them from the room, closed the door, and returned to the bedside. On being excluded, the old ladies changed their tone, and cried through the keyhole that old Sally was drunk; which, indeed, was not unlikely, since, in addition to a moderate dose of opium prescribed by the apothecary, she was labouring under the effects of a final taste of gin and water, which had been privily administered in the openness of their hearts by the worthy old ladies themselves.

'Now listen to me!' said the dying woman aloud, as if making a great effort to revive one latent spark of energy. 'In this very room – in this very bed – I once nursed a pretty young creetur', that was brought into the house with her feet cut and bruised with walking, and all soiled with dust and blood. She gave birth to a boy, and died. Let me think – What was the year again?'

'Never mind the year,' said the impatient auditor; 'what about her?'

'Ay,' murmured the sick woman, relapsing into her former drowsy state, 'what about her? – what about – I know!' she cried, jumping fiercely up, her face flushed, and her eyes starting from her head, – 'I robbed her, so I did! She wasn't cold – I tell you she wasn't cold when I stole it!'

'Stole what, for God's sake?' cried the matron, with a gesture as if she would call for help.

'*It!*' – replied the woman, laying her hand over the other's mouth, – 'the only thing she had! She wanted clothes to keep her warm, and food to eat; but she had kept it safe, and had it in her bosom. It was gold, I tell you! – rich gold, that might have saved her life!'

'Gold!' echoed the matron, bending eagerly over the woman as she fell back. 'Go on, go on – yes – what of it? Who was the mother? – when was it?'

'She charged me to keep it safe,' replied the woman with a groan, 'and trusted me as the only woman about her. I stole it in my heart when she first showed it me hanging round her neck; and the child's death, perhaps, is on me besides! They would have treated him better if they had known it all!'

'Known what?' asked the other. 'Speak!'

'The boy grew so like his mother,' said the woman, rambling on and not heeding the question, 'that I could never forget it when I saw his face. Poor girl! poor girl! – she was so young, too! – such a gentle lamb! – Wait; there's more to tell. I have not told you all, have I?'

'No, no,' replied the matron, inclining her head to catch the words as they came more faintly from the dying woman. – 'Be quick, or it may be too late.'

'The mother,' said the woman, making a more violent effort than before, – 'the mother, when the pains of death first came upon her, whispered in my ear, that if her baby was born alive, and thrived, the day might come when it would not feel disgraced to hear its poor young mother named. "And oh, my God!" she said, folding her thin hands together, "whether it be boy or girl, raise up some friends for it in this troubled world, and take pity upon a lonely desolate child abandoned to its mercy!"'

'The boy's name?' demanded the matron.

'They *called* him Oliver,' replied the woman feebly. 'The gold I stole was—'

'Yes, yes – what?' cried the other.

She was bending eagerly over the woman to hear her reply, but drew back instinctively as she once again rose slowly and stiffly into a sitting posture, and, clutching the coverlet with both hands, muttered some indistinct sounds in her throat, and fell lifeless on the bed.

*　　*　　*　　*　　*

'Stone dead!' said one of the old women, hurrying in as soon as the door was opened.

'And nothing to tell, after all,' rejoined the matron, walking carelessly away.

The two crones were to all appearance too busily occupied in the preparations for their dreadful duties to make any reply, and were left alone hovering about the body.

CHAPTER THE THIRD

WHEREIN THIS HISTORY REVERTS TO MR FAGIN AND COMPANY

Where these things were passing in the country workhouse, Mr Fagin sat in the old den, – the same from which Oliver had been removed by the girl – brooding over a dull smoky fire. He held a pair of bellows upon his knee, with which he had apparently been endeavouring to rouse it into more cheerful action; but he had fallen into deep thought, and with his arms folded upon them, and his chin resting on his thumbs, fixed his eyes abstractedly on the rusty bars.

At a table behind him sat the Artful Dodger, Master Charles Bates, and Mr Chitling, all intent upon a game of whist; the Artful taking dummy against Master Bates and Mr Chitling. The countenance of the first-named gentleman, peculiarly intelligent at all times, acquired great additional interest from his close observance of the game, and his attentive perusal of Mr Chitling's hand, upon which, from time to time, as occasion served, he bestowed a variety of earnest glances, wisely regulating his own play by the result of his observations upon his neighbour's cards. It being a cold night, the Dodger wore his hat, as, indeed, was often his custom within doors. He also sustained a clay pipe between his teeth, which he only removed for a brief space, when he deemed it necessary to apply for refreshment to a quart-pot upon the table, which stood ready filled with gin and water for the accommodation of the company.

Master Bates was also attentive to the play; but, being of a more excitable nature than his accomplished friend, it was observable that he more frequently applied himself to the gin and water, and moreover indulged in many jests and irrelevant remarks, all highly unbecoming a scientific rubber. Indeed, the Artful, presuming upon their close attachment, more than once took occasion to reason gravely with his companion upon these improprieties: all of which remonstrances Master Bates took in extremely good part, merely requesting his friend to be 'blowed,' or to insert his hand in a sack, or replying with some other neatly-turned witticism of a similar kind, the happy application of which excited considerable admiration in the mind of Mr Chitling. It was remarkable that the latter gentleman and his partner invariably lost; and that the circumstance, so far from angering Master Bates, appeared to afford him the highest amusement, inasmuch as he laughed most uproariously at the end of every deal, and protested that he had never seen such a jolly game in all his born days.

'That's two doubles and the rub,'¹ said Mr Chitling with a very long face, as he drew half-a-crown from his waistcoat pocket. 'I never see such a feller as you, Jack; you win everything. Even when we've good cards, Charley and I can't make nothing of 'em.'

Either the matter or manner of this remark, which was made very ruefully, delighted Charley Bates so much, that his consequent shout of laughter roused the Jew from his reverie, and induced him to inquire what was the matter.

'Matter, Fagin!' cried Charley. 'I wish you had watched the play. Tommy Chitling hasn't won a point, and I went partners with him against the Artful and dum.'

'Ay, ay?' said the Jew with a grin, which sufficiently demonstrated that he was at no loss to understand the reason. 'Try 'em again, Tom; try 'em again.'

'No more of it for me, thankee, Fagin,' replied Mr Chitling; 'I've had enough. That 'ere Dodger has such a run of luck, that there's no standing again' him.'

'Ha! ha! my dear,' replied the Jew, 'you must get up very early in the morning to win against the Dodger.'

'Morning!' said Charley Bates; 'you must put your boots on over night, and have a telescope at each eye, and a opera-glass between your shoulders, if you want to come over him.'

Mr Dawkins received these handsome compliments with much philosophy, and offered to cut any gentleman in company for the first picture-card at a shilling a time. Nobody accepting the challenge, and his pipe being by this time smoked out, he proceeded to amuse himself by sketching a ground-plan of Newgate on the table with the piece of chalk which had served him in lieu of counters, whistling meantime with peculiar shrillness.

'How precious dull you are, Tommy!' said the Dodger, stopping short when there had been a long silence, and addressing Mr Chitling. 'What do you think he's thinking of, Fagin?'

'How should I know, my dear?' replied the Jew, looking round as he plied the bellows. 'About his losses, maybe, – or the little retirement in the country that he's just left, eh? – Ha! ha! Is that it, my dear?'

'Not a bit of it,' replied the Dodger, stopping the subject of discourse as Mr Chitling was about to reply. 'What do *you* say, Charley?'

'*I* should say,' replied Master Bates with a grin, 'that he was uncommon sweet upon Betsy. See how he's a-blushing! Oh, my eye! here's a merry-go-rounder! – Tommy Chitling's in love! – Oh, Fagin, Fagin! what a spree!'

Thoroughly overpowered with the notion of Mr Chitling being the victim of the tender passion, Master Bates threw himself back in his chair with such violence, that he lost his balance, and pitched over upon the floor, where (the accident abating nothing of his merriment) he lay at full length till his laugh was over, when he resumed his former position and began another.

'Never mind him, my dear,' said the Jew, winking at Mister Dawkins, and giving Master Bates a reproving tap with the nozzle of the bellows. 'Betsy's a fine girl. Stick up to her, Tom; stick up to her.'

'What I mean to say, Fagin,' replied Mr Chitling, very red in the face, 'is, that that isn't anything to anybody here.'

'No more it is,' replied the Jew: 'Charley will talk. Don't mind him, my dear; don't mind him. Betsy's a fine girl. Do as she bids you, Tom, and you'll make your fortune.'

'So I *do* do as she bids me,' replied Mr Chitling; 'I shouldn't have been milled if it hadn't been for her advice. But it turned out a good job for you; didn't it, Fagin? And what's six weeks of it? It must come some time or another, – and why not in the winter time, when you don't want to go out a-walking so much; eh, Fagin?'

'Ah, to be sure, my dear,' replied the Jew.

'You wouldn't mind it again, Tom, would you,' asked the Dodger, winking upon Charley and the Jew, 'if Bet was all right?'

'I mean to say that I shouldn't,' replied Tom angrily; 'there, now! Ah! Who'll say as much as that, I should like to know; eh, Fagin?'

'Nobody, my dear,' replied the Jew; 'not a soul, Tom. I don't know one of 'em that would do it besides you; not one of 'em, my dear.'

'I might have got clear off if I'd split upon her; mightn't I, Fagin?' angrily pursued the poor half-witted dupe. 'A word from me would have done it; wouldn't it, Fagin?'

'To be sure it would, my dear,' replied the Jew.

'But I didn't blab it; did I, Fagin?' demanded Tom, pouring question upon question with great volubility.

'No, no, to be sure,' replied the Jew; 'you were too stout-hearted for that, – a deal too stout, my dear.'

'Perhaps I was,' rejoined Tom, looking round; 'and if I was, what's to laugh at in that; eh, Fagin?'

The Jew, perceiving that Mr Chitling was considerably roused, hastened to assure him that nobody was laughing, and, to prove the gravity of the company, appealed to Master Bates, the principal offender; but unfortunately Charley, in opening his mouth to reply that he was never more serious in his life, was unable to prevent the escape of such a violent roar, that the abused Mr Chitling, without any preliminary ceremonies, rushed across the room and aimed a blow at the offender, who, being skilful in evading pursuit, ducked to avoid it, and chose his time so well, that it lighted on the chest of the merry old gentleman, and caused him to stagger to the wall, where he stood panting for breath, while Mr Chitling looked on in intense dismay.

'Hark!' cried the Dodger at this moment, 'I heard the tinkler.' Catching up the light, he crept softly up stairs.

The bell rang again with some impatience while the party were in darkness. After a short pause, the Dodger reappeared, and whispered Fagin mysteriously.

'What!' cried the Jew, 'alone?'

The Dodger nodded in the affirmative, and, shading the flame of the candle with his hand, gave Charley Bates a private intimation in dumb show that he had better not be funny just then. Having performed this friendly office, he fixed his eyes on the Jew's face, and awaited his directions.

The old man bit his yellow fingers, and meditated for some seconds, his face working with agitation the while, as if he dreaded something, and feared to know the worst. At length he raised his head.

'Where is he?' he asked.

The Dodger pointed to the floor above, and made a gesture as if to leave the room.

'Yes,' said the Jew, answering the mute inquiry; 'bring him down. Hush! – Quiet, Charley! – gently, Tom! Scarce, scarce!'

This brief direction to Charley Bates and his recent antagonist to retire, was softly and immediately obeyed. There was no sound of their whereabout when the Dodger descended the stairs bearing the light in his hand, and followed by a man in a coarse smock-frock, who, after casting a hurried glance round the room, pulled off a large shawl which had concealed the lower portion of his face, and disclosed – all haggard, unwashed, and unshaven, – the features of flash Toby Crackit.

'How are you, Fagey?' said the worthy, nodding to the Jew. 'Pop that shawl away in my castor, Dodger, so that I may know where to find it when I cut; that's the time of day! You'll be a fine young cracksman afore the old file now!'

With these words he pulled up the smock-frock, and, winding it round his middle, drew a chair to the fire, and placed his feet upon the hob.

'See there, Fagey,' he said, pointing disconsolately to his top-boots; 'not a drop of Day and Martin[2] since you know when; not a bubble of blacking, by——! but don't look at me in that way, man. All in good time; I can't talk about business till I've eat and drank; so produce the sustainance, and let's have a quiet fill-out for the first time these three days!'

The Jew motioned to the Dodger to place what eatables there were, upon the table: and, seating himself opposite the housebreaker, waited his leisure.

To judge from appearances, Toby was by no means in a hurry to open the conversation. At first the Jew contented himself with patiently watching his countenance, as if to gain from its expression some clue to the intelligence he brought; but in vain. He looked tired and worn, but there was the same complacent repose upon his features that they always wore, and through dirt, and beard, and whisker, there still shone unimpaired the self-satisfied smirk of flash Toby Crackit. Then the Jew in an agony of impatience watched every morsel he put into his mouth, pacing up and down the room meanwhile in irrepressible excitement. It was all of no use. Toby continued to eat with the utmost outward indifference until he could eat no more; and then, ordering the Dodger out, closed the door, mixed a glass of spirits and water, and composed himself for talking.

'First and foremost, Fagey,' said Toby.

'Yes, yes!' interposed the Jew, drawing up his chair.

Mr Crackit stopped to take a draught of spirits and water, and to declare that the gin was excellent; and then placing his feet against the low mantelpiece, so as to bring his boots to about the level of his eye, quietly resumed.

'First and foremost, Fagey,' said the housebreaker, 'how's Bill?'

'What!' screamed the Jew, starting from his seat.

'Why, you don't mean to say—' began Toby, turning pale.

'Mean!' cried the Jew, stamping furiously on the ground. 'Where are they? – Sikes and the boy – where are they? – where have they been? – where are they hiding? – why have they not been here?'

'The crack failed,' said Toby faintly.

'I know it,' replied the Jew, tearing a newspaper from his pocket and pointing to it. 'What more?'

'They fired, and hit the boy. We cut over the fields at the back with him between us – straight as the crow flies – through hedge and ditch. They gave chase. D— me! the whole country was awake, and the dogs upon us!'

'The boy!' gasped the Jew.

'Bill had him on his back, and scudded like the wind. We stopped to take him again between us; his head hung down, and he was cold. They were close upon our heels: every man for himself, and each from the gallows! We parted company, and left the youngster lying in a ditch. Alive or dead, that's all I know of him.'

The Jew stopped to hear no more; but uttering a loud yell, and twining his hands in his hair, rushed from the room and from the house.

*

CHAPTER THE FOURTH

IN WHICH A MYSTERIOUS CHARACTER
APPEARS UPON THE SCENE, AND MANY
THINGS INSEPARABLE FROM THIS
HISTORY ARE DONE AND PERFORMED

The old man had gained the street corner before he began to recover the effect of Toby Crackit's intelligence. He had relaxed nothing of his unusual speed, but was still pressing onward in the same wild and disordered manner, when the sudden dashing past of a carriage, and a boisterous cry from the foot-passengers who saw his danger, drove him back upon the pavement. Looking hastily round, as if uncertain whither he had been hurrying, he paused for a few moments, and turned away in quite an opposite direction to that in which he had before proceeded. Avoiding as much as possible all the main streets, and skulking only through the by ways and alleys, he at length emerged on Snow Hill. Here he walked even faster than before; nor did he linger until he had again turned into a court, when, as if conscious that he was now in his proper element, he fell into his usual shuffling pace, and seemed to breathe more freely.

Near to the spot on which Snow Hill and Holborn Hill meet, there opens, upon the right hand as you come out of the city, a narrow and dismal alley leading to Saffron Hill. In its filthy shops are exposed for sale huge bunches of second-hand silk handkerchiefs of all sizes and patterns – for here reside the traders who purchase them from pickpockets. Hundreds of these handkerchiefs hang dangling from pegs outside the windows, or flaunting from the door-posts; and the shelves within are piled with them. Confined as the limits of Field Lane[1] are, it has its barber, its coffee-shop, its beer-shop, and its fried-fish warehouse. It is a commercial colony of itself, the emporium of petty larceny, visited at early morning and setting-in of dusk by silent merchants, who traffic in dark back-parlours, and go as strangely as they came. Here the clothesman, the shoe-vamper,[2] and the rag-merchant display their goods as sign-boards to the petty thief; and stores of old iron and bones, and heaps of mildewy fragments of woollen-stuff and linen, rust and rot in the grimy cellars.

It was into this place that the Jew turned. He was well-known to the sallow denizens of the lane, for such of them as were on the look-out to buy or sell, nodded familiarly as he passed along. He replied to their salutations in the same way, but bestowed no closer recognition until he reached the further end of the alley, when he stopped to address a salesman of small stature, who had squeezed as much of his person into a child's chair as the chair would hold, and was smoking a pipe at his warehouse-door.

'Why, the sight of you, Mister Fagin, would cure the hoptalmy!'³ said this respectable trader, in acknowledgment of the Jew's inquiry after his health.

'The neighbourhood was a little too hot, Lively!' said Fagin, elevating his eyebrows, and crossing his hands upon his shoulders.

'Well! I've heerd that complaint of it once or twice before,' replied the trader, 'but it soon cools down again; don't you find it so?'

Fagin nodded in the affirmative, and, pointing in the direction of Saffron Hill, inquired whether any one was up yonder to-night.

'At the Cripples?'⁴ inquired the man.

The Jew nodded.

'Let me see!' pursued the merchant, reflecting. 'Yes; there's some half-dozen of 'em gone in, that I knows on. I don't think your friend's there.'

'Sikes is not, I suppose?' inquired the Jew, with a disappointed countenance.

'*Non istwentus*, as the lawyers say,'⁵ replied the little man, shaking his head, and looking amazingly sly. 'Have you got anything in my line to-night?'

'Nothing to-night,' said the Jew, turning away.

'Are you going up to the Cripples, Fagin?' cried the little man, calling after him. 'Stop! I don't mind if I have a drain there with you!'

But as the Jew, looking back, waved his hand to intimate that he preferred being alone; and, moreover, as the little man could not very easily disengage himself from the chair, the sign of the Cripples was, for a time, bereft of the advantage of Mr Lively's presence. By the time he had got upon his legs the Jew had disappeared; so Mr Lively, after ineffectually standing on tip-toe, in the hope of catching sight of him, again forced himself into the little chair, and, exchanging a shake of the head with a lady in the opposite shop, in which doubt and mistrust were plainly mingled, resumed his pipe with a grave demeanour.

The Three Cripples, or rather the Cripples, which was the sign by which the establishment was familiarly known to its patrons, was the same public-house in which Mr Sikes and his dog have already figured. Merely making a sign to a man in the bar, Fagin walked straight up stairs, and opening the door of a room, and softly insinuating himself into the chamber, looked anxiously about, shading his eyes with his hand, as if in search of some particular person.

The room was illuminated by two gas-lights, the glare of which was prevented, by the barred shutters and closely-drawn curtains of faded red, from being visible outside. The ceiling was blackened, to prevent its colour being injured by the flaring of the lamps; and the place was so full of dense tobacco-smoke, that at first it was scarcely possible to discern anything further. By degrees, however, as some of it cleared away through the open door, an assemblage of heads, as confused as the noises that greeted the ear, might be made out; and, as the eye grew more accustomed to the scene, the spectator gradually became aware of the presence of a numerous company, male and female, crowded round a long table, at the upper end of which sat a chairman with a hammer of office in his hand, while a professional gentleman, with a bluish nose, and his face tied up for the benefit of a tooth-ache, presided at a jingling piano in a remote corner.

As Fagin stepped softly in, the professional gentleman, running over the keys by way of prelude, occasioned a general cry of order for a song; which having subsided, a young lady proceeded to entertain the company with a ballad in four verses, between each of which the accompanyist played the melody all through as loud as he could. When this was over, the chairman gave a sentiment;[6] after which, the professional gentlemen on the chairman's right and left volunteered a duet, and sang it with great applause.

It was curious to observe some faces which stood out prominently from among the group. There was the chairman himself, the landlord of the house: a coarse, rough, heavy-built fellow, who, while the songs were proceeding, rolled his eyes hither and thither, and, seeming to give himself up to joviality, had an eye for everything that was done, and an ear for everything that was said, – and sharp ones, too. Near him were the singers, receiving with professional indifference the compliments of the company, and applying themselves in turn to a dozen proffered glasses of spirits and water tendered by their more boisterous admirers, whose countenances, expressive of almost every vice in almost every grade, irresistibly attracted the attention by their very repulsiveness. Cunning, ferocity, and drunkenness in all its stages were there in their strongest aspects; and women – some with the last lingering tinge of their early freshness almost fading as you looked, and others with every mark and stamp of their sex utterly beaten out, and presenting but one loathsome blank of profligacy and crime; some mere girls, others but young women, and none past the prime of life, – formed the darkest and saddest portion of this dreary picture.

Fagin, troubled by no grave emotions, looked eagerly from face to face while these proceedings were in progress, but apparently without meeting that of which he was in search. Succeeding at length in catching the eye of the man who occupied the chair, he beckoned to him slightly, and left the room as quietly as he had entered it.

'What can I do for you, Mr Fagin?' softly inquired the man as he followed him out to the landing. 'Won't you join us? They'll be delighted, every one of 'em.'

The Jew shook his head impatiently, and said in a whisper, 'Is *he* here?'

'No,' replied the man.

'And no news of Barney?' inquired Fagin.

'None,' replied the landlord of the Cripples, for it was he. 'He won't stir till it's all safe. Depend on it that they're on the scent down there, and that if he moved he'd blow upon the thing at once. He's all right enough, Barney is; else I should have heard of him. I'll pound it that Barney's managing properly. Let him alone for that.'

'Will *he* be here to-night?' asked the Jew, laying the same emphasis on the pronoun as before.

'Monks do you mean?' inquired the landlord, hesitating.

'Hush!' said the Jew. 'Yes.'

'Certain,' replied the man, drawing a gold watch from his fob; 'I expected him here before now. If you'll wait ten minutes, he'll be—'

'No, no,' said the Jew hastily, as though, however desirous he might be to see the person in question, he was nevertheless relieved by his absence. 'Tell him I came here to see him, and that he must come to me to-night; no, say to-morrow. As he is not here, to-morrow will be time enough.'

'Good!' said the man. 'Nothing more?'

'Not a word now,' said the Jew, descending the stairs.

'I say,' said the other, looking over the rails, and speaking in a hoarse whisper; 'what a time this would be for a sell! I've got Phil Barker here, so drunk, that a boy might take him.'

'Aha! But it's not Phil Barker's time,' said the Jew, looking up. 'Phil has something more to do before we can afford to part with him; so go back to the company, my dear, and tell them to lead merry lives — *while they last.* Ha! ha! ha!'

The landlord reciprocated the old man's laugh, and returned to his guests. The Jew was no sooner alone than his countenance resumed its former expression of anxiety and thought. After a brief reflection, he called a hack-cabriolet, and bade the man drive towards Bethnal Green. He dismissed him within some quarter of a mile of Mr Sikes's residence, and performed the short remainder of the distance on foot.

'Now,' muttered the Jew as he knocked at the door, 'if there is any deep play here, I shall have it out of you, my girl, cunning as you are.'

She was in her room, the woman said; so Fagin crept softly up-stairs, and entered it without any previous ceremony. The girl was alone, lying with her head upon the table, and her hair straggling over it. 'She has been drinking,' thought the Jew coolly, 'or perhaps she is only miserable.'

The old man turned to close the door as he made this reflection, and the noise thus occasioned roused the girl. She eyed his crafty face narrowly as she inquired whether there was any news, and listened to his recital of Toby Crackit's story. When it was concluded, she sunk into her former attitude, but spoke not a word. She pushed the candle impatiently away, and once or twice, as she feverishly changed her position, shuffled her feet upon the ground; but this was all.

During this silence, the Jew looked restlessly about the room, as if to assure himself that there were no appearances of Sikes having covertly returned. Apparently satisfied with his inspection, he coughed twice or thrice, and made as many efforts to open a conversation; but the girl heeded him no more than if he had been made of stone. At length he made another attempt, and, rubbing his hands together, said, in his most conciliatory tone,

'And where should you think Bill was now, my dear; eh?'

The girl moaned out some scarcely intelligible reply, that she could not tell; and seemed, from the half-smothered noise that escaped her, to be crying.

'And the boy, too,' said the Jew, straining his eyes to catch a glimpse of her face. 'Poor leetle child! – left in a ditch, Nance; only think!'

'The child,' said the girl, suddenly looking up, 'is better where he is, than among us: and, if no harm comes to Bill from it, I hope he lies dead in the ditch, and that his young bones may rot there.'

'What!' cried the Jew in amazement.

'Ay, I do,' returned the girl, meeting his gaze. 'I shall be glad to have him away from my eyes, and to know that the worst is over. I can't bear to have him about me: the sight of him turns me against myself and all of you.'

'Pooh!' said the Jew scornfully. 'You're drunk, girl.'

'Am I?' cried the girl bitterly. 'It's no fault of yours if I am not; you'd never have me anything else if you had your will, except now! – the humour doesn't suit you, doesn't it?'

'No!' rejoined the Jew furiously. 'It does not!'

'Change it, then!' responded the girl with a laugh.

'Change it!' exclaimed the Jew, exasperated beyond all bounds by his companion's unexpected obstinacy and the vexation of the night,

'I will change it! Listen to me, you drab![7] listen to me, who with six words can strangle Sikes as surely as if I had his bull's throat between my fingers now. If he comes back, and leaves that boy behind him, — if he gets off free, and, dead or alive, fails to restore him to me, murder him yourself if you would have him escape Jack Ketch,[8] and do it the moment he sets foot in this room, or, mind me, it will be too late!'

'What is all this?' cried the girl involuntarily.

'What is it!' pursued Fagin, mad with rage. 'This! When the boy's worth hundreds of pounds to me, am I to lose what chance threw me in the way of getting safely, through the whims of a drunken gang that I could whistle away the lives of — and me bound, too, to a born devil that only wants the will, and has got the power to, to —'

Panting for breath, the old man stammered for a word, and in that one instant checked the torrent of his wrath, and changed his whole demeanour. A moment before, his clenched hands had grasped the air, his eyes had dilated, and his face grown livid with passion; but now he shrunk into a chair, and, cowering together, trembled with the apprehension of having himself disclosed some hidden villany. After a short silence he ventured to look round at his companion, and appeared somewhat reassured on beholding her in the same listless attitude from which he had first roused her.

'Nancy dear!' croaked the Jew in his usual voice. 'Did you mind me, dear?'

'Don't worry me now, Fagin!' replied the girl, raising her head languidly. 'If Bill has not done it this time, he will another: he has done many a good job for you, and will do many more when he can; and when he can't, he won't, and so no more about that.'

'Regarding this boy, my dear?' said the Jew, rubbing the palms of his hands nervously together.

'The boy must take his chance with the rest,' interrupted Nancy hastily; 'and I say again, I hope he is dead, and out of harm's way, and out of yours, — that is, if Bill comes to no harm; and, if Toby got clear off, he's pretty sure to, for he's worth two of him any time.'

'And about what I was saying, my dear?' observed the Jew, keeping his glistening eye steadily upon her.

'You must say it all over again if it's anything you want me to do,' rejoined Nancy; 'and if it is, you had better wait till to-morrow. You put me up for a minute, but now I'm stupid again.'

Fagin put several other questions, all with the same drift of ascertaining whether the girl had profited by his unguarded hints; but she answered them so readily, and was withal so utterly unmoved by his searching looks, that his original impression of her being more than a trifle in liquor was fully confirmed. Miss Nancy, indeed, was not exempt from a failing which was very common among the Jew's female pupils, and in which in their tenderer years they were rather encouraged than checked. Her disordered appearance, and a wholesome perfume of Geneva⁹ which pervaded the apartment, afforded strong confirmatory evidence of the justice of the Jew's supposition; and when, after indulging in the temporary display of violence above described, she subsided, first into dullness, and afterwards into a compound of feelings, under the influence of which she shed tears one minute, and in the next gave utterance to various exclamations of 'Never say die!' and divers calculations as to what might be the amount of the odds so long as a lady or gentleman were happy, Mr Fagin, who had had considerable experience of such matters in his time, saw with great satisfaction that she was very far gone indeed.

Having eased his mind by this discovery, and accomplished his two-fold object of imparting to the girl what he had that night heard, and ascertaining with his own eyes that Sikes had not returned, Mr Fagin again turned his face homeward, leaving his young friend asleep with her head upon the table.

It was within an hour of midnight, and the weather being dark and piercing cold, he had no great temptation to loiter. The sharp wind that scoured the streets seemed to have cleared them of passengers as of dust and mud, for few people were abroad, and they were to all appearance hastening fast home. It blew from the right quarter for the Jew, however; and straight before it he went, trembling and shivering as every fresh gust drove him rudely on his way.

He had reached the corner of his own street, and was already fumbling in his pocket for the door-key, when a dark figure emerged from a projecting entrance which lay in deep shadow, and, crossing the road, glided up to him unperceived.

'Fagin!' whispered a voice close to his ear.

'Ah!' said the Jew, turning quickly round. 'Is that—'

'Yes!' interrupted the stranger harshly. 'I have been lingering here these two hours. Where the devil have you been?'

'On your business, my dear,' replied the Jew, glancing uneasily at his companion, and slackening his pace as he spoke. 'On your business all night.'

'Oh, of course!' said the stranger, with a sneer. 'Well; and what's come of it?'

'Nothing good,' said the Jew.

'Nothing bad, I hope!' said the stranger, stopping short, and turning a startled look upon his companion.

The Jew shook his head, and was about to reply, when the stranger, interrupting him, motioned to the house, before which they had by this time arrived, and remarked that he had better say what he had got to say, under cover, for his blood was chilled with standing about so long, and the wind blew through him.

Fagin looked as if he could have willingly excused himself from taking home a visitor at that unseasonable hour, and muttered something about having no fire; but, his companion repeating his request in a peremptory manner, he unlocked the door, and requested him to close it softly, while he got a light.

'It's as dark as the grave,' said the man, groping forward a few steps. 'Make haste; I hate this!'

'Shut the door,' whispered Fagin from the end of the passage. As he spoke, it closed with a loud noise.

'That wasn't my doing,' said the other man, feeling his way. 'The wind blew it to, or it shut of its own accord; one or the other. Look sharp with the light, or I shall knock my brains out against something in this confounded hole.'

Fagin stealthily descended the kitchen stairs, and, after a short absence, returned with a lighted candle, and the intelligence that Toby Crackit was asleep in the back-room below, and the boys in the front one. Beckoning the other man to follow him, he led the way up stairs.

'We can say the few words we've got to say, in here, my dear,' said the Jew, throwing open a door on the first floor; 'and as there are holes in the shutters, and we never show lights to our neighbours, we'll set the candle on the stairs. There!'

With these words, the Jew, stooping down, placed the candle on an upper flight of stairs exactly opposite the room door, and led the way into the apartment, which was destitute of all movables save a broken arm-chair, and an old couch or sofa, without covering, which stood behind the door. Upon this piece of furniture the stranger flung himself with the air of a weary man; and, the Jew drawing up the arm-chair opposite, they sat face to face. It was not quite dark, for the door was partially open, and the candle outside threw a feeble reflection on the opposite wall.

They conversed for some time in whispers; and, although nothing of the conversation was distinguishable beyond a few disjointed words here and there, a listener might easily have perceived that Fagin appeared to be defending himself against some remarks of the stranger, and that the latter was in a state of considerable irritation. They might have been talking thus for a quarter of an hour or more, when Monks – by which name the Jew had designated the strange man several times in the course of their colloquy – said, raising his voice a little,

'I tell you again it was badly planned. Why not have kept him here among the rest, and made a sneaking, snivelling pickpocket of him at once?'

'Only hear him!' exclaimed the Jew, shrugging his shoulders.

'Why; do you mean to say you couldn't have done it if you had chosen?' demanded Monks sternly. 'Haven't you done it with other boys scores of times? If you had had patience for a twelvemonth at most, couldn't you have got him convicted and sent safely out of the kingdom, perhaps for life?'

'Whose turn would that have served, my dear?' inquired the Jew humbly.

'Mine,' replied Monks.

'But not mine,' said the Jew submissively. 'When there are two parties to a bargain, it is only reasonable that the interest of both should be consulted; is it, my good friend?'

'What then?' demanded Monks sulkily.

'I saw it was not easy to train him to the business,' replied the Jew; 'he was not like other boys in the same circumstances.'

'Curse him, no!' muttered the man, 'or he would have been a thief long ago.'

'I had no hold upon him to make him worse,' pursued the Jew, anxiously watching the countenance of his companion; 'his hand was not in; I had nothing to frighten him with; which we always must have in the beginning, or we labour in vain. What could I do? Send him out with the Dodger and Charley? We had enough of that at first, my dear; I trembled for us all.'

'*That* was not my doing,' observed Monks.

'No, no, my dear!' renewed the Jew, 'and I don't quarrel with it now; because, if it had never happened, you might never have clapped eyes upon the boy to notice him, and so led to the discovery that it was him you were looking for. Well; I got him back for you by means of the girl, and then *she* begins to favour him.'

'Throttle the girl!' said Monks impatiently.

'Why, we can't afford to do that just now, my dear,' replied the Jew, smiling; 'and, besides, that sort of thing is not in our way, or one of these days I might be glad to have it done. I know what these girls are, Monks, well; as soon as the boy begins to harden, she'll care no more for him than for a block of wood. You want him made a thief: if he is alive, I can make him one from this time; and if – if –' said the Jew, drawing nearer to the other – 'it's not likely, mind, – but if the worst comes to the worst, and he is dead—'

'It's no fault of mine if he is!' interposed the other man with a look of terror, and clasping the Jew's arm with trembling hands. 'Mind that, Fagin! I had no hand in it. Anything but his death, I told you from the first. I won't shed blood; it's always found out, and haunts a man besides! If they shot him dead, I was not the cause; do you hear me? Fire this infernal den! – what's that?'

'What!' cried the Jew, grasping the coward round the body with both arms as he sprung to his feet. 'Where?'

'Yonder!' replied the man, glaring at the opposite wall. 'The shadow – I saw the shadow of a woman in a cloak and bonnet pass along the wainscot like a breath!'

The Jew released his hold, and they rushed tumultuously from the room. The candle, wasted by the draught, was standing where it had been placed, and showed them the empty staircases, and their own white faces. They listened intently, but a profound silence reigned throughout the house.

'It's your fancy,' said the Jew, taking up the light, and turning to his companion.

'I'll swear I saw it!' replied Monks, trembling violently. 'It was bending forward when I saw it first, and when I spoke it darted away.'

The Jew glanced contemptuously at the pale face of his associate, and, telling him he could follow if he pleased, ascended the stairs. They looked into all the rooms; they were cold, bare, and empty. They descended to the passage, and thence into the cellars below. The green damp hung upon the low walls, and the tracks of the snail and slug glistened in the light, but all was still as death.

'What do you think now, my dear?' said the Jew, when they had regained the passage. 'Besides ourselves, there's not a creature in the house except Toby and the boys, and they're safe enough. See here!'

As a proof of the fact, the Jew drew forth two keys from his pocket; and explained that when he first went down stairs he had locked them in, to prevent any intrusion on the conference.

This accumulated testimony effectually staggered Mr Monks. His protestations had gradually become less and less vehement as they proceeded in their search without making any discovery; and now he gave vent to several very grim laughs, and confessed it could only have been his excited imagination. He declined any renewal of the conversation however for that night, suddenly remembering that it was past one o'clock; and so the amiable couple parted.

CHAPTER THE FIFTH

ATONES FOR THE UNPOLITENESS OF A FORMER CHAPTER, WHICH DESERTED A LADY MOST UNCEREMONIOUSLY

As it would be by no means seemly in a humble author to keep so mighty a personage as a beadle waiting with his back to a fire, and the skirts of his coat gathered up under his arms, until such time as it might suit his pleasure to relieve him; and as it would still less become his station or his gallantry to involve in the same neglect a lady on whom that beadle had looked with an eye of tenderness and affection, and in whose ear he had whispered sweet words, which, coming from such a quarter, might well thrill the bosom of maid or matron of whatsoever degree; the faithful historian whose pen traces these words, trusting that he knows his place, and entertains a becoming reverence for those upon earth to whom high and important authority is delegated, hastens to pay them that respect which their position demands, and to treat them with all that duteous ceremony which their exalted rank and (by consequence) great virtues imperatively claim at his hands. Towards this end, indeed, he had purposed to introduce in this place a dissertation touching the divine right of beadles, and elucidative of the position that a beadle can do no wrong, which could not fail to have been both pleasurable and profitable to the right-minded reader, but which he is unfortunately compelled by want of time and space to postpone to some more convenient and fitting opportunity; on the arrival of which, he will be prepared to show that a beadle properly constituted – that is to say, a parochial beadle attached to the parochial workhouse, and attending in his official capacity the parochial church, – is, in right and virtue of his office, possessed of all the excellencies and best qualities of humanity; and that to none of those excellencies can mere companies' beadles, or court-of-law beadles, or even chapel-of-ease beadles (save the last in a very lowly and inferior degree), lay the remotest sustainable claim.

Mr Bumble had re-counted the tea-spoons, re-weighed the sugar-tongs, made a closer inspection of the milk-pot, and ascertained to a nicety the exact condition of the furniture down to the very horse-hair seats of the chairs, and had repeated each process full half-a-dozen times, before he began to think that it was time for Mrs Corney to return. Thinking begets thinking; and, as there were no sounds of Mrs Corney's approach, it occurred to Mr Bumble that it would be an innocent and virtuous way of spending the time, if he were further to allay his curiosity by a cursory glance at the interior of Mrs Corney's chest of drawers.

Having listened at the key-hole to assure himself that nobody was approaching the chamber, Mr Bumble, beginning at the bottom, proceeded to make himself acquainted with the contents of the three long drawers; which, being filled with various garments of good fashion and texture, carefully preserved between two layers of old newspaper speckled with dried lavender, seemed to yield him exceeding satisfaction. Arriving in course of time at the right-hand corner drawer (in which was the key), and beholding therein a small padlocked box, which, being shaken, gave forth a pleasant sound as of the chinking of coin, Mr Bumble returned with a stately walk to the fire-place, and, resuming his old attitude, said, with a grave and determined air, 'I'll do it!' He followed up this remarkable declaration by shaking his head in a waggish manner for ten minutes, as though he were remonstrating with himself for being such a pleasant dog; and then took a view of his legs in profile with much seeming pleasure and interest.

He was still placidly engaged in this latter survey when Mrs Corney, hurrying into the room, threw herself in a breathless state on a chair by the fire-side, and covering her eyes with one hand, placed the other over her heart, and gasped for breath.

'Mrs Corney,' said Mr Bumble, stooping over the matron, 'what is this, ma'am? has anything happened, ma'am? Pray answer me; I'm on – on –' Mr Bumble in his alarm could not immediately think of the word 'tenterhooks,'[1] so he said 'broken bottles.'

'Oh, Mr Bumble!' cried the lady, 'I have been so dreadfully put out!'

'Put out, ma'am!' exclaimed Mr Bumble; 'who has dared to –? I know!' said Mr Bumble, checking himself with native majesty, 'this is them wicious paupers!'

'It's dreadful to think of!' said the lady, shuddering.

'Then *don't* think of it, ma'am,' rejoined Mr Bumble.

'I can't help it,' whimpered the lady.

'Then take something, ma'am,' said Mr Bumble soothingly. 'A little of the wine?'

'Not for the world!' replied Mrs Corney. 'I couldn't – oh! The top shelf in the right-hand corner – oh!' Uttering these words, the good lady pointed distractedly to the cupboard, and underwent a convulsion from internal spasms. Mr Bumble rushed to the closet, and, snatching a pint green-glass bottle[2] from the shelf thus incoherently indicated, filled a tea-cup with its contents, and held it to the lady's lips.

'I'm better now,' said Mrs Corney, falling back after drinking half of it.

Mr Bumble raised his eyes piously to the ceiling in thankfulness, and, bringing them down again to the brim of the cup, lifted it to his nose.

'Peppermint,' explained Mrs Corney in a faint voice, smiling gently on the beadle as she spoke. 'Try it; there's a little – a little something else in it.'

Mr Bumble tasted the medicine with a doubtful look; smacked his lips, took another taste, and put the cup down empty.

'It's very comforting,' said Mrs Corney.

'Very much so indeed, ma'am,' said the beadle. As he spoke, he drew a chair beside the matron, and tenderly inquired what had happened to distress her.

'Nothing,' replied Mrs Corney. 'I am a foolish, excitable, weak creetur.'

'Not weak, ma'am,' retorted Mr Bumble, drawing his chair a little closer. 'Are you a weak creetur, Mrs Corney?'

'We are all weak creeturs,' said Mrs Corney, laying down a general principle.

'So we are,' said the beadle.

Nothing was said on either side for a minute or two afterwards; and by the expiration of that time Mr Bumble had illustrated the position by removing his left arm from the back of Mrs Corney's chair, where it had previously rested, to Mrs Corney's apron-string, round which it gradually became entwined.

'We are all weak creeturs,' said Mr Bumble.

Mrs Corney sighed.

'Don't sigh, Mrs Corney,' said Mr Bumble.

'I can't help it,' said Mrs Corney; and she sighed again.

'This is a very comfortable room, ma'am,' said Mr Bumble, looking round. 'Another room and this, ma'am, would be a complete thing.'

'It would be too much for one,' murmured the lady.

'But not for two, ma'am,' rejoined Mr Bumble in soft accents. 'Eh, Mrs Corney?'

Mrs Corney drooped her head when the beadle said this, and the beadle drooped his to get a view of Mrs Corney's face. Mrs Corney with great propriety turned her head away, and released her hand to get at her pocket-handkerchief, but insensibly replaced it in that of Mr Bumble.

'The board allow you coals, don't they, Mrs Corney?' affectionately inquired the beadle, pressing her hand.

'And candles,' replied Mrs Corney, slightly returning the pressure.

'Coals, candles, and house-rent free,' said Mr Bumble. 'Oh, Mrs Corney, what a angel you are!'

The lady was not proof against this burst of feeling. She sunk into Mr Bumble's arms; and that gentleman, in his agitation, imprinted a passionate kiss upon her chaste nose.

'Such porochial perfection!' exclaimed Mr Bumble rapturously. 'You know that Mr Slout is worse to-night, my fascinator?'

'Yes,' replied Mrs Corney bashfully.

'He can't live a week, the doctor says,' pursued Mr Bumble. 'He is the master of this establishment; his death will cause a wacancy; that wacancy must be filled up. Oh, Mrs Corney, what a prospect this opens! What a opportunity for a joining of hearts and housekeeping!'

Mrs Corney sobbed.

'The little word?' said Mr Bumble, bending over the bashful beauty. 'The one little, little, little word, my blessed Corney?'

'Ye – ye – yes!' sighed out the matron.

'One more,' pursued the beadle; 'compose your darling feelings for only one more. When is it to come off?'

Mrs Corney twice essayed to speak, and twice failed. At length, summoning up courage, she threw her arms round Mr Bumble's neck, and said it might be as soon as ever he pleased, and that he was 'a irresistible duck.'

Matters being thus amicably and satisfactorily arranged, the contract was solemnly ratified in another tea-cup-full of the peppermint mixture, which was rendered the more necessary by the flutter and agitation of the lady's spirits. While it was being disposed of, she acquainted Mr Bumble with the old woman's decease.

'Very good,' said that gentleman, sipping his peppermint. 'I'll call at Sowerberry's as I go home, and tell him to send to-morrow morning. Was it that as frightened you, love?'

'It wasn't anything particular, dear,' said the lady evasively.

'It must have been something, love,' urged Mr Bumble. 'Won't you tell your own B.?'

'Not now,' rejoined the lady; 'one of these days, – after we're married, dear.'

'After we're married!' exclaimed Mr Bumble. 'It wasn't any impudence from any of them male paupers as —'

'No, no, love!' interposed the lady hastily.

'If I thought it was,' continued Mr Bumble, – 'if I thought any one of 'em had dared to lift his wulgar eyes to that lovely countenance –'

'They wouldn't have dared to do it, love,' responded the lady.

'They had better not!' said Mr Bumble, clenching his fist. 'Let me see any man, porochial or extra-porochial, as would presume to do it, and I can tell him that he wouldn't do it a second time!'

Unembellished by any violence of gesticulation, this might have sounded as no very high compliment to the lady's charms; but, as Mr Bumble accompanied the threat with many warlike gestures, she was much touched with this proof of his devotion, and protested with great admiration that he was indeed a dove.

The dove then turned up his coat-collar, and put on his cocked-hat, and, having exchanged a long and affectionate embrace with his future partner, once again braved the cold wind of the night; merely pausing for a few minutes in the male paupers' ward to abuse them a little, with the view of satisfying himself that he could fill the office of workhouse-master with needful acerbity. Assured of his qualifications, Mr Bumble left the building with a light heart, and bright visions of his future promotion, which served to occupy his mind until he reached the shop of the undertaker.

Now, Mr and Mrs Sowerberry having gone out to tea and supper, and Noah Claypole not being at any time disposed to take upon himself a greater amount of physical exertion than is necessary to a convenient performance of the two functions of eating and drinking, the shop was not closed, although it was past the usual hour of shutting-up. Mr Bumble tapped with his cane on the counter several times; but, attracting no attention, and beholding a light shining through the glass-window of the little parlour at the back of the shop, he made bold to peep in and see what was going forward; and, when he saw what was going forward, he was not a little surprised.

The cloth was laid for supper, and the table was strewed with bread and butter, plates and glasses, a porter-pot, and a wine-bottle. At the upper end of the table Mr Noah Claypole lolled negligently in an easy-chair with his legs thrown over one of the arms, an open clasp-knife in one hand, and a mass of buttered bread in the other; close beside him stood Charlotte, opening oysters from a barrel,[3] which Mr Claypole condescended to swallow with remarkable avidity. A more than ordinary redness in the region of the young gentleman's nose, and a kind of fixed wink in his right eye, denoted that he was in a slight degree intoxicated; and these symptoms were confirmed by the intense relish with which he took his oysters, for which nothing but a strong appreciation of their cooling properties in cases of internal fever could have sufficiently accounted.

'Here's a delicious fat one, Noah dear!' said Charlotte; 'try him, do; only this one.'

'What a delicious thing is a oyster!' remarked Mr Claypole after he had swallowed it. 'What a pity it is a number of 'em should ever make you feel uncomfortable, isn't it, Charlotte?'

'It's quite a cruelty,' said Charlotte.

'So it is,' acquiesced Mr Claypole. 'Ain't yer fond of oysters?'

'Not overmuch,' replied Charlotte. 'I like to see you eat 'em, Noah dear, better than eating them myself.'

'Lor'!' said Noah reflectively; 'how queer!'

'Have another?' said Charlotte. 'Here's one with such a beautiful, delicate beard!'

Mr Claypole as he appeared when his master was out

'I can't manage any more,' said Noah. 'I'm very sorry. Come here, Charlotte, and I'll kiss yer.'

'What!' said Mr Bumble, bursting into the room. 'Say that again, sir.'

Charlotte uttered a scream, and hid her face in her apron; while Mr Claypole, without making any further change in his position than suffering his legs to reach the ground, gazed at the beadle in drunken terror.

'Say it again, you vile, owdacious fellow!' said Mr Bumble. 'How dare you mention such a thing, sir? and how dare you encourage him, you insolent minx? Kiss her!' exclaimed Mr Bumble in strong indignation. 'Faugh!'

'I didn't mean to do it!' said Noah, blubbering. 'She's always a-kissing of me, whether I like it or not.'

'Oh, Noah!' cried Charlotte reproachfully.

'Yer are, yer know yer are!' retorted Noah. 'She's always a-doing of it, Mr Bumble, sir; she chucks me under the chin, please sir, and makes all manner of love!'

'Silence!' cried Mr Bumble sternly. 'Take yourself down stairs, ma'am! Noah, you shut up the shop, and say another word till your master comes home at your peril; and, when he does come home, tell him that Mr Bumble said he was to send a old woman's shell after breakfast to-morrow morning. Do you hear, sir? Kissing!' cried Mr Bumble, holding up his hands. 'The sin and wickedness of the lower orders in this porochial district is frightful; if parliament don't take their abominable courses under consideration, this country's ruined, and the character of the peasantry gone for ever!' With these words the beadle strode, with a lofty and gloomy air, from the undertaker's premises.

And now that we have accompanied him so far on his road home, and have made all necessary preparations for the old woman's funeral, let us set on foot a few inquiries after young Oliver Twist, and ascertain whether he be still lying in the ditch where Toby Crackit left him.

*

CHAPTER THE SIXTH

LOOKS AFTER OLIVER, AND PROCEEDS WITH HIS ADVENTURES

'Wolves tear your throats!' muttered Sikes, grinding his teeth; 'I wish I was among some of you; you'd howl the hoarser for it.'

As Sikes growled forth this imprecation with the most desperate ferocity that his desperate nature was capable of, he rested the body of the wounded boy across his bended knee, and turned his head for an instant to look back at his pursuers.

There was little to be made out in the mist and darkness; but the loud shouting of men vibrated through the air, and the barking of the neighbouring dogs, roused by the sound of the alarm bell, resounded in every direction.

'Stop, you white-livered hound!' cried the robber, shouting after Toby Crackit who, making the best use of his long legs, was already ahead, – 'stop!'

The repetition of the word brought Toby to a dead standstill, for he was not quite satisfied that he was beyond the range of pistol shot, and Sikes was in no mood to be played with.

'Bear a hand with the boy,' roared Sikes, beckoning furiously to his confederate. 'Come back!'

Toby made a show of returning, but ventured in a low voice, broken for want of breath, to intimate considerable reluctance as he came slowly along.

'Quicker!' cried Sikes, laying the boy in a dry ditch at his feet, and drawing a pistol from his pocket. 'Don't play the booby with me.'

At this moment the noise grew louder, and Sikes again looking round, could discern that the men who had given chase were already climbing the gate of the field in which he stood, and that a couple of dogs were some paces in advance of them.

'It's all up, Bill,' cried Toby, 'drop the kid and show 'em your heels.' With this parting advice, Mr Crackit, preferring the chance of being shot by his friend to the certainty of being taken by his enemies, fairly turned tail, and darted off at full speed. Sikes clenched his teeth, took one look round, threw over the prostrate form of Oliver the cape in which he had been hurriedly muffled, ran along the front of the hedge as if to distract the attention of those behind, from the spot where the boy lay, paused for a second before another hedge which met it at right angles, and whirling his pistol high into the air, cleared it at a bound and was gone.

'Ho, ho, there!' cried a tremulous voice in the rear. 'Pincher, Neptune, come here, come here!'

The dogs, which in common with their masters, seemed to have no particular relish for the sport in which they were engaged, readily answered to this command: and three men, who had by this time advanced some distance into the field, stopped to take counsel together.

'My advice, or leastways I should say, my *orders* is,' said the fattest man of the party, 'that we 'mediately go home again.'

'I am agreeable to anything which is agreeable to Mr Giles,' said a shorter man, who was by no means of a slim figure, and who was very pale in the face, and very polite, as frightened men frequently are.

'I shouldn't wish to appear ill-mannered, gentlemen,' said the third, who had called the dogs back, 'Mr Giles ought to know.'

'Certainly,' replied the shorter man; 'and whatever Mr Giles says, it isn't our place to contradict him. No, no, I know my sitiwation, – thank my stars I know my sitiwation.' To tell the truth, the little man *did* seem to know his situation, and to know perfectly well that it was by no means a desirable one, for his teeth chattered in his head as he spoke.

'You are afraid, Brittles,' said Mr Giles.

'I ain't,' said Brittles.

'You are,' said Giles.

'You're a falsehood, Mr Giles,' said Brittles.

'You're a lie, Brittles,' said Mr Giles.

Now, these four retorts arose from Mr Giles's taunt, and Mr Giles's taunt had arisen from his indignation at having the responsibility of going home again imposed upon himself under cover of a compliment. The third man brought the dispute to a close most philosophically.

'I'll tell you what it is, gentlemen,' said he, 'we're all afraid.'

'Speak for yourself, sir,' said Mr Giles, who was the palest of the party.

'So I do,' replied the man. 'It's natural and proper to be afraid, under such circumstances: *I* am.'

'So am I,' said Brittles, 'only there's no call to tell a man he is, so bounceably.'

These frank admissions softened Mr Giles, who at once owned that *he* was afraid; upon which they all three faced about and ran back again with the completest unanimity, till Mr Giles (who had the shortest wind of the party, and was encumbered with a pitchfork) most handsomely insisted upon stopping to make an apology for his hastiness of speech.

'But it's wonderful,' said Mr Giles, when he had explained, 'what a man will do when his blood is up. I should have committed murder, I know I should, if we'd caught one of the rascals.'

As the other two were impressed with a similar presentiment, and their blood, like his, had all gone down again, some speculation ensued upon the cause of this sudden change in their temperament.

'I know what it was,' said Mr Giles; 'it was the gate.'

'I shouldn't wonder if it was,' exclaimed Brittles, catching at the idea.

'You may depend upon it,' said Giles, 'that that gate stopped the flow of the excitement. I felt all mine suddenly going away as I was climbing over it.'

By a remarkable coincidence the other two had been visited with the same unpleasant sensation at that precise moment; so that it was quite conclusive that it was the gate, especially as there was no doubt regarding the time at which the change had taken place, because all three remembered that they had come in sight of the robbers at the very instant of its occurrence.

This dialogue was held between the two men who had surprised the burglars, and a travelling tinker,[1] who had been sleeping in an outhouse, and who had been roused, together with his two mongrel curs, to join in the pursuit. Mr Giles acted in the double capacity of butler and steward to the old lady of the mansion, and Brittles was a lad of all work, who having entered her service a mere child, was treated as a promising young boy still, though he was something past thirty.

Encouraging each other with such converse as this, but keeping very close together notwithstanding, and looking apprehensively round whenever a fresh gust rattled through the boughs, the three men hurried back to a tree, behind which they had left their lantern, lest its light should inform the thieves in what direction to fire. Catching up the light, they made the best of their way home at a good round trot; and long after their dusky forms had ceased to be discernible, it might have been seen twinkling and dancing in the distance, like some exhalation of the damp and gloomy atmosphere through which it was swiftly borne.

The air grew colder as day came slowly on, and the mist rolled along the ground like a dense cloud of smoke; the grass was wet, the pathways and low places were all mire and water, and the damp breath of an unwholesome wind went languidly by with a hollow moaning. Still Oliver lay motionless and insensible on the spot where Sikes had left him.

Morning drew on apace; the air became more sharp and piercing as its first dull hue – the death of night rather than the birth of day – glimmered faintly in the sky. The objects which had looked dim and terrible in the darkness grew more and more defined, and gradually resolved into their familiar shapes. The rain came down thick and fast, and pattered noisily among the leafless bushes. But Oliver felt it not, as it beat against him, for he still lay stretched, helpless and unconscious, on his bed of clay.

At length a low cry of pain broke the stillness that prevailed, and uttering it, the boy awoke. His left arm, rudely bandaged in a shawl, hung heavy and useless at his side, and the bandage was saturated with blood. He was so weak that he could scarcely raise himself into a sitting posture, and when he had done so, he looked feebly round for help and groaned with pain. Trembling in every joint from cold and exhaustion, he made an effort to stand upright, but shuddering from head to foot, fell prostrate on the ground.

After a short return of the stupor in which he had been so long plunged, Oliver, urged by a creeping sickness at his heart, which seemed to warn him that if he lay there he must surely die, got upon his feet and essayed to walk. His head was dizzy, and he staggered to and fro like a drunken man; but he kept up nevertheless, and, with his head drooping languidly on his breast, went stumbling onward he knew not whither.

And now, hosts of bewildering and confused ideas came crowding on his mind. He seemed to be still walking between Sikes and Crackit, who were angrily disputing, for the very words they said sounded in his ears: and when he caught his own attention, as it were, by making some violent effort to save himself from falling, he found that he was talking to them. Then he was alone with Sikes plodding on as they had done the previous day, and as shadowy people passed them by, he felt the robber's grasp upon his wrist. Suddenly he started back at the report of fire-arms, and there rose into the air loud cries and shouts; lights gleamed before his eyes, and all was noise and tumult as some unseen hand bore him hurriedly away. Through all these rapid visions there ran an undefined, uneasy, consciousness of pain which wearied and tormented him incessantly.

Thus he staggered on, creeping almost mechanically between the bars of gates, or through hedge-gaps as they came in his way, until he reached a road; and here the rain began to fall so heavily that it roused him.

He looked about, and saw that at no great distance there was a house, which perhaps he could reach. Seeing his condition they might have compassion on him, and if they did not, it would be better, he thought, to die near human beings than in the lonely open fields. He summoned up all his strength for one last trial, and bent his faltering steps towards it.

As he drew nearer to this house, a feeling came over him that he had seen it before. He remembered nothing of its details, but the shape and aspect of the building seemed familiar to him. That garden wall! On the grass inside he had fallen on his knees last night, and prayed the two men's mercy. It was the very same house they had attempted to rob.

Oliver felt such fear come over him when he recognised the place, that for the instant he forgot the agony of his wound, and thought only of flight. Flight! He could scarcely stand; and if he were in full possession of all the best powers of his slight and youthful frame, where could he fly to? He pushed against the garden gate; it was unlocked and swung open on its hinges. He tottered across the lawn, climbed the steps, knocked faintly at the door, and his whole strength failing him, sunk down against one of the pillars of the little portico.

It happened that about this time Mr Giles, Brittles, and the tinker were recruiting themselves after the fatigues and terrors of the night, with tea and sundries in the kitchen. Not that it was Mr Giles's habit to admit to too great familiarity the humbler servants, towards whom it was rather his wont to deport himself with a lofty affability, which, while it gratified, could not fail to remind them of his superior position in society. But death, fires, and burglary make all men equals; and Mr Giles sat with his legs stretched out before the kitchen fender, leaning his left arm on the table, while with his right he illustrated a circumstantial and minute account of the robbery, to which his hearers (but especially the cook and housemaid, who were of the party) listened with breathless interest.

'It was about half-past two,' said Mr Giles, 'or I wouldn't swear that it mightn't have been a little nearer three, when I woke up, and turning round in my bed, as it might be so, (here Mr Giles turned round in his chair, and pulled the corner of the table-cloth over him to imitate bed-clothes,) I fancied I heerd a noise.'

At this point of the narrative the cook turned pale, and asked the housemaid to shut the door, who asked Brittles, who asked the tinker, who pretended not to hear.

'Heerd a noise,' continued Mr Giles, 'I says at first, "this is illusion;" and was composing myself off to sleep when I heerd the noise again, distinct.'

'What sort of a noise?' asked the cook.

'A kind of a busting² noise,' replied Mr Giles, looking round him.

'More like the noise of powdering a iron bar on a nutmeg-grater,' suggested Brittles.

'It was, when *you* heerd it, sir,' rejoined Mr Giles; 'but at this time it had a busting sound. I turned down the clothes,' continued Giles, rolling back the table-cloth, 'sat up in bed, and listened.'

The cook and housemaid simultaneously ejaculated, 'Lor!' and drew their chairs closer together.

'I heard it now, quite apparent,' resumed Mr Giles.

'"Somebody," I says, "is forcing of a door or window, what's to be done! I'll call up that poor lad, Brittles, and save him from being murdered in his bed; or his throat," I says, "may be cut from his right ear to his left, without his ever knowing it."'

Here all eyes were turned upon Brittles, who fixed his upon the speaker, and stared at him with his mouth wide open, and his face expressive of the most unmitigated horror.

'I tossed off the clothes,' said Giles, throwing away the table-cloth, and looking very hard at the cook and housemaid, 'got softly out of bed, drew on a pair of –'

'Ladies present, Mr Giles,' murmured the tinker.

'– Of *shoes*, sir,' said Giles, turning upon him, and laying great emphasis on the word, 'seized the loaded pistol that always goes up stairs with the plate-basket, and walked on tip-toes to his room. "Brittles," I says, when I had woke him, "don't be frightened!"'

'So you did,' observed Brittles, in a low voice.

'"We're dead men, I think, Brittles, I says,"' continued Giles, '"but don't be under any alarm."'

'*Was* he frightened?' asked the cook.

'Not a bit of it,' replied Mr Giles. 'He was as firm – ah! pretty near as firm as I was.'

'I should have died at once, I'm sure, if it had been me,' observed the housemaid.

'You're a woman,' retorted Brittles, plucking up a little.

'Brittles is right,' said Mr Giles, nodding his head approvingly; 'from a woman nothing else was to be expected. But we, being men, took a dark lantern that was standing on Brittles's hob, and groped our way down stairs in the pitch dark, – as it might be so.'

Mr Giles had risen from his seat and taken two steps with his eyes shut to accompany his description with appropriate action, when he started violently in common with the rest of the company, and hurried back to his chair. The cook and housemaid screamed.

'It was a knock,' said Mr Giles, assuming perfect serenity; 'open the door, somebody.'

Nobody moved.

'It seems a strange sort of thing, a knock coming at such a time in the morning,' said Mr Giles, surveying the pale faces which surrounded him, and looking very blank himself; 'but the door must be opened. Do you hear, somebody?'

Mr Giles, as he spoke, looked at Brittles; but that young man being naturally modest, probably considered himself nobody, and so held that the inquiry could not have any application to him. At all events he tendered no reply. Mr Giles directed an appealing glance at the tinker, but he had suddenly fallen asleep. The women were out of the question.

'If Brittles would rather open the door in the presence of witnesses,' said Mr Giles, after a short silence, 'I am ready to make one.'

'So am I,' said the tinker, waking up as suddenly as he had fallen asleep.

Brittles capitulated on these terms; and the party being somewhat re-assured by the discovery (made on throwing open the shutters) that it was now broad day, took their way up stairs with the dogs in front, and the two women, who were afraid to stop below, bringing up the rear. By the advice of Mr Giles they all talked very loud, to warn any evil-disposed person outside that they were strong in numbers; and by a masterstroke of policy, originating in the brain of the same ingenious gentleman, the dog's tails were well pinched in the hall to make them bark savagely.

These precautions having been taken, Mr Giles held on fast by the tinker's arm, (to prevent his running away, as he pleasantly said), and gave the word of command to open the door. Brittles obeyed, and the group peeping timorously over each other's shoulder, beheld no more formidable object than poor little Oliver Twist, speechless and exhausted, who raised his heavy eyes, and mutely solicited their compassion.

'A boy!' exclaimed Mr Giles, valiantly pushing the tinker into the

Oliver Twist at Mrs Maylie's door

background. 'What's the matter with the – eh? – Why – Brittles – look here – don't you know?'

Brittles, who had got behind the door to open it, no sooner saw Oliver, than he uttered a loud cry of recognition. Mr Giles seizing the boy by one leg and one arm – fortunately not the broken limb – lugged him straight into the hall, and deposited him at full length on the floor thereof. 'Here he is!' bawled Giles, calling in a great state of excitement up the staircase; 'here's one of the thieves, ma'am! Here's a thief, miss – wounded, miss! I shot him, miss, and Brittles held the light.'

'In a lantern, miss,' cried Brittles, applying one hand to the side of his mouth, so that his voice might travel the better.

The two women servants ran up stairs to carry the intelligence that Mr Giles had captured a robber; and the tinker busied himself in endeavouring to restore Oliver, lest he should die before he could be hung. In the midst of all this noise and commotion there was heard a sweet female voice which quelled it in an instant.

'Giles!' whispered the voice from the stairhead.

'I'm here, miss,' replied Mr Giles. 'Don't be frightened, miss; I ain't much injured. He didn't make a very desperate resistance, miss; I was soon too many for him.'

'Hush!' replied the young lady; 'you frighten my aunt almost as much as the thieves did. Is the poor creature severely hurt?'

'Wounded desperate, miss,' replied Giles, with indescribable complacency.

'He looks as if he was a-going, miss,' bawled Brittles, in the same manner as before. 'Wouldn't you like to come and look at him, miss, in case he should –?'

'Hush, pray, there's a good man!' rejoined the young lady. 'Wait quietly one instant while I speak to aunt.'

With a footstep as soft and gentle as the voice, the speaker tripped away, and soon returned with the direction that the wounded person was to be carried carefully up stairs to Mr Giles's room, and that Brittles was to saddle the pony and betake himself instantly to Chertsey, from which place he was to despatch with all speed a constable and doctor.

'But won't you take one look at him first, miss?' said Giles, with as much pride as if Oliver were some bird of rare plumage that he had skilfully brought down. 'Not one little peep, miss.'

'Not now for the world,' replied the young lady. 'Poor fellow! oh! treat him kindly, Giles, if it is only for my sake!'

The old servant looked up at the speaker, as she turned away, with a glance as proud and admiring as if she had been his own child. Then bending over Oliver, he helped to carry him up stairs with the care and solicitude of a woman.

CHAPTER THE SEVENTH

HAS AN INTRODUCTORY ACCOUNT OF THE INMATES OF THE HOUSE TO WHICH OLIVER RESORTED, AND RELATES WHAT THEY THOUGHT OF HIM

In a handsome room – though its furniture had rather the air of old-fashioned comfort, than of modern elegance – there sat two ladies at a well-spread breakfast table. Mr Giles, dressed with scrupulous care in a full suit of black, was in attendance upon them. He had taken his station some half-way between the sideboard and the breakfast-table, and with his body drawn up to its full height, his head thrown back and inclined the merest trifle on one side, his left leg advanced, and his right hand thrust into his waistcoat, while his left hung down by his side grasping a waiter,[1] looked like one who laboured under a very agreeable sense of his own merits and importance.

Of the two ladies, one was well advanced in years, but the high-backed oaken chair in which she sat was not more upright than she. Dressed with the utmost nicety and precision in a quaint mixture of bygone costume, with some slight concessions to the prevailing taste, which rather served to point the old style pleasantly than to impair its effect, she sat in a stately manner with her hands folded on the table before her, and her eyes, of which age had dimmed but little of their brightness, attentively fixed upon her young companion.

The younger lady was in the lovely bloom and spring-time of womanhood; at that age when, if ever angels be for God's good purposes enthroned in mortal forms, they may be without impiety supposed to abide in such as hers.

She was not past seventeen. Cast in so slight and exquisite a mould, so mild and gentle, so pure and beautiful, that earth seemed not her element, nor its rough creatures her fit companions. The very intelligence that shone in her deep blue eye and was stamped upon her noble head, seemed scarcely of her age or of the world, and yet the changing expression of sweetness and good humour, the thousand lights that played about the face and left no shadow there; above all, the smile – the cheerful happy smile – were entwined with the best sympathies and affections of our nature.

She was busily engaged in the little offices of the table, and chancing to raise her eyes as the elder lady was regarding her, playfully put back her hair, which was simply braided on her forehead, and threw into one beaming look such a gush of affection and artless loveliness, that blessed spirits might have smiled to look upon her.

The elder lady smiled; but her heart was full, and she brushed away a tear as she did so.

'And Brittles has been gone upwards of an hour, has he?' asked the old lady after a pause.

'An hour and twelve minutes, ma'am;' replied Mr Giles, referring to a silver watch which he drew forth by a black ribbon.

'He is always slow,' remarked the old lady.

'Brittles always was a slow boy, ma'am,' replied the attendant. And seeing, by-the-by, that Brittles had been a slow boy for upwards of thirty years, there appeared no great probability of his ever being a fast one.

'He gets worse instead of better, I think,' said the elder lady.

'It is very inexcusable in him if he stops to play with any other boys,' said the young lady, smiling.

Mr Giles was apparently considering the propriety of indulging in a respectful smile himself, when a gig[2] drove up to the garden-gate, out of which there jumped a fat gentleman, who ran straight up to the door, and getting quickly into the house by some mysterious process, burst into the room, and nearly overturned Mr Giles and the breakfast table together.

'I never heard of such a thing!' exclaimed the fat gentleman. 'My dear Mrs Maylie – bless my soul – in the silence of night too – I *never* heard of such a thing!'

With these expressions of condolence, the fat gentleman shook hands with both ladies, and drawing up a chair, inquired how they found themselves.

'You ought to be dead – positively dead with the fright,' said the fat gentleman. 'Why didn't you send? Bless me, my man should have come in a minute, or I myself and my assistant would have been delighted, or anybody: I'm sure, under such circumstances; dear, dear – so unexpected – in the silence of night too!'

The doctor seemed especially troubled by the fact of the robbery having been unexpected, and attempted in the night time, as if it were the established custom of gentlemen in the housebreaking way to transact business at noon, and to make an appointment by the twopenny post[3] a day or two previous.

'And you, Miss Rose,' said the doctor, turning to the young lady, 'I—'

'Oh! very much so, indeed,' said Rose, interrupting him; 'but there is a poor creature up stairs whom aunt wishes you to see.'

'Ah! to be sure,' replied the doctor, 'so there is. That was your handy-work, Giles, I understand.'

Mr Giles, who had been feverishly putting the tea-cups to rights, blushed very red, and said that he had had that honour.

'Honour, eh?' said the doctor; 'well, I don't know, perhaps it's as honourable to hit a thief in a back kitchen, as to hit your man at twelve paces. Fancy that he fired in the air, and you've fought a duel, Giles.'

Mr Giles, who thought this light treatment of the matter an unjust attempt at diminishing his glory, answered respectfully, that it was not for the like of him to judge about that, but he rather thought it was no joke to the opposite party.

' 'Gad, that's true!' said the doctor. 'Where is he? Show me the way. I'll look in again as I come down, Mrs Maylie. That's the little window that he got in at, eh? Well, I couldn't have believed it.' Talking all the way, he followed Mr Giles up stairs; and while he is going up stairs the reader may be informed, that Mr Losberne, a surgeon, in the neighbourhood, known through a circuit of ten miles round as 'the doctor,' had grown fat more from good humour than from good living, and was as kind and hearty, and withal as eccentric an old bachelor as will be found in five times that space by any explorer alive.

The doctor was absent much longer than either he or the ladies had anticipated. A large flat box was fetched out of the gig, and a bed-room bell was rung very often, and the servants ran up and down stairs perpetually, from which tokens it was justly concluded that something important was going on above. At length he returned; and in reply to an anxious inquiry after his patient, looked very mysterious, and closed the door carefully.

'This is a very extraordinary thing, Mrs Maylie,' said the doctor, standing with his back to the door as if to keep it shut.

'He is not in danger, I hope?' said the old lady.

'Why, that would not be an extraordinary thing, under the circumstances,' replied the doctor, 'though I don't think he is. Have you seen this thief?'

'No,' rejoined the old lady.

'Nor heard anything about him?'

'No.'

'I beg your pardon, ma'am,' interposed Mr Giles; 'but I was going to tell you about him when Doctor Losberne came in.'

The fact was, that Mr Giles had not at first been able to bring his mind to the avowal that he had only shot a boy. Such commendations had been bestowed upon his bravery, that he could not for the life of him help postponing the explanation for a few delicious minutes, during which he had flourished in the very zenith of a brief reputation for undaunted courage.

'Rose wished to see the man,' said Mrs Maylie, 'but I wouldn't hear of it.'

'Humph!' rejoined the doctor. 'There's nothing very alarming in his appearance. Have you any objection to see him in my presence?'

'If it be necessary,' replied the old lady, 'certainly not.'

'Then I think it is necessary,' said the doctor; 'at all events I am quite sure that you would deeply regret not having done so, if you postponed it. He is perfectly quiet and comfortable now. Allow me – Miss Rose, will you permit me? not the slightest fear, I pledge you my honour.'

With many more loquacious assurances that they would be agreeably surprised in the aspect of the criminal, the doctor drew the young lady's arm through one of his, and offering his disengaged hand to Mrs Maylie, led them with much ceremony and stateliness up stairs.

'Now,' said the doctor in a whisper as he softly turned the handle of a bed-room door, 'let us hear what you think of him. He has not been shaved very recently, but he doesn't look at all ferocious notwithstanding. Stop, though: let me see that he is in visiting order first.'

Stepping before them, he looked into the room, and motioning them to advance, closed the door when they had entered, and gently drew back the curtains of the bed. Upon it, in lieu of the dogged, black-visaged ruffian they had expected to behold, there lay a mere child, worn with pain and exhaustion and sunk into a deep sleep. His wounded arm, bound and splintered up, was crossed upon his breast, and his head reclined upon the other, which was half hidden by his long hair as it streamed over the pillow.

The honest gentleman held the curtain in his hand, and looked on for a minute or so, in silence. Whilst he was watching the patient thus, the younger lady glided softly past, and seating herself in a chair by the bedside gathered Oliver's hair from his face, and as she stooped over him, her tears fell upon his forehead.

The boy stirred and smiled in his sleep, as though these marks of pity and compassion had awakened some pleasant dream of a love and affection he had never known; as a strain of gentle music, or the rippling of water in a silent place, or the odour of a flower, or even the mention of a familiar word, will sometimes call up sudden dim remembrances of scenes that never were, in this life, which vanish like a breath, and which some brief memory of a happier existence long gone by, would seem to have awakened, for no power of the human mind can ever recal them.

'What can this mean!' exclaimed the elder lady. 'This poor child can never have been the pupil of robbers.'

'Vice,' sighed the surgeon, replacing the curtain, 'takes up her abode in many temples, and who can say that a fair outside shall not enshrine her?'

'But at so early an age,' urged Rose.

'My dear young lady,' rejoined the surgeon, mournfully shaking his head, 'crime, like death, is not confined to the old and withered alone. The youngest and fairest are too often its chosen victims.'

'But, can you – oh, sir! can you, really believe that this delicate boy has been the voluntary associate of the worst outcasts of society?' said Rose anxiously.

The surgeon shook his head in a manner which intimated that he feared it was very possible; and observing that they might disturb the patient, led the way into an adjoining apartment.

'But even if he has been wicked,' pursued Rose, 'think how young he is; think that he may never have known a mother's love, or even the comfort of a home, and that ill-usage and blows, or the want of bread, may have driven him to herd with the men who have forced him to guilt. Aunt, dear aunt, for mercy's sake think of this before you let them drag this sick child to a prison, which in any case must be the grave of all his chances of amendment. Oh! as you love me, and know that I have never felt the want of parents in your goodness and affection, but that I might have done so, and might have been equally helpless and unprotected with this poor child, have pity upon him before it is too late.'

'My dear love!' said the elder lady, as she folded the weeping girl to her bosom; 'do you think I would harm a hair of his head?'

'Oh, no!' replied Rose, eagerly, 'not you, aunt, not you!'

'No;' said the old lady with a trembling lip, 'my days are drawing to their close, and may mercy be shown to me as I show it to others. What can I do to save him, sir?'

'Let me think, ma'am,' said the doctor, 'let me think.'

Mr Losberne thrust his hands into his pockets and took several turns up and down the room, often stopping and balancing himself on his toes and frowning frightfully. After various exclamations of 'I've got it now,' and 'no, I haven't,' and as many renewals of the walking and frowning, he at length made a dead halt, and spoke as follows: –

'I think if you give me a full and unlimited commission to bully Giles and that little boy, Brittles, I can manage it. He is a faithful fellow and an old servant, I know; but you can make it up to him in a thousand ways, and reward him for being such a good shot besides. You don't object to that?'

'Unless there is some other way of preserving the child,' replied Mrs Maylie.

'There is no other,' said the doctor. 'No other, take my word for it.'

'Then aunt invests you with full power,' said Rose, smiling through her tears; 'but pray don't be harder upon the poor fellows than is indispensably necessary.'

'You seem to think,' retorted the doctor, 'that everybody is disposed to be hard-hearted to-day except yourself. I only hope, for the sake of the rising male sex generally, that you may be found in as vulnerable and soft-hearted a mood by the very first eligible young fellow who appeals to your compassion; and I wish *I* were a young fellow that I might avail myself on the spot of such a favourable opportunity for doing so, as the present.'

'You are as great a boy as poor Brittles himself,' returned Rose, blushing.

'Well,' said the doctor, laughing heartily, 'that is no very difficult matter. But to return to this boy: the great point of our agreement is yet to come. He will wake in an hour or so, I dare say; and although I have told that thick-headed constable fellow[4] down stairs that he musn't be moved or spoken to, on peril of his life, I think we may converse with him without danger. Now, I make this stipulation – that I shall examine him in your presence, and that if from what he says, we judge, and I can show to the satisfaction of your cool reason, that he is a real and thorough bad one, (which is more than possible,) he shall be left to his fate, without any further interference, on my part, at all events.'

'Oh, no, aunt!' entreated Rose.

'Oh, yes, aunt!' said the doctor. 'Is it a bargain?'

'He cannot be hardened in vice,' said Rose; 'it is impossible.'

'Very good,' retorted the doctor; 'then so much the more reason for acceding to my proposition.'

Finally the treaty was entered into, and the parties thereto sat down to wait with some impatience until Oliver should wake.

The patience of the two ladies was destined to undergo a longer trial than Mr Losberne had led them to expect, for hour after hour passed on, and still Oliver slumbered heavily. It was evening, indeed, before the kind-hearted doctor brought them the intelligence that he had at length roused sufficiently to be spoken to. The boy was very ill, he said, and weak from the loss of blood; but his mind was so troubled with anxiety to disclose something, that he deemed it better to give him the opportunity than to insist upon his remaining quiet until next morning, which he should otherwise have done.

The conference was a long one, for Oliver told them all his simple history, and was often compelled to stop by pain and want of strength. It was a solemn thing to hear, in the darkened room, the feeble voice of the sick child recounting a weary catalogue of evils and calamities which hard men had brought upon him. Oh! if, when we oppress and grind our fellow-creatures, we bestowed but one thought on the dark evidences of human error, which, like dense and heavy clouds are rising slowly, it is true, but not less surely, to heaven, to pour their after-vengeance on our heads – if we heard but one instant in imagination the deep testimony of dead men's voices, which no power can stifle and no pride shut out, where would be the injury and injustice, the suffering, misery, cruelty, and wrong, that each day's life brings with it!

Oliver's pillow was smoothed by woman's hands that night, and loveliness and virtue watched him as he slept. He felt calm and happy, and could have died without a murmur.

The momentous interview was no sooner concluded, and Oliver composed to rest again, than the doctor, after wiping his eyes and condemning them in the usual phrase for being weak all at once, betook himself down stairs to open upon Mr Giles. And finding nobody about the parlours, it occurred to him that he could perhaps originate the proceedings with better effect in the kitchen; so into the kitchen he went.

There were assembled in that lower house of the domestic parliament, the women servants, Mr Brittles, Mr Giles, the tinker, (who had received a special invitation to regale himself for the remainder of the day in consideration of his services,) and the constable. The latter gentleman had a large staff, a large head, large features, and large half-boots, and looked as if he had been taking a proportionate allowance of ale, as indeed he had.

The adventures of the previous night were still under discussion, for Mr Giles was expatiating upon his presence of mind when the doctor entered; and Mr Brittles, with a mug of ale in his hand, was corroborating everything before his superior said it.

'Sit still,' said the doctor, waving his hand.

'Thank you, sir,' said Mr Giles. 'Misses wished some ale to be given out, sir, and as I felt noways inclined for my own little room, sir, and disposed for company, I am taking mine among 'em here.'

Brittles headed a low murmur by which the ladies and gentlemen generally, were understood to express the gratification they derived from Mr Giles's condescension; and Mr Giles looked round with a patronising air, as much as to say, that so long as they behaved properly, he would never desert them.

'How is the patient to-night, sir?' asked Giles.

'So-so;' returned the doctor. 'I am afraid you have got yourself into a scrape there, Mr Giles.'

'I hope you don't mean to say, sir,' said Mr Giles, trembling, 'that he's going to die. If I thought it, I should never be happy again. I wouldn't cut a boy off, no, not even Brittles here, not for all the plate in the country, sir.'

'That's not the point,' said the doctor mysteriously. 'Mr Giles, are you a Protestant?'

'Yes, sir, I hope so;' faltered Mr Giles, who had turned very pale.

'And what are you, boy?' said the doctor, turning sharply upon Brittles.

'Lord bless me, sir!' replied Brittles, starting violently; 'I'm the same as Mr Giles, sir.'

'Then tell me this,' said the doctor fiercely, 'both of you – both of you: are you going to take upon yourselves to swear that that boy up stairs is the boy that was put through the little window last night! Out with it! Come; we are prepared for you.'

The doctor, who was universally considered one of the best-tempered creatures on earth, made this demand in such a dreadful tone of anger, that Giles and Brittles, who were considerably muddled by ale and excitement, stared at each other in a state of stupefaction.

'Pay attention to the reply, constable, will you,' said the doctor, shaking his forefinger with great solemnity of manner, and tapping the bridge of his nose with it, to bespeak the exercise of that worthy's utmost acuteness. 'Something may come of this before long.'

The constable looked as wise as he could, and took up his staff of office which had been reclining indolently in the chimney-corner.

'It's a simple question of identity, you will observe,' said the doctor.

'That's what it is, sir,' replied the constable, coughing with great violence; for he had finished his ale in a hurry, and some of it had gone the wrong way.

'Here's a house broken into,' said the doctor, 'and a couple of men catch one moment's glimpse of a boy in the midst of gunpowder smoke, and in all the distraction of alarm and darkness. Here's a boy comes to that very same house next morning, and because he happens to have his arm tied up, those men lay violent hands upon him – by doing which, they place his life in great danger – and swear he is the thief. Now, the question is, whether those men are justified by the fact, and if not, what situation do they place themselves in?'

The constable nodded profoundly, and said that if that wasn't law, he should be glad to know what was.

'I ask you again,' thundered the doctor, 'are you on your solemn oaths able to identify that boy?'

Brittles looked doubtfully at Mr Giles, Mr Giles looked doubtfully at Brittles; the constable put his hand behind his ear to catch the reply; the two women and the tinker leant forward to listen; and the doctor glanced keenly round, when a ring was heard at the gate, and at the same moment the sound of wheels.

'It's the runners!' cried Brittles, to all appearance much relieved.

'The what!' exclaimed the doctor, aghast in his turn.

'The Bow-street officers,[5] sir,' replied Brittles, taking up a candle, 'me and Mr Giles sent for 'em this morning.'

'What!' cried the doctor.

'Yes,' replied Brittles, 'I sent a message up by the coachman, and I only wonder they weren't here before, sir.'

'You did, did you. Then confound and damn your — slow coaches down here; that's all,' said the doctor, walking away.

*

CHAPTER THE EIGHTH

INVOLVES A CRITICAL POSITION

'Who's that?' inquired Brittles, opening the door a little way with the chain up, and peeping out, shading the candle with his hand.

'Open the door,' replied a man outside: 'it's the officers from Bow-street that was sent to, to-day.'

Much comforted by this assurance, Brittles opened the door to its full width, and confronted a portly man in a great coat, who walked in without saying anything more, and wiped his shoes on the mat as coolly as if he lived there.

'Just send somebody out to relieve my mate, will you, young man?' said the officer: 'he's in the gig minding the prad. Have you got a coach'us here that you could put it up in for five or ten minutes?'

Brittles, replying in the affirmative, and pointing out the building, the portly man stepped back to the garden gate, and helped his companion to put up the gig, while Brittles lighted them in a state of great admiration. This done, they returned to the house, and, being shown into a parlour, took off their great-coats and hats, and showed like what they were. The man who had knocked at the door was a stout personage of middle height, aged about fifty, with shiny black hair, cropped pretty close, half-whiskers, a round face, and sharp eyes. The other was a red-headed bony man, in top-boots, with a rather ill-favoured countenance, and a turned-up sinister-looking nose.

'Tell your governor that Blathers and Duff is here, will you?' said the stouter man, smoothing down his hair, and laying a pair of handcuffs on the table. 'Oh! Good evening, master. Can I have a word or two with you in private, if you please?'

This was addressed to Mr Losberne, who now made his appearance; and that gentleman, motioning Brittles, to retire, brought in the two ladies and shut the door.

'This is the lady of the house,' said Mr Losberne, motioning towards Mrs Maylie.

Mr Blathers made a bow, and, being desired to sit down, put his hat upon the floor, and, taking a chair, motioned Duff to do the same. The latter gentleman, who did not appear quite so much accustomed to good society, or quite so much at his ease in it, one of the two, seated himself, after undergoing several muscular affections of the limbs, and forced the head of his stick into his mouth with some embarrassment.

'Now, with regard to this here robbery, master,' said Blathers. 'What are the circumstances?'

Mr Losberne, who appeared desirous of gaining time, recounted them at great length and with much circumlocution: Messrs Blathers and Duff looking very knowing meanwhile, and occasionally exchanging a nod.

'I can't say for certain till I see the place, of course,' said Blathers; 'but my opinion at once is, — I don't mind committing myself to that extent, — that this wasn't done by a yokel — eh, Duff?'

'Certainly not,' replied Duff.

'And, translating the word yokel for the benefit of the ladies, I apprehend your meaning to be that this attempt was not made by a countryman?' said Mr Losberne with a smile.

'That's it, master,' replied Blathers. 'This is all about the robbery, is it?'

'All,' replied the doctor.

'Now, what is this about this here boy that the servants are talking of?' said Blathers.

'Nothing at all,' replied the doctor. 'One of the frightened servants chose to take it into his head that he had something to do with this attempt to break into the house; but it's nonsense – sheer absurdity.'

'Wery easy disposed of it is,' remarked Duff.

'What he says is quite correct,' observed Blathers, nodding his head in a confirmatory way, and playing carelessly with the handcuffs, as if they were a pair of castanets. 'Who is the boy? What account does he give of himself? Where did he come from? He didn't drop out of the clouds, did he, master?'

'Of course not,' replied the doctor with a nervous glance at the two ladies. 'I know his whole history; – but we can talk about that presently. You would like to see the place where the thieves made their attempt, first, I suppose?'

'Certainly,' rejoined Mr Blathers. 'We had better inspect the premises first, and examine the servants arterwards. That's the usual way of doing business.'

Lights were then procured, and Messrs Blathers and Duff, attended by the native constable, Brittles, Giles, and everybody else in short, went into the little room at the end of the passage, and looked out at the window, and afterwards went round by way of the lawn, and looked in at the window, and after that had a candle handed out to inspect the shutter with, and after that a lantern to trace the footsteps with, and after that a pitchfork to poke the bushes with. This done amidst the breathless interest of all beholders, they came in again, and Mr Giles and Brittles were put through a melo-dramatic representation of their share in the previous night's adventures, which they performed some six times over, contradicting each other in not more than one important respect the first time, and in not more than a dozen the last. This consummation being arrived at, Blathers and Duff cleared the room, and held a long council together, compared with which, for secrecy and solemnity, a consultation of great doctors on the knottiest point in medicine would be mere child's play.

Meanwhile the doctor walked up and down the next room in a very uneasy state, and Mrs Maylie and Rose looked on with anxious faces.

'Upon my word,' he said, making a halt after a great number of very rapid turns, 'I hardly know what to do.'

'Surely,' said Rose, 'the poor child's story, faithfully repeated to these men, will be sufficient to exonerate him.'

'I doubt it, my dear young lady,' said the doctor, shaking his head. 'I don't think it would exonerate him, either with them or with legal functionaries of a higher grade. What is he, after all, they would say – a runaway. Judged by mere worldly considerations and probabilities, his story is a very doubtful one.'

'You credit it, surely?' interrupted Rose in haste.

'*I* believe it, strange as it is, and perhaps may be an old fool for doing so,' rejoined the doctor; 'but I don't think it is exactly the tale for a practised police officer, nevertheless.'

'Why not?' demanded Rose.

'Because, my pretty cross-examiner,' replied the doctor, 'because, viewed with their eyes, there are so many ugly points about it; he can only prove the parts that look bad, and none of those that look well. Confound the fellows, they will have the why and the wherefore, and take nothing for granted. On his own showing, you see, he has been the companion of thieves for some time past; he has been carried to a police-office on a charge of picking a gentleman's pocket, and is taken away forcibly from that gentleman's house to a place which he cannot describe or point out, and of the situation of which he has not the remotest idea. He is brought down to Chertsey by men who seem to have taken a violent fancy to him, whether he will or no, and put through a window to rob a house, and then, just at the very moment when he is going to alarm the inmates, and so do the very thing that would set him all to rights, there rushes into the way that blundering dog of a half-bred butler and shoots him, as if on purpose to prevent his doing any good for himself. Don't you see all this?'

'I see it, of course,' replied Rose, smiling at the doctor's impetuosity; 'but still I do not see anything in it to criminate the poor child.'

'No,' replied the doctor; 'of course not! Bless the bright eyes of your sex! They never see, whether for good or bad, more than one side of any question; and that is, invariably, the one which first presents itself to them.'

Having given vent to this result of experience, the doctor put his hands into his pockets, and walked up and down the room with even greater rapidity than before.

'The more I think of it,' said the doctor, 'the more I see that it will occasion endless trouble and difficulty to put these men into possession of the boy's real story. I am certain it will not be believed; and, even if they can do nothing to him in the end, still the dragging it forward, and giving publicity to all the doubts that will be cast upon it, must interfere materially with your benevolent plan of rescuing him from misery.'

'Oh! what is to be done?' cried Rose. 'Dear, dear! why did they send for these people?'

'Why, indeed!' exclaimed Mrs Maylie. 'I would not have had them here for the world!'

'All I know is,' said Mr Losberne at last, sitting down with a kind of desperate calmness, 'that we must try and carry it off with a bold face, that's all! The object is a good one, and that must be the excuse. The boy has strong symptoms of fever upon him, and is in no condition to be talked to any more; that's one comfort. We must make the best of it we can; and, if bad's the best, it's no fault of ours. Come in.'

'Well, master,' said Blathers, entering the room, followed by his colleague, and making the door fast before he said any more. 'This warn't a put-up thing.'

'And what the devil's a put-up thing!' demanded the doctor impatiently.

'We call it a put-up robbery, ladies,' said Blathers, turning to them, as if he compassioned their ignorance, but had a contempt for the doctor's, 'when the servants is in it.'

'Nobody suspected them in this case,' said Mrs Maylie.

'Wery likely not, ma'am,' replied Blathers, 'but they might have been in it, for all that.'

'More likely on that wery account,' said Duff.

'We find it was a town hand,' said Blathers, continuing his report; 'for the style of work is first-rate.'

'Wery pretty indeed, it is,' remarked Duff in an under tone.

'There was two of 'em in it,' continued Blathers, 'and they had a boy with 'em; that's plain, from the size of the window. That's all to be said at present. We'll see this lad that you've got up stairs at once, if you please.'

'Perhaps they will take something to drink first, Mrs Maylie?' said the doctor, his face brightening up as if some new thought had occurred to him.

'Oh! To be sure!' exclaimed Rose eagerly. 'You shall have it immediately, if you will.'

'Why, thank you, Miss!' said Blathers, drawing his coat-sleeve across his mouth: 'it's dry work this sort of duty. Anything that's handy, Miss; don't put yourself out of the way on our accounts.'

'What shall it be?' asked the doctor, following the young lady to the sideboard.

'A little drop of spirits, master, if it's all the same,' replied Blathers. 'It's a cold ride from London, ma'am, and I always find that spirits comes home warmer to the feelings.'

This interesting communication was addressed to Mrs Maylie, who received it very graciously. While it was being conveyed to her, the doctor slipped out of the room.

'Ah!' said Mr Blathers, not holding his wine-glass by the stem, but grasping the bottom between the thumb and forefinger of his left hand, and placing it in front of his chest. 'I have seen a good many pieces of business like this in my time, ladies.'

'That crack down in the back lane at Edmonton, Blathers,' said Mr Duff, assisting his colleague's memory.

'That was something in this way, warn't it?' rejoined Mr Blathers; 'that was done by Conkey Chickweed, that was.'

'You always gave that to him,' replied Duff. 'It was the Family Pet, I tell you, and Conkey hadn't any more to do with it than I had.'

'Get out!' retorted Mr Blathers: 'I know better. Do you mind that time Conkey was robbed of his money, though? What a start that was! better than any novel-book I ever see!'

'What was that?' inquired Rose, anxious to encourage any symptoms of good humour in the unwelcome visitors.

'It was a robbery, Miss, that hardly anybody would have been down upon,' said Blathers. 'This here Conkey Chickweed—'

'Conkey means Nosey, ma'am,' interposed Duff.

'Of course the lady knows that, don't she?' demanded Mr Blathers. 'Always interrupting you are, partner. This here Conkey Chickweed, Miss, kept a public-house over Battle-bridge way, and had a cellar where a good many young lords went to see cockfighting, and badger-drawing,[1] and that; and a wery intellectual manner the sports was conducted in, for I've seen 'em off'en. He warn't one of the family at that time; and one night he was robbed of three hundred and twenty-seven guineas in a canvas-bag, that was stole out of his bedroom in the dead of night by a tall man with a black patch over his eye, who had concealed himself under the bed, and, after committing the robbery, jumped slap out of window, which was only a story high. He was wery quick about it. But Conkey was quick, too, for he was woke by the noise, and, darting out of bed, fired a blunderbuss[2] arter him, and roused the neighbourhood. They set up a hue-and-cry directly, and, when they came to look about 'em, found that Conkey had hit the robber; for there was traces of blood all the way to some palings a good distance off, and there they lost 'em. However he had made off with the blunt, and, consequently, the name of Mr Chickweed, licensed witler, appeared in the Gazette[3] among the other bankrupts; and all manner of benefits and subscriptions, and I don't know what all, was got up for the poor man, who was in a wery low state of mind about his loss, and went up and down the streets for three or four days, pulling his hair off in such a desperate manner that many people was afraid he might be going to make away with himself. One day he come up to the office all in a hurry, and had a private interview with the magistrate, who, after a good deal of talk, rings the bell, and orders Jem Spyers in, (Jem was a active officer,) and tells him to go and assist Mr Chickweed in apprehending the man that robbed his house. "I see him, Spyers," said Chickweed, "pass my house yesterday morning." – "Why didn't you up, and collar him?" says Spyers. – "I was so struck all of a heap that you might have fractured my skull with a toothpick," says the poor man; "but we're sure to have him, for between ten and eleven o'clock at night he passed again." Spyers no sooner heard this, than he put some clean linen and a comb in his pocket, in case he should have to stop a day or two; and away he goes, and sets himself down at one of the public-house windows behind a little red curtain, with his hat on, all ready to bolt at a moment's notice. He was smoking his pipe here late at night, when all of a sudden Chickweed roars out – "Here he is! Stop thief! Murder!" Jem Spyers dashed out; and there he sees Chickweed tearing down the street full-cry. Away goes Spyers; on keeps Chickweed; round turn the people; everybody roars out "Thieves!" and Chickweed himself keeps on shouting all the time like mad. Spyers loses sight of him a minute as he turns a corner, – shoots round – sees a little crowd – dives in. "Which is the man?" – "D – me!" says Chickweed, "I've lost him again!"

'It was a remarkable occurrence, but he warn't to be seen nowhere, so they went back to the public house, and next morning Spyers took his old place, and looked out from behind the curtain for a tall man with a black patch over his eye, till his own two eyes ached again. At last he couldn't help shutting 'em to ease 'em a minute, and the wery moment he did so, he hears Chickweed roaring out, "Here he is!" Off he starts once more, with Chickweed half way down the street ahead of him; and, after twice as long a run as the yesterday's one, the man's lost again! This was done once or twice more, till one half the neighbours gave out that Mr Chickweed had been robbed by the devil who was playing tricks with him arterwards, and the other half that poor Mr Chickweed had gone mad with grief.'

'What did Jem Spyers say?' inquired the doctor, who had returned to the room shortly after the commencement of the story.

'Jem Spyers,' resumed the officer, 'for a long time said nothing at all, and listened to everything without seeming to, which showed he understood his business. But one morning he walked into the bar, and, taking out his snuff-box, said, "Chickweed, I've found out who's done this here robbery." – "Have you?" said Chickweed. "Oh, my dear Spyers, only let me have wengeance, and I shall die contented! Oh, my dear Spyers, where is the villain?" – "Come!" said Spyers, offering him a pinch of snuff, "none of that gammon! You did it yourself." So he had, and a good bit of money he had made by it, too; and nobody would ever have found it out if he hadn't been so precious anxious to keep up appearances, that's more!' said Mr Blathers, putting down his wine-glass, and clinking the handcuffs together.

'Very curious, indeed,' observed the doctor. 'Now, if you please, you can walk up stairs.'

'If *you* please, sir,' returned Mr Blathers. And, closely following Mr Losberne, the two officers ascended to Oliver's bedroom, Mr Giles preceding the party with a lighted candle.

Oliver had been dozing, but looked worse, and was more feverish than he had appeared yet. Being assisted by the doctor, he managed to sit up in bed for a minute or so, and looked at the strangers without at all understanding what was going forward, and, in fact, without seeming to recollect where he was, or what had been passing.

'This,' said Mr Losberne, speaking softly, but with great vehemence notwithstanding, 'this is the lad, who, being accidentally wounded by a spring-gun in some boyish trespass on Mr What-d'ye-call-him's grounds at the back here, comes to the house for assistance this morning, and is immediately laid hold of, and maltreated by that ingenious gentleman with the candle in his hand, who has placed his life in considerable danger, as I can professionally certify.'

Messrs Blathers and Duff looked at Mr Giles as he was thus recommended to their notice, and the bewildered butler gazed from them towards Oliver, and from Oliver towards Mr Losberne, with a most ludicrous mixture of fear and perplexity.

'You don't mean to deny that, I suppose?' said the doctor, laying Oliver gently down again.

'It was all done for the – for the best, sir!' answered Giles. 'I am sure I thought it was the boy, or I wouldn't have meddled with him. I am not of an inhuman disposition, sir.'

'Thought it was what boy?' inquired the senior officer.

'The housebreaker's boy, sir!' replied Giles. 'They – they certainly had a boy.'

'Well, do you think so now?' inquired Blathers.

'Think what, now?' replied Giles, looking vacantly at his questioner.

'Think it's the same boy, stupid-head?' rejoined Mr Blathers impatiently.

'I don't know; I really don't know,' said Giles, with a rueful countenance. 'I couldn't swear to him.'

'What do you think?' asked Mr Blathers.

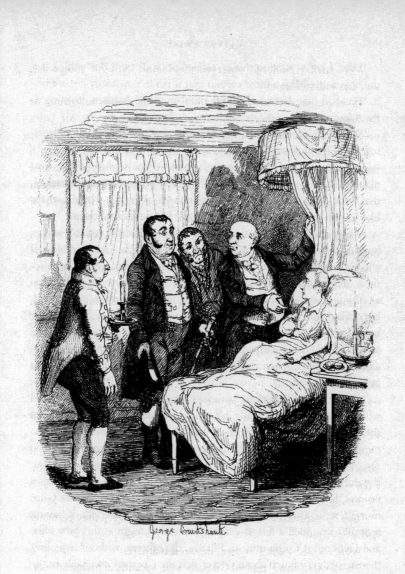

Oliver waited on by the Bow Street Runners

'I don't know what to think,' replied poor Giles. 'I don't think it is the boy; indeed I'm almost certain that it isn't. You know it can't be.'

'Has this man been a-drinking, sir?' inquired Blathers, turning to the doctor.

'What a precious muddle-headed chap you are!' said Duff, addressing Mr Giles with supreme contempt.

Mr Losberne had been feeling the patient's pulse during this short dialogue; but he now rose from the chair by the bedside, and remarked, that if the officers had any doubts upon the subject they would perhaps like to step into the next room, and have Brittles before them.

Acting upon this suggestion, they accordingly adjourned to a neighbouring apartment, where Mr Brittles being called in, involved himself and his respected superior in such a wonderful maze of fresh contradictions and impossibilities as tended to throw no particular light upon anything save the fact of his own strong mystification; except, indeed, his declarations that he shouldn't know the real boy if he were put before him that instant; that he had only taken Oliver to be he because Mr Giles had said he was, and that Mr Giles had five minutes previously admitted in the kitchen that he began to be very much afraid he had been a little too hasty.

Among other ingenious surmises, the question was then raised whether Mr Giles had really hit anybody, and upon examination of the fellow pistol to that which he had fired, it turned out to have no more destructive loading than gunpowder and brown paper: – a discovery which made a considerable impression on everybody but the doctor, who had drawn the ball about ten minutes before. Upon no one, however, did it make a greater impression than on Mr Giles himself, who, after labouring for some hours under the fear of having mortally wounded a fellow-creature, eagerly caught at this new idea, and favoured it to the utmost. Finally, the officers, without troubling themselves very much about Oliver, left the Chertsey constable in the house, and took up their rest for that night in the town, promising to return next morning.

With the next morning there came a rumour that two men and a boy were in the cage at Kingston,[4] who had been apprehended overnight under suspicious circumstances; and to Kingston Messrs Blathers and Duff journeyed accordingly. The suspicious circumstances, however, resolving themselves, on investigation, into the one fact that they had been discovered sleeping under a haystack, which, although a great crime, is only punishable by imprisonment,[5] and is, in the merciful eye of the English law, and its comprehensive love of all the King's subjects, held to be no satisfactory proof in the absence of all other evidence, that the sleeper or sleepers have committed burglary accompanied with violence, and have therefore rendered themselves liable to the punishment of death, – Messrs Blathers and Duff came back again as wise as they went.

In short, after some more examination, and a great deal more conversation, a neighbouring magistrate was readily induced to take the joint bail of Mrs Maylie and Mr Losberne for Oliver's appearance if he should ever be called upon; and Blathers and Duff, being rewarded with a couple of guineas,[6] returned to town with divided opinions on the subject of their expedition: the latter gentleman, on a mature consideration of all the circumstances, inclining to the belief that the burglarious attempt had originated with the Family Pet, and the former being equally disposed to concede the full merit of it to the great Mr Conkey Chickweed.

Meanwhile Oliver gradually throve and prospered under the united care of Mrs Maylie, Rose, and the kind-hearted Mr Losberne. If fervent prayers gushing from hearts overcharged with gratitude be heard in heaven, – and if they be not, what prayers are? – the blessings which the orphan child called down upon them, sunk into their souls, diffusing peace and happiness.

CHAPTER THE NINTH

OF THE HAPPY LIFE OLIVER BEGAN TO LEAD WITH HIS KIND FRIENDS

Oliver's ailings were neither slight nor few. In addition to the pain and delay attendant upon a broken limb, his exposure to the wet and cold had brought on fever and ague, which hung about him for many weeks, and reduced him sadly. But at length he began by slow degrees to get better, and to be able to say sometimes, in a few tearful words, how deeply he felt the goodness of the two sweet ladies, and how ardently he hoped that when he grew strong and well again he could do something to show his gratitude; only something which would let them see the love and duty with which his breast was full; something, however slight, which would prove to them that their gentle kindness had not been cast away, but that the poor boy, whom their charity had rescued from misery or death, was eager and anxious to serve them with all his heart and soul.

'Poor fellow!' said Rose, when Oliver had been one day feebly endeavouring to utter the words of thankfulness that rose to his pale lips. 'You shall have many opportunities of serving us, if you will. We are going into the country, and my aunt intends that you shall accompany us. The quiet place, the pure air, and all the pleasures and beauties of spring, will restore you in a few days, and we will employ you in a hundred ways when you can bear the trouble.'

'The trouble!' cried Oliver. 'Oh! dear lady, if I could but work for you, – if I could only give you pleasure by watering your flowers, or watching your birds, or running up and down the whole day long to make you happy, what would I give to do it!'

'You shall give nothing at all,' said Miss Maylie smiling; 'for, as I told you before, we shall employ you in a hundred ways; and if you only take half the trouble to please us that you promise now, you will make me very happy indeed.'

'Happy, ma'am!' cried Oliver: 'oh, how kind of you to say so!'

'You will make me happier than I can tell you,' replied the young lady. 'To think that my dear good aunt should have been the means of rescuing any one from such sad misery as you have described to us, would be an unspeakable pleasure to me; but to know that the object of her goodness and compassion was sincerely grateful and attached in consequence, would delight me more than you can well imagine. Do you understand me?' she inquired, watching Oliver's thoughtful face.

'Oh, yes, ma'am, yes!' replied Oliver eagerly; 'but I was thinking that I am ungrateful now.'

'To whom?' inquired the young lady.

'To the kind gentleman and the dear old nurse who took so much care of me before,' rejoined Oliver. 'If they knew how happy I am, they would be pleased, I am sure.'

'I am sure they would,' rejoined Oliver's benefactress; 'and Mr Losberne has already been kind enough to promise that when you are well enough to bear the journey he will carry you to see them.'

'Has he, ma'am!' cried Oliver, his face brightening with pleasure. 'I don't know what I shall do for joy when I see their kind faces once again!'

In a short time Oliver was sufficiently recovered to undergo the fatigue of this expedition; and one morning he and Mr Losberne set out accordingly in a little carriage which belonged to Mrs Maylie. When they came to Chertsey Bridge, Oliver turned very pale, and uttered a loud exclamation.

'What's the matter with the boy!' cried the doctor, as usual all in a bustle. 'Do you see anything – hear anything – feel anything – eh?'

'That, sir,' cried Oliver, pointing out of the carriage window. 'That house!'

'Yes; well, what of it? Stop, coachman. Pull up here,' cried the doctor. 'What of the house, my man – eh?'

'The thieves – the house they took me to,'[1] whispered Oliver.

'The devil it is!' cried the doctor. 'Halloa, there! let me out!' But before the coachman could dismount from his box he had tumbled out of the coach by some means or other, and, running down to the deserted tenement, began kicking at the door like a madman.

'Halloa!' said a little ugly hump-backed man, opening the door so suddenly that the doctor, from the very impetus of his last kick, nearly fell forward into the passage. 'What's the matter here?'

'Matter!' exclaimed the other, collaring him without a moment's reflection. 'A good deal. Robbery is the matter.'

'There'll be murder too,' replied the hump-backed man coolly, 'if you don't take your hands off. Do you hear me?'

'I hear you,' said the doctor, giving his captive a hearty shake. 'Where's – confound the fellow, what's his rascally name – Sikes – that's it. Where's Sikes, you thief?'

The hump-backed man stared as if in excess of amazement and indignation; and, twisting himself dexterously from the doctor's grasp, growled forth a volley of horrid oaths, and retired into the house. Before he could shut the door, however, the doctor had passed into the parlour without a word of parley. He looked anxiously round: not an article of furniture, not a vestige of anything, animate or inanimate, not even the position of the cupboards, answered Oliver's description!

'Now,' said the hump-backed man, who had watched him keenly, 'what do you mean by coming into my house in this violent way? Do you want to rob me, or to murder me? – which is it?'

'Did you ever know a man come out to do either in a chariot and pair,[2] you ridiculous old vampire?' said the irritable doctor.

'What do you want then?' demanded the hunchback fiercely. 'Will you take yourself off before I do you a mischief? curse you!'

'As soon as I think proper,' said Mr Losberne, looking into the other parlour, which, like the first, bore no resemblance whatever to Oliver's account of it. 'I shall find you out some day, my friend.'

'Will you?' sneered the ill-favoured cripple. 'If you ever want me, I'm here. I haven't lived here mad, and all alone, for five-and-twenty years, to be scared by you. You shall pay for this; you shall pay for this.' And so saying, the misshapen little demon set up a hideous yell, and danced upon the ground as if frantic with rage.

'Stupid enough, this,' muttered the doctor to himself: 'the boy must have made a mistake. There; put that in your pocket, and shut yourself up again.' With these words he flung the hunchback a piece of money, and returned to the carriage.

The man followed to the chariot door, uttering the wildest imprecations and curses all the way; but as Mr Losberne turned to speak to the driver, he looked into the carriage, and eyed Oliver for an instant with a glance so sharp and fierce, and at the same time so furious and vindictive, that, waking or sleeping, he could not forget it for months afterwards. He continued to utter the most fearful imprecations until the driver had resumed his seat, and when they were once more on their way, they could see him some distance behind, beating his feet upon the ground, and tearing his hair in transports of frenzied rage.

'I am an ass!' said the doctor after a long silence. 'Did you know that before, Oliver?'

'No, sir.'

'Then don't forget it another time.'

'An ass,' said the doctor again after a further silence of some minutes. 'Even if it had been the right place, and the right fellows had been there, what could I have done single-handed? And if I had had assistance, I see no good that I should have done except leading to my own exposure, and an unavoidable statement of the manner in which I have hushed up this business. That would have served me right, though. I am always involving myself in some scrape or other by acting upon these impulses, and it might have done me good.'

Now the fact was, that the excellent doctor had never acted upon anything else but impulse all through his life; and it was no bad compliment to the nature of the impulses which governed him, that so far from being involved in any peculiar troubles or misfortunes, he had the warmest respect and esteem of all who knew him. If the truth must be told, he was a little out of temper for a minute or two at being disappointed in procuring corroborative evidence of Oliver's story on the very first occasion on which he had a chance of obtaining any. He soon came round again, however, and finding that Oliver's replies to his questions were still as straight-forward and consistent, and still delivered with as much apparent sincerity and truth, as they had ever been, he made up his mind to attach full credence to them from that time forth.

As Oliver knew the name of the street in which Mr Brownlow

resided, they were enabled to drive straight thither. When the coach turned into it, his heart beat so violently that he could scarcely draw his breath.

'Now, my boy, which house is it?' inquired Mr Losberne.

'That, that!' replied Oliver, pointing eagerly out of the window. 'The white house. Oh! make haste! Pray make haste! I feel as if I should die: it makes me tremble so.'

'Come, come!' said the good doctor, patting him on the shoulder. 'You will see them directly, and they will be over-joyed to find you safe and well.'

'Oh! I hope so!' cried Oliver. 'They were so good to me; so very, very good to me, sir.'

The coach rolled on. It stopped. No; that was the wrong house. The next door. It went on a few paces, and stopped again. Oliver looked up at the windows with tears of happy expectation coursing down his face.

Alas! the white house was empty, and there was a bill in the window – 'To Let.'

'Knock at the next door,' cried Mr Losberne, taking Oliver's arm in his. 'What has become of Mr Brownlow, who used to live in the adjoining house, do you know?'

The servant did not know; but would go and enquire. She presently returned, and said that Mr Brownlow had sold off his goods, and gone to the West Indies six weeks before. Oliver clasped his hands, and sank feebly backwards.

'Has his housekeeper gone too?' inquired Mr Losberne, after a moment's pause.

'Yes, sir,' replied the servant. 'The old gentleman, the housekeeper, and a gentleman, a friend of Mr Brownlow's, all went together.'

'Then turn towards home again,' said Mr Losberne to the driver, 'and don't stop to bait the horses till you get out of this confounded London!'

'The book-stall keeper, sir?' said Oliver. 'I know the way there. See him, pray sir! Do see him!'

'My poor boy, this is disappointment enough for one day,' said the doctor. 'Quite enough for both of us. If we go to the book-stall keeper's we shall certainly find that he is dead, or has set his house on fire, or run away. No; home again straight!' And, in obedience to the doctor's first impulse, home they went.

This bitter disappointment caused Oliver much sorrow and grief even in the midst of his happiness; for he had pleased himself many times during his illness with thinking of all that Mr Brownlow and Mrs Bedwin would say to him, and what delight it would be to tell them how many long days and nights he had passed in reflecting upon what they had done for him, and bewailing their cruel separation. The hope of eventually clearing himself with them, too, and explaining how he had been forced away, had buoyed him up and sustained him under many of his recent trials; and now the idea that they should have gone so far, and carried with them the belief that he was an impostor and robber, – a belief which might remain uncontradicted to his dying day, – was almost more than he could bear.

The circumstance occasioned no alteration, however, in the behaviour of his benefactors. After another fortnight, when the fine warm weather had fairly begun, and every tree and flower was putting forth its young leaves and rich blossoms, they made preparations for quitting the house at Chertsey for some months. Sending the plate which had so excited the Jew's cupidity to the banker's, and leaving Giles and another servant in care of the house, they departed for a cottage some distance in the country, and took Oliver with them.

Who can describe the pleasure and delight, the peace of mind and soft tranquillity, which the sickly boy felt in the balmy air, and among the green hills and rich woods of an inland village! Who can tell how scenes of peace and quietude sink into the minds of pain-worn dwellers in close and noisy places, and carry their own freshness deep into their jaded hearts? Men who have lived in crowded pent-up streets, through whole lives of toil, and never wished for change; men to whom custom has indeed been second nature, and who have come almost to love each brick and stone that formed the narrow boundaries of their daily walks – even they with the hand of death upon them, have been known to yearn at last for one short glimpse of Nature's face, and carried far from the scenes of their old pains and pleasures, have seemed to pass at once into a new state of being, and crawling forth from day to day to some green sunny spot, have had such memories wakened up within them by the mere sight of sky, and hill, and plain, and glistening water, that a foretaste of Heaven itself has soothed their quick decline, and they have sunk into their tombs as peacefully as the sun, whose setting they watched from their lonely chamber window but a few hours before, faded from their dim and feeble sight! The memories which peaceful country scenes call up, are not of this world, or of its thoughts or hopes. Their gentle influence may teach us to weave fresh garlands for the graves of those we loved, may purify our thoughts, and bear down before it old enmity and hatred; but, beneath all this there lingers in the least reflective mind a vague and half-formed consciousness of having held such feelings long before in some remote and distant time, which calls up solemn thoughts of distant times to come, and bends down pride and worldliness beneath it.

It was a lovely spot to which they repaired, and Oliver, whose days had been spent among squalid crowds, and in the midst of noise and brawling, seemed to enter upon a new existence there. The rose and honey-suckle clung to the cottage walls, the ivy crept round the trunks of the trees, and the garden-flowers perfumed the air with delicious odours. Hard by, was a little churchyard: not crowded with tall, unsightly gravestones, but full of humble mounds covered with fresh turf and moss, beneath which the old people of the village lay at rest. Oliver often wandered here, and, thinking of the wretched grave in which his mother lay, would sometimes sit him down and sob unseen; but, as he raised his eyes to the deep sky overhead, he would cease to think of her as lying in the ground, and weep for her sadly, but without pain.

It was a happy time. The days were peaceful and serene, and the nights brought with them no fear or care, no languishing in a wretched prison, or associating with wretched men: nothing but pleasant and happy thoughts. Every morning he went to a white-headed old gentle-man, who lived near the little church, who taught him to read better and to write, and spoke so kindly, and took such pains, that Oliver could never try enough to please him. Then he would walk with Mrs Maylie and Rose, and hear them talk of books, or perhaps sit near them in some shady place, and listen whilst the young lady read, which he could have done till it grew too dark to see the letters. Then he had his own lesson for the next day to prepare, and at this he would work hard in a little room which looked into the garden, till evening came slowly on, when the ladies would walk out again, and he with them: listening with such pleasure to all they said, and so happy if they wanted a flower that he could climb to reach, or had forgotten anything he could run to fetch, that he could never be quick enough about it. When it became quite dark, and they returned home, the young lady would sit down to the piano, and play some melancholy air, or sing in a low and gentle voice some old song which it pleased her aunt to hear. There would be no candles at such times as these, and Oliver would sit by one of the windows, listening to the sweet music, while tears of tranquil joy stole down his face.

And, when Sunday came, how differently the day was spent from any manner in which he had ever spent it yet! and how happily, too, like all the other days in that most happy time! There was the little church in the morning, with the green leaves fluttering at the windows, the birds singing without, and the sweet-smelling air stealing in at the low porch, and filling the homely building with its fragrance. The poor people were so neat and clean, and knelt so reverently in prayer, that it seemed a pleasure, not a tedious duty, their assembling there together; and, though the singing might be rude, it was real, and sounded more musical (to Oliver's ears at least) than any he had ever heard in church before. Then there were the walks as usual, and many calls at the clean houses of the labouring men; and at night Oliver read a chapter or two from the Bible, which he had been studying all the week, and in the performance of which duty he felt more proud and pleased than if he had been the clergyman himself.

In the morning Oliver would be a-foot by six o'clock, roaming the fields and surveying the hedges far and wide, for nosegays of wild flowers, with which he would return laden home, and which it took great care and consideration to arrange to the best advantage for the embellishment of the breakfast-table. There was fresh groundsel,[3] too, for Miss Maylie's birds, with which Oliver, – who had been studying the subject under the able tuition of the village clerk – would decorate the cages in the most approved taste. When the birds were made all spruce and smart for the day, there was usually some little commission of charity to execute in the village, or failing that, there was always something to do in the garden, or about the plants, to which Oliver – who had studied this science also under the same master, who was a gardener by trade, – applied himself with hearty good-will till Miss Rose made her appearance, when there were a thousand commendations to be bestowed upon all he had done, for which one of those light-hearted beautiful smiles was an ample recompense.

So three months glided away; three months which, in the life of the most blessed and favoured of mortals, would have been unmixed happiness; but which, in Oliver's troubled and clouded dawn, were felicity indeed. With the purest and most amiable generosity on one side, and the truest, and warmest, and most soul-felt gratitude on the other, it is no wonder that, by the end of that short time, Oliver Twist had become completely domesticated with the old lady and her niece, and that the fervent attachment of his young and sensitive heart was repaid by their pride in, and attachment to, himself.

*

CHAPTER THE TENTH

WHEREIN THE HAPPINESS OF OLIVER AND HIS FRIENDS EXPERIENCES A SUDDEN CHECK

Spring flew swiftly by, and summer came; and if the village had been beautiful at first, it was now in the full glow and luxuriance of its richness. The great trees, which had looked shrunken and bare in the earlier months, had now burst into strong life and health, and, stretching forth their green arms over the thirsty ground, converted open and naked spots into choice nooks, where was a deep and pleasant shade from which to look upon the wide prospect, steeped in sunshine, which lay stretched out beyond. The earth had donned her mantle of brightest green, and shed her richest perfumes abroad. It was the prime and vigour of the year, and all things were glad and flourishing.

Still the same quiet life went on at the little cottage, and the same cheerful serenity prevailed among its inmates. Oliver had long since grown stout and healthy; but health or sickness made no difference in his warm feelings to those about him, (though they do in the feelings of a great many people,) and he was still the same gentle, attached, affectionate creature, that he had been when pain and suffering had wasted his strength, and he was dependent for every slight attention and comfort on those who tended him.

One beautiful night they had taken a longer walk than was customary with them, for the day had been unusually warm, and there was a brilliant moon, and a light wind had sprung up, which was unusually refreshing. Rose had been in high spirits too, and they had walked on in merry conversation until they had far exceeded their ordinary bounds. Mrs Maylie was fatigued, and they returned more slowly home. The young lady, merely throwing off her simple bonnet, sat down to the piano as usual; after running abstractedly over the keys for a few minutes, she fell into a low and very solemn air, and as she played it they heard her sob as if she were weeping.

'Rose, my dear?' said the elder lady.

Rose made no reply, but played a little quicker, as though the sound had roused her from some painful thoughts.

'Rose, my love!' cried Mrs Maylie, rising hastily, and bending over her. 'What is this? Your face is bathed in tears. My dear child, what distresses you?'

'Nothing, aunt, – nothing,' replied the young lady. 'I don't know what it is; I can't describe it; but I feel so low to-night, and —'

'Not ill, my love?' interposed Mrs Maylie.

'No, no! Oh, not ill!' replied Rose, shuddering as though some deadly chillness were passing over her while she spoke; 'at least, I shall be better presently. Close the window, pray.'

Oliver hastened to comply with the request; and the young lady, making an effort to recover her cheerfulness, strove to play some livelier tune. But her fingers dropped powerless on the keys, and, covering her face with her hands, she sank upon a sofa, and gave vent to the tears which she was now unable to repress.

'My child!' said the elder lady, folding her arms about her, 'I never saw you thus before.'

'I would not alarm you if I could avoid it,' rejoined Rose; 'but indeed I have tried very hard, and cannot help this. I fear I *am* ill, aunt.'

She was, indeed; for, when candles were brought, they saw that in the very short time which had elapsed since their return home, the hue of her countenance had changed to a marble whiteness. Its expression had lost nothing of its beauty, but yet it was changed, and there was an anxious haggard look about that gentle face which it had never worn before. Another minute, and it was suffused with a crimson flush, and a heavy wildness came over the soft blue eye; again this disappeared like the shadow thrown by a passing cloud, and she was once more deadly pale.[1]

Oliver, who watched the old lady anxiously, observed that she was alarmed by these appearances, and so, in truth, was he; but, seeing that she affected to make light of them, he endeavoured to do the same, and they so far succeeded that when Rose was persuaded by her aunt to retire for the night, she was in better spirits, and appeared even in better health, and assured them that she felt certain she would wake in the morning quite well.

'I hope, ma'am,' said Oliver when Mrs Maylie returned, 'that nothing serious is the matter. Miss Maylie doesn't look well to-night, but—'

The old lady motioned him not to speak, and, sitting herself down in a dark corner of the room, remained silent for some time. At length she said, in a trembling voice, –

'I hope not, Oliver. I have been very happy with her for some years – too happy, perhaps, and it may be time that I should meet with some misfortune; but I hope it is not this.'

'What misfortune, ma'am?' inquired Oliver.

'The heavy blow,' said the old lady almost inarticulately, 'of losing the dear girl who has so long been my comfort and happiness.'

'Oh! God forbid!' exclaimed Oliver hastily.

'Amen to that, my child!' said the old lady, wringing her hands.

'Surely there is no danger of anything so dreadful!' said Oliver. 'Two hours ago she was quite well.'

'She is very ill now,' rejoined Mrs Maylie, 'and will be worse, I am sure. My dear, dear Rose! Oh, what should I do without her!'

The lady sank beneath her desponding thoughts, and gave way to such great grief that Oliver, suppressing his own emotion, ventured to remonstrate with her, and to beg earnestly that for the sake of the dear young lady herself she would be more calm.

'And consider, ma'am,' said Oliver, as the tears forced themselves into his eyes despite his efforts to the contrary; 'oh! consider how young and good she is, and what pleasure and comfort she gives to all about her. I am sure – certain – quite certain – that for your sake, who are so good yourself, and for her own, and for the sake of all she makes so happy, she will not die. God will never let her die yet.'

'Hush!' said Mrs Maylie, laying her hand on Oliver's head. 'You think like a child, poor boy; and although what you say may be natural, it is wrong. But you teach me my duty, notwithstanding. I had forgotten it for a moment, Oliver, and I hope I may be pardoned, for I am old, and have seen enough of illness and death to know the pain they leave to those behind. I have seen enough, too, to know that it is not always the youngest and best who are spared to those that love them; but this should give us comfort rather than sorrow, for Heaven is just, and such things teach us impressively that there is a far brighter world than this, and that the passage to it is speedy. God's will be done! but I love her, and He alone knows how well!'

Oliver was surprised to see that as Mrs Maylie said these words she checked her lamentations as though by one struggle, and, drawing herself up as she spoke, became quite composed and firm. He was still more astonished to find that this firmness lasted, and that under all the care and watching which ensued, Mrs Maylie was ever ready and collected, performing all the duties which devolved upon her steadily, and, to all external appearance, even cheerfully. But he was young, and did not know what strong minds are capable of under trying circumstances. How should he, indeed, when their possessors so seldom know themselves?

An anxious night ensued, and when morning came Mrs Maylie's predictions were but too well verified. Rose was in the first stage of a high and dangerous fever.

'We must be active, Oliver, and not give way to useless grief,' said Mrs Maylie, laying her finger on her lip as she looked steadily into his face; 'this letter must be sent with all possible expedition to Mr Losberne. It must be carried to the market-town, which is not more than four miles off by the foot-path across the fields, and thence despatched by an express on horseback straight to Chertsey. The people at the inn will undertake to do this, and I can trust you to see it done, I know.'

Oliver could make no reply, but looked his anxiety to be gone at once.

'Here is another letter,' said Mrs Maylie, pausing to reflect; 'but whether to send it now, or wait until I see how Rose goes on, I scarcely know. I would not forward it unless I feared the worst.'

'Is it for Chertsey, too, ma'am?' inquired Oliver, impatient to execute his commission, and holding out his trembling hand for the letter.

'No,' replied the old lady, giving it him mechanically. Oliver glanced at it, and saw that it was directed to Harry Maylie Esquire, at some lord's house in the country; where, he could not make out.

'Shall it go, ma'am?' asked Oliver, looking up impatiently.

'I think not,' replied Mrs Maylie, taking it back. 'I will wait till to-morrow.'

With these words she gave Oliver her purse, and he started off without more delay at the greatest speed he could muster.

Swiftly he ran across the fields, and down the little lanes which sometimes divided them, now almost hidden by the high corn on either side, and now emerging into an open field where the mowers and haymakers were busy at their work; nor did he stop once, save now and then for a few seconds to recover breath, until he emerged in a great heat, and covered with dust, on the little market-place of the market-town.

Here he paused, and looked about for the inn. There was a white bank, and a red brewery, and a yellow town-hall; and in one corner a large house with all the wood about it painted green, before which was the sign of 'The George,'[2] to which he hastened directly it caught his eye.

Oliver spoke to a postboy who was dozing under the gateway, and who, after hearing what he wanted, referred him to the hostler; who, after hearing all he had to say again, referred him to the landlord, who was a tall gentleman in a blue neckcloth, a white hat, drab breeches, and boots with tops to match, and was leaning against a pump by the stable-door, picking his teeth with a silver tooth-pick.

This gentleman walked with much deliberation to the bar to make out the bill, which took a long time making out, and after it was ready, and paid, a horse had to be saddled, and a man to be dressed, which took up ten good minutes more; meanwhile Oliver was in such a desperate state of impatience and anxiety that he felt as if he could have jumped upon the horse himself, and galloped away full tear to the next stage. At length all was ready, and the little parcel having been handed up, with many injunctions and entreaties for its speedy delivery, the man set spurs to his horse, and, rattling over the uneven paving of the market-place, was out of the town, and galloping along the turnpike-road in a couple of minutes.

It was something to feel certain that assistance was sent for, and that no time had been lost. Oliver hurried up the inn-yard with a somewhat lighter heart, and was turning out of the gateway when he accidentally stumbled against a tall man wrapped in a cloak, who was that moment coming out at the inn-door.

'Hah!' cried the man, fixing his eyes on Oliver, and suddenly recoiling. 'What the devil's this?'

'I beg your pardon, sir,' said Oliver; 'I was in a great hurry to get home, and didn't see you were coming.'

'Death!' muttered the man to himself, glaring at the boy with his large dark eyes. 'Who'd have thought it! Grind him to ashes! he'd start up from a marble coffin to come in my way!'

'I am sorry, sir,' stammered Oliver, confused by the strange man's wild look. 'I hope I have not hurt you?'

'Rot his bones!' murmured the man in a horrible passion between his clenched teeth, 'if I had only had the courage to say the word, I might have been free of him in a night. Curses light upon your head, and black death upon your heart, you imp! What are you doing here?'

The man shook his fist, and gnashed his teeth, as he uttered these words incoherently, and advancing towards Oliver as if with the intention of aiming a blow at him, fell violently on the ground, writhing and foaming, in a fit.

Oliver gazed for a moment at the fearful struggles of the madman, (for such he supposed him to be,) and then darted into the house for help. Having seen him safely carried into the hotel, he turned his face homewards, running as fast as he could to make up for lost time, and recalling, with a great deal of astonishment and some fear, the extraordinary behaviour of the person from whom he had just parted.

The circumstance did not dwell in his recollection long, however; for when he reached the cottage there was enough to occupy his mind, and to drive all considerations of self completely from his memory.

Rose Maylie had rapidly grown worse, and before midnight was delirious. A medical practitioner, who resided on the spot, was in constant attendance upon her, and, after first seeing the patient, he had taken Mrs Maylie aside, and pronounced her disorder to be one of a most alarming nature. 'In fact,' he said, 'it would be little short of a miracle if she recovered.'

How often did Oliver start from his bed that night, and, stealing out with noiseless footstep to the staircase, listen for the slightest sound from the sick chamber! How often did a tremble shake his frame, and cold drops of terror start upon his brow, when a sudden trampling of feet caused him to fear that something too dreadful to think of had even then occurred. And what had been the fervency of all the prayers he had ever uttered, compared with those he poured forth now, in the agony and passion of his supplication, for the life and health of the gentle creature who was tottering on the deep grave's verge!

The suspense, the fearful acute suspense, of standing idly by while the life of one we dearly love is trembling in the balance – the racking thoughts that crowd upon the mind, and make the heart beat violently, and the breath come thick, by the force of the images they conjure up before it – the desperate anxiety *to be doing something* to relieve the pain, or lessen the danger which we have no power to alleviate; and the sinking of soul and spirit which the sad remembrance of our helplessness produces, – what tortures can equal these, and what reflections or efforts can, in the full tide and fever of the time, allay them!

Morning came; and the little cottage was lonely and still. People spoke in whispers; anxious faces appeared at the gate from time to time, and women and children went away in tears. All the livelong day, and for hours after it had grown dark, Oliver paced softly up and down the garden, raising his eyes every instant to the sick-chamber, and shuddering to see the darkened window looking as if death lay stretched inside. Late at night Mr Losberne arrived. 'It is hard,' said the good doctor, turning away as he spoke, 'so young – so much beloved – but there is very little hope.'

Another morning the sun shone brightly, – as brightly as if it looked upon no misery or care; and, with every leaf and flower in full bloom about her, – with life, and health, and sounds and sights of joy surrounding her on every side, the fair young creature lay wasting fast. Oliver crept away to the old churchyard, and, sitting down on one of the green mounds, wept for her in silence.

There was such peace and beauty in the scene, so much of brightness and mirth in the sunny landscape, such blithesome music in the songs of the summer birds, such freedom in the rapid flight of the rook careering overhead, so much of life and joyousness in all, that when the boy raised his aching eyes, and looked about, the thought instinctively occurred to him that this was not a time for death; that Rose could surely never die when humbler things were all so glad and gay; that graves were for cold and cheerless winter, not for sunlight and fragrance. He almost thought that shrouds were for the old and shrunken, and never wrapped the young and graceful form within their ghastly folds.

A knell from the church-bell broke harshly on these youthful thoughts. Another – again! It was tolling for the funeral service. A group of humble mourners entered the gate, and they wore white favours,[3] for the corpse was young. They stood, uncovered, by a grave; and there was a mother – a mother once – among the weeping train. But the sun shone brightly, and the birds sang on.

Oliver turned homewards, thinking on the many kindnesses he had received from the young lady, and wishing that the time could come over again, that he might never cease showing her how grateful and attached he was. He had no cause for self-reproach on the score of neglect or want of thought, for he had been devoted to her service; and yet a hundred little occasions rose up before him on which he fancied he might have been more zealous and more earnest, and wished he had been. We need be careful how we deal with those about us, for every death carries with it to some small circle of survivors thoughts of so much omitted, and so little done; of so many things forgotten, and so many more which might have been repaired, that such recollections are among the bitterest we can have. There is no remorse so deep as that which is unavailing; if we would be spared its tortures let us remember this in time.

When he reached home Mrs Maylie was sitting in the little parlour. Oliver's heart sank at sight of her, for she had never left the bedside of her niece, and he trembled to think what change could have driven her away. He learnt that she had fallen into a deep sleep, from which she would waken again either to recovery and life, or to bid them farewell, and die.

They sat, listening, and afraid to speak, for hours. The untasted meal was removed; and, with looks which showed that their thoughts were elsewhere, they watched the sun as he sank lower and lower, and at length cast over sky and earth those brilliant hues which herald his departure. Their quick ears caught the sound of an approaching footstep, and they both involuntarily darted towards the door as Mr Losberne entered.

'What of Rose?' cried the old lady. 'Tell me at once. I can bear it; anything but suspense. Oh, tell me! in the name of Heaven!'

'You must compose yourself,' said the doctor, supporting her. 'Be calm, my dear ma'am, pray.'

'Let me go, in God's name!' gasped Mrs Maylie. 'My dear child! She is dead! She is dying!'

'No!' cried the doctor passionately. 'As He is good and merciful, she will live to bless us all for years to come.'

The lady fell upon her knees, and tried to fold her hands together;

but the energy which had supported her so long fled to Heaven with her first thanksgiving, and she sunk back into the friendly arms which were extended to receive her.

CHAPTER THE ELEVENTH

CONTAINS SOME INTRODUCTORY PARTICULARS RELATIVE TO A YOUNG GENTLEMAN WHO NOW ARRIVES UPON THE SCENE, AND A NEW ADVENTURE WHICH HAPPENED TO OLIVER

It was almost too much happiness to bear. Oliver felt stunned and stupified by the unexpected intelligence; he could not weep, or speak, or rest. He had scarcely the power of understanding anything that had passed, until after a long ramble in the quiet evening air a burst of tears came to his relief, and he seemed to awaken all at once to a full sense of the joyful change that had occurred, and the almost insupportable load of anguish which had been taken from his breast.

The night was fast closing in when he returned homewards, laden with flowers which he had culled with peculiar care for the adornment of the sick chamber. As he walked briskly along the road, he heard behind him the noise of some vehicle approaching at a furious pace. Looking round, he saw that it was a post-chaise[1] driven at great speed; and as the horses were galloping, and the road was narrow, he stood leaning against a gate until it should have passed him by.

As it dashed on, Oliver caught a glimpse of a man in a white nightcap, whose face seemed familiar to him, although his view was so brief that he could not identify the person. In another second or two the nightcap was thrust out of the chaise window, and a stentorian voice bellowed to the driver to stop, which he did as soon as he could pull up his horses, when the nightcap once again appeared, and the same voice called Oliver by his name.

'Here!' cried the voice. 'Master Oliver, what's the news? Miss Rose – Master O-li-ver.'

'Is it you, Giles?' cried Oliver, running up to the chaise door.

Giles popped out his nightcap again, preparatory to making some reply, when he was suddenly pulled back by a young gentleman who occupied the other corner of the chaise, and who eagerly demanded what was the news.

'In a word,' cried the gentleman, 'better or worse?'

'Better – much better,' replied Oliver hastily.

'Thank Heaven!' exclaimed the gentleman. 'You are sure?'

'Quite, sir,' replied Oliver; 'the change took place only a few hours ago, and Mr Losberne says that all danger is at an end.'

The gentleman said not another word, but opening the chaise-door leaped out, and, taking Oliver hurriedly by the arm, led him aside.

'This is quite certain? – there is no possibility of any mistake on your part, my boy, is there?' demanded the gentleman in a tremulous voice. 'Pray do not deceive me by awakening any hopes that are not to be fulfilled.'

'I would not for the world, sir,' replied Oliver. 'Indeed you may believe me. Mr Losberne's words were, that she would live to bless us all for many years to come. I heard him say so.'

The tears stood in Oliver's eyes as he recalled the scene which was the beginning of so much happiness, and the gentleman turned his face away, and remained silent for some minutes. Oliver thought he heard him sob more than once, but he feared to interrupt him by any farther remark, – for he could well guess what his feelings were, – and so stood apart, feigning to be occupied with his nosegay.

All this time Mr Giles, with the white nightcap on, had been sitting upon the steps of the chaise, supporting an elbow on each knee, and wiping his eyes with a blue cotton pocket-handkerchief dotted with white spots. That the honest fellow had not been feigning emotion was abundantly demonstrated by the very red eyes with which he regarded the young gentleman, when he turned round and addressed him.

'I think you had better go on to my mother's in the chaise, Giles,' said he. 'I would rather walk slowly on, so as to gain a little time before I see her. You can say I am coming.'

'I beg your pardon, Mr Harry,' said Giles, giving a final polish to his ruffled countenance with the handkerchief, 'but if you would leave the postboy to say that, I should be very much obliged to you. It wouldn't be proper for the maids to see me in this state, sir; I should never have any more authority with them if they did.'

'Well,' rejoined Harry Maylie, smiling, 'you can do as you like. Let him go on with the portmanteaus, if you wish it, and do you follow with us. Only first exchange that nightcap for some more appropriate covering, or we shall be taken for madmen.'

Mr Giles, reminded of his unbecoming costume, snatched off and pocketed his nightcap, and substituted a hat of grave and sober shape which he took out of the chaise. This done, the postboy drove off, and Giles, Mr Maylie, and Oliver followed at their leisure.

As they walked along, Oliver glanced from time to time with much interest and curiosity at the new-comer. He seemed about five-and-twenty years of age, and was of the middle height; his countenance was frank and handsome, and his demeanour singularly easy and prepossessing. Notwithstanding the differences between youth and age, he bore so strong a likeness to the old lady, that Oliver would have had no great difficulty in imagining their relationship, even if he had not already spoken of her as his mother.

Mrs Maylie was anxiously waiting to receive her son when he reached the cottage, and the meeting did not take place without great emotion on both sides.

'Oh, mother,' whispered the young man, 'why did you not write before?'

'I did write,' replied Mrs Maylie; 'but, on reflection, I determined to keep back the letter until I had heard Mr Losberne's opinion.'

'But why,' said the young man, 'why run the chance of that occurring which so nearly happened? If Rose had – I cannot utter that word now – if this illness had terminated differently, how could you ever have forgiven yourself, or I been happy again?'

'If that *had* been the case, Harry,' said Mrs Maylie, 'I fear your happiness would have been effectually blighted, and that your arrival here a day sooner or a day later would have been of very, very little import.'

'And who can wonder if it be so, mother?' rejoined the young man; 'or why should I say *if?* – It is – it is – you know it, mother – you must know it.'

'I know that she well deserves the best and purest love that the heart of man can offer,' said Mrs Maylie; 'I know that the devotion and affection of her nature require no ordinary return, but one that shall be deep and lasting. If I did not feel this, and know, besides, that a changed behaviour in one she loved would break her heart, I should not feel my task so difficult of performance, or have to encounter so many struggles in my own bosom, when I take what seems to me to be the strict line of duty.'

'This is unkind, mother,' said Harry. 'Do you still suppose that I am so much a boy as not to know my own mind, or to mistake the impulses of my own soul?'

'I think, my dear fellow,' returned Mrs Maylie, laying her hand upon his shoulder, 'that youth has many generous impulses which do not last, and that among them are some which, being gratified, become only the more fleeting. Above all, I think,' said the lady, fixing her eyes on her son's face, 'that if an enthusiastic, ardent, ambitious young man has a wife on whose name is a stain, which, though it originate in no fault of hers, may be visited by cold and sordid people upon her, and upon his children also, and, in exact proportion to his success in the world, be cast in his teeth, and made the subject of sneers against him, he may – no matter how generous and good his nature – one day repent of the connection he formed in early life, and she may have the pain and torture of knowing that he does so.'

'Mother,' said the young man impatiently, 'he would be a mere selfish brute, unworthy alike of the name of man and of the woman you describe, who acted thus.'

'You think so now, Harry,' replied his mother.

'And ever will,' said the young man. 'The mental agony I have suffered during the last two days wrings from me the undisguised avowal to you of a passion which, as you well know, is not one of yesterday, nor one I have lightly formed. On Rose, sweet gentle girl, my heart is set as firmly as ever heart of man was set on woman. I have no thought, or view, or hope in life beyond her; and if you oppose me in this great stake, you take my peace and happiness in your hands and cast them to the wind. Mother, think better of this, and of me, and do not disregard the warm feelings of which you seem to think so little.'

'Harry,' said Mrs Maylie, 'it is because I think so much of warm and sensitive hearts that I would spare them from being wounded. But we have said enough, and more than enough, on this matter just now.'

'Let it rest with Rose, then,' interposed Harry. 'You will not press these overstrained opinions of yours so far as to throw any obstacle in my way?'

'I will not,' rejoined Mrs Maylie; 'but I would have you consider—'

'I *have* considered,' was the impatient reply, – 'I have considered for years – considered almost since I have been capable of serious reflection. My feelings remain unchanged, as they ever will; and why should I suffer the pain of a delay in giving them vent, which can be productive of no earthly good? No. Before I leave this place Rose shall hear me.'

'She shall,' said Mrs Maylie.

'There is something in your manner which would almost imply that she will hear me coldly, mother,' said the young man anxiously.

'Not coldly,' rejoined the old lady; 'far from it.'

'How then?' urged the young man. 'She has formed no other attachment?'

'No, indeed,' replied his mother. 'You have, or I mistake, too strong a hold on her affections already.'

'What I would say,' resumed the old lady, stopping her son as he was about to speak, 'is this. Before you stake your all on this chance, – before you suffer yourself to be carried to the highest point of hope, reflect for a few moments, my dear child, on Rose's history, and consider what effect the knowledge of her doubtful birth may have on her decision, – devoted as she is to us with all the intensity of her noble mind, and that perfect sacrifice of self which in all matters, great or trifling, has always been her characteristic.'

'What do you mean?'

'That I leave to you to discover,' replied Mrs Maylie. 'I must go back to Rose. God bless you!'

'I shall see you again to-night?' said the young man eagerly.

'By and by,' replied the lady, 'when I leave Rose.'

'You will tell her I am here?' said Harry.

'Of course,' replied Mrs Maylie.

'And say how anxious I have been, and how much I have suffered, and how I long to see her – you will not refuse to do this, mother?'

'No,' said the old lady, 'I will tell her that;' and, pressing her son's hand affectionately, she hastened from the room.

Mr Losberne and Oliver had remained at another end of the apartment while this hurried conversation was proceeding. The former now held out his hand to Harry Maylie, and hearty salutations were exchanged between them. The doctor then communicated, in reply to multifarious questions from his young friend, a precise account of his patient's situation, which was quite as consolatory and full of promise as Oliver's statement had encouraged him to hope, and to the whole of which Mr Giles, who affected to be busy about the luggage, listened with greedy ears.

'Have you shot anything particular lately, Giles?' inquired the doctor, when he had concluded.

'Nothing particular, sir,' replied Mr Giles, colouring up to the eyes.

'Nor catching any thieves, nor identifying any housebreakers?' said the doctor maliciously.

'None at all, sir,' replied Mr Giles with much gravity.

'Well,' said the doctor, 'I am sorry to hear it, because you do that sort of thing so well. Pray, how is Brittles?'

'The boy is very well, sir,' said Mr Giles, recovering his usual tone of patronage, 'and sends his respectful duty, sir.'

'That's well,' said the doctor. 'Seeing you here, reminds me, Mr Giles, that on the day before that on which I was called away so hurriedly, I executed, at the request of your good mistress, a small commission in your favour. Just step into this corner a moment, will you?'

Mr Giles walked into the corner with much importance and some wonder, and was honoured with a short whispering conference with the doctor, on the termination of which he made a great many bows, and retired with steps of unusual stateliness. The subject matter of this conference was not disclosed in the parlour, but the kitchen was speedily enlightened concerning it; for Mr Giles walked straight thither, and having called for a mug of ale, announced, with an air of majestic mystery which was highly effective, that it had pleased his mistress, in consideration of his gallant behaviour on the occasion of that attempted robbery, to deposit in the local savings bank the sum of twenty-five pounds for his sole use and benefit. At this the two women servants lifted up their hands and eyes, and supposed that Mr Giles would begin to be quite proud now; whereunto Mr Giles, pulling out his shirt-frill, replied, 'No, no' – and that if they observed at any time that he was at all haughty to his inferiors, he would thank them to tell him so. And then he made a great many other remarks, no less illustrative of his humility, which were received with equal favour and applause, and were withal as original and as much to the purpose as the remarks of great men commonly are.

Above stairs, the remainder of the evening passed cheerfully away, for the doctor was in high spirits, and however fatigued or thoughtful Harry Maylie might have been at first, he was not proof against the worthy gentleman's good humour, which displayed itself in a great variety of sallies and professional recollections, and an abundance of small jokes, which struck Oliver as being the drollest things he had ever heard, and caused him to laugh proportionately, to the evident satisfaction of the doctor, who laughed immoderately at himself, and made Harry laugh almost as heartily by the very force of sympathy. So they were as pleasant a party as, under the circumstances, they could well have been, and it was late before they retired, with light and thankful hearts, to take that rest of which, after the doubt and suspense they had recently undergone, they stood so much in need.

Oliver rose next morning in better heart, and went about his usual early occupations with more hope and pleasure than he had known for many days. The birds were once more hung out to sing in their old places, and the sweetest wild flowers that could be found were once more gathered to gladden Rose with their beauty and fragrance. The melancholy which had seemed to the sad eyes of the anxious boy to hang for days past over every object, beautiful as they all were, was dispelled as though by magic. The dew seemed to sparkle more brightly on the green leaves, the air to rustle among them with a sweeter music, and the sky itself to look more blue and bright. Such is the influence which the condition of our own thoughts exercises even over the appearance of external objects. Men who look on nature and their fellow men, and cry that all is dark and gloomy, are in the right; but the sombre colours are reflections from their own jaundiced eyes and hearts. The real hues are delicate, and require a clearer vision.

It is worthy of remark, and Oliver did not fail to note at the time, that his morning expeditions were no longer made alone. Harry Maylie, after the very first morning when he met Oliver coming laden home, was seized with such a passion for flowers, and displayed such a taste in their arrangement, as left his young companion far behind. If Oliver were behind-hand in these respects, however, he knew where the best were to be found, and morning after morning they scoured the country together, and brought home the fairest that blossomed. The window of the young lady's chamber was opened now, for she loved to feel the rich summer air stream in and revive her with its freshness; but there always stood in water, just inside the lattice, one particular little bunch which was made up with great care every morning. Oliver could not help noticing that the withered flowers were never thrown away, although the little vase was regularly replenished; nor could he help observing that whenever the doctor came into the garden he invariably cast his eyes up to that particular corner, and nodded his head most expressively as he set forth on his morning's walk. Pending these observations, the days were flying by, and Rose was rapidly and surely recovering.

Nor did Oliver's time hang heavy upon his hands, although the young lady had not yet left her chamber, and there were no evening walks, save now and then for a short distance with Mrs Maylie. He applied himself with redoubled assiduity to the instructions of the white-headed old gentleman, and laboured so hard that his quick progress surprised even himself. It was while he was engaged in this pursuit that he was greatly startled and distressed by a most unexpected occurrence.

The little room in which he was accustomed to sit when busy at his books was on the ground-floor, at the back of the house. It was quite a cottage-room, with a lattice-window, around which were clusters of jessamine and honey-suckle, that crept over the casement, and filled the place with their delicious perfume. It looked into a garden, whence a wicket-gate opened into a small paddock; all beyond was fine meadow-land and wood. There was no other dwelling near, in that direction, and the prospect it commanded was very extensive.

One beautiful evening, when the first shades of twilight were beginning to settle upon the earth, Oliver sat at this window intent upon his books. He had been poring over them for some time; and as the day had been uncommonly sultry and he had exerted himself a great deal, it is no disparagement to the authors, whoever they may have been, to say that gradually and by slow degrees he fell asleep.

There is a kind of sleep[2] that steals upon us sometimes which, while it holds the body prisoner, does not free the mind from a sense of things about it, and enable it to ramble as it pleases. So far as an overpowering heaviness, a prostration of strength, and an utter inability to control our thoughts or power of motion can be called sleep, this is it; and yet we have a consciousness of all that is going on about us, and even if we dream, words which are really spoken, or sounds which really exist at the moment, accommodate themselves with surprising readiness to our visions, until reality and imagination become so strangely blended that it is afterwards almost a matter of impossibility to separate the two. Nor is this the most striking phenomenon incidental to such a state. It is an ascertained fact, that although our senses of touch and sight be for the time dead, yet our sleeping thoughts, and the visionary scenes that pass before us, will be influenced, and materially influenced, by the *mere silent presence* of some external object which may not have been near us when we closed our eyes, and of whose vicinity we have had no waking consciousness.

Oliver knew perfectly well that he was in his own little room, that his books were lying on the table before him, and that the sweet air was stirring among the creeping plants outside, – and yet he was asleep. Suddenly the scene changed, the air became close and confined, and he thought with a glow of terror that he was in the Jew's house

Monks and the Jew

again. There sat the hideous old man in his accustomed corner pointing at him, and whispering to another man with his face averted, who sat beside him.

'Hush, my dear!' he thought he heard the Jew say; 'it is him, sure enough. Come away.'

'He!' the other man seemed to answer; 'could I mistake him, think you? If a crowd of devils were to put themselves into his exact shape, and he stood amongst them, there is something that would tell me how to point him out. If you buried him fifty feet deep, and took me across his grave, I should know, if there wasn't a mark above it, that he lay buried there. Wither his flesh, I should!'

The man seemed to say this with such dreadful hatred, that Oliver awoke with the fear and started up.

Good God! what was that which sent the blood tingling to his heart, and deprived him of voice or power to move! There – there – at the window – close before him – so close, that he could have almost touched him before he started back – with his eyes peering into the room, and meeting his – there stood the Jew – and beside him, white with rage, or fear, or both, were the scowling features of the very man who had accosted him at the inn yard!

It was but an instant, a glance, a flash before his eyes, and they were gone. But they had recognised him, and he them, and their look was as firmly impressed upon his memory as if it had been deeply carved in stone, and set before him from his birth. He stood transfixed for a moment, and then, leaping from the window into the garden, called loudly for help.

*

CHAPTER THE TWELFTH

CONTAINING THE UNSATISFACTORY RESULT OF OLIVER'S ADVENTURE, AND A CONVERSATION OF SOME IMPORTANCE BETWEEN HARRY MAYLIE AND ROSE

When the inmates of the house, attracted by Oliver's cries, hurried to the spot from which they proceeded, they found him, pale and agitated, pointing in the direction of the meadows behind the house, and scarcely able to articulate the words 'The Jew! the Jew!'

Mr Giles was at a loss to comprehend what this outcry meant; but Harry Maylie, whose perceptions were something quicker, and who had heard Oliver's history from his mother, understood it at once.

'What direction did he take?' he asked, catching up a heavy stick which was standing in a corner.

'That,' replied Oliver, pointing out the course the men had taken. 'I missed them all in an instant.'

'Then they are in the ditch!' said Harry. 'Follow, and keep as near me as you can.' So saying he sprang over the hedge, and darted off with a speed which rendered it matter of exceeding difficulty for the others to keep near him.

Giles followed as well as he could, and Oliver followed too, and in the course of a minute or two, Mr Losberne, who had been out walking, and just then returned, tumbled over the hedge after them, and picking himself up with more agility than he could have been supposed to possess, struck into the same course at no contemptible speed, shouting all the while most prodigiously to know what was the matter.

On they all went; nor stopped they once to breathe until the leader, striking off into an angle of the field indicated by Oliver, began to search narrowly the ditch and hedge adjoining, which afforded time for the remainder of the party to come up, and for Oliver to communicate to Mr Losberne the circumstances that had led to so vigorous a pursuit.

The search was all in vain. There were not even the traces of recent footsteps to be seen. They stood now on the summit of a little hill, commanding the open fields in every direction for three or four miles. There was the village in the hollow on the left; but, in order to gain that, after pursuing the track Oliver had pointed out, the men must have made a circuit of open ground which it was impossible they could have accomplished in so short a time. A thick wood skirted the meadow-land in another direction; but they could not have gained that covert for the same reason.

'It must have been a dream, Oliver?' said Harry Maylie, taking him aside.

'Oh no, indeed, sir,' replied Oliver, shuddering at the very recollection of the old wretch's countenance; 'I saw him too plainly for that. I saw them both as plainly as I see you now.'

'Who was the other?' inquired Harry and Mr Losberne together.

'The very same man that I told you of, who came upon me so suddenly at the inn,' said Oliver. 'We had our eyes fixed full upon each other, and I could swear to him.'

'They took this way?' demanded Harry; 'are you certain of that?'

'As I am that the men were at the window,' replied Oliver, pointing down as he spoke to the hedge which divided the cottage-garden from the meadow. 'The tall man leaped over just there; and the Jew, running a few paces to the right, crept through that gap.'

The two gentlemen watched Oliver's earnest face as he spoke, and looking from him to each other, seemed to feel satisfied of the accuracy of what he said. Still, in no direction were there any appearances of the trampling of men in hurried flight. The grass was long, but it was trodden down nowhere save where their own feet had crushed it. The sides and brinks of the ditches were of damp clay, but in no one place could they discern the print of men's shoes, or the slightest mark which would indicate that any feet had pressed the ground for hours before.

'This is strange!' said Harry.

'Strange?' echoed the doctor. 'Blathers and Duff themselves could make nothing of it.'

Notwithstanding the evidently inefficacious nature of their search, however, they did not desist until the coming on of night rendered its further prosecution hopeless, and even then they gave it up with reluctance. Giles was despatched to the different alehouses in the village, furnished with the best description Oliver could give of the appearance and dress of the strangers; of whom the Jew was at all events sufficiently remarkable to be remembered supposing he had been seen drinking, or loitering about; but he returned without any intelligence calculated to dispel or lessen the mystery.

On the next day further search was made, and the enquiries renewed, but with no better success. On the day following, Oliver and Mr Maylie repaired to the market-town, in the hope of seeing or hearing something of the men there; but this effort was equally fruitless; and, after a few days the affair began to be forgotten, as most affairs are, when wonder, having no fresh food to support it, dies away of itself.

Meanwhile Rose was rapidly recovering. She had left her room, was able to go out, and, mixing once more with the family, carried joy with the hearts of all.

But although this happy change had a visible effect on the little circle, and although cheerful voices and merry laughter were once more heard in the cottage, there was at times an unwonted restraint upon some there – even upon Rose herself – which Oliver could not fail to remark. Mrs Maylie and her son were often closeted together for a long time, and more than once Rose appeared with traces of tears upon her face. After Mr Losberne had fixed a day for his departure to Chertsey, these symptoms increased, and it became evident that something was in progress which affected the peace of the young lady and of somebody else besides.

At length one morning, when Rose was alone in the breakfast parlour, Harry Maylie entered, and with some hesitation begged permission to speak with her for a few moments.

'A few – a very few – will suffice, Rose,' said the young man, drawing his chair towards her. 'What I shall have to say has already presented itself to your mind; the most cherished hopes of my heart are not unknown to you, though from my lips you have not yet heard them stated.'

Rose had been very pale from the moment of his entrance, although that might have been the effect of her recent illness. She merely bowed, and bending over some plants that stood near, waited in silence for him to proceed.

'I – I – ought to have left here before,' said Harry.

'You should indeed,' replied Rose. 'Forgive me for saying so, but I wish you had.'

'I was brought here by the most dreadful and agonizing of all apprehensions,' said the young man, 'the fear of losing the one dear being on whom my every wish and hope are centred. You had been dying – trembling between earth and heaven. We know that when the young, the beautiful, and good,[1] are visited with sickness, their pure spirits insensibly turn towards their bright home of lasting rest, and hence it is that the best and fairest of our kind so often fade in blooming.'

There were tears in the eyes of the gentle girl as these words were spoken, and when one fell upon the flower over which she bent, and glistened brightly in its cup, making it more beautiful, it seemed as though the outpourings of a fresh young heart claimed common kindred with the loveliest things in nature.

'An angel,' continued the young man passionately, 'a creature as fair and innocent of guile as one of God's own angels, fluttered between life and death. Oh! who could hope, when the distant world to which she was akin half opened to her view, that she would return to the sorrow and calamity of this! Rose, Rose, to know that you were passing away like some soft shadow, which a light from above casts upon the earth – to have no hope that you would be spared to those who linger here, and to know no reason why you should – to feel that you belonged to that bright sphere whither so many gifted creatures in infancy and youth have winged their early flight – and yet to pray, amid all these consolations, that you might be restored to those who loved you – these are distractions almost too great to bear. They were mine by day and night, and with them came such a rushing torrent of fears and apprehensions, and selfish regrets lest you should die and never know how devotedly I loved you, as almost bore down sense and reason in its course. You recovered – day by day, and almost hour by hour, some drop of health came back, and mingling with the spent and feeble stream of life which circulated languidly within you, swelled it again to a high and rushing tide. I have watched you change almost from death to life, with eyes that moistened with their own eagerness and deep affection. Do not tell me that you wish I had lost this; for it has softened my heart to all mankind.'

'I did not mean that,' said Rose weeping; 'I only wished you had left here, that you might have turned to high and noble pursuits again – to pursuits well worthy of you.'

'There is no pursuit more worthy of me – more worthy of the highest nature that exists – than the struggle to win such a heart as yours,' said the young man, taking her hand. 'Rose, my own dear Rose, for years – for years I have loved you, hoping to win my way to fame, and then come proudly home and tell you it had been sought, only for you to share; thinking in my day dreams how I would remind you in that happy moment of the many silent tokens I had given of a boy's attachment, and rally you who had blushed to mark them, and then claim your hand, as if in redemption of some old mute contract that had been sealed between us. That time has not arrived; but here, with no fame won and no young vision realized, I give to you the heart so long your own, and stake my all upon the words with which you greet the offer.'

'Your behaviour has ever been kind and noble,' said Rose, mastering the emotions by which she was agitated. 'As you believe that I am not insensible or ungrateful, so hear my answer.'

'It is that I may endeavour to deserve you – is it, dear Rose?'

'It is,' replied Rose, 'that you must endeavour to forget me – not as your old and dearly-attached companion, for that would wound me deeply, but as the object of your love. Look into the world, think how many hearts you would be equally proud to gain are there. Confide some other passion to me if you will, and I will be the truest, warmest, most faithful friend you have.'

There was a pause, during which Rose, who had covered her face with one hand, gave free vent to her tears. Harry still retained the other.

'And your reasons, Rose,' he said at length in a low voice, 'your reasons for this decision – may I ask them?'

'You have a right to know them,' rejoined Rose. 'You can say nothing to alter my resolution. It is a duty that I must perform. I owe it alike to others, and to myself.'

'To yourself?'

'Yes, Harry, I owe it to myself that I, a friendless, portionless girl, with a blight upon my name, should not give the world reason to suspect that I had sordidly yielded to your first passion, and fastened myself, a clog, upon all your hopes and projects. I owe it to you and yours to prevent you from opposing, in the warmth of your generous nature, this great obstacle to your progress in the world.'

'If your inclinations chime with your sense of duty—' Harry began.

'They do not,' replied Rose, colouring deeply.

'Then you return my love?' said Harry. 'Say but that, Rose; say but that, and soften the bitterness of this hard disappointment.'

'If I could have done so without doing heavy wrong to him I loved,' rejoined Rose, 'I could have—'

'Have received this declaration very differently?' said Harry with great eagerness. 'Do not conceal that from me at least, Rose.'

'I could,' said Rose. 'Stay,' she added, disengaging her hand. 'Why should we prolong this painful interview; most painful to me, and yet productive of lasting happiness notwithstanding; for it *will* be happiness to know that I once held the high place in your regard which I now occupy, and every triumph you achieve in life will animate me with new fortitude and firmness. Farewell, Harry! for as we have met to-day, we meet no more: but in other relations than those in which this conversation would have placed us, may we be long and happily entwined; and may every blessing that the prayers of a true and earnest heart can call down from where all is truth and sincerity, cheer and prosper you.'

'Another word, Rose,' said Harry. 'Your reason in your own words. From your own lips let me hear it.'

'The prospect before you,' answered Rose firmly, 'is a brilliant one; all the honours to which great talents and powerful connexions can help men in public life are in store for you. But those connexions are proud, and I will neither mingle with such as hold in scorn the mother who gave me life, nor bring disgrace or failure upon the son of her who has so well supplied that mother's place. In a word,' said the young lady, turning away as her temporary firmness forsook her, 'there is a stain upon my name which the world visits on innocent heads; I will carry it into no blood but my own and the reproach shall rest alone on me.'

'One word more, Rose – dear Rose, one more,' cried Harry throwing himself before her. 'If I had been less, less fortunate, as the world would call it, – if some obscure and peaceful life had been my destiny, – if I had been poor, sick, helpless, – would you have turned from me then? or has my probable advancement to riches and honour given this scruple birth?'

'Do not press me to reply,' answered Rose. 'The question does not arise, and never will. It is unfair, unkind, to urge it.'

'If your answer be what I almost dare to hope it is,' retorted Harry, 'it will shed a gleam of happiness upon my lonely way, and light the dreary path before me. It is not an idle thing to do so much, by the utterance of a few brief words, for one who loves us beyond all else. Oh, Rose, in the name of my ardent and enduring attachment, – in the name of all I have suffered for you, and all you doom me to undergo, – answer me that one question.'

'Then if your lot had been differently cast,' rejoined Rose; 'if you had been even a little, but not so far above me; if I could have been a help and comfort to you in some humble scene of peace and retirement, and not a blot and drawback in ambitious and distinguished crowds; I should have been spared this trial. I have every reason to be happy, very happy, now; but then, Harry, I own I should have been happier.'

Busy recollections of old hopes, cherished as a girl long ago, crowded into the mind of Rose while making this avowal; but they brought tears with them, as old hopes will when they come back withered, and they relieved her.

'I cannot help this weakness, and it makes my purpose stronger,' said Rose extending her hand. 'I must leave you now, indeed.'

'I ask one promise,' said Harry. 'Once, and only once more, – say within a year, but it may be much sooner, – let me speak to you again on this subject for the last time.'

'Not to press me to alter my right determination,' replied Rose with a melancholy smile: 'it will be useless.'

'No,' said Harry; 'to hear you repeat it, if you will; finally repeat it. I will lay at your feet whatever of station or fortune I may possess, and if you still adhere to your present resolution, will not seek by word or act to change it.'

'Then let it be so,' rejoined Rose. 'It is but one pang the more, and by that time I may be enabled to bear it better.'

She extended her hand again, but the young man caught her to his bosom, and, imprinting one kiss upon her beautiful forehead, hurried from the room.

CHAPTER THE THIRTEENTH

IS A VERY SHORT ONE, AND MAY APPEAR
OF NO GREAT IMPORTANCE IN ITS PLACE,
BUT IT SHOULD BE READ
NOTWITHSTANDING, AS A SEQUEL TO
THE LAST, AND A KEY TO ONE THAT WILL
FOLLOW WHEN ITS TIME ARRIVES

'And so you are resolved to be my travelling-companion this morning – eh?' said the doctor, as Harry Maylie joined him and Oliver at the breakfast-table. 'Why, you are not in the same mind or intention two half hours together.'

'You will tell me a different tale one of these days,' said Harry, colouring without any perceptible reason.

'I hope I may have good cause to do so,' replied Mr Losberne; 'though I confess I don't think I shall. But yesterday morning you had made up your mind in a great hurry to stay here, and accompany your mother, like a dutiful son, to the sea-side; before noon you announce that you are going to do me the honour of accompanying me as far as

I go on your road to London; and at night you urge me with great mystery to start before the ladies are stirring, the consequence of which is, that young Oliver here is pinned down to his breakfast when he ought to be ranging the meadows after botanical phenomena of all kinds. Too bad, isn't it, Oliver?'

'I should have been very sorry not to have been at home when you and Mr Maylie went away, sir,' rejoined Oliver.

'That's a fine fellow,' said the doctor; 'you shall come and see me when you return. But, to speak seriously, Harry, has any communication from the great nobs produced this sudden anxiety on your part to be gone?'

'The great nobs,' replied Harry, 'under which designation, I presume, you include my most stately uncle, have not communicated with me at all since I have been here, nor, at this time of the year, is it likely that anything would occur to render necessary my immediate attendance among them.'

'Well,' said the doctor, 'you are a queer fellow. But of course they will get you into Parliament at the election before Christmas, and these sudden shiftings and changes are no bad preparation for political life. There's something in that; good training is always desirable, whether the race be for place, cup or sweepstakes.'[1]

Harry Maylie looked as if he could have followed up this short dialogue by one or two remarks that would have staggered the doctor not a little, but he contented himself with saying, 'We shall see,' and pursued the subject no further. The post-chaise drove up to the door shortly afterwards, and Giles coming in for the luggage, the good doctor bustled out to see it packed away.

'Oliver,' said Harry Maylie in a low voice, 'let me speak a word with you.'

Oliver walked into the window-recess to which Mr Maylie beckoned him; much surprised at the mixture of sadness and boisterous spirits, which his whole behaviour displayed.

'You can write well now,' said Harry, laying his hand upon his arm.

'I hope so, sir,' replied Oliver.

'I shall not be at home again, perhaps for some time; I wish you would write to me – say once a fortnight, every alternate Monday, to the General Post Office in London:[2] will you?' said Mr Maylie.

'Oh! certainly sir; I shall be proud to do it,' exclaimed Oliver, greatly delighted with the commission.

'I should like to know how – how my mother and Miss Maylie are,' said the young man; 'and you can fill up a sheet by telling me what walks you take, and what you talk about, and whether she – they, I mean, seem happy and quite well. You understand me?'

'Oh! quite sir, quite,' replied Oliver.

'I would rather you did not mention it to them,' said Harry, hurrying over his words. 'Because it might make my mother anxious to write to me oftener, and it is a trouble and worry to her. Let it be a secret between you and me, and mind you tell me everything; I depend upon you.'

Oliver, quite elated and honoured by a sense of his importance, faithfully promised to be secret and explicit in his communications, and Mr Maylie took leave of him with many warm assurances of his regard and protection.

The doctor was in the chaise; Giles (who, it had been arranged, should be left behind,) held the door open in his hand; and the women servants were in the garden looking on. Harry cast one slight glance at the latticed window, and jumped into the carriage.

'Drive on!' he cried, 'hard, fast, full gallop. Nothing short of flying will keep pace with me to-day.'

'Halloa!' cried the doctor, letting down the front glass in a great hurry, and shouting to the postilion,[3] 'something very far short of flying will keep pace with me. Do you hear?'

Jingling and clattering till distance rendered its noise inaudible, and its rapid progress only perceptible to the eye, the vehicle wound its way along the road almost hidden in a cloud of dust, now wholly disappearing, and now becoming visible again, as intervening objects or the intricacies of the way permitted. It was not until even the dusty cloud was no longer to be seen, that the gazers dispersed.

And there was one looker-on, who remained with eyes fixed upon the spot where the carriage had disappeared, long after it was many miles away; for behind the white curtain which had shrouded her from view, when Harry raised his eyes towards the window, sat Rose herself.

'He seems in high spirits and happy,' she said at length. 'I feared for a time he might be otherwise. I was mistaken. I am very, very glad.'

Tears are signs of gladness as well as grief, but those which coursed down Rose's face as she sat pensively at the window, still gazing in the same direction, seemed to tell more of sorrow than of joy.

CHAPTER THE FOURTEENTH

IN WHICH THE READER, IF HE OR SHE RESORT TO THE FIFTH CHAPTER OF THIS SECOND BOOK, WILL PERCEIVE A CONTRAST NOT UNCOMMON IN MATRIMONIAL CASES

Mr Bumble sat in the workhouse parlour, with his eyes moodily fixed on the cheerless grate, whence, as it was summer time, no brighter gleam proceeded than the reflection of certain sickly rays of the sun, which were sent back from its cold and shining surface. A paper fly-cage dangled from the ceiling, to which he occasionally raised his eyes in gloomy thought; and, as the heedless insects hovered round the gaudy net-work, Mr Bumble would heave a deep sigh, while a more gloomy shadow overspread his countenance. Mr Bumble was meditating, and it might be that the insects brought to mind some painful passage in his own past life.

Nor was Mr Bumble's gloom the only thing calculated to awaken a pleasing melancholy in the bosom of a spectator. There were not wanting other appearances, and those closely connected with his own person, which announced that a great change had taken place in the position of his affairs. The laced coat and the cocked hat, where were they? He still wore knee-breeches and dark cotton stockings on his nether limbs, but they were not *the* breeches. The coat was wide-skirted, and in that respect like *the* coat, but, oh, how different! The mighty cocked-hat was replaced by a modest round one. Mr Bumble was no longer a beadle.

There are some promotions in life which, independent of the more substantial rewards they offer, acquire peculiar value and dignity from the coats and waistcoats connected with them. A field-marshal has his uniform, a bishop his silk apron, a counsellor his silk gown, a beadle his cocked hat. Strip the bishop of his apron, or the beadle of his cocked hat and gold lace, what are they? Men, – mere men. Dignity, and even holiness too, sometimes, are more questions of coat and waistcoat than some people imagine.

Mr Bumble had married Mrs Corney, and was master of the work-house. Another beadle had come into power, and on him the cocked hat, gold-laced coat, and staff, had all three descended.

'And to-morrow two months it was done!' said Mr Bumble with a sigh. 'It seems a age.'

Mr Bumble might have meant that he had concentrated a whole existence of happiness into the short space of eight weeks; but the sigh – there was a vast deal of meaning in the sigh.

'I sold myself,' said Mr Bumble, pursuing the same train of reflection, 'for six teaspoons, a pair of sugar-tongs, and a milk-pot, with a small quantity of second-hand furniter, and twenty pound in money. I went very reasonable – cheap, dirt cheap.'

'Cheap!' cried a shrill voice in Mr Bumble's ear: 'You would have been dear at any price; and dear enough I paid for you, Lord above knows that.'

Mr Bumble turned and encountered the face of his interesting consort, who, imperfectly comprehending the few words she had overheard of his complaint, had hazarded the foregoing remark at a venture.

'Mrs Bumble, ma'am!' said Mr Bumble, with sentimental sternness.

'Well,' cried the lady.

'Have the goodness to look at me,' said Mr Bumble, fixing his eyes upon her.

'If she stands such a eye as that,' said Mr Bumble to himself, 'she can stand anything. It is a eye I never knew to fail with paupers, and if it fails with her my power is gone.'

Whether an exceedingly small expansion of eye is sufficient to quell paupers, who, being lightly fed, are in no very high condition, or whether the late Mrs Corney was particularly proof against eagle glances, are matters of opinion. The matter of fact is, that the matron was in no way overpowered by Mr Bumble's scowl, but, on the contrary, treated it with great disdain, and even raised a laugh thereat, which sounded as though it were genuine.

On hearing this most unexpected sound, Mr Bumble looked first incredulous, and afterwards amazed. He then relapsed into his former state; nor did he rouse himself until his attention was again awakened by the voice of his partner.

'Are you going to sit snoring there all day?' inquired Mrs Bumble.

'I am going to sit here as long as I think proper, ma'am,' rejoined Mr Bumble; 'and although I was *not* snoring, I shall snore, gape, sneeze, laugh, or cry, as the humour strikes me, such being my prerogative.'

'Your prerogative!' sneered Mrs Bumble with ineffable contempt.

'I said the word, ma'am,' observed Mr Bumble. 'The prerogative of a man is to command.'

'And what's the prerogative of a woman, in the name of goodness?' cried the relict of Mr Corney deceased.

'To obey, ma'am,' thundered Mr Bumble. 'Your late unfort'nate husband should have taught it you, and then, perhaps, he might have been alive now. I wish he was, poor man!'

Mrs Bumble, seeing at a glance that the decisive moment had now arrived, and that a blow struck for the mastership on one side or other must necessarily be final and conclusive, no sooner heard this allusion to the dead and gone, than she dropped into a chair, and, with a loud scream that Mr Bumble was a hard-hearted brute, fell into a paroxysm of tears.

But tears were not the things to find their way to Mr Bumble's soul; his heart was waterproof. Like washable beaver hats,[1] that improve with rain, his nerves were rendered stouter and more vigorous by showers of tears, which, being tokens of weakness, and so far tacit admissions of his own power, pleased and exalted him. He eyed his good lady with looks of great satisfaction, and begged in an encouraging manner that she would cry her hardest, the exercise being looked upon by the faculty as strongly conducive to health.

'It opens the lungs, washes the countenance, exercises the eyes, and softens down the temper,' said Mr Bumble; 'so cry away.'

As he discharged himself of this pleasantry, Mr Bumble took his hat from a peg, and putting it on rather rakishly on one side, as a man might do who felt he had asserted his superiority in a becoming manner, thrust his hands into his pockets, and sauntered towards the door with much ease and waggishness depicted in his whole appearance.

Now Mrs Corney, that was, had tried the tears, because they were less troublesome than a manual assault; but she was quite prepared to make trial of the latter mode of proceeding, as Mr Bumble was not long in discovering.

The first proof he experienced of the fact was conveyed in a hollow sound, immediately succeeded by the sudden flying off of his hat to the opposite end of the room. This preliminary proceeding laying bare his head, the expert lady, clasping him tight round the throat with one hand, inflicted a shower of blows (dealt with singular vigour and dexterity) upon it with the other. This done, she created a little variety by scratching his face and tearing his hair off, and having by this time inflicted as much punishment as she deemed necessary for the offence, she pushed him over a chair, which was luckily well situated for the purpose, and defied him to talk about his prerogative again if he dared.

'Get up,' said Mrs Bumble in a voice of command, 'and take yourself away from here, unless you want me to do something desperate.'

Mr Bumble rose with a very rueful countenance, wondering much what something desperate might be, and picking up his hat, looked towards the door.

'Are you going?' demanded Mrs Bumble.

'Certainly, my dear, certainly,' rejoined Mr Bumble, making a quicker motion towards the door. 'I didn't intend to – I'm going, my dear – you are so very violent, that really I —'

At this instant Mrs Bumble stepped hastily forward to replace the carpet, which had been kicked up in the scuffle, and Mr Bumble immediately darted out of the room without bestowing another thought on his unfinished sentence, leaving the late Mrs Corney in full possession of the field.

Mr Bumble was fairly taken by surprise, and fairly beaten. He had a decided bullying propensity, derived no inconsiderable pleasure from the exercise of petty cruelty, and consequently was (it is needless to say) a coward. This is by no means a disparagement to his character; for many official personages, who are held in high respect and admiration, are the victims of similar infirmities. The remark is made, indeed, rather in his favour than otherwise, and with the view of impressing the reader with a just sense of his qualifications for office.

But the measure of his degradation was not yet full. After making a tour of the house, and thinking for the first time that the poor laws really were too hard upon people, and that men who ran away from their wives, leaving them chargeable to the parish, ought in justice to be visited with no punishment at all, but rather rewarded as meritorious individuals who had suffered much, Mr Bumble came to a room where some of the female paupers were usually employed in washing the parish linen, and whence the sound of voices in conversation now proceeded.

'Hem!' said Mr Bumble, summoning up all his native dignity. 'These women at least shall continue to respect the prerogative. Hallo! hallo there! – what do you mean by this noise, you hussies?'

With these words Mr Bumble opened the door, and walked in with a very fierce and angry manner, which was at once exchanged for a most humiliated and cowering air as his eyes unexpectedly rested on the form of his lady wife.

'My dear,' said Mr Bumble, 'I didn't know you were here.'

'Didn't know I was here!' repeated Mrs Bumble. 'What do *you* do here?'

'I thought they were talking rather too much to be doing their work properly, my dear,' replied Mr Bumble, glancing distractedly at a couple of old women at the wash-tub, who were comparing notes of admiration at the workhouse-master's humility.

'You thought they were talking too much?' said Mrs Bumble. 'What business is it of yours?'

'Why, my dear –' urged Mr Bumble submissively.

'What business is it of yours?' demanded Mrs Bumble again.

'It's very true you're matron here, my dear,' submitted Mr Bumble; 'but I thought you mightn't be in the way just then.'

'I'll tell you what, Mr Bumble,' returned his lady, 'we don't want any of your interference, and you're a great deal too fond of poking your nose into things that don't concern you, making everybody in the house laugh the moment your back is turned, and making yourself look like a fool every hour in the day. Be off; come!'

Mr Bumble, seeing with excruciating feelings the delight of the two old paupers who were tittering together most rapturously, hesitated for an instant. Mrs Bumble, whose patience brooked no delay, caught up a bowl of soap-suds, and motioning him towards the door, ordered him instantly to depart, on pain of receiving the contents upon his portly person.

What could Mr Bumble do? He looked dejectedly round, and slunk away; and as he reached the door the titterings of the paupers broke into a shrill chuckle of irrepressible delight. It wanted but this. He was degraded in their eyes; he had lost caste and station before the very paupers; he had fallen from all the height and pomp of beadleship to the lowest depth of the most snubbed hen-peckery.

'All in two months!' said Mr Bumble, filled with dismal thoughts. 'Two months – not more than two months ago I was not only my own master, but everybody else's, so far as the porochial workhouse was concerned, and now! – '

It was too much. Mr Bumble boxed the ears of the boy who opened the gate for him, (for he had reached the portal in his reverie,) and walked distractedly into the street.

He walked up one street and down another until exercise had abated the first passion of his grief, and then the revulsion of feeling made him thirsty. He passed a great many public-houses, and at length paused before one in a bye-way, whose parlour, as he gathered from a hasty peep over the blinds, was deserted save by one solitary customer. It began to rain heavily at the moment, and this determined him; Mr Bumble stepped in, and ordering something to drink as he passed the bar, entered the apartment into which he had looked from the street.

Mr Bumble degraded in the eyes of the Paupers

The man who was seated there was tall and dark, and wore a large cloak. He had the air of a stranger, and seemed, by a certain haggardness in his look, as well as by the dusty soils on his dress, to have travelled some distance. He eyed Bumble askance as he entered, but scarcely deigned to nod his head in acknowledgment of his salutation.

Mr Bumble had quite dignity enough for two, supposing even that the stranger had been more familiar, so he drank his gin-and-water in silence, and read the paper with great show of pomp and importance.

It so happened, however, – as it will happen very often when men fall into company under such circumstances, – that Mr Bumble felt every now and then a powerful inducement, which he could not resist, to steal a look at the stranger, and that whenever he did so he withdrew his eyes in some confusion, to find that the stranger was at that moment stealing a look at him. Mr Bumble's awkwardness was enhanced by the very remarkable expression of the stranger's eye, which was keen and bright, but shadowed by a scowl of distrust and suspicion unlike anything he had ever observed before, and most repulsive to behold.

When they had encountered each other's glance several times in this way, the stranger, in a harsh, deep voice, broke silence.

'Were you looking for me,' he said, 'when you peered in at the window?'

'Not that I am aware of, unless you're Mr —' Here Mr Bumble stopped short, for he was curious to know the stranger's name, and thought in his impatience he might supply the blank.

'I see you were not,' said the stranger, an expression of quiet sarcasm playing about his mouth, 'or you would have known my name. You don't know it, and I should recommend you not to inquire.'

'I meant no harm, young man,' observed Mr Bumble majestically.

'And have done none,' said the stranger.

Another silence succeeded this short dialogue, which was again broken by the stranger.

'I have seen you before, I think,' said he. 'You were differently dressed at that time, and I only passed you in the street, but I should know you again. You were beadle here once, were you not?'

'I was,' said Mr Bumble, in some surprise. 'Porochial beadle.'

'Just so,' rejoined the other, nodding his head. 'It was in that character I saw you. What are you now?'

'Master of the workhouse,' rejoined Mr Bumble slowly and impressively, to check any undue familiarity the stranger might otherwise assume. 'Master of the workhouse, young man!'

'You have the same eye to your own interest that you always have had, I doubt not?' resumed the stranger, looking keenly into Mr Bumble's eyes as he raised them in astonishment at the question. 'Don't scruple to answer freely, man. I know you pretty well, you see.'

'I suppose a married man,' replied Mr Bumble, shading his eyes with his hand, and surveying the stranger from head to foot in evident perplexity, 'is not more averse to turning an honest penny when he can than a single one. Porochial officers are not so well paid that they can afford to refuse any little extra fee, when it comes to them in a civil and proper manner.'

The stranger smiled, and nodded his head again, as much as to say he found he had not mistaken his man: then rang the bell.

'Fill this glass again,' he said, handing Mr Bumble's empty tumbler to the landlord. 'Let it be strong and hot. You like it so, I suppose?'

'Not too strong,' replied Mr Bumble, with a delicate cough.

'You understand what that means, landlord!' said the stranger drily.

The host smiled, disappeared, and shortly afterwards returned with a steaming jorum,[2] of which the first gulph brought the water into Mr Bumble's eyes.

'Now listen to me,' said the stranger, after closing the door and window. 'I came down to this place to-day to find you out, and, by one of those chances which the devil throws in the way of his friends sometimes, you walked into the very room I was sitting in while you were uppermost in my mind. I want some information from you, and don't ask you to give it for nothing, slight as it is. Put up that to begin with.'

As he spoke he pushed a couple of sovereigns across the table to his companion carefully, as though unwilling that the chinking of money should be heard without; and when Mr Bumble had scrupulously examined the coins to see that they were genuine, and put them up with much satisfaction in his waistcoat-pocket, he went on.

'Carry your memory back – let me see – twelve years last winter.'

'It's a long time,' said Mr Bumble. 'Very good. I've done it.'

'The scene the workhouse.'

'Good!'

'And the time night.'

'Yes.'

'And the place the crazy hole, wherever it was, in which miserable drabs brought forth the life and health so often denied to themselves – gave birth to puling children for the parish to rear, and hid their shame, rot 'em, in the grave.'

'The lying-in room, I suppose that means?' said Mr Bumble, not quite following the stranger's excited description.

'Yes,' said the stranger. 'A boy was born there.'

'A many boys,' observed Mr Bumble, shaking his head despondingly.

'A murrain on the young devils!' cried the stranger impatiently; 'I speak of one, a meek-looking pale-faced hound, who was apprenticed, down here, to a coffin-maker, (I wish he had made his coffin, and screwed his body in it,) and who afterwards ran away to London, as it was supposed.'

'Why, you mean Oliver – young Twist?' said Mr Bumble; 'I remember him of course. There wasn't a obstinater young rascal—'

'It's not of him I want to hear; I've heard enough of him,' said the stranger, stopping Mr Bumble in the very outset of a tirade on the subject of poor Oliver's vices. 'It's of a woman, the hag that nursed his mother. Where is she?'

'Where is she?' said Mr Bumble, whom the gin and water had rendered facetious. 'It would be hard to tell. There's no midwifery there, whichever place she's gone to; so I suppose she's out of employment any way.'

'What do you mean?' demanded the stranger, sternly.

'That she died last winter,' rejoined Mr Bumble.

The man looked fixedly at him when he had given this information, and although he did not withdraw his eyes for some time afterwards, his gaze gradually became vacant and abstracted, and he seemed lost in thought. For some time he appeared doubtful whether he ought to be relieved or disappointed by the intelligence, but at length he breathed more freely, and withdrawing his eyes, observed that it was no great matter, and rose as if to depart.

Mr Bumble was cunning enough, and he at once saw that an opportunity was opened for the lucrative disposal of some secret in the possession of his better half. He well remembered the night of old Sally's death, which the occurrences of that day had given him good reason to recollect as the occasion on which he had proposed to Mrs Corney, and although that lady had never confided to him the disclosure of which she had been the solitary witness, he had heard enough to know that it related to something that had occurred in the old woman's attendance as workhouse nurse, upon the young mother of Oliver Twist. Hastily calling this circumstance to mind, he informed the stranger with an air of mystery, that one woman had been closeted with the old harridan shortly before she died, and that she could, as he had reason to believe, throw some light on the subject of his inquiry.

'How can I find her?' said the stranger, thrown off his guard, and plainly showing that all his fears (whatever they were) were aroused afresh by the intelligence.

'Only through me,' rejoined Mr Bumble.

'When?' cried the stranger, hastily.

'To-morrow,' rejoined Bumble.

'At nine in the evening,' said the stranger, producing a scrap of paper, and writing down an obscure address, by the water-side, upon it, in characters that betrayed his agitation, 'at nine in the evening, bring her to me there. I needn't tell you to be secret, for it's your interest.'

With these words he led the way to the door, after stopping to pay for the liquor that had been drunk; and shortly remarking that their roads were different, departed without more ceremony than an emphatic repetition of the hour of appointment for the following night.

On glancing at the address, the parochial functionary observed that it contained no name. The stranger had not gone far, so he made after him to ask it.

'Who's that?' cried the man turning quickly round as Bumble touched him on the arm. 'Following me!'

'Only to ask a question,' said the other, pointing to the scrap of paper. 'What name am I to ask for?'

'Monks!' rejoined the man, and strode hastily away.

THE END OF THE SECOND BOOK

*

CHAPTER THE FIRST

CONTAINING AN ACCOUNT OF WHAT
PASSED BETWEEN MR AND MRS BUMBLE
AND MONKS AT THEIR NOCTURNAL
INTERVIEW

It was a dull, close, overcast summer evening, when the clouds, which
had been threatening all day, spread out in a dense and sluggish mass
of vapour, already yielded large drops of rain, and seemed to presage
a violent thunder-storm, as Mr and Mrs Bumble, turning out of the
main street of the town, directed their course towards a scattered little
colony of ruinous houses, distant from it some mile and a half, or
thereabouts, and erected on a low unwholesome swamp, bordering
upon the river.

They were both wrapped in old and shabby outer garments, which
might perhaps serve the double purpose of protecting their persons
from the rain, and sheltering them from observation; the husband
carried a lantern, from which, however, no light yet shone, and trudged
on a few paces in front, as though – the way being dirty – to give his
wife the benefit of treading in his heavy foot-prints. They went on in
profound silence; every now and then Mr Bumble relaxed his pace,
and turned his head round, as if to make sure that his helpmate was
following, and, discovering that she was close at his heels, mended his
rate of walking, and proceeded at a considerable increase of speed
towards their place of destination.

This was far from being a place of doubtful character, for it had
long been known as the residence of none but low and desperate
ruffians, who, under various pretences of living by their labour,

subsisted chiefly on plunder and crime. It was a collection of mere hovels, some hastily built with loose bricks, and others of old worm-eaten ship timber, jumbled together without any attempt at order or arrangement, and planted, for the most part, within a few feet of the river's bank. A few leaky boats drawn up on the mud, and made fast to the dwarf wall which skirted it, and here and there an oar or coil of rope, appeared at first to indicate that the inhabitants of these miserable cottages pursued some avocation on the river; but a glance at the shattered and useless condition of the articles thus displayed would have led a passer-by without much difficulty to the conjecture that they were disposed there, rather for the preservation of appearances than with any view to their being actually employed.

In the heart of this cluster of huts, and skirting the river, which its upper stories overhung, stood a large building formerly used as a manufactory of some kind, and which had in its day probably furnished employment to the inhabitants of the surrounding tenements. But it had long since gone to ruin. The rat, the worm, and the action of the damp, had weakened and rotted the piles on which it stood, and a considerable portion of the building had already sunk down into the water beneath, while the remainder, tottering and bending over the dark stream, seemed but to wait a favourable opportunity of following its old companion, and involving itself in the same fate.

It was before this ruinous building that the worthy couple paused as the first peal of distant thunder reverberated in the air, and the rain commenced pouring violently down.

'The place should be somewhere here,' said Bumble, consulting a scrap of paper he held in his hand.

'Halloa there!' cried a voice from above.

Following the sound, Bumble raised his head, and descried a man looking out of a door, breast-high, on the second story.

'Stand still a minute,' cried the voice; 'I'll be with you directly.' With which the head disappeared, and the door closed.

'Is that the man?' asked Mr Bumble's good lady.

Mr Bumble nodded in the affirmative.

'Then, mind what I told you,' said the matron, 'and be careful to say as little as you can, or you'll betray us at once.'

Mr Bumble, who had eyed the building with very rueful looks, was apparently about to express some doubts relative to the advisability of proceeding any farther with the enterprise just then, when he was prevented by the appearance of Monks, who opened a small door, near which they stood, and beckoned them inwards.

'Come!' he cried impatiently, stamping his foot upon the ground. 'Don't keep me here!'

The woman, who had hesitated at first, walked boldly in without any further invitation, and Mr Bumble, who was ashamed, or afraid to hang behind, followed, obviously very ill at his ease, and with scarcely any of that remarkable dignity which was usually his chief characteristic.

'What the devil made you stand lingering there in the wet?' said Monks, turning round, and addressing Bumble, after he had bolted the door behind them.

'We – we were only cooling ourselves,' stammered Bumble, looking apprehensively about him.

'Cooling yourselves!' retorted Monks. 'Not all the rain that ever fell, or ever will fall, will put as much of hell's fire out as a man can carry about with him. You won't cool yourself so easily, don't think it!'

With this agreeable speech Monks turned short upon the matron, and bent his fierce gaze upon her, till even she who was not easily cowed, was fain to withdraw her eyes, and turn them towards the ground.

'This is the woman, is it?' demanded Monks.

'Hem! That is the woman,' replied Mr Bumble, mindful of his wife's caution.

'You think women never can keep secrets, I suppose?' said the matron, interposing, and returning as she spoke the searching look of Monks.

'I know they will always keep *one* till it's found out,' said Monks contemptuously.

'And what may that be?' asked the matron in the same tone.

'The loss of their own good name,' replied Monks: 'so, by the same rule, if a woman's a party to a secret that might hang or transport her,

I'm not afraid of her telling it to anybody, not I. Do you understand me?'

'No,' rejoined the matron, slightly colouring as she spoke.

'Of course you don't!' said Monks ironically. 'How should you?'

Bestowing something half-way between a sneer and a scowl upon his two companions, and again beckoning them to follow him, the man hastened across the apartment, which was of considerable extent, but low in the roof, and was preparing to ascend a steep staircase, or rather ladder, leading to another floor of warehouses above, when a bright flash of lightning streamed down the aperture, and a peal of thunder followed, which shook the crazy building to its centre.

'Hear it!' he cried, shrinking back. 'Hear it rolling and crashing away as if it echoed through a thousand caverns, where the devils are hiding from it. Fire the sound! I hate it.'

He remained silent for a few moments, and then removing his hands suddenly from his face, showed, to the unspeakable discomposure of Mr Bumble, that it was much distorted, and nearly blank.

'These fits come over me now and then,' said Monks, observing his alarm, 'and thunder sometimes brings them on. Don't mind me now; it's all over for this once.'

Thus speaking, he led the way up the ladder, and hastily closing the window-shutter of the room into which it led, lowered a lantern which hung at the end of a rope and pulley passed through one of the heavy beams in the ceiling, and which cast a dim light upon an old table and three chairs that were placed beneath it.

'Now,' said Monks, when they had all three seated themselves, 'the sooner we come to our business, the better for all. The woman knows what it is, does she?'

The question was addressed to Bumble; but his wife anticipated the reply, by intimating that she was perfectly acquainted with it.

'He is right in saying that you were with this hag the night she died, and that she told you something –'

'About the mother of the boy you named,' replied the matron interrupting him. 'Yes.'

'The first question is, of what nature was her communication?' said Monks.

'That's the second,' observed the woman with much deliberation. 'The first is, what may the communication be worth?'

'Who the devil can tell that, without knowing of what kind it is?' asked Monks.

'Nobody better than you, I am persuaded,' answered Mrs Bumble, who did not want for spirit, as her yokefellow could abundantly testify.

'Humph!' said Monks significantly, and with a look of eager inquiry, 'there may be money's worth to get, eh?'

'Perhaps there may,' was the composed reply.

'Something that was taken from her,' said Monks eagerly; 'something that she wore – something that –'

'You had better bid,' interrupted Mrs Bumble. 'I have heard enough already to assure me that you are the man I ought to talk to.'

Mr Bumble, who had not yet been admitted by his better half into any greater share of the secret than he had originally possessed, listened to this dialogue with outstretched neck and distended eyes, which he directed towards his wife and Monks by turns in undisguised astonishment; increased, if possible, when the latter sternly demanded what sum was required for the disclosure.

'What's it worth to you?' asked the woman, as collectedly as before.

'It may be nothing; it may be twenty pounds,' replied Monks; 'speak out, and let me know which.'

'Add five pounds to the sum you have named; give me five-and-twenty pounds in gold,' said the woman, 'and I'll tell you all I know – not before.'

'Five-and-twenty pounds!' exclaimed Monks, drawing back.

'I spoke as plainly as I could,' replied Mrs Bumble, 'and it's not a large sum either.'

'Not a large sum for a paltry secret, that may be nothing when it's told!' cried Monks impatiently, 'and which has been lying dead for twelve years past, or more!'

'Such matters keep well, and, like good wine, often double their value in course of time,' answered the matron, still preserving the resolute indifference she had assumed. 'As to lying dead, there are those who will lie dead for twelve thousand years to come, or twelve million, for anything you or I know, who will tell strange tales at last.'

'What if I pay it for nothing?' asked Monks, hesitating.

'You can easily take it away again,' replied the matron. 'I am but a woman, alone here, and unprotected.'

'Not alone, my dear, nor unprotected neither,' submitted Mr Bumble, in a voice tremulous with fear; '*I* am here, my dear. And besides,' said Mr Bumble, his teeth chattering as he spoke, 'Mr Monks is too much of a gentleman to attempt any violence on porochial persons. Mr Monks is aware that I am not a young man, my dear, and also that I am a little run to seed, as I may say; but he has heerd – I say I have no doubt Mr Monks has heerd, my dear – that I am a very determined officer, with very uncommon strength, if I'm once roused. I only want a little rousing, that's all.'

As Mr Bumble spoke, he made a melancholy feint of grasping his lantern with fierce determination, and plainly showed, by the alarmed expression of every feature, that he did want a little rousing, and not a little, prior to making any very warlike demonstration, unless, indeed, against paupers, or other person or persons trained down for the purpose.

'You are a fool,' said Mrs Bumble in reply, 'and had better hold your tongue.'

'He had better have cut it out before he came, if he can't speak in a lower tone,' said Monks grimly. 'So he's your husband, eh?'

'He my husband!' tittered the matron, parrying the question.

'I thought as much when you came in,' rejoined Monks, marking the angry glance which the lady darted at her spouse as she spoke. 'So much the better; I have less hesitation in dealing with two people, when I find that there's only one will between them. I'm in earnest – see here.'

He thrust his hand into a side-pocket, and producing a canvass bag, told out twenty-five sovereigns on the table, and pushed them over to the woman.

'Now,' he said, 'gather them up; and when this cursed peal of thunder, that I feel is coming up to break over the house-top, is gone, let's hear your story.'

The roar of thunder, which seemed in fact much nearer, and to shiver and break almost over their heads, having subsided, Monks, raising his face from the table, bent forward to listen to what the woman should say. The faces of the three nearly touched as the two men leant over the small table in their eagerness to hear, and the woman also leant forward to render her whisper audible. The sickly rays of the suspended lantern falling directly upon them, aggravated the paleness and anxiety of their countenances, which, encircled by the deepest gloom and darkness, looked ghastly in the extreme.

'When this woman, that we called old Sally, died,' the matron began, 'she and I were alone.'

'Was there no one by?' asked Monks in the same hollow whisper, 'no sick wretch or idiot in some other bed? – no one who could hear, and might by possibility understand?'

'Not a soul,' replied the woman; 'we were alone: *I* stood alone beside the body when death came over it.'

'Good,' said Monks, regarding her attentively: 'go on.'

'She spoke of a young creature,' resumed the matron, 'who had brought a child into the world some years before: not merely in the same room, but in the same bed in which she then lay dying.'

'Ay?' said Monks with quivering lip, and glancing over his shoulder. 'Blood! How things come about at last!'

'The child was the one you named to him last night,' said the matron, nodding carelessly towards her husband; 'the mother this nurse had robbed.'

'In life?' asked Monks.

'In death,' replied the woman with something like a shudder. 'She stole from the corpse, when it had hardly turned to one, that which the dead mother had prayed her with her last breath to keep for the infant's sake.'

'She sold it?' cried Monks with desperate eagerness; 'did she sell it? – where? – when? – to whom? – how long before?'

'As she told me with great difficulty that she had done this,' said the matron, 'she fell back and died.'

'Without saying more?' cried Monks in a voice which, from its very suppression, seemed only the more furious. 'It's a lie! I'll not be played with. She said more – I'll tear the life out of you both, but I'll know what it was.'

'She didn't utter another word,' said the woman, to all appearance unmoved (as Mr Bumble was very far from being) by the strange man's violence; 'but she clutched my gown violently with one hand, which was partly closed, and when I saw that she was dead, and so removed the hand by force, I found it clasped a scrap of dirty paper.'

'Which contained –' interposed Monks, stretching forward.

'Nothing,' replied the woman; 'it was a pawnbroker's duplicate.'

'For what?' demanded Monks.

'In good time I'll tell you,' said the woman. 'I judge that she had kept the trinket for some time, in the hope of turning it to better account, and then pawned it, and saved or scraped together money to pay the pawnbroker's interest year by year, and prevent its running out, so that if anything came of it, it could still be redeemed. Nothing had come of it; and, as I tell you, she died with the scrap of paper, all worn and tattered, in her hand. The time was out in two days; I thought something might one day come of it too, and so redeemed the pledge.'

'Where is it now?' asked Monks quickly.

'*There*,' replied the woman. And, as if glad to be relieved of it, she hastily threw upon the table a small kid bag scarcely large enough for a French watch, which Monks pouncing upon, tore open with trembling hands. It contained a little gold locket, in which were two locks of hair, and a plain gold wedding ring.

'It has the word "Agnes" engraved on the inside,' said the woman. 'There is a blank left for the surname, and then follows the date, which is within a year before the child was born; I found out that.'

'And this is all?' said Monks, after a close and eager scrutiny of the contents of the little packet.

'All,' replied the woman.

Mr Bumble drew a long breath, as if he were glad to find that the story was over, and no mention made of taking the five-and-twenty pounds back again; and now took courage to wipe off the perspiration, which had been trickling over his nose unchecked during the whole of the previous conversation.

'I know nothing of the story beyond what I can guess at,' said his wife, addressing Monks after a short silence, 'and I want to know nothing, for it's safer not. But I may ask you two questions, may I?'

'You may ask,' said Monks, with some show of surprise, 'but whether I answer or not is another question.'

'– Which makes three,' observed Mr Bumble, essaying a stroke of facetiousness.

'Is that what you expected to get from me?' demanded the matron.

'It is,' replied Monks. 'The other question? –'

'What you propose to do with it. Can it be used against me?'

'Never,' rejoined Monks; 'nor against me either. See here; but don't move a step forward, or your life's not worth a bulrush!'

With these words he suddenly wheeled the table aside, and pulling an iron ring in the boarding, threw back a large trap-door which opened close at Mr Bumble's feet, and caused that gentleman to retire several paces backward with great precipitation.

'Look down,' said Monks, lowering the lantern into the gulf. 'Don't fear me. I could have let you down[1] quietly enough when you were seated over it, if that had been my game.'

Thus encouraged, the matron drew near to the brink, and even Mr Bumble himself, impelled by curiosity, ventured to do the same. The turbid water, swollen by the heavy rain, was rushing rapidly on below, and all other sounds were lost in the noise of its plashing and eddying against the green and slimy piles. There had once been a water-mill beneath, and the tide foaming and chafing round the few rotten stakes, and fragments of machinery, that yet remained, seemed to dart onward with a new impulse when freed from the obstacles which had unavailingly attempted to stem its headlong course.

'If you flung a man's body down there, where would it be to-morrow morning?' said Monks, swinging the lantern to and fro in the dark well.

'Twelve miles down the river, and cut to pieces besides,' replied Bumble, recoiling at the very notion.

Monks drew the little packet from his breast, into which he had hurriedly thrust it, and tying it firmly to a leaden weight which had

The evidence destroyed

formed a part of some pulley, and was lying on the floor, dropped it into the stream. It fell straight, and true as a die, clove the water with a scarcely audible splash, and was gone.

The three looked into each other's faces, and seemed to breathe more freely.

'There!' said Monks, closing the trap-door, which fell heavily back into its former position. 'If the sea ever gives up its dead – as books say it will[2] – it will keep its gold and silver to itself, and that trash among it. We have nothing more to say, and may break up our pleasant party.'

'By all means,' observed Mr Bumble with great alacrity.

'You'll keep a quiet tongue in your head, will you?' said Monks, with a threatening look. 'I am not afraid of your wife.'

'You may depend upon me, young man,' answered Mr Bumble, bowing himself gradually towards the ladder with excessive politeness. 'On everybody's account, young man; on my own, you know, Mr Monks.'

'I am glad for your sake to hear it,' remarked Monks. 'Light your lantern, and get away from here as fast as you can.'

It was fortunate that the conversation terminated at this point, or Mr Bumble, who had bowed himself to within six inches of the ladder, would infallibly have pitched headlong into the room below. He lighted his lantern from that which Monks had detached from the rope, and now carried in his hand, and, making no effort to prolong the discourse, descended in silence, followed by his wife. Monks brought up the rear, after pausing on the steps to satisfy himself that there were no other sounds to be heard than the beating of the rain without, and the rushing of the water.

They traversed the lower room slowly, and with caution, for Monks started at every shadow, and Mr Bumble, holding his lantern a foot above the ground, walked not only with remarkable care, but with a marvellously light step for a gentleman of his figure: looking nervously about him for hidden trap-doors. The gate at which they had entered was softly unfastened and opened by Monks, and merely exchanging a nod with their mysterious acquaintance, the married couple emerged into the wet and darkness outside.

They were no sooner gone, than Monks, who appeared to entertain an invincible repugnance to being left alone, called to a boy who had been hidden somewhere below, and bidding him go first, and bear the light, returned to the chamber he had just quitted.

CHAPTER THE SECOND

INTRODUCES SOME RESPECTABLE CHARACTERS WITH WHOM THE READER IS ALREADY ACQUAINTED, AND SHOWS HOW MONKS AND THE JEW LAID THEIR WORTHY HEADS TOGETHER

It was about two hours earlier on the evening following that upon which the three worthies mentioned in the last chapter disposed of their little matter of business as therein narrated, when Mr William Sikes, awakening from a nap, drowsily growled forth an inquiry what time of night it was.

The room in which Mr Sikes propounded this question was not one of those he had tenanted previous to the Chertsey expedition, although it was in the same quarter of the town, and was situated at no great distance from his former lodgings. It was not in appearance so desirable a habitation as his old quarters, being a mean and badly-furnished apartment of very limited size, lighted only by one small window in the shelving roof, and abutting upon a close and dirty lane. Nor were there wanting other indications of the good gentleman's having gone down in the world of late; for a great scarcity of furniture, and total absence of comfort, together with the disappearance of all such small moveables as spare clothes and linen, bespoke a state of extreme poverty, while the meagre and attenuated condition of Mr Sikes himself would have fully confirmed these symptoms if they had stood in need of corroboration.

The housebreaker was lying on the bed wrapped in his white great coat, by way of dressing-gown, and displaying a set of features in no degree improved by the cadaverous hue of illness, and the addition of a soiled nightcap, and a stiff, black beard of a week's growth. The dog sat at the bedside, now eyeing his master with a wistful look, and now pricking his ears, and uttering a low growl as some noise in the street, or in the lower part of the house, attracted his attention. Seated by the window, busily engaged in patching an old waistcoat which formed a portion of the robber's ordinary dress, was a female, so pale and reduced with watching and privation that there would have been considerable difficulty in recognizing her as the same Nancy who has already figured in this tale, but for the voice in which she replied to Mr Sikes's question.

'Not long gone seven,' said the girl. 'How do you feel to-night, Bill?'

'As weak as water,' replied Mr Sikes, with an imprecation on his eyes and limbs. 'Here; lend us a hand, and let me get off this thundering bed, anyhow.'

Illness had not improved Mr Sikes's temper, for, as the girl raised him up, and led him to a chair, he muttered various curses upon her awkwardness, and struck her.

'Whining, are you?' said Sikes. 'Come; don't stand snivelling there. If you can't do anything better than that, cut off altogether. D'ye hear me?'

'I hear you,' replied the girl, turning her face aside, and forcing a laugh. 'What fancy have you got in your head now?'

'Oh! you've thought better of it, have you?' growled Sikes, marking the tear which trembled in her eye. 'All the better for you, you have.'

'Why, you don't mean to say you'd be hard upon me to-night, Bill?' said the girl, laying her hand upon his shoulder.

'No!' cried Mr Sikes. 'Why not?'

'Such a number of nights,' said the girl, with a touch of woman's tenderness, which communicated something like sweetness of tone even to her voice, – 'such a number of nights as I've been patient with you, nursing and caring for you as if you had been a child, and this the first that I've seen you like yourself; you wouldn't have served me as you did just now, if you'd thought of that, would you? Come, come; say you wouldn't.'

'Well, then,' rejoined Mr Sikes, 'I wouldn't. Why, damme, now, the girl's whining again!'

'It's nothing,' said the girl, throwing herself into a chair. 'Don't you seem to mind me, and it'll soon be over.'

'What'll be over?' demanded Mr Sikes in a savage voice. 'What foolery are you up to now again? Get up, and bustle about, and don't come over me with your woman's nonsense.'

At any other time this remonstrance, and the tone in which it was delivered, would have had the desired effect; but the girl being really weak and exhausted, dropped her head over the back of the chair, and fainted, before Mr Sikes could get out a few of the appropriate oaths with which on similar occasions he was accustomed to garnish his threats. Not knowing very well what to do in this uncommon emergency, for Miss Nancy's hysterics were usually of that violent kind which the patient fights and struggles out of without much assistance, Mr Sikes tried a little blasphemy, and, finding that mode of treatment wholly ineffectual, called for assistance.

'What's the matter here, my dear?' said the Jew, looking in.

'Lend a hand to the girl, can't you?' replied Sikes impatiently, 'and don't stand chattering and grinning at me!'

With an exclamation of surprise Fagin hastened to the girl's assistance, while Mr John Dawkins, (otherwise the Artful Dodger,) who had followed his venerable friend into the room, hastily deposited on the floor a bundle with which he was laden, and, snatching a bottle from the grasp of Master Charles Bates who came close at his heels, uncorked it in a twinkling with his teeth, and poured a portion of its contents down the patient's throat; previously taking a taste himself to prevent mistakes.

'Give her a whiff of fresh air with the bellows, Charley,' said Mr Dawkins; 'and you slap her hands, Fagin, while Bill undoes the petticuts.'

These united restoratives, administered with great energy, especially that department consigned to Master Bates, who appeared to consider his share in the proceeding a piece of unexampled pleasantry, were not

Mr Fagin and his pupil recovering Nancy

long in producing the desired effect. The girl gradually recovered her senses, and, staggering to a chair by the bedside, hid her face upon the pillow, leaving Mr Sikes to confront the new-comers, in some astonishment at their unlooked-for appearance.

'Why, what evil wind has blowed you here?' he asked of Fagin.

'No evil wind at all, my dear,' replied the Jew; 'for ill winds blow nobody any good, and I've brought something good with me that you'll be glad to see. Dodger, my dear, open the bundle, and give Bill the little trifles that we spent all our money on this morning.'

In compliance with Mr Fagin's request, the Artful untied his bundle, which was of large size, and formed of an old table-cloth, and handed the articles it contained, one by one, to Charley Bates, who placed them on the table, with various encomiums on their rarity and excellence.

'Sitch a rabbit pie, Bill!' exclaimed that young gentleman, disclosing to view a huge pasty; 'sitch delicate creeturs, with sitch tender limbs, Bill, that the wery bones melt in your mouth, and there's no occasion to pick 'em; half a pound of seven and sixpenny green,[1] so precious strong that if you mix it with boiling water, it'll go nigh to blow the lid of the teapot off; a pound and a half of moist sugar that the niggers didn't work at all at afore they got it to sitch a pitch of goodness, – oh no! two half-quartern brans; pound of best fresh; piece of double Glo'ster,[2] and, to wind up all, some of the rightest sort you ever lushed.' Uttering this last panegyric, Master Bates produced from one of his extensive pockets a full-sized wine-bottle, carefully corked, while Mr Dawkins at the same instant poured out a wine-glassful of raw spirits from the bottle he carried, which the invalid tossed down his throat without a moment's hesitation.

'Ah!' said the Jew, rubbing his hands with great satisfaction. 'You'll do, Bill; you'll do now.'

'Do!' exclaimed Mr Sikes; 'I might have been done for twenty times over, afore you'd have done anything to help me. What do you mean by leaving a man in this state three weeks and more, you false-hearted wagabond?'

'Only hear him, boys!' said the Jew, shrugging his shoulders; 'and us come to bring him all these beautiful things.'

'The things is well enough in their way,' observed Mr Sikes, a little soothed as he glanced over the table; 'but what have you got to say for yourself why you should leave me here, down in the mouth, health, blunt, and everything else, and take no more notice of me all this mortal time than if I was that ere dog. – Drive him down, Charley.'

'I never see such a jolly dog as that,' cried Master Bates, doing as he was desired. 'Smelling the grub like a old lady a-going to market! He'd make his fortun' on the stage that dog would, and rewive the drayma besides.'

'Hold your din,' cried Sikes, as the dog retreated under the bed, still growling angrily. 'And what have you got to say for yourself, you withered old fence, eh?'

'I was away from London a week and more, my dear, on a plant,' replied the Jew.

'And what about the other fortnight?' demanded Sikes. 'What about the other fortnight that you've left me lying here, like a sick rat in his hole?'

'I couldn't help it, Bill,' replied the Jew. 'I can't go into a long explanation before company; but I couldn't help it, upon my honour.'

'Upon your what?' growled Sikes with excessive disgust. 'Here, cut me off a piece of the pie, one of you boys, to take the taste of that out of my mouth, or it'll choke me dead.'

'Don't be out of temper, my dear,' urged the Jew submissively. 'I have never forgot you, Bill; never once.'

'No, I'll pound it, that you han't,' replied Sikes with a bitter grin. 'You've been scheming and plotting away every hour that I've laid shivering and burning here; and Bill was to do this, and Bill was to do that, and Bill was to do it all dirt cheap, as soon as he got well, and was quite poor enough for your work. If it hadn't been for the girl, I might have died.'

'There now, Bill,' remonstrated the Jew, eagerly catching at the word. 'If it hadn't been for the girl! Who was the means of your having such a handy girl about you but me?'

'He says true enough there, God knows!' said Nancy, coming hastily forward. 'Let him be, let him be.'

Nancy's appearance gave a new turn to the conversation, for the boys, receiving a sly wink from the wary old Jew, began to ply her with liquor, of which, however, she partook very sparingly; while Fagin, assuming an unusual flow of spirits, gradually brought Mr Sikes into a better temper, by affecting to regard his threats as a little pleasant banter, and, moreover, laughing very heartily at one or two rough jokes, which, after repeated applications to the spirit-bottle, he condescended to make.

'It's all very well,' said Mr Sikes; 'but I must have some blunt from you to-night.'

'I haven't a piece of coin about me,' replied the Jew.

'Then you've got lots at home,' retorted Sikes, 'and I must have some from there.'

'Lots!' cried the Jew holding up his hands. 'I haven't so much as would—'

'I don't know how much you've got, and I dare say you hardly know yourself, as it would take a pretty long time to count it,' said Sikes; 'but I must have some to-night, and that's flat.'

'Well, well,' said the Jew with a sigh, 'I'll send the Artful round presently.'

'You won't do nothing of the kind,' rejoined Mr Sikes. 'The Artful's a deal too artful, and would forget to come, or lose his way, or get dodged by traps and so be perwented, or anything for an excuse, if you put him up to it. Nancy shall go to the ken and fetch it, to make all sure, and I'll lie down and have a snooze while she's gone.'

After a great deal of haggling and squabbling, the Jew beat down the amount of the required advance from five pounds to three pounds four and sixpence, protesting with many solemn asseverations that that would only leave him eighteenpence to keep house with; Mr Sikes, sullenly remarking that if he couldn't get any more he must be content with that, Nancy prepared to accompany him home, while the Dodger and Master Bates put the eatables in the cupboard. The Jew then, taking leave of his affectionate friend, returned homewards, attended by Nancy and the boys, Mr Sikes meanwhile flinging himself on the bed, and composing himself to sleep away the time until the young lady's return.

In due time they arrived at the Jew's abode, where they found Toby Crackit and Mr Chitling intent upon their fifteenth game at cribbage, which it is scarcely necessary to say the latter gentleman lost, and with it his fifteenth and last sixpence, much to the amusement of his young friends. Mr Crackit, apparently somewhat ashamed at being found relaxing himself with a gentleman so much his inferior in station and mental endowments, yawned heavily, and, inquiring after Sikes, took up his hat to go.

'Has nobody been, Toby?' asked the Jew.

'Not a living leg,' answered Mr Crackit, pulling up his collar: 'it's been as dull as swipes. You ought to stand something handsome, Fagin, to recompense me for keeping house so long. Damme, I'm as flat as a juryman, and should have gone to sleep as fast as Newgate, if I hadn't had the good natur' to amuse this youngster. Horrid dull, I'm blessed if I an't.'

With these and other ejaculations of the same kind, Mr Toby Crackit swept up his winnings, and crammed them into his waistcoat pocket with a haughty air, as though such small pieces of silver were wholly beneath the consideration of a man of his figure, and swaggered out of the room with so much elegance and gentility, that Mr Chitling, bestowing numerous admiring glances on his legs and boots till they were out of sight, assured the company that he considered his acquaintance cheap at fifteen sixpences an interview, and that he didn't value his losses the snap of a little finger.

'Wot a rum chap you are, Tom,' said Master Bates, highly amused by this declaration.

'Not a bit of it,' replied Mr Chitling: 'am I, Fagin?'

'A very clever fellow, my dear,' said the Jew, patting him on the shoulder, and winking to his other pupils.

'And Mr Crackit *is* a heavy swell, an't he, Fagin?' asked Tom.

'No doubt at all of that, my dear,' replied the Jew.

'And it *is* a creditable thing to have his acquaintance, an't it, Fagin?' pursued Tom.

'Very much so indeed, my dear,' replied the Jew. 'They're only jealous, Tom, because he won't give it to them.'

'Ah!' cried Tom triumphantly, 'that's where it is. He has cleaned me out; but I can go and earn some more when I like, – can't I, Fagin?'

'To be sure you can,' replied the Jew; 'and the sooner you go, the better, Tom; so make up your loss at once, and don't lose any more time. Dodger, Charley, it's time you were on the lay: – come, it's near ten, and nothing done yet.'

In obedience to this hint, the boys nodding to Nancy, took up their hats and left the room; the Dodger and his vivacious friend indulging as they went in many witticisms at the expense of Mr Chitling, in whose conduct, it is but justice to say, there was nothing very conspicuous or peculiar, inasmuch as there are a great number of spirited young bloods upon town who pay a much higher price than Mr Chitling for being seen in good society, and a great number of fine gentlemen (composing the good society aforesaid) who establish their reputation upon very much the same footing as flash Toby Crackit.

'Now,' said the Jew, when they had left the room, 'I'll go and get you that cash, Nancy. This is only the key of a little cupboard where I keep a few odd things the boys get, my dear. I never lock up my money, for I've got none to lock up, my dear – ha! ha! ha! – none to lock. It's a poor trade, Nancy, and no thanks; but I'm fond of seeing the young people about me, and I bear it all; I bear it all. Hush!' he said, hastily concealing the key in his breast; 'who's that? Listen!'

The girl, who was sitting at the table with her arms folded, appeared in no way interested in the arrival, or to care whether the person, whoever he was, came or went, until the murmur of a man's voice reached her ears. The instant she caught the sound she tore off her bonnet and shawl with the rapidity of lightning, and thrust them under the table. The Jew turning round immediately afterwards, she muttered a complaint of the heat in a tone of languor that contrasted very remarkably with the extreme haste and violence of this action, which, however, had been unobserved by Fagin, who had his back towards her at the time.

'Bah!' whispered the Jew, as though nettled by the interruption; 'it's the man I expected before; he's coming down stairs. Not a word about the money while he's here, Nance. He won't stop long – not ten minutes, my dear.'

Laying his skinny fore-finger upon his lip, the Jew carried a candle to the door as a man's step was heard upon the stairs without, and reached it at the same moment as the visitor, who coming hastily into the room, was close upon the girl before he observed her.

It was Monks.

'Only one of my young people,' said the Jew, observing that Monks drew back on beholding a stranger. 'Don't move, Nancy.'

The girl drew closer to the table, and glancing at Monks with an air of careless levity, withdrew her eyes; but as he turned his towards the Jew, she stole another look, so keen and searching, and full of purpose, that if there had been any bystander to observe the change he could hardly have believed the two looks to have proceeded from the same person.

'Any news?' inquired the Jew.

'Great.'

'And – and – good?' asked the Jew hesitatingly, as though he feared to vex the other man by being too sanguine.

'Not bad any way,' replied Monks with a smile. 'I have been prompt enough this time. Let me have a word with you.'

The girl drew closer to the table, and made no offer to leave the room, although she could see that Monks was pointing to her. The Jew – perhaps fearing that she might say something aloud about the money, if he endeavoured to get rid of her – pointed upwards, and took Monks out of the room.

'Not that infernal hole we were in before,' she could hear the man say as they went up-stairs. The Jew laughed, and making some reply which did not reach her, seemed by the creaking of the boards to lead his companion to the second story.

Before the sound of their footsteps had ceased to echo through the house, the girl had slipped off her shoes, and drawing her gown loosely over her head, and muffling her arms in it, stood at the door listening with breathless interest. The moment the noise ceased she glided from the room, ascended the stairs with incredible softness and silence, and was lost in the gloom above.

The room remained deserted for a quarter of an hour or more; the girl glided back with the same unearthly tread, and immediately afterwards the two men were heard descending. Monks went at once into the street, and the Jew crawled up stairs again for the money. When he returned, the girl was adjusting her shawl and bonnet, as if preparing to be gone.

'Why, Nance,' exclaimed the Jew, starting back as he put down the candle, 'how pale you are!'

'Pale!' echoed the girl, shading her eyes with her hand as if to look steadily at him.

'Quite horrible,' said the Jew. 'What have you been doing to yourself?'

'Nothing that I know of, except sitting in this close place for I don't know how long and all,' replied the girl carelessly. 'Come, let me get back; that's a dear.'

With a sigh for every piece of money, Fagin told the amount into her hand, and they parted without more conversation than interchanging a 'good-night.'

When the girl got into the open street she sat down upon a door-step, and seemed for a few moments wholly bewildered and unable to pursue her way. Suddenly she arose, and hurrying on in a direction quite opposite to that in which Sikes was awaiting her return, quickened her pace, until it gradually resolved into a violent run. After completely exhausting herself, she stopped to take breath, and, as if suddenly recollecting herself, and deploring her inability to do something she was bent upon, wrung her hands, and burst into tears.

It might be that her tears relieved her, or that she felt the full hopelessness of her condition; but she turned back, and hurrying with nearly as great rapidity in the contrary direction, partly to recover lost time, and partly to keep pace with the violent current of her own thoughts, soon reached the dwelling where she had left the house-breaker.

If she betrayed any agitation by the time she presented herself to Mr Sikes, he did not observe it; for merely inquiring if she had brought the money, and receiving a reply in the affirmative, he laid his head upon his pillow, and resumed the slumbers which her arrival had interrupted.

*

CHAPTER THE THIRD[1]

A STRANGE INTERVIEW, WHICH IS A SEQUEL TO THE LAST CHAPTER

It was fortunate for the girl that the possession of money occasioned Mr Sikes so much employment next day in the way of eating and drinking, and withal had so beneficial an effect in smoothing down the asperities of his temper that he had neither time nor inclination to be very critical upon her behaviour and deportment. That she had all the abstracted and nervous manner of one who is on the eve of some bold and hazardous step, which it has required no common struggle to resolve upon, would have been obvious to his lynx-eyed friend, the Jew, who would most probably have taken the alarm at once; but Mr Sikes lacking the niceties of discrimination, and being troubled with no more subtle misgivings than those which resolve themselves into a dogged roughness of behaviour towards everybody; and being, furthermore, in an unusually amiable condition, as has been already observed, saw nothing unusual in her demeanour, and, indeed, troubled himself so little about her, that, had her agitation been far more perceptible than it was, it would have been very unlikely to have awakened his suspicions.

As the day closed in the girl's excitement increased, and, when night came on, and she sat by, watching till the housebreaker should drink himself asleep, there was an unusual paleness in her cheek, and fire in her eye, that even Sikes observed with astonishment.

Mr Sikes, being weak from the fever, was lying in bed, taking hot water with his gin to render it less inflammatory, and had pushed his glass towards Nancy to be replenished for the third or fourth time, when these symptoms first struck him.

'Why, burn my body!' said the man, raising himself on his hands as he stared the girl in the face. 'You look like a corpse come to life again. What's the matter?'

'Matter!' replied the girl. 'Nothing. What do you look at me so hard for?'

'What foolery is this?' demanded Sikes, grasping her by the arm, and shaking her roughly. 'What is it? What do you mean? What are you thinking of, ha?'

'Of many things, Bill,' replied the girl, shuddering, and as she did so pressing her hands upon her eyes. 'But, Lord! what odds in that?'

The tone of forced gaiety in which the last words were spoken seemed to produce a deeper impression on Sikes than the wild and rigid look which had preceded them.

'I tell you wot it is,' said Sikes, 'If you haven't caught the fever and got it comin' on now, there's something more than usual in the wind, and something dangerous too. You're not a-going to—No, damme! you wouldn't do that!'

'Do what?' asked the girl.

'There ain't,' said Sikes, fixing his eyes upon her, and muttering the words to himself, 'there ain't a stauncher-hearted gal going, or I'd have cut her throat three months ago. She's got the fever coming on; that's it.'

Fortifying himself with this assurance, Sikes drained the glass to the bottom, and then, with many grumbling oaths, called for his physic. The girl jumped up with great alacrity, poured it quickly out, but with her back towards him: and held the vessel to his lips while he drank it off.

'Now,' said the robber, 'come and sit aside of me, and put on your own face, or I'll alter it so that you won't know it again when you *do* want it.'

The girl obeyed, and Sikes, locking her hand in his, fell back upon the pillow, turning his eyes upon her face. They closed, opened again; closed once more, again opened; the housebreaker shifted his position restlessly, and, after dozing again and again for two or three minutes, and as often springing up with a look of terror, and gazing vacantly about him, was suddenly stricken, as it were, while in the very attitude of rising, into a deep and heavy sleep. The grasp of his hand relaxed, the upraised arm fell languidly by his side, and he lay like one in a profound trance.

'The laudanum has taken effect at last,' murmured the girl as she rose from the bedside. 'I may be too late even now.'

She hastily dressed herself in her bonnet and shawl, looking fearfully round from time to time as if, despite the sleeping draught, she expected every moment to feel the pressure of Sikes's heavy hand upon her shoulder; then stooping softly over the bed, she kissed the robber's lips, and opening and closing the room-door with noiseless touch, hurried from the house.

A watchman was crying half-past nine[2] down a dark passage through which she had to pass in gaining the main thoroughfare.

'Has it long gone the half hour?' asked the girl.

'It'll strike the hour in another quarter,' said the man, raising his lantern to her face.

'And I cannot get there in less than an hour or more,' muttered Nancy, brushing swiftly past him and gliding rapidly down the street.

Many of the shops were already closing in the back lanes and avenues through which she tracked her way in making from Spitalfields towards the West-End of London. The clock struck ten, increasing her impatience. She tore along the narrow pavement, elbowing the passengers from side to side and darting almost under the horses' heads, crossed crowded streets, where clusters of persons were eagerly watching their opportunity to do the like.

'The woman is mad!' said the people, turning to look after her as she rushed away.

When she reached the more wealthy quarter of the town, the streets were comparatively deserted, and here her headlong progress seemed to excite a greater curiosity in the stragglers whom she hurried past. Some quickened their pace behind, as though to see whither she was hastening at such an unusual rate; and a few made head upon her, and looked back, surprised at her undiminished speed, but they fell off one by one; and when she neared her place of destination she was alone.

It was a family hotel in a quiet but handsome street near Hyde Park.[3] As the brilliant light of the lamp which burnt before its door guided her to the spot, the clock struck eleven. She had loitered for a few paces as though irresolute, and making up her mind to advance; but the sound determined her, and she stepped into the hall. The porter's seat was vacant. She looked round with an air of incertitude, and advanced towards the stairs.

'Now, young woman,' said a smartly-dressed female, looking out from a door behind her, 'who do you want here?'

'A lady who is stopping in this house,' answered the girl.

'A lady!' was the reply, accompanied with a scornful look. 'What lady, pray?'

'Miss Maylie,' said Nancy.

The young woman, who had by this time noted her appearance, replied only by a look of virtuous disdain, and summoned a man to answer her. To him Nancy repeated her request.

'What name am I to say?' asked the waiter.

'It's of no use saying any,' replied Nancy.

'Nor business?' said the man.

'No, nor that neither,' rejoined the girl. 'I must see the lady.'

'Come,' said the man, pushing her towards the door, 'none of this! Take yourself off, will you?'

'I shall be carried out if I go!' said the girl violently, 'and I can make that a job that two of you won't like to do. Isn't there anybody here,' she said, looking round, 'that will see a simple message carried for a poor wretch like me?'

This appeal produced an effect on a good-tempered-faced man-cook, who with some other of the servants was looking on, and who stepped forward to interfere.

'Take it up for her, Joe, can't you?' said this person.

'What's the good?' replied the man. 'You don't suppose the young lady will see such as her, do you?'

This allusion to Nancy's doubtful character raised a vast quantity of chaste wrath in the bosoms of four housemaids, who remarked with great fervour that the creature was a disgrace to her sex, and strongly advocated her being thrown ruthlessly into the kennel.

'Do what you like with me,' said the girl, turning to the men again; 'but do what I ask you first; and I ask you to give this message for God Almighty's sake.'

The soft-hearted cook added his intercession, and the result was that the man who had first appeared undertook its delivery.

'What's it to be?' said the man, with one foot on the stairs.

'That a young woman earnestly asks to speak to Miss Maylie alone,' said Nancy; 'and, that if the lady will only hear the first word she has to say, she will know whether to hear her business, or have her turned out of doors as an impostor.'

'I say,' said the man, 'you're coming it strong!'

'You give the message,' said the girl firmly, 'and let me hear the answer.'

The man ran up stairs, and Nancy remained pale and almost breathless, listening with quivering lip to the very audible expressions of scorn, of which the chaste housemaids were very prolific; and became still more so when the man returned, and said the young woman was to walk up stairs.

'It's no good being proper in this world,' said the first house-maid.

'Brass can do better than the gold what has stood the fire,' said the second.

The third contented herself with wondering 'what ladies was made of;' and the fourth took the first in a quartette of 'Shameful!' with which the Dianas[4] concluded.

Regardless of all this — for she had weightier matters at heart — Nancy followed the man with trembling limbs to a small anti-chamber, lighted by a lamp from the ceiling, in which he left her, and retired.

The girl's life had been squandered in the streets, and the most noisome of the stews[5] and dens of London, but there was something of the woman's original nature left in her still; and when she heard a light step approaching the door opposite to that by which she had entered, and thought of the wide contrast which the small room would in another moment contain, she felt burdened with the sense of her own deep shame, and shrunk as though she could scarcely bear the presence of her with whom she had sought this interview.

But struggling with these better feelings was pride, — the vice of the lowest and most debased creatures no less than of the high and self-assured. The miserable companion of thieves and ruffians, the fallen outcast of low haunts, the associate of the scourings of the jails and hulks,[6] living within the shadow of the gallows itself, — even this degraded being felt too proud to betray one feeble gleam of the womanly feeling which she thought a weakness, but which alone connected her with that humanity, of which her wasting life had obliterated all outward traces when a very child.

She raised her eyes sufficiently to observe that the figure which presented itself was that of a slight and beautiful girl, and then bending them on the ground, tossed her head with affected carelessness as she said,

'It's a hard matter to get to see you, lady. If I had taken offence, and gone away, as many would have done, you'd have been sorry for it one day, and not without reason either.'

'I am very sorry if any one has behaved harshly to you,' replied Rose, 'Do not think of it; but tell me why you wished to see me. I am the person you inquired for.'

The kind tone of this answer, the sweet voice, the gentle manner, the absence of any accent of haughtiness or displeasure, took the girl completely by surprise, and she burst into tears.

'Oh, lady, lady!' she said, clasping her hands passionately before her face, 'if there was more like you, there would be fewer like me, – there would – there would!'

'Sit down,' said Rose earnestly; 'you distress me. If you are in poverty or affliction I shall be truly happy to relieve you if I can, – I shall indeed. Sit down.'

'Let me stand, lady,' said the girl, still weeping, 'and do not speak to me so kindly till you know me better. It is growing late. Is – is – that door shut?'

'Yes,' said Rose, recoiling a few steps, as if to be nearer assistance in case she should require it. 'Why?'

'Because,' said the girl, 'I am about to put my life and the lives of others in your hands. I am the girl that dragged little Oliver back to old Fagin's, the Jew's, on the night he went out from the house in Pentonville.'

'You!' said Rose Maylie.

'I, lady,' replied the girl. 'I am the infamous creature you have heard of, that lives among the thieves, and that never from the first moment I can recollect my eyes and senses opening on London streets have known any better life, or kinder words than they have given me, so help me God! Do not mind shrinking openly from me, lady. I am younger than you would think, to look at me, but I am well used to it; the poorest women fall back as I make my way along the crowded pavement.'

'What dreadful things are these!' said Rose, involuntarily falling from her strange companion.

'Thank Heaven upon your knees, dear lady,' cried the girl, 'that you had friends to care for and keep you in your childhood, and that you were never in the midst of cold and hunger, and riot and drunkenness, and – and something worse than all – as I have been from my cradle; I may use the word, for the alley and the gutter were mine, as they will be my deathbed.'

'I pity you!' said Rose in a broken voice. 'It wrings my heart to hear you!'

'God bless you for your goodness!' rejoined the girl. 'If you knew what I am sometimes you would pity me, indeed. But I have stolen away from those who would surely murder me if they knew I had been here to tell you what I have overheard. Do you know a man named Monks?'

'No,' said Rose.

'He knows you,' replied the girl; 'and knew you were here, for it was by hearing him tell the place that I found you out.'

'I never heard the name,' said Rose.

'Then he goes by some other amongst us,' rejoined the girl, 'which I more than thought before. Some time ago, and soon after Oliver was put into your house on the night of the robbery, I – suspecting this man – listened to a conversation held between him and Fagin in the dark. I found out from what I heard that Monks – the man I asked you about, you know –'

'Yes,' said Rose, 'I understand.'

' – That Monks,' pursued the girl, 'had seen him accidentally with two of our boys on the day we first lost him, and had known him directly to be the same child that he was watching for, though I couldn't make out why. A bargain was struck with Fagin, that if Oliver was got back he should have a certain sum; and he was to have more for making him a thief, which this Monks wanted for some purpose of his own.'

'For what purpose?' asked Rose.

'He caught sight of my shadow on the wall as I listened in the hope of finding out,' said the girl; 'and there are not many people besides me that could have got out of their way in time to escape discovery. But I did; and I saw him no more till last night.'

'And what occurred then?'

'I'll tell you, lady. Last night he came again. Again they went up stairs, and I, wrapping myself up so that my shadow should not betray me, again listened at the door. The first words I heard Monks say were these. "So the only proofs of the boy's identity lie at the bottom of the river, and the old hag that received them from the mother is rotting in her coffin." They laughed, and talked of his success in doing this; and Monks, talking on about the boy, and getting very wild, said, that though he had got the young devil's money safely now, he'd rather have had it the other way; for, what a game it would have been to have brought down the boast of the father's will, by driving him through every jail in town, and then hauling him up for some capital felony, which Fagin could easily manage, after having made a good profit of him besides.'

'What is all this!' said Rose.

'The truth, lady, though it comes from my lips,' replied the girl. 'Then he said, with oaths common enough in my ears, but strangers to yours, that if he could gratify his hatred by taking the boy's life without bringing his own neck in danger, he would; but, as he couldn't, he'd be upon the watch to meet him at every turn in life, and if he took advantage of his birth and history, he might harm him yet. "In short, Fagin," he says, "Jew as you are, you never laid such snares as I'll contrive for my young brother, Oliver."'

'His brother!' exclaimed Rose, clasping her hands.

'Those were his words,' said Nancy, glancing uneasily round, as she had scarcely ceased to do since she began to speak, for a vision of Sikes haunted her perpetually. 'And more. When he spoke of you and the other lady, and said it seemed contrived by heaven, or the devil, against him, that Oliver should come into your hands, he laughed, and said there was some comfort in that too, for how many thousands and hundreds of thousands of pounds would you not give, if you had them, to know who your two-legged spaniel was.'

'You do not mean,' said Rose, turning very pale, 'to tell me that this was said in earnest.'

'He spoke in hard and angry earnest, if a man ever did,' replied the girl, shaking her head. 'He is an earnest man when his hatred is up. I know many who do worse things; but I'd rather listen to them all a dozen times than to that Monks once. It is growing late, and I have to reach home without suspicion of having been on such an errand as this. I must get back quickly.'

'But what can I do?' said Rose. 'To what use can I turn this communication without you? Back! Why do you wish to return to companions you paint in such terrible colours? If you repeat this information to a gentleman whom I can summon in one instant from the next room, you can be consigned to some place of safety without half an hour's delay.'

'I wish to go back,' said the girl. 'I must go back, because – how can I tell such things to an innocent lady like you? – because among the men I have told you of, there is one the most desperate among them all that I can't leave; no – not even to be saved from the life I am leading now.'

'Your having interfered in this dear boy's behalf before,' said Rose; 'your coming here at so great a risk to tell me what you have heard; your manner, which convinces me of the truth of what you say; your evident contrition, and sense of shame, all lead me to believe that you might be yet reclaimed. Oh!' said the earnest girl, folding her hands as the tears coursed down her face, 'do not turn a deaf ear to the entreaties of one of your own sex; the first – the first, I do believe, who ever appealed to you in the voice of pity and compassion. Do hear my words, and let me save you yet for better things.'

'Lady,' cried the girl, sinking on her knees, 'dear, sweet, angel lady, you *are* the first that ever blessed me with such words as these, and if I had heard them years ago, they might have turned me from a life of sin and sorrow; but it is too late – it is too late.'

'It is never too late,' said Rose, 'for penitence and atonement.'

'It is,' cried the girl, writhing in the agony of her mind; 'I cannot leave him now – I could not be his death.'

'Why should you be?' asked Rose.

'Nothing could save him,' cried the girl. 'If I told others what I have told you, and led to their being taken, he would be sure to die. He is the boldest, and has been so cruel.'

'Is it possible,' cried Rose, 'that for such a man as this you can resign every future hope, and the certainty of immediate rescue? It is madness.'

'I don't know what it is,' answered the girl; 'I only know that it is so, and not with me alone, but with hundreds of others as bad and wretched as myself. I must go back. Whether it is God's wrath for the wrong I have done, I do not know; but I am drawn back to him through every suffering and ill usage, and should be, I believe, if I knew that I was to die by his hand at last.'

'What am I to do?' said Rose. 'I should not let you depart from me thus.'

'You should, lady, and I know you will,' rejoined the girl, rising. 'You will not stop my going because I have trusted in your goodness, and forced no promise from you, as I might have done.'

'Of what use, then, is the communication you have made?' said Rose. 'This mystery must be investigated, or how will its disclosure to me benefit Oliver, whom you are anxious to serve?'

'You must have some kind gentleman about you that will hear it as a secret, and advise you what to do,' rejoined the girl.

'But where can I find you again when it is necessary?' asked Rose. 'I do not seek to know where these dreadful people live, but where you will be walking or passing at any settled period from this time?'

'Will you promise me that you will have my secret strictly kept, and come alone, or with the only other person that knows it, and that I shall not be watched or followed?' asked the girl.

'I promise you solemnly,' answered Rose.

'Every Sunday night, from eleven until the clock strikes twelve,' said the girl without hesitation, 'I will walk on London Bridge[7] if I am alive.'

'Stay another moment,' interposed Rose, as the girl moved hurriedly towards the door. 'Think once again on your own condition, and the opportunity you have of escaping from it. You have a claim on me: not only as the voluntary bearer of this intelligence, but as a woman lost almost beyond redemption. Will you return to this gang of robbers and to this man, when a word can save you? What fascination is it that can take you back, and make you cling to wickedness and misery? Oh! is there no chord in your heart that I can touch – is there nothing left to which I can appeal against this terrible infatuation?'

'When ladies as young, and good, and beautiful as you are,' replied the girl steadily, 'give away your hearts, love will carry you all lengths – even such as you who have home, friends, other admirers, everything to fill them. When such as me, who have no certain roof but the coffin-lid, and no friend in sickness or death but the hospital nurse, set our rotten hearts on any man, and let him fill the place that parents, home, and friends filled once, or that has been a blank through all our wretched lives, who can hope to cure us? Pity us, lady, – pity us for having only one feeling of the woman left, and for having that turned by a heavy judgment from a comfort and a pride into a new means of violence and suffering.'

'You will,' said Rose, after a pause, 'take some money from me, which may enable you to live without dishonesty – at all events until we meet again?'

'Not a penny,' replied the girl, waving her hand.

'Do not close your heart against all my efforts to help you,' said Rose, stepping gently forward. 'I wish to serve you indeed.'

'You would serve me best, lady,' replied the girl, wringing her hands, 'if you could take my life at once; for I have felt more grief to think of what I am to-night than I ever did before, and it would be something not to die in the same hell in which I have lived. God bless you, sweet lady, and send as much happiness on your head as I have brought shame on mine!'

Thus speaking, and sobbing aloud, the unhappy creature turned away; while Rose Maylie, overpowered by this extraordinary interview, which bore more the semblance of a rapid dream than an actual occurrence, sank into a chair, and endeavoured to collect her wandering thoughts.

CHAPTER THE FOURTH

CONTAINING FRESH DISCOVERIES, AND
SHOWING THAT SURPRISES, LIKE
MISFORTUNES, SELDOM COME ALONE

Her situation was indeed one of no common trial and difficulty, for while she felt the most eager and burning desire to penetrate the mystery in which Oliver's history was enveloped, she could not but hold sacred the confidence which the miserable woman with whom she had just conversed had reposed in her, as a young and guileless girl. Her words and manner had touched Rose Maylie's heart, and mingled with her love for her young charge, and scarcely less intense in its truth and fervour, was her fond wish to win the outcast back to repentance and hope.

They only proposed remaining in London three days, prior to departing for some weeks to a distant part of the coast. It was now midnight of the first day. What course of action could she determine upon which could be adopted in eight-and-forty hours? or how could she postpone the journey without exciting suspicion?

Mr Losberne was with them, and would be for the next two days; but Rose was too well acquainted with the excellent gentleman's impetuosity, and foresaw too clearly the wrath with which, in the first explosion of his indignation, he would regard the instrument of Oliver's re-capture to trust him with the secret, when her representations in the girl's behalf could be seconded by no experienced person. These were all reasons for the greatest caution and most circumspect behaviour in communicating it to Mrs Maylie, whose first impulse would infallibly be to hold a conference with the worthy doctor on the subject. As to resorting to any legal adviser, even if she had known how to do so, it was scarcely to be thought of, for the same reasons. Once the thought occurred to her of seeking assistance from Harry; but this awakened the recollection of their last parting, and it seemed unworthy of her to call him back, when – the tears rose to her eyes as she pursued this train of reflection – he might have by this time learnt to forget her, and to be happier away.

Disturbed by these different reflections, and inclining now to one course and then to another, and again recoiling from all as each successive consideration presented itself to her mind, Rose passed a sleepless and anxious night, and, after more communing with herself next day, arrived at the desperate conclusion of consulting Harry Maylie.

'If it be painful to him,' she thought, 'to come back here, how painful will it be to me! But perhaps he will not come; he may write, or he may come himself, and studiously abstain from meeting me – he did when he went away. I hardly thought he would; but it was better for us both – a great deal better.' And here Rose dropped the pen and turned away, as though the very paper which was to be her messenger should not see her weep.

She had taken up the same pen and laid it down again fifty times, and had considered and re-considered the very first line of her letter without writing the first word, when Oliver, who had been walking in the streets with Mr Giles for a body-guard, entered the room in such breathless haste and violent agitation, as seemed to betoken some new cause of alarm.

'What makes you look so flurried?' asked Rose, advancing to meet him. 'Speak to me, Oliver.'

'I hardly know how; I feel as if I should be choked,' replied the boy. 'Oh dear! to think that I should see him at last, and you should be able to know that I have told you all the truth!'

'I never thought you had told us anything but the truth, dear,' said Rose, soothing him. 'But what is this? – of whom do you speak?'

'I have seen the gentleman,' replied Oliver, scarcely able to articulate, 'the gentleman who was so good to me – Mr Brownlow, that we have so often talked about.'

'Where?' asked Rose.

'Getting out of a coach,' replied Oliver, shedding tears of delight, 'and going into a house. I didn't speak to him – I couldn't speak to him, for he didn't see me, and I trembled so, that I was not able to go up to him. But Giles asked for me whether he lived there, and they said he did. Look here,' said Oliver, opening a scrap of paper, 'here it is; here's where he lives – I'm going there directly. Oh, dear me, dear me! what shall I do when I come to see him and hear him speak again!'

With her attention not a little distracted by these and a great many other incoherent exclamations of joy, Rose read the address, which was Craven Street, in the Strand,[1] and very soon determined upon turning the discovery to account.

'Quick!' she said, 'tell them to fetch a hackney-coach, and be ready to go with me. I will take you there directly, without a minute's loss of time. I will only tell my aunt that we are going out for an hour, and be ready as soon as you are.'

Oliver needed no prompting to despatch, and in little more than five minutes they were on their way to Craven Street. When they arrived there, Rose left Oliver in the coach under pretence of preparing the old gentleman to receive him, and sending up her card by the servant, requested to see Mr Brownlow on very pressing business. The servant soon returned to beg that she would walk up stairs, and, following him into an upper room, Miss Maylie was presented to an elderly gentleman of benevolent appearance, in a bottle-green coat; at no great distance from whom was seated another old gentleman, in nankeen breeches and gaiters, who did not look particularly benevolent, and was sitting with his hands clasped on the top of a thick stick, and his chin propped thereupon.

'Dear me,' said the gentleman in the bottle-green coat, hastily rising with great politeness, 'I beg your pardon, young lady – I imagined it was some importunate person who – I beg you will excuse me. Be seated, pray.'

'Mr Brownlow, I believe, sir?' said Rose, glancing from the other gentleman to the one who had spoken.

'That is my name,' said the old gentleman. 'This is my friend, Mr Grimwig. Grimwig, will you leave us for a few minutes?'

'I believe,' interposed Miss Maylie, 'that at this period of our interview I need not give that gentleman the trouble of going away. If I am correctly informed, he is cognizant of the business on which I wish to speak to you.'

Mr Brownlow inclined his head, and Mr Grimwig, who had made

one very stiff bow, and risen from his chair, made another very stiff bow, and dropped into it again.

'I shall surprise you very much, I have no doubt,' said Rose, naturally embarrassed; 'but you once showed great benevolence and goodness to a very dear young friend of mine; and I am sure you will take an interest in hearing of him again.'

'Indeed!' said Mr Brownlow. 'May I ask his name?'

'Oliver Twist you knew him as,' replied Rose.

The words no sooner escaped her lips than Mr Grimwig, who had been affecting to dip into a large book that lay on the table, upset it with a great crash, and falling back in his chair, discharged from his features every expression but one of the most unmitigated wonder, and indulged in a prolonged and vacant stare; then, as if ashamed of having betrayed so much emotion, he jerked himself, as it were, by a convulsion into his former attitude, and looking out straight before him emitted a long, deep whistle, which seemed at last not to be discharged on empty air, but to die away in the inmost recesses of his stomach.

Mr Brownlow was no less surprised, although his astonishment was not expressed in the same eccentric manner. He drew his chair nearer to Miss Maylie's, and said,

'Do me the favour, my dear young lady, to leave entirely out of the question that goodness and benevolence of which you speak, and of which nobody else knows anything, and if you have it in your power to produce any evidence which will alter the unfavourable opinion I was once induced to entertain of that poor child, in Heaven's name put me in possession of it.'

'A bad one – I'll eat my head if he is not a bad one,' growled Mr Grimwig, speaking by some ventriloquial power, without moving a muscle of his face.

'He is a child of a noble nature and a warm heart,' said Rose, colouring; 'and that Power which has thought fit to try him beyond his years has planted in his breast affections and feelings which would do honour to many who have numbered his days six times over.'

'I'm only sixty-one,' said Mr Grimwig with the same rigid face, 'and, as the devil's in it if this Oliver is not twelve at least, I don't see the application of that remark.'

'Do not heed my friend, Miss Maylie,' said Mr Brownlow; 'he does not mean what he says.'

'Yes, he does,' growled Mr Grimwig.

'No, he does not,' said Mr Brownlow, obviously rising in wrath as he spoke.

'He'll eat his head if he doesn't,' growled Mr Grimwig.

'He would deserve to have it knocked off, if he does,' said Mr Brownlow.

'And he'd uncommonly like to see any man offer to do it,' responded Mr Grimwig, knocking his stick upon the floor.

Having gone thus far, the two old gentlemen severally took snuff, and afterwards shook hands, according to their invariable custom.

'Now, Miss Maylie,' said Mr Brownlow, 'to return to the subject in which your humanity is so much interested. Will you let me know what intelligence you have of this poor child: allowing me to premise that I exhausted every means in my power of discovering him, and that since I have been absent from this country, my first impression that he had imposed upon me, and been persuaded by his former associates to rob me, has been considerably shaken.'

Rose, who had had time to collect her thoughts, at once related in a few natural words all that had befallen Oliver since he left Mr Brownlow's house, reserving Nancy's information for that gentleman's private ear, and concluding with the assurance that his only sorrow for some months past had been the not being able to meet with his former benefactor and friend.

'Thank God!' said the old gentleman; 'this is great happiness to me, great happiness. But you have not told me where he is now, Miss Maylie. You must pardon my finding fault with you, – but why not have brought him?'

'He is waiting in a coach at the door,' replied Rose.

'At this door!' cried the old gentleman. With which he hurried out of the room, down the stairs, up the coach-steps, and into the coach, without another word.

When the room-door closed behind him, Mr Grimwig lifted up his head, and converting one of the hind legs of his chair into a pivot described three distinct circles with the assistance of his stick and the table: sitting in it all the time. After performing this evolution, he rose and limped as fast as he could up and down the room at least a dozen times, and then stopping suddenly before Rose, kissed her without the slightest preface.

'Hush!' he said, as the young lady rose in some alarm at this unusual proceeding, 'don't be afraid; I'm old enough to be your grandfather. You're a sweet girl – I like you. Here they are.'

In fact, as he threw himself at one dexterous dive into his former seat, Mr Brownlow returned accompanied by Oliver, whom Mr Grimwig received very graciously; and if the gratification of that moment had been the only reward for all her anxiety and care in Oliver's behalf, Rose Maylie would have been well repaid.

'There is somebody else who should not be forgotten, by the bye,' said Mr Brownlow, ringing the bell. 'Send Mrs Bedwin here, if you please.'

The old housekeeper answered the summons with all despatch, and dropping a curtsy at the door, waited for orders.

'Why, you get blinder every day, Bedwin,' said Mr Brownlow, rather testily.

'Well, that I do, sir,' replied the old lady. 'People's eyes, at my time of life, don't improve with age, sir.'

'I could have told you that,' rejoined Mr Brownlow; 'but put on your glasses, and see if you can't find out what you were wanted for, will you?'

The old lady began to rummage in her pocket for her spectacles; but Oliver's patience was not proof against this new trial, and yielding to his first impulse, he sprung into her arms.

'God be good to me!' cried the old lady, embracing him; 'it is my innocent boy!'

'My dear old nurse!' cried Oliver.

'He would come back – I knew he would,' said the old lady, holding him in her arms. 'How well he looks, and how like a gentleman's son he is dressed again. Where have you been this long, long while? Ah! the same sweet face, but not so pale; the same soft eye, but not so sad. I have never forgotten them or his quiet smile, but seen them every day side by side with those of my own dear children, dead and gone since I was a young lightsome creature.' Running on thus, and now holding Oliver from her to mark how he had grown, now clasping him to her and passing her fingers fondly through his hair, the poor soul laughed and wept upon his neck by turns.

Leaving her and Oliver to compare notes at leisure, Mr Brownlow led the way into another room, and there heard from Rose a full narration of her interview with Nancy, which occasioned him no little surprise and perplexity. Rose also explained her reasons for not making a confident of her friend Mr Losberne in the first instance; the old gentleman considered that she had acted prudently, and readily undertook to hold solemn conference with the worthy doctor himself. To afford him an early opportunity for the execution of this design, it was arranged that he should call at the hotel at eight o'clock that evening, and that in the mean time Mrs Maylie should be cautiously informed of all that had occurred. These preliminaries adjusted, Rose and Oliver returned home.

Rose had by no means overrated the measure of the good doctor's wrath, for Nancy's history was no sooner unfolded to him than he poured forth a shower of mingled threats and execrations; threatened to make her the first victim of the combined ingenuity of Messrs Blathers and Duff, and actually put on his hat preparatory to sallying forth immediately to obtain the assistance of those worthies. And doubtless he would, in this first outbreak, have carried the intention into effect without a moment's consideration of the consequences if he had not been restrained, in part, by corresponding violence on the side of Mr Brownlow, who was himself of an irascible temperament, and partly by such arguments and representations as seemed best calculated to dissuade him from his hot-brained purpose.

'Then what the devil is to be done?' said the impetuous doctor, when they had rejoined the two ladies. 'Are we to pass a vote of thanks to all these vagabonds, male and female, and beg them to accept a hundred pounds or so apiece as a trifling mark of our esteem, and some slight acknowledgment of their kindness to Oliver?'

'Not exactly that,' rejoined Mr Brownlow laughing, 'but we must proceed gently and with great care.'

'Gentleness and care!' exclaimed the doctor. 'I'd send them one and all to —'

'Never mind where,' interposed Mr Brownlow. 'But reflect whether sending them anywhere is likely to attain the object we have in view.'

'What object?' asked the doctor.

'Simply the discovery of Oliver's parentage, and regaining for him the inheritance of which, if this story be true, he has been fraudulently deprived.'

'Ah!' said Mr Losberne, cooling himself with his pocket-handkerchief; 'I almost forgot that.'

'You see,' pursued Mr Brownlow, 'placing this poor girl entirely out of the question, and supposing it were possible to bring these scoundrels to justice without compromising her safety, what good should we bring about?'

'Hanging a few of them at least, in all probability,' suggested the doctor, 'and transporting the rest.'

'Very good,' replied Mr Brownlow smiling, 'but no doubt they will bring that about themselves in the fulness of time, and if we step in to forestall them, it seems to me that we shall be performing a very Quixotic act in direct opposition to our own interest, or at least to Oliver's, which is the same thing.'

'How?' inquired the doctor.

'Thus. It is quite clear that we shall have the most extreme difficulty in getting to the bottom of this mystery, unless we can bring this man, Monks, upon his knees. That can only be done by stratagem, and by catching him when he is not surrounded by these people. For, suppose he were apprehended, we have no proof against him. He is not even (so far as we know, or as the facts appear to us,) concerned with the gang in any of their robberies. If he were not discharged, it is very unlikely that he could receive any further punishment than being committed to prison as a rogue and vagabond, and of course ever afterwards his mouth is so obstinately closed that he might as well, for our purposes, be deaf, dumb, blind, and an idiot.'

'Then,' said the doctor impetuously, 'I put it to you again, whether you think it reasonable that this promise to the girl should be considered binding; a promise made with the best and kindest intentions, but really –'

'Do not discuss the point, my dear young lady, pray,' said Mr

Brownlow interrupting Rose as she was about to speak. 'The promise shall be kept. I don't think it will in the slightest degree interfere with our proceedings. But before we can resolve upon any precise course of action, it will be necessary to see the girl, to ascertain from her whether she will point out this Monks on the understanding that she is to be dealt with by us, and not by the law; or if she will not or cannot do that, to procure from her such an account of his haunts and description of his person as will enable us to identify him. She cannot be seen until next Sunday night; this is Tuesday. I would suggest that, in the mean time, we remain perfectly quiet, and keep these matters secret even from Oliver himself.'

Although Mr Losberne received with many wry faces a proposal involving a delay of five whole days, he was fain to admit that no better course occurred to him just then; and as both Rose and Mrs Maylie sided very strongly with Mr Brownlow, that gentleman's proposition was carried unanimously.

'I should like,' he said, 'to call in the aid of my friend Grimwig. He is a strange creature, but a shrewd one, and might prove of material assistance to us; I should say that he was bred a lawyer, and quitted the bar in disgust because he had only one brief and a motion of course[2] in ten years, though whether that is a recommendation or not, you must determine for yourselves.'

'I have no objection to your calling in your friend if I may call in mine,' said the doctor.

'We must put it to the vote,' replied Mr Brownlow, 'who may he be?'

'That lady's son, and this young lady's – very old friend,' said the doctor, motioning towards Mrs Maylie, and concluding with an expressive glance at her niece.

Rose blushed deeply, but she did not make any audible objection to this motion (possibly she felt in a hopeless minority) and Harry Maylie and Mr Grimwig were accordingly added to the committee.

'We stay in town of course,' said Mrs Maylie, 'while there remains the slightest prospect of prosecuting this inquiry with a chance of success. I will spare neither trouble nor expense in behalf of the object in whom we are all so deeply interested, and I am content to remain here, if it be for twelve months, so long as you assure me that any hope remains.'

'Good,' rejoined Mr Brownlow, 'and as I see on the faces about me a disposition to inquire how it happened that I was not in the way to corroborate Oliver's tale, and had so suddenly left the kingdom, let me stipulate that I shall be asked no questions until such time as I may deem it expedient to forestall them by telling my own story. Believe me that I make this request with good reason, for I might otherwise excite hopes destined never to be realized, and only increase difficulties and disappointments already quite numerous enough. Come; supper has been announced, and young Oliver, who is all alone in the next room, will have begun to think, by this time, that we have wearied of his company, and entered into some dark conspiracy to thrust him forth upon the world.'

With these words the old gentleman gave his hand to Mrs Maylie, and escorted her into the supper room. Mr Losberne followed, leading Rose, and the council was for the present effectually broken up.

*

CHAPTER THE FIFTH

*AN OLD ACQUAINTANCE OF OLIVER'S,
EXHIBITING DECIDED MARKS OF GENIUS,
BECOMES A PUBLIC CHARACTER IN THE
METROPOLIS*

Upon the very same night when Nancy, having lulled Mr Sikes to sleep, hurried on her self-imposed mission to Rose Maylie, there advanced towards London by the Great North Road two persons, upon whom it is expedient that this history should bestow some attention.

They were a man and woman, or perhaps they would be better described as a male and female; for the former was one of those long-limbed, knock-kneed, shambling, bony figures, to whom it is difficult to assign any precise age, – looking as they do, when they are yet boys, like under-grown men, and when they are almost men, like overgrown boys. The woman was young, but of a robust and hardy make, as she need have been to bear the weight of the heavy bundle which was strapped to her back. Her companion was not encumbered with much luggage, as there merely dangled from a stick which he carried over his shoulder a small parcel wrapped in a common handkerchief, and apparently light enough. This circumstance, added to the length of his legs, which were of unusual extent, enabled him with much ease to keep some half dozen paces in advance of his companion, to whom he occasionally turned with an impatient jerk of the head, as if reproaching her tardiness, and urging her to greater exertion.

Thus they toiled along the dusty road, taking little heed of any object within sight, save when they stepped aside to allow a wider passage for the mail-coaches which were whirling out of town, until they passed through Highgate archway,[1] when the foremost traveller stopped and called impatiently to his companion,

'Come on, can't yer?' – What a lazybones yer are, Charlotte!'

'It's a heavy load, I can tell you,' said the female, coming up, almost breathless with fatigue.

'Heavy! What are yer talking about? – what are yer made for?' rejoined the male traveller, changing his own little bundle as he spoke to the other shoulder. 'Oh! there yer are, resting again! Well, if you ain't enough to tire anybody's patience out, I don't know what is.'

'Is it much farther?' asked the woman, resting herself on a bank, and looking up with the perspiration streaming from her face.

'Much farther! – Yer as good as there,' said the long-legged tramper, pointing out before him. 'Look there – those are the lights of London.'

'They're a good two mile off at least,' said the woman despondingly.

'Never mind whether they're two mile off or twenty,' said Noah Claypole, for he it was; 'but get up and come on, or I'll kick yer; and so I give yer notice.'

As Noah's red nose grew redder with anger, and as he crossed the road while speaking, as if fully prepared to put his threat into execution, the woman rose without any farther remark, and trudged onwards by his side.

'Where do you mean to stop for the night, Noah?' she asked, after they had walked a few hundred yards.

'How should I know?' replied Noah, whose temper had been considerably impaired by walking.

'Near, I hope,' said Charlotte.

'No, not near,' replied Mr Claypole; 'there – not near; so don't think it.'

'Why not?'

'When I tell yer that I don't mean to do a thing, that's enough, without any why, or because either,' replied Mr Claypole with dignity.

'Well, you needn't be so cross,' said his companion.

'A pretty thing it would be, wouldn't it, to go and stop at the very first public house outside the town, so that Sowerberry, if he come up after us, might poke in his old nose, and have us taken back in a cart with handcuffs on,' said Mr Claypole in a jeering tone. 'No. I shall go and lose myself among the narrowest streets I can find, and not stop till we come to the very out-of-the-wayest house I can set eyes on. 'Cod, you may thank your stars I've got a head on; for if we hadn't gone at first the wrong road on purpose, and come back across country, you'd have been locked up hard and fast a week ago, my lady, and serve you right for being a fool.'

'I know I an't as cunning as you are,' replied Charlotte; 'but don't put all the blame on me, and say I should have been locked up. You would have been if I had been, any way.'

'Yer took the money from the till, yer know yer did,' said Mr Claypole.

'I took it for you, Noah, dear,' rejoined Charlotte.

'Did I keep it?' asked Mr Claypole.

'No; you trusted in me, and let me carry it like a dear, and so you are,' said the lady, chucking him under the chin, and drawing her arm through his.

This was indeed the case; but, as it was not Mr Claypole's habit to repose a blind and foolish confidence in anybody, it should be observed, in justice to that gentleman, that he had trusted Charlotte to this extent, in order that, if they were pursued, the money might be found on her, which would leave him an opportunity of asserting his utter innocence of any theft, and greatly facilitate his chances of escape. Of course, he entered at this juncture into no explanation of his motives, and they walked on very lovingly together.

In pursuance of his cautious plan, Mr Claypole went on without halting until he arrived at the Angel at Islington, where he wisely judged, from the crowd of passengers and number of vehicles, that London began in earnest. Just pausing to observe which appeared the most crowded streets, and consequently the most to be avoided, he crossed into Saint John's Road, and was soon deep in the obscurity of the intricate and dirty ways which, lying between Gray's Inn Lane and Smithfield, render that part of the town one of the lowest and worst that improvement has left in the midst of London.[2]

Through these streets Noah Claypole walked, dragging Charlotte after him, now stepping into the kennel to embrace at a glance the whole external character of some small public house, and now jogging on again as some fancied appearance induced him to believe it too public for his purpose. At length he stopped in front of one more humble in appearance and more dirty than any he had yet seen; and having crossed over and surveyed it from the opposite pavement, graciously announced his intention of putting up there for the night.

'So give us the bundle,' said Noah, unstrapping it from the woman's shoulders, and slinging it over his own; 'and don't yer speak except when yer spoken to. What's the name of the house – t-h-r – three what?'

'Cripples,' said Charlotte.

'Three Cripples,' repeated Noah, 'and a very good sign too. Now, then, keep close at my heels, and come along.' With these injunctions, he pushed the rattling door with his shoulder, and entered the house, followed by his companion.

There was nobody in the bar but a young Jew, who, with his two elbows on the counter, was reading a dirty newspaper. He stared very hard at Noah, and Noah stared very hard at him.

If Noah had been attired in his charity-boy's dress, there might have been some reason for the Jew's opening his eyes so wide; but as he had discarded the coat and badge, and wore a short smock-frock over his leathers, there seemed no particular reason for his appearance exciting so much attention in a public house.

'Is this the Three Cripples?' asked Noah.

'That is the dabe of this house,' replied the Jew.

'A gentleman we met on the road coming up from the country recommended us here,' said Noah, nudging Charlotte, perhaps to call her attention to this most ingenious device for attracting respect, and perhaps to warn her to betray no surprise. 'We want to sleep here to-night.'

'I'b dot certaid you cad,' said Barney, who was the attendant sprite; 'but I'll idquire.'

'Show us the tap, and give us a bit of cold meat and a drop of beer, while yer inquiring, will yer?' said Noah.

Barney complied by ushering them into a small back-room, and setting the required viands before them; having done which, he informed the travellers that they could be lodged that night, and left the amiable couple to their refreshment.

Now, this back-room was immediately behind the bar, and some steps lower, so that any person connected with the house, undrawing a small curtain which concealed a single pane of glass fixed in the wall of the last-named apartment, about five feet from its flooring, could not only look down upon any guests in the back-room without any great hazard of being observed, (the glass being in a dark angle of the wall, between which and a large upright beam the observer had to thrust himself,) but could, by applying his ear to the partition, ascertain with tolerable distinctness, their subject of conversation. The landlord of the house had not withdrawn his eye from this place of espial for five minutes, and Barney had only just returned from making the communication above related, when Fagin, in the course of his evening's business, came into the bar to inquire after some of his young pupils.

'Hush!' said Barney: 'stradegers id the next roob.'

'Strangers!' repeated the old man in a whisper.

'Ah! ad rub uds too,' added Barney. 'Frob the cuttry, but subthig in your way, or I'b bistaked.'

Fagin appeared to receive this communication with great interest, and, mounting on a stool, cautiously applied his eye to the pane of glass, from which secret post he could see Mr Claypole taking cold beef from the dish, and porter from the pot, and administering homœopathic doses[3] of both to Charlotte, who sat patiently by, eating and drinking at his pleasure.

'Aha!' whispered the Jew, looking round to Barney, 'I like this fellow's looks. He'd be of use to us; he knows how to train the girl already. Don't make as much noise as a mouse, my dear, and let me hear 'em talk – let me hear 'em.'

The Jew again applied his eye to the glass, and turning his ear to the partition, listened attentively, with a subtle and eager look upon his face that might have appertained to some old goblin.

'So I mean to be a gentleman,' said Mr Claypole, kicking out his legs, and continuing a conversation, the commencement of which Fagin had arrived too late to hear. 'No more jolly old coffins, Charlotte, but a gentleman's life for me; and, if yer like, yer shall be a lady.'

'I should like that well enough, dear,' replied Charlotte; 'but tills an't to be emptied every day, and people to get clear off after it.'

'Tills be blowed!' said Mr Claypole; 'there's more things besides tills to be emptied.'

'What do you mean?' asked his companion.

'Pockets, women's ridicules,[4] houses, mail-coaches, banks,' said Mr Claypole, rising with the porter.

'But you can't do all that, dear,' said Charlotte.

'I shall look out to get into company with them as can,' replied Noah. 'They'll be able to make us useful some way or another. Why, you yourself are worth fifty women; I never see such a precious sly and deceitful creetur as yer can be when I let yer.'

'Lor, how nice it is to hear you say so,' exclaimed Charlotte, imprinting a kiss upon his ugly face.

'There, that'll do; don't yer be too affectionate, in case I'm cross with yer,' said Noah, disengaging himself with great gravity. 'I should like to be the captain of some band, and have the whopping of 'em, and follering 'em about, unbeknown to themselves. That would suit me, if there was good profit; and if we could only get in with some gentlemen of this sort, I say it would be cheap at that twenty-pound note you've got – especially as we don't very well know how to get rid of it ourselves.'

After expressing this opinion, Mr Claypole looked into the porter pot with an aspect of deep wisdom, and having well shaken its contents, nodded condescendingly to Charlotte, and took a draught, wherewith he appeared greatly refreshed. He was meditating another, when the sudden opening of the door and appearance of a stranger interrupted him.

The stranger was Mr Fagin, and very amiable he looked, and a very low bow he made as he advanced, and, sitting himself down at the nearest table, ordered something to drink of the grinning Barney.

'A pleasant night, sir, but cool for the time of year,' said Fagin, rubbing his hands. 'From the country, I see, sir?'

'How do yer see that?' asked Noah Claypole.

'We have not so much dust as that in London,' replied the Jew, pointing from Noah's shoes to those of his companion, and from them to the two bundles.

'Yer a sharp feller,' said Noah. 'Ha! ha! – only hear that, Charlotte!'

'Why, one need be sharp in this town, my dear,' replied the Jew, sinking his voice to a confidential whisper, 'and that's the truth.'

The Jew followed up this remark by striking the side of his nose with his right fore-finger, – a gesture which Noah attempted to imitate, though not with complete success, in consequence of his own nose not being large enough for the purpose. However, Mr Fagin seemed to interpret the endeavour as expressing a perfect coincidence with his opinion, and put about the liquor which Barney re-appeared with, in a very friendly manner.

'Good stuff that,' observed Mr Claypole, smacking his lips.

'Dear,' said Fagin. 'A man need be always emptying a till, or a pocket, or a woman's reticule, or a house, or a mail-coach, or a bank, if he drinks it regularly.'

Mr Claypole no sooner heard this extract from his own remarks than he fell back in his chair, and looked from the Jew to Charlotte with a countenance of ashy paleness and excessive terror.

'Don't mind me, my dear,' said Fagin, drawing his chair closer. 'Ha! ha! – it was lucky it was only me that heard you by chance. It was very lucky it was only me.'

'I didn't take it,' stammered Noah, no longer stretching out his legs like an independent gentleman, but coiling them up as well as he could under his chair; 'it was all her doing; yer've got it now, Charlotte, yer know yer have.'

'No matter who's got it, or who did it, my dear!' replied Fagin, glancing, nevertheless, with a hawk's eye at the girl and the two bundles. 'I'm in that way myself, and I like you for it.'

'In what way?' asked Mr Claypole, a little recovering.

'In that way of business,' rejoined Fagin, 'and so are the people of this house. You've hit the right nail upon the head, and are as safe here as you could be. There is not a safer place in all this town than is the Cripples; that is, when I like to make it so, and I've taken a fancy to you and the young woman; so I've said the word, and you may make your minds easy.'

Noah Claypole's mind might have been at ease after this assurance, but his body certainly was not, for he shuffled and writhed about into various uncouth positions, eyeing his new friend meanwhile with mingled fear and suspicion.

'I'll tell you more,' said the Jew, after he had re-assured the girl, by dint of friendly nods and muttered encouragements. 'I have got a friend that I think can gratify your darling wish and put you in the right way, where you can take whatever department of the business you think will suit you best at first, and be taught all the others.'

'Yer speak as if yer were in earnest,' replied Noah.

'What advantage would it be to me to be anything else?' inquired the Jew, shrugging his shoulders. 'Here. Let me have a word with you outside.'

'There's no occasion to trouble ourselves to move,' said Noah, getting his legs by gradual degrees abroad again. 'She'll take the luggage up stairs the while. Char-lotte, see to them bundles.'

This mandate, which had been delivered with great majesty, was obeyed without the slightest demur; and Charlotte made the best of

The Jew & Morris Bolter begin to understand each other

her way off with the packages, while Noah held the door open, and watched her out.

'She's kept tolerably well under, ain't she, sir?' he asked, as he resumed his seat, in the tone of a keeper who has tamed some wild animal.

'Quite perfect,' rejoined Fagin, clapping him on the shoulder. 'You're a genius, my dear.'

'Why, I suppose if I wasn't, I shouldn't be here,' replied Noah. 'But, I say, she'll be back if yer lose time.'

'Now, what do you think?' said the Jew. 'If you was to like my friend, could you do better than join him?'

'Is he in a good way of business, that's where it is?' responded Noah, winking one of his little eyes.

'The top of the tree,' said the Jew, 'employs a power of hands, and has the very best society in the profession.'

'Regular town-maders?' asked Mr Claypole.

'Not a countryman among 'em; and I don't think he'd take you even on my recommendation if he didn't run rather short of assistants just now,' replied the Jew.

'Should I have to hand over?' said Noah, slapping his breeches' pocket.

'It couldn't possibly be done without,' replied Fagin, in a most decided manner.

'Twenty pound, though, – it's a lot of money!'

'Not when it's in a note you can't get rid of,' retorted Fagin. 'Number and date taken, I suppose; payment stopped at the Bank? Ah! It's not worth much to him; it'll have to go abroad, and he couldn't sell it for a great deal in the market.'

'When could I see him?' asked Noah doubtfully.

'To-morrow morning,' replied the Jew.

'Where?'

'Here.'

'Um!' said Noah. 'What's the wages?'

'Live like a gentleman, – board and lodging, pipes and spirits free, – half of all you earn, and half of all the young woman earns,' replied Mr Fagin.

Whether Noah Claypole, whose rapacity was none of the least comprehensive, would have acceded even to these glowing terms, had he been a perfectly free agent, is very doubtful; but as he recollected that, in the event of his refusal, it was in the power of his new acquaintance to give him up to justice immediately, (and more unlikely things had come to pass,) he gradually relented, and said he thought that would suit him.

'But, yer see,' observed Noah, 'as she will be able to do a good deal, I should like to take something very light.'

'A little fancy-work?' suggested Fagin.

'Ah! something of that sort,' replied Noah. 'What do you think would suit me now? Something not too trying for the strength, and not very dangerous, you know; – that's the sort of thing!'

'I heard you talk of something in the spy way upon the others, my dear?' said the Jew. 'My friend wants somebody who would do that well very much.'

'Why, I did mention that, and I shouldn't mind turning my hand to it sometimes,' rejoined Mr Claypole slowly; 'but it wouldn't pay by itself, you know.'

'That's true!' observed the Jew, ruminating, or pretending to ruminate. 'No, it might not.'

'What do you think, then?' asked Noah, anxiously regarding him. 'Something in the sneaking-way, where it was pretty sure work, and not much more risk than being at home.'

'What do you think of the old ladies?' asked the Jew. 'There's a good deal of money made in snatching their bags and parcels, and running round the corner.'

'Don't they holler out a good deal, and scratch sometimes?' asked Noah, shaking his head. 'I don't think that would answer my purpose. Ain't there any other line open?'

'Stop,' said the Jew, laying his hand on Noah's knee. 'The kinchin lay.'

'What's that?' demanded Mr Claypole.

'The kinchins, my dear,' said the Jew, 'is the young children that's sent on errands by their mothers, with sixpences and shillings, and the lay is just to take their money away – they've always got it ready in their hands, – and then knock 'em into the kennel, and walk off very slow, as if there was nothing else the matter but a child fallen down and hurt itself. Ha! ha! ha!'

'Ha! ha!' roared Mr Claypole, kicking up his legs in an ecstacy. 'Lord, that's the very thing!'

'To be sure it is,' replied Fagin; 'and you can have a few good beats chalked out in Camden-Town, and Battle-Bridge,[5] and neighbour-hoods like that, where they're always going errands, and upset as many kinchins as you want, any hour in the day. Ha! ha! ha!' With this, Fagin poked Mr Claypole in the side, and they joined in a burst of laughter both long and loud.

'Well, that's all right!' said Noah when he had recovered himself, and Charlotte had returned. 'What time to-morrow shall we say?'

'Will ten do?' asked the Jew, adding, as Mr Claypole nodded assent, 'What name shall I tell my good friend?'

'Mr Bolter,' replied Noah, who had prepared himself for such an emergency. 'Mr Morris Bolter. This is Mrs Bolter.'

'Mrs Bolter's humble servant,' said Fagin, bowing with grotesque politeness. 'I hope I shall know her better very shortly.'

'Do you hear the gentleman, Char-lotte?' thundered Mr Claypole.

'Yes, Noah, dear,' replied Mrs Bolter, extending her hand.

'She calls me Noah, as a sort of fond way of talking,' said Mr Morris Bolter, late Claypole, turning to the Jew. 'You understand?'

'Oh, yes, I understand, – perfectly,' replied Fagin, telling the truth for once. 'Good night! Good night!'

CHAPTER THE SIXTH

WHEREIN IS SHOWN HOW THE ARTFUL DODGER GOT INTO TROUBLE

'And so it was you that was your own friend, was it?' asked Mr Claypole, otherwise Bolter, when, by virtue of the compact entered into between them, he had removed next day to the Jew's house. 'Cod, I thought as much last night!'

'Every man's his own friend,' replied Fagin.[1] 'Some conjurors say that number three is the magic number, and some say number seven. It's neither, my friend, neither. It's number one.'[2]

'Ha! ha!' cried Mr Bolter. 'Number one for ever!'

'In a little community like ours,' said the Jew, who felt it necessary to qualify this position, 'we have a general number one; that is, you can't consider yourself as number one without considering me too as the same, and all the other young people.'

'Oh, the devil!' exclaimed Mr Bolter.

'You see,' pursued the Jew, affecting to disregard this interruption, 'we are so mixed up together, and identified in our interests, that it must be so. For instance, it's your object to take care of number one – meaning yourself.'

'Certainly,' replied Mr Bolter. 'Yer about right there.'

'Well, you can't take care of yourself, number one, without taking care of me, number one.'

'Number two, you mean,' said Mr Bolter, who was largely endowed with the quality of selfishness.

'No, I don't!' retorted the Jew. 'I'm of the same importance to you as you are to yourself.'

'I say,' interrupted Mr Bolter, 'yer a very nice man, and I'm very fond of yer; but we ain't quite so thick together as all that comes to.'

'Only think,' said the Jew, shrugging his shoulders, and stretching out his hands, 'only consider. You've done what's a very pretty thing, and what I love you for doing; but what at the same time would put the cravat round your throat that's so very easily tied, and so very difficult to unloosen, – in plain English, the halter!'

Mr Bolter put his hand to his neckerchief, as if he felt it inconveniently tight, and murmured an assent, qualified in tone, but not in substance.

'The gallows,' continued Fagin, 'the gallows, my dear, is an ugly finger-post, which points out a very short and sharp turning that has stopped many a bold fellow's career on the broad highway. To keep in the easy road, and keep it at a distance, is object number one with you.'

'Of course it is,' replied Mr Bolter. 'What do yer talk about such things for?'

'Only to show you my meaning clearly,' said the Jew, raising his eyebrows. 'To be able to do that, you depend upon me; to keep my little business all snug, I depend upon you. The first is your number one, the second my number one. The more you value your number one, the more careful you must be of mine; so we come at last to what I told you at first – that a regard for number one holds us all together, and must do so unless we would all go to pieces in company.'

'That's true,' rejoined Mr Bolter thoughtfully. 'Oh! yer a cunning old codger!'

Mr Fagin saw with delight that this tribute to his powers was no mere compliment, but that he had really impressed his recruit with a sense of his wily genius, which it was most important that he should entertain in the outset of their acquaintance. To strengthen an impression so desirable and useful, he followed up the blow by acquainting him in some detail with the magnitude and extent of his operations; blending truth and fiction together as best served his purpose, and bringing both to bear with so much art that Mr Bolter's respect visibly increased, and became tempered, at the same time, with a degree of wholesome fear, which it was highly desirable to awaken.

'It's this mutual trust we have in each other that consoles me under heavy losses,' said the Jew. 'My best hand was taken from me yesterday morning.'

'What, I suppose he was—'

'Wanted,' interposed the Jew. 'Yes, he was wanted.'

'Very particular?' inquired Mr Bolter.

'No,' replied the Jew, 'not very. He was charged with attempting to pick a pocket, and they found a silver snuff-box on him, – his own, my dear, his own, for he took snuff himself, and was very fond of it. They remanded him till to-day, for they thought they knew the owner. Ah! he was worth fifty boxes, and I'd give the price of as many to have him back. You should have known the Dodger, my dear; you should have known the Dodger.'

'Well, but I shall know him I hope; don't yer think so?' said Mr Bolter.

'I'm doubtful about it,' replied the Jew, with a sigh. 'If they don't get any fresh evidence it'll only be a summary conviction, and we shall have him back again after six weeks or so; but, if they do, it's a case of lagging. They know what a clever lad he is; he'll be a lifer: they'll make the Artful nothing less than a lifer.'

'What do yer mean by lagging and a lifer?' demanded Mr Bolter. 'What's the good of talking in that way to me; why don't yer speak so as I can understand yer?'

Fagin was about to translate these mysterious expressions into the vulgar tongue, and, being interpreted, Mr Bolter would have been informed that they represented that combination of words, 'transportation for life,' when the dialogue was cut short by the entry of Master Bates with his hands in his breeches' pockets, and his face twisted into a look of semi-comical woe.

'It's all up, Fagin,' said Charley, when he and his new companion had been made known to each other.

'What do you mean?' asked the Jew with trembling lips.

'They've found the gentleman as owns the box; two or three more's a coming to 'dentify him, and the Artful's booked for a passage out,' replied Master Bates. 'I must have a full suit of mourning, Fagin, and a hatband, to wisit him in, afore he sets out upon his travels. To think of Jack Dawkins – lummy Jack – the Dodger – the Artful Dodger – going abroad for a common twopenny-halfpenny sneeze-box! I never thought he'd ha' done it under a gold watch, chain, and seals, at the lowest. Oh! why didn't he rob some rich old gentleman of all his walables, and go out *as* a gentleman, and not like a common prig, without no honour nor glory!'

With this expression of feeling for his unfortunate friend, Master Bates sat himself on the nearest chair with an aspect of chagrin and despondency.

'What do you talk about his having neither honour nor glory for!' exclaimed Fagin, darting an angry look at his pupil. 'Wasn't he always top-sawyer among you all? – is there one of you that could touch him, or come near him, on any scent – eh?'

'Not one,' replied Master Bates, in a voice rendered husky by regret, – 'not one.'

'Then what do you talk of?' replied the Jew angrily; 'what are you blubbering for?'

''Cause it isn't on the rec-ord, is it?' said Charley, chafed into perfect defiance of his venerable friend by the current of his regrets; ''cause it can't come out in the indictment; 'cause nobody will never know half of what he was. How will he stand in the Newgate Calendar? P'raps not be there at all. Oh, my eye, my eye, wot a blow it is!'

'Ha! ha!' cried the Jew, extending his right hand, and turning to Mr Bolter in a fit of chuckling which shook him as though he had the palsy; 'see what a pride they take in their profession, my dear. Isn't it beautiful?'

Mr Bolter nodded assent; and the Jew, after contemplating the grief of Charley Bates for some seconds with evident satisfaction, stepped up to that young gentleman, and patted him on the shoulder.

'Never mind, Charley,' said Fagin soothingly; 'it'll come out, it'll be sure to come out. They'll all know what a clever fellow he was; he'll show it himself, and not disgrace his old pals and teachers. Think how young he is too! What a distinction, Charley, to be lagged at his time of life!'

'Well, it is a honour, – that is!' said Charley, a little consoled.

'He shall have all he wants,' continued the Jew. 'He shall be kept in the Stone Jug, Charley, like a gentleman – like a gentleman, with his beer every day, and money in his pocket to pitch and toss with, if he can't spend it.'

'No, shall he though?' cried Charley Bates.

'Ay, that he shall,' replied the Jew, 'and we'll have a big-wig, Charley, – one that's got the greatest gift of the gab, – to carry on his defence, and he shall make a speech for himself too, if he likes, and we'll read it all in the papers – "Artful Dodger – shrieks of laughter – here the court was convulsed" – eh, Charley, eh?'

'Ha! ha!' laughed Master Bates, 'what a lark that would be, wouldn't it, Fagin? I say, how the Artful would bother 'em, wouldn't he?'

'Would!' cried the Jew. 'He shall – he will!'

'Ah, to be sure, so he will,' repeated Charley, rubbing his hands.

'I think I see him now,' cried the Jew, bending his eyes upon his pupil.

'So do I,' cried Charley Bates – 'ha! ha! ha! – so do I. I see it all afore me – upon my soul I do, Fagin. What a game! what a regular game! All the big-wigs trying to look solemn, and Jack Dawkins addressing of 'em as intimate and comfortable as if he was the judge's own son, making a speech arter dinner – ha! ha! ha!'

In fact, the Jew had so well humoured his young friend's eccentric disposition, that Master Bates, who had at first been disposed to consider the imprisoned Dodger rather in the light of a victim, now looked upon him as the chief actor in a scene of most uncommon and exquisite humour, and felt quite impatient for the arrival of the time when his old companion should have so favourable an opportunity of displaying his abilities.

'We must know how he gets on to-day by some handy means or other,' said Fagin. 'Let me think.'

'Shall I go?' asked Charley.

'Not for the world,' replied the Jew. 'Are you mad, my dear; stark mad, that you'd walk into the very place where – No, Charley, no – one is enough to lose at a time.'

'You don't mean to go yourself, I suppose?' said Charley with a humorous leer.[3]

'That wouldn't quite fit,' replied Fagin, shaking his head.

'Then why don't you send this new cove?' asked Master Bates, laying his hand on Noah's arm; 'nobody knows him.'

'Why, if he didn't mind,' observed the Jew.

'Mind!' interposed Charley. 'What should *he* have to mind?'

'Really nothing, my dear,' said Fagin, turning to Mr Bolter, 'really nothing.'

'Oh, I dare say about that, yer know,' observed Noah, backing towards the door, and shaking his head with a kind of sober alarm. 'No, no – none of that. It's not in my department, that isn't.'

'Wot department has he got, Fagin?' inquired Master Bates, surveying Noah's lanky form with much disgust. 'The cutting away when there's anything wrong, and the eating all the wittles when there's everything right; is that his branch?'

'Never mind,' retorted Mr Bolter; 'and don't yer take liberties with yer superiors, little boy, or yer'll find yerself in the wrong shop.'

Master Bates laughed so vehemently at this magnificent threat, that it was some time before Fagin could interpose and represent to Mr Bolter that he incurred no possible danger in visiting the police-office; that, inasmuch as no account of the little affair in which he had been engaged, nor any description of his person, had yet been forwarded to the metropolis, it was very probable that he was not even suspected of having resorted to it for shelter; and that, if he were properly disguised, it would be as safe a spot for him to visit as any in London, inasmuch as it would be of all places the very last to which he could be supposed likely to resort of his own free will.

Persuaded, in part, by these representations, but overborne in a much greater degree by his fear of the Jew, Mr Bolter at length consented, with a very bad grace, to undertake the expedition. By Fagin's directions he immediately substituted for his own attire a waggoner's frock, velveteen breeches, and leather leggings, all of which articles the Jew had at hand. He was likewise furnished with a felt hat, well garnished with turnpike tickets, and a carter's whip. Thus equipped, he was to saunter into the office as some country fellow from Covent Garden market might be supposed to do for the gratification of his curiosity; and as he was as awkward, ungainly, and raw-boned a fellow as need be, Mr Fagin had no fear but that he would look the part to perfection.

These arrangements completed, he was informed of the necessary signs and tokens by which to recognise the artful Dodger, and conveyed by Master Bates through dark and winding ways to within a very short distance of Bow-street. Having described the precise situation of the office, and accompanied it with copious directions how he was to walk straight up the passage, and, when he got into the yard, take the door up the steps on the right-hand side, and pull off his hat as he went into the room, Charley Bates bade him hurry on alone, and promised to bide his return on the spot of their parting.

Noah Claypole, or Morris Bolter, as the reader pleases, punctually followed the directions he had received, which – Master Bates being pretty well acquainted with the locality – were so exact that he was enabled to gain the magisterial presence without asking any question, or meeting with any interruption by the way. He found himself jostled among a crowd of people, chiefly women, who were huddled together in a dirty, frowsy room, at the upper end of which was a raised platform railed off from the rest, with a dock for the prisoners on the left hand against the wall, a box for the witnesses in the middle, and a desk for the magistrates on the right; the awful locality last-named being screened off by a partition which concealed the bench from the common gaze, and left the vulgar to imagine (if they could) the full majesty of justice.

There were only a couple of women in the dock, who were nodding to their admiring friends, while the clerk read some depositions to a couple of policemen and a man in plain clothes who leant over the table. A jailer stood reclining against the dock-rail, tapping his nose listlessly with a large key, except when he repressed an undue tendency to conversation among the idlers, by proclaiming silence, or looked sternly up to bid some woman 'Take that baby out,' when the gravity of justice was disturbed by feeble cries, half-smothered in the mother's shawl, from some meagre infant. The room smelt close and unwholesome; the walls were dirt-discoloured, and the ceiling blackened. There was an old smoky bust over the mantel-shelf, and a dusty clock above the dock – the only thing present that seemed to go on as it ought; for depravity, or poverty, or an habitual acquaintance with both, had left a taint on all the animate matter, hardly less unpleasant than the thick greasy scum on every inanimate object that frowned upon it.

Noah looked eagerly about him for the Dodger, but although

there were several women who would have done very well for that distinguished character's mother or sister, and more than one man who might be supposed to bear a strong resemblance to his father, nobody at all answering the description given him of Mr Dawkins was to be seen. He waited in a state of much suspense and uncertainty until the women, being committed for trial, went flaunting out, and then was quickly relieved by the appearance of another prisoner, whom he felt at once could be no other than the object of his visit.

It was indeed Mr Dawkins, who, shuffling into the office with the big coat sleeves tucked up as usual, his left hand in his pocket and his hat in his right, preceded the jailer with a rolling gait altogether indescribable, and taking his place in the dock requested in an audible voice to know what he was placed in that 'ere disgraceful sitivation for.[4]

'Hold your tongue, will you?' said the jailer.

'I'm an Englishman, an't I?' rejoined the Dodger. 'Where are my priwileges?'

'You'll get your privileges soon enough,' retorted the jailer, 'and pepper with 'em.'

'We'll see wot the Secretary of State for the Home Affairs has got to say to the beaks, if I don't,' replied Mr Dawkins. 'Now then, wot is this here business? — I shall thank the madg'strates to dispose of this here little affair, and not to keep me while they read the paper, for I've got an appintment with a genelman in the city, and as I'm a man of my word, and wery punctual in bisness matters, he'll go away if I ain't there to my time, and then pr'aps there won't be an action for damage against them as kept me away. Oh no, certainly not!'

At this point, the Dodger, with a show of being very particular with a view to proceedings to be had thereafter, desired the jailer to communicate 'the names of them two old files as was on the bench,' which so tickled the spectators that they laughed almost as heartily as Master Bates could have done if he had heard the request.

'Silence there!' cried the jailer.

'What is this?' inquired one of the magistrates.

'A pick-pocketing case, your worship.'

'Has that boy ever been here before?'

'He ought to have been a many times,' replied the jailer. 'He has been pretty well everywhere else. *I* know him well, your worship.'

'Oh! you know me, do you?' cried the Artful, making a note of the statement. 'Wery good. That's a case of deformation of character, any way.'

Here there was another laugh, and another cry of silence.

'Now then, where are the witnesses?' said the clerk.

'Ah! that's right,' added the Dodger. 'Where are they? – I should like to see 'em.'

This wish was immediately gratified, for a policeman stepped forward who had seen the prisoner attempt the pocket of an unknown gentleman in a crowd, and indeed take a handkerchief therefrom, which being a very old one, he deliberately put back again, after trying it on his own countenance. For this reason he took the Dodger into custody as soon as he could get near him, and the said Dodger being searched had upon his person a silver snuff-box, with the owner's name engraved upon the lid. This gentleman had been discovered on reference to the Court Guide,[5] and being then and there present, swore that the snuff-box was his, and that he had missed it on the previous day, the moment he had disengaged himself from the crowd before referred to. He had also remarked a young gentleman in the throng particularly active in making his way about, and that young gentleman was the prisoner before him.

'Have you anything to ask this witness, boy?' said the magistrate.

'I wouldn't abase myself by descending to hold any conversation with him,' replied the Dodger.

'Have you anything to say at all?'

'Do you hear his worship ask if you've anything to say?' inquired the jailer, nudging the silent Dodger with his elbow.

'I beg your pardon,' said the Dodger, looking up with an air of abstraction. 'Did you address yourself to me, my man?'

'I never see such an out-and-out young wagabond, your worship,' observed the officer with a grin. 'Do you mean to say anything, you young shaver?'

'No,' replied the Dodger, 'not here, for this ain't the shop for justice; besides which, my attorney is a breakfasting this morning with the

Wice President of the House of Commons,[6] but I shall have something to say elsewhere, and so will he, and so will a wery numerous and respectable circle of acquaintance as 'll make them beaks wish they'd never been born, or that they'd got their footman to hang 'em up to their own hat-pegs 'afore they let 'em come out this morning to try it on upon me. I'll —'

'There, he's fully committed!' interposed the clerk. 'Take him away.'

'Come on,' said the jailer.

'Oh, ah! I'll come on,' replied the Dodger, brushing his hat with the palm of his hand. 'Ah! (to the Bench) it's no use your looking frightened; I won't show you no mercy, not a ha'porth of it. *You'll* pay for this, my fine fellers; I wouldn't be you for something. I wouldn't go free now, if you wos to fall down on your knees and ask me. Here, carry me off to prison. Take me away.'

With these last words the Dodger suffered himself to be led off by the collar, threatening till he got into the yard to make a parliamentary business of it, and then grinning in the officer's face with great glee and self-approval.

Having seen him locked up by himself in a little cell, Noah made the best of his way back to where he had left Master Bates. After waiting here some time, he was joined by that young gentleman, who had prudently abstained from showing himself until he had looked carefully abroad from a snug retreat, and ascertained that his new friend had not been followed by any impertinent person.

The two hastened back together, to bear to Mr Fagin the animating news that the Dodger was doing full justice to his bringing-up, and establishing for himself a glorious reputation.

*

CHAPTER THE SEVENTH

*THE TIME ARRIVES FOR NANCY TO
REDEEM HER PLEDGE TO ROSE MAYLIE.
SHE FAILS. NOAH CLAYPOLE IS
EMPLOYED BY FAGIN ON A SECRET
MISSION*

Adept as she was in all the arts of cunning and dissimulation, the girl Nancy could not wholly conceal the effect which the knowledge of the step she had taken, worked upon her mind. She remembered that both the crafty Jew and the brutal Sikes had confided to her schemes, which had been hidden from all others, in the full confidence that she was trustworthy, and beyond the reach of their suspicion; and vile as those schemes were, desperate as were their originators, and bitter as were her feelings towards the Jew, who had led her step by step deeper and deeper down into an abyss of crime and misery, whence was no escape, still there were times when even towards him she felt some relenting, lest her disclosure should bring him within the iron grasp he had so long eluded, and he should fall at last – richly as he merited such a fate – by her hand.

But these were the mere wanderings of a mind unable wholly to detach itself from old companions and associations, though enabled to fix itself steadily on one object, and resolved not to be turned aside by any consideration. Her fears for Sikes would have been more powerful inducements to recoil while there was yet time; but she had stipulated that her secret should be rigidly kept – she had dropped no clue which could lead to his discovery – she had refused, even for his sake, a refuge from all the guilt and wretchedness that encompassed her – and what more could she do? She was resolved.

Though every mental struggle terminated in this conclusion, they forced themselves upon her again and again, and left their traces too. She grew pale and thin even within a few days. At times she took no heed of what was passing before her, or no part in conversations where once she would have been the loudest. At others she laughed without merriment, and was noisy without cause or meaning. At others – often within a moment afterwards – she sat silent and dejected, brooding with her head upon her hands, while the very effort by which she roused herself told more forcibly than even these indications that she was ill at ease, and that her thoughts were occupied with matters very different and distant from those in course of discussion by her companions.

It was Sunday night, and the bell of the nearest church struck the hour. Sikes and the Jew were talking, but they paused to listen. The girl looked up from the low seat on which she crouched, and listened too, intently. Eleven.

'An hour this side of midnight,' said Sikes, raising the blind to look out, and returning to his seat. 'Dark and heavy it is too. A good night for business this.'

'Ah!' replied the Jew. 'What a pity, Bill, my dear, that there's none quite ready to be done.'

'You're right for once,' replied Sikes gruffly. 'It is a pity, for I'm in the humour too.'

The Jew sighed and shook his head despondingly.

'We must make up for lost time when we've got things into a good train; that's all I know,' said Sikes.

'That's the way to talk, my dear,' replied the Jew, venturing to pat him on the shoulder. 'It does me good to hear you.'

'Does you good, does it!' cried Sikes. 'Well, so be it.'

'Ha! ha! ha!' laughed the Jew, as if he were relieved by even this concession. 'You're like yourself to-night, Bill – quite like yourself.'

'I don't feel like myself when you lay that withered old claw on my shoulder, so take it away,' said Sikes, casting off the Jew's hand.

'It makes you nervous, Bill, – reminds you of being nabbed, does it?' said the Jew, determined not to be offended.

'Reminds me of being nabbed by the devil,' returned Sikes, 'not by a trap. There never was another man with such a face as yours, unless it was your father, and I suppose *he* is singeing his grizzled red beard by this time, unless you came straight from the old 'un without any father at all betwixt you, which I shouldn't wonder at a bit.'

Fagin offered no reply to this compliment; but, pulling Sikes by the sleeve, pointed his finger towards Nancy, who had taken advantage of the foregoing conversation to put on her bonnet, and was now leaving the room.

'Hallo!' cried Sikes. 'Nance. Where's the gal going at this time of night?'

'Not far.'

'What answer's that!' returned Sikes. 'Where are you going?'

'I say, not far.'

'And I say where?' retorted Sikes in a loud voice. 'Do you hear me?'

'I don't know where,' replied the girl.

'Then I do,' said Sikes, more in the spirit of obstinacy than because he had any real objection to the girl going where she listed. 'Nowhere. Sit down.'

'I'm not well. I told you that before,' rejoined the girl. 'I want a breath of air.'

'Put your head out of the winder, and take it there,' replied Sikes.

'There's not enough there,' said the girl. 'I want it in the street.'

'Then you won't have it,' replied Sikes; with which assurance he rose, locked the door, took the key out, and, pulling her bonnet from her head, flung it up to the top of an old press.[1] 'There,' said the robber. 'Now stop quietly where you are, will you?'

'It's not such a matter as a bonnet would keep me,' said the girl, turning very pale. 'What do you mean, Bill? Do you know what you're doing?'

'Know what I'm—Oh!' cried Sikes, turning to Fagin, 'she's out of her senses, you know, or she daren't talk to me in that way.'

'You'll drive me on to something desperate,' muttered the girl, placing both hands upon her breast, as though to keep down by force some violent outbreak. 'Let me go, will you, – this minute – this instant –'

'No!' roared Sikes.

'Tell him to let me go, Fagin. He had better. It'll be better for him. Do you hear me?' cried Nancy, stamping her foot upon the ground.

'Hear you!' repeated Sikes, turning round in his chair to confront her. 'Ay, and if I hear you for half a minute longer, the dog shall have such a grip on your throat as 'll tear some of that screaming voice out. Wot has come over you, you jade[2] – wot is it?'

'Let me go,' said the girl with great earnestness; then, sitting herself down on the floor before the door, she said –' Bill, let me go; you don't know what you're doing – you don't, indeed. For only one hour – do – do!'

'Cut my limbs off one by one!' cried Sikes, seizing her roughly by the arm – 'if I don't think the gal's stark raving mad. Get up!'

'Not till you let me go – not till you let me go. – Never – never!' screamed the girl. Sikes looked on for a minute, watching his opportunity, and, suddenly pinioning her hands, dragged her, struggling and wrestling with him by the way, into a small room adjoining, where he sat himself on a bench, and thrusting her into a chair, held her down by force. She struggled and implored by turns until twelve o'clock had struck, and then, wearied and exhausted, ceased to contest the point any further. With a caution, backed by many oaths, to make no more efforts to go out that night, Sikes left her to recover at leisure, and rejoined the Jew.

'Phew!' said the housebreaker, wiping the perspiration from his face. 'Wot a precious strange gal that is!'

'You may say that, Bill,' replied the Jew thoughtfully. 'You may say that.'

'Wot did she take it into her head to go out to-night for, do you think?' asked Sikes. 'Come; you should know her better than me – wot does it mean?'

'Obstinacy – woman's obstinacy, I suppose, my dear,' replied the Jew, shrugging his shoulders.

'Well, I suppose it is,' growled Sikes. 'I thought I had tamed her, but she's as bad as ever.'

'Worse,' said the Jew thoughtfully. 'I never knew her like this, for such a little cause.'

'Nor I,' said Sikes. 'I think she's got a touch of that fever in her blood yet, and it won't come out – eh?'

'Like enough,' replied the Jew.

'I'll let her a little blood without troubling the doctor,[3] if she's took that way again,' said Sikes.

The Jew nodded an expressive approval of this mode of treatment.

'She was hanging about me all day and night too when I was stretched on my back; and you, like a black-hearted wolf as you are, kept yourself aloof,' said Sikes. 'We was very poor too all the time, and I think one way or other it's worried and fretted her, and that being shut up here so long has made her restless – eh?'

'That's it, my dear,' replied the Jew in a whisper. – 'Hush!'

As he uttered these words, the girl herself appeared and resumed her former seat. Her eyes were swollen and red; she rocked herself to and fro, tossed her head, and after a little time burst out laughing.

'Why, now she's on the other tack!' exclaimed Sikes, turning a look of excessive surprise upon his companion.

The Jew nodded to him to take no further notice just then, and in a few minutes the girl subsided into her accustomed demeanour. Whispering Sikes that there was no fear of her relapsing, Fagin took up his hat and bade him good-night. He paused when he reached the door, and looking round, asked if somebody would light him down the dark stairs.

'Light him down,' said Sikes, who was filling his pipe. 'It's a pity he should break his neck himself, and disappoint the sight-seers. There; show him a light.'

Nancy followed the old man down stairs with the candle. When they reached the passage he laid his finger on his lip, and drawing close to the girl, said in a whisper,

'What is it, Nancy, dear?'

'What do you mean?' replied the girl in the same tone.

'The reason of all this,' replied Fagin. 'If *he*' – he pointed with his skinny fore-finger up the stairs – 'is so hard with you, (he's a brute, Nance, a brute-beast) why don't you—'

'Well!' said the girl, as Fagin paused, with his mouth almost touching her ear, and his eyes looking into hers.

'No matter just now,' said the Jew; 'we'll talk of this again. You have a friend in me, Nance; a staunch friend. I have the means at hand, quiet and close. If you want revenge on those that treat you like a dog – like a dog! worse than his dog, for he humours him sometimes – come to me. I say, come to me. He is the mere hound of a day; but you know me of old, Nance – of old.'

'I know you well,' replied the girl, without manifesting the least emotion. 'Good night.'

She shrunk back as Fagin offered to lay his hand on hers, but said good night again in a steady voice, and, answering his parting look with a nod of intelligence, closed the door between them.

Fagin walked towards his own home, intent upon the thoughts that were working within his brain. He had conceived the idea – not from what had just passed, though that had tended to confirm him, but slowly and by degrees – that Nancy, wearied of the housebreaker's brutality, had conceived an attachment for some new friend. Her altered manner, her repeated absences from home alone, her comparative indifference to the interests of the gang for which she had once been so zealous, and, added to these, her desperate impatience to leave home that night at a particular hour, all favoured the supposition, and rendered it, to him at least, almost a matter of certainty. The object of this new liking was not among his myrmidons. He would be a valuable acquisition with such an assistant as Nancy, and must (thus Fagin argued) be secured without delay.

There was another and a darker object to be gained. Sikes knew too much, and his ruffian taunts had not galled the Jew the less because the wounds were hidden. The girl must know well that if she shook him off, she could never be safe from his fury, and that it would be surely wreaked – to the maiming of limbs, or perhaps the loss of life – on the object of her more recent fancy. 'With a little persuasion,' thought Fagin, 'what more likely than that she would consent to poison him? Women have done such things, and worse, to secure the same object before now. There would be the dangerous villain – the man I hate – gone; another secured in his place; and my influence over the girl, with the knowledge of this crime to back it, unlimited.'

These things passed through the mind of Fagin during the short time he sat alone in the housebreaker's room; and with them uppermost in his thoughts, he had taken the opportunity afterwards afforded him of sounding the girl in the broken hints he threw out at parting. There was no expression of surprise, no assumption of an inability to understand his meaning. The girl clearly comprehended it. Her glance at parting showed *that*.

But perhaps she would recoil from a plot to take the life of Sikes, and that was one of the chief ends to be attained. 'How,' thought the Jew, as he crept homewards, 'can I increase my influence with her? what new power can I acquire?'

Such brains are fertile in expedients. If, without extracting a confession from herself, he laid a watch, discovered the object of her altered regard, and threatened to reveal the whole history to Sikes (of whom she stood in no common fear) unless she entered into his designs, could he not secure her compliance?

'I can,' said Fagin almost aloud. 'She durst not refuse me then – not for her life, not for her life! I have it all. The means are ready, and shall be set to work. I shall have you yet.'

He cast back a dark look and a threatening motion of the hand towards the spot where he had left the bolder villain, and went on his way, busying his bony hands in the folds of his tattered garment, which he wrenched tightly in his grasp as though there were a hated enemy crushed with every motion of his fingers.

He rose betimes[4] next morning, and waited impatiently for the appearance of his new associate, who, after a delay which seemed interminable, at length presented himself, and commenced a voracious assault upon the breakfast.

'Bolter,' said the Jew, drawing up a chair and seating himself opposite to him.

'Well, here I am,' returned Noah. 'What's the matter? Don't yer ask me to do anything till I have done eating. That's a great fault in this place. Yer never get time enough over yer meals.'

'You can talk as you eat, can't you?' said Fagin, cursing his dear young friend's greediness from the very bottom of his heart.

'Oh yes, I can talk; I get on better when I talk,' said Noah, cutting a monstrous slice of bread. 'Where's Charlotte?'

'Out,' said Fagin. 'I sent her out this morning with the other young woman, because I wanted us to be alone.'

'Oh!' said Noah, 'I wish yer'd ordered her to make some buttered toast first. Well. Talk away. Yer won't interrupt me.'

There seemed indeed no great fear of anything interrupting him, as he had evidently sat down with a determination to do a great deal of business.

'You did well yesterday, my dear,' said the Jew, 'beautiful! Six shillings and ninepence halfpenny on the very first day! The kinchin lay will be a fortune to you.'

'Don't yer forget to add three pint-pots and a milk-can,' said Mr Bolter.

'No, no, my dear,' replied the Jew. 'The pint-pots were great strokes of genius, but the milk-can was a perfect masterpiece.'

'Pretty well, I think, for a beginner,' remarked Mr Bolter complacently. 'The pots I took off airy railings, and the milk-can was standing by itself outside a public-house, so I thought it might get rusty with the rain, or catch cold, yer know. Ha! ha! ha!'

The Jew affected to laugh very heartily; and Mr Bolter, having had his laugh out, took a series of large bites which finished his first hunk of bread and butter, and assisted himself to a second.

'I want you, Bolter,' said Fagin, leaning over the table, 'to do a piece of work for me, my dear, that needs great care and caution.'

'I say,' rejoined Bolter, 'don't yer go shoving me into danger, or sending me to any more police-offices. That don't suit me, that don't; and so I tell yer.'

'There's not the smallest danger in it – not the very smallest,' said the Jew; 'it's only to dodge a woman.'

'An old woman?' demanded Mr Bolter.

'A young one,' replied Fagin.

'I can do that pretty well, I know,' said Bolter. 'I was a regular cunning sneak when I was at school. What am I to dodge her for? not to —'

'Not to do anything,' interrupted the Jew, 'but to tell me where she goes to, who she sees, and, if possible, what she says; to remember the street, if it is a street, or the house, if it is a house, and to bring me back all the information you can.'

'What'll yer give me?' asked Noah, setting down his cup, and looking his employer eagerly in the face.

'If you do it well, a pound, my dear – one pound,' said Fagin, wishing to interest him in the scent as much as possible. 'And that's what I never gave yet for any job of work where there wasn't valuable consideration to be gained.'

'Who is she?' inquired Noah.

'One of us.'

'Oh Lor!' cried Noah, curling up his nose. 'Yer doubtful of her, are yer?'

'She has found out some new friends, my dear, and I must know who they are,' replied the Jew.

'I see,' said Noah. 'Just to have the pleasure of knowing them, if they're respectable people, eh? – Ha! ha! ha! I'm your man.'

'I knew you would be,' cried Fagin, elated by the success of his proposal.

'Of course, of course,' replied Noah. 'Where is she? Where am I to wait for her? When am I to go?'

'All that, my dear, you shall hear from me. I'll point her out at the proper time,' said Fagin. 'You keep ready, and leave the rest to me.'

That night, and the next, and the next again, the spy sat booted and equipped in his carter's dress, ready to turn out at a word from Fagin. Six nights passed, – six long weary nights, – and on each Fagin came home with a disappointed face, and briefly intimated that it was not yet time. On the seventh he returned earlier, and with an exultation he could not conceal. It was Sunday.

'She goes abroad[5] to-night,' said Fagin, 'and on the right errand, I'm sure; for she has been alone all day, and the man she is afraid of will not be back much before daybreak. Come with me. Quick.'

Noah started up without saying a word, for the Jew was in a state of such intense excitement that it infected him. They left the house stealthily, and, hurrying through a labyrinth of streets, arrived at length before a public-house, which Noah recognised as the same in which he had slept on the night of his arrival in London.

It was past eleven o'clock, and the door was closed. It opened softly on its hinges as the Jew gave a low whistle. They entered without noise, and the door was closed behind them.

Scarcely venturing to whisper, but substituting dumb show for words, Fagin and the young Jew who had admitted them pointed out the pane of glass to Noah, and signed to him to climb up and observe the person in the adjoining room.

'Is that the woman?' he asked, scarcely above his breath.

The Jew nodded yes.

'I can't see her face well,' whispered Noah. 'She is looking down, and the candle is behind her.'

'Stay there,' whispered Fagin. He signed to Barney, who withdrew. In an instant the lad entered the room adjoining, and, under pretence of snuffing the candle, moved it into the required position, and, speaking to the girl, caused her to raise her face.

'I see her now,' cried the spy.

'Plainly?' asked the Jew.

'I should know her among a thousand.'

He hastily descended as the room-door opened, and the girl came out. Fagin drew him behind a small partition which was curtained off, and they held their breaths as she passed within a few feet of their place of concealment, and emerged by the door at which they had entered.

'Hist!' cried the lad who held the door. 'Now.'

Noah exchanged a look with Fagin, and darted out.

'To the left,' whispered the lad; 'take the left hand, and keep on the other side.'

He did so, and by the light of the lamps saw the girl's retreating figure already at some distance before him. He advanced as near as he considered prudent, and kept on the opposite side of the street, the better to observe her motions. She looked nervously round twice or thrice, and once stopped to let two men, who were following close behind her, pass on. She seemed to gather courage as she advanced, and to walk with a steadier and firmer step. The spy preserved the same relative distance between them, and followed with his eye upon her.

CHAPTER THE EIGHTH

THE APPOINTMENT KEPT

The church clocks chimed three quarters past eleven as two figures emerged on London Bridge. One, which advanced with a swift and rapid step, was that of a woman, who looked eagerly about her as though in quest of some expected object; the other figure was that of a man, who slunk along in the deepest shadow he could find, and at some distance, accommodated his pace to her's, stopping when she stopped, and, as she moved again, creeping stealthily on, but never allowing himself, in the ardour of his pursuit, to gain upon her footsteps. Thus they crossed the bridge from the Middlesex to the Surrey shore, when the woman, apparently disappointed in her anxious scrutiny of the foot-passengers, turned back. The movement was sudden, but he who watched her was not thrown off his guard by it, for shrinking into one of the recesses which surmount the piers of the bridge, and leaning over the parapet the better to conceal his figure, he suffered her to pass by on the opposite pavement, and when she was about the same distance in advance as she had been before, he slipped quietly down and followed her again. At nearly the centre of the bridge she stopped. The man stopped too.

It was a very dark night. The day had been unfavourable, and at that hour and place there were few people stirring. Such as there were hurried quickly past, very possibly without seeing, but certainly without noticing, either the woman or the man who kept her in view. Their appearance was not calculated to attract the importunate regards of such of London's destitute population as chanced to take their way over the bridge that night in search of some cold arch or doorless hovel wherein to lay their heads; they stood there in silence, neither speaking nor spoken to by any one who passed.

A mist hung over the river, deepening the red glare of the fires that burnt upon the small craft moored off the different wharfs, and rendering darker and more indistinct the mirky buildings on the banks.

The old smoke-stained storehouses on either side rose heavy and dull from the dense mass of roofs and gables, and frowned sternly upon water too black to reflect even their lumbering shapes. The tower of old Saint Saviour's church, and the spire of Saint Magnus,[1] so long the giant-warders of the ancient bridge, were visible in the gloom; but the forest of shipping below bridge, and the thickly scattered spires of churches above, were nearly all hidden from the sight.

The girl had taken a few restless turns to and fro – closely watched meanwhile by her hidden observer – when the heavy bell of St Paul's tolled for the death of another day. Midnight had come upon the crowded city. The palace, the night-cellar,[2] the jail, the madhouse; the chambers of birth and death, of health and sickness; the rigid face of the corpse and the calm sleep of the child – midnight was upon them all.

The hour had not struck two minutes, when a young lady, accompanied by a grey-haired gentleman, alighted from a hackney-carriage within a short distance of the bridge, and, having dismissed the vehicle, walked straight towards it. They had scarcely set foot upon its pavement when the girl started, and immediately made towards them.

They walked onwards, looking about them with the air of persons who entertained some very slight expectation which had little chance of being realised, when they were suddenly joined by this new associate. They halted with an exclamation of surprise, but suppressed it immediately, for a man in the garments of a countryman came close up – brushed against them, indeed – at the precise moment.

'Not here,' said Nancy hurriedly. 'I am afraid to speak to you here. Come away – out of the public road – down the steps yonder.'

As she uttered these words, and indicated with her hand the direction in which she wished them to proceed, the countryman looked round, and roughly asking what they took up the whole pavement for, passed on.

The steps to which the girl had pointed were those which, on the Surrey bank, and on the same side of the bridge as Saint Saviour's church, form a landing-stairs from the river. To this spot the man bearing the appearance of a countryman hastened unobserved; and after a moment's survey of the place, he began to descend.

The stairs are a part of the bridge; they consist of three flights. Just below the end of the second, going down, the stone wall on the left terminates in an ornamental pier or pedestal facing towards the Thames. At this point the lower steps widen, so that a person turning that angle of the wall is necessarily unseen by any others on the stairs who chance to be above him, if only a step. The countryman looked hastily round when he reached this point, and as there seemed no better place of concealment, and the tide being out there was plenty of room, he slipped aside, with his back to the pier, and there waited pretty certain that they would come no lower, and that even if he could not hear what was said, he could follow them again with safety.

So tardily stole the time in this lonely place, and so eager was the spy to penetrate the motives of an interview so different from what he had been led to expect, that he more than once gave the matter up for lost, and persuaded himself either that they had stopped far above, or resorted to some entirely different spot to hold their mysterious conversation. He was on the very point of emerging from his hiding-place, and regaining the road above, when he heard the sound of footsteps, and directly afterwards of voices, almost close at his ear.

He drew himself straight upright against the wall, and, scarcely breathing, listened attentively.

'This is far enough,' said a voice, which was evidently that of the gentleman. 'I will not suffer this young lady to go any further. Many people would have distrusted you too much to have come even so far, but you see I am willing to humour you.'

'To humour me!' cried the voice of the girl whom he had followed. 'You're considerate, indeed, sir. To humour me! Well, well, it's no matter.'

'Why, for what,' said the gentleman in a kinder tone, 'for what purpose can you have brought us to this strange place? Why not have let me speak to you above there, where it is light, and there is something stirring, instead of bringing us to this dark and dismal hole?'

'I told you before,' replied Nancy, 'that I was afraid to speak to you there. I don't know why it is,' said the girl, shuddering, 'but I have such a fear and dread upon me to-night that I can hardly stand.'

'A fear of what?' asked the gentleman, who seemed to pity her.

The Meeting

'I scarcely know of what,' replied the girl. 'I wish I did. Horrible thoughts of death, and shrouds with blood upon them, and a fear that has made me burn as if I were on fire, have been upon me all day. I was reading a book to-night to wile the time away, and the same things came into the print.'

'Imagination,' said the gentleman, soothing her.

'No imagination,' replied the girl in a hoarse voice. 'I'll swear I saw "coffin" written in every page of the book in large black letters, – ay, and they carried one close to me in the streets to-night.'

'There is nothing unusual in that,' said the gentleman. 'They have passed me often.'

'*Real ones*,' rejoined the girl. 'This was not.'

There was something so uncommon in her manner that the flesh of the concealed listener crept as he heard the girl utter these words, and the blood chilled within him. He had never experienced a greater relief than hearing the sweet voice of the young lady as she begged her to be calm, and not allow herself to become the prey of such fearful fancies.

'Speak to her kindly,' said the young lady to her companion. 'Poor creature! She seems to need it.'

'Your haughty religious people would have held their heads up to see me as I am to-night, and preached of flames and vengeance,' cried the girl. 'Oh, dear lady, why ar'n't those, who claim to be God's own folks, as gentle and as kind to us poor wretches as you, who, having youth and beauty and all that they have lost, might be a little proud, instead of so much humbler!'

'Ah!' said the gentleman, 'a Turk turns his face, after washing it well, to the East when he says his prayers; these good people, after giving their faces such a rub with the World as takes the smiles off, turn with no less regularity to the darkest side of Heaven. Between the Mussulman and the Pharisee,[3] commend me to the first.'

These words appeared to be addressed to the young lady, and were perhaps uttered with the view of affording Nancy time to recover herself. The gentleman shortly afterwards addressed himself to her.

'You were not here last Sunday night,' he said.

'I couldn't come,' replied Nancy; 'I was kept by force.'

'By whom?'

'Bill – him that I told the young lady of before.'

'You were not suspected of holding any communication with anybody on the subject which has brought us here to-night, I hope?' asked the old gentleman anxiously.

'No,' replied the girl, shaking her head. 'It's not very easy for me to leave him unless he knows why; I couldn't have seen the lady when I did, but that I gave him a drink of laudanum before I came away.'

'Did he awake before you returned?' inquired the gentleman.

'No; and neither he nor any of them suspect me.'

'Good,' said the gentleman. 'Now listen to me.'

'I am ready,' replied the girl, as he paused for a moment.

'This young lady,' the gentleman began, 'has communicated to me and some other friends who can be safely trusted, what you told her nearly a fortnight since. I confess to you that I had doubts at first whether you were to be implicitly relied upon, but now I firmly believe you are.'

'I am,' said the girl earnestly.

'I repeat that I firmly believe it. To prove to you that I am disposed to trust you, I tell you without reserve, that we propose to extort the secret, whatever it may be, from the fears of this man Monks. But if – if –' said the gentleman, 'he cannot be secured, or, if secured, cannot be acted upon as we wish, you must deliver up the Jew.'

'Fagin!' cried the girl, recoiling.

'That man must be delivered up by you,' said the gentleman.

'I will not do it – I will never do it,' replied the girl. 'Devil that he is, and worse than devil as he has been to me, I will never do that.'

'You will not?' said the gentleman, who seemed fully prepared for this answer.

'Never!' returned the girl.

'Tell me why?'

'For one reason,' rejoined the girl firmly, 'for one reason, that the lady knows and will stand by me in, I know she will, for I have her promise; and for this other reason besides, that, bad life as he has led,

I have led a bad life too; there are many of us who have kept the same courses together, and I'll not turn upon them, who might – any of them – have turned upon me, but didn't, bad as they are.'

'Then,' said the gentleman quickly, as if this had been the point he had been aiming to attain – 'put Monks into my hands, and leave him to me to deal with.'

'What if he turns against the others?'

'I promise you that in that case, if the truth is forced from him, there the matter will rest; there must be circumstances in Oliver's little history which it would be painful to drag before the public eye, and if the truth is once elicited, they shall go scot free.'

'And if it is not?' suggested the girl.

'Then,' pursued the gentleman, 'this Jew shall not be brought to justice without your consent. In such a case I could show you reasons, I think, which would induce you to yield it.'

'Have I the lady's promise for that?' asked the girl eagerly.

'You have,' replied Rose. 'My true and faithful pledge.'

'Monks would never learn how you knew what you do?' said the girl, after a short pause.

'Never,' replied the gentleman. 'The intelligence should be so brought to bear upon him, that he could never even guess.'

'I have been a liar, and among liars, from a little child,' said the girl after another interval of silence, 'but I will take your words.'

After receiving an assurance from both that she might safely do so, she proceeded in a voice so low that it was often difficult for the listener to discover even the purport of what she said, to describe by name and situation the public-house whence she had been followed that night. From the manner in which she occasionally paused, it appeared as if the gentleman were making some hasty notes of the information she communicated. When she had thoroughly explained the localities of the place, the best position from which to watch it without exciting observation, and the night and hour on which Monks was most in the habit of frequenting it, she seemed to consider a few moments for the purpose of recalling his features and appearance more forcibly to her recollection.

'He is tall,' said the girl, 'and a strongly made man, but not stout;

he has a lurking walk, and as he walks, constantly looks over his shoulder, first on one side and then on the other. Don't forget that, for his eyes are sunk in his head so much deeper than any other man's, that you might almost tell him by that alone. His face is dark, like his hair and eyes, but, although he can't be more than six or eight and twenty, withered and haggard. His lips are often discoloured and disfigured with the marks of teeth, for he has desperate fits, and sometimes even bites his hands and covers them with wounds – why did you start?' said the girl, stopping suddenly.

The gentleman replied in a hurried manner that he was not conscious of having done so, and begged her to proceed.

'Part of this,' said the girl, 'I've drawn out from other people at the house I tell you of, for I have only seen him twice, and both times he was covered up in a large cloak. I think that's all I can give you to know him by. Stay though,' she added. 'Upon his throat, so high that you can see a part of it below his neckerchief when he turns his face, there is –'

'A broad red mark, like a burn or scald,' cried the gentleman.

'How's this!' said the girl. 'You know him!'

The young lady uttered a cry of extreme surprise, and for a few moments they were so still that the listener could distinctly hear them breathe.

'I think I do,' said the gentleman, breaking silence. 'I should, by your description. We shall see. Many people are singularly like each other though, – it may not be the same.'

As he expressed himself to this effect with assumed carelessness, he took a step or two nearer the concealed spy, as the latter could tell from the distinctness with which he heard him mutter, 'It must be he!'

'Now,' he said, returning, so it seemed by the sound, to the spot where he had stood before, 'you have given us most valuable assistance, young woman, and I wish you to be the better for it. What can I do to serve you?'

'Nothing,' replied Nancy.

'You will not persist in saying that,' rejoined the gentleman with a voice and emphasis of kindness that might have touched a much harder and more obdurate heart. 'Think now. Tell me.'

'Nothing, sir,' rejoined the girl, weeping. 'You can do nothing to help me. I am past all hope, indeed.'

'You put yourself beyond its pale,' said the gentleman: 'the past has been a dreary waste with you, of youthful energies mis-spent, and such priceless treasures lavished as the Creator bestows but once, and never grants again, but for the future you may hope. I do not say that it is in our power to offer you peace of heart and mind, for that must come as you seek it; but a quiet asylum, either in England, or, if you fear to remain here, in some foreign country, it is not only within the compass of our ability but our most anxious wish to secure to you. Before the dawn of morning, before this river wakes to the first glimpse of daylight, you shall be placed as entirely beyond the reach of your former associates, and leave as utter an absence of all traces behind you, as if you were to disappear from the earth this moment. Come. I would not have you go back to exchange one word with any old companion, or take one look at any old haunt, or breathe the very air which is pestilence and death to you. Quit them all, while there is time and opportunity.'

'She will be persuaded now,' cried the young lady. 'She hesitates, I am sure.'

'I fear not, my dear,' said the gentleman.

'No, sir, I do not,' replied the girl after a short struggle. 'I am chained to my old life. I loathe and hate it now, but I cannot leave it. I must have gone too far to turn back, – and yet I don't know, for if you had spoken to me so, some time ago, I should have laughed it off. But,' she said, looking hastily round, 'this fear comes over me again. I must go home.'

'Home!' repeated the young lady, with great stress upon the word.

'Home, lady,' rejoined the girl. 'To such a home as I have raised for myself with the work of my whole life. Let us part. I shall be watched or seen. Go, go. If I have done you any service, all I ask is, that you leave me and let me go my way alone.'

'It is useless,' said the gentleman with a sigh. 'We compromise her safety perhaps by staying here. We may have detained her longer than she expected already.'

'Yes, yes,' urged the girl. 'You have.'

'What,' cried the young lady, 'can be the end of this poor creature's life!'

'What!' repeated the girl. 'Look before you, lady. Look at that dark water. How many times do you read of such as me who spring into the tide, and leave no living thing to care for or bewail them. It may be years hence, or it may be only months, but I shall come to that at last.'

'Do not speak thus, pray,' returned the young lady, sobbing.

'It will never reach your ears, dear lady, and God forbid such horrors should –' replied the girl. 'Good night, good night.'

The gentleman turned away.

'This purse,' cried the young lady. 'Take it for my sake, that you may have some resource in an hour of need and trouble.'

'No, no,' replied the girl. 'I have not done this for money. Let me have that to think of. And yet – give me something that you have worn: I should like to have something – no, no, not a ring – your gloves or handkerchief – anything that I can keep as having belonged to you, sweet lady. There. Bless you – God bless you! Good night, good night!'

The violent agitation of the girl, and the apprehension of some discovery which would subject her to ill-usage and violence, seemed to determine the gentleman to leave her as she requested. The sound of retreating footsteps was audible, and the voices ceased.

The two figures of the young lady and her companion soon afterwards appeared upon the bridge. They stopped at the summit of the stairs.

'Hark!' cried the young lady, listening. 'Did she call! I thought I heard her voice.'

'No, my love,' replied Mr Brownlow, looking sadly back. 'She has not moved, and will not till we are gone.'

Rose Maylie lingered, but the old gentleman drew her arm through his, and led her with gentle force away. As they disappeared, the girl sunk down nearly at her full length upon one of the stone stairs, and vented the anguish of her heart in bitter tears.

After a time she rose, and with feeble and tottering steps ascended to the street. The astonished listener remained motionless on his post for some minutes afterwards, and having ascertained with many cautious glances round him that he was again alone, crept slowly from his hiding-place, and returned, stealthily and in the shade of the wall, in the same manner as he had descended.

Peeping out more than once when he reached the top, to make sure that he was unobserved, Noah Claypole darted away at his utmost speed, and made for the Jew's house as fast as his legs would carry him.

*

CHAPTER THE NINTH

FATAL CONSEQUENCES

It was nearly two hours before daybreak – the time which in the autumn of the year may be truly called the dead of night; when the streets are silent and deserted, when even sound appears to slumber, and profligacy and riot have staggered home to dream – it was at this still and silent hour that the Jew sat watching in his old lair, with face so distorted and pale, and eyes so red and bloodshot, that he looked less like a man than some hideous phantom, moist from the grave, and worried by an evil spirit

He sat crouching over a cold hearth, wrapped in an old torn coverlet, with his face turned towards a wasting candle that stood upon a table by his side. His right hand was raised to his lips, and as, absorbed in thought, he bit his long black nails, he disclosed among his toothless gums a few such fangs as should have been a dog's or rat's.

Stretched on a mattress upon the floor lay Noah Claypole fast asleep. Towards him the old man sometimes directed his eyes for an instant, then brought them back again to the candle, which, with long-burnt wick drooping almost double, and hot grease falling down in clots upon the table, plainly showed that his thoughts were busy elsewhere.

Indeed they were. Mortification at the overthrow of his notable scheme, hatred of the girl who had dared to palter with strangers, an utter distrust of the sincerity of her refusal to yield him up, bitter disappointment at the loss of his revenge on Sikes, the fear of detection, and ruin, and death, and a fierce and deadly rage kindled by all, – these were the passionate considerations which, following close upon each other with rapid and ceaseless whirl, shot through the brain of Fagin, as every evil thought and blackest purpose lay working at his heart.

He sat without changing his attitude in the least, or appearing to take the smallest heed of time, until his quick ear seemed to be attracted by a footstep in the street.

'At last,' muttered the Jew, wiping his dry and fevered mouth. 'At last.'

The bell rang gently as he spoke. He crept up stairs to the door, and presently returned, accompanied by a man muffled to the chin, who carried a bundle under one arm. Sitting down, and throwing back his outer coat, the man displayed the burly frame of Sikes.

'There,' he said, laying the bundle on the table. 'Take care of that, and do the most you can with it. It's been trouble enough to get; I thought I should have been here three hours ago.'

Fagin laid his hand upon the bundle, and, locking it in the cupboard, sat down again without speaking. But he did not take his eyes off the robber for an instant during this action, and now that they sat over against each other, face to face, he looked fixedly at him, with his lips quivering so violently, and his face so altered by the emotions which had mastered him, that the housebreaker involuntarily drew back his chair, and surveyed him with a look of real affright.

'Wot now?' cried Sikes. 'Wot do you look at a man so for? – Speak, will you?'

The Jew raised his right hand, and shook his trembling forefinger in the air, but his passion was so great that the power of speech was for the moment gone.

'D—me!' said Sikes, feeling in his breast with a look of alarm. 'He's gone mad. I must look to myself here.'

'No, no,' rejoined Fagin, finding his voice. 'It's not – you're not the person, Bill. I've no – no fault to find with you.'

'Oh, you haven't, haven't you?' said Sikes, looking sternly at him, and ostentatiously passing a pistol into a more convenient pocket. 'That's lucky – for one of us. Which one that is, don't matter.'

'I've got that to tell you, Bill,' said the Jew, drawing his chair nearer, 'will make you worse than me.'

'Ay?' returned the robber, with an incredulous air. 'Tell away. Look sharp, or Nance will think I'm lost.'

'Lost!' cried Fagin. 'She has pretty well settled that in her own mind already.'

Sikes looked with an aspect of great perplexity into the Jew's face, and reading no satisfactory explanation of the riddle there, clenched his coat collar in his huge hand, and shook him soundly.

'Speak, will you!' he said; 'or if you don't, it shall be for want of breath. Open your mouth, and say wot you've got to say in plain words. Out with it, you thundering old cur, out with it.'

'Suppose that lad that's lying there—' Fagin began.

Sikes turned round to where Noah was sleeping, as if he had not previously observed him. 'Well,' he said, resuming his former position.

'Suppose that lad,' pursued the Jew, 'was to peach – blow upon us all – first seeking out the right folks for the purpose, and then having a meeting with 'em in the street to paint our likenesses, describe every mark that they might know us by, and the crib where we might be most easily taken. Suppose he was to do all this, and, besides, to blow upon a plant we've all been in, more or less – of his own fancy; not grabbed, trapped, tried, earwigged by the parson, and brought to it on bread and water – but of his own fancy; to please his own taste; stealing out at nights to find those most interested against us, and peaching to them. Do you hear me?' cried the Jew, his eyes flashing with rage. 'Suppose he did all this, what then?'

'What then!' replied Sikes with a tremendous oath. 'If he was left alive till I came, I'd grind his skull under the iron heel of my boot into as many grains as there are hairs upon his head.'

'What if *I* did it!' cried the Jew, almost in a yell. '*I*, that know so much, and could hang so many besides myself!'

'I don't know,' replied Sikes, clenching his teeth, and turning white at the mere suggestion. 'I'd do something in the jail that 'ud get me put in irons; and if I was tried along with you, I'd fall upon you with them in the open court, and beat your brains out afore the people, I should have such strength,' muttered the robber, poising his brawny arm, 'that I could smash your head as if a loaded waggon had gone over it.'

'You would?'

'Would I!' said the housebreaker. 'Try me.'

'If it was Charley, or the Dodger, or Bet, or—'

'I don't care who,' replied Sikes impatiently. 'Whoever it was, I'd serve them the same.'

Fagin again looked hard at the robber, and motioning him to be silent, stooped over the bed upon the floor, and shook the sleeper to rouse him. Sikes leant forward in his chair, looking on, with his hands upon his knees, as if wondering much what all this questioning and preparation was to end in.

'Bolter! Bolter! Poor lad!' said Fagin, looking up with an expression of devilish anticipation, and speaking slowly, and with marked emphasis. 'He's tired – tired with watching for *her* so long, – watching for *her*, Bill.'

'Wot d'ye mean?' asked Sikes, drawing back.

The Jew made no answer, but bending over the sleeper again, hauled him into a sitting posture. When his assumed name had been repeated several times, Noah rubbed his eyes, and giving a heavy yawn, looked sleepily about him.

'Tell me that again – once again, just for him to hear,' said the Jew, pointing to Sikes as he spoke.

'Tell yer what?' asked the sleepy Noah, shaking himself pettishly.

'That about – NANCY,' said the Jew, clutching Sikes by the wrist, as if to prevent his leaving the house before he had heard enough. 'You followed her!'

'Yes.'

'To London Bridge?'

'Yes.'

'Where she met two people?'

'So she did.'

'A gentleman, and a lady that she had gone to of her own accord before, who asked her to give up all her pals and Monks first, which she did; and to describe him, which she did; and to tell her what house it was that we meet at, and go to, which she did; and where it could be best watched from, which she did; and what time the people went there, which she did. She did all this. She told it all, every word, without a threat, without a murmur – she did – didn't she?' cried the Jew, half mad with fury.

'All right,' replied Noah, scratching his head. 'That's just what it was.'

'What did they say about last Sunday?' demanded the Jew.

'About last Sunday,' replied Noah, considering. 'Why, I told yer that before.'

'Again. Tell it again!' cried Fagin, tightening his grasp on Sikes, and brandishing his other hand aloft as the foam flew from his lips.

'They asked her,' said Noah, who, as he grew more wakeful, seemed to have a dawning perception who Sikes was, 'they asked her why she didn't come last Sunday as she promised. She said she couldn't –'

'Why – why?' interrupted the Jew, triumphantly. 'Tell him that.'

'Because she was forcibly kept at home by Bill, the man she had told them of before,' replied Noah.

'What more of him?' cried the Jew. 'What more of the man she had told them of before. Tell him that – tell him that.'

'Why, that she couldn't very easily get out of doors unless he knew where she was going to,' said Noah; 'and so the first time she went to see the lady, she – ha! ha! ha! it made me laugh when she said it, that did, – she gave him a drink of laudanum.'

'Hell's fire!' cried Sikes, breaking fiercely from the Jew. 'Let me go!'

Flinging the old man from him, he rushed from the room, and darted wildly and furiously up the stairs.

'Bill, Bill!' cried the Jew, following him hastily. 'A word. Only a word.'

The word would not have been exchanged, but that the housebreaker was unable to open the door, on which he was expending fruitless oaths and violence when the Jew came panting up.

'Let me out!' said Sikes. 'Don't speak to me – it's not safe. Let me out, I say.'

'Hear me speak a word,' rejoined the Jew, laying his hand upon the lock, 'you won't be—'

'Well,' replied the other.

'You won't be – too – violent, Bill?' whined the Jew.

The day was breaking, and there was light enough for the men to see each other's faces. They exchanged one brief glance; there was a fire in the eyes of both which could not be mistaken.

'I mean,' said Fagin, showing that he felt all disguise was now useless, 'not too violent for safety. Be crafty, Bill, and not too bold.'

Sikes made no reply, but, pulling open the door, of which the Jew had turned the lock, dashed into the silent streets.

Without one pause or moment's consideration, without once turning his head to the right or left, or raising his eyes to the sky, or lowering them to the ground, but looking straight before him with savage resolution, his teeth so tightly compressed that the strained jaw seemed starting through his skin, the robber held on his headlong course, nor muttered a word, nor relaxed a muscle, until he reached his own door. He opened it softly with a key, strode lightly up the stairs, and entering his own room, double-locked the door, and, lifting a heavy table against it, drew back the curtain of the bed.

The girl was lying half-dressed upon it. He had wakened her from her sleep, for she raised herself with a hurried and startled look.

'Get up,' said the man.

'It *is* you, Bill,' said the girl, with an expression of pleasure at his return.

'It is,' was the reply. 'Get up.'

There was a candle burning, but the man hastily drew it from the candlestick, and hurled it under the grate. Seeing the faint light of early day without, the girl rose to undraw the curtain.

'Let it be,' said Sikes, thrusting his hand before her. 'There's light enough for wot I've got to do.'

'Bill,' said the girl, in the low voice of alarm, 'why do you look like that at me?'

The robber sat regarding her for a few seconds with dilated nostrils and heaving breast, and then, grasping her by the head and throat, dragged her into the middle of the room, and, looking once towards the door, placed his heavy hand upon her mouth.

'Bill, Bill –' gasped the girl, wrestling with the strength of mortal fear, '– I – I won't scream, or cry – not once, – hear me – speak to me – tell me what I have done!'

'You know, you she-devil!' returned the robber, suppressing his breath. 'You were watched to-night; every word you said was heard.'

'Then, spare my life, for the love of Heaven, as I spared yours,' rejoined the girl, clinging to him. 'Bill, dear Bill! you cannot have the heart to kill me! Oh, think of all I have given up only this one night for you! You *shall* have time to think, and save yourself this crime! I will not loose my hold; you cannot throw me off. Bill! Bill! for dear God's sake, for your own, for mine, stop before you spill my blood. I have been true to you; upon my guilty soul I have.'

The man struggled violently to release his arms, but those of the girl were clasped round his, and, tear her as he would, he could not tear them away.

'Bill,' cried the girl, striving to lay her head upon his breast, 'the gentleman, and that dear lady, told me to-night of a home in some foreign country, where I could end my days in solitude and peace. Let me see them again, and beg them on my knees to show the same mercy and goodness to you, and let us both leave this dreadful place, and far apart lead better lives, and forget how we have lived, except in prayers, and never see each other more. It is never too late to repent. They told me so – I feel it now – but we must have time – a little, little time!'

The housebreaker freed one arm, and grasped his pistol. The certainty of immediate detection if he fired, flashed across his mind, even in the midst of his fury, and he beat it twice with all the force he could summon, upon the upturned face that almost touched his own.

She staggered and fell, nearly blinded with the blood that rained down from a deep gash in her forehead, but raising herself with difficulty on her knees, drew from her bosom a white handkerchief –

Rose Maylie's own – and holding it up in her folded hands as high towards Heaven as her feeble strength would let her, breathed one prayer for mercy to her Maker.

It was a ghastly figure to look upon. The murderer staggering backward to the wall, and shutting out the sight with his hand, seized a heavy club and struck her down.

CHAPTER THE TENTH

THE FLIGHT OF SIKES

Of all bad deeds that under cover of the darkness had been committed within wide London's bounds since night hung over it, that was the worst; – of all the horrors that rose with an ill scent upon the morning air, that was the foulest and most cruel.

The sun – the bright sun, that brings back not light alone, but new life, and hope, and freshness to man – burst upon the crowded city in clear and radiant glory. Through costly-coloured glass and paper-mended window, through cathedral dome and rotten crevice, it shed its equal ray. It lighted up the room where the murdered woman lay. It did. He tried to shut it out, but it would stream in. If the sight had been a ghastly one in the dull morning, what was it now in all that brilliant light!

He had not moved: he had been afraid to stir. There had been a moan and motion of the hand; and with terror added to hate he had struck and struck again. Once he threw a rug over it; but it was worse to fancy the eyes, and imagine them moving towards him, than to see them glaring upwards, as if watching the reflection of the pool of gore that quivered and danced in the sunlight on the ceiling. He had plucked it off again. And there was the body – mere flesh and blood, no more – but *such* flesh, and *such* blood!

He struck a light, kindled a fire, and thrust the club into it. There was human hair upon the end which blazed and shrunk into a light cinder, and, caught by the air, whirled up the chimney. Even that frightened him, sturdy as he was; but he held the weapon till it broke, and then piled it on the coals to burn away, and smoulder into ashes. He washed himself and rubbed his clothes; there were spots that would not be removed, but he cut the pieces out, and burnt them. How those stains were dispersed about the room! The very feet of the dog were bloody.

All this time he had never once turned his back upon the corpse; no, not for a moment. Such preparations completed, he moved backwards towards the door, dragging the dog with him, lest he should carry out new evidences of the crime into the streets. He shut the door softly, locked it, took the key, and left the house.

He crossed over, and glanced up at the window, to be sure that nothing was visible from the outside. There was the curtain still drawn, which she would have opened to admit the light she never saw again. It lay nearly under there. *He* knew that. God, how the sun poured down upon the very spot!

The glance was instantaneous. It was a relief to have got free of the room. He whistled on the dog, and walked rapidly away.

He went through Islington; strode up the hill at Highgate, on which stands the stone in honour of Whittington; turned down to Highgate Hill, unsteady of purpose, and uncertain where to go; struck off to the right again almost as soon as he began to descend it, and taking the foot-path across the fields, skirted Caen Wood, and so came out on Hampstead Heath. Traversing the hollow by the Vale of Health, he mounted the opposite bank, and crossing the road which joins the villages of Hampstead and Highgate, made along the remaining portion of the heath to the fields at North End,[1] in one of which he laid himself down under a hedge and slept.

Soon he was up again, and away – not far into the country, but back towards London by the high-road – then back again – then over another part of the same ground as he had already traversed – then wandering up and down in fields, and lying on ditches' brinks to rest, and starting up to make for some other spot and do the same, and ramble on again.

Where could he go, that was near and not too public, to get some meat and drink? Hendon. That was a good place, not far off, and out of most people's way. Thither he directed his steps, – running sometimes, and sometimes, with a strange perversity, loitering at a snail's pace, or stopping altogether and idly breaking the hedges with his stick. But when he got there, all the people he met – the very children at the doors – seemed to view him with suspicion. Back he turned again, without the courage to purchase bit or drop, though he had tasted no food for many hours; and once more he lingered on the heath, uncertain where to go.

He wandered over miles and miles of ground, and still came back to the old place; morning and noon had passed, and the day was on the wane, and still he rambled to and fro, and up and down, and round and round, and still lingered about the same spot. At last he got away, and shaped his course for Hatfield.[2]

It was nine o'clock at night when the man, quite tired out, and the dog limping and lame from the unaccustomed exercise, turned down the hill by the church of the quiet village, and plodding along the little street, crept into a small public-house, whose scanty light had guided them to the spot. There was a fire in the tap-room, and some country labourers were drinking before it. They made room for the stranger, but he sat down in the farthest corner, and ate and drank alone, or rather with his dog, to whom he cast a morsel of food from time to time.

The conversation of the men assembled here, turned upon the neighbouring land and farmers, and, when those topics were exhausted, upon the age of some old man who had been buried on the previous Sunday; the young men present considering him very old, and the old men present declaring him to have been quite young – not older, one white-haired grandfather said, than he was – with ten or fifteen years of life in him at least – if he had taken care; if he had taken care.

There was nothing to attract attention or excite alarm in this. The robber, after paying his reckoning, sat silent and unnoticed in his corner, and had almost dropped asleep, when he was half wakened by the noisy entrance of a new-comer.

This was an antic fellow, half pedlar and half mountebank, who travelled about the country on foot to vend hones, strops, razors, wash-balls,[3] harness-paste, medicines for dogs and horses, cheap perfumery, cosmetics, and such like wares, which he carried in a case slung to his back. His entrance was the signal for various homely jokes with the countrymen, which slackened not until he had made his supper, and opened his box of treasures, when he ingeniously contrived to unite business with amusement.

'And what be that stoof – good to eat, Harry?' asked a grinning countryman, pointing to some composition cakes in one corner.

'This,' said the fellow, producing one, 'this is the infallible and invaluable composition for removing all sorts of stain, rust, dirt, mildew, spick, speck, spot, or spatter, from silk, satin, linen, cambric, cloth, crape, stuff, carpet, merino, muslin, bombazeen,[4] or woollen stuff. Wine-stains, fruit-stains, beer-stains, water-stains, paint-stains, pitch-stains, any stains – all come out at one rub with the infallible and invaluable composition. If a lady stains her honour,[5] she has only need to swallow one cake, and she's cured at once – for it's poison. If a gentleman wants to prove his, he has only need to bolt one little square, and he has put it beyond question – for it's quite as satisfactory as a pistol-bullet, and a great deal nastier in the flavour, consequently the more credit in taking it. One penny a-square. With all these virtues, one penny a square.'

There were two buyers directly, and more of the listeners plainly hesitated. The vender observing this, increased in loquacity.

'It's all bought up as fast as it can be made,' said the fellow. 'There are fourteen water-mills, six steam-engines, and a galvanic battery always a-working upon it, and they can't make it fast enough, though the men work so hard that they die off, and the widows is pensioned directly with twenty pound a-year for each of the children, and a premium of fifty for twins. One penny a square – two halfpence is all the same, and four farthings is received with joy. One penny a square. Wine-stains, fruit-stains, beer-stains, water-stains, paint-stains, pitch-stains, mud-stains, blood-stains – here is a stain upon the hat of a gentleman in company that I'll take clean out before he can order me a pint of ale.'

'Ha!' cried Sikes starting up. 'Give that back.'

'I'll take it clean out, sir,' replied the man, winking to the company, 'before you can come across the room to get it. Gentlemen all, observe the dark stain upon this gentleman's hat, no wider than a shilling, but thicker than a half-crown. Whether it is a wine-stain, fruit-stain, beer-stain, water-stain, paint-stain, pitch-stain, mud-stain, or blood-stain –'

The man got no farther, for Sikes with a hideous imprecation overthrew the table, and tearing the hat from him, burst out of the house.

With the same perversity of feeling, and irresolution that had fastened upon him, despite himself, all day, the murderer, finding that he was not followed, and that they most probably considered him some drunken sullen fellow, turned back up the town, and getting out of the glare of the lamps of a stage-coach that was standing in the street, was walking past, when he recognized the mail from London, and saw that it was standing at the little post-office.[6] He almost knew what was to come, but he crossed over and listened.

The guard was standing at the door waiting for the letter-bag. A man dressed like a gamekeeper came up at the moment, and he handed him a basket which lay ready on the pavement.

'That's for your people,' said the guard. 'Now, look alive in there, will you. Damn that 'ere bag, it warn't ready night afore last: this won't do, you know.'

'Anything new up in town, Ben?' asked the gamekeeper, drawing back to the window-shutters, the better to admire the horses.

'No, nothing that I knows on,' replied the man, pulling on his gloves. 'Corn's up a little. I heerd talk of a murder, too, down Spitalfields way, but I don't reckon much upon it.'

'Oh, that's quite true,' said a gentleman inside, who was looking out of the window. 'And a very dreadful murder it was.'

'Was it, sir?' rejoined the guard, touching his hat. 'Man or woman, pray, sir?'

'A woman,' replied the gentleman. 'It is supposed –'

'Now, Ben,' cried the coachman impatiently.

'Damn that 'ere bag,' said the guard; 'are you gone to sleep in there?'

'Coming,' cried the office-keeper, running out.

'Coming,' growled the guard. 'Ah, and so's the young 'ooman of property that's going to take a fancy to me, but I don't know when. Here, give hold. All ri—ight!'

The horn sounded a few cheerful notes, and the coach was gone.

Sikes remained standing in the street, apparently unmoved by what he had just heard, and agitated by no stronger feeling than a doubt where to go. At length he went back again, and took the road which leads from Hatfield to St Albans.[7]

He went on doggedly; but as he left the town behind him, and plunged further and further into the solitude and darkness of the road, he felt a dread and awe creeping upon him which shook him to the core. Every object before him, substance or shadow, still or moving, took the semblance of some fearful thing; but these fears were nothing, compared to the sense that haunted him of that morning's ghastly figure following at his heels. He could trace its shadow in the gloom, supply the smallest item of the outline, and note how stiff and solemn it seemed to stalk along. He could hear its garments rustling in the leaves, and every breath of wind came laden with that last low cry. If he stopped, it did the same. If he ran, it followed – not running too, that would have been a relief, but like a corpse endowed with the mere machinery of life, and borne upon one slow melancholy wind that never rose or fell.

At times he turned with desperate determination, resolved to beat this phantom off, though it should look him dead; but the hair rose from his head, and his blood stood still; for it had turned with him, and was behind him then. He had kept it before him that morning, but it was behind him now – always. He leant his back against a bank, and felt that it stood above him, visibly out against the cold night-sky. He threw himself upon the road – on his back upon the road. At his head it stood, silent, erect, and still – a living grave-stone, with its epitaph in blood.

Let no man talk of murderers escaping justice, and hint that Providence must sleep. There were twenty score of violent deaths in one long minute of that agony of fear.

There was a shed in a field he passed that offered shelter for the night. Before the door were three tall poplar trees, which made it very dark within, and the wind moaned through them with a dismal wail. He *could not* walk on till daylight came again, and here he stretched himself close to the wall – to undergo new torture.

For now a vision came before him, as constant and more terrible than that from which he had escaped. Those widely-staring eyes, so lustreless and so glassy, that he had better borne to see than think upon, appeared in the midst of the darkness; light in themselves, but giving light to nothing. There were but two, but they were everywhere. If he shut out the sight, there came the room with every well-known object – some, indeed, that he would have forgotten if he had gone over its contents from memory – each in its accustomed place. The body was in *its* place, and its eyes were as he saw them when he stole away. He got up and rushed into the field without. The figure was behind him. He re-entered the shed, and shrunk down once more. The eyes were there before he had lain himself along.

And here he remained in such terror as none but he can know, trembling in every limb, and the cold sweat starting from every pore, when suddenly there arose upon the night-wind the noise of distant shouting, and the roar of voices mingled in alarm and wonder. Any sound of men in that lonely place, even though it conveyed a real cause of alarm, was something to him. He regained his strength and energy at the prospect of personal danger, and springing to his feet, rushed into the open air.

The broad sky seemed on fire. Rising into the air with showers of sparks, and rolling one above the other, were sheets of flame, lighting the atmosphere for miles round, and driving clouds of smoke in the direction where he stood. The shouts grew louder as new voices swelled the roar, and he could hear the cry of Fire mingled with the ringing of an alarm-bell, the fall of heavy bodies, and the crackling of flames as they twined round some new obstacle, and shot aloft as though refreshed by food. The noise increased as he looked. There were people there – men and women – light, bustle. It was like new life to him. He darted onward – straight, headlong – dashing through brier and brake, and leaping gate and fence as madly as the dog who careered with loud and sounding bark before him.

He came upon the spot. There were half-dressed figures tearing to and fro, some endeavouring to drag the frightened horses from the stables, others driving the cattle from the yard and out-houses, and others coming laden from the burning pile amidst a shower of falling sparks, and the tumbling down of red-hot beams. The apertures, where doors and windows stood an hour ago, disclosed a mass of raging fire; walls rocked and crumbled into the burning well; the molten lead and iron poured down, white-hot, upon the ground. Women and children shrieked, and men encouraged each other with noisy shouts and cheers. The clanking of the engine-pumps, and the spirting and hissing of the water as it fell upon the blazing wood, added to the tremendous roar. He shouted too till he was hoarse; and flying from memory and himself, plunged into the thickest of the throng.

Hither and thither he dived that night – now working at the pumps, and now hurrying through the smoke and flame, but never ceasing to engage himself wherever noise and men were thickest. Up and down the ladders, upon the roofs of buildings, over floors that quaked and trembled with his weight, to under the lee of falling bricks and stones, – in every part of that great fire was he; but he bore a charmed life,[8] and had neither scratch nor bruise, nor weariness nor thought, till morning dawned again, and only smoke and blackened ruins remained.

This mad excitement over, there returned with tenfold force the dreadful consciousness of his crime. He looked suspiciously about him, for the men were conversing in groups, and he feared to be the subject of their talk. The dog obeyed the significant beck of his finger, and they drew off stealthily together. He passed near an engine where some men were seated, and they called to him to share in their refreshment. He took some bread and meat; and as he drank a draught of beer, heard the firemen, who were from London,[9] talking about the murder. 'He has gone to Birmingham, they say,' said one: 'but they'll have him yet, for the scouts are out, and by to-morrow night there'll be a cry all through the country.'

He hurried off and walked till he almost dropped upon the ground, then lay down in a lane, and had a long, but broken and uneasy sleep. He wandered on again, irresolute and undecided, and oppressed with the fear of another solitary night.

Sikes attempting to destroy his dog

Suddenly he took the desperate resolution of going back to London.

'There's somebody to speak to there, at all events,' he thought. 'A good hiding-place, too. They'll never expect to nab me there after this country scent. Why can't I lay by for a week or so, and forcing blunt from Fagin, get abroad to France! D—me, I'll risk it.'

He acted upon this impulse without delay, and choosing the least frequented roads began his journey back, resolved to lie concealed within a short distance of the metropolis, and entering it at dusk by a circuitous route, to proceed straight to that part of it which he had fixed on for his destination.

The dog, though, – if any descriptions of him were out, it would not be forgotten that the dog was missing, and had probably gone with him. This might lead to his apprehension as he passed along the streets. He resolved to drown him, and walked on looking about for a pond; picking up a heavy stone, and tying it to his handkerchief as he went.

The animal looked up into his master's face while these preparations were making, – and, whether his instinct apprehended something of their purpose, or the robber's sidelong look at him was sterner than ordinary, – skulked a little farther in the rear than usual, and cowered as he came more slowly along. When his master halted at the brink of a pool, and looked round to call him, he stopped outright.

'Do you hear me call "come here?"' cried Sikes, whistling.

The animal came up from the very force of habit; but as Sikes stooped to attach the handkerchief to his throat, he uttered a low growl and started back.

'Come back,' said the robber, stamping on the ground. The dog wagged his tail, but moved not. Sikes made a running noose, and called him again.

The dog advanced, retreated, paused an instant, turned and scoured away at his hardest speed.

The man whistled again and again, and sat down and waited in the expectation that he would return. But no dog appeared, and he resumed his journey.

CHAPTER THE ELEVENTH

MONKS AND MR BROWNLOW AT LENGTH MEET. THEIR CONVERSATION, AND THE INTELLIGENCE THAT INTERRUPTS IT

The twilight was beginning to close in, when Mr Brownlow alighted from a hackney-coach[1] at his own door, and knocked softly. The door being opened, a sturdy man got out of the coach and stationed himself on one side of the steps, while another man who had been seated on the box dismounted too, and stood upon the other side. At a sign from Mr Brownlow, they helped out a third man, and taking him between them, hurried him into the house. This man was Monks.

They walked in the same manner up the stairs without speaking, and Mr Brownlow, preceding them, led the way into a back-room. At the door of this apartment, Monks, who had ascended with evident reluctance, stopped. The two men looked to the old gentleman, as if for instructions.

'He knows the alternative,' said Mr Brownlow. 'If he hesitates or moves a finger but as you bid him, drag him into the street, call for the aid of the police, and impeach him as a felon in my name.'

'How dare you say this of me?' said Monks.

'How dare you urge me to it, young man?' replied Mr Brownlow, confronting him with a steady look. 'Are you mad enough to leave this house? Unhand him. There, sir. You are free to go, and we to follow. But I warn you, by all I hold most solemn and most sacred, that the instant you set foot in the street, that instant will I have you apprehended on a charge of fraud and robbery. I am resolute and immoveable. If you are determined to be the same, your blood be upon your own head!'

'By what authority am I kidnapped in the street, and brought here by these dogs?' asked Monks, looking from one to the other of the men who stood beside him.

'By mine,' replied Mr Brownlow. 'Those persons are indemnified by me. If you complain of being deprived of your liberty – you had power and opportunity to retrieve it as you came along, but you deemed it advisable to remain quiet – I say again, throw yourself for protection upon the law. I will appeal to the law too; but when you have gone too far to recede, do not sue to me for leniency when the power will have passed into other hands, and do not say I plunged you down the gulf into which you rushed yourself.'

Monks was plainly disconcerted, and alarmed besides. He hesitated.

'You will decide quickly,' said Mr Brownlow, with perfect firmness and composure. 'If you wish me to prefer my charges publicly, and consign you to a punishment, the extent of which, although I can, with a shudder, foresee, I cannot control, once more, I say, you know the way. If not, and you appeal to my forbearance, and the mercy of those you have deeply injured, seat yourself without a word in that chair. It has waited for you two whole days.'

Monks muttered some unintelligible words, but wavered still.

'You will be prompt,' said Mr Brownlow. 'A word from me, and the alternative has gone for ever.'

Still the man hesitated.

'I have not the inclination to parley farther,' said Mr Brownlow, 'and, as I advocate the dearest interests of others, I have not the right.'

'Is there –' demanded Monks with a faltering tongue, – 'is there – no middle course?'

'None; emphatically none.'

Monks looked at the old gentleman with an anxious eye; but, reading in his countenance nothing but severity and determination, walked into the room, and, shrugging his shoulders, sat down.

'Lock the door on the outside,' said Mr Brownlow to the attendants, 'and come when I ring.'

The men obeyed, and the two were left alone together.

'This is pretty treatment, sir,' said Monks, throwing down his hat and cloak, 'from my father's oldest friend.'

'It is because I was your father's oldest friend, young man,' returned Mr Brownlow. 'It is because the hopes and wishes of young and happy years were bound up with him, and that fair creature of his blood and kindred who rejoined her God in youth, and left me here a solitary, lonely man; it is because he knelt with me beside his only sister's death-bed when he was yet a boy, on the morning that would – but Heaven willed otherwise – have made her my young wife; it is because my seared heart clung to him from that time forth through all his trials and errors, till he died; it is because old recollections and associations fill my heart, and even the sight of you brings with it old thoughts of him; it is all these things that move me to treat you gently now – yes, Edward Leeford, even now – and blush for your unworthiness who bear the name.'

'What has the name to do with it?' asked the other, after contemplating, half in silence, and half in dogged wonder, the agitation of his companion. 'What is the name to me?'

'Nothing,' replied Mr Brownlow, 'nothing to you. But it was *hers;* and even at this distance of time brings back to me, an old man, the glow and thrill which I once felt only to hear it repeated by a stranger. I am very glad you have changed it – very – very.'

'This is all mighty fine,' said Monks (to retain his assumed designation) after a long silence, during which he had jerked himself in sullen defiance to and fro, and Mr Brownlow had sat shading his face with his hand. 'But, what do you want with me?'

'You have a brother,' said Mr Brownlow, rousing himself, ' – a brother, the whisper of whose name in your ear, when I came behind you in the street, was in itself almost enough to make you accompany me hither in wonder and alarm.'

'I have no brother,' replied Monks. 'You know I was an only child. Why do you talk to me of brothers? You know that as well as I.'

'Attend to what I do know, and you may not,' said Mr Brownlow. 'I shall interest you by and by. I know that of the wretched marriage, into which family pride, and the most sordid and narrowest of all ambition, forced your unhappy father when a mere boy, you were the sole and most unnatural issue,' returned Mr Brownlow.

'I don't care for hard names,' interrupted Monks, with a jeering laugh. 'You know the fact, and that's enough for me.'

'But I also know,' pursued the old gentleman, 'the misery, the slow torture, the protracted anguish of that ill-assorted union; I know how listlessly and wearily each of that wretched pair dragged on their heavy chain through a world that was poisoned to them both; I know how cold formalities were succeeded by open taunts; how indifference gave place to dislike, dislike to hate, and hate to loathing, until at last they wrenched the clanking bond asunder, and retiring a wide space apart, carried each a galling fragment, of which nothing but death could break the rivets, to hide it in new society, beneath the gayest looks they could assume. Your mother succeeded; she forgot it soon: but it rusted and cankered at your father's heart for years.'

'Well, they were separated,' said Monks, 'and what of that?'

'When they had been separated for some time,' returned Mr Brownlow, 'and your mother, wholly given up to continental frivolities, had utterly forgotten the young husband ten good years her junior, who, with prospects blighted, lingered on at home, he fell among new friends. *This* circumstance, at least, you know already.'

'Not I,' said Monks, turning away his eyes, and beating his foot upon the ground, as a man who is determined to deny everything. 'Not I.'

'Your manner, no less than your actions, assures me that you have never forgotten it, or ceased to think of it with bitterness,' returned Mr Brownlow. 'I speak of fifteen years ago, when you were not more than eleven years old, and your father but one-and-thirty – for he was, I repeat, a boy, when *his* father ordered him to marry. Must I go back to events that cast a shade upon the memory of your parent, or will you spare it, and disclose to me the truth?'

'I have nothing to disclose,' rejoined Monks in evident confusion. 'You must talk on if you will.'

'These new friends, then,' said Mr Brownlow, 'were a naval officer, retired from active service, whose wife had died some half a year before, and left him with two children – there had been more, but, of all their family happily but two survived. They were both daughters; one a beautiful creature of nineteen, and the other a mere child of two or three years old.'

'What's this to me?' asked Monks.

'They resided,' said Mr Brownlow, without seeming to hear the interruption, 'in a part of the country to which your father, in his wandering, had repaired, and where he had taken up his abode. Acquaintance, intimacy, friendship, fast followed on each other. Your father was gifted as few men are – he had his sister's soul and person. As the old officer knew him more and more, he grew to love him. I would that it had ended there. His daughter did the same.'

The old gentleman paused; Monks was biting his lips, with his eyes fixed upon the floor; seeing this, he immediately resumed.

'The end of a year found him contracted, solemnly contracted, to that daughter; the object of the first true, ardent, only passion of a guileless, untried girl.'

*

'Your tale is of the longest,' observed Monks, moving restlessly in his chair.

'It is a true tale of grief, and trial, and sorrow, young man,' returned Mr Brownlow, 'and such tales usually are; if it were one of unmixed joy and happiness, it would be very brief. At length one of those rich relations, to strengthen whose interest and importance your father had been sacrificed, as others are often, – it is no uncommon case, – died, and to repair the misery he had been instrumental in occasioning, left him *his* panacea for all griefs – money. It was necessary that he should immediately repair to Rome, whither this man had sped for health, and where he had died, leaving his affairs in great confusion. He went, was seized with mortal illness there, was followed the moment the intelligence reached Paris by your mother, who carried you with her; he died the day after her arrival, leaving no will – *no will* – so that the whole property fell to her and you.'

At this part of the recital Monks held his breath, and listened with a face of intense eagerness, though his eyes were not directed towards the speaker. As Mr Brownlow paused he changed his position, with the air of one who has experienced a sudden relief, and wiped his hot face and hands.

'Before he went abroad, and as he passed through London on his way,' said Mr Brownlow slowly, and fixing his eyes upon the other's face, 'he came to me.'

'I never heard of that,' interrupted Monks, in a tone intended to appear incredulous, but savouring more of disagreeable surprise.

'He came to me; and left with me, among some other things, a picture – a portrait painted by himself – a likeness of this poor girl – which he did not wish to leave behind, and could not carry forward on his hasty journey. He was worn by anxiety and remorse almost to a shadow; talked in a wild, distracted way of ruin and dishonour worked by him; confided to me his intention to convert his whole property, at any loss, into money, and, having settled on his wife and you a portion of his recent acquisition, to fly the country – I guessed too well he would not fly alone – and never see it more. Even from me, his old and early friend, whose strong attachment had taken root in the earth that covered one most dear to both – even from me he withheld any more particular confession, promising to write, and tell me all, and after that to see me once again, for the last time on earth. Alas! *That* was the last time. I had no letter, and I never saw him more.

'I went,' said Mr Brownlow after a short pause, – 'I went when all was over to the scene of his – I will use the term the world would use, for harshness or favour are now alike to him – of his guilty love; resolved that, if my fears were realized, that erring child should find one heart and home open to shelter and compassionate her. The family had left that part a week before; they had called in such trifling debts as were outstanding, discharged them, and left the place by night. Why, or whither, none could tell.'

Monks drew his breath yet more freely, and looked round with a smile of triumph.

'When your brother,' said Mr Brownlow, drawing nearer to the other's chair, – 'When your brother – a feeble, ragged, neglected child, – was cast in my way by a stronger hand than chance, and rescued by me from a life of vice and infamy –'

'What!' cried Monks, starting.

'By me,' said Mr Brownlow. 'I told you I should interest you before long. I say by me. I see that your cunning associate suppressed my name, although, for aught he knew, it would be quite strange to your ears. When he was rescued by me, then, and lay recovering from sickness in my house, his strong resemblance to this picture I have spoken of struck me with astonishment. Even when I first saw him, in all his dirt and misery, there was a lingering expression in his face that came upon me like a glimpse of some old friend flashing on one in a vivid dream. I need not tell you he was snared away before I knew his history –'

'Why not?' asked Monks hastily.

'Because you know it well.'

'I!'

'Denial to me is vain,' replied Mr Brownlow. 'I shall show you that I know more than that.'

'You – you – can't prove anything against me,' stammered Monks. 'I defy you to do it!'

'We shall see,' returned the old gentleman, with a searching glance. 'I lost the boy, and no efforts of mine could recover him. Your mother being dead, I knew that you alone could solve the mystery if anybody could; and as, when I had last heard of you, you were on your own estate in the West Indies, – whither, as you well know, you retired upon your mother's death, to escape the consequences of vicious courses here, – I made the voyage. You had left it months before, and were supposed to be in London, but no one could tell where. I returned. Your agents had no clue to your residence. You came and went, they said, as strangely as you had ever done, sometimes for days together, and sometimes not for months, keeping to all appearance the same low haunts, and mingling with the same infamous herd who had been your associates when a fierce ungovernable boy. I wearied them with new applications. I paced the streets by night and day; but, until two hours ago, all my efforts were fruitless, and I never saw you for an instant.'

'And now you do see me,' said Monks, rising boldly, 'what then? Fraud and robbery are high-sounding words – justified, you think, by a fancied resemblance in some young imp to an idle daub of a dead man's. Brother! You don't even know that a child was born of this maudlin pair; you don't even know that.'

'I *did not*,' replied Mr Brownlow, rising too; 'but within the last fortnight I have learnt it all. You have a brother; you know it, and him. There was a will, which your mother destroyed, leaving the secret and the gain to you at her own death. It contained a reference to some child likely to be the result of this sad connection; which child was born, and accidentally encountered by you, when your suspicions were first awakened by his resemblance to his father. You repaired to the place of his birth. There existed proofs – proofs long suppressed – of his birth and parentage. Those proofs were destroyed by you; and now, in your own words to your accomplice, the Jew, "*the only proofs of the boy's identity lie at the bottom of the river, and the old hag that received them from the mother is rotting in her coffin.*" Unworthy son, coward, liar, – you, who hold your councils with thieves and murderers in dark rooms at night, – you, whose plots and wiles have hurled a violent death upon the head of one worth millions such as you, – you, who from your cradle were gall and bitterness to your own father's heart, and in whom all evil passions, vice, and profligacy festered till they found a vent in a hideous disease which has made your face an index even to your mind,[2] – you, Edward Leeford, do you brave me still!'

'No, no, no!' returned the coward, overwhelmed by these accumulated charges.

'Every word!' cried the old gentleman, 'every word that has passed between you and this detested villain is known to me. Shadows on the wall have caught your whispers, and brought them to my ear; the sight of the persecuted child has turned vice itself, and given it the courage, and almost the attributes of virtue. Murder has been done, to which you were morally, if not really, a party.'

'No, no,' interposed Monks. 'I – I – know nothing of that; I was going to inquire the truth of the story when you overtook me. I didn't know the cause; I thought it was a common quarrel.'

'It was the partial disclosure of your secrets,' replied Mr Brownlow. 'Will you disclose the whole?'

'Yes, I will.'

'Set your hand to a statement of truth and facts, and repeat it before witnesses?'

'That I promise too.'

'Remain quietly here until such a document is drawn up, and

proceed with me to such a place as I may deem most advisable, for the purpose of attesting it?'

'If you insist upon that, I'll do that also,' replied Monks.

'You must do more than that,' said Mr Brownlow. 'Make restitution to an innocent and unoffending child; for such he is, although the offspring of a guilty and most miserable love. You have not forgotten the provisions of the will. Carry them into execution so far as your brother is concerned, and then go where you please. In this world you need meet no more.'

While Monks was pacing up and down, meditating with dark and evil looks on this proposal, and the possibilities of evading it, – torn by his fears on the one hand and his hatred on the other, – the door was hurriedly unlocked, and Mr Losberne entered the room in violent agitation.

'The man will be taken,' he cried. 'He will be taken to-night.'

'The murderer?' asked Mr Brownlow.

'Yes, yes,' replied the other. 'His dog has been seen lurking about some old haunt, and there seems little doubt that his master either is, or will be, there, under cover of the darkness. Spies are hovering about in every direction; I have spoken to the men who are charged with his capture, and they tell me he can never escape. A reward of a hundred pounds is proclaimed by Government to-night.'

'I will give fifty more,' said Mr Brownlow, 'and proclaim it with my own lips upon the spot if I can reach it. Where is Mr Maylie?'

'Harry – as soon as he had seen your friend here safe in a coach with you, he hurried off to where he heard this,' replied the doctor, 'and, mounting his horse, sallied forth to join the first party at some place in the outskirts agreed upon between them.'

'The Jew' – said Mr Brownlow; 'what of him?'

'When I last heard, he had not been taken; but he will be, or is, by this time. They're sure of him.'

'Have you made up your mind?' asked Mr Brownlow, in a low voice, of Monks.

'Yes,' he replied. 'You – you – will be secret with me?'

'I will. Remain here till I return. It is your only hope of safety.'

They left the room, and the door was again locked.

'What have you done?' asked the doctor in a whisper.

'All that I could hope to do, and even more. Coupling the poor girl's intelligence with my previous knowledge, and the result of our good friend's inquiries on the spot, I left him no loophole of escape, and laid bare the whole villany, which by these lights became plain as day. Write, and appoint the evening after to-morrow at seven, for the meeting. We shall be down there a few hours before, but shall require rest, and especially the young lady, who *may* have greater need of firmness than either you or I can quite foresee just now. But my blood boils to avenge this poor murdered creature. Which way have they taken?'

'Drive straight to the office, and you will be in time,' replied Mr Losberne. 'I will remain here.'

The two gentlemen hastily separated, each in a fever of excitement wholly uncontrollable.

CHAPTER THE TWELFTH

THE PURSUIT AND ESCAPE

Near to that part of the Thames on which the church at Rotherhithe abuts, where the buildings on the banks are dirtiest and the vessels on the river blackest with the dust of colliers and the smoke of close-built low-roofed houses, there exists, at the present day, the filthiest, the strangest, the most extraordinary of the many localities that are hidden in London, wholly unknown, even by name, to the great mass of its inhabitants.[1]

To reach this place, the visitor has to penetrate through a maze of close, narrow, and muddy streets, thronged by the roughest and poorest of water-side people, and devoted to the traffic they may be supposed to occasion. The cheapest and least delicate provisions are heaped in the shops; the coarsest and commonest articles of wearing apparel dangle at the salesman's door, and stream from the house-parapet and windows. Jostling with unemployed labourers of the lowest class, ballast-heavers, coal-whippers, brazen women,[2] ragged children, and the very raff and refuse of the river, he makes his way with difficulty along, assailed by offensive sights and smells from the narrow alleys which branch off on the right and left, and deafened by the clash of ponderous waggons which bear great piles of merchandise from the stacks of warehouses that rise from every corner. Arriving at length in streets remoter and less frequented than those through which he has passed, he walks beneath tottering house-fronts projecting over the pavement, dismantled walls that seem to totter as he passes, chimneys half crushed, half hesitating to fall, windows guarded by rusty iron bars that time and dirt have almost eaten away, and every imaginable sign of desolation and neglect.

In such a neighbourhood, beyond Dockhead in the Borough of Southwark, stands Jacob's Island, surrounded by a muddy ditch, six or eight feet deep and fifteen or twenty wide when the tide is in, once called Mill Pond, but known in these days as Folly Ditch. It is a creek or inlet from the Thames, and can always be filled at high water by opening the sluices at the Lead Mills from which it took its old name. At such times, a stranger, looking from one of the wooden bridges thrown across it at Mill-lane,[3] will see the inhabitants of the houses on either side lowering from their back doors and windows, buckets, pails, domestic utensils of all kinds, in which to haul the water up; and, when his eye is turned from these operations to the houses themselves, his utmost astonishment will be excited by the scene before him. Crazy wooden galleries common to the backs of half-a-dozen houses, with holes from which to look upon the slime beneath; windows broken and patched, with poles thrust out on which to dry the linen that is never there; rooms so small, so filthy, so confined, that the air would seem too tainted even for the dirt and squalor which they shelter; wooden chambers thrusting themselves out above the mud and threatening to fall into it — as some have done; dirt-besmeared walls and decaying foundations; every repulsive lineament of poverty, every loathsome indication of filth, rot, and garbage; — all these ornament the banks of Folly Ditch.

In Jacob's Island the warehouses are roofless and empty; the walls are crumbling down; the windows are windows no more; the doors are falling into the street; the chimneys are blackened, but they yield no smoke. Thirty or forty years ago, before losses and chancery suits[4] came upon it, it was a thriving place; but now it is a desolate island indeed. The houses have no owners; they are broken open, and entered upon by those who have the courage, and there they live and there they die. They must have powerful motives for a secret residence, or be reduced to a destitute condition indeed, who seek a refuge in Jacob's Island.

In an upper room of one of these houses[5] – a detached house of fair size, ruinous in other respects, but strongly defended at door and window – of which the back commanded the ditch in manner already described, there were assembled three men, who, regarding each other every now and then with looks expressive of perplexity and expectation, sat for some time in profound and gloomy silence. One of these was Toby Crackit, another Mr Chitling, and the third a robber of fifty years, whose nose had been almost beaten in, in some old scuffle, and whose face bore a frightful scar which might probably be traced to the same occasion. This man was a returned transport,[6] and his name was Kags.

'I wish,' said Toby, turning to Mr Chitling, 'that you had picked out some other crib when the two old ones got too warm, and not come here, my fine feller.'

'Why didn't you, blunder-head?' said Kags.

'Well, I thought you'd have been a little more glad to see me than this,' replied Mr Chitling, with a melancholy air.

'Why look'e, young gentleman,' said Toby, 'when a man keeps himself so very ex-clusive as I have done, and by that means has a snug house over his head with nobody prying and smelling about it, it's rather a startling thing to have the honour of a wisit from a young gentleman (however respectable and pleasant a person he may be to play cards with at conweniency) circumstanced as you are.'

'Especially when the exclusive young man has got a friend stopping with him that's arrived sooner than was expected from foreign parts, and is too modest to want to be presented to the Judges on his return,' added Kags.

There was a short silence; after which Toby Crackit, seeming to abandon as hopeless any further effort to maintain his usual devil-may-care swagger, turned to Chitling and said –

'When was Fagin took then?'

'Just at dinner-time – two o'clock this afternoon,' was the reply. 'Charley and I made our lucky up the wash'us chimney; and Bolter got into the empty water-butt, head downwards, but his legs were so precious long that they stuck out at the top, and so they took him too.'

'And Bet?'

'Poor Bet! She went to see the body, to speak to who it was,' replied Chitling, his countenance falling more and more, 'and went off mad, screaming and raving, and beating her head against the boards; so they put a strait weskut on her and took her to the hospital – and there she is.'

'Wot's come of young Bates?' demanded Kags.

'He hung about, not to come over here afore dark; but he'll be here soon,' replied Chitling. 'There's nowhere else to go to now, for the people at the Cripples are all in custody, and the bar of the ken – I went up there and saw it with my own eyes – is filled with traps.'

'This is a smash,' observed Toby, biting his lips. 'There's more than one will go with this.'

'The sessions are on,' said Kags: 'if they get the inquest over; if Bolter turns King's evidence, as of course he will from what he's said already – and they can prove Fagin an accessory before the fact, and get the trial on on Friday, he'll swing in six days from this,[7] by G –!'

'You should have heard the people groan,' said Chitling; 'the officers fought like devils, or they'd have torn him away. He was down once, but they made a ring round him, and fought their way along. You should have seen how he looked about him, all muddy and bleeding, and clung to them as if they were his dearest friends. I can see 'em now, not able to stand upright with the pressing of the mob, and dragging him along amongst 'em; I can see the people jumping up, one behind another, and snarling with their teeth, and making at him like wild beasts; I can see the blood upon his hair and beard, and hear the dreadful cries with which the women worked themselves into the centre of the crowd at the street corner, and swore they'd tear his heart out!' The horror-stricken witness of this scene pressed his hands upon his ears, and with his eyes fast closed got up and paced violently to and fro like one distracted.

Whilst he was thus engaged, and the two men sat by in silence with their eyes fixed upon the floor, a pattering noise was heard upon the stairs, and Sikes's dog bounded into the room. They ran to the window, down stairs, and into the street. The dog had jumped in at an open window; he made no attempt to follow them, nor was his master to be seen.

'What's the meaning of this!' said Toby, when they had returned. 'He can't be coming here. I – I – hope not.'

'If he was coming here, he'd have come with the dog,' said Kags, stooping down to examine the animal, who lay panting on the floor. 'Here; give us some water for him; he has run himself faint.'

'He's drunk it all up, every drop,' said Kags, after watching the dog some time in silence. 'Covered with mud – lame – half-blind – he must have come a long way.'

'Where can he have come from!' exclaimed Toby. 'He's been to the other kens of course, and finding them filled with strangers come on here, where he's been many a time and often. But where can he have come from first, and how comes he here alone, without the other!'

'He' (none of them called the murderer by his old name) – 'He can't have made away with himself. What do you think?' said Chitling.

Toby shook his head.

'If he had,' said Kags, 'the dog 'ud want to lead us away to where he did it. No. I think he's got out of the country, and left the dog behind. He must have given him the slip somehow, or he wouldn't be so easy.'

This solution appearing the most probable one was adopted as the right; and, the dog creeping under a chair, coiled himself up to sleep, without further notice from anybody.

It being now dark, the shutter was closed, and a candle lighted and placed upon the table. The terrible events of the two days had made a deep impression upon all three, increased by the danger and uncertainty of their own position. They drew their chairs closer together, starting at every sound. They spoke little, and that in whispers, and were as silent and awestricken as if the remains of the murdered woman lay in the next room.

They had sat thus some time, when suddenly was heard a hurried knocking at the door below.

'Young Bates,' said Kags, looking angrily round to check the fear he felt himself.

The knocking came again. No, it wasn't he. He never knocked like that.

Crackit went to the window, and, shaking all over, drew in his head. There was no need to tell them who it was; his pale face was enough. The dog too was on the alert in an instant, and ran whining to the door.

'We must let him in,' he said, taking up the candle.

'Isn't there any help for it?' asked the other man in a hoarse voice.

'None. He *must* come in.'

'Don't leave us in the dark,' said Kags, taking down a candle from the chimney-piece, and lighting it with such a trembling hand that the knocking was twice repeated before he had finished.

Crackit went down to the door, and returned followed by a man with the lower part of his face buried in a handkerchief, and another tied over his head under his hat. He drew them slowly off – blanched face, sunken eyes, hollow cheeks, beard of three days' growth, wasted flesh, short thick breath; it was the very ghost of Sikes.

He laid his hand upon a chair which stood in the middle of the room; but shuddering as he was about to drop into it, and seeming to glance over his shoulder, dragged it back close to the wall – as close as it would go – ground it against it – and sat down.

Not a word had been exchanged. He looked from one to another in silence. If an eye was furtively raised and met his, it was instantly averted. When his hollow voice broke silence they all three started. They had never heard its tones before.

'How came that dog here?' he asked.

'Alone. Three hours ago.'

'To-night's paper says that Fagin's taken. Is it true, or a lie?'

'Quite true.'

They were silent again.

'Damn you all,' said Sikes, passing his hand across his forehead. 'Have you nothing to say to me?'

There was an uneasy movement among them, but nobody spoke.

'You that keep this house,' said Sikes, turning his face to Crackit, 'do you mean to sell me, or to let me lie here till this hunt is over?'

'You must stop here if you think it safe,' returned the person addressed, after some hesitation.

Sikes carried his eyes slowly up the wall behind him, rather trying to turn his head than actually doing it, and said, 'Is – it – the body – is it buried?'

They shook their heads.

'Why isn't it!' said the man with the same glance behind him. 'Wot do they keep such ugly things as *that*, above the ground for? – Who's that knocking?'

Crackit intimated by a motion of his hand as he left the room that there was nothing to fear, and directly came back with Charley Bates behind him. Sikes sat opposite the door, so that the moment the boy entered the room he encountered his figure.

'Toby,' said the boy, falling back as Sikes turned his eyes towards him, 'why didn't you tell me this down stairs?'

There had been something so tremendous in the shrinking off of the three, that the wretched man was willing to propitiate even this lad. Accordingly he nodded, and made as though he would shake hands with him.

'Let me go into some other room,' said the boy retreating still further.

'Why, Charley!' said Sikes stepping forward. 'Don't you – don't you know me?'

'Don't come nearer me,' answered the boy, still retreating and looking with horror in his eyes upon the murderer's face. 'You monster!'

The man stopped half-way, and they looked at each other; but Sikes's eyes sunk gradually to the ground.

'Witness you three,' cried the boy, shaking his clenched fist, and becoming more and more excited as he spoke. 'Witness you three – I'm not afraid of him – if they come here after him, I'll give him up; I will. I tell you out at once; he may kill me for it if he likes, or if he dares, but if I'm here I'll give him up. I'd give him up if he was to be boiled alive. Murder! Help! If there's the pluck of a man among you three, you'll help me. Murder! Help! Down with him!'

Pouring out these cries, and accompanying them with violent gesticulation, the boy actually threw himself single-handed upon the strong man, and in the intensity of his energy and the suddenness of his surprise brought him heavily to the ground.

The three spectators seemed quite transfixed and stupefied. They offered no interference, and the boy and man rolled on the ground together, the former heedless of the blows that showered upon him, wrenching his hands tighter and tighter in the garments about the murderer's breast, and never ceasing to call for help with all his might.

The contest, however, was too unequal to last long. Sikes had him down and his knee was on his throat, when Crackit pulled him back with a look of alarm and pointed to the window. There were lights gleaming below, voices in loud and earnest conversation, the tramp of hurried footsteps – endless they seemed in number – crossing the nearest wooden-bridge. One man on horseback seemed to be among the crowd, for there was the noise of hoofs rattling on the uneven pavement; the gleam of lights increased, the footsteps came more thickly and noisily on. Then came a loud knocking at the door, and then a hoarse murmur from such a multitude of angry voices as would have made the boldest quail.

'Help!' shrieked the boy in a voice that rent the air. 'He's here; he's here! Break down the door.'

'In the King's name,'[8] cried voices without; and the hoarse cry arose again, but louder.

'Break down the door,' screamed the boy. 'I tell you they'll never open it. Run straight to the room where the light is. Break down the door.'

Strokes thick and heavy rattled upon the door and lower window-shutters as he ceased to speak, and a loud huzza burst from the crowd; – giving the listener for the first time some adequate idea of its immense extent.

'Open the door of some place where I can lock this screeching Hell-babe,' cried Sikes fiercely; running to and fro, and dragging the

boy, now, as easily as if he were an empty sack. 'That door. Quick!'
He flung him in, bolted it, and turned the key. 'Is the down-stairs door
fast?'

'Double-locked and chained,' replied Crackit, who, with the other
two men, still remained quite helpless and bewildered.

'The panels – are they strong?'

'Lined with sheet-iron.'

'And the windows too?'

'Yes, and the windows.'

'Damn you!' cried the desperate ruffian, throwing up the sash and
menacing the crowd. 'Do your worst; I'll cheat you yet!'

Of all the terrific yells that ever fell on mortal ears none could
exceed the cry of that infuriated throng. Some shouted to those who
were nearest to set the house on fire; others roared to the officers to
shoot him dead. Among them all, none showed such fury as the man
on horseback, who, throwing himself out of the saddle, and bursting
through the crowd as if he were parting water, cried beneath the
window, in a voice that rose above all others, 'Twenty guineas to the
man who brings a ladder!'

The nearest voices took up the cry, and hundreds echoed it. Some
called for ladders, some for sledge-hammers; some ran with torches to
and fro as if to seek them, and still came back and roared again; some
spent their breath in impotent curses and execrations; some pressed
forward with the ecstasy of madmen, and thus impeded the progress
of those below; some among the boldest attempted to climb up by the
water-spout and crevices in the wall; and all waved to and fro in the
darkness beneath like a field of corn moved by an angry wind, and
joined from time to time in one loud furious roar.

'The tide,' cried the murderer, as he staggered back into the room,
and shut the faces out, 'the tide was in as I came up. Give me a rope,
a long rope! They're all in front. I may drop into the Folly Ditch, and
clear off that way. Give me a rope, or I shall do three more murders
and kill myself at last.'

The panic-stricken men pointed to where such articles were kept;
the murderer, hastily selecting the longest and strongest cord, hurried
up to the house-top.

All the windows in the rear of the house had been long ago bricked up, except one small trap in the room where the boy was locked, and that was too small even for the passage of his body. But from this aperture he had never ceased to call on those without to guard the back, and thus when the murderer emerged at last on the house-top by the door in the roof, a loud shout proclaimed the fact to those in front, who immediately began to pour round, pressing upon each other in one unbroken stream.

He planted a board which he had carried up with him for the purpose so firmly against the door that it must be matter of great difficulty to open it from the inside, and creeping over the tiles, looked over the low parapet.

The water was out, and the ditch a bed of mud.

The crowd had been hushed during these few moments, watching his motions and doubtful of his purpose, but the instant they perceived it and knew it was defeated, they raised a cry of triumphant execration to which all their previous shouting had been whispers. Again and again it rose. Those who were at too great a distance to know its meaning, took up the sound; it echoed and re-echoed; it seemed as though the whole city had poured its population out to curse him.

On pressed the people from the front – on, on, on, in one strong struggling current of angry faces, with here and there a glaring torch to light them up and show them out in all their wrath and passion. The houses on the opposite side of the ditch had been entered by the mob; sashes were thrown up, or torn bodily out; there were tiers and tiers of faces in every window, and cluster upon cluster of people clinging to every house-top. Each little bridge (and there were three in sight) bent beneath the weight of the crowd upon it; and still the current poured on to find some nook or hole from which to vent their shouts, and only for an instant see the wretch.

'They have him now,' cried a man on the nearest bridge. 'Hurrah!'

The crowd grew light with uncovered heads, and again the shout uprose.

'I promise fifty pounds,' cried an old gentleman from the same quarter, 'fifty pounds to the man who takes him alive. I will remain here till he comes to ask me for it.'

There was another roar. At this moment the word was passed among the crowd that the door was forced at last, and that he who had first called for the ladder had mounted into the room. The stream abruptly turned as this intelligence ran from mouth to mouth, and the people at the windows, seeing those upon the bridges pouring back, quitted their stations, and, running into the street, joined the concourse that now thronged pell-mell to the spot they had left, each man crushing and striving with his neighbour, and all panting with impatience to get near the door and look upon the criminal as the officers brought him out. The cries and shrieks of those who were pressed almost to suffocation, or trampled down and trodden under foot in the confusion, were dreadful; the narrow ways were completely blocked up; and at this time, between the rush of some to regain the space in front of the house and the unavailing struggles of others to extricate themselves from the mass, the immediate attention was distracted from the murderer, although the universal eagerness for his capture was, if possible, increased.

The man had shrunk down, thoroughly quelled by the ferocity of the crowd and the impossibility of escape; but seeing this sudden change with no less rapidity than it occurred, he sprang upon his feet, determined to make one last effort for his life by dropping into the ditch, and, at the risk of being stifled, endeavouring to creep away in the darkness and confusion.

Roused into new strength and energy, and stimulated by the noise within the house, which announced that an entrance had really been effected, he set his foot against the stack of chimneys, fastened one end of the rope tightly and firmly round it, and with the other made a strong running noose by the aid of his hands and teeth almost in a second. He could let himself down by the cord to within a less distance of the ground than his own height, and had his knife ready in his hand to cut it then, and drop.

At the very instant that he brought the loop over his head, previous to slipping it beneath his arm-pits, and when the old gentleman before-mentioned (who had clung so tight to the railing of the bridge as to resist the force of the crowd and retain his position) earnestly warned those about him that the man was about to lower himself down

The Last Chance

– at that very instant the murderer, looking behind him on the roof, threw his arms above his head, and uttered a yell of terror.

'The eyes again!' he cried in an unearthly screech. Staggering as if struck by lightning, he lost his balance and tumbled over the parapet; the noose was at his neck; it ran up with his weight tight as a bow-string, and swift as the arrow it speeds. He fell for five-and-thirty feet. There was a sudden jerk, a terrific convulsion of the limbs, and there he hung, with the open knife clenched in his stiffening hand.

The old chimney quivered with the shock, but stood it bravely. The murderer swung lifeless against the wall, and the boy, thrusting aside the dangling body which obscured his view, called to the people to come and take him out for God's sake.

A dog, which had lain concealed till now, ran backwards and forwards on the parapet with a dismal howl, and collecting himself for a spring, jumped for the dead man's shoulders. Missing his aim, he fell into the ditch, turning completely over as he went, and striking his head against a stone, dashed out his brains.

CHAPTER THE THIRTEENTH

*AFFORDING AN EXPLANATION OF MORE
MYSTERIES THAN ONE, AND
COMPREHENDING A PROPOSAL OF
MARRIAGE WITH NO WORD OF
SETTLEMENT OR PIN-MONEY*

The events narrated in the last chapter were yet but two days old, when Oliver found himself, at three o'clock in the afternoon, in a travelling-carriage rolling fast towards his native town. Mrs Maylie and Rose and Mrs Bedwin and the good doctor were with him; and Mr Brownlow followed in a post-chaise, accompanied by one other person whose name had not been mentioned.

They had not talked much upon the way, for Oliver was in a flutter of agitation and uncertainty which deprived him of the power of collecting his thoughts, and almost of speech, and appeared to have scarcely less effect on his companions, who shared it in at least an equal degree. He and the two ladies had been very carefully made acquainted by Mr Brownlow with the nature of the admissions which had been forced from Monks, and although they knew that the object of their present journey was to complete the work which had been so well begun, still the whole matter was enveloped in enough of doubt and mystery to leave them in endurance of the most intense suspense.

The same kind friend had, with Mr Losberne's assistance, cautiously stopped all channels of communication through which they could receive intelligence of the dreadful occurrences that had so recently taken place. 'It was quite true,' he said, 'that they must know them before long, but it might be at a better time than the present, and it could not be at a worse.' So they travelled on in silence, each busied with reflections on the object which had brought them together, and no one disposed to give utterance to the thoughts which crowded upon all.

But if Oliver, under these influences, had remained silent while they journeyed towards his birth-place by a road he had never seen, how the whole current of his recollections ran back to old times, and what a crowd of emotions were wakened up in his breast, when they turned into that which he had traversed on foot a poor houseless wandering boy, without a friend to help him or a roof to shelter his head!

'See there, there —' cried Oliver, eagerly clasping the hand of Rose, and pointing out at the carriage window, — 'that's the stile I came over, there are the hedges I crept behind for fear any one should overtake me and force me back, yonder is the path across the fields leading to the old house where I was a little child. Oh Dick, Dick, my dear old friend, if I could only see you now!'

'You will see him soon,' replied Rose, gently taking his folded hands between her own. 'You shall tell him how happy you are, and how rich you are grown, and that in all your happiness you have none so great as the coming back to make him happy too.'

'Yes, yes,' said Oliver, 'and we'll — we'll take him away from here, and have him clothed and taught, and send him to some quiet country place where he may grow strong and well, – shall we?'

Rose nodded 'yes,' for the boy was smiling through such happy tears that she could not speak.

'You will be kind and good to him, for you are to every one,' said Oliver. 'It will make you cry, I know, to hear what he can tell; but never mind, never mind, it will be all over, and you will smile again – I know that too – to think how changed he is; you did the same with me. He said "God bless you" to me when I ran away,' cried the boy with a burst of affectionate emotion; 'and I will say "God bless *you*" now, and show him how I love him for it!'

As they approached the town and at length drove through its narrow streets, it became matter of no small difficulty to restrain the boy within reasonable bounds. There was Sowerberry, the undertaker's, just as it used to be, only smaller and less imposing in appearance than he remembered it – all the well-known shops and houses, with almost every one of which he had some slight incident connected – Gamfield's cart, the very cart he used to have, standing at the old public-house door – the workhouse, the dreary prison of his youthful days, with its dismal windows frowning on the street – the same lean porter standing at the gate, at sight of whom Oliver involuntarily shrunk back, and then laughed at himself for being so foolish, – then cried, then laughed again – scores of faces at the doors and windows that he knew quite well – nearly everything as if he had left it but yesterday and all his recent life had been but a happy dream.

But it was pure, earnest, joyful reality. They drove straight to the door of the chief hotel (which Oliver used to stare up at with awe, and think a mighty palace, but which had somehow fallen off in grandeur and size); and here was Mr Grimwig all ready to receive them, kissing the young lady, and the old one too, when they got out of the coach, as if he were the grandfather of the whole party, all smiles and kindness, and not offering to eat his head – no, not once; not even when he contradicted a very old postboy about the nearest road to London, and maintained he knew it best, though he had only come that way once, and that time fast asleep. There was dinner prepared, and there were bed-rooms ready, and everything was arranged as if by magic.

Notwithstanding all this, when the hurry of the first half hour was over, the same silence and constraint prevailed that had marked their journey down. Mr Brownlow did not join them at dinner, but remained in a separate room. The two other gentlemen hurried in and out with anxious faces, and, during the short intervals that they were present, conversed apart. Once Mrs Maylie was called away, and after being absent for nearly an hour, returned with eyes swollen with weeping. All these things made Rose and Oliver, who were not in any new secrets, nervous and uncomfortable. They sat wondering in silence, or, if they exchanged a few words, spoke in whispers, as if they were afraid to hear the sound of their own voices.

At length, when nine o'clock had come and they began to think they were to hear no more that night, Mr Losberne and Mr Grimwig entered the room, followed by Mr Brownlow and a man whom Oliver almost shrieked with surprise to see; for they told him it was his brother, and it was the same man he had met at the market town and seen looking in with Fagin at the window of his little room. He cast a look of hate, which even then he could not dissemble, at the astonished boy, and sat down near the door. Mr Brownlow who had papers in his hand, walked to a table near which Rose and Oliver were seated.

'This is a painful task,' said he, 'but these declarations, which have been signed in London before many gentlemen, must be in substance repeated here. I would have spared you the degradation, but we must hear them from your own lips before we part, and you know why.'

'Go on,' said the person addressed, turning away his face. 'Quick! I have done enough. Don't keep me here.'

'This child,' said Mr Brownlow, drawing Oliver to him, and laying his hand upon his head, 'is your half-brother; the illegitimate son of your father and my dear friend Edwin Leeford, by poor young Agnes Fleming, who died in giving him birth.'

*

'Yes,' said Monks, scowling at the trembling boy, the beating of whose heart he might have heard. 'That is their bastard child.'

'The term you use,' said Mr Brownlow sternly, 'is a reproach to those who long since passed beyond the feeble censure of this world. It reflects true disgrace on no one living, except you who use it. Let that pass. He was born in this town?'

'In the workhouse of this town,' was the sullen reply. 'You have the story there.' He pointed impatiently to the papers as he spoke.

'I must have it here too,' said Mr Brownlow, looking round upon the listeners.

'Listen then,' returned Monks. 'His father being taken ill at Rome, as you know, was joined by his wife, my mother, from whom he had been long separated, who went from Paris and took me with her – to look after his property, for what I know, for she had no great affection for him, nor he for her. He knew nothing of us, for his senses were gone, and he slumbered on till next day, when he died. Among the papers in his desk were two, dated on the night his illness first came on, directed to yourself, and enclosed in a few short lines to you, with an intimation on the cover of the package that it was not to be forwarded till after he was dead. One of these papers was a letter to this girl Agnes, and the other a will.'

'What of the letter?' asked Mr Brownlow.

'The letter? – A sheet of paper crossed and crossed again,[1] with a penitent confession, and prayers to God to help her. He had palmed a tale on the girl that some secret mystery – to be explained one day – prevented his marrying her just then, and so she had gone on trusting patiently to him until she trusted too far, and lost what none could ever give her back. She was at that time within a few months of her confinement. He told her all he had meant to do to hide her shame, if he had lived, and prayed her, if he died, not to curse his memory or think the consequences of their sin would be visited on her or their young child; for all the guilt was his. He reminded her of the day he had given her the little locket and the ring with her christian name engraved upon it, and a blank left for that which he hoped one day to have bestowed upon her – prayed her yet to keep it, and wear it next her heart, as she had done before – and then ran on wildly in the same words, over and over again, as if he had gone distracted – as I believe he had.'

'The will,' said Mr Brownlow, as Oliver's tears fell fast.

Monks was silent.

'The will,' said Mr Brownlow, speaking for him, 'was in the same spirit as that letter. He talked of miseries which his wife had brought upon him, of the rebellious disposition, vice, malice, and premature bad passions of you, his only son, who had been trained to hate him; and left you and your mother each an annuity of eight hundred pounds. The bulk of his property he divided into two equal portions – one for Agnes Fleming; and the other for their child, if it should be born alive and ever come of age. If it was a girl, it was to come into the money unconditionally; but if a boy, only on the stipulation that in his minority he should never have stained his name with any public act of dishonour, meanness, cowardice, or wrong. He did this, he said, to mark his confidence in the mother, and his conviction – only strengthened by approaching death – that the child would share her gentle heart and noble nature. If he was disappointed in this expectation, then the money was to come to you; for then, and not till then, when both children were equal, would he recognize your prior claim upon his purse, who had none upon his heart, but had from an infant repulsed him with coldness and aversion.'

'My mother,' said Monks in a louder tone, 'did what a woman should have done – she burnt this will. The letter never reached its destination, but that and other proofs she kept, in case they ever tried to lie away the blot. The girl's father had the truth from her with every aggravation that her violent hate – I love her for it now – could add. Goaded by shame and dishonour, he fled with his children into a remote corner of Wales, changing his very name that his friends might never know of his retreat; and here, no great while afterwards, he was found dead in his bed. The girl had left her home in secret some weeks before; he had searched for her on foot in every town and village near, and it was on the night that he returned home, assured that she had destroyed herself to hide her shame and his, that his old heart broke.'

There was a short silence here, until Mr Brownlow took up the thread of the narrative.

'Years after this,' he said, 'this man's – Edward Leeford's – mother came to me. He had left her when only eighteen, robbed her of jewels and money, gambled, squandered, forged, and fled to London, where for two years he had associated with the lowest outcasts. She was sinking under a painful and incurable disease, and wished to recover him before she died. Inquiries were set on foot; strict searches made, unavailing for a long time, but ultimately successful; and he went back with her to France.'

'There she died,' said Monks, 'after a lingering illness; and on her death-bed she bequeathed these secrets to me, together with her unquenchable and deadly hatred of all whom they involved, though she need not have left me that, for I had inherited it long before. She would not believe that the girl had destroyed herself and the child too, but was filled with the impression that a male child had been born, and was alive. I swore to her if ever it crossed my path to hunt it down, never to let it rest, to pursue it with the bitterest and most unrelenting animosity, to vent upon it the hatred that I deeply felt, and to spit upon the empty vaunt of that insulting will by dragging it, if I could, to the very gallows-foot. She was right. He came in my way at last; I began well, and but for babbling drabs I would have finished as I began; I would, I would!'

As the villain folded his arms tight together, and muttered curses on himself in the impotence of baffled malice, Mr Brownlow turned to the terrified group beside him, and explained that the Jew, who had been his old accomplice and confident, had a large reward for keeping Oliver ensnared, of which some part was to be given up in the event of his being rescued, and that a dispute on this head had led to their visit to the country house for the purpose of identifying him.

'The locket and ring?' said Mr Brownlow, turning to Monks.

'I bought them from the man and woman I told you of, who stole them from the nurse, who stole them from the corpse,' answered Monks without raising his eyes. 'You know what became of them.'

Mr Brownlow merely nodded to Mr Grimwig, who, disappearing with great alacrity, shortly returned, pushing in Mrs Bumble, and dragging her unwilling consort after him.

'Do my hi's deceive me!' cried Mr Bumble with ill-feigned enthusiasm, 'or is that little Oliver? Oh O-li-ver, if you know'd how I've been a-grieving for you – !'

'Hold your tongue, fool,' murmured Mrs Bumble.

'Isn't natur, natur, Mrs Bumble!' remonstrated the workhouse master. 'Can't I be supposed to feel – I as brought him up porochially – when I see him a-setting here among ladies and gentlemen of the very affablest description! I always loved that boy as if he'd been my – my – my own grandfather,' said Mr Bumble, halting for an appropriate comparison. 'Master Oliver, my dear, you remember the blessed gentleman in the white waistcoat? Ah! he went to heaven last week in a oak coffin with plated handles, Oliver.'

'Come, sir,' said Mr Grimwig tartly, 'suppress your feelings.'

'I will do my endeavours, sir,' replied Mr Bumble. 'How do you do, sir? I hope you are very well.'

This salutation was addressed to Mr Brownlow, who had stepped up to within a short distance of the respectable couple, and who inquired, as he pointed to Monks, –

'Do you know that person?'

'No,' replied Mrs Bumble flatly.

'Perhaps *you* don't?' said Mr Brownlow, addressing her spouse.

'I never saw him in all my life,' said Mr Bumble.

'Nor sold him anything, perhaps?'

'No,' replied Mrs Bumble.

'You never had, perhaps, a certain gold locket and ring?' said Mr Brownlow.

'Certainly not,' replied the matron. 'What are we brought here to answer to such nonsense as this for?'

Again Mr Brownlow nodded to Mr Grimwig, and again that gentleman limped away with extraordinary readiness. But not again did he return with a stout man and wife, for this time he led in two palsied women, who shook and tottered as they walked.

'You shut the door the night old Sally died,' said the foremost one, raising her shrivelled hand, 'but you couldn't shut out the sound nor stop the chinks.'

'No, no,' said the other, looking round her and wagging her toothless jaws. 'No, no, no.'

'We heard her try to tell you what she'd done, and saw you take a paper from her hand, and watched you too, next day, to the pawn-broker's shop,' said the first.

'Yes,' added the second, 'and it was "a locket and gold ring." We found out that, and saw it given you. We were by. Oh! we were by.'

'And we know more than that,' resumed the first, 'for she told us often, long ago, that the young mother had told her that, feeling she should never get over it, she was on her way, at the time that she was taken ill, to die near the grave of the father of the child.'

'Would you like to see the pawnbroker himself?' asked Mr Grimwig with a motion towards the door.

'No,' replied the woman; 'if he' – she pointed to Monks – 'has been coward enough to confess, as I see he has, and you have sounded all these hags till you found the right ones, I have nothing more to say. I *did* sell them, and they're where you'll never get them. What then?'

'Nothing,' replied Mr Brownlow, 'except that it remains for us to take care that you are neither of you employed in a situation of trust again. You may leave the room.'

'I hope,' said Mr Bumble, looking about him with great ruefulness as Mr Grimwig disappeared with the two old women, 'I hope that this unfortunate little circumstance will not deprive me of my porochial office?'

'Indeed it will,' replied Mr Brownlow; 'you must make up your mind to that, and think yourself well off besides.'

'It was all Mrs Bumble – she *would* do it –' urged Mr Bumble; first looking round to ascertain that his partner had left the room.

'That is no excuse,' returned Mr Brownlow. 'You were present on the occasion of the destruction of these trinkets, and, indeed, are the more guilty of the two in the eye of the law, for the law supposes that your wife acts under your direction.'

'If the law supposes that,' said Mr Bumble, squeezing his hat emphatically in both hands, 'the law is a ass – a idiot. If that is the eye of the law, the law's a bachelor, and the worst I wish the law is, that his eye may be opened by experience – by experience.'

Laying great stress on the repetition of these two words, Mr Bumble fixed his hat on very tight, and putting his hands in his pockets followed his helpmate down stairs.

'Young lady,' said Mr Brownlow, turning to Rose, 'give me your hand. Do not tremble; you need not fear to hear the few remaining words we have to say.'

'If they have – I do not know how they can, but if they have – any reference to me,' said Rose, 'pray let me hear them at some other time. I have not strength or spirits now.'

'Nay,' returned the old gentleman, drawing her arm through his; 'you have more fortitude than this, I am sure. Do you know this young lady, sir?'

'Yes,' replied Monks.

'I never saw you before,' said Rose faintly.

'I have seen you often,' returned Monks.

'The father of the unhappy Agnes had *two* daughters,' said Mr Brownlow. 'What was the fate of the other – the child?'

'The child,' replied Monks, 'when her father died in a strange place, in a strange name, without a letter, book, or scrap of paper that yielded the faintest clue by which his friends or relatives could be traced – the child was taken by some wretched cottagers, who reared it as their own.'

'Go on,' said Mr Brownlow, signing to Mrs Maylie to approach. 'Go on!'

'You couldn't find the spot to which these people had repaired,' said Monks, 'but where friendship fails, hatred will often force a way. My mother found it after a year of cunning search – ay, and found the child.'

'She took it, did she?'

'No. The people were poor, and began to sicken – at least the man did – of their fine humanity; so she left it with them, giving them a small present of money which would not last long, and promising more, which she never meant to send. She didn't quite rely, however, on their discontent and poverty for the child's unhappiness, but told the history of the sister's shame with such alterations as suited her, bade them take good heed of the child, for she came of bad blood, and told them she was illegitimate, and sure to go wrong one time or other. The circumstances countenanced all this; the people believed it; and there the child dragged on an existence miserable enough even to satisfy us, until a widow lady, residing then at Chester,[2] saw the girl by chance, pitied her, and took her home. There was some cursed spell against us, for in spite of all our efforts she remained there and was happy: I lost sight of her two or three years ago, and saw her no more until a few months back.'

'Do you see her now?'

'Yes – leaning on your arm.'

'But not the less my niece,' cried Mrs Maylie, folding the fainting girl in her arms, – 'not the less my dearest child. I would not lose her now for all the treasures of the world. My sweet companion, my own dear girl –'

'The only friend I ever had,' cried Rose, clinging to her, – 'the kindest, best of friends. My heart will burst. I cannot – cannot – bear all this.'

'You have borne more, and been through all the best and gentlest creature that ever shed happiness on every one she knew,' said Mrs Maylie, embracing her tenderly. 'Come, come, my love, remember who this is who waits to clasp you in his arms, poor child, – see here – look, look, my dear!'

'Not aunt,' cried Oliver, throwing his arms about her neck: 'I'll never call her aunt – sister, my own dear sister, that something taught my heart to love so dearly from the first – Rose, dear, darling Rose.'

Let the tears which fell, and the broken words which were exchanged in the long close embrace between the orphans, be sacred. A father, sister, and mother, were gained and lost in that one moment. Joy and grief were mingled in the cup, but there were no bitter tears, for even grief itself arose so softened, and clothed in such sweet and tender recollections, that it became a solemn pleasure, and lost all character of pain.

They were a long, long time alone. A soft tap at the door at length announced that some one was without. Oliver opened it, glided away, and gave place to Harry Maylie.

'I know it all,' he said, taking a seat beside the lovely girl. 'Dear Rose, I know it all.'

'I am not here by accident,' he added after a lengthened silence; 'nor have I heard all this to-night, for I knew it yesterday – only yesterday. Do you guess that I have come to remind you of a promise?'

'Stay,' said Rose, – 'you *do* know all?'

'All. You gave me leave, at any time within a year, to renew the subject of our last discourse.'

'I did.'

'Not to press you to alter your determination,' pursued the young man, 'but to hear you repeat it, if you would. I was to lay whatever of station or fortune I might possess at your feet, and if you still adhered to your former determination, I pledged myself by no word or act to seek to change it.'

'The same reasons which influenced me then will influence me now,' said Rose firmly. 'If I ever owed a strict and rigid duty to her, whose goodness saved me from a life of indigence and suffering, when should I ever feel it as I should to-night? It is a struggle,' said Rose, 'but one I am proud to make; it is a pang, but one my heart shall bear.'

'The disclosure of to-night –' Harry began.

'The disclosure of to-night,' replied Rose softly, 'leaves me in the same position, with reference to you, as that in which I stood before.'

'You harden your heart against me, Rose,' urged her lover.

'Oh, Harry, Harry,' said the young lady, bursting into tears, 'I wish I could, and spare myself this pain.'

'Then why inflict it on yourself?' said Harry, taking her hand. 'Think, dear Rose, think what you have heard to-night.'

'And what have I heard! what have I heard!' cried Rose. 'That a sense of his deep disgrace so worked upon my own father that he shunned all – there, we have said enough, Harry, we have said enough.'

'Not yet, not yet,' said the young man, detaining her as she rose. 'My hopes, my wishes, prospects, feelings – every thought in life except my love for you – have undergone a change. I offer you, now, no distinction among a bustling crowd, no mingling with a world of malice and detraction, where the blood is called into honest cheeks by aught but real disgrace and shame; but a home – a heart and home – yes, dearest Rose, and those, and those alone, are all I have to offer.'

'What does this mean?' faltered the young lady.

'It means but this – that when I left you last, I left you with the firm determination to level all fancied barriers between yourself and me; resolved that if my world could not be yours, I would make yours mine; that no pride of birth should curl the lip at you, for I would turn from it. This I have done. Those who have shrunk from me because of this, have shrunk from you, and proved you so far right. Such power and patronage – such relatives of influence and rank – as smiled upon me then, look coldly now; but there are smiling fields and waving trees in England's richest county, and by one village church – mine, Rose, my own – there stands a rustic dwelling which you can make me prouder of than all the hopes I have renounced, measured a thousandfold. This is *my* rank and station now, and here I lay it down.'

* * * * *

'It's a trying thing waiting supper for lovers,' said Mr Grimwig, waking up, and pulling his pocket-handkerchief from over his head.

Truth to tell, the supper had been waiting a most unreasonable time. Neither Mrs Maylie, nor Harry, nor Rose (who all came in together), could offer a word in extenuation.

'I had serious thoughts of eating my head to-night,' said Mr Grimwig, 'for I began to think I should get nothing else. I'll take the liberty, if you'll allow me, of saluting the bride that is to be.'

Mr Grimwig lost no time in carrying this notice into effect upon the blushing girl; and the example being contagious, was followed both by the doctor and Mr Brownlow. Some people affirm that Harry Maylie had been observed to set it originally in a dark room adjoining; but the best authorities consider this downright scandal, he being young and a clergyman.

'Oliver, my child,' said Mrs Maylie, 'where have you been, and why do you look so sad? There are tears stealing down your face at this moment. What is the matter?'

It is a world of disappointment – often to the hopes we most cherish, and hopes that do our nature the greatest honour.

Poor Dick was dead!

*

CHAPTER THE FOURTEENTH

THE JEW'S LAST NIGHT ALIVE

The court[1] was paved from floor to roof with human faces. Inquisitive and eager eyes peered from every inch of space; from the rail before the dock, away into the sharpest angle of the smallest corner in the galleries, all looks were fixed upon one man – the Jew. Before him and behind, above, below, on the right and on the left – he seemed to stand surrounded by a firmament all bright with beaming eyes.

He stood there, in all this glare of living light, with one hand resting on the wooden slab before him, the other held to his ear, and his head thrust forward to enable him to catch with greater distinctness every word that fell from the presiding judge, who was delivering his charge to the jury. At times he turned his eyes sharply upon them to observe the effect of the slightest feather-weight in his favour; and when the points against him were stated with terrible distinctness, looked towards his counsel in mute appeal that he would even then urge something in his behalf. Beyond these manifestations of anxiety, he stirred not hand or foot. He had scarcely moved since the trial began; and now that the judge ceased to speak, he still remained in the same strained attitude of close attention, with his gaze bent on him as though he listened still.

A slight bustle in the court recalled him to himself, and looking round, he saw that the jurymen had turned together to consider of their verdict. As his eyes wandered to the gallery, he could see the people rising above each other to see his face: some hastily applying their glasses to their eyes, and others whispering their neighbours with looks expressive of abhorrence. A few there were who seemed unmindful of him, and looked only to the jury in impatient wonder how they could delay, but in no one face – not even among the women, of whom there were many there – could he read the faintest sympathy with him, or any feeling but one of all-absorbing interest that he should be condemned.

As he saw all this in one bewildered glance, the death-like stillness came again, and looking back, he saw that the jurymen had turned towards the judge. Hush!

They only sought permission to retire.

He looked wistfully into their faces, one by one, when they passed out, as though to see which way the greater number leant; but that was fruitless. The jailer touched him on the shoulder. He followed mechanically to the end of the dock, and sat down on a chair. The man pointed it out, or he should not have seen it.

He looked up into the gallery again. Some of the people were eating, and some fanning themselves with handkerchiefs, for the crowded place was very hot. There was one young man sketching his face in a little note-book. He wondered whether it was like, and looked on when the artist broke his pencil-point and made another with his knife, as any idle spectator might have done.

In the same way, when he turned his eyes towards the judge, his mind began to busy itself with the fashion of his dress, and what it cost, and how he put it on. There was an old fat gentleman on the bench, too, who had gone out some half an hour before, and now came back. He wondered within himself whether this man had been to get his dinner, what he had had, and where he had had it, and pursued this train of careless thought until some new object caught his eye and roused another.

Not that all this time his mind was for an instant free from one oppressive, overwhelming sense of the grave that opened at his feet; it was ever present to him, but in a vague and general way, and he could not fix his thoughts upon it. Thus, even while he trembled and turned, burning hot at the idea of speedy death, he fell to counting the iron spikes before him, and wondering how the head of one had been broken off, and whether they would mend it or leave it as it was. Then he thought of all the horrors of the gallows and the scaffold, and stopped to watch a man sprinkling the floor to cool it – and then went on to think again.

At length there was a cry of silence, and a breathless look from all towards the door. The jury returned and passed him close. He could glean nothing from their faces; they might as well have been of stone. Perfect stillness ensued – not a rustle – not a breath – Guilty.

The building rang with a tremendous shout, and another, and another, and then it echoed deep loud groans, that gathered strength as they swelled out, like angry thunder. It was a peal of joy from the populace outside, greeting the news that he would die on Monday.

The noise subsided, and he was asked if he had anything to say why sentence of death should not be passed upon him. He had resumed his listening attitude, and looked intently at his questioner while the demand was made, but it was twice repeated before he seemed to hear it, and then he only muttered that he was an old man – an old man – an old man – and so dropping into a whisper, was silent again.

The judge assumed the black cap,[2] and the prisoner still stood with the same air and gesture. A woman in the gallery uttered some exclamation, called forth by this dread solemnity; he looked hastily up, as if angry at the interruption, and bent forward yet more attentively. The address was solemn and impressive, the sentence fearful to hear; but he stood like a marble figure, without the motion of a nerve. His haggard face was still thrust forward, his under-jaw hanging down, and his eyes staring out before him, when the jailer put his hand upon his arm, and beckoned him away. He gazed stupidly about him for an instant, and obeyed.

They led him through a paved room under the court, where some prisoners were waiting till their turns came, and others were talking to their friends, who crowded round a grate which looked into the open yard. There was nobody there to speak to *him;* but as he passed, the prisoners fell back to render him more visible to the people who were clinging to the bars, and they assailed him with opprobrious names, and screeched and hissed. He shook his fist, and would have spat upon them; but his conductors hurried him on through a gloomy passage, lighted by a few dim lamps, into the interior of the prison.

Here he was searched, that he might not have about him the means of anticipating the law; this ceremony performed, they led him to one of the condemned cells,[3] and left him there – alone.

He sat down on a stone bench opposite the door, which served for seat and bedstead, and casting his bloodshot eyes upon the ground, tried to collect his thoughts. After a while he began to remember a few disjointed fragments of what the judge had said, though it had

Fagin in the condemned Cell

seemed to him at the time that he could not hear a word. These gradually fell into their proper places, and by degrees suggested more, so that in a little time he had the whole almost as it was delivered. To be hanged by the neck till he was dead – that was the end. To be hanged by the neck till he was dead.

As it came on very dark, he began to think of all the men he had known who had died upon the scaffold – some of them through his means. They rose up in such quick succession that he could hardly count them. He had seen some of them die – and joked too, because they died with prayers upon their lips. With what a rattling noise the drop went down; and how suddenly they changed from strong and vigorous men to dangling heaps of clothes!

Some of them might have inhabited that very cell – sat upon that very spot. It was very dark; why didn't they bring a light? The cell had been built for many years – scores of men must have passed their last hours there – it was like sitting in a vault strewn with dead bodies – the cap, the noose, the pinioned arms – the faces that he knew even beneath that hideous veil – Light, light!

At length when his hands were raw with beating against the heavy door and walls, two men appeared, one bearing a candle, which he thrust into an iron candlestick fixed against the wall, and the other dragging in a mattress on which to pass the night, for the prisoner was to be left alone no more.

Then came night – dark, dismal, silent night. Other watchers are glad to hear the church-clocks strike, for they tell of life and coming day. To the Jew they brought despair. The boom of every iron bell came laden with the one deep hollow sound – Death. What availed the noise and bustle of cheerful morning, which penetrated even there, to him? It was another form of knell, with mockery added to the warning.

The day passed off – day, there was no day; it was gone as soon as come – and night came on again; night so long and yet so short; long in its dreadful silence, and short in its fleeting hours. One time he raved and blasphemed, and at another howled and tore his hair. Venerable men of his own persuasion had come to pray beside him, but he had driven them away with curses. They renewed their charitable efforts, and he beat them off.

Saturday night; he had only one night more to live. And as he thought of this, the day broke — Sunday.

It was not until the night of this last awful day that a withering sense of his helpless desperate state came in its full intensity upon his blighted soul; not that he had ever held any defined or positive hopes of mercy, but that he had never been able to consider more than the dim probability of dying so soon. He had spoken little to either of the two men who relieved each other in their attendance upon him, and they, for their parts, made no effort to rouse his attention. He had sat there awake, but dreaming. Now he started up every minute, and with gasping mouth and burning skin hurried to and fro, in such a paroxysm of fear and wrath, that even they — used to such sights — recoiled from him with horror. He grew so terrible at last in all the tortures of his evil conscience, that one man could not bear to sit there, eyeing him alone, and so the two kept watch together.

He cowered down upon his stone bed, and thought of the past. He had been wounded with some missiles from the crowd on the day of his capture, and his head was bandaged with a linen cloth. His red hair hung down upon his bloodless face; his beard was torn and twisted into knots; his eyes shone with a terrible light; his unwashed flesh crackled with the fever that burnt him up. Eight — nine — ten. If it was not a trick to frighten him, and those were the real hours treading on each other's heels, where would he be when they came round again! Eleven. Another struck ere the voice of the hour before had ceased to vibrate. At eight he would be the only mourner in his own funeral train; at eleven——

Those dreadful walls of Newgate, which have hidden so much misery and such unspeakable anguish, not only from the eyes, but too often and too long from the thoughts of men, never held so dread a spectacle as that. The few who lingered as they passed and wondered what the man was doing who was to be hung to-morrow, would have slept but ill that night, if they could have seen him then.

From early in the evening until nearly midnight, little groups of two and three presented themselves at the lodge-gate, and inquired with anxious faces whether any reprieve had been received. These being answered in the negative, communicated the welcome intelligence to clusters in the street, who pointed out to one another the door from which he must come out, and showed where the scaffold would be built, and, walking with unwilling steps away, turned back to conjure up the scene. By degrees they fell off one by one, and for an hour in the dead of night the street was left to solitude and darkness.

The space before the prison was cleared, and a few strong barriers, painted black, had been already thrown across the road to break the pressure of the expected crowd, when Mr Brownlow and Oliver appeared at the wicket, and presented an order of admission to the prisoner, signed by one of the sheriffs. They were immediately admitted into the lodge.

'Is the young gentleman to come too, sir?' said the man whose duty it was to conduct them. 'It's not a sight for children, sir.'

'It is not indeed, my friend,' rejoined Mr Brownlow, 'but my business with this man is intimately connected with him, and as this child has seen him in the full career of his success and villany, I think it better — even at the cost of some pain and fear — that he should see him now.'

These few words had been said apart, so as to be inaudible to Oliver. The man touched his hat, and glancing at him with some curiosity, opened another gate opposite to that at which they had entered, and led them on through dark and winding ways towards the cells.

'This,' said the man, stopping in a gloomy passage where a couple of workmen were making some preparations in profound silence, — 'this is the place he passes through. If you step this way, you can see the door he goes out at.'

He led them into a stone kitchen, fitted with coppers for dressing the prison food, and pointed to a door. There was an open grating above it, through which came the sound of men's voices, mingled with the noise of hammering and the throwing down of boards. They were putting up the scaffold.

From this place they passed through several strong gates, opened by other turnkeys from the inner side, and having entered an open yard, ascended a flight of narrow steps, and came into a passage with a row of strong doors on the left hand. Motioning them to remain where they were, the turnkey knocked at one of these with his bunch of keys. The two attendants after a little whispering came out into the passage, stretching themselves as if glad of the temporary relief, and motioned the visitors to follow the jailer into the cell. They did so.

The condemned criminal was seated on his bed, rocking himself from side to side, with a countenance more like that of a snared beast than the face of a man. His mind was evidently wandering to his old life, for he continued to mutter, without seeming conscious of their presence otherwise than as a part of his vision.

'Good boy, Charley – well done!' – he mumbled. 'Oliver too, ha! ha! ha! Oliver too – quite the gentleman now – quite the – take that boy away to bed.'

The jailer took the disengaged hand of Oliver, and whispering him not to be alarmed, looked on without speaking.

'Take him away to bed' – cried the Jew. 'Do you hear me, some of you? He has been the – the – somehow the cause of all this. It's worth the money to bring him up to it – Bolter's throat. Bill; never mind the girl – Bolter's throat as deep as you can cut. Saw his head off.'

'Fagin,' said the jailer.

'That's me!' cried the Jew, falling instantly into precisely the same attitude of listening that he had assumed upon his trial. 'An old man, my Lord; a very old, old man.'

'Here,' said the turnkey, laying his hand upon his breast to keep him down. 'Here's somebody wants to see you, to ask you some questions, I suppose. Fagin, Fagin. Are you a man?'

'I shan't be one long,' replied the Jew, looking up with a face retaining no human expression but rage and terror. 'Strike them all dead! – what right have they to butcher me?'

As he spoke he caught sight of Oliver and Mr Brownlow, and shrinking to the furthest corner of the seat, demanded to know what they wanted there.

'Steady,' said the turnkey, still holding him down. 'Now, sir, tell him what you want – quick, if you please, for he grows worse as the time gets on.'

'You have some papers,' said Mr Brownlow advancing, 'which were placed in your hands for better security, by a man called Monks.'

'It's all a lie together,' replied the Jew. 'I haven't one – not one.'

'For the love of God,' said Mr Brownlow solemnly, 'do not say that now, upon the very verge of death; but tell me where they are. You know that Sikes is dead; that Monks has confessed; that there is no hope of any further gain. Where are these papers?'

'Oliver,' cried the Jew, beckoning to him. 'Here, here. Let me whisper to you.'

'I am not afraid,' said Oliver in a low voice, as he relinquished Mr Brownlow's hand.

'The papers,' said the Jew, drawing him towards him, 'are in a canvass bag, in a hole a little way up the chimney in the top front-room. I want to talk to you, my dear – I want to talk to you.'

'Yes, yes,' returned Oliver. 'Let me say a prayer. Do. Let me say one prayer; say only one upon your knees with me, and we will talk till morning.'

'Outside, outside,' replied the Jew, pushing the boy before him towards the door, and looking vacantly over his head. 'Say I've gone to sleep – they'll believe *you*. You can get me out if you take me so. Now then, now then.'

'Oh! God forgive this wretched man!' cried the boy with a burst of tears.

'That's right, that's right,' said the Jew. 'That'll help us on. This door first; if I shake and tremble as we pass the gallows, don't you mind, but hurry on. Now, now, now.'

'Have you nothing else to ask him, sir?' inquired the turnkey.

'No other question,' replied Mr Brownlow. 'If I hoped we could recall him to a sense of his position –'

'Nothing will do that, sir,' replied the man, shaking his head. 'You had better leave him.'

The door of the cell opened, and the attendants returned.

'Press on, press on,' cried the Jew. 'Softly, but not so slow. Faster, faster!'

The men laid hands upon him, and disengaging Oliver from his grasp, held him back. He writhed and struggled with the power of desperation, and sent up shriek upon shriek that penetrated even those massive walls, and rang in their ears until they reached the open yard.

It was some time before they left the prison, for Oliver nearly swooned after this frightful scene, and was so weak, that for an hour or more he had not the strength to walk.

Day was dawning when they again emerged. A great multitude had already assembled; the windows were filled with people smoking and playing cards to beguile the time; the crowd were pushing, quarrelling, and joking. Every thing told of life and animation, but one dark cluster of objects in the very centre of all – the black stage, the cross-beam, the rope, and all the hideous apparatus of death.

CHAPTER THE FIFTEENTH

AND LAST

The fortunes of those who have figured in this tale are nearly closed, and what little remains to their historian to relate is told in few and simple words.

Before three months had passed, Rose Fleming and Harry Maylie were married in the village church, which was henceforth to be the scene of the young clergyman's labours; on the same day they entered into possession of their new and happy home.

Mrs Maylie took up her abode with her son and daughter-in-law, to enjoy, during the tranquil remainder of her days, the greatest felicity that age and worth can know – the contemplation of the happiness of those on whom the warmest affections and tenderest cares of a well-spent life have been unceasingly bestowed.

It appeared, on a full and careful investigation, that if the wreck of property remaining in the custody of Monks (which had never prospered either in his hands or in those of his mother) were equally divided between himself and Oliver, it would yield to each little more than three thousand pounds. By the provisions of his father's will, Oliver would have been entitled to the whole; but Mr Brownlow, unwilling to deprive the elder son of the opportunity of retrieving his former vices and pursuing an honest career, proposed this mode of distribution, to which his young charge most joyfully acceded.

Monks, still bearing that assumed name, retired with his portion to a distant part of the New World, where, having quickly squandered it, he once more fell into his old courses, and, after undergoing a long confinement for some fresh act of fraud and knavery, at length sunk under an attack of his old disorder, and died in prison. As far from home died the chief remaining members of his friend Fagin's gang.

Mr Brownlow adopted Oliver as his own son, and removing with him and the old housekeeper to within a mile of the parsonage house, where his dear friends resided, gratified the only remaining wish of Oliver's warm and earnest heart, and thus linked together a little society, whose condition approached as nearly to one of perfect happiness as can ever be known in this changing world.

Soon after the marriage of the young people, the worthy doctor returned to Chertsey, where, bereft of the presence of his old friends, he would have been discontented if his temperament had admitted of such a feeling, and would have turned quite peevish if he had known how. For two or three months he contented himself with hinting that he feared the air began to disagree with him, and then finding that the place really was to him no longer what it had been before, settled his business on his assistant, took a bachelor's cottage just outside the village of which his young friend was pastor, and instantaneously recovered. Here he took to gardening, planting, fishing, carpentering, and various other pursuits of a similar kind, all undertaken with his characteristic impetuosity; and in each and all, he has since become famous throughout the neighbourhood as a most profound authority.

Before his removal, he had managed to contract a strong friendship for Mr Grimwig, which that eccentric gentleman cordially reciprocated. He is accordingly visited by him a great many times in the course of the year, and on all such occasions Mr Grimwig plants, fishes, and carpenters with great ardour, doing everything in a very singular and unprecedented manner; but always maintaining, with his favourite asseveration, that his mode is the right one. On Sundays, he never fails to criticise the sermon to the young clergyman's face, always informing Mr Losberne in strict confidence afterwards, that he considers it an excellent performance, but thinks it as well not to say so. It is a standing and very favourite joke for Mr Brownlow to rally him on his old prophecy concerning Oliver, and to remind him of the night on which they sat with the watch between them waiting his return; but Mr Grimwig contends that he was right in the main, and in proof thereof remarks that Oliver *did not come back*, after all, which always calls forth a laugh on his side, and increases his good humour.

Mr Noah Claypole, receiving a free pardon from the crown in consequence of being admitted approver[1] against the Jew, and considering his profession not altogether as safe a one as he could wish, was for some little time at a loss for the means of a livelihood, not burdened with too much work. After some consideration he went into business as an informer,[2] in which calling he realizes a genteel subsistence. His plan is to walk out once a-week during church time, attended by Charlotte in respectable attire. The lady faints away at the doors of charitable publicans, and the gentleman being accommodated with threepenny-worth of brandy to restore her, lays an information next day, and pockets half the penalty. Sometimes Mr Claypole faints himself, but the result is the same.

Mr and Mrs Bumble, deprived of their situations, were gradually reduced to great indigence and misery, and finally became paupers in that very same workhouse in which they had once lorded it over others. Mr Bumble has been heard to say, that in this reverse and degradation he has not even spirits to be thankful for being separated from his wife.

As to Mr Giles and Brittles, they still remain in their old posts, although the former is bald, and the last-named boy quite grey. They sleep at the parsonage, but divide their attentions so equally between its inmates, and Oliver, and Mr Brownlow, and Mr Losberne, that to this day the villagers have never been able to discover to which establishment they properly belong.

Master Charles Bates, appalled by Sikes's crime, fell into a train of reflection whether an honest life was not, after all, the best. Arriving at the conclusion that it certainly was, he turned his back upon the scenes of the past, resolved to amend it in some new sphere of action.

He struggled hard and suffered much for some time; but having a contented disposition and a good purpose, succeeded in the end; and, from being a farmer's drudge and a carrier's lad, is now the merriest young grazier[3] in all Northamptonshire.

And now the hand that traces these words falters as it approaches the conclusion of its task, and would weave for a little longer space the thread of these adventures.

I would fain linger yet with a few of those among whom I have so long moved, and share their happiness by endeavouring to depict it. I would show Rose Maylie in all the bloom and grace of early womanhood, shedding upon her secluded path in life such soft and gentle light, as fell on all who trod it with her, and shone into their hearts, – I would paint her the life and joy of the fireside circle and the lively summer group; I would follow her through the sultry fields at noon, and hear the low tones of her sweet voice in the moonlit evening walk; I would watch her in all her goodness and charity abroad, and the smiling untiring discharge of domestic duties at home; I would paint her and her dead sister's child happy in their mutual love, and passing whole hours together in picturing the friends whom they had so sadly lost; I would summon before me once again those joyous little faces that clustered round her knee, and listen to their merry prattle; I would recall the tones of that clear laugh, and conjure up the sympathising tear that glistened in that soft blue eye. These, and a thousand looks and smiles and turns of thought and speech – I would fain recall them every one.

How Mr Brownlow went on from day to day, filling the mind of his adopted child with stores of knowledge, and becoming attached to him more and more as his nature developed itself, and showed the thriving seeds of all he could wish him to become – how he traced in him new traits of his early friend, that awakened in his own bosom old remembrances, melancholy and yet sweet and soothing – how the two orphans, tried by adversity, remembered its lessons in mercy to others, and mutual love, and fervent thanks to Him who had protected and preserved them – these are all matters which need not to be told; for I have said that they were truly happy; and without strong affection, and humanity of heart, and gratitude to that Being whose code is

Rose Maylie and Oliver

mercy, and whose great attribute is benevolence to all things that breathe, true happiness can never be attained.

Within the altar of the old village church there stands a white marble tablet, which bears as yet but one word, – 'Agnes!' There is no coffin in that tomb; and may it be many, many years before another name is placed above it. But if the spirits of the Dead ever come back to earth to visit spots hallowed by the love – the love beyond the grave – of those whom they knew in life, I do believe that the shade of that poor girl often hovers about that solemn nook – ay, though it *is* a church, and she was weak and erring.

THE AUTHOR'S INTRODUCTION TO THE
THIRD EDITION (1841)

'Some of the author's friends cried, "Lookee, gentlemen, the man is a villain; but it is Nature for all that;" and the young critics of the age, the clerks, apprentices, &c., called it low, and fell a groaning.'

FIELDING.[1]

The greater part of this Tale was originally published in a magazine. When I completed it, and put it forth in its present form three years ago, I fully expected it would be objected to on some very high moral grounds in some very high moral quarters.[2] The result did not fail to prove the justice of my anticipations.

I embrace the present opportunity of saying a few words in explanation of my aim and object in its production. It is in some sort a duty with me to do so, in gratitude to those who sympathised with me and divined my purpose at the time, and who, perhaps, will not be sorry to have their impression confirmed under my own hand.

It is, it seems, a very coarse and shocking circumstance, that some of the characters in these pages are chosen from the most criminal and degraded of London's population; that Sikes is a thief, and Fagin a receiver of stolen goods; that the boys are pick-pockets, and the girl is a prostitute.

I confess I have yet to learn that a lesson of the purest good may not be drawn from the vilest evil. I have always believed this to be a recognized and established truth, laid down by the greatest men the world has ever seen, constantly acted upon by the best and wisest natures, and confirmed by the reason and experience of every thinking mind. I saw no reason, when I wrote this book, why the very dregs of life, so long as their speech did not offend the ear, should not serve the purpose of a moral, at least as well as its froth and cream. Nor did I doubt that there lay festering in Saint Giles's as good materials towards the Truth as any flaunting in Saint James's.[3]

In this spirit, when I wished to show, in little Oliver, the principle of Good surviving through every adverse circumstance, and triumphing at last; and when I considered among what companions I could try him best, having regard to that kind of men into whose hands he would most naturally fall; I bethought myself of those who figure in these volumes. When I came to discuss the subject more maturely with myself, I saw many strong reasons for pursuing the course to which I was inclined. I had read of thieves by scores — seductive fellows (amiable for the most part), faultless in dress, plump in pocket, choice in horseflesh, bold in bearing, fortunate in gallantry, great at a song, a bottle, pack of cards or dice-box, and fit companions for the bravest. But I had never met (except in HOGARTH)[4] with the miserable reality. It appeared to me that to draw a knot of such associates in crime as really do exist; to paint them in all their deformity, in all their wretchedness, in all the squalid poverty of their lives; to show them as they really are, for ever skulking uneasily through the dirtiest paths of life, with the great, black, ghastly gallows closing up their prospect, turn them where they may; it appeared to me that to do this, would be to attempt a something which was greatly needed, and which would be a service to society. And therefore I did it, as I best could.

In every book I know, where such characters are treated of at all, certain allurements and fascinations are thrown around them. Even in the Beggars' Opera,[5] the thieves are represented as leading a life which is rather to be envied than otherwise; while MACHEATH, with all the captivations of command, and the devotion of the most beautiful girl and only pure character in the piece, is as much to be admired and emulated by weak beholders, as any fine gentleman in a red coat who has purchased, as VOLTAIRE says, the right to command a couple of thousand men, or so, and to affront death at their head.[6] Johnson's question,[7] whether any man will turn thief because Macheath is reprieved, seems to me beside the matter. I ask myself, whether any man will be deterred from turning thief because of his being sentenced to death, and because of the existence of Peachum and Lockit; and remembering the captain's roaring life, and great appearance, and vast success, and strong advantages, I feel assured that nobody having a bent that way will take any warning from him, or will see anything in the play but a very flowery and pleasant road, conducting an honourable ambition, in course of time, to Tyburn Tree.[8]

In fact, Gay's witty satire on society had a general object, which made him careless of example in this respect, and gave him other, wider, and higher aims. The same may be said of Sir Edward Bulwer's admirable and most powerful novel of Paul Clifford,[9] which cannot be fairly considered as having, or being intended to have, any bearing on this part of the subject, one way or other.

What manner of life is that which is described in these pages, as the every-day existence of a Thief? What charms has it for the young and ill-disposed, what allurements for the most jolter-headed of juveniles? Here are no canterings upon moonlit heaths, no merry-makings in the snuggest of all possible caverns, none of the attractions of dress, no embroidery, no lace, no jack-boots, no crimson coats and ruffles, none of the dash and freedom with which 'the road' has been, time out of mind, invested. The cold, wet, shelterless midnight streets of London; the foul and frowsy dens, where vice is closely packed and lacks the room to turn; the haunts of hunger and disease, the shabby rags that scarcely hold together; where are the attractions of these things? Have they no lesson, and do they not whisper something beyond the little-regarded warning of a moral precept?

But there are people of so refined and delicate a nature, that they cannot bear the contemplation of these horrors. Not that they turn instinctively from crime; but that criminal characters, to suit them, must be, like their meat, in delicate disguise. A Massaroni in green velvet is quite an enchanting creature; but a Sikes in fustian is insupportable. A Mrs Massaroni,[10] being a lady in short petticoats and a fancy dress, is a thing to imitate in tableaux and have in lithograph on pretty songs; but a Nancy, being a creature in a cotton gown and cheap shawl, is not to be thought of. It is wonderful how Virtue turns from dirty stockings; and how Vice, married to ribbons and a little gay attire, changes her name, as wedded ladies do, and becomes Romance.

Now, as the stern and plain truth, even in the dress of this – in novels – much exalted race, was a part of the purpose of this book, I will not, for these readers, abate one hole in the Dodger's coat, or one scrap of curl-paper in the girl's dishevelled hair. I have no faith in the delicacy which cannot bear to look upon them. I have no desire to make proselytes among such people. I have no respect for their opinion, good or bad; do not covet their approval; and do not write for their amusement. I venture to say this without reserve; for I am not aware of any writer in our language having a respect for himself, or held in any respect by his posterity, who has ever descended to the taste of this fastidious class.

On the other hand, if I look for examples, and for precedents, I find them in the noblest range of English literature. Fielding, De Foe, Goldsmith, Smollett, Richardson, Mackenzie[11] – all these for wise purposes, and especially the two first, brought upon the scene the very scum and refuse of the land. Hogarth, the moralist and censor of his age – in whose great works the times in which he lived, and the characters of every time, will never cease to be reflected – did the like, without the compromise of a hair's breadth; with a power and depth of thought which belonged to few men before him, and will probably appertain to fewer still in time to come. Where does this giant stand now in the estimation of his countrymen? and yet, if I turn back to the days in which he or any of these men flourished, I find the same reproach levelled against them every one, each in his turn, by the insects of the hour, who raised their little hum, and died, and were forgotten.

Cervantes[12] laughed Spain's chivalry away, by showing Spain its impossible and wild absurdity. It was my attempt, in my humble and far-distant sphere, to dim the false glitter surrounding something which really did exist, by showing it in its unattractive and repulsive truth. No less consulting my own taste, than the manners of the age, I endeavoured, while I painted it in all its fallen and degraded aspect, to banish from the lips of the lowest character I introduced, any expression that could by possibility offend; and rather to lead to the unavoidable inference that its existence was of the most debased and vicious kind, than to prove it elaborately by words and deeds. In the case of the girl, in particular, I kept this intention constantly in view. Whether it is apparent in the narrative, and how it is executed, I leave my readers to determine.

It has been observed of this girl, that her devotion to the brutal housebreaker does not seem natural, and it has been objected to Sikes in the same breath – with some inconsistency, as I venture to think – that he is surely over-drawn, because in him there would appear to be none of those redeeming traits which are objected to as unnatural in his mistress. Of the latter objection I will merely say, that I fear there are in the world some insensible and callous natures that do become, at last, utterly and irredeemably bad. But whether this be so or not, of one thing I am certain: that there are such men as Sikes, who, being closely followed through the same space of time, and through the same current of circumstances, would not give, by one look or action of a moment, the faintest indication of a better nature. Whether every gentler human feeling is dead within such bosoms, or the proper chord to strike has rusted and is hard to find, I do not know; but that the fact is so, I am sure.

It is useless to discuss whether the conduct and character of the girl seems natural or unnatural, probable or improbable, right or wrong. IT IS TRUE. Every man who has watched these melancholy shades of life knows it to be so. Suggested to my mind long ago – long before I dealt in fiction – by what I often saw and read of, in actual life around me, I have, for years, tracked it through many profligate and noisome ways, and found it still the same. From the first introduction of that poor wretch, to her laying her bloody head upon the robber's breast, there is not one word exaggerated or over-wrought. It is emphatically God's truth, for it is the truth He leaves in such depraved and miserable breasts; the hope yet lingering behind; the last fair drop of water at the bottom of the dried-up weed-choked well. It involves the best and worst shades of our common nature; much of its ugliest hues, and something of its most beautiful; it is a contradiction, an anomaly, an apparent impossibility, but it is a Truth. I am glad to have had it doubted, for in that circumstance I find a sufficient assurance that it needed to be told.

DEVONSHIRE TERRACE,
April, 1841.

APPENDIX B

PREFACE TO THE 'CHEAP EDITION' (1850)

Dickens wrote a special Preface to Oliver Twist *for the Cheap Edition of his novels, at the height of the controversies over sanitary reform in which he was embroiled. His longstanding opponent, Sir Peter Laurie, the former Lord Mayor and proud introducer of a new patented scaffold, whom he had previously satirized in* The Chimes *(1844), incorrectly alleged in February 1850 that Dickens had admitted Jacob's Island 'ONLY existed in a work of fiction'. Dickens's Preface, written in the same month, ironically retorts by turning against Laurie himself his apparent reasoning that whatever appeared in a work of fiction could not be fact. (For Jacob's Island, see III, 12 and notes.)*

At page 267 of this present edition of OLIVER TWIST, there is a description of 'the filthiest, the strangest, the most extraordinary, of the many localities that are hidden in London.' And the name of this place is JACOB'S ISLAND.

Eleven or twelve years have elapsed, since the description was first published. I was as well convinced then, as I am now, that nothing effectual can be done for the elevation of the poor in England, until their dwelling-places are made decent and wholesome. I have always been convinced that this Reform must precede all other Social Reforms; that it must prepare the way for Education, even for Religion; and that, without it, those classes of the people which increase the fastest, must become so desperate and be made so miserable, as to bear within themselves the certain seeds of ruin to the whole community.

The Metropolis (of all places under Heaven) being excluded from the provisions of the Public Health Act, passed last year, a society has been formed called the Metropolitan Sanitary Association, with the view of remedying this grievous mistake. The association held its first public meeting at Freemason's Hall, on Wednesday the sixth of February last: the Bishop of London presiding. It happened that this very place, JACOB'S ISLAND, had lately attracted the attention of the Board of Health, in consequence of its having been ravaged by cholera; and that the Bishop of London had in his hands the result of an inquiry under the Metropolitan Sewers Commission, shewing, by way of proof of the cheapness of sanitary improvements, an estimate of the probable cost at which the houses in JACOB'S ISLAND could be rendered fit for human habitation – which cost was stated at about a penny three farthings per week per house. The Bishop referred to this paper, with the moderation and forbearance which pervaded all his observations, and did me the honour to mention that I had described JACOB'S ISLAND. When I subsequently made a few observations myself, I confessed that soft impeachment.

Now, the vestry of Marylebone parish, meeting on the following Saturday, had the honour to be addressed by SIR PETER LAURIE; a gentleman of infallible authority, of great innate modesty, and of a most sweet humanity. This remarkable alderman, as I am informed by *The Observer* newspaper, then and there delivered himself (I quote the passage without any correction) as follows:

'Having touched upon the point of saving to the poor, he begged to illustrate it by reading for them the particulars of a survey that had been made in a locality called "Jacob's Island" – [a laugh] – where, according to the surveyor, 1,300 houses were erected on forty acres of ground. The surveyor asserted and laid down that each house could be supplied with a constant supply of pure water – secondly, that each house could be supplied with a sink – thirdly, a water-closet – fourthly, a drain – fifthly, a foundation drain – and, sixthly, the accommodation of a dust bin [laughter], and all at the average rate of 13s. 4d. per week [oh, oh, and laughter].

'Mr G. Bird: Can Sir Peter Laurie tell the vestry where "Jacob's Island" is [laughter].

'Sir P. Laurie: That was just what he was about to tell them. The Bishop of London, poor soul, in his simplicity, thought there really was such a place, which he had been describing so minutely, *whereas it turned out that it ONLY existed in a work of fiction, written by Mr Charles Dickens ten years ago* [roars of laughter]. *The fact was admitted by Mr Charles Dickens himself at the meeting*, and he (Sir P. Laurie) had extracted his words from the same paper, the

Morning Herald. Mr Dickens said "Now the first of these classes proceeded generally on the supposition that the compulsory improvement of these dwellings, when exceedingly defective, would be very expensive. But that was a great mistake, for nothing was cheaper than good sanitary improvements, as they knew in this case of 'Jacob's Island' [laughter], which he had described in a work of fiction some ten or eleven years ago." '

When I came to read this, I was so much struck by the honesty, by the truth, and by the wisdom of this logic, as well as by the fact of the sagacious vestry, including members of parliament, magistrates, officers, chemists, and I know not who else listening to it meekly (as became them), that I resolved to record the fact here, as a certain means of making it known to, and causing it to be reverenced by, many thousands of people. Reflecting upon this logic, and its universal application; remembering that when FIELDING described Newgate, the prison immediately ceased to exist; that when SMOLLETT took Roderick Random to Bath, that city instantly sank into the earth; that when SCOTT exercised his genius on Whitefriars, it incontinently glided into the Thames; that an ancient place called Windsor was entirely destroyed in the reign of Queen Elizabeth by two Merry Wives of that town, acting under the direction of a person of the name of SHAKESPEARE; and that MR POPE, after having at a great expense completed his grotto at Twickenham,[1] incautiously reduced it to ashes by writing a poem upon it; – I say, when I came to consider these things, I was inclined to make this preface the vehicle of my humble tribute of admiration to SIR PETER LAURIE. But, I am restrained by a very painful consideration – by no less a consideration than the impossibility of *his* existence. For SIR PETER LAURIE having been himself described in a book (as I understand he was, one Christmas time, for his conduct on the seat of Justice), it is but too clear that there CAN be no such man!

Otherwise, I should have been quite sure of his concurrence in the following passage, written thirty years ago by my late lamented friend the Reverend SYDNEY SMITH,[2] that great master of wit, and terror of noodles; but singularly applicable to the present occasion.

'We have been thus particular in stating the case, that we may make an answer to those profligate persons who are always ready to fling an air of ridicule upon the labours of humanity, because they are desirous that what they have not the virtue to do themselves, should appear to be foolish and romantic when done by others. A still higher degree of depravity than this, is to want every sort of compassion for human misery, when it is accompanied by filth, poverty, and ignorance. To regulate humanity by the income tax, and to deem the bodily wretchedness and the dirty tears of the poor, a fit subject for pleasantry and contempt. We should have been loth to believe that such deep-seated and disgusting immorality existed in these days; but the notice of it is forced upon us.'

DEVONSHIRE TERRACE

March, 1850.

GLOSSARY OF THIEVES' CANT AND SLANG
AND SOME UNUSUAL WORDS

'He then in cant terms, with which his whole conversation was plentifully besprinkled, but which would be quite unintelligible if they were recorded here, demanded a glass of liquor' (I, 13). Dickens uses cant terms much less heavily, in particular with Bill Sikes, than his contemporary and friend William Harrison Ainsworth in his gothic historical novel *Rookwood* (1834), where Dick Turpin the legendary highwayman and his associates from the *Newgate Calendar*, as well as a picturesque crew of gypsies, speak and even sing in 'flash' a good deal, mostly to comic effect.

Rookwood may indeed be one source for Dickens in this respect, though also a case to react against. Of the cant terms in this glossary, by my rough count, nearly half are used by Ainsworth; his characters revel in their patois, rejoicing 'in our own respective names, as High Pads and Low Pads, Rum Gills and Queer Gills, Patricos, Palliads, Priggers, Whip Jacks, and Jarkmen, from the Arch Rogue to the Needy Mizzler . . .' (II, p.331). Dick Turpin tells a lady at one point, 'I want a little ready cash in Rumville' – then apologizes: 'beg pardon, Ma'am, London I mean; but my ears have been so stunned with those Romany patterers, I almost *think* in flash' (III, p.27 – 'Romany' meaning 'gypsy'). A good deal of Ainsworth's knowledge may be antiquarian and bookish; at one point he gives what amounts to a learned reference for a piece of cant: '(*crede* [take it on the authority of] James Hardy Vaux)' (III, p.212) – Vaux, an ex-convict, being the author of 'A new and comprehensive vocabulary of the flash language' (1812).

Though consulting throughout Kathleen Tillotson's pioneering glossary in the Clarendon edition of *Oliver Twist*, I have quoted where possible definitions from Dickens's own period, trying to give more of the flavour of the period and milieu, and more sense of how Dickens actively manipulates a language which is drawn both from the street and from a long lexicographical tradition. I have tried to avoid an excessive reliance on context and thus sometimes on guesswork in determining meanings.

Where Fagin describes how an imprisoned criminal can be brought to betray his associates – 'grabbed, trapped, tried, earwigged by the parson, and brought to it on bread and water' (III, 9) – 'earwigged' has been glossed by previous editors as 'to coax into confessing', or 'to worm a confidence out of someone'. 'Coax' and 'worm' are in the right area, but I have found no source to justify the further 'confessing' and 'confidence', which also render Dickens's phrasing tautological. I cite two sources to convey the metaphorical and associative force of Dickens's word (see entry below).

I have been careful to maintain the dictionary-makers' distinction, nicely put by John Camden Hotten in 1860: 'CANT, apart from religious hypocrisy, refers to the old secret language, by allegory or distinct terms, of Gipseys, thieves, tramps, and beggars. SLANG represents that evanescent, vulgar language, ever changing with fashion and taste, which has principally come into vogue during the last seventy or eighty years, spoken by persons in every grade of life, rich and poor, honest and dishonest' (*A Dictionary of Modern Slang, Cant, and Vulgar Words*, p. 6). I have mostly accepted Partridge's authority as to whether a given usage is cant or slang at the time of *Oliver Twist* (though the fashion for low life, in for instance Pierce Egan's *Life in London* (1821), and the 'Newgate Novel', was bringing many cant terms into general currency). Many of the historical instances and definitions quoted derive from Partridge's awe-inspiring *Dictionary of the Underworld*. I have also referred to the *Oxford English Dictionary* ('*OED*', 10 vols., 1884–1928), especially for recondite words not strictly cant or slang.

I give the page-reference for the first occurrence of the words glossed, on the ground that Dickens's vocabulary is of interest in its own right.

ABBREVIATIONS

Farmer   John S. Farmer and W. E. Henley, *Slang and its Analogues, Past and Present: A Dictionary, Historical and Comparative, of the Heterodox Speech of All Classes of Society for More than Three Hundred Years* (London: 1890–1903)

Grose   Captain Francis Grose (1730/31–91), *A Classical Dictionary of the Vulgar Tongue* (3rd edn, 1796; reprinted London: Scholartis Press, 1931)

Hotten   John Camden Hotten, *A Dictionary of modern slang, cant, and vulgar words, used at the present day in the streets of London, the universities, etc.*, 2nd edn (London: 1860)

Kent   E. Kent, *A modern Flash Dictionary* (1825?), in *Sinks of London Laid Open: A Pocket Companion for the Uninitiated, to which is added a Modern Flash Dictionary containing all the Cant Words, Slang Terms and Flash Phrases now in vogue, with A List of the Sixty Orders of Prime Coves, The whole Forming a True Picture of London Life, Cadging Made Easy, the He-She Man, Doings of the Modern Greeks, Snooking Kens Depicted, the Common Lodging-house Gallants, Lessons to Lovers of Dice, the Gaming Table, etc. Embellished with Humorous Illustrations by George Cruikshank* (London: J. Duncombe, 1848)

Lexicon   Grose, *Classical Dictionary*, reprinted as *Lexicon Balatronicum* (1811; reprinted with a foreword by Max Harris (London: Papermac, 1981))

Partridge   Eric Partridge, *A Dictionary of Slang and Unconventional English*, rev. (London: 1949)

Underworld   Eric Partridge, *A Dictionary of the Underworld, British and American: Being the Vocabularies of Crooks, Criminals, Racketeers; Beggars and Tramps; Convicts; The Commercial Underworld; The Drug Traffic; The White Slave Traffic; Spivs* (London: Routledge & Kegan Paul, 1949)

Vaux   James Hardy Vaux, 'A new and comprehensive vocabulary of the flash language' (1812) *airy* [377] area (i.e. open well in front of town house; e.g. 'tossing them down areas' (I, 10)) (classed by Farmer as 'vulgar').

barkers [178] pistols. Not recorded before Scott, *Guy Mannering* (1815) ('barkers and slashers'), but cf. Grose: 'BARKING IRONS. Pistols, from their explosion resembling the bow-wow or barking of a dog.'

beak [61] magistrate (formerly policeman). (*Underworld*: 'Origin: the prominent noses of dominant magistrates and judges.')

big-wig [364] evidently used here to mean barrister. (*Underworld*: 'A magistrate . . . With a ref. to a judge's wig.')

bit or drop [399] evidently food or drink: cf. Charles Kingsley, *The Water Babies* (1863): 'Some one will give me a bit and a sup' (not cant).

blab, to [104] Kent: 'to nose, to chatter, to tell secrets'.

blow upon, to [99] to inform upon or betray; or [as p. 156] give away by mistake. (*Underworld*: '*Blow up*, v. To reveal the illicit practices or activities of (a person, a gang, a house, a neighborhood).')

blowing-up [by women] [168] scolding or telling-off (colloquial).

blunt [250] ready money (cant).

bob [61] shilling (formerly cant; *Underworld*: 'by 1830 at latest, it was slang').

booby [224] Samuel Johnson, *A Dictionary of the English Language*, 2 vols. (1755): 'A dull, heavy, stupid fellow: a lubber'.

booty, to play [68] to play falsely, betray (by 'cheating play, where the player purposely avoids winning' (Grose)).

bounceably [226] swaggeringly (Kent: 'Bounceable, proud, saucy'; Grose: to bounce is to brag or hector).

castor [202] man's hat (slang).

centre-bit [157] *OED*: 'An instrument turning on a projecting centre-point, used for making cylindrical holes. (Noted as a burglar's tool.)'

cleaned out [324] Vaux: 'said of a gambler who has lost his last stake at play; also, of a flat who has been stript of all his money' (slang).

codger, old [361] with 'old': an old fellow (low colloquialism, usually grotesque or whimsical).

Common Garden [160] Covent Garden (slang).

Conkey [249] Hotten: 'CONKY, having a projecting or remarkable nose.'

cove, covey [60] Grose: 'A man, a fellow, a rogue'. Often in combinations, e.g. 'Flash-Cove = a thief or swindler', 'Downy-Cove = shrewd man' (Farmer).

crack [177] burglary (Grose: 'The Crack Lay, of late is used, in the cant language, to signify the art and mystery of house-breaking').

crack, to [157] *Underworld*: 'to break open burglariously'.

cracksman [202] *Lexicon*: 'The kiddy is a clever cracksman; the young fellow is a very expert house-breaker' (cant).

crape [179] *OED* sb. 2b.: 'A piece of crape drawn over the face as a disguise'; *The Examiner* (1813): 'He [a highwayman] pulled down a crape over his face.'

crib [119] Vaux: 'A house, sometimes applied to shops' (cant).

cry [404] *OED* sb. 7: 'Rumour, public report'; a 'cry' is also a pack of dogs.

cut, to [202]; *cutting away* [365]; *cut off* [318] to run away, to make off (slang).

darkies (darky or darkee) [179] bull's-eyes, or 'dark lanthorn[s] used by housebreakers' (*Lexicon*) (cant).

dodge, to [377]; *dodged, get* [323]; *Dodger* [62] follow; get followed; follower. *Underworld*: '"to track one in a stealthy manner" (as in Dickens's *Oliver Twist*), is not, I think, cant; probably slang. In *The London Guide*, 1818, it is defined as "to follow at a distance". There is undoubtedly some reference to or reminiscence of "to *dog*".'

downiest [148] most artful; most knowing. (*Underworld*: '*downy cove*, "a shrewd or very alert fellow".' Partridge thinks probably not cant but slang, possibly from boxing.)

drain [178] drink (usually gin; from *c.* 1800) (slang).

earwigged [392] pestered or influenced. Hotten: 'EARWIG, a clergyman, also one who prompts another maliciously.' (Farmer: 'From the popular delusion that the earwig lodges itself in the ear with a view to working its way into the brain when it causes death' (slang).)

Ecod [174; cf. ''Cod', 350] a mild oath, possibly from 'Egad' (itself probably from 'Ah God!').

family [250] Vaux: 'Thieves, sharpers, and all others who get their living *upon the cross* [by dishonest means], are comprehended under the title of "*The Family*".'

fancy-work [358] Exact meaning unclear. Hotten: 'the paramour of a prostitute is still called her FANCY-MAN' (slang). Tillotson's speculation, followed by most subsequent editors, 'living on the proceeds of prostitution' seems based on Farmer, quoted in *OED*, to take in fancy work, 'to be addicted to secret prostitution'. If this *is* Fagin's meaning, Noah either ignores or misses it. A fancy-house is a brothel.

fence [98] Grose: 'FENCE, or FENCING CULLY [= rogue]. A receiver of stolen goods.'

file, old; file [202] Formerly a pickpocket (cant); Vaux declares this sense obsolete. But *Lexicon*: 'A person who has had a long course of experience in the arts of fraud, so as to have become an adept, is termed *an old file upon the town*.'

flash [61] *OED*: 'Connected with or pertaining to the class of thieves, tramps, and prostitutes'. Or knowing, wide-awake, 'smart', 'fly' (slang). Or gaudy, dashing, ostentatious.

flat [150] *Underworld*: 'A dupe, a gullible person . . . Hence, any person ignorant of the wiles of the underworld' (cant).

fogles [150]; *fogle-hunter* [79] silk handkerchiefs (possibly from Italian, *foglia*, a leaf); stealer of handkerchiefs (Bulwer-Lytton, *Paul Clifford* (1830): 'Who's here so base as would be a *fogle-hunter*?').

fork out, to [61] to produce money (Grose: 'FORK. A pickpocket. Let us fork him; let us pick his pocket') (*Underworld* says low slang, not cant).

gallows [79] (as noun) From Grose: 'GALLOWS BIRD. A thief, or pickpocket; also one that associates with them' (slang); (as adverb, p. 542); implied [154] Hotten: 'very, or exceedingly – a disgusting exclamation; "GALLOWS poor," very poor.'

gammon [118] Hotten: 'deceit, humbug, a false and ridiculous story' (slang).

glim [127] Grose: 'A candle, or dark lantern, used in housebreaking.'

grabbed [129] Hotten: 'caught, apprehended'.

green [61] Hotten: 'ignorant, not wide awake, inexperienced'.

Greenland [64] the land of greenhorns (earlier than first recorded use in *Underworld*).

grub [61] Grose: 'Victuals. To grub: to dine'.

heavy-swell [128] *Underworld*: swell, 'n. [As] a "gentleman", "a well-dressed man", seems to have been cant until c. 1815.' But *OED* cites Lady Glanville's *Letters* (1830): 'The people at Melton ... asking "who's that heavy swell?"'

Jack Ketch [210] Grose: 'a general name for the finishers of the law, or hangmen, ever since the year 1682, when the office was filled by a famous practitioner of that name [*fl.* 1663–86], of whom his wife said, that any bungler might put a man to death, but only her husband knew how to make a gentleman die sweetly.'

japanning [146] making black and glossy (here, blacking boots; from the colour of varnished and decorated 'japan' ware).

jemmies [169] Crowbars: 'A crow(bar). This instrument is much used by housebreakers. Sometimes called Jemmy Rook' (*Lexicon* 1820). Also, though not thieves' cant but sporting slang, sheeps' heads: 'JEMMY (bloody) – a sheep's head; so called from a great dealer in these delicious *morceaux*' (Jon. Bee [John Badcock], *Dictionary of the Turf* (1823)).

jiggered [100] *OED*: 'Used as a vague substitute for a profane oath or imprecation, especially in asseverations. (Only in passive)'. The first citation is Marryat (1837); the second, *Great Expectations*: 'This penalty of being jiggered was a favourite suppositious case of his. He attached no definite meaning to the word that I am aware of' (ch. xvii).

ken [104] house (recorded 1566); a flash ken: Grose: 'a house that harbours thieves'.

kennel [74] street gutter.

kinchin lay, the [358] *Underworld*: 'Robbing children – especially young
 or innocent children – of their money as they walk along the street
 with it in their hands, and then jostling them to make it appear that
 they have fallen down.'

kinchins [358] 'a little child'. (B.E., *A New Dictionary of the Terms
 Ancient and Modern of the Canting Crew* (London: W. Hawes,
 1699).)

lagged, lagging [129] transported; transportation (as convict) (*Lexicon*:
 'The cove was lagged for a drag. The man was transported for
 stealing something out of a waggon.').

lay [358] Grose: 'Enterprise, pursuit or attempt'; an underworld scheme
 or means of livelihood.

lay, on the [325] on the job, engaged in crime.

leg-bail, to give someone [160] to escape someone; literally, to be
 indebted to one's legs for flight (Grose: 'To give leg-bail and
 land-security; to run away' (according to *OED*, 'jocular')).

life-preserver [155] *OED*: 'A stick or bludgeon loaded with lead,
 intended for self-defence. Often referred to as a frequent weapon
 of burglars.' *Annual Register* (1837): 'The prisoner was given in
 charge to the police, a life-preserver having been found upon him.'

lifer [362] Hotten: 'A convict who is sentenced to transportation *for
 life*'.

line, to get into a [156] Vaux: 'To *get* a person *in a line*, or *in a string*,
 is to engage them in a conversation, while your confederate is
 robbing their person or premises'; here, probably, to persuade to
 become an accomplice in a crime (a sense not recorded in any of
 the period sources).

lucky, made our [149] escaped (low slang).

lummy [362] first-class (low slang).

lushed [321] drank (*Lexicon*: 'To lush at Freeman's quay; to drink at
 another's cost').

magpie [61] halfpenny (probably from *mag* or *meg*, a halfpenny) (*Oliver
 Twist* is first instance in *Underworld* of this sense).

mill, on the [61] the treadmill: Dickens may also have in mind an old sense, cited in *Underworld*: 'those that go upon the *Mill*, which are called House-Breakers' (1676, Anon.).

milled [200] jailed, sent to the treadmill (*Oliver Twist* is first instance in *Underworld* of this sense).

morrice, to [61] to decamp, get going (Kent: 'Morriss off, to run away'; Goldsmith, *She Stoops to Conquer* (1773): 'Zounds, here they are! Morrice! Prance! (*Exit Hastings*)') (slang).

move [149] motive of scheme (Vaux: 'the secret spring by which any project is conducted, as, There is a *move* in that Business which you are not *down to*.').

mug [177] the face (slang).

mull [see p. 548] Farmer: 'a muddle: a result of mismanagement' (colloquial or slang). Pierce Egan, *Life in London* (1821): 'Somebody must make a mull – but Randall's the man.'

murrain [303] a plague. *OED*: 'In imprecations . . . "may a murrain or pestilence fall upon (some one)".'

nabbed [371] 'B. E.', *The Canting Crew* (1699): '*Nab'd*, Apprehended . . . or Arrested'.

nightcap [118] A horse's nightcap is a halter; to die in a horse's nightcap, to be hanged (low slang).

pad the hoof, to [71] to walk (Anon., *The New Fol de rol Tit* (or *The Flash Man of St Giles*) (*c.* 1773): 'I padded the hoof for many miles / To show the strength of my flame').

passengers [123] in former sense, *OED*: 'a passer by or through', or 'a traveller (usually on foot), a wayfarer'.

paviour [77] one who paves, or lays pavements.

peach, to; peached [67] to turn informer; informed. (Grose: 'To impeach; called also to blow the gab, squeak, or turn stag' (slang).)

persuaders [178] Kent: 'Persuaders, cudgels or spurs' (slang).

pins [61] legs (slang).

plant [156]; *a prime plant* [74] a criminal scheme; a fine target for plunder (Vaux: 'A person's money, or valuables, secreted about his house or person, is called his plant').

play booty, to [68] to play falsely, betray; seems a metaphorical application of gambling cant term: *Underworld*: 'to play with intention to lose, so that one shares in one's opponent's winnings from that simpleton whom one has partnered'.

Plummy [63] *Lexicon*: 'It is all plummy; i.e. all is right, or as it ought to be'; here in phrase as password (see also 'slam').

pound it, I'll [207] I'll wager (from cockfights) (slang).

prad [244] Bee's *Dictionary of the Turf* (1823): '*Prads* – are riding-horses of any description, ponies included' (cant).

prig [147] Humphrey Potter, *A New Dictionary of All the Cod and Flash Languages* (London: B. Crosby, 1797): '*Prigg*, a pickpocket'.

put up [211] *OED*: '(Hunting) To cause (game) to rise from cover; to rouse, start'.

put-up job, put-up thing [156] Vaux: '*Put up Affair*, any preconcerted plan or scheme to effect a robbery, &c., undertaken at the suggestion of another person, who possessing a knowledge of the premises, is competent to advise the principal how best to succeed'.

row, what's the [60] what's the matter? (slang).

sack; insert his hand in a sack [198] a pocket; pick a pocket (Grose: 'To dive into the sack; to pick a pocket').

scouts [404] Farmer: 'a spy, esp. a police-spy'.

scragged [150] hanged. Partridge, in his edition of Grose: 'the hanging terms are all cant: *scrag* or *crag*, a neck; *scragboy*, hangman; *scrag*, *scrag-squeeʒer*, *scragging-post*, the gallows; *scrag'em Fair*, a public execution'.

sell [208] an act of betrayal; Vaux: 'To *sell* a man is to betray him, by giving information against him, or otherwise to injure him clandestinely for the sake of interest . . . A man who falls a victim to any treachery of this kind, is said to have been *sold like a bullock in Smithfield*.'

shaver [368] Grose: 'A cunning shaver; a subtle fellow, one who trims close, an acute cheat. A young shaver; a boy. *Sea term*' (slang not cant, according to Partridge).

shell [223] *OED*: 'A wooden coffin, especially a rough or temporary

one. Also a thin coffin of lead or other material to be enclosed in a
more substantial one.'

shiners [157] guineas (21 shillings); or after *c.* 1825, sovereigns (£1, or
20 shillings).

shopped [125] Grose: 'SHOP. A prison. Shopped; confined, imprisoned.'

slam [63] a trick, a swindling piece of cheating; used as password (see
also 'plummy').

sneaking-way [358] to sneak is to pilfer (John Poulter, *Discoveries*
(1753): '*I'm a Sneak for Chinks or Feeders*; I'm a Thief for Tankards
and Spoons').

sneeze-box [362] snuff-box. 'Sneezing-coffer' and 'sneezing-scoop' were
also cant terms for a snuff-box; *Oliver Twist* is the earliest instance
of 'sneeze-box' in *OED*.

split upon, to [201] Vaux: 'To *split upon* a person, or *turn split*, is
synonymous with *nosing*, *snitching*, or *turning nose*. To *split* signifies
generally to tell of any thing you hear, or see transacted.'

spring-gun [252] *OED*: 'A gun capable of being discharged by one
coming in contact with it, or with a wire or the like attached to the
trigger; formerly used as a guard against trespassers or poachers,
and placed in concealment for this purpose.' (It was made illegal
by an Act of Parliament in 1827.)

stick up to, to [200] *OED*: '*Dialect*: to make love to.'

Stone Jug [363] Grose: 'Newgate, or any other prison'. (Hence 'jug'
for gaol.) Vaux: 'Newgate in London is called by various names,
as the *pitcher*, *the stone pitcher*, *the start*, and *the stone jug*, according
to the humour of the speaker.'

stones, [to get] *off the* [160] to get out of London.

'Stow [118] leave off, withhold. (Grose: 'Stow you; be silent, or hold
your peace. Stow your whidds [words] and plant 'em, for the cove
of the ken can cant 'em: you have said enough, the man of the
house understands you.')

stump, to [61] to pay, hand over (slang).

swag [160] Vaux: 'Booty . . . of any kind . . . except money'. Related
to 'Grose: A shop. Rum swag; a shop full of rich goods.'

swell see 'heavy swell'.

swipes [324] flat or small beer. Joseph Wright, *English Dialect Dictionary*

(1898–1905): 'The name given by the seamen to the beer that (in the Navy) was formerly issued as a ration. The quantity was generous – four quarts a day while it lasted – but the quality and conditions were appalling.' (slang).

tickers [150] watches. *The Oracle* (1800): 'They secured three gold tickers'.

time of day [167] the right way (rhyming slang) (Kent: 'Time o' day, quite right, the thing').

tinkler [119] bell. (*Underworld*: 'As "a bell", this has never, I think, been English cant, despite Dickens's apparent belief (see *Oliver Twist*, 1838) that it was.')

togs [128] Potter (1797): '*Toges* or *toggs*, cloaths for both sexes' (cant).

top-sawyer [363] Barrère & Leland, *Dictionary of Slang, Jargon and Cant*, 2 vols. (Edinburgh: Ballantyne Press, 1889–90): 'an expert thief' (according to Partridge, not cant but slang).

town-maders [357] Perhaps from 'town-made', 'made or manufactured in a town' (*OED*).

traps [97] Vaux: '*Traps*, police officers, or runners, are properly so called; but it is common to include constables of any description under this title.'

trotter-cases [146] (or 'trotting-cases') boots or shoes (low slang).

up, to be; up to [168] *Underworld* quotes Humphrey Potter's *Dictionary* (1797). '*Upp*, being acquainted with what is going forward', and says, '*up to*, "equal to", "alert to the tricks or the illicit or criminal intentions of"', may itself have, originally, been cant'.

up, it's all [224], *U. P., it's all* [193] *OED*, up (adv) 12e: '*All up*, completely done or finished; quite over' (earliest example given is 1825). Also in euphemistic or emphatic form, 'U. P.'

when the wind's low [61] when money is short (Grose: 'To raise the wind; to procure money').

Winkin [148] Meaning obscure. Grose: 'to tip one the wink; to give a signal by winking the eye.' 'Like winkin': suddenly or vigorously.

wipes [64] handkerchiefs, usually cotton (cant; replaced *wiper c.* 1790)
  (Grose: 'WIPER DRAWER. A pickpocket, one who steals handkerchiefs').
wittles [148] Cockney for victuals; food.

younker [177] Hotten: 'in street language, a lad or boy'.

APPENDIX D

LIST OF CHAPTERS

CONTENTS

BOOK THE FIRST

478

BOOK THE SECOND

MAP OF LONDON IN 1837

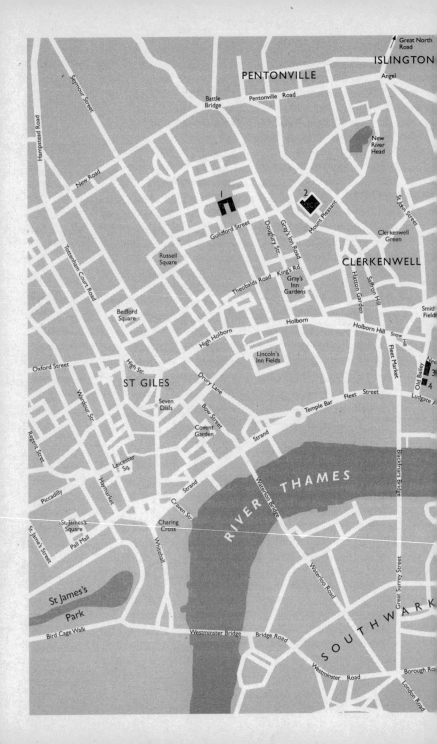

New North Road

Hackney Road

City Road

Bethnal Green Road

Old Street

City Road

Shoreditch

Kingsland Road

BETHNAL

GREEN

Finsbury
Square

Barbican

Brick Lane

Aldersgate Str.

London Wall

Moorfields

Finsbury
Circus

Bishopsgate Street

Petticoat Lane

Whitechapel Road

London Wall

Houndsditch

Whitechapel Road

Commercial Road

Str.

6

Cheapside

5

Watling Str.

Cornhill

Lombard Str.

Aldgate High Str.

Fenchurch Street

Minories

Cable Street

Queen Str.

Cannon Str.

Rosemary Lane

Wellclose
Square

Upper Thames Street

7

Lower Thames Street

Tower
of London

East Smithfield

London
Docks

Bank Side

Southwark Bridge

London Bridge

St Catherine's
Dock

RIVER THAMES

Bridge Str.

Tooley Street

Jacob's Island

Borough High Street

Lant Str.

8

Bermondsey Street

Newington Road

Long Lane

1 Foundling Hospital
2 House of Correction
3 Newgate Prison
4 Central Criminal Court

5 St Paul's Cathedral
6 General Post Office
7 Monument
8 Marshalsea Prison

NOTES

The following notes are indebted to ranks of previous editors; though it may be invidious to name any in particular, it would be wrong not to mention Kathleen Tillotson, the foremost authority on *Oliver Twist*; the editors of the Pilgrim Edition of *The Letters of Charles Dickens*; Dennis Walder, editor of the Penguin Classics *Sketches by Boz*; Peter Fairclough, editor of the previous Penguin Classics edition of *Oliver Twist*; Edward Guiliano and Philip Collins, editors of *The Annotated Dickens*; Stephen Gill, editor of the Oxford World's Classics edition; and for much rich detail, David Paroissien, author of the extraordinary *Companion to 'Oliver Twist'*, a provocative treasure-house of research and speculation.

Abbreviations:

Dixon   W. Hepworth Dixon, *The London Prisons* (London: 1850)
DJ   *Dickens' Journalism*, ed. Michael Slater, 4 vols. (London: J. M. Dent, 1993–)
Fitzgerald   Percy Fitzgerald, *Bozland: Dickens' Places and People* (London: —, 1895)
OED   *The Oxford English Dictionary*, 10 vols. (1884–1928)
Paroissien   David Paroissien, *Companion to 'Oliver Twist'* (Edinburgh: Edinburgh University Press, 1992)

Most modern readers need help with Britain's pre-decimal currency, pounds, shillings and pence (£.s.d.). There were 20 shillings to a pound, and 12 pence to a shilling. A farthing was the smallest coin, a quarter of a penny; there were also halfpennies, pennies, threepenny bits, sixpenny pieces, shillings, florins (two-shilling pieces), half-crowns and crowns (two-shilling-and-six-penny and five-shilling pieces); and then sovereigns worth one pound.

For identification of the editions of *Oliver Twist*, see Selected Textual Variants, p. 535.

[BOOK THE FIRST]

CHAPTER THE FIRST

TREATS OF THE PlACE WHERE OLIVER TWIST
WAS BORN

1. *the town of Mudfog*: The town which conditions Oliver Twist's early years is only named once, and only in *Bentley's Miscellany*, the text used here (other occurrences in the manuscript are cancelled). From the three-volume first edition (*1838*) it becomes 'a certain town which for many reasons it will be prudent to refrain from mentioning, and to which I will assign no fictitious name'. In the previous (first) number of *Bentley's Miscellany* (January 1837) – of which he was editor – Dickens had contributed 'Public Life of Mr Tulrumble, Once Mayor of Mudfog', using the name for a riverside town with 'an agreeable scent of pitch, tar, coals, and rope-yarn', probably based on Chatham, in Kent, south-east of London (where Dickens had lived for five years as a child). That piece concludes, 'Perhaps, at some future period, we may venture to open the chronicles of Mudfog', but the shared name seems a red herring: the novel's Mudfog turns out to be about 75 miles north of London, beyond Barnet on the Great North Road (see note 3 to I, 8). Fitzgerald identified it as either Peterborough or Grantham. Alfred Rimmer (*About England with Dickens*) favours Peterborough, but also mentions Market Harborough. Kathleen Tillotson suggested Northampton and Kettering. All these are some way inland, though Grantham, Peterborough and Market Harborough were all linked to the busy canal network.

2. *workhouse*: Since 1601 England had had houses of correction for the poor and miscreants, and since 1647 'houses of industry' of a less punitive kind, where the poor could labour profitably. The Poor Law Amendment Act, or New Poor Law, of 1834 (hereafter '1834 Act'), following the recommendations of a commission appointed two years earlier, made changes which are reflected in the early chapters of *Oliver Twist*. Disturbed by the increase in the taxation burden of the poor rate, the commissioners found that 'the great source of abuse was the outdoor relief afforded to the able-bodied on their own account or on that of their families, given either in kind or in money'. The Act reinforced the distinction made under the original statute, dating from the reign of Elizabeth I, between relief to all able-bodied persons given in workhouses, and 'outdoor relief' (allowing a pauper to live at home) given only to the demonstrably 'impotent'. Many austere new workhouses were erected as a result of the 1834 Act; the one in Mudfog appears however to predate it. The Act cut the cost of relief from £7 million in 1831 to £4.6 million ten years later.

3. *item of mortality*: 'Bills of mortality', periodically published, gave official returns of the deaths in particular districts. Beginning in 1592, they were brought out weekly for 109 parishes in the London area by the London Company of Parish Clerks (Paroissien).

4. *the parish surgeon*: Parishes often made arrangements with local surgeons, usually those putting forward the lowest tenders, and frequently incompetent or inexperienced, to provide medical attention for all in the workhouse. Until 1745 surgeons had been classed, demeaningly, with barbers, as treating only external ailments; physicians, more trained and educated, monopolized internal ills. The third category of medical practitioner, the apothecaries, dispensed drugs; in the first half of the nineteenth century they were coming under increasing regulation.

5. *gruel*: A kind of porridge made with oatmeal, groats or grits (ground Indian corn).

6. *by the overseer's order*: The office of parish overseer, created in 1597, involved responsibility for making, assessing, collecting and distributing the fund for the relief of the poor.

CHAPTER THE SECOND

TREATS OF OLIVER TWIST'S GROWTH

1. *brought up by hand*: Hand-fed from a bottle, rather than breast-fed.

2. *'farmed,'* ... *poor-laws*: A local matron, that is, has contracted with the parish to take care of a number of infants. The 1834 Act attempted to reform the existing often corrupt and scandalous system, but there was much local variation and many diverse institutions were permitted under it, with great freedom to be as generous or as mean as they pleased. It was contradictory in its view of workhouses, wishing them to be humane to the ailing and helpless, but also, punitively, to deter by unpleasantness the able-bodied poor. Children were often placed in the already existing baby-farms, where the mortality rate, in large towns, could be as high as 90%.

3. *finding in the lowest depth a deeper still*: Compare Satan in Milton's *Paradise Lost* (1667), IV, 75–8: 'Which way I fly is Hell; myself am Hell; / And in the lowest deep a lower deep / Still threat'ning to devour me opens wide, / To which the Hell I suffer seems a Heav'n.'

4. *experimental philosopher . . . horse being able to live without eating*: A scientist, in particular an adherent of the 'political science' or 'political economy' which is Dickens's target in these early chapters and which was partly embodied in the 1834 Act – based on a commission report by Edwin Chadwick (1800–1890), former secretary of the great Utilitarian thinker Jeremy Bentham (1748–1832). See also note 7 to I, 4. The Act resembled proposals in Bentham's unfinished *Constitutional Code* (published 1830–41). The experimental philosopher who starves his horse is apparently a fictitious case, but in the spirit of early-nineteenth-century experimentation on animals.

5. *the beadle*: An elaborately-uniformed parish official whose duties included operating the poor laws, keeping order in church and punishing minor offenders. Cf. the first chapter ('The Beadle – The Parish Engine – The Schoolmaster') of *Sketches by Boz* (1836–7): 'The parish beadle is one of the most, perhaps *the* most, important member of the local administration . . . The dignity of his office is never impaired by the absence of efforts on his part to maintain it . . .' And at church: 'How pompously he marshals the children into their places! and how demurely the little urchins look at him askance as he surveys them when they are all seated, with a glare of the eye peculiar to beadles!'

6. *the board*: Such bodies, of what Dickens later calls 'long-headed' (shrewd) men, were an innovation of the 1834 Act, intended to improve on corrupt or inefficient local management of poor relief by Justices of the Peace and parish officers. They formed part of a newly constituted administrative structure of local Boards of (mostly annually elected) Guardians, replacing the 'vestry' of elected parish officers as responsible for the local poor, and answerable for Unions of parishes to three Poor Law Commissioners in London.

7. *Oliver Twist's eighth birth-day*: In *1838* Dickens made this Oliver's ninth birthday (and altered his age in I, 5). This reduced from three years to one what, even so, remains a discrepancy in the novel's time-scheme, the nebulous period, described as 'three months' in *Bentley's* and 'six months' from *1838* onwards, that Oliver spends in the workhouse – an inconsistency perhaps caused by Dickens's writing in parts. As Kathleen Tillotson says, 'No version of the novel gives us a time-scheme that is completely consistent on the literal level, and in these [*1838*] revisions Dickens altered only those inconsistencies which would become most obvious to readers (as they did to the writer re-reading) when the novel was read straight through instead of in monthly portions' (Clarendon edition of *Oliver Twist*, pp. xxxiv–xxxv). See also Selected Textual Variants for I, 2 and I, 5.

8. *threshing*: An alternative spelling of 'thrashing'. (The Captain Swing Riots of 1830–31 by the rural poor were partly directed at the new threshing machines which threatened traditional winter employment.)

9. *the blessed infants' Daffy*: The seventeenth-century cleric Thomas Daffy invented Daffy's Elixir Salutis, a medicine for adults and children which used senna (the leaves of a tropical shrub with purgative properties). 'Daffy' became slang for unmixed gin.

10. *half-baptised*: In a shortened baptism not in a church and without the full service, when the full service was inconvenient or impossible.

11. *who is his father, or what is his mother's settlement, name, or condition*: Until the 1834 Act, fathers of illegitimate children – once identified – could be made to contribute to their support, reducing the cost to the parish. Thereafter responsibility was placed in effect more heavily on the mother. A 'settlement' was 'legal residence or establishment in a particular parish, entitling a person to relief from the poor rates; the right to relief acquired by such residence' (*OED*). 'Condition' is rank.

12. *pick oakum*: Not a 'useful trade': oakum-picking (a set amount per day) was a common activity of convicts and inmates of workhouses. Oakum, a loose fibre obtained by untwisting and picking apart old rope, was used to caulk ships' seams, stop up leaks and dress wounds. Dixon remarks: 'The fact is, the old criminals, having been often in gaol, have acquired, by long practice, a knack of getting the oakum through their fingers very quickly. As a punishment, it is very unequal. To the young offender it is a severe punishment, breaking his nails, and tearing the flesh off his finger-ends.' Three and a half tons a week were picked in the Coldbath Fields House of Correction.

13. *regulations having reference to the ladies*: The 1834 Act was partly of Malthusian inspiration, that is, concerned not to permit population growth, and so couples were separated and stringent rules punished any workhouse inmate attempting to enter the quarters of another class of pauper.

14. *to divorce poor married people . . . a suit in Doctors' Commons*: The 'divorce' is not legal, but the physical separation of married couples in the workhouse. (In 1847 a further Act prohibited the separation of husbands and wives in workhouses if over the age of sixty.) Dickens had observed as a young shorthand writer for the proctors of Doctors' Commons, from 1829 to 1831, the workings of the centuries-old Consistory Court, where he was in an office at 5 Bell Yard, just south of St Paul's Cathedral. Until the creation of a civil divorce-court in 1857 it was the one institution 'whose decrees can even unloose the bonds of matrimony' ('Doctors' Commons', ch. 8, *Sketches by Boz*). David Copperfield starts his training as a lawyer in these courts.

15. *a copper at one end*: *OED*: 'A vessel made of copper, particularly a large boiler for cooking or laundry purposes, originally made of copper, but now more often of iron.' This one – as is confirmed by Cruikshank's illustration – seems to be mounted above a fire in a brick housing.

16. *per diem*: Each day (Latin).

CHAPTER THE THIRD

RELATES HOW OLIVER TWIST WAS VERY NEAR GETTING A PLACE

1. *register stoves . . . This here boy, sir, wot the parish wants to 'prentis*: On a register stove metal plates could be opened and closed to regulate the passage of air, heat and smoke. Until 1842, when Lord Ashley (later Lord Shaftesbury) and other philanthropists made it illegal to force anyone under 21 to enter a chimney, the longstanding use of young boys as chimney-sweeps (to clean out soot from narrow chimneys) was a glaring abuse, attacked for example by William Blake (1757–1827) in the poem 'The Chimney Sweeper' (1794). 'Climbing Boys' might suffocate or be burned, and were liable to a variety of occupational diseases. The 1834 Act for the Better Regulation of Chimney Sweepers and Their Apprentices made the minimum age for apprenticeship as a chimney-sweep ten years (by a householder; Gamfield is in arrears with rent, thus only a tenant, so strictly Oliver should be 14). Since 1788 the minimum had been eight years (in 1840 it became 16). Technically, that is, Oliver is still too young.

2. *the magistrate*: Parish officials had the power to apprentice any orphan child between 12 and 21 to any master or factory-owner willing to relieve the parish of the child's upkeep, for a premium anywhere between £2 and £10. A necessary part of this process was the sanctioning of the indentures (contract) of apprenticeship (by which a child was 'bound') by local magistrates, respectable citizens without legal training responsible for committing offenders to trial, for sentencing in minor cases and for enforcing various laws. (Strictly, the 1834 Chimney Sweep Act required a two-month trial period before indentures were signed.)

3. *to take snuff*: Tobacco ground, moistened with salt, fermented, dried and flavoured – then snorted. Smoking – in cigars and pipes – was the more fashionable use of tobacco by the nineteenth century.

4. *He seems to want it*: This can mean both that, having been deprived of kind treatment, in the older sense, he suffers the want – lack – of it, has occasion for it, needs or requires it; and that, in the more modern sense, dating from the early eighteenth century, he desires or has a wish for it.

OLIVER, BEING OFFERED ANOTHER PLACE

1. *possession, reversion, remainder, or expectancy*: Dickens's time as a law clerk and reporter had taught him this standard (and tautological) phrase covering all contingencies. A expectancy here is 'anything in expectancy; anything which a person is entitled to expect' (*OED*). The jurist Sir William Blackstone declared in his *Commentaries* (1765–9): 'Of expectancies there are two sorts; one . . . called a remainder; the other . . . called a reversion.' A remainder is 'The residual or further interest remaining over from a particular estate coming into effect when this has determined, and created by the same conveyance by which the estate itself was granted' [*sic*]. A reversion is 'the return of an estate to the donor or grantor, or his heirs, after the expiry of the grant' (*OED*).

2. *shipping off Oliver Twist in some small trading vessel*: Local authorities had long been able to apprentice boys to the mercantile marine: a brutal and insanitary life. Some commentators argue that Bumble's mission to look for a captain 'clearly' assumes a maritime town like Chatham – though how long his trip has taken is not specified.

3. *Birmingham*: At this time a new industrial centre in the Midlands, 100 miles north-west of London, linked to much of the rest of the country by an elaborate system of canals.

4. *a millstone*: Christ says in Matthew 18:6 (Authorized Version): 'But whoso shall offend one of these little ones . . . it were better for him that a millstone were hanged about his neck, and that he were drowned in the depth of the sea.'

5. *the Good Samaritan healing the sick and bruised man*: In Luke 10:30–37, Christ's parable about charity shows a man robbed and left for dead on the roadside being passed by a priest and by a Levite before a Samaritan, from whom as a non-Jew nothing would be expected, has compassion on him and stops to tend to his wounds, carry him to an inn and heal him. Mr Gradgrind, the embodiment of political economy in *Hard Times* (1854), describes the Good Samaritan as 'a bad economist'. In Fielding's *Joseph Andrews* (1742), Book I, ch. xii, there is a darkly ironic reworking of the parable in modern England, in which a coachload of respectable travellers refuses help or covering to the naked, bleeding Joseph until 'the Postillion (a Lad who hath been since transported for robbing a Hen-roost) . . . voluntarily stript off a great Coat, his only Garment, at the same time swearing a great Oath, (for which he was rebuked by the Passengers) "that he would rather ride in his Shirt all his Life, than suffer a Fellow-Creature to lie in so miserable a Condition".' The episode may have prompted Oliver's unhappy experience with the coach on the London road (I, 8). Stephen Gill notes that Cruikshank places a picture of the Good Samaritan on Mr Brownlow's wall in the sixth plate.

6. *the relieving officer*: The overseer, appointed by the board of guardians to administer poor relief; named in II, 1 as 'Mr Grannet'.

7. *political economy*: This term was applied to Utilitarian social thinking at least from the publication of *Elements of Political Economy* (1821) by James Mill (1773–1836), follower of Bentham, which was concerned with 'two grand objects, the Consumption of the Community, and that supply upon which the consumption depends'. Bentham wished to promote the influence of sympathy, but regarded it as a fact that 'In *every* human breast (rare and shortlived ebulliations, the result of some extraordinarily strong stimulus or excitement, excepted) self-regarding interest is predominant over social interest; each person's own individual interest over the interests of all other persons taken together' (*Book of Fallacies*).

8. *day-book*: A book used in accounting to record commercial transactions day by day.

CHAPTER THE FIFTH

OLIVER MINGLES WITH NEW ASSOCIATES

1. *Coffin-plates . . . two mutes*: Metal plates set on the lid of a coffin for names and dates of birth and death. It was Victorian practice for two men, 'mutes' because silent, wearing black frock coats, black gloves and top hats draped with black silk streamers ('hat-bands'), to be hired to stand on either side of the doorway of a house of the dead, awaiting the funeral procession which they would then lead. Dickens was against such costly and elaborate ritual, and satirized it in *Great Expectations* (1860–61), ch. 35; his will insisted that 'I be buried in an inexpensive, unostentatious, and strictly private manner'.

2. *charity-boy*: Charity schools were funded by subscriptions which entitled subscribers to nominate orphaned or impoverished pupils for admission. Their distinctive uniforms of coats and badges, flat woollen 'muffin-caps' and leather breeches – Noah's leather 'smalls', his small-clothes or short trousers, are yellow, hence the taunt of 'leathers' – painfully singled out the wearers as recipients of charity. 'I don't', declared Dickens in 1857, 'by any means like

schools in leather breeches, and with mortified straw baskets for bonnets, which file along the streets to churches in long melancholy rows under the escort of that surprising British monster, a beadle' (*The Speeches of Charles Dickens*, ed. K, J. Fielding (Brighton: Harvester Wheatsheaf, 1988)). The education they offered was usually unsystematic and often woefully inadequate – and according to Dickens its crude methods produced hypocrites. Noah is the first of Dickens's many unlikeable alumni of these institutions (others include Rob the Charitable Grinder in *Dombey and Son* (1846–8), Uriah Heep in *David Copperfield* (1849–50) and Grandfather Smallweed in *Bleak House* (1852–3)).

3. *antimonial*: Antimony takes the form of a metallic silvery white crystal; the word 'antimonial' was sometimes used to describe spoiled wine that served as an emetic.

4. *houseless wretches*: In *King Lear*, III.iv.28–30, Lear in the storm refers to 'Poor naked wretches' and the exposure of their 'houseless heads'.

5. *The kennel was stagnant and filthy*: The kennel was an open street-gutter, which in poorer areas would often be polluted by the overflow from privies.

6. *I begged for her in the streets, and they sent me to prison*: The 1824 Vagrancy Act made offences specially characteristic of vagrancy, such as begging and sleeping out, punishable on summary conviction by imprisonment with hard labour for fourteen days, or on conviction by a petty sessional court by a fine of £5 or a month's imprisonment with or without hard labour. As the 1911 *Encyclopaedia Britannica* summarizes the law on 'Vagrancy': 'Any person sleeping out without visible means of subsistence is a rogue and vagabond, or on second conviction an incorrigible rogue, while an ordinary beggar is an idle and disorderly person.'

7. *a half-quartern loaf*: The 'outdoor relief' offered here, which continued even after the 1834 Law's attempt to outlaw it, takes the form of a loaf just under two pounds (a quartern loaf was just under four pounds), a standard size at the time. In I, 8 the Dodger buys a half-quartern loaf, which he refers to as a 'four penny bran'.

8. *the parish graves*: Dickens later said he had based this episode on a hurried and undignified pauper's funeral he had seen near Chatham. The details given, such as the piling-up of coffins in a common grave, are authenticated practice for the period.

CHAPTER THE SIXTH

OLIVER, BEING GOADED BY THE TAUNTS OF NOAH

1. *Bridewell, or transported*: The original Bridewell, near Blackfriars in London, long a prison for vagrants, prostitutes, and political and religious criminals, pioneered the use of hard labour, making it the first house of correction, and the first reformatory in England. Apprentices were also trained there. The term came to mean any prison or house of correction. From the late sixteenth till halfway through the nineteenth century, many criminals – some as young as seven – were transported to the 'penal colonies' in America and Australia.

CHAPTER THE SEVENTH

OLIVER CONTINUES REFRACTORY

1. *the wax-end which was twisted round the bottom of his cane*: Wax-end is 'thread coated with cobblers' wax, used by shoemakers' (*OED*). In *Nicholas Nickleby* (1838–9), Mr Squeers the schoolmaster has 'a fearful instrument of flagellation, strong, supple, wax-ended, and new' (ch. 13).

CHAPTER THE EIGHTH

OLIVER WALKS TO LONDON

1. *post-boys*: A post-boy was either a messenger ('a man or boy who rides post', that is, carrying and delivering mail) or 'the postilion of a stage-coach, post-chaise, or hired carriage' (*OED*).
2. *turnpike-man*: Livestock and vehicles with wheels passing along a privately maintained road with a 'turnpike' – a barrier – would pay tolls to the keeper of the tollbooth, who would issue a receipt or ticket.
3. *the little town of Barnet*: Ten and a quarter miles north of London, with a population of 507 in 1831, Barnet in Hertfordshire was a significant coaching-station and market town on the Great North Road; see also Selected Variants. Paroissien notes that Barnet's annual fair as well as the market and the flood of coaches made it a focus for criminals.

4. *bluchers*: Strong leather half-boots, so called after Gerhart von Blücher (1742–1819), a Prussian field marshal who played a large part in the defeat of Napoleon at the Battle of Waterloo.

5. *a small public-house*: B. W. Matz suggests this may have been based on the Red Lion, where Dickens sometimes dined with his friends on riding excursions from London along one of his favourite routes, the Great North Road (*Dickensian Inns and Taverns* (1922)).

6. *the turnpike at Islington . . . Saffron-hill the Great*: The Angel was an inn and a London landmark at the bottom of the Great North Road, in Islington, formerly a village but just recently joined to London by the spread of new building. John Cary's 1812 *New and Accurate Plan of London and Westminster* shows open fields around Sadler's Wells Theatre, the adjoining 'Islington Spa' and the 'New River Head' waterworks, but by 1831, Samuel Lewis refers to 'the recent laying-out of Spa-fields and the New River Company's estate, in a variety of new streets and squares' (*Topographical Dictionary of England*, 4 vols. (London: B. Lewis & Co., 1831)). The London conurbation was rushing out to meet those like the Dodger and Oliver coming in from the country. Alexander Pope's visionary London satire *The Dunciad* (1742), I.222, in its picture of artistic mediocrities perpetrated by 'the Smithfield Muses', refers to 'This Mess, toss'd up of Hockley-hole and White's' (a coffee-house), and its editor James Sutherland comments: 'Hockley-in-the-hole, a place near Clerkenwell-Green, famous for the baiting of bulls and bears, dog-fights, trials of skill, etc.' (Twickenham Edition (London: Methuen, 1953)). *Dunciad* IV.321 gives a view of the disastrous effect of the European Grand Tour of Classical sites on a young gentleman's education: 'All Classic learning lost on Classic ground'. The 'little court by the side of [Clerkenwell] workhouse' connecting Coppice-row and Little Saffron-hill was probably Crawford's Passage – one of the streets mentioned here that do not survive. (Some that do have changed their name.)

7. *the lowest orders of Irish (who are generally the lowest orders of anything)*: As F. H. W. Sheppard says, 'Irish migrants had been coming to London for centuries, but in the 1820s and 1830s their numbers mounted rapidly . . . They were generally poor, unskilled, and often destitute' (*London, 1808–70*). By 1841 3% of the total population of the capital was Irish.

8. *Field-lane*: This narrow street, where Fagin has his headquarters, was the continuation of Saffron-hill at the south end, debouching onto Holborn Hill. It had been the location of the hide-out of the notorious eighteenth-century thief Jonathan Wild. Its shops were well known for selling silk handkerchiefs bought from pickpockets: in October 1834 Dickens, complaining in a letter about a literary piracy, declared that 'It is very little consolation to me to know, when my handkerchief is gone, that I may see it flaunting with renovated beauty in Field-lane'. In *The London Prisons*, Dixon describes walking through it:

The lane is narrow enough for [one] to reach across from house to house, and the buildings so lofty that a very bright sun is required to send light to the surface. The dwellings on either side are dark; in some of them candles or gas is burning all day long. The stench is awful. Along the middle of the narrow lane runs a gutter, into which every sort of poisonous liquid is poured. This thoroughfare is occupied entirely by receivers of stolen goods, which goods are openly spread out for sale. Here you may *re*-purchase your own hat, boots, or umbrella; and, unless you take especial precaution, you may have one of the importunate saleswomen – daughters of Israel . . . – attempting to seduce you into the purchase of the very handkerchief which you had in your pocket at the entrance.

9. *a very old shrivelled Jew*: In 1860, Dickens sold Tavistock House for 2000 guineas (£2100) to James Phineas Davis, a solicitor, whom he first described as 'a Jew Money-Lender' – only to be surprised by how 'satisfactory, considerate and trusting' the 'money-dealings' between them were. Later Mrs Davis remonstrated with Dickens for having made Fagin a Jew, and he replied that such criminals were almost invariably Jewish (see Introduction, p. xxxix). Peter Fairclough cites a contemporary report: 'A Jew seldom thieves, but is worse than a thief; he encourages others to thieve. In every town there is a Jew, resident or tramping; . . . if a robbery is effected, the property is hid till a Jew is found, and a bargain is then made.' It was thought until recently, indeed, that Fagin was at least loosely based on a famous Jewish fence, Ikey Solomons. At any rate the severe restrictions on Jewish occupations and property-holding did push a number of Jews into illegal activities. Dickens also says in response to Mrs Davis, 'firstly, that all the wicked dramatis personae are Christians; and secondly, that he is called "The Jew", not because of his religion, but because of his race' (letter of 10 July 1843). He did however respond by putting a sympathetic Jewish character, Mr Riah, into *Our Mutual Friend* (1865); and in *1867* he changed most references to 'the Jew'.

CHAPTER THE NINTH

CONTAINING FURTHER PARTICULARS CONCERNING THE PLEASANT OLD GENTLEMAN

1. *It was late*: There had been no instalment of *Oliver Twist*, nor of *The Pickwick Papers*, in June 1837, which caused rumours about 'Boz' to abound. Dickens had been stunned by the sudden death on 7 May of his wife's sister, Mary Hogarth (1819–37), who had frequently been a member of their household. 'She went up stairs to bed at about one o'Clock in perfect health and her usual delightful spirits; was taken ill before she had undressed; and died in my arms next afternoon at 3 o'Clock. Everything that could be done *was* done but nothing could save her. The medical men imagine it was a disease of the heart.' In the same letter, Dickens wrote that 'I have lost the dearest friend I ever had . . . She had not a single fault, and was in life almost as far above the foibles and vanity of her sex and age as she is now in Heaven.'

2. *the execution that morning*: Executions outside Newgate Prison, using the 'new drop' (see note 1 to III, 14), took place on Monday mornings at eight o'clock; so Oliver and the Dodger have arrived at Fagin's on a Sunday night. Dixon says that 'an execution is as good as a lord-mayor's show to the race of pickpockets'; he estimated that at a given hanging the arrests would number some thirty to fifty, the robberies several hundred.

3. *note-case . . . guard-chain*: A note-case was a wallet; a guard-chain was supposed to secure a pocket-watch to a gentleman's clothing.

CHAPTER THE TENTH

OLIVER BECOMES BETTER ACQUAINTED WITH THE CHARACTERS OF HIS NEW ASSOCIATES

1. *the open square in Clerkenwell . . . 'The Green'*: Clerkenwell, less than a third of a mile north of Field Lane, was known at this time for the highest murder-rate and the greatest concentration of criminality in London. In *The London Prisons*, Dixon states: 'The constant conflict of its turbulent population with the guardians of the public peace, has given it a universal reputation. It is low London *of* low London.' There had not for at least a century been a 'Green' in the open space by the Sessions House in Clerkenwell – where Mr Bumble

later comes to attend a case. Clerkenwell Green was a site of political meetings and became a starting-point for Chartist processions.

2. *a powdered head*: That he powders his hair, a habit more prevalent in the eighteenth century than the nineteenth, identifies Mr Brownlow as an old-fashioned gentleman.

3. *a whole audience desert Punch in the very thickest of the plot*: In the brutally comic Punch and Judy puppet-show, a nineteenth-century reworking of the Pulcinella in the Italian *commedia dell'arte*, Mr Punch usually insults, beats and kills a succession of characters, including his wife, Judy, and generally avoids a bad end by tricking, and hanging, the hangman.

4. *a police officer (who is always the last person to arrive in such cases)*: In *A New Study of Police History* (1956), Charles Reith says that by the early nineteenth century: 'The complete breakdown in London of the old parish-constable system had spread to all parts of the country.' One response came in the shape of the London police force, established in 1829 by the Home Secretary Robert Peel's Metropolitan Police Act. Taking over from the locally organized parish-constables, it only gradually superseded the Bow Street Runners (see below, note 5 to II, 7 and note 4 to III, 6), 'The principal object to be attained is the Prevention of Crime', as its original manifesto stated. It was uniformed, poorly paid, and was to provide a free centralized public service, unlike the Runners who were paid by the private individuals who hired them. For years there was intense public resistance to the police (as a threat to English liberty) and a fierce Press campaign against them, with which this remark is in keeping, though crime and disorder in London visibly decreased.

CHAPTER THE ELEVENTH

TREATS OF MR FANG THE POLICE MAGISTRATE

1. *a very notorious metropolitan police-office . . . a place called Mutton-hill . . . summary justice*: Mutton-hill is now Vine Hill, and Oliver is taken to the Hatton Garden Police Office (or court) at 52–3 Hatton Street. Cases concerning minor offences (e.g. vagrancy, drunkenness, minor larceny and prostitution) were tried not by jury but 'summarily', by magistrate.

2. *the renowned Mr Fang*: Dickens wrote to Thomas Haines, an influential police reporter, on 3 June 1837 that

In my next number of Oliver Twist, I must have a magistrate; and casting about for a magistrate whose harshness and insolence would render him a fit subject to be 'shewn up' I have, as a necessary consequence, stumbled upon Mr Laing of Hatton Garden celebrity. I know the man's character perfectly well, but as it would be necessary to describe his appearance also, I ought to have seen him, which (fortunately or unfortunately as the case may be) I have never done. In this dilemma it occurred to me that perhaps I might under your auspices be smuggled into the Hatton Garden office for a few moments some morning.

Allan Stewart Laing (1788–1862), appointed as a police magistrate in 1820, had been much attacked as outrageously severe in Gilbert à Beckett's satirical weekly *Figaro in London* and elsewhere in 1835–6. On 1 January 1838 Laing was dismissed from the Bench by the Home Secretary, Lord John Russell, having been forced to pay damages following a collision in the street with a doctor whom he struck, called a 'damned blackguard' and had taken into custody. Dickens may have been following Smollett, who in *Roderick Random* (1748) satirizes an angry bullying justice 'not many miles distant from Covent Garden' (ch. 17).

3. *three months, – hard labour*: Fang appears to apply a maximum sentence under the 1824 Vagrancy Act (for loitering in a street 'with intent to commit a felony'), thus avoiding the need for a jury trial.

CHAPTER THE TWELFTH

IN WHICH OLIVER IS TAKEN BETTER CARE OF

1. *down Mount Pleasant and up Exmouth-street . . . a quiet shady street near Pentonville*: With the spread of the city, Mount Pleasant, north of Hatton Garden, was already a misleadingly pastoral name. Pentonville, to the west of Islington and north-east of where King's Cross station now stands, was then a fashionable suburb, developed in 1773 on the estate of Henry Penton, MP, from which clerks would commute the short distance to the City. George Cruikshank (1792–1878), Dickens's friend, and the illustrator of this book, lived at 23 Myddelton Terrace, Pentonville.

2. *rushlight-shade*: A cylindrical metal shade pierced with holes around a weak rush candle, and thus a good night-light.

3. *The man that invented the machine for taking likenesses*: As Dickens was writing, photography was in the experimental stages of its development. 'The man' might be the Frenchman Louis Jacques Mandé Daguerre (1789–1851), who made his first successful photograph in 1837 but only made his work

public in 1839; or the Englishman William Henry Fox Talbot (1800–1877), who made the first photographic negative in 1835; but more probably another Frenchman, Joseph Nicéphor Niépce (1765–1833), who produced his first heliograph (a faint image made through a chemical process with a camera obscura on a metal plate) in 1826 and had addressed the Royal Society in 1827. Alternatively, Paroissien suggests Joseph Tussaud's profile machine, referred to by Sam Weller in *Pickwick Papers*, ch. 33.

4. *slops*: Invalids' weak liquid food, usually unappetizing.

CHAPTER THE THIRTEENTH

REVERTS TO THE MERRY OLD GENTLEMAN AND HIS YOUTHFUL FRIENDS

1. *Thus, to do a great right, you may do a little wrong*: In Shakespeare's *The Merchant of Venice*, IV.i. 210–12, Bassanio addresses Portia (disguised as a judge, Balthasar) about Shylock: 'Wrest once the law to your authority; / To do a great right do a little wrong, / And curb this cruel devil of his will'. Portia replies, 'It must not be.'

2. *Toor rul lol loo, gammon and spinnage, the frog he wouldn't, and high cockolorum*: 'Toor rul lol loo': untraced. 'Gammon and spinach' and the frog are from the refrain of the nursery rhyme, 'A Frog He Would a-Wooing Go'. 'High cockolorum' is a boys' game with two teams, one of which jumps on the opposition's backs and sits there till they collapse.

3. *done the River Company every quarter*: The New River Company had supplied water from Hertfordshire to North London since the seventeenth century. This slightly obscure expression may imagine Fagin collecting quarterly dues like the River Company; or, Gill suggests, cheating the company.

4. *belcher handkerchief*: A dark blue neckerchief mottled with white spots, named after the boxer Jim Belcher (1781–1811).

5. *it would come out rather worse for you than it would for me*: Despite Fagin's threat, fences – receivers of stolen goods – had since Robert Peel's 1827 Larceny Act lost their previous comparative impunity, and in felony cases could be tried as accessories after the fact or as felons themselves.

6. *genteel suburb of Ratcliffe*: Ratcliff Highway, a riverside district in the East End, notorious for the seven bloody Ratcliff Highway Murders in 1811: 'that reservoir of dirt, drunkenness, and drabs: thieves, oysters, baked potatoes, and pickled salmon – Ratcliff-highway' ('Brokers and Marine-store Shops', Ch. 21, *Sketches by Boz*).

7. *a miserable shoeless criminal, who had been taken up for playing the flute*: In November 1835 Dickens had joined the mockery of Laing, who had had a muffin-boy taken up for ringing a muffin-bell in Hatton Garden while Laing's court was sitting.

8. *so much breath to spare, it would be much more wholesomely expended on the treadmill*: The treadmill was introduced at Brixton Prison in 1817, and abolished only in the Prisons Act of 1898: convicts, who called the activity 'grinding the wind', trod exhaustingly and unproductively, in compartments like 'the stalls at a public urinal' (Henry Mayhew and John Binney, *The Criminal Prisons of London*), up the steps of an elongated heavy revolving wheel, thus working a giant fan outside. Dixon notes: 'The wheel does find work for the muscles, but it is in itself, in spite of its one advantage of compelling to exertion, useless, profitless, disgusting, and demoralising.' In 1850, seemingly influenced by Thomas Carlyle's attack that year on 'Model Prisons' in *Latter-Day Pamphlets*, Dickens was in favour of it, precisely for its waste of effort: 'Is it no part of the legitimate consideration of this important point of work, to discover what kind of work the people always filtering through the gaols of large towns – the pickpocket, the sturdy vagrant, the habitual drunkard, and the begging-letter impostor – like least, and to give them that work to do in preference to any other?' ('Pet Prisoners', *DJ*, II).

9. *in defiance of the Stamp-office*: This government department marked papers, including vendors' licences and newspapers, to guarantee that the appropriate duty ('stamp-duty') had been paid.

CHAPTER THE FOURTEENTH

COMPRISING FURTHER PARTICULARS OF OLIVER'S STAY AT MR BROWNLOW'S

1. *cribbage*: A card game for two. First to reach 61, 121 or 181 points, depending on the number of cards dealt, is the winner; therefore once, twice or three times round the board.

2. *sell them to a Jew*: I.e. to a second-hand clothes dealer. Of Holywell-street, parallel to the Strand, which was demolished to make the present-day Aldwych, Dickens had written in *Sketches by Boz*: 'Holywell-street we despise; the red-headed and red-whiskered Jews who forcibly haul you into their squalid houses, and thrust you into a suit of clothes, whether you will or not, we detest' (ch. 6, 'Meditations in Monmouth-street').

3. *it would be a much better thing to be a bookseller*: When Dickens wrote this in August 1837, he was in dispute with Bentley, and much oppressed by the contractually fixed disproportion between his publisher's earnings from his books and his own. In January 1839, he told his friend Forster why he could not yet bring himself to write *Barnaby Rudge*:

The immense profits which *Oliver* has realised to its publisher, and is still realising; the paltry, wretched, miserable sum it brought to me (not equal to what is every day paid for a novel that sells fifteen hundred copies at most); the recollection of this, and the consciousness that I have still the slavery and drudgery of another work on the same journeyman-terms; the consciousness that my books are enriching everybody connected with them but myself, and that I, with such a popularity as I have acquired, am struggling in old toils, and wasting my energies in the very height and freshness of my fame, and the best part of my life, to fill the pockets of others, while for those who are nearest and dearest to me I can realise little more than a genteel subsistence: all this puts me out of heart and spirits . . .

4. *nankeen*: A yellow cotton cloth, very 'respectable' and hard-wearing.

5. *I won't be ten minutes*: From anywhere in Pentonville, Oliver, eager as he is, would have to run very fast to get to Clerkenwell Green and back in ten minutes.

CHAPTER THE FIFTEENTH

SHEWING HOW VERY FOND OF OLIVER TWIST

1. *If it did not come strictly within the scope . . . no part of my original intention so to do*: This passage, which looks back to the eighteenth-century digressions of Fielding and Sterne, was cut from *1838* (see introduction to Selected Textual Variants). 'This prose epic' may deliberately recall Fielding's preface to *Joseph Andrews* (1742) as describing it as a 'comic Epic-Poem in Prose'.

2. *There must always be two parties . . . adage*: Thomas Fuller's *Gnomologia: Adagies and Proverbs* (1732), n. 4942: 'There must be two at least to a quarrel.'

3. *nightcap . . . If I go, you go*: In low slang, a 'horse's nightcap' is a halter; 'to die in a horse's nightcap' is to be hanged. It had become usual to put a hood over the head of the criminal on the scaffold. Sikes may be referring to the change in the law with Peel's 1827 Larceny Act (see note 5 to I, 13).

4. *the interesting pages of the Hue and Cry*: First issued in 1772 from Bow Street by the magistrate Sir John Fielding, half-brother to Henry Fielding, what became *The Public* – then *The Weekly* – *Hue-and-Cry* was a police bulletin describing crimes committed and criminals wanted. From 1828 it was a weekly

called *The Police Gazette; or, Hue and Cry*, containing advertisements offering rewards for the recovery of stolen property and the apprehension of criminals (hence perhaps Fagin's interest).

5. *gas-lamps*: Gas street-lighting had been introduced in London as early as 1807 in Pall Mall, and within twenty years had displaced oil lamps in most central districts. It was not much used domestically till the 1830s.

CHAPTER THE SIXTEENTH

RELATES WHAT BECAME OF OLIVER TWIST

1. *The narrow streets*: This chapter begins the November 1837 instalment of the novel; there had been no instalment in October, and a notice appeared on the magazine's wrapper: 'Oliver Twist will be continued by Mr. Dickens in the next number of the Miscellany, and after that from month to month as usual. The great length of the proceedings of the Mudfog Association prevents the insertion of the usual continuation this month.' This refers to Dickens's 'Full Report of the First Meeting of the Mudfog Association for the Advancement of Everything', the first of two satires on the annual meetings of the British Association. Forster suggested that the delay was caused by a contractual dispute with Bentley over whether *Oliver Twist* counted as the second new novel in their agreement.

2. *Smithfield . . . Grosvenor Square*: Smithfield was London's main livestock market (held on Mondays and Thursdays till 1855), as well as a long-established site of public executions and religious martyrdoms – Sir William Wallace was executed there in 1305. It was also home to Bartholomew Fair, already a focus for fraudsters and pickpockets in Ben Jonson's 1614 comedy of the same name, held every year for three days, starting on 3 September (new calendar), the feast of St Bartholomew (Sikes's 'Bartlemy time'). The fair was discontinued in 1855, and Dickens was later active in his journal *Household Words* against the 'Beast Market', and unhygienic nearby 'slaughter-houses in the heart of a city' ('A Monument of French Folly' (1851), *DJ*, II). In *Great Expectations* the young Pip, wandering into it, finds that 'the shameful place, being all asmear with filth and fat and blood and foam, seemed to stick to me'; he flees, only to run into Newgate and the Old Bailey, where a drunken official shows him where the gallows is kept and informs him four people are to be hanged 'the day after tomorrow at eight in the morning' (ch. 20). See also I, 21. The mansions of Grosvenor Square are quite at the other, smart, West End of town, just south of Oxford Street.

3. *when I was shopped*: Sikes is shopped or imprisoned in the notorious Newgate Prison (see note 2 to I, 18), well within earshot of Smithfield, which was just north up Giltspur Street.

4. *a very filthy narrow street, nearly full of old-clothes shops*: Sikes, Nancy and Oliver take 'a full half-hour' to get to 'the other ken' in Whitechapel, over in the East End and north-east of the Tower of London, a mile and a half or so. Fagin's alternative, more derelict headquarters is in an area that has come down in the world, with a 'Rag Fair' or old-clothes market in Whitechapel Road and Petticoat Lane. Mayhew and Binny lists known receivers of stolen goods in this district: in Middlesex Street, Brick Lane, Whitechapel Road, Commercial Road and Rosemary Lane.

5. *when I was a child not half as old as this . . . for twelve years since*: Guiliano and Collins comment: 'If Nancy came under Fagin's influence when she was half Oliver's age, say five years old, and since she has been at it for twelve years, she is therefore seventeen years old.'

CHAPTER THE SEVENTEENTH

OLIVER'S DESTINY CONTINUING UNPROPITIOUS

1. *all good, murderous melodramas, to present the tragic and the comic scenes in as regular alternation*: In *Sketches by Boz*, Dickens evokes 'a melo-drama (with three murders and a ghost), a pantomime, a comic song, an overture, and some incidental music, all done in five-and-twenty minutes' ('Greenwich Fair', ch. 12). One could also see this same principle of alternation at work in Shakespeare's tragedies (perhaps most notably and controversially with the Porter's scene in *Macbeth* just after Duncan's murder). It applies also to the popular novel *Rookwood* (1834), by Dickens's friend William Harrison Ainsworth, in which there are many comic songs interspersed with life-threatening captivities and indeed scenes in 'church vaults'; see also Introduction.

2. *before the quarter-sessions at Clerkinwell*: The quarterly sessions of the court at Clerkenwell at which people were tried for minor offences. Those found guilty were usually sentenced to the nearby Middlesex House of Correction in Coldbath Fields. Mr Bumble's reference to the Sessions coming 'off rather worse than they expected' seems to mean that a rival parish – or the London court itself – will end up with responsibility for the two paupers in the case.

3. *his place on the outside of the coach*: Such seats were considerably cheaper and more uncomfortable than those inside.

CHAPTER THE EIGHTEENTH

HOW OLIVER PASSED HIS TIME IN THE IMPROVING SOCIETY OF HIS REPUTABLE FRIENDS

1. *the crying sin of ingratitude*: Cf. *Macbeth*, I. iv. 14–16, where the generous King Duncan says to the treacherous Macbeth: 'O worthiest cousin, / The sin of my ingratitude even now / Was heavy on me.'

2. *hung at the Old Bailey*:

There, in the very core of London, in the heart of its business and animation, in the midst of a whirl of noise and motion: stemming as it were the giant currents of life that flow ceaselessly on from different quarters, and meet beneath its walls, stands Newgate; and in that crowded street on which it frowns so darkly – within a few feet of the squalid tottering houses – upon the very spot on which the vendors of soup and fish and damaged fruit are now plying their trades – scores of human beings, amidst a roar of sounds to which even the tumult of a great city is as nothing, four, six, or eight strong men at a time, have been hurried violently and swiftly from the world, when the scene has been rendered frightful with excess of human life; when curious eyes have glared from casement, and house-top, and wall and pillar, and when, in the mass of white and up-turned faces, the dying wretch, in his all-comprehensive look of agony, has met not one – not one – that bore the impress of pity or compassion.

This is from the first instalment of *Nicholas Nickleby* (ch. 4), published on 31 March 1838, while Dickens was still writing *Oliver Twist*. The Central Criminal Court of England in the Old Bailey, a street running from Ludgate Hill to Newgate, with the adjacent Newgate Prison, was burnt down in the Gordon Riots of 1780, later fictionalized by Dickens in *Barnaby Rudge* (1841); both were rebuilt in 1809. Hangings had taken place on a scaffold erected against its walls since 1783, when they were discontinued at the previous site, Tyburn, and continued till public executions were abolished in 1868.

3. *it had belonged to better people . . . dismal and dreary as it looked now*: With the changes in fashion and growth of such suburbs as Pentonville, formerly grand residences in such areas as Whitechapel, in and around the City, had fallen into decline. The City never really recovered as a residential district from the Great Fire of London in 1666. When Mr Pickwick's coach drives through a 'crowded and filthy street' in Whitechapel, Sam Weller remarks, 'Not a wery nice neighbourhood this, sir' (*Pickwick Papers*, ch. 22).

4. *the ball of St Paul's Cathedral*: On 28 February 1837, Dickens had written

to his friend Thomas Beard suggesting a walk: 'The top of the Monument is one of my longings; the ditto of St. Paul's, another.' The dome of Christopher Wren's cathedral, high above the City (like the 202-foot Monument not far off, a column near London Bridge erected in memory of the Great Fire), is surmounted by a hollow globe with a golden cross on top; it was formerly possible for visitors to go inside the globe, which accommodates about a dozen people.

5. *fumigating clothes up yonder*: Tom Chitling has come from 'the house of correction', a generic term for local prisons under the control of local magistrates, used for minor offenders sentenced to anything from one week to three years, but here probably the one at Coldbath Fields, Clerkenwell. Rebuilt in 1794 and subsequently extended, controlled by the Middlesex Magistrates, it was probably the largest prison in the world at the time and very near Dickens's house in Doughty Street. ('Among other advantages of situation, we have the inestimable one of living in the immediate neighbourhood of the House of Correction,' as he wrote to Ainsworth in June 1837.) Dickens went over it on 5 November 1835: 'I was immensely interested in everything I saw.' In 1834 its reformist governor, George Laval Chesterton (d. 1868), later Dickens's friend, introduced the 'Silent System', whereby prisoners could work together, but not communicate. Chitling's clothes are fumigated with brimstone (sulphur).

CHAPTER THE NINETEENTH

IN WHICH A NOTABLE PLAN IS DISCUSSED AND DETERMINED ON

1. *like some loathsome reptile, engendered in the slime and darkness*: Paroissien cites Byron's verse-drama *Cain* (1821), II.ii. 95–8, where in Hades Lucifer tells Cain that 'the rest / Of your poor attributes is such as suits / Reptiles engendered out of the subsiding / Slime of a mighty universe'. (One of the descriptive headlines introduced by Dickens in 1867, for Sikes's flight near the end, is 'The Curse of Cain'.)

2. *Spitalfields . . . Bethnal Green*: A slum area, to the east of the City of London, Spitalfields was built up in the late seventeenth century; it had been a major location for the weaving industry, and in 1763 several thousand journeymen weavers had rioted there. Bethnal Green was infamous for its slums, taverns and social disorder.

3. *another adjective, derived from the name of an unpleasant instrument of death*

... *ears polite*: 'Gallows', really used here as an adverb: see Appendix C. Pope's *Epistle IV: To Burlington* (1735), ll. 147–8, evokes the comfortable chapel of a rich nobleman: 'To rest, the Cushion and soft Dean invite, / Who never mentions Hell to ears polite'.

4. *Chertsey*: A small town in Surrey beside the River Thames, about 20 miles west-south-west of central London, with a population in 1831 of 4279; even decades later it was described by Charles Dickens Junior as 'an old-fashioned country town – one of the most characteristic still remaining in the immediate neighborhood of London. The country around is well-wooded, hilly, and exceedingly picturesque ...' (*Dickens's Dictionary of London, 1879: An Unconventional Handbook*). Paroissien notes that the creation of the Metropolitan Police in 1829 tended to drive thieves out of London for their criminal targets.

5. *the Juvenile Delinquent Society*: Dickens's 1850 article 'A December Vision' would offer a nightmarish view of the problem of juvenile delinquency, especially in London, which taxed him greatly: 'I saw Thirty Thousand children, hunted, flogged, imprisoned, but not taught – who might have been nurtured by the wolf or bear, so little of humanity had they, within them or without – all joining in this doleful cry' (*DJ*, II, 307). The Society to Inquire into Causes of Juvenile Delinquency was founded in 1815.

6. *Common Garden*: Covent Garden was until 1970 London's main fruit, vegetable and flower market, and was also a refuge for the homeless.

CHAPTER THE TWENTIETH

WHEREIN OLIVER IS DELIVERED OVER TO MR WILLIAM SIKES

1. *a history of the lives and trials of great criminals*: Almost certainly what Oliver reads, when he has 'snuffed' (here, trimmed) the candle, is *The Newgate Calendar, or Malefactors' Bloody Register* (1728), published in five volumes in 1773–4, in six volumes in 1795 and 1800, and again in four in 1824–8. It was a popular collection of narratives of notorious criminals' lives, exploits, trials and last days in Newgate. It is mentioned by name in III, 6.

2. *A hackney cabriolet*: Pulled by a single hackney, a light breed of trotting-horse, such vehicles were light, two-wheeled carriages for hire, seating four and with a folding leather hood.

CHAPTER THE TWENTY-FIRST

THE EXPEDITION

1. *St Andrew's church*: As Sikes and Oliver pass from the City into the West End, they look up at the clock on the Wren-designed St Andrew's on the south side of Holborn Hill (very close to Fagin's Field-lane lair).

2. *'Hounslow'* . . . *the Coach and Horses*: Hounslow at this time was a town outside London, 9½ miles west-south-west, on the main coaching route to Bristol and the West Country; Isleworth (9 miles west-south-west) is on the west side of the Thames, and Twickenham lies south of it. Sikes and Oliver head steadily south-west towards Chertsey, following the main roads as they accommodate the bends of the river. The Coach and Horses is a particularly common name for inns along the traditional coaching routes, and this one at Isleworth is described by the Dickensian pub-scholar B. W. Matz as 'a huge four-square lump of a place' with 'rather a dour and forbidding aspect' (*Dickensian Inns and Taverns*).

3. *Twickenham* . . . *an old public-house*: In *1846* Dickens leaves out the mention of Twickenham and, perhaps to fill the hours of their long day, has Sikes and Oliver 'linger about, in the fields, for some hours' before going to the public-house. Hampton, 13½ miles west-south-west of London, with a population of 3549 in 1831, lies south of Twickenham on the north bank of the winding Thames; thereafter the trip to Chertsey is more direct. (The Red Lion was still a landmark in Hampton a century later.)

4. *Lower Halliford* . . . *Shepperton*: To follow the north bank of the Thames to Chertsey Sikes and Oliver must head south and west through Sunbury, a couple of miles on to Lower Halliford and then another mile or so to the village of Shepperton (population 782 in 1831), across the flat ground by the river – from where Chertsey was another 2½ miles.

CHAPTER THE TWENTY-SECOND

THE BURGLARY

1. *shawl-pattern*: A paisley pattern: Scots weavers in Paisley appropriated a distinctive Indian and Persian design of fruit and pine-cones.

2. *large dark shawls*: At this period a 'shawl' could mean a scarf worn round the neck as protection from cold.

3. *the bridge . . . Chertsey . . . the church bell*: F. A. H. Lambert's 1903 guide *Surrey* says 'Chertsey Bridge – one of the most picturesque on the river – is worth a visit for its own sake as well as for the view to be obtained from it.' St Peter's church contains one of the oldest bells in the county, taken from the ancient abbey formerly in the town. Fitzgerald stated that 'Years ago there was a ruined hovel standing by the bridge which was pointed out as the house in question [i.e. Toby's house], but it has since disappeared.'

4. *a detached house surrounded by a wall*: Fitzgerald says this is Pycroft House, 'a charming old Queen Anne structure' in pleasant grounds, and that the lattice where Oliver climbs in became known as 'Oliver's window'.

5. *a dark lantern*: A lantern with a sliding front that can be closed by turning the top of the lantern, thus shutting off the light when necessary without putting out the candle. When Mr Pickwick uses one in ch. 39 of *The Pickwick Papers*, Sam Weller gives his opinion of them: 'Wery nice things, if they're managed properly, sir, . . . but if you don't want to be seen, I think they're more useful arter the candle's gone out, than wen it's alight.'

BOOK THE SECOND

CHAPTER THE FIRST

WHICH CONTAINS THE SUBSTANCE OF A PLEASANT CONVERSATION BETWEEN MR BUMBLE AND A LADY

1. *yet them paupers are not contented*: What is offered here is a newly parsimonious form of 'out-of-door relief', a kind of support with which the Poor Law Commissioners were forced to continue by temporarily severe conditions and full workhouses, despite the 1834 Act's original intention to restrict relief to the workhouse.

2. *real fresh, genuine port wine . . . no sediment . . . shaken it well*: Good, vintage port – the deep-red fortified wine from northern Portugal – is aged for many years before drinking, and is better when it *has* a sediment – and thus ought not to be shaken.

CHAPTER THE SECOND

TREATS OF A VERY POOR SUBJECT

1. *the parish apothecary's apprentice*: As in the opening chapter, the medical care provided in the workhouse is relatively unskilled, because the Board does everything on the cheap. Here the apprentice is unqualified, and into the bargain neglectful of his duties.

CHAPTER THE THIRD

WHEREIN THIS HISTORY REVERTS TO MR FAGIN AND COMPANY

1. *game of whist . . . taking dummy . . . a scientific rubber . . . two doubles and the rub*: Whist had become a very popular card game in the eighteenth century. It can be played as here with a dummy or 'dum' when there is not an even number of players: one of them can be partnered by an imaginary player, whose exposed hand of cards is controlled by him. The best of three games at whist is a 'rubber'. 'Two doubles and the rub' is two tricks making ten points while the opponents score under three, and the best of three games.

2. *Day and Martin*: This firm, rivals of Warren's where Dickens worked as a child, made a popular liquid shoe polish, or blacking. Sam Weller uses it in *The Pickwick Papers*, ch. 10. The name was also slang for cheap port.

CHAPTER THE FOURTH

IN WHICH A MYSTERIOUS CHARACTER APPEARS UPON THE SCENE

1. *Snow Hill and Holborn Hill . . . Field Lane*: At this time Holborn Viaduct had not yet been built (which happened 1863–9); the area was known as Holborn Bridge. Snow Hill ran steeply down from Smithfield; Holborn Hill up from what had been the Fleet Ditch on the other side. Field Lane, the alley at the bottom of Saffron Hill, Fagin's original base in I, 8, is now fully described.

2. *the shoe-vamper*: The vamp is the front upper part of a shoe. The *OED*

cites Carlyle, *The French Revolution* (1837): 'Skilfullest vamper-up of old rotten leather, to make it look like new'.

3. *the hoptalmy*: Ophthalmia, an inflammation of the eyes.

4. *the Cripples*: This particular pub, a 'flash house' or resort of criminals, is fictitious, as Matz says, though doubtless based on those in the area (*Dickensian Inns and Taverns*).

5. *Non istwentus, as the lawyers say*: Garbled attempt at *non est inventus*, Latin legal phrase: 'not to be found'.

6. *gave a sentiment*: Made a toast.

7. *drab*: *OED*: 'a harlot, prostitute, strumpet'. Cf. *Macbeth*, IV.i. 31: 'Birth-strangled babe, / Ditch-delivered by a drab'.

8. *Jack Ketch*: See Appendix C. The neighbourhood round Fagin's lair in Field Lane was sometimes known in the eighteenth century as 'Jack Ketch's Warren'.

9. *perfume of Geneva*: 'Gin' is a shortened form of the Dutch word 'genever', meaning juniper; the word was often spelt thus and written with capital G by confusion with the city in Switzerland.

CHAPTER THE FIFTH

ATONES FOR THE UNPOLITENESS OF A FORMER CHAPTER

1. *'tenterhooks'*: Literally, hooks or bent nails on a 'tenter' or wood frame across which cloth is stretched after it has been milled, in order to set or dry evenly and without shrinking. To be on tenterhooks is thus to be in suspense.

2. *green-glass bottle*: According to the traditional colour coding for bottles by druggists or chemists, green was the colour for peppermint.

3. *opening oysters from a barrel*: At this time oysters were plentiful and eaten by all classes; they were thought to serve as aphrodisiacs.

CHAPTER THE SIXTH

LOOKS AFTER OLIVER

1. *a travelling tinker*: A mender of pots and pans.

2. *busting*: *OED* says this can be a dialect word for 'beating'.

CHAPTER THE SEVENTH

HAS AN INTRODUCTORY ACCOUNT OF THE INMATES OF THE HOUSE TO WHICH OLIVER RESORTED

1. *a waiter*: A waiter here is a small tray.

2. *a gig*: A light carriage with two wheels drawn by a single horse.

3. *the twopenny post*: The government took over London's postal service in 1801 from the private Penny Post, and increased the rate to twopence. The postmaster Rowland Hill introduced a standard penny rate in January 1840.

4. *that thick-headed constable fellow*: This is a parish-constable, part of the old-fashioned rural system of law-enforcement that is mocked by Shakespeare in the figure of Dogberry, the constable in charge of the watch in *Much Ado about Nothing* (1599), a man of many wrong words and all-round incompetence. In ch. 24 of *The Pickwick Papers*, rioting Ipswich schoolboys 'pelted the constabulary – an elderly gentleman in top-boots, who . . . had been a peace-officer, man and boy, for half a century at least' and 'who was chiefly remarkable for a bottle-nose, a hoarse voice, snuff-coloured surtout, and a wandering eye'. He carries 'a short truncheon, surmounted by a brazen crown' – part of his official regalia, referred to here in *Oliver Twist* as his 'staff of office'.

5. *the runners . . . The Bow-street officers*: The Bow Street Runners had operated as a detective force out of the Bow Street Magistrates' Court since the mid-eighteenth century. In 1829, the modernizing Peel founded the Metropolitan Police (see note 4 to I, 10); and in 1839, the Runners were disbanded, though it was another three years till the Metropolitan Police had their own Detective department. In an 1850 article, 'A Detective Police Party', describing Dickens's close relation with members of the Detective Branch (founded in 1842), he declares that

> We are not by any means devout believers in the Old Bow-Street Police. To say the truth, we think there was a vast amount of humbug about those worthies. Apart from many of them being men of very indifferent character, and far too much in the habit of concerting with thieves and the like, they never lost a public occasion of jobbing and trading in mystery and making the most of themselves. (*DJ*, II)

It has though been suggested by Philip Collins (*Dickens and Crime*) and others that Dickens's allegations about their corruption and inefficiency were not altogether fair.

CHAPTER THE EIGHTH

INVOLVES A CRITICAL POSITION

1. *Edmonton . . . Battle-bridge . . . badger-drawing*: Edmonton was in 1831 a pleasant little town of 7900 inhabitants on the Lea river, 7 miles north of London. Battle Bridge, in the eighteenth century a small village, was the name for the district (down the hill from Mr Brownlow in Pentonville) now known as King's Cross – from the short-lived monument bearing a statue of George IV that was erected in 1836 and removed, having been widely deplored, by 1845 (see also note 5 to III, 5). The father of one of Dickens's earliest friends, Thomas Mitton, was, like Conkey Chickweed, a publican there. Cockfighting and badger-drawing (both outlawed in 1849) were popular blood sports. In cockfighting two male fowl fought to the death with strapped-on spurs; in badger-drawing a badger was put in a hole, most often a barrel, and a dog was set after it. Spectators would bet on the outcome.

2. *blunderbuss*: A short, large-bore gun with a wide muzzle, that fired many balls or slugs rather than a single bullet; 'capable of doing execution within a limited range without exact aim' (*OED*).

3. *the Gazette*: Published twice a week, the *London Gazette* contained public notices, lists of government appointments and the names of bankrupts.

4. *the cage at Kingston*: A temporary jail where suspects were detained before being brought to court. Kingston-upon-Thames is a market town in Surrey, several miles towards London from Chertsey.

5. *sleeping under a haystack . . . a great crime . . . punishable by imprisonment*: Vagrancy and trespass, as said above, were both serious enough offences at this time to warrant imprisonment. When Oliver runs away from Mr Sowerberry's, he immediately breaks the law by sleeping 'under a hay-rick'.

6. *rewarded with a couple of guineas*: The Bow Street Runners, as Philip Collins says, 'depended upon rewards and private fees for most of their income, and their activities . . . sometimes included the arrangement of compromises whereby stolen cash or goods were restored to their owners without prosecutions being entered' (*Dickens and Crime*). Their usual rate for a job outside London was a guinea a day, with fourteen shillings a day to cover living expenses, plus a reward in the case of a successful prosecution.

CHAPTER THE NINTH

OF THE HAPPY LIFE OLIVER BEGAN TO LEAD WITH HIS KIND FRIENDS

1. *Chertsey Bridge . . . The thieves – the house they took me to*: Heading back eastwards towards London from the Maylies' house, which appears to be just west of Chertsey, Oliver and Mr Losberne presumably pass back through the town and then over Chertsey Bridge before Oliver recognizes, or thinks he does, the 'solitary house all ruinous and decayed' where he, Sikes and Toby Crackit have waited, and from which, in I, 22, 'They crossed the bridge . . . towards the lights'.

2. *chariot and pair*: A light four-wheeled vehicle drawn by two horses.

3. *groundsel*: *OED*: 'A common European weed, which is given as food to cage-birds'.

CHAPTER THE TENTH

WHEREIN THE HAPPINESS OF OLIVER AND HIS FRIENDS EXPERIENCES A SUDDEN CHECK

1. *she was once more deadly pale*: Dickens's account of Rose Maylie's illness was praised by the *British Medical Journal* as having 'found its way into more than one standard work in both medicine and surgery'. It is 'hectic', a fever accompanying consumption and other wasting diseases, characterized by wide swings in temperature which recur daily, and numbering among its symptoms flushed cheeks and hot dry skin.

2. *the little market-place of the market-town . . . 'The George'*: Fitzgerald says that Dickens, economizing on research, has actually based the unnamed 'little town' here, supposedly many miles from Chertsey because only four miles from the Maylies' country cottage, on Chertsey itself. Guildford Street, Chertsey, has also an inn called 'The George' and a red brewery dated 1703. Paroissien identifies the unnamed town near the unlocated cottage as Petersham, where Dickens had spent four or five weeks in 1836.

3. *white favours*: White ribbons symbolize the innocence of the child who has died.

CHAPTER THE ELEVENTH

CONTAINS SOME INTRODUCTORY PARTICULARS RELATIVE TO A YOUNG GENTLEMAN WHO NOW ARRIVES UPON THE SCENE

1. *a post-chaise*: A rapid travelling carriage holding two or four passengers.
2. *There is a kind of sleep*: Paroissien cites *The Philosophy of Sleep* (1830) by Robert Macnish (1802–37), whose work Dickens knew, which describes a state of half-sleep where the sleeper, without waking, can hear conversations and 'although not awakened by such circumstances, may recollect them afterwards. These impressions, caught by the sense, often . . . form the groundwork of the most extraordinary dreams.'

CHAPTER THE TWELFTH

CONTAINING THE UNSATISFACTORY RESULT OF OLIVER'S ADVENTURE

1. *the young, the beautiful, and good*: Dickens, the year before, wrote the inscription for the headstone of his sister-in-law: 'MARY SCOTT HOGARTH / DIED 7TH MAY 1837 / YOUNG BEAUTIFUL AND GOOD / GOD IN HIS MERCY / NUMBERED HER WITH HIS ANGELS / AT THE EARLY AGE OF / SEVENTEEN.'

CHAPTER THE THIRTEENTH

IS A VERY SHORT ONE

1. *place, cup or sweepstakes*: Kinds of prize in horse racing: the first three to finish win a prize which they are awarded on how they place; a cup goes to the outright winner; in sweepstakes, all the entrants put up stakes for the winner's pot before the race.
2. *the General Post Office in London*: The new post office in St Martin's le Grand in the City, opened in 1829, had a Poste Restante Office where visitors without a permanent London address could pick up letters marked 'To be called for'.

3. *postilion*: *OED*: 'One who rides the near horse of the leaders (or formerly sometimes, each of the riders of the near horses) when four or more are used in carriage or post-chaise; especially one who rides the near horse when one pair only is used and there is no driver on the box.'

CHAPTER THE FOURTEENTH

IN WHICH THE READER, IF HE OR SHE RESORT TO THE FIFTH CHAPTER OF THIS SECOND BOOK

1. *washable beaver hats*: Hats had been made of beaver fur for centuries, and early nineteenth-century advertising played up the waterproof qualities of the latest versions.

2. *jorum*: *OED*: 'A large drinking-bowl or vessel; also, the contents of this; especially a bowl of punch.' *OED*'s earliest three citations come from Fielding, Goldsmith and Francis Grose's *Classical Dictionary of the Vulgar Tongue*.

BOOK THE THIRD

CHAPTER THE FIRST

CONTAINING AN ACCOUNT OF WHAT PASSED BETWEEN MR AND MRS BUMBLE AND MONKS AT THEIR NOCTURNAL INTERVIEW

1. *I could have let you down*: Cruikshank's illustration shows a trapdoor that opens upwards, falsifying Monks's claim. Dickens too contradicts this when Monks closes the trapdoor, for it '*fell* heavily back into its former position'.

2. *If the sea ever gives up its dead – as books say it will*: Revelation 20:12–13: 'And the sea gave up the dead which were in it; and death and hell delivered up the dead which were in them; and they were judged every man according to their works.'

CHAPTER THE SECOND

INTRODUCES SOME RESPECTABLE CHARACTERS WITH WHOM THE READER IS ALREADY ACQUAINTED

1. *seven and sixpenny green*: There was a special customs duty on green tea, which was a luxury at seven shillings and sixpence a pound.

2. *pound of best fresh; piece of double Glo'ster*: Butter; Double Gloucester cheese.

CHAPTER THE THIRD

A STRANGE INTERVIEW

1. *CHAPTER THE THIRD*: There was no instalment in the September 1838 *Bentley's*; Dickens produced instead a third Mudfog paper, 'Full Report of the Second Mudfog Association for the advancement of everything'. The delay seems to have been partly calculated to increase the appeal of the book form of the novel, published on 9 November 1838 (with five instalments still to appear).

2. *A watchman was crying half-past nine*: Guiliano and Collins (in *The Annotated Dickens*) say: 'Watchmen called the hour and the half-hour throughout the night. They would periodically call out the last half hour to be struck until the next one was nearly due. The practice was abolished by Peel's Police Act of 1829.' But it appears to be still going here, several years later; only in 1839 was the old watch system abolished in the City of London, where Peel's Metropolitan Police at first had no jurisdiction.

3. *from Spitalfields towards the West-End of London . . . a family hotel in a quiet but handsome street near Hyde Park*: Nancy's journey of a couple of miles thus takes her west and up in the social world, from the poorest slum (Spitalfields) to the most elegant district (Mayfair), near Hyde Park and thus probably off Park Lane.

4. *the Dianas*: Diana was the Roman goddess of chastity and the moon.

5. *stews*: Brothels. The archaism for Nancy's place of work is Dickens's way of avoiding, in his phrase from the later Preface, 'any expression that could by possibility offend'.

6. *hulks*: The Hulks were disused ships that were first adapted in 1779 to serve only as temporary prisons for prisoners awaiting transportation to the 'penal colonies' during the American War of Independence (1776–83), but continued in use until 1858. It was a common punishment, and the prisoners worked in the dockyards at Woolwich and Chatham. There were high mortality rates and Mayhew and Binney speak of 'crimes impossible to be mentioned being frequently perpetrated' in the cramped conditions (*The Criminal Prisons*). When the convict Magwitch encounters the young hero Pip at the beginning of *Great Expectations* (1860–61), he has just escaped from a Hulk.

7. *London Bridge*: There have been a succession of London Bridges joining the north bank (Middlesex) to the south (Surrey). Just before *Oliver Twist* a modern one, designed by John Rennie, was constructed 1824–31. Opened by William IV on 1 August 1831, it remained in place till 1968, when it was moved to Arizona.

CHAPTER THE FOURTH

CONTAINING FRESH DISCOVERIES

1. *Craven Street, in the Strand*: Mr Brownlow's new house is in the West End, in a street leading down from the western extremity of the Strand to the Thames. E. Beresford Chancellor, *The London of Charles Dickens* (1924), identified Mr Brownlow's house as number 39, saying this was 'generally accepted as the correct one'.

2. *a motion of course*: Grimwig as counsel had made an application to the court for a rule or order of court without which a legal action cannot proceed, or run its 'course'.

CHAPTER THE FIFTH

AN OLD ACQUAINTANCE OF OLIVER'S

1. *the Great North Road . . . mail-coaches . . . Highgate archway*: On its way down from Mudfog to the Angel at Islington, the Great North Road (linking London and York) passed under an arched viaduct, built in 1813 to a design by John Nash, to span a steep cutting made in Highgate Hill. (In 1897 a steel bridge was put in its place.)

2. *Saint John's Road . . . the lowest and worst that improvement has left in the midst of London*: The area of Clerkenwell and Smithfield that Noah and

Charlotte end up in, retracing Oliver's footsteps, is Fagin's territory, containing Saffron Hill and Field Lane. 'Improvement' refers to the modernization of London, particularly the creation of Regent Street by John Nash between 1813 and 1820.

3. *homœopathic doses*: In *OED*, homoeopathy is defined as 'a system of medical practice founded by Hahnemann of Leipzig about 1796, according to which diseases are treated by the administration (usually in very small doses) of drugs which would produce in a healthy person symptoms closely resembling those of the disease treated'. Here, small portions of food seem intended to prevent Charlotte from getting hungry – the metaphor not quite making sense, but the point being the tiny helpings.

4. *ridicules*: Reticules, or bags.

5. *Camden-Town, and Battle-Bridge*: Camden Town, just north of Regent's Park, was a newly developed residential district in the nineteenth century, where Dickens had lived, when himself a 'kinchin', in 1823 (at 16 Bayham Street); Battle Bridge adjoined it to the south and east (see also note 1 to II, 8).

CHAPTER THE SIXTH

WHEREIN IS SHOWN HOW THE ARTFUL DODGER GOT INTO TROUBLE

1. *replied Fagin*: See Selected Textual Variants for the full passage in MS and *1838*.

2. *It's number one*: K. J. Fielding cites the 1839 review by Richard Ford in the *Quarterly Review*, which calls Fagin in this scene 'a modern sophist, whose trade is to make mankind wise, by teaching them the utilitarian principle of Mr Jeremy Bentham – *alias*, the golden rule of number one'.

3. *'Are you mad ... humorous leer*: The cut in the *Bentley's* text makes a confusing nonsense, and has been emended to follow *1838*. See Selected Textual Variants, and for III, 11 and III, 14.

4. *what he was placed in that 'ere disgraceful sitivation for*: The Dodger has been arrested and remanded in custody, and now is facing a magistrate to be committed for trial. Dickens bases the scene on one at the Old Bailey he had recorded in *Sketches by Boz*:

A boy of thirteen is tried, say for picking the pocket of some subject of her Majesty, and the offence is about as clearly proved as an offence can be. He is called upon for his defence, and contents himself with a little declamation about the jurymen and his country – asserts that all the witnesses have committed perjury, and hints that the police force generally, have entered into a conspiracy 'agin' him ... The boy is sentenced, perhaps to seven years' transportation ... As he declines to take the trouble of walking from the dock, he is forthwith carried out by two men, congratulating himself on having succeeded in giving every body as much trouble as possible. ('Criminal Courts', ch. 24)

5. *the Court Guide*: One of a number of social directories of the genteel, of 'Noblemen and gentlemen' published at the time.
6. *the Wice President of the House of Commons*: The House of Commons has never had either a President or a Vice-President.

CHAPTER THE SEVENTH

THE TIME ARRIVES FOR NANCY TO REDEEM HER PLEDGE TO ROSE MAYLIE

1. *an old press*: A clothes-press or large cupboard.
2. *jade*: *OED*: 'a contemptuous name for a horse', or 'a term of reprobation applied to a woman'.
3. *let her a little blood without troubling the doctor*: Bloodletting was a long-standing medical technique, designed to thin the blood and thus relieve or cure a number of illnesses, especially fevers.
4. *He rose betimes* From 1869 Dickens began his famous, passionate performance of what he called 'Sikes and Nancy' here, as a highlight of his extraordinary public readings, starting 'Fagin the receiver of stolen goods was up ...'
5. *She goes abroad*: The older sense of out-of-doors.

CHAPTER THE EIGHTH

THE APPOINTMENT KEPT

1. *The tower of old Saint Saviour's church, and the spire of Saint Magnus*: Saint Saviour's church (now Southwark Cathedral) stood with its tower and pinnacles at the south (Surrey) end of the bridge; St Magnus Martyr, in Lower Thames Street, rebuilt by Wren after the great Fire, and mentioned for its 'Inexplicable splendour of Ionian white and gold' in T. S. Eliot's *The Waste Land* (1922) III.265, raised its spire at the north (Middlesex).

2. *the night-cellar*: *OED*: 'A cellar serving as a tavern or place of resort during the night for persons of the lowest class.' In *Barnaby Rudge*, Dickens refers to 'Night-cellars . . . for the reception and entertainment of the most abandoned of both sexes' (ch. xvi).

3. *Between the Mussulman and the Pharisee*: Muslims (Mussulmans), including Turks, turn to face Mecca when they pray. The way the sect of Pharisees is shown in the New Testament caused the term to be used for people of unbending religious strictness.

CHAPTER THE TENTH

THE FLIGHT OF SIKES

1. *through Islington . . . the fields at North End*: Sikes heads at first directly north-west up what is now the Holloway Road; but turns back, then strikes west to the Vale of Health, and going over the east–west Hampstead–Highgate road heads north to North End (where Dickens had rented a cottage after the death of Mary Hogarth), a good six or seven miles' walk from his starting-point. The real Richard Whittington (1358–1423) was four times Lord Mayor of London, but in the popular legend (e.g. in *Dombey and Son* about Walter Gay) is an orphaned kitchen boy who puts his cat, his sole possession, on board his master's ship, hoping it will be traded and make him money. Then running away from London by the Great North Road, Dick is halted at Highgate Hill, looking back over London, by the sound of Bow Bells telling him, inaccurately, 'Turn again, Whittington, thrice Mayor of London'. He returns to discover that the King of rat-infested Morocco has paid a fortune for his cat and made him rich enough to marry his master's daughter, etc. A monument to Whittington and cat stands by the roadside on Highgate Hill.

2. *Hendon . . . Hatfield*: From North End to the village of Hendon was only about a mile north-west; Hatfield, in Hertfordshire, a town of 3,215 in 1831, is much further north up the Great North Road, 19 miles north-north-west of central London. Dickens's particularity about Sikes's wayward movements on the northern fringes of London emphasizes his loss of direction, in contrast to the expedition to Chertsey. In the next paragraph, the church is St Etheldreda's; and the pub is 'no doubt the Eight Bells, a picturesque old house . . . on the spot where Dickens accurately located it' (Matz, *Dickensian Inns and Taverns*).

3. *half pedlar and half mountebank . . . hones, strops, razors, wash-balls*: Pedlars were itinerant sellers of small goods, mountebanks sold their wares to an audience (often quack medicines) through a more theatrical performance. Hones are stones for sharpening blades; strops are leather straps for the same purpose, used on razors; washballs are balls of soap.

4. *cambric . . . merino . . . bombazeen*: Fine white linen; soft wool from the merino sheep; black, twill-woven silk fabric.

5. *If a lady stains her honour*: A joke-allusion to Alexander Pope, *The Rape of the Lock* (1714), Canto II: the sylph Ariel, one of those whose 'humbler province is to tend the Fair', describes the emergencies that may befall women: 'Whether the Nymph shall break *Diana*'s Law, / Or some frail *China* Jar receive a Flaw, / Or stain her Honour, or her new Brocade . . .' (II. 91. 105–7).

6. *the little post-office*: 'At the time, this adjoined the Salisbury Arms, another public house in Hatfield' (Paroissien).

7. *to St Albans*: Sikes is heading west to the cathedral town of St Albans, on the site of the Roman city of Verulam, about six miles from Hatfield, and which lies on the line of the old Roman Road.

8. *he bore a charmed life*: Compare the murderer-hero's claim to Macduff in *Macbeth*, V.x.12: 'I bear a charmèd life.'

9. *the firemen, who were from London*: In 1832 London insurance firms created a professional fire brigade of about 100 men, divided into 5 fire districts, and serving an area stretching 15 miles beyond London. If a fire was reported on the horizon, an engine would set out and relays of post-horses be used to get rapidly to the blaze.

CHAPTER THE ELEVENTH

MONKS AND MR BROWNLOW AT LENGTH MEET

1. *a hackney-coach*: A hirable four-wheeled vehicle, larger than a hackney cabriolet, with a box for the driver and a couple of exterior passengers.

2. *a hideous disease which has made your face an index even to your mind*: Epilepsy, which causes among other symptoms spasm of the muscles. Compare the medically trained novelist Charles Lever in his *Jack Hinton the Guardsman* (1843), ch. 34: 'His features worked like one in a fit of epilepsy.'

CHAPTER THE TWELFTH

THE PURSUIT AND ESCAPE

1. *that part of the Thames on which the church at Rotherhithe abuts ... wholly unknown, even by name, to the great mass of its inhabitants*: St Mary's, Rotherhithe, stands opposite Wapping and its docks, and was downriver in this busy waterfront area from Jacob's Island, also on the south bank, the controversial area of 300 or 400 houses here evoked. (It was not far from the Marshalsea Prison.) In mid century controversies about Sanitary Reform, involving Dickens and Henry Mayhew, Jacob's Island figured as a *cause célèbre*: see Appendix B.

2. *ballast-heavers, coal-whippers, brazen women*: The 'ballast-heavers' are dock-labourers who shovel ballast – heavy matter like lead, stones, or gravel – into the hold of an unladen ship to balance and lower it to sailing depth in the water. Mayhew and Binney: 'The *coalwhippers* generally work in gangs of nine. During their labour of whipping the coals from the hold of the colliers in the river, they raise during the day 1½ cwt. (or 18⅔ lbs. for each man) very nearly eight miles high, or four times as high as a balloon ordinarily mounts in the air' (*The Criminal Prisons*). They used pulleys to swing coal between a ship's hold and barges. 'Brazen women' is carefully poised in this list between euphemistically describing a profession and merely characterizing an attitude.

3. *beyond Dockhead in the Borough of Southwark, stands Jacob's Island ... Mill-lane*: Dickens leads us from Dockhead, a street at the head of St Saviour's Dock, down Mill-lane riverwards into what had been for some decades a strange damp slum itself, striking for its tanneries, its ditch and its slime. (Dog dung was purchased by tanners for purifying leather.) The Mill Pond had once driven a tidal mill grinding the corn for the long-demolished Bermondsey Abbey. The stream running from the Abbey to the Thames was the Neckinger, so-called from its outlet at Neckinger Wharf, which, as Nicholas Barton says in *The Lost Rivers of London* (1962), 'appears on a map of 1740 as the "Devol's Neckenger": this is supposed to derive from the fact that Thames pirates were executed there, and the rope which was used to hang them became known as the Devil's neckcloth or "neckinger"'. The vicinity was described as 'the Venice of drains' by Henry Mayhew, in an account of an 1849 visit, 'The Homes of the People in Jacob's Island'. Mayhew says it has 'the look of a Flemish street, flanking a sewer instead of a canal', and – there was a cholera epidemic at the time – 'the air has literally the smell of a graveyard' (collected in *Meliora, or Better Times to Come*, ed. Viscount Inegstre, 1852). In January 1853, having returned to Jacob's Island, Dickens reported that Folly Ditch 'has since been filled up'.

4. *chancery suits*: The particular dereliction of Jacob's Island is caused by its involvement in a 'chancery suit' – anticipating Tom-All-Alone's later in *Bleak House* (1853) – Chancery being a powerful but inefficient court with jurisdiction over disputed wills and estates, which could take expensive years and even decades to be decided while the disputants, and their putative property, were held in suspense by the court.

5. *one of these houses*: According to E. Beresford Chancellor, 'The actual house . . . has been identified as being at the back of 18 Eckell Street, in Metcalf Yard, now used as stables' (*The London of Charles Dickens* (1924)).

6. *a returned transport*: As successive colonies refused to accept any more convicts, the practice of punishment by transportation would come to a halt by 1852. Until 1835 the punishment for a convict returning home was death. In *Great Expectations*, Magwitch seems to lie under sentence of death for what was no longer in fact a capital offence.

7. *an accessory before the fact . . . he'll swing in six days from this*: As Paroissien says, Noah Claypole presumably gives testimony establishing Fagin as 'One who, being absent at the time a crime is committed, yet assists, procures, counsels, incites, induces, encourages, engages, or commands another to commit it.' Conviction as an accessory before the fact to murder could mean death under the Offences Against the Person Act of 1828. Old Bailey trials, after an Act of 1834, moved rapidly: a prisoner could be arrested one day, committed for trial the next and the day after that tried, convicted and sentenced. It seems to be a Tuesday, since hangings, as noted above, took place on Monday mornings.

8. *In the King's name*: An indication that at this late stage in the novel we are still in the reign of William IV, who died in June 1837.

CHAPTER THE THIRTEENTH

AFFORDING AN EXPLANATION OF MORE MYSTERIES THAN ONE

1. *A sheet of paper crossed and crossed again*: Because of the cost of paper and postage at this period, people would commonly finish writing a page in horizontal lines, rotate it ninety degrees, and write across it vertically. Sometimes a third, diagonal, 'crossing' was superimposed.

2. *Chester*: The walled and picturesque county town of Cheshire, 181 miles north-west of London, and not far from the Welsh border, Chester had a population of nearly 20,000 in 1831.

CHAPTER THE FOURTEENTH

THE JEW'S LAST NIGHT ALIVE

1. *the court*: No doubt the Old Bailey, visited by Dickens for *Sketches by Boz*, where he describes a prisoner in the dock of the Old Court, who 'watches the countenances of the jury, as a dying man, clinging to life to the very last, vainly looks in the face of his physician for one slight ray of hope. They turn round to consult; you can almost hear the man's heart beat . . .' ('Criminal Courts'). From the prisoners' dock stairs descended to a covered passageway which led through the Press Yard (where prisoners had formerly been pressed to death, and where executions would be held when public hangings were abolished) to Newgate. In the next, widely praised, *Boz* sketch, 'A Visit to Newgate', Dickens enters the condemned cell and incites us with him to 'Conceive the situation of a man, spending his last night on earth in this cell', before being taken out to the so-called new drop, first used outside the walls of Newgate in 1783, and evoked by Byron in 1817 as 'the vulgar and ungentlemanly dirty "new drop" & dog-like agony of infliction upon the sufferers of the English sentence' (*Byron's Letters*, ed. Leslie Marchand (London: John Murray, 1976), vol.5, pp. 229–30). Dickens conjures up scenes from the wretch's last fevered dream: 'He is on his trial again: there are the judge and jury, and prosecutors, and witnesses, just as they were before. How full the court is – what a sea of heads – with a gallows, too, and a scaffold – and how all those people stare at *him*! Verdict, "Guilty."'

2. *the black cap*: The judge would normally carry the square black cap in his hand as part of his ceremonial paraphernalia, and would place it on his head only when pronouncing sentence of death.

3. *the condemned cells*: Described by W. Hepworth Dixon in *The London Prisons*:

The condemned cells are built in the oldest part of the prison – at the back. There are fifteen of them in all; five on each of the three floors. The port-holes in Newgate-street let light into the galleries, into which the cell-doors open; and the man confined in the farthest dungeon on the ground-floor is within a yard of the passer-by. All the death-cells are vaulted, and about nine feet high, nine deep, and six broad. High up, in each cell, is a small window, doubly grated. The doors are four inches thick.

CHAPTER THE FIFTEENTH

AND LAST

1. *being admitted approver*: *OED*: 'One who proves or offers to prove (another) guilty; hence, an informer, an accuser'. Increasingly restricted to 'One who confesses a felony and gives evidence against his accomplices in order to secure their conviction.' This was the legal term for 'King's evidence'.

2. *went into business as an informer*: Informers were entitled to part of any fines imposed on offenders sentenced as a result of their 'laying an information' before the authorities.

3. *grazier*: One who grazes or feeds cattle to get them ready for market.

APPENDIX A

THE AUTHOR'S INTRODUCTION TO THE THIRD EDITION (1841)

1. *FIELDING*: The epigraph is from *The History of Tom Jones, A Foundling* (1749) by Henry Fielding (1707–54), Book VII, ch. i, 'A comparison between the World and the Stage', where Fielding as author writes about different views on poetic justice expressed in response to a character's bad action in the novel's preceding Book: 'The Pit, as usual, was no doubt divided: Those who delight in heroic Virtue and perfect Character, objected to the producing such instances of Villainy, without punishing them very severely for the Sake of Example. Some of the Author's Friends, cry'd . . .'

2. *objected to . . . in some very high moral quarters*: See the Introduction for an account of the controversy over the 'Newgate Novel' which arose when Thackeray attacked Dickens, Ainsworth and others in his parody-novel *Catherine*.

3. *Saint Giles's . . . Saint James's*: It was proverbial in the nineteenth century to contrast the parish of Giles-in-the-Fields, the poorest and one of the most criminally active in the city, containing the 'Rookery' and Seven Dials, with that of St James, the heart of society and fashion around St James's Square.

St Giles had been the setting of William Hogarth's great satirical print 'Gin Lane', where gin's disastrous effects were contrasted with the healthy English honesty of 'Beer Street' (see also next note).

4. *HOGARTH*: William Hogarth (1697–1764), artist and friend of Fielding, best known for his satirical narrative panoramas of English conduct and institutions ('The Rake's Progress', 'The Harlot's Progress', 'Marriage à la Mode'), which portray a world of venality and foolishness in unflinching detail.

5. *the Beggar's Opera*: The most famous of the works of John Gay (1685–1732), one of the Scriblerus Club. *The Beggar's Opera* (1728), a 'Newgate Pastoral', immensely successful in its day, is a parody of fashionable Italian opera and a serious satire, whose hero Captain Macheath is a highwayman and head of a gang of thieves. He is beloved by the beautiful Polly Peachum, daughter of the self-seeking fence Mr Peachum – like Fagin a turner-in of his own gang when it profits him, and betrayer of Macheath. The Newgate jailer is Mr Lockit. After many complications Macheath's death sentence is dropped, and he is released at the behest of an indulgent crowd.

6. *as VOLTAIRE says . . . at their head*: In the philosophical tale *Le monde comme il va* (1748: 'The World As It Goes'), by Voltaire (1694–1778), one of the objects of satire is the purchase of army commissions; a young officer declares, 'I myself purchased the right of braving death at the head of two thousand men who are under my command.'

7. *Johnson's question*: Not in fact a question. What Samuel Johnson (1709–84) says in his *Lives of the Poets* essay on 'John Gay' (1779) is more complex, and relevant to the dispute about the 'Newgate Novel':

Swift commended it for the excellence of its morality, as a piece that *placed all kinds of vice in the strongest and most odious light*; but others . . . censured it as giving encouragement not only to vice but to crimes, by making a highwayman the hero, and dismissing him at last unpunished . . .

   Both these decisions are surely exaggerated. The play, like many others, was plainly written only to divert, without any moral purpose, and is therefore not likely to do good; nor can it be conceived, without more speculation than human life requires or admits, to be productive of much evil. Highwaymen and housebreakers seldom frequent the playhouse, or mingle in any elegant diversion; nor is it possible for any one to imagine that he may rob with safety, because he sees Macheath reprieved upon the stage.

8. *Tyburn Tree*: Until 1783, Tyburn (near the present Marble Arch) was the main place in London for public executions (on the 'gallows-tree'). An execution was first recorded as occurring there in 1196.

9. *higher aims . . . Sir Edward Bulwer's . . . novel of Paul Clifford*: *Paul Clifford* (1830), by Edward Bulwer-Lytton (1803–73), the story of a highway robber, was said in Lytton's 1840 Preface to have been meant to

draw attention to two errors in our penal institutions, viz., a vicious Prison-discipline, and a sanguinary Criminal Code, – the habit of corrupting the boy by the very punishment that ought to redeem him, and then hanging the man, at the first occasion, as the easiest way of getting rid of our own blunders. Between the example of crime which the tyro learns from the felons in the prison-yard, and the horrible levity with which the mob gather round the drop at Newgate, there is a connection.

10. *Massaroni . . . Mrs Massaroni*: Alessandro Massaroni is the hero of *The Brigand: A Romantic Drama in Two Acts* (1829) by James Robinson Planché (1796–1880), based on a French original. In the original Drury Lane production, as described in the printed text of the play, this 'Italian Robin Hood' wore 'green velvet jacket and breeches', 'red striped waistcoat', 'pistols, stilettoes, etc.' His wife, Maria Grazie, was attired in 'red petticoat, trimmed with black velvet – white apron, with gold binding and fringe, red silk stockings . . .'

11. *Fielding, De Foe, Goldsmith, Smollett, Richardson, Mackenzie*: Fielding's *Life of Jonathan Wild the Great* (1743) was his contribution to the flourishing eighteenth-century genre of the criminal novel. The prolific Daniel Defoe (1661?–1731), was author of *Robinson Crusoe* (1719), one of Dickens's favourite books, but also of *Moll Flanders* and *Colonel Jack* (both 1722), which dealt with 'Newgate' or criminal subjects. Oliver Goldsmith (1728–74) wrote *The Vicar of Wakefield* (1766), another favourite of Dickens's. Tobias Smollett (1721–71) reproduced low life in *Peregrine Pickle* (1751) and *Ferdinand Count Fathom* (1753). Samuel Richardson (1689–1761), author of *Clarissa* (1747–48), created a great villain in the rake and rapist Lovelace. Henry Mackenzie (1745–1831) has a gleeful corruptor in *The Man of Feeling* (1771).

12. *Cervantes*: Miguel de Cervantes Saavedra (1547–1616), author of *Don Quixote* (1605, 1615), a complex burlesque of medieval chivalric romance, whose eponymous hero attempts to apply his reading in a series of incongruous quests through the modern world. Like Ainsworth in *Rookwood* (1834), Dickens misquotes Byron, who says in *Don Juan* (xiii. 11) that 'Cervantes smiled Spain's chivalry away'.

APPENDIX B:

PREFACE TO THE 'CHEAP EDITION' (1850)

1. *when FIELDING described Newgate ... grotto at Twickenham*: Fielding in *Jonathan Wild* (1743). Smollett in ch. 55 of *Roderick Random* (1748). Scott in *The Fortunes of Nigel* (1822). Shakespeare's last play to use Falstaff, the comedy *The Merry Wives of Windsor*, dates from 1602. Pope writes about his grotto in his Twickenham retreat at some length in *Satire I* (1733).

2. *the Reverend SYDNEY SMITH*: Sydney Smith (1771–1845), canon of St Paul's, educated at Winchester and Oxford, was a famous eccentric intellectual and wit, compelled to take clerical orders by his father when he wished to follow the law.

As the Note on the Text explains, the textual history of *Oliver Twist* is complicated.

MS AND *BENTLEY'S*

Only parts of the manuscript (MS) for the novel survive (at the Victoria and Albert Museum), and where they do it is often not possible to determine the exact sequence of cancellation and revision, but I have attempted to distinguish between readings that stand in the manuscript and others that are cancelled ('MS originally read'). I have given all the longer passages, and examples of phrasings, that appear in the MS but not in the serial version in *Bentley's Miscellany* (hereafter '*Bentley's*') to suggest something of Dickens's creative process. The MS shows, for instance, that he tried calling Rose Maylie 'Emily', and Duff, the second Bow Street Runner, 'Dubb'. Certain changes seem to reflect narrative strategy: thus at the end of II, 6 Brittles in the MS is told not only to get 'a constable and doctor' but also to 'ride on to London' for 'an experienced police officer'. *Bentley's* omits this latter instruction altogether, so that when the Bow Street Runners, threateningly for Oliver, arrive late in II,7 (at the end of an instalment), called in on Giles's and Brittles's own initiative, it is a minor dramatic coup.

It is sometimes hard to judge how far cuts made between the MS and *Bentley's* represent artistic choices and how far they simply reflect the mechanical necessity of trimming an excessively long instalment to the requisite dimensions (16 *Bentley's* pages; exceeded only once, in October 1838, when an instalment ran over by half a page). The heaviest section of cut passages in the MS is in the instalment of July 1838 (II, 12–14), with a certain amount also in the next instalment (III, 1–2). There is consequently a certain amount more of – if not much more *to* – Harry Maylie in the MS than in any of the printed versions, posturing romantically with Rose (II, 12) and joshing in a sub-Pickwickian way with Dr Losberne (II, 13). We lose some energetic comic writing in the portrait of the soured Bumble marriage and Mr Bumble's witty – probably too witty – remark about Mrs Bumble's use of the word 'sacrifice' (II, 14).

Occasionally a cancellation seems meant to prevent too self-exposing a show of feeling: the narrator of the novel as printed no longer refers us sanctimoniously to 'the real colours of this lovely world that once was Paradise' (II, 11), nor so obviously displays Dickens's worship of his late sister-in-law Mary Hogarth (II, 7). An exchange between Monks and Bumble about Old Sally is cut, and its vivid phrasing saved for *A Christmas Carol*: '"Dead!" cried the stranger. / "As a door-nail" said Mr Bumble' (II, 14). And an interesting cut in III, 2 removes a somewhat repetitious and uncharacteristically long speech to Fagin by Bill Sikes, complaining about his illness and Fagin's neglect after the failed Chertsey burglary.

BENTLEY'S AND 1838

When Dickens revised for the first book edition (*1838*) – on proof-sheets which had been set up directly from the pages of all the instalments already published in *Bentley's* – he made a number of minor adjustments of phrasing and punctuation, correcting and regularizing. In III, 5, for instance, *Bentley's* begins with Noah Claypole addressing Charlotte as 'yer', but slips back into occasional 'you'; *1838* established consistency on this score. Few of these changes greatly affect the reading experience.

On the other hand, a number of longer passages were excluded, with more ponderable effects. We lose the opening two paragraphs of I, 15, an ironic passage on the theme of benevolence and self-interest which, with its Fieldingesque digressiveness and reference to 'this prose epic', and equally Fieldingesque topic of the rarity of disinterested kindness, suggests a connection between the eighteenth-century roots of *Oliver Twist* and its more modern concern with political economy and the ethics of self-interest. Another cut in the third paragraph of I, 17 is a digression which applies the famous image of 'the tragic and the comic scenes in as regular alternation as the layers of red and white in a side of streaky, well-cured bacon' to the narrative shift Dickens is making from Fagin's recapture of Oliver back to Bumble and the town of Oliver's birth. Part of its point seems to be to emphasize (in what is thus only rhetorically a 'digression') that the switch back to the scene of Bumble's power is part of a unified plot in which all details are pertinent, rather than what readers might have expected, a Pickwickian, picaresque, starting of another hare in the chase after amusement.

Some sentences in *Bentley's* cut from *1838* seem full of implications. Only in *Bentley's*, I, 19, does 'Miss Nancy' prefix 'to the word "cold" another adjective, derived from the name of an unpleasant instrument of death, which, as the word is seldom mentioned to ears polite in any other form than as a substantive, I have omitted in this chronicle' (the word being 'gallows'; see Notes and Glossary). This sentence uses the ironically distancing title of 'Miss Nancy', whereas *1838* prefers to call her 'Nancy'. In its learnedly self-conscious, periphrastically witty way, the gallows reference brings back the inescapability of 'the drop' in the very daily language of these low-life characters, and its skirting around crude slang and its signalled avoidance of offence suggest (especially with the Pope allusion) some sarcasm about the terms on which Dickens's readers are prepared to contemplate the criminals about whom they are so curious. In cutting the sentence Dickens in *1838* probably also wants not to disgust readers whose sympathy for 'Miss Nancy' is later to be demanded. Another sentence is intriguingly omitted when Fagin hears that Oliver has been shot, perhaps fatally, in the burglary at Chertsey, and rushes distractedly into the street in II, 4, nearly getting himself run over. In *Bentley's* Fagin then changes his mind: 'Looking hastily round, as if uncertain whither he had been hurrying, he paused for a few moments, and turned away in quite an opposite direction to that in which he had before proceeded.' The exact point is unclear; but Fagin's uncertainty soon afterwards as to whether he should seek out Monks or Sikes, and his apparent suspicion that his secret scheme with Monks is perhaps being deliberately thwarted, may be clues.

It should be noted that the division of the novel into three Books in *Bentley's* is lost in *1838*, where the chapters are numbered in a single sequence. It may be of interest that each of the three Books in *Bentley's* begins with a chapter set in the town of the Bumbles and the workhouse.

1846

In the novel's most thorough revision for the major revised edition of *1846*, Dickens further cut out certain expressions of what could seem exaggerated reaction. Thus when the portrait of Agnes in Mr Brownlow's is recognized as the image of Oliver, *Bentley's* (and all editions up to *1846*) makes this miraculous: it is as if 'copied with an accuracy which was perfectly unearthly' (I, 12). But *1846* tones it down: 'with a startling accuracy' (and omits the picture from the chapter title). In the same chapter *1846* cuts the further, passionately charged, description of 'the dry and wasting heat of fever' as 'that heat which, like the subtle acid that gnaws into the very heart of hardest iron, burns only to corrode and to destroy' – which seems to be Dickens recalling Mary Hogarth's fatal illness less than three months before. I have in the list of variants attempted to suggest Dickens's reduction of colouring adjectives and adverbs, seemingly aimed at dramatically showing rather than judgementally or sentimentally telling.

In places *1846* brings *Oliver Twist* closer in tone or rhetorical patterning to the later Dickensian novel. On the crucial and controversial matter of Nancy's residual moral instinct, which in a descriptive running head added for *1867* is called 'Soul of Goodness in Things Evil', *Bentley's* and the early editions refer to Nancy's 'humanity, of which her wasting life had obliterated all outward traces when a very child' (III, 3). This points to her protective formation of a hard public surface. But *1846* makes it, with a pious catch in the voice, 'of which her wasting life had obliterated so many, many traces when a very child'. Another later Dickensian repetition for pathos comes in when Oliver returns to 'Mudfog' with Mr Brownlow in III, 13: where *Bentley's* introduces the remembered places and items with just one 'There was . . .', *1846* takes off into the enumerative mode Dickens loved: 'There was . . . there were . . . there was . . . there was . . . there was . . . there were . . . there was . . .'

In III, 12, *Bentley's* has a strange moment where Sikes's dog Bull's-eye has arrived in the Jacob's Island refuge before his master, and the assembled crooks are watching him:

'If he was coming here, he'd have come with the dog,' said Kags, stooping down to examine the animal, who lay panting on the floor. 'Here; give us some water for him; he has run himself faint.'

'He's drunk it all up, every drop,' said Kags, after watching the dog some time in silence.

We can read this as a startlingly modern temporal effect, making us jump forward to the same speaker's second utterance, *then* explaining ('after . . . some time') the nervous, disjunctive movement of the scene. If this was meant, then in *1846*, at any rate, Dickens either feared the appearance of a mistake or missed his own point, and attributed the second speech to Chitling. *1846* heavily revises the novel's punctuation, with a powerful cumulative effect on the way it reads. Dickens typically took longer sentences consisting of clauses loosely joined by conjunctions and turned them into sequences of shorter sentences. He was in *1846* moreover punctuating, temporarily, in a very idiosyncratic and emphatic way, perhaps to stress the rhythms of his prose when read aloud, profusely inserting colons instead of commas, as at the end of I, 15, where Oliver on his errand has been recaptured by Nancy and Sikes. *Bentley's* and the early editions read: 'and still the two old gentlemen sat perseveringly in the dark parlour, with the watch between them', while *1846* reads: 'and still the two old gentlemen sat, perseveringly, in the dark parlour: with the watch between them'. I have not attempted to convey the cumulative difference of effect in the following selection of variants. (Interested readers can compare this text with Stephen Gill's World's Classics edition, which reprints the Clarendon text based on *1846*. The Clarendon edition does not record accidentals.)

Dickens's rearrangement of chapter divisions in *1846* seems specifically intended for its serial publication (see entries in I, 12; II, 7; III, 3; and III, 7).

1850

For the *1850* 'Cheap Edition', Dickens wrote a new, short, topical Preface (included here as Appendix B). In the novel he changed some of the unusual colons and semi-colons to commas again, though this may be compositorial normalizing rather than authorial rethinking. Otherwise the edition tones down some more phrasing, introduces errors and adds in a footnote a change in the regulations about police-courts like Fang's being closed to the public: 'Or were virtually, then.' (I, 11).

1867

The constant reference to Fagin as 'the Jew' is certain to cause pain, as it did, but less widely, in Dickens's time. It is only in the *1867* 'Charles Dickens Edition', and only at a certain point in the text, with the reference to 'the Jew's cupidity' in II, 9, that Dickens starts to change 'the Jew' to 'Fagin' or 'he' – as if moving from an external and racial to a more intimate and personal view of him – and it is only from III, 2 that the changes become consistent (the penultimate chapter becomes 'Fagin's Last Night Alive'). See also note 9 to I, 8. The language is toned down in other respects also: Sikes loses his mild swearword in 'Damnation, how the boy bleeds!' (I, 22). And descriptive running heads come in, nudging the book further towards tonal consistency with the Dickensian *oeuvre*: 'Mischievous effects of Meat', 'Silent, for the Girl's Sake', 'Goading the Wild Beast', 'The Curse of Cain'.

EMENDATION OF *BENTLEY'S*

The main problem with *Bentley's* as a copy-text results from the comparative lack of care taken over the last instalments, from November 1838 when *1838* came out. These instalments were set directly from the book, and there are a few short but regrettable cuts in the November issue (see entries for III, 5 and 6), probably made hastily due to the frantic setting and proofing of the book at exactly the same time. I have emended *Bentley's* on three occasions where cuts or haste produced nonsense: III, 6 and 13 from the reading of *MS* and *1838*; and III, 11 from *1846*.

In the list of variants I give the exact form of each revision or different version as it first appears in the edition whose date is given. The exception is all readings have single quotation marks. (The instalments in *Bentley's* are indicated in the novel with an asterisk.)

ABBREVIATIONS FOR TEXTS

MS = Manuscript, Forster Collection, Victoria and Albert Museum

Bentley's = *Bentley's Miscellany*, 24 instalments (February 1837–April 1839)

1838 = 'Boz' issue of *Oliver Twist: or, the Parish Boy's Progress*, 3 volumes (London: Richard Bentley, [9 November] 1838)

1846 = 'A New Edition, Revised and Corrected', *The Adventures of Oliver Twist; or, The Parish Boy's Progress*, in ten monthly parts and one volume (London: Bradbury & Evans, [26 September] 1846)

1850 = Cheap Edition, *The Adventures of Oliver Twist*, in weekly and monthly parts and one volume (London: Chapman & Hall, [20 April] 1850)

1858 = Library Edition, *The Adventures of Oliver Twist*, one volume (London: Chapman & Hall and Bradbury & Evans, [4 December] 1858)

1867 = Charles Dickens Edition, *The Adventures of Oliver Twist*, one volume (London: Chapman & Hall, [1 August] 1867)

< > = cancelled phrasing in MS

[BOOK THE FIRST]

CHAPTER THE FIRST

3 in the town of Mudfog,] *1838*: in a certain town which for many reasons it will be prudent to refrain from mentioning, and to which I will assign no fictitious name,

3 it boasts of one which is common to most towns great or small,] *1846*: there is one anciently common to most towns great or small:

CHAPTER THE SECOND

7 eighth birth-day] *1838*: ninth birth-day

8 aware,] *1846*: aweer,

9 It's gin.] *1846*: It's gin. I'll not deceive you, Mr. B. It's gin.

9 eight years old] *1838*: nine year old

12 waistcoat, in a very decided tone . . . an opinion on the matter.] *1846*: waistcoat.

14 first three months] *1838*: first six months

17 will be a long or a short piece of biography.] *1838*: had this violent termination or no.

CHAPTER THE FOURTH

32 don't be cross to me. I feel as if I had been cut here, sir, and it was all bleeding away;' and the child] *1838*: don't, don't pray be cross to me.' The child

CHAPTER THE FIFTH

35 Eleven,] *1838*: Ten,

44 in a fit.] *1838*: in a swoon.

CHAPTER THE SIXTH

45 It was a nice sickly] *1838*: The month's trial over, Oliver was formally apprenticed. It was a nice sickly season
46 for some weeks] *1838*: for many months
50 some very audible tears] *1838*: some affecting tears

CHAPTER THE SEVENTH

54 replied Oliver, sullenly.] *1838*: replied Oliver.
57 and sufferings of his after life, through all the troubles and changes of many weary years,] *1838*: and sufferings, and troubles, and changes of his after life,

CHAPTER THE EIGHTH

60 crouching on the step for some time,] *1838*: crouching on the step for some time, wondering at the great number of public-houses (every other house in Barnet is a tavern, large or small),
60 three feet six,] *1838*: four feet six,
63 Irish (who are generally the lowest orders of anything)] *1846*: Irish
63 that it was all right;] *1838*: that all was right;

CHAPTER THE NINTH

68 The prospect of the gallows, too, makes them hardy and bold.] *1838*: *omitted*

CHAPTER THE TENTH

73 For eight or ten days] *1838*: For many days
76 a handkerchief, which he handed to Charley Bates, and with which they both ran away] *1846*: a handkerchief! To see him hand the same to Charley Bates; and finally to behold them, both, running away
77 the pursuers, and made this reply to their anxious inquiries. / 'Yes,' said the gentleman in a benevolent voice,] *1846*: the pursuers. / 'Yes,' said the gentleman,

CHAPTER THE ELEVENTH

80 there were others that the grave had changed to ghastly trophies of death,]
1846: there were faces that the grave had changed and closed upon,
81 a middle-sized man,] *1846*: a lean, long-backed, stiff-necked, middle-sized
man,
81 and consequently in strong contrast to Mr Fang,] *1838*: *omitted*
84 the daily press,] *1850*: [CD's footnote:] Or were virtually, then.

CHAPTER THE TWELFTH

86 *WITH SOME PARTICULARS CONCERNING A CERTAIN
PICTURE*] *1846*: *AND IN WHICH THE NARRATIVE REVERTS
TO THE MERRY OLD GENTLEMAN AND HIS YOUTHFUL
FRIENDS*
86 heat of fever, – that heat which . . . and to destroy.] *1846*: heat of fever.
89 a small Prayer Book] *MS*: a small Bible
93 'Gracious God, what's this! Bedwin, look, look there!'] *1846*: 'Why! what's
this? Bedwin, look there!'
93 copied with an accuracy which was perfectly unearthly.] *1846*: copied with
a startling accuracy.

CHAPTER THE THIRTEENTH

93 he fainted away. / CHAPTER THE THIRTEENTH . . . When the Dodger
and his accomplished friend Master Bates joined] *1846*: he fainted away. A
weakness on his part, which affords the narrative an opportunity of relieving
the reader from suspense, in behalf of the two young pupils of the Merry Old
Gentleman; and of recording / That when the Dodger, and his accomplished
friend Master Bates, joined [In *1846 Chapter XII continues to p. 71*, '. . . the
Dodger and Charley Bates entered and closed it behind them.']
94 described with great perspicuity . . . regard for themselves:] *1846*:
described, they were actuated by a very laudable and becoming regard for
themselves;
95 Thus, to do a great right . . . impartial view of his own particular case.]
MS originally read: In proof of which proposition I need hardly appeal to
everybody's experience of every day and every school.

97 'Speak out, or] *MS*: "Speak out, damn you, or
97 D—me] *MS*: Damme
100 desire to be 'jiggered'] *1838*: desire to be 'blessed'
100 he turned to the other young lady . . . and yellow curl-papers.] *1838*: he turned from this young lady, who was gaily, not to say gorgeously attired, in a red gown, green boots, and yellow curl-papers; to the other female.
101 replied Miss Nancy] *1838*: replied Nancy
101 bawled Nancy.] *1846*: said Nancy.
104 stop his windpipe yet.] *1846*: stop his mouth yet.

CHAPTER THE FOURTEENTH

108 Deep affliction has only made them stronger; it ought, I think, for it should refine our nature.] *1846*: Deep affliction has but strengthened and refined them.
109 quite still, almost afraid to breathe.] *1846*: quite still.
109 and if I find you have committed no crime, you will never be friendless] *1846*: and you shall not be friendless
110 this cursed poor-surgeon's-friend] *1838*: this poor-surgeon's-friend
115 Of such contradictions is human nature made up!] *1846*: *omitted*

CHAPTER THE FIFTEENTH

115 If it did not come . . . it forms no part of my original intention so to do.] *1838*: *omitted*
120 might be lying dead] *1838*: might be weeping bitterly
123 struck him violently] *1846*: struck him

CHAPTER THE SIXTEENTH

124 Oliver's throat, and uttering a savage oath;] *1846*: Oliver's throat;
125 foggy, and it was just beginning to rain.] *1838*: foggy.
126 very few people, for it now rained heavily,] *1838*: very few people:
131 that, my dear.] *1838*: that, my young master.

CHAPTER THE SEVENTEENTH

135 But I have set it ... ask him to accompany me] *1838*: If so, let it be considered a delicate intimation on the part of the historian that he is going back directly to the town in which Oliver Twist was born; the reader taking it for granted that there are good and substantial reasons for making the journey, or he would not be invited to proceed upon such an expedition

139 demoralised] *1846*: demogalized

141 His great-coat is a parochial cut, and he looks a beadle all over.] *1846*: A beadle all over!

143 retorted the old gentleman sharply.] *1846*: retorted the old gentleman.

CHAPTER THE EIGHTEENTH

145 neither unnoticed nor unrelished by the wary villain.] *1846*: neither unnoticed, nor unrelished by, that wary old gentleman.

148 breed! Winkin!] *1838*: breed! –

CHAPTER THE NINETEENTH

154 Miss Nancy prefixed to the word ... omitted in this chronicle.] *1838*: *omitted*

155 D– your eyes! wot] *1846*: Wot

157 suddenly rousing himself as if from a trance.] *1846*: as suddenly rousing himself.

157 Jew, grasping the other's hand, his eyes glistening] *1846*: Jew; his eyes glistening

157 Jew, biting his lip.] *1846*: Jew.

CHAPTER THE TWENTIETH

163 'Good-night, sir!' replied Oliver softly.] *1846*: 'Good night!' replied Oliver, softly.

165 and then, wringing her hands violently,] *1838*: *omitted*

165 The girl burst into a fit of loud laughter, beating her hands] *1838*: The girl beat her hands

168 new *protégé*,] *1846*: new pupil,
168 replied Oliver, trembling.] *1846*: replied Oliver.
168 repress a shriek;] *1846*: repress a start;

CHAPTER THE TWENTY-FIRST

173 way, and at length crossing a little bridge . . . a narrow street, walked straight to an old public-house] *1846*: way: and stopping for nothing but a little beer, until they reached a town. Here against the wall of a house, Oliver saw, written up in pretty large letters, 'Hampton.' They lingered about, in the fields, for some hours. At length, they came back into the town; and turning into an old public-house [In *1838*: Here they lingered about in the fields for some hours. At length they came back into the town, and keeping on past a public-house which bore the sign of the Red Lion, and by the river-side for a short distance, they came to an old public-house]

CHAPTER THE TWENTY-SECOND

181 a savage look.] *1838*: a threatening look.
183 Damnation, how] *1867*: How

BOOK THE SECOND

CHAPTER THE FIRST

186 'My God!'] *1846*: 'My heart!'
187 wine, only out of the cask this afternoon, –] *1846*: wine; only out of the cask this forenoon;

CHAPTER THE SECOND

197 would not feel disgraced to hear its poor young mother named.] *MS*: would hear of its birth without shame.

CHAPTER THE THIRD

202 a large shawl] *1838*: a large wrapper
203 gasped the Jew.] *1867*: *omitted*

CHAPTER THE FOURTH

204 Looking hastily round . . . in which he had before proceeded.] *1838*: *omitted*
209 The girl moaned out some scarcely intelligible reply,] *MS* originally read: 'In hell for anything I know' replied the girl without raising her face.
209 looking up,] *MS*: looking up, and striking her hand upon the table with a force that made it rattle again
212 'Make haste; I hate this!'] *MS* originally read: 'Make haste. I hate this! I say, I had better leave the door ajar till you've got the glim.'; *1846*: 'Make haste!'
213 of the kingdom, perhaps for life?] *MS* originally read: of the kingdom. Ten to one but if the big wigs knew of his being one of your boys and you [three words illegible] could have managed that well enough he would have been lagged for life.
215 now, my dear?] *1838*: now?

CHAPTER THE FIFTH

219 Mrs Corney sighed.] *MS* originally read: 'Bold man' murmured Mrs Corney.
220 satisfactorily arranged,] *MS* originally read: satisfactorily arranged, a little more embracing ensued.
223 the peasantry] *MS*: the Mudfog peasantry

CHAPTER THE SIXTH

224 'Wolves tear your throats!' muttered Sikes, grinding his teeth;] *MS*: 'Wolves tear your <gallows> cursed throats!' muttered Sikes, grinding his teeth with rage 'It's half worth swinging for.
224 play the booby] *1846*: play booty

233 a constable and doctor.] *MS*: a constable and a doctor. Having done this, he was to ride on to London, if no better conveyance offered, and to request the immediate attendance of an experienced police officer.

CHAPTER THE SEVENTH

234 *HOUSE TO WHICH OLIVER RESORTED, AND RELATES WHAT THEY THOUGHT OF HIM*] *1846*: *HOUSE TO WHICH OLIVER RESORTED.*

235 such as hers.] *MS* originally read: such as hers. Oh! Where are the hearts <that> which following some halting description of youth and beauty, do not recal a loved original that <Death> Time has sadly changed, or Death resolved to dust.

235 the cheerful happy smile – were entwined with the best sympathies and affections of our nature.] *1846*: the cheerful, happy smile; were made for Home; for fireside peace and happiness.

235 The elder lady smiled; but her heart was full, and she brushed away a tear as she did so.] *1846*: *omitted*

238 With many more] *1846*: CHAPTER XXX / *RELATES WHAT OLIVER'S NEW VISITORS THOUGHT OF HIM.* / With many more

239 for no power of the human mind] *1846*: for no voluntary exertion of the mind

239 eagerly, 'not you, aunt, not you!'] *1846*: eagerly.

240 to-day except yourself.] *1846*: to-day, except yourself Miss Rose.

241 by woman's hands that night,] *1846*: by gentle hands that night;

243 said the doctor fiercely,] *1846*: said the doctor,

243 'Pay attention to the reply . . . should be glad to know what was.] not in *MS*

244 Then confound and damn your – slow] *1838*: Then confound your – slow

CHAPTER THE EIGHTH

248 'The more I think of it . . . had them here for the world!'] added in *MS*

CHAPTER THE NINTH

258 demanded the hunchback fiercely.] *1846*: demanded the hunchback.
260 so very, very good to me, sir.] *1846*: so very very good to me.

262 lay at rest.] *MS* originally read: lay at rest, while the birds sang sweetly and violets bloomed above them.

262 the deep sky overhead,] *MS* originally read: the deep sky overhead <and remembered that there was a home beyond, to which>

263 some melancholy air,] *1846*: some pleasant air,

263 music, while tears of tranquil joy stole down his face.] *1846*: music, in a perfect rapture.

264 upon all he had done, for which one of those light-hearted beautiful smiles was an ample recompense.] *1846*: on all he had done.

CHAPTER THE TENTH

266 Miss Maylie doesn't look well] *1846*: She don't look well

266 'What misfortune, ma'am?'] *1846*: 'What?'

267 The lady sank beneath her desponding thoughts, and gave way] *1846*: She gave way

267 boy; and although what you say may be natural, it is wrong.] *1846*: boy.

268 directed to Harry Maylie Esquire, at some lord's house in the country;] *MS*: directed to <the Reverend> Harry Maylie <near Taunton Somersetshire> Esquire Trinity College Cambridge

269 Grind him to ashes!] *MS*: Blast him!

270 foaming, in a fit.] *MS*: foaming, in an epileptic fit.

272 repaired, that such recollections are among the bitterest we can have.] *1846*: repaired.

272 gasped Mrs Maylie.] *1846*: *omitted*

CHAPTER THE ELEVENTH

276 my dear fellow,] *1846*: my dear son,

278 said the doctor maliciously.] *1846*: said the doctor.

280 eyes and hearts.] *MS* originally read: eyes and hearts and are not the real colours of this lovely world that once was Paradise.

283 Wither his flesh,] *1846*: *omitted*

283 Good God!] *1846*: Good Heaven!

283 called loudly for help.] *MS*: called loudly for help and followed in the direction which he supposed the two men had taken.

CHAPTER THE TWELFTH

285 dream, Oliver?' said Harry Maylie, taking him aside.] *1846*: dream, Oliver,' said Harry Maylie.

286 the mystery.] *MS*: the mystery. No persons at all answering the description given, had been seen by anyone with whom he had fallen in.

288 Rose, for years – for years I have loved you] *MS* originally read: Rose if true, honest, ardent love were ever felt by man, it is the love I bear to you. Tell me if I may make some effort to deserve you <tell me you have not forgotten that you know how I have loved you>

289 rejoined Rose. 'You can say nothing to alter my resolution. It is a duty that I must perform.] *MS*: rejoined Rose. / 'Not if they give you pain' – interrupted her lover 'I do know them already indeed; you communicated them to my mother, and she has more than hinted them to me. What can I say, Rose, to shew you their futility?' / 'Oh Harry, dear Harry' – cried the beautiful girl, half yielding to and half repelling his caress, 'You can say nothing to alter my resolution. It is a duty that I must perform.' / 'Nay' – urged Harry Maylie 'but hear reason.' / 'I have heard reason' replied Rose. 'I have reasoned with myself, painfully and long, and to this decision I have been impelled by every consideration of duty, gratitude, and honor. <I am' – said Rose, rising with dignity as she spoke, and taking a few steps towards the door 'I am <of doubt> a nameless orphan upon whom there hangs a stain.' / 'A stain!' exclaimed Harry impetuously. / 'The world calls it so' – replied Rose gently, 'and visits its punishment upon the innocent head that bears it'>

CHAPTER THE THIRTEENTH

291 'And so you are resolved to be my travelling-companion . . . intention two half hours together.'] *MS*: 'And so you still continue in the same mind, and are resolved to be my travelling companion this morning eh?' said the doctor as Harry Maylie joined him and Oliver at the breakfast table. / 'If you will give me a seat in your chaise' was the reply 'Did you think I had altered my mind?' / 'Why, to tell you the truth I thought it by no means impossible' returned the doctor, 'for you young fellows are so whimsical that the church weathercock yonder which spins round in rapid circles whenever there is any wind blowing, is constancy itself compared with you. It always turns round, at least, while you move in squares, angles, and ingenious zigzags of all kinds.' / 'You older heads being so very remarkable for gravity and steadiness of purpose, have a licence to twit us for our misdeeds,' retorted Harry smiling. / 'If I run about after mysterious ruffians, jew and christian, with greater speed than beseems my solemn profession and elderly legs,' said the doctor 'and eight or ten times a week amuse my acquaintance by doing something exceedingly preposterous, that is the extent of my irregularities, but you – you are not in the same mind or intention two half-hours together.'

292 or sweepstakes.'] *MS*: or sweepstakes.' / 'But suppose the person training, or the horse entered (to carry out your felicitous illustration) has no intention of running at all' – said Harry 'what then?' / 'Why then he is no horse, but an ass to take so much trouble about what don't concern him' – returned Mr. Losberne 'and as that supposition does not concern you, who are entered and sure to run, I have no delicacy in assigning him his proper place in natural history.'

293 pace with me. Do you hear?'] *MS*: pace with me so have the goodness to go soberly and steadily. Do you hear?' / The man smiled, touched his hat, and away they went, although at a pace more in compliance with Harry's orders than those of Mr. Losberne whose head was very soon thrust out of the window in violent but ineffectual remonstrance.

CHAPTER THE FOURTEENTH

295 mere men.] *MS*: mere men. Promote them, raise them to higher and different offices in the state; and divested of their black silk aprons and cocked hats they shall still lack their old dignity and be somewhat shorn of their influence with the multitude.

295 at a venture.] *MS*: at a venture. / 'Is that' – said Mr. Bumble with sentimental sternness 'is that the woice as called me a irresistible duck in the small one-pair? Is that the creetur that was all meekness, mildness, and sensibility?' / 'It is indeed, worse luck' – replied his helpmate; 'not much of sensibility though, or I should have had more sense than to make the sacrifice I did.' / 'The sacrifice Mrs. Bumble?' – said the gentleman with great asperity. / 'You may well repeat the word' rejoined the lady 'It ought to be never out of my mouth gracious knows.' / 'I am not aware that it ever is Ma'am' – retorted Mr. Bumble. 'It's always coming out of your mouth Ma'am, but is always there. Mrs. Bumble, Ma'am.'

295 eyes upon her.] *MS*: eyes upon her. The lady did as she was requested, and after some seconds withdrew her gaze with a contemptuous laugh.

297 Now Mrs Corney, that was,] *MS*: Now Mrs. Corney, that was, had great experience in matrimonial tactics having, previous to the bestowal of her hand on Mr. Corney, been united to another worthy gentleman also departed. She **298** possession of the field.] *MS*: possession of the field. / 'I couldn't have believed it' said Mr. Bumble as he crawled down the passage arranging his disordered dress 'She didn't seem one of that sort at all. If the paupers knew of this, I should be a porochial bye-word.'

301 known my name. You don't know it, and I should recommend] *MS*: known my name.' / 'Perhaps I do' – said Mr. Bumble, determined to pump his companion. / 'Perhaps so' rejoined the stranger gravely. 'If you do, you don't need to be told it. If you don't, I should recommend

301 broken by the stranger.] *MS*: broken by the stranger who pushed away the old newspaper he had previously kept before him, and took up the conversation again.

302 I saw you. What are you now?'] *MS*: I saw you.' / 'Aye aye?' said Mr. Bumble regarding the stranger attentively, and running over in his mind all the unmarried fathers, rate-paying defaulters, and other offenders against the poor laws whose appearance he could call to mind 'I don't recollect you.' / 'It would be a miracle if you did' observed the other coolly. 'What are you now?'

302 workhouse, young man!'] *MS*: workhouse, young man!' / 'Married?' enquired the stranger. / 'Yes' – said Mr. Bumble with an uneasy movement on his seat. 'Two months tomorrow.' / 'You married rather late in life' – said the stranger 'Well; better late than never.' / Mr. Bumble was on the point of reversing the axiom, and expressing his opinion that for the correct guidance of mankind it ought to stand 'better never than late,' when the stranger interrupted him.

302 water into Mr Bumble's eyes.] *MS*: water into Mr. Bumble's eyes. <Strong as it was, he swallowed more than half of it in the short interval the stranger employed in closing the door and windows>

302 in my mind. I want some information] *MS*: in my mind. Be quick in answering what I ask you, for I want to reach the place I am to sleep in, before the cursed black night comes on; the way is lonely and the night is dark, and I hate both when I am alone. Do you mind me?' / 'I hear you' – said Mr. Bumble applying to his gin and water as though for a solution of the mystery, 'but to say I understand you, you know, would be rather stretching a point, at present.' / 'I shall be plain enough' – said the stranger. 'I want some information

303 rejoined Mr Bumble.] *MS* rejoined Mr. Bumble. / 'Dead!' cried the stranger. / 'As a door-nail' said Mr. Bumble.

BOOK THE THIRD

CHAPTER THE FIRST

309 Fire the sound! I hate it!'] *1846*: I hate the sound!

309 and nearly blank.] *1846*: and discoloured.

316 you know, Mr Monks.'] *MS*: you know, Mr. Monks.' / 'You may as well teach yourself to drop that name, do you mind?' said the person whom he had addressed. / 'Certainly' – answered Mr. Bumble, still retreating. / 'And if we meet again anywhere there's no call for us to know each other – you understand?' said Monks frowning. / 'You may depend upon my not saying a word to you, young man, or about you, on no account' – said Mr. Bumble.

CHAPTER THE SECOND

317 It was about two hours earlier on] *1846*: On

318 and struck her.] *MS*: and struck her <in the face>

319 say you wouldn't.'] *MS*: say you wouldn't. A good word's as easy to speak as a bad one.'

319 bustle about, and] *MS*: bustle about <or I'll beat it out of you> and

322 the drayma besides.'] *MS*: the drayma besides.' / After indulging in this humorous effusion Master Bates laughed so loudly at his own joke as to throw the redoubtable Bullseye (who was a dog of misanthropical temperament) into a perfect convulsion of barking, which it required all the influence of his master to stop.

322 choke me dead.'] *MS*: choke me dead. / Being hastily accommodated with a large mess of pie, Mr. Sikes exercised his knife and fork for some time in silence, and at length pushing his plate away and swallowing another glassful from the Dodger's bottle, he addressed the Jew to the following effect. / 'I'll tell you wot it is Fagin. I caught the ague in your service lurking about in the wet so long and keeping out of the way arter that precious mull that you got me into which might have cost me my neck and you the best hand that ever helped to pile up gold in your mouldy old sacks. You've left me to starve and dwindle down here till such time as I should be brought low enough to do any job you've got on hand, at any price. Don't say you haven't, for you have, and know you have. All I say is serve me so again and the game's up. I'd as soon swing as be so hard up again, and a great deal sooner to feel the pleasure of having you dangling from the same beam. Serve me so again and we two'll dance upon nothing in less than six weeks arterwards, or you an't a wiper, and my name an't Bill Sikes, and more I can't say.'

323 'It's all very well,' said Mr Sikes;] *MS*: 'It's all very well laughing' – said Mr. Sikes stopping short in the conversation at a sign from Nancy

325 I bear it all. Hush!'] *MS*: I bear it all.' / Nancy nodded her head in a manner which seemed to say that she knew what the trade was worth, as well as the Jew did. Fagin, lighting a candle and taking the key in his hand prepared to go up stairs when he was suddenly stopped by hearing that the boys in going out, had encountered some person at the street door. / 'Hush!'

326 the same person.] *MS*: the same person. / 'When did you return to town?' added the Jew, turning the light he held in his hand. / 'Two hours back' – answered Monks. / 'Did you see him?' asked the Jew. / 'I did' replied the other with an inclination of the head, which, as well as the tone in which he made the reply, appeared full of meaning.

326 muffling her arms in it,] *MS*: muffling her arms in it so that if she cast any shadow as she went, its shape might not betray her,

327 preparing to be gone.] *MS*: preparing to be gone. / 'How long you've been Fagin' – she said impatiently 'I shall have Bill in a fine humour when I get back.' / 'I couldn't help it my dear' – said the Jew – 'a matter of business about a small quantity of silk and velvet that the gentleman wants to get rid of, without being asked questions. Ha! ha!'

CHAPTER THE THIRD

329 thinking of, ha?'] *1846*: thinking of?'

332 The girl's life] *1846*: CHAPTER XL / *A STRANGE INTERVIEW, WHICH IS A SEQUEL TO THE LAST CHAPTER* / The girl's life [*In 1846 no new chapter at p. 328.*]

333 had obliterated all outward traces] *1846*: had obliterated so many, many traces

336 I have to reach home] *MS* originally read: my life depends on my reaching home

336 of her mind;] *MS* originally read: of her mind and beating her hands together;

338 that parents, home, and friends filled once, or] *1846*: omitted

CHAPTER THE FOURTH

342 not twelve at least] *MS*: not eleven at least
343 said the old gentleman;] *MS*: said the old gentleman with moistened eyelids;
347 in ten years,] *1846*: in twenty years,
347 said the doctor.] *MS*: said the doctor laughing.

CHAPTER THE FIFTH

355 make it so,] *MS*: make it so, my dear,
357 of hands,] *MS*: of hands my dear,
358 fancy-work?] *MS*: fancy work, my dear?
359 'Good night! Good night!'] *MS* and *1838*: 'Good night! Good night!' /
With many adieus and good wishes Mr. Fagin went his way; and Noah
Claypole, bespeaking his good lady's attention, proceeded to enlighten her
relative to the arrangement he had made, with all that haughtiness and air of
superiority, becoming, not only a member of the sterner sex, but a gentleman
who appreciated the dignity of a special appointment on the kinchin lay in
London and its vicinity.

CHAPTER THE SIXTH

360 *WHEREIN IS SHOWN HOW THE ARTFUL DODGER GOT
INTO TROUBLE*] *MS* originally read: *WHEREIN THE ARTFUL
DODGER IS EXHIBITED IN A TRYING SITUATION*
360 replied Fagin. 'Some conjurors] *MS* and *1838*: replied Fagin, with his most
insinuating grin. 'He hasn't as good a one as himself anywhere.' / 'Except
sometimes,' replied Morris Bolter, assuming the air of a man of the world. 'Some
people are nobody's enemies but their own, yer know.' / 'Don't believe that,'
said the Jew. 'When a man's his own enemy, it's only because he's too much his
own friend; not because he's careful for every body but himself. Pooh! pooh!
There ain't such a thing in nature.' / 'There oughtn't to be, if there is,' replied
Mr. Bolter. / 'That stands to reason,' said the Jew. 'Some conjurors
360 like ours] *MS* and *1838*: like ours, my dear,
364 'Are you mad, my dear; . . . Charley with a humorous leer.] *Bentley's*:
omitted [The Penguin text follows *MS* and *1838*]
366 up the steps] *MS*: up the three steps

CHAPTER THE SEVENTH

370 *NOAH CLAYPOLE IS EMPLOYED BY FAGIN ON A SECRET MISSION*] *1846*: omitted

371 by the devil,' returned Sikes, 'not by a trap. There] *1846*: by the devil,' returned Sikes. 'There

372 retorted Sikes in a loud voice.] *1846*: retorted Sikes.

376 He rose betimes] *1846*: CHAPTER XLV /*NOAH CLAYPOLE IS EMPLOYED BY FAGIN ON A SECRET MISSION*/ The old man was up, betimes,

379 'Now.'] *1846*: 'Dow.'

379 left hand, and keep on the other] *1846*: left had, and keep od the other

CHAPTER THE EIGHTH

385 asked the old gentleman anxiously.] *1846*: asked the old gentleman.

CHAPTER THE NINTH

391 – Speak, will you?] *1846*: omitted

CHAPTER THE TENTH

397 but *such* flesh, and *such* blood!] *1846*: but such flesh, and so much blood!

398 he should carry out new evidences] *1846*: he should soil his feet anew and carry out new evidences

CHAPTER THE ELEVENTH

408 'None; emphatically none.'] *1846*: 'None.'

409 issue,' returned Mr Brownlow.] *1846*: issue.'

410 rejoined Monks in evident confusion.] *1846*: rejoined Monks.

410 old.' / 'What's this to me?' asked Monks. / 'They *Bentley's*: old They [The Penguin text follows *1838*]. "Your tale is of the longest" (p. 411) begins an instalment.

412 cried Monks, starting.] *1846*: cried Monks.

CHAPTER THE TWELFTH

416 there exists, at the present day,] *1867*: there exists
417 known in these days as] *1867*: known in the days of this story as
420 drop,' said Kags,] *1846*: drop,' said Chitling,
421 They had never heard] *1846*: They seemed never to have heard
423 'He's here; he's here!] *1846*: 'He's here!
424 of that infuriated] *1846*: of the infuriated

CHAPTER THE THIRTEENTH

430 all the well-known ... nearly everything *1846*: there were all the well-known ... there was Gamfield's ... there was the workhouse ... there was the same ... there were scores ... there was nearly everything. ' "Yes," said Monks' (p. 431) begins a new instalment.
432 'Listen then,'] *1846*: 'Listen then! You!'
432 to yourself, and enclosed] *1846*: to yourself;' he addressed himself to Mr. Brownlow; 'and enclosed
432 fell fast. / Monks was silent. / 'The will,' said Mr Brownlow, speaking for him, 'was] *Bentley's*: fell fast. / 'I will go on to that.' / 'The will was [The Penguin text follows *1846*]

CHAPTER THE FOURTEENTH

441 a firmament all bright with beaming eyes.] *1846*: a firmament, all bright with gleaming eyes.
449 He writhed and struggled with the power of desperation, and sent up shriek upon shriek that] *1846*: He struggled with the power of desperation, for an instant; and then, sent up cry upon cry that

CHAPTER THE FIFTEENTH

455 I do believe that the shade of that poor girl often hovers about that solemn nook – ay, though it *is* a church,] *1846*: I believe that the shade of Agnes sometimes hovers round that solemn nook. I believe it none the less, because that nook is in a Church,

APPENDIX A

THE AUTHOR'S INTRODUCTION TO THE THIRD EDITION (1841)

456 Some . . . FIELDING.] *1867: omitted*

456 The greater part of this Tale . . . under my own hand.] *1867: omitted* The result did not fail . . . under my own hand.] *1858: omitted*

456 It is, it seems, a very coarse] *1858*: It was, it seemed, a coarse; *1867*: Once upon a time it was held to be a coarse

456 that Sikes is a thief . . . every thinking mind.] *1867: omitted*

456 I saw no reason . . . its froth and cream.] *1867*: As I saw no reason, when I wrote this book, why the dregs of life, so long as their speech did not offend the ear, should not serve the purpose of a moral, as well as its froth and cream, I made bold to believe that this same Once upon a time would not prove to be All-time or even a long time.

456 Nor did I doubt . . . who figure in these volumes.] *1867: omitted*

458 other, wider, and higher aims.] *1858*: other aims. *1867*: other and wider aims.

459 in the girl's dishevelled hair.] *1867*: in Nancy's dishevelled hair.

459 I venture to say this without reserve . . . I leave my readers to determine.] *1867: omitted*

460 become, at last, utterly and irredeemably bad.] *1867*: become utterly and incurably bad.

460 Suggested to my mind long ago . . . found it still the same.] *1867: omitted*

460 told.] *1867*: told. In the year one thousand eight hundred and fifty, it was publicly declared in London by an amazing Alderman, that Jacob's Island did not exist, and never had existed. Jacob's Island continues to exist (like an ill-bred place as it is) in the year one thousand eight hundred and sixty-seven, though improved and much changed.

APPENDIX B

PREFACE TO THE 'CHEAP EDITION' (1850)

The MS is in the J. F. Dexter Collection.

461 ISLAND.] *MS*: Island. <I have the honor to belong to the constituent body represented, for parochial purposes, by the sagacious vestry of Marylebone – an honor which I hope I bear meekly. This vestry>

461 wholesome] *MS* originally read: wholesome <I have ever since been, to the best of my power an advocate of what is now call[ed] the Sanitary cause I was a member of the late [?] Metropolitan Health of Towns>

461 desperate] *MS*: degraded

461 The Metropolis . . . Public Health Act] *MS*: The Government constitutionally nervous, being more frightened as to Sanitary questions, than it need have been, by the noise of the noisiest members of a few metropolitan vestries and other such bodies; and having in consequence excluded the Metropolis (of all places under Heaven) from the Public Health Act

462 the Bishop of London had . . . proof of the cheapness] *MS*: Mr. CHADWICK had placed in the hands of the Bishop of London, as an instance of the cheapness

462 Saturday] *MS*: Saturday <. I have the honour to be one of the constituents of this sagacious [word illegible] and I hope I bear it meekly>

462 (I quote the passage without any correction)] not in *MS*

462 'Having touched . . . some ten or eleven years ago] [In *MS* the passage is a pasted-in newspaper cutting with ink underlining, which continues: 'and where the improvements had been made at a cost of less than the price of a pint of porter or of two glasses of gin a week to each inhabitant [laughter]. Now he did hope that this industrial training scheme would not turn out like "Jacob's Island", *all fiction*.']

463 struck by the honesty, by the truth,] *MS*: struck by the truth,

463 making it known to, and causing it to be reverenced by, many] *MS*: making it known to many

464 upon us.] *MS* [deleted in proof by John Forster]: upon us./If any person, in a diseased appetite for notoriety, should henceforth assume the name and title of SIR PETER LAURIE that person will please to take notice (after the precedent of John Partridge and Isaac Bickerstaff) that he is dead.